The Grey World
Author: Jordan Simpson

The Grey World

A World So Cold Universe, Volume 3

Jordan Simpson

Published by Jordan Simpson, 2025.

This is a work of fiction. Similarities to real people, places, or events are entirely coincidental.

THE GREY WORLD

First edition. February 1, 2025.

Copyright © 2025 Jordan Simpson.

ISBN: 979-8230867845

Written by Jordan Simpson.

Also by Jordan Simpson

A World So Cold Universe
Worlds Apart
Worlds Collide
The Grey World

Standalone
Vicious Circle

To my family and friends who have followed me on this journey so far; Thank you.

Book 3 of the Drake Miller Saga

Copyright 2025

Prologue

1-2 The sizzle of bacon punctuated the morning air, a familiar symphony that Drake Miller had heard countless times before. Yet today, it stirred something deeper within him—a sense of unease that clung to the edges of his consciousness like cobwebs in a forgotten attic.

He leaned against the counter, cool marble pressing against his palms as he flipped through the stack of papers crammed into his briefcase. The weight of the documents felt heavier than usual, each page a reminder of the monumental case that awaited him at the office.

"You remembered to sign that permission slip, right, Harry?" Linda's voice floated across the kitchen, her blonde hair catching the sunlight as she turned from the stove.

Drake's gaze shifted to Harrison, hunched over his phone at the table. The boy's tie hung loose around his neck; sneakers untied—a portrait of teenage nonchalance.

"Mhmm," Harrison mumbled, thumbs tapping furiously at his screen.

Drake suppressed a sigh. How many mornings had played out like this? The routine felt both comforting and suffocating, a stark contrast to the turmoil that roiled beneath his composed exterior.

"You know," Drake began, his voice cutting through the domestic tableau, "there was a time when I thought mornings like this were impossible."

Linda paused, spatula hovering above the pan. "What do you mean, honey?"

Drake's fingers tightened around the edge of his briefcase. How could he explain the weight of alternate realities, of choices unmade and paths untraveled? "Just... appreciating what we have," he said instead, forcing a smile that didn't quite reach his eyes.

Harrison glanced up, curiosity momentarily outweighing the allure of his game. "Dad, you're being weird again."

A chuckle escaped Drake's lips, tinged with a sadness he couldn't quite suppress. "Weird is relative, kiddo. One day, you might understand."

As he spoke, Drake's gaze swept across the kitchen, drinking in every detail. The golden stripes of sunlight on the floor, the steam rising from Linda's coffee mug, the faint smudge of syrup on Harrison's cheek. Each element felt both precious and precarious, as if it might dissolve at any moment.

"I should get going," Drake announced, straightening his already impeccable suit. He moved to kiss Linda's cheek, inhaling the scent of her shampoo—lavender and something uniquely her. "I love you," he whispered, the words carrying the weight of universes.

Linda's blue eyes met his, a flicker of concern passing through them. "I love you too. Are you sure you're alright?"

Drake nodded, swallowing past the lump in his throat. "Never better," he lied, the taste of it bitter on his tongue.

As he ruffled Harrison's hair and headed for the door, Drake couldn't shake the feeling that he was leaving something vital behind. The morning light caught his wedding ring, and for a moment, he saw not gold but the glimmer of infinite possibilities—each one a reminder of what he stood to lose.

With one last look at his family, Drake stepped into the world beyond, carrying with him the warmth of the kitchen and the crushing responsibility of a man who knew too much about the fragility of happiness.

3 - 4

"You're going to be late if you don't hustle," Linda said without turning, her tone somewhere between teasing and stern. The words hung in the air, weighted with an urgency that Drake felt in his bones.

He watched Harrison, hunched over his phone, fingers flying across the screen. The boy's dirty blonde hair fell over his forehead, obscuring eyes that Drake knew were wide and expressive. A pang of longing struck him, sharp and sudden. How many mornings had he missed, buried in case files and depositions?

"I'm fine," Harrison mumbled, not looking up from his phone. The nonchalance in his voice was so achingly familiar, so perfectly teenage, that Drake felt his throat constrict.

Linda's spatula clinked against the pan, a steady rhythm that seemed to count down the precious seconds. Drake found himself torn between the desire to freeze this moment in amber and the pressing need to shepherd his son out the door, into a world that suddenly felt fraught with unseen dangers.

He opened his mouth to speak, to urge Harrison along, but the words died on his tongue. What could he say that wouldn't betray the storm of emotions roiling beneath his carefully composed exterior? Instead, he watched, heart heavy, as Linda's shoulders tensed slightly, her nurturing instincts battling with the need to let her child stumble and learn.

The morning light caught a wisp of Linda's blonde hair, turning it to spun gold. Drake's mind raced, grasping at the beauty of this ordinary moment, desperate to commit every detail to memory. The scent of bacon, the warmth of sunlight, the soft rustle of Harrison's clothing as he shifted in his seat – each sensation etched itself into Drake's consciousness with painful clarity.

"Time's ticking, champ," Drake finally managed, his voice rougher than he intended. He cleared his throat, pushing down the surge of protectiveness that threatened to overwhelm him. "Your future's out there waiting."

If only they knew how true those words were, how many futures hung in the balance of this seemingly mundane morning. Drake's fingers tightened on his briefcase, anchoring himself to this reality even as his mind whispered of countless others.

5 - 6

Linda's blue eyes flickered with concern as she glanced over her shoulder, one eyebrow arching in a familiar expression of maternal exasperation. "Harry, I'm serious," she said, her voice carrying a weight that belied her calm exterior. "Mike's waiting, and you know how I feel about that boy's car."

The spatula in her hand paused mid-flip, a droplet of grease sizzling as it hit the stovetop. Drake watched her, marveling at the strength that radiated from her slender frame, even in this mundane moment. How many times had he seen her like this, poised between nurturing and stern? And yet, in this world – this perfect, fragile reality – it felt both achingly familiar and hauntingly new.

Harrison's sigh cut through Drake's reverie. "Mom, I'm sixteen," the boy groused, his fingers still tapping away at his phone screen. "You don't have to call me Harry anymore."

Drake felt a pang in his chest at the petulant tone, so typical of a teenager and yet so precious in its normalcy. He wanted to freeze this moment, to hold onto the irritation in his son's voice, the exasperation in Linda's eyes, the mundane argument over names and cars and time slipping away.

"Sixteen or sixty, you'll always be our Harry," Drake found himself saying, the words escaping before he could stop them. He swallowed hard, fighting against the lump in his throat. How many mornings like this had he missed? How many would he have left?

The weight of unseen realities pressed down on him, making the bright kitchen feel suddenly claustrophobic. Drake loosened his tie, his mind racing with the knowledge of alternate worlds, of paths not taken and choices yet to be made. In this moment, watching his wife and son bicker over breakfast, he felt both intensely present and achingly distant, a silent guardian of a fragile peace.

7 - 8

Linda's lips quirked into a playful smirk as she flipped the last piece of bacon onto the plate with a satisfying sizzle. The aroma of crispy pork and coffee enveloped the kitchen, a comforting blanket of domesticity that Drake desperately wanted to wrap himself in.

"You're right," Linda conceded, her blue eyes twinkling with mischief. "It's either Harry or pumpkin. Take your pick."

Harrison's groan was muffled by the piece of toast he'd shoved unceremoniously into his mouth. Drake watched, a bittersweet ache in his chest, as his son stood up, lankier than he remembered, those once-chubby cheeks now sharpening into the angles of adulthood.

"Harry it is," Harrison mumbled around his mouthful, crumbs spilling onto his untucked shirt. He swallowed hard, a grin spreading across his face as he darted towards the door. "Later, pumpkin!"

Linda's laugh rang out, bright and clear, as she brandished a dish towel at their retreating son. Harrison's own laughter echoed back as he ducked out of reach, the sound fading as the front door slammed shut behind him.

Drake closed his eyes for a moment, committing every detail to memory: the lingering warmth of Linda's laughter, the fading echoes of Harrison's footsteps, the mingled scents of breakfast and the coming day. How fragile it all was, this perfect morning suspended in time. He felt the weight of unseen worlds pressing down on him, countless realities where this simple joy might never exist.

"Earth to Drake," Linda's voice cut through his thoughts, tinged with fond exasperation. "You're going to be late if you keep daydreaming."

He opened his eyes, drinking in the sight of her – the slight furrow of concern between her brows, the wisp of blonde hair that had escaped her ponytail. "Just savoring the moment," he said softly, willing his voice not to betray the storm of emotions roiling beneath the surface.

9 - 10

"You're impossible!" Linda called after Harrison's retreating form, shaking her head as she turned back to the stove. The sizzle of bacon grease filled the air as she muttered under her breath, "Teenagers."

Drake watched her, a bittersweet ache settling in his chest. The familiarity of the scene before him felt both comforting and unsettling, like a vivid dream he couldn't quite shake. He snapped his briefcase shut with a decisive click, the sound grounding him in the present moment.

"He's got your sass, you know," Drake chuckled, his voice low and tinged with an affection that surprised even him. The words felt right on his tongue, yet a part of him wondered if they truly belonged to him or to some other version of himself.

Linda turned, raising an eyebrow at him. "Oh, so it's my fault he's a smart mouth?"

Drake's lips quirked into a half-smile. "I didn't say that" he replied, his mind racing ahead to all the possible outcomes of this conversation, all the ways it could diverge from the reality he desperately wanted to cling to. "But you have to admit, the apple doesn't fall far from the tree."

As Linda laughed, Drake found himself cataloging every detail: the crinkles at the corners of her eyes, the way her shoulders shook slightly, the warmth that spread through him at the sound. He wondered, not for the first time, how many versions of this moment existed across the multiverse, and how many of them ended in tragedy.

11 - 12

"And your stubbornness," Linda replied, meeting his gaze with a playful glare. Her blue eyes sparkled with mirth, a stark contrast to the shadows that haunted Drake's memories.

Drake felt a tug in his chest, a mixture of love and an inexplicable sense of loss. He leaned in, drawn by an instinct that felt both familiar and foreign, brushing a kiss against her temple. The scent of her shampoo – lavender and vanilla – enveloped him, stirring a whirlpool of emotions he struggled to contain.

"You love it," he murmured, his voice husky with suppressed feeling. As the words left his lips, Drake was struck by their double meaning. Did she love his stubbornness, or did she love him? In this reality, in this moment, were they the same thing?

Linda's smile softened, and she leaned into his touch. Drake's mind raced, grappling with the dissonance between the warmth of her skin against his lips and the cold dread that lurked at the edges of his consciousness. He wanted to lose himself in this moment, to believe that this was his life, his family, his world. But the weight of his mission, the knowledge of what was at stake, pressed down on him like a physical force.

"I do," Linda whispered, her words barely audible above the gentle hum of the kitchen appliances. "God help me, but I do."

Drake closed his eyes, savoring the closeness, even as part of him screamed that it wasn't real, that it couldn't last. How many times had he lived this moment? How many times would he have to lose it all again?

13 - 14

Linda sighed, her breath warm against Drake's neck. "Most days, anyway," she added with a wry smile, her eyes twinkling with a mixture of affection and exasperation.

Drake chuckled, the sound rumbling deep in his chest. He watched as Linda turned back to the stove, her movements graceful and practiced. The sizzle of bacon, the aroma of coffee, the soft clink of dishes – it all wove together into a tapestry of domesticity that felt both achingly familiar and strangely surreal.

"You okay?" Linda asked, glancing over her shoulder. "You've got that look again."

Drake blinked, forcing a smile. "What look?"

"Like you're seeing ghosts," she replied, her brow furrowing slightly.

He swallowed hard, fighting back the surge of emotions her words evoked. "Just... appreciating the moment," he managed, his voice rough.

Outside, leaves rustled in a gentle breeze, their whispers seeming to carry echoes of countless mornings just like this one. The dishwasher hummed quietly, its rhythm a steady counterpoint to the beating of Drake's heart.

"Dad!" Harrison's voice cut through the air, distant but clear. "Tell Mike his car's a death trap!"

Drake's lips quirked in a half-smile, even as a chill ran down his spine. Perfect, he thought. It's all so perfect. But why does it feel like I've lived this before?

The sense of déjà vu pricked at the edges of his mind, insistent and unsettling. He pushed it aside, focusing instead on the warmth in his chest as he watched Linda bustle about the kitchen. This was his family, his life. This was real.

Wasn't it?

15 - 16

The morning sun painted the city in hues of gold, its warmth a stark contrast to the chill that had settled in Drake's bones. As he navigated the thinning traffic, his eyes were drawn to the towering glass facade of Miller

& Co Law Firm. The building's reflective surface caught the light, creating a dazzling display that made Drake's breath catch in his throat.

"Christ," he muttered, his knuckles whitening on the steering wheel. The scene before him – the glinting glass, the faint buzz of the awakening city – struck him with an eerie familiarity that sent his mind reeling.

He shook his head, trying to dispel the sensation. "Get it together, Miller," he chastised himself. "It's just another day."

But as he pulled into his parking spot, the unease lingered. Drake sat for a moment, his eyes closed, willing his racing heart to slow. When he opened them, his reflection in the rearview mirror startled him – the shadows under his eyes seemed deeper, his face more haggard than he remembered.

"Too many late nights," he muttered, running a hand through his disheveled hair. "That's all it is."

The lobby bustled with its usual morning activity as Drake strode through, his footsteps echoing on the polished marble floor. The cacophony of ringing phones and clacking keyboards washed over him, a familiar symphony that should have been comforting. Instead, it only intensified the gnawing sense of wrongness that had plagued him since leaving home.

As he approached his office, he spotted Sarah waiting by the door, her posture as impeccable as always. The stack of files in her hands seemed to mock him, a physical manifestation of the weight pressing down on his shoulders.

"Good morning, Mr. Miller," Sarah greeted him, her voice cutting through his thoughts. "I have the files you requested."

Drake forced a smile, hoping it didn't look as strained as it felt. "Thanks, Sarah. You're a lifesaver, as always."

As he reached for the files, a wave of vertigo hit him, nearly causing him to stumble. For a split second, the world seemed to shimmer around him, like heat rising from asphalt on a scorching day.

"Mr. Miller?" Sarah's concerned voice seemed to come from far away. "Are you alright?"

Drake blinked hard, the sensation passing as quickly as it had come. "Fine," he managed, straightening up. "Just... a bit tired. Nothing to worry about."

But as he pushed open his office door, Drake couldn't shake the feeling that something was terribly, irrevocably wrong. The day stretched before him, a familiar path that suddenly seemed fraught with unseen dangers. And deep in his gut, a voice whispered that this was more than simple fatigue or stress.

This was something else entirely.

17 - 18

Sarah's voice cut through Drake's unsettling thoughts, her chipper tone a stark contrast to the unease roiling in his stomach.

"Morning, Mr. Miller," she chirped, her smile bright but eyes betraying a hint of concern. "Here are the deposition notes for the Parker case. Mr. Vega's already in the conference room."

Drake's fingers brushed against the cool surface of the manila folder as he accepted it, the weight oddly comforting in its familiarity. He forced a brief smile, hoping it didn't look as strained as it felt. "Thanks, Sarah."

As he turned towards the conference room, Drake's mind raced. The Parker case—it should have been straightforward, but something nagged at him. A detail just out of reach, like a word on the tip of his tongue. He flexed his fingers, fighting the urge to loosen his tie as the corridor seemed to stretch endlessly before him.

Why did everything feel so... off? The fluorescent lights overhead buzzed faintly, casting harsh shadows that made the familiar hallway seem alien. Drake's footsteps echoed hollowly, each one carrying him closer to Vega and whatever awaited him in that conference room.

A chill ran down his spine as he approached the door. What was waiting for him on the other side? The rational part of his brain insisted it was just another day, another case. But the growing knot in his stomach whispered otherwise. Something was different. Something had changed.

With a deep breath, Drake squared his shoulders and reached for the door handle, steeling himself for whatever lay ahead.

19 - 20

Drake pushed open the heavy oak door, stepping into the expansive conference room. The polished wood gleamed under the morning light that poured through the floor-to-ceiling windows, casting long shadows across the plush carpet. Below, the city pulsed with life, a stark contrast to the stillness within.

At the head of the long table sat Richard Vega, his posture impossibly straight, as if the weight of his impeccable suit could anchor him to reality. His eyes, sharp and calculating, remained fixed on the file before him, not acknowledging Drake's entrance. The perfect coif of his dark hair seemed almost too pristine, like a mask hiding something beneath.

Drake's gaze lingered on Vega, a strange sense of unease creeping over him. Had his colleague's jaw always been so tense? Were those new lines etched around his eyes?

"Cutting it close," Vega's voice cut through the silence, still not looking up. "I was about to start without you."

The words hung in the air, laden with an unspoken tension. Drake's mind raced, searching for the right response. Was this their usual banter, or was there an edge to Vega's tone he'd never noticed before?

"Traffic," Drake offered lamely, sliding into a chair. He studied Vega's face, looking for any hint of... what? Deception? Worry? "Anything I should know before we dive in?"

Vega's eyes flickered up, meeting Drake's gaze for a split second. In that moment, Drake saw something that made his blood run cold – a flicker of guilt, quickly masked by Vega's usual professional demeanor.

"Nothing out of the ordinary," Vega replied smoothly, sliding a document across the table. "Just another day at Miller & Co, isn't it?"

Drake nodded, forcing a smile that didn't reach his eyes. As he reached for the paper, he couldn't shake the feeling that he was missing something crucial, something that could change everything. The conference room suddenly felt too small, too confining, as if the walls themselves were closing in on a truth he wasn't ready to face.

21 - 22

Drake slid into the chair beside him, smirking to mask the unease churning in his gut. "You'd enjoy the spotlight too much." The words felt hollow, rehearsed, as if he were an actor in a play he couldn't quite remember.

Vega's eyes met his, a flicker of something—recognition? fear? —passing between them before it vanished behind his professional facade. "Damn right," he replied, the faintest smirk tugging at his lips. It didn't reach his eyes.

The polished wood of the conference table reflected Drake's distorted image as Vega slid a file across its surface. The rustling papers seemed unnaturally loud in the quiet room, each page turned into a whispered secret.

"Client wants to push for an early settlement," Vega continued, his voice tight with an urgency Drake couldn't quite place. "But we both know that's a terrible idea. If we settle, we lose the chance to set a precedent. This case could define corporate liability in AI."

Drake nodded, his mind racing. The words made sense, yet something felt off, like a painting hung slightly askew. He glanced out the floor-to-ceiling windows, the bustling street below suddenly alien and unfamiliar.

*Why does this feel wrong? * He wondered, a chill creeping up his spine. *We've had this conversation before, haven't we? Or... have we? *

His fingers brushed against the file, hesitating. In that moment, the weight of unseen choices pressed down on him, suffocating in their intensity. Drake forced himself to focus, to play the role expected of him, even as doubt gnawed at the edges of his reality.

23 - 24

Drake's gaze swept over the file, his sharp mind sifting through the legal jargon with practiced ease. The negligence clause jumped out at him, a beacon of opportunity amidst the dense text. He looked up at Vega, their eyes meeting across the polished expanse of the table.

"We emphasize the negligence clause," Drake said, his voice steady despite the lingering unease in his gut. "Point out how they prioritized profits over public safety. Juries won't side with a company cutting corners."

As he spoke, Drake's fingers traced the edge of the file, the tactile sensation grounding him in the present moment. Yet, a part of him felt detached, as if he were watching the scene unfold from afar.

Vega leaned back in his chair, a rare note of approval coloring his tone. "Exactly," he said, his eyes narrowing slightly as he studied Drake. "See? That's why I tolerate you."

The words hung in the air between them, laden with unspoken history. Drake felt the weight of their complicated relationship pressing down on him, a tangle of alliance and mistrust that seemed to stretch across lifetimes.

*How many times have we been here? * Drake wondered, the thought unbidden and unsettling. *How many versions of this conversation have we had? *

He pushed the feeling aside, forcing a wry smile. "High praise indeed," Drake quipped, his tone light but his eyes searching Vega's face for... something. A clue, a tell, anything to explain the persistent sense of déjà vu that clung to him like a shroud.

25 - 26

Drake chuckled; the sound hollow even to his own ears. "Good to know I'm more than just a pretty face," he said, his attempt at levity falling flat in the charged atmosphere of the conference room.

The words felt scripted, as if he'd uttered them a thousand times before. Drake's gaze drifted to the window, where the city sprawled beneath them, a maze of glass and steel that suddenly seemed alien and overwhelming. His reflection stared back at him; a ghost superimposed over the bustling metropolis.

Vega leaned back in his chair, the leather creaking softly. The sound drew Drake's attention back to his colleague, and he found himself caught in Vega's penetrating stare. There was something in those eyes—a flicker of recognition, perhaps, or a hint of shared unease—that sent a chill down Drake's spine.

"You alright?" Vega asked, his voice uncharacteristically soft. "You seem... off."

The question hung in the air, heavy with implications, Drake couldn't quite grasp. He opened his mouth to respond, but the words caught in his throat. How could he explain the persistent fog of unreality that clung to his thoughts? The nagging sensation that this moment—this entire life—was somehow wrong?

Instead, Drake forced a smile, his fingers drumming an anxious rhythm on the polished wood of the conference table. "Just a long night," he lied, the taste of deceit bitter on his tongue. "Nothing a strong coffee won't fix."

But even as he spoke, Drake couldn't shake the feeling that he was missing something crucial. That beneath the veneer of this perfect life—successful career, loving family—lurked a truth too terrible to face.

27 - 28

Drake frowned, caught off guard by Vega's persistent scrutiny. "Off?" he echoed, his voice barely above a whisper. The word hung in the air, laden with unspoken tension.

His mind raced, grasping for an explanation that would satisfy Vega without revealing the turmoil churning beneath the surface. How could he articulate the sense of displacement that had plagued him all morning? The eerie familiarity of scenes he couldn't possibly have witnessed before?

Vega's piercing gaze bore into him, as if trying to peel away layers of carefully constructed normalcy. "Yeah," he said, leaning forward slightly. "Like you've seen a ghost or something."

The phrase sent a jolt through Drake's system, his heart hammering against his ribcage. For a fleeting moment, he saw not Vega's face, but a flickering image of... himself? Older, haunted, desperate. It vanished as quickly as it had appeared, leaving Drake reeling.

He gripped the edge of the table, knuckles white with the effort of maintaining composure. "I..." he began, then faltered. How could he explain what he didn't understand himself? The weight of unremembered guilt, the shadow of a life unlived?

Drake swallowed hard, forcing himself to meet Vega's eyes. "Just a strange dream," he lied, the words tasting like ash in his mouth. "Nothing more."

But even as he spoke, a part of him wondered if perhaps he was the ghost – a spectral intruder in a life that didn't truly belong to him.

29 - 30

Drake's fingers tapped a restless rhythm on the polished conference table, his mind racing to dispel the lingering unease. "Long night," he offered with a forced smile, the lie settling uncomfortably on his tongue. "Let's focus on the case."

Vega's eyes narrowed, but he nodded, returning his attention to the files spread before them. As they delved into legal strategies, Drake found himself grateful for the familiar terrain of corporate law, a lifeline amidst the surreal undercurrent of his day.

Hours slipped by in a blur of depositions and client calls. The satisfaction of a productive workday gradually pushed back the shadows of uncertainty, though they never fully retreated. As Drake packed his briefcase, the setting sun cast long fingers of golden light across his office, reminding him of his dinner plans.

"Heading out to meet Linda and Harrison," he called to Sarah as he strode past her desk. She responded with a cheerful wave, her normalcy a balm to his frayed nerves.

The crisp evening air carried hints of salt and brine as Drake made his way to The Lighthouse. The cozy seafood restaurant sat perched on the edge of the bay, its windows offering sweeping views of the water. As he approached, Drake caught sight of Linda and Harrison already seated at their usual table.

"There's my two favorite people," Drake announced, sliding into his seat. Linda's blue eyes sparkled as she reached across to squeeze his hand, while Harrison offered a playful eye roll.

"Geez, Dad, tone down the cheese factor," Harrison quipped, but his grin betrayed his affection.

Drake chuckled, drinking in the sight of his family. The nagging sense of wrongness that had plagued him all day seemed to recede in their presence. And yet... a faint whisper of unease persisted, like a discordant note in an otherwise perfect melody.

"How was your day, honey?" Linda asked, her voice warm and familiar.

Drake hesitated, weighing his response. Should he burden them with his inexplicable feelings of displacement? No, he decided. This moment was too precious to taint with his own inner turmoil.

"Productive," he replied instead, forcing a lightness into his tone. "Though not nearly as exciting as whatever scheme I'm sure Harrison cooked up at school today."

As Harrison launched into an animated tale of classroom hijinks, Drake found himself studying his son's face. The boy's enthusiasm was infectious, his brown eyes alight with mischief. And yet, a part of Drake couldn't shake the feeling that he was seeing Harrison through a veil – as if this vibrant, living version of his son was somehow... less real than another he couldn't quite recall.

Drake shook his head, willing away the unsettling thoughts. He focused on the menu, on the comforting aroma of garlic and herbs wafting from the kitchen, on the gentle lapping of waves against the pier outside. This was his life, his family. Real and solid and present.

And if a small voice in the back of his mind whispered that something wasn't quite right, well... he would just have to ignore it.

31 - 32

The soft clink of cutlery against China filled the air as their meals arrived, steaming plates of seafood perfection laid before them. Drake inhaled deeply, allowing the rich aromas to ground him in the present moment.

"This place always gets it right," Linda said, her fingers brushing against Drake's across the table. The warm smile she gave him made the faint tension in his chest ease, if only slightly. Her blue eyes sparkled in the soft lighting, a beacon of comfort amidst his inner turmoil.

Drake squeezed her hand gently, savoring the familiar softness of her skin. "Always," he agreed, his voice low and intimate. He paused, studying the lines of her face, committing every detail to memory. "Good to slow down, isn't it?"

As the words left his lips, a peculiar sense of déjà vu washed over him. Had they had this exact conversation before? In this very restaurant? Drake's brow furrowed imperceptibly as he wrestled with the sensation.

Linda's thumb traced small circles on the back of his hand, drawing him back to the present. "You seem distracted, love," she murmured, concern etching her features. "Is everything alright?"

Drake hesitated, torn between honesty and the desire to preserve this moment of apparent normalcy. How could he explain the gnawing feeling that something fundamental was... off? That this perfect family dinner felt both achingly familiar and oddly hollow?

"Just... savoring the moment," he finally replied, offering a smile that didn't quite reach his eyes. He lifted his glass, the amber liquid within catching the light. "To family," he toasted, pushing down the inexplicable sense of loss that threatened to overwhelm him.

33 - 34

Harrison's groan cut through Drake's reverie, the teenager's face contorting in exaggerated disgust. "You two are being mushy again," he interjected, pulling a face that was equal parts amusement and teenage rebellion. "I'm begging you, stop."

Drake felt a rush of affection for his son, mixed with a strange, bittersweet ache he couldn't quite place. Harrison's unruly blonde hair fell across his forehead, reminding Drake of countless mornings spent urging the boy to use a comb. The thought brought a lump to his throat.

Linda's laughter, warm and melodious, filled the air. She rolled her eyes, her expression a perfect blend of exasperation and fondness. "Teenagers," she said, shaking her head. The word carried layers of meaning – love, frustration, and a hint of nostalgia for simpler times.

"What?" Harrison protested; his brown eyes wide with feigned innocence. "I'm just trying to protect my delicate sensibilities."

Drake chuckled, but something about the moment felt fragile, as if it might shatter at any second. He studied Harrison's face, drinking in every detail. Had his son always had that tiny scar above his left eyebrow? Why did it feel so important to remember?

"Your delicate sensibilities, huh?" Drake managed, forcing levity into his voice. "I seem to recall a certain someone's colorful language when he stubbed his toe this morning."

Harrison grinned sheepishly, and for a fleeting instant, Drake saw the little boy he once was, gap-toothed and mischievous. The image sent a jolt of panic through him, though he couldn't fathom why.

35 - 36

The waiter approached, notepad in hand, and Drake welcomed the distraction from his unsettling thoughts.

"The usual for everyone?" Linda asked, her eyes scanning the familiar menu.

Drake nodded, forcing a smile. "Fried calamari to start, then clam chowder for me."

"Crab cakes," Harrison chimed in, his voice brimming with anticipation. "And extra lemon, please."

As the waiter jotted down their order, Drake's gaze drifted to the window. The bay stretched out before them, its waters painted in hues of orange and pink by the setting sun. It was beautiful, serene – and yet, a nagging sense of unease persisted.

"So, Harry," Linda began, leaning forward with interest, "how was school today? Any exciting news?"

Harrison's eyes lit up, a grin spreading across his face. "Oh man, you won't believe what Mike did in Mr. Stevenson's class!"

As Harrison launched into his tale, his hands gesticulating wildly, Drake found himself hanging on every word. The story itself – something about a well-timed whoopee cushion and an oblivious substitute teacher – wasn't particularly remarkable. But Harrison's animated retelling, the way his eyes sparkled with mischief, the infectious laughter that punctuated his words – it all felt precious beyond measure.

Drake glanced at Linda, catching her eye. They exchanged a look of amused exasperation, a silent conversation passing between them. How many times had they sat in the principal's office, trying to keep straight faces while being informed of their son's latest escapade?

"And then," Harrison continued, barely pausing for breath, "Mr. Stevenson walks in right as the sub is yelling at Mike, and he just loses it!"

Drake chuckled, shaking his head. "I hope you weren't involved in this mastermind plan, Harry."

"Me?" Harrison placed a hand over his heart, the picture of wounded innocence. "I would never."

Linda snorted, reaching out to ruffle Harrison's hair. "Sure, sweetie. We believe you."

As their food arrived, steam rising invitingly from the plates, Drake was struck by how perfect everything felt. The warmth of the restaurant, the gentle murmur of conversation around them, the love evident in every glance and gesture between his family members – it was everything he could have ever wanted.

And yet...

A chill ran down Drake's spine, unbidden and inexplicable. He looked at Linda, radiant in the soft lighting, then at Harrison, happily digging into his crab cakes. Why did he suddenly feel as though he was trying to memorize their faces? Why did the contentment of the moment feel so fragile, so fleeting?

"Drake?" Linda's voice cut through his reverie, concern evident in her tone. "Is everything okay?"

He forced a smile, pushing the disquiet aside. "Everything's perfect," he replied, even as a voice in the back of his mind whispered that it was all too perfect, too good to be true.

37 - 38

The crab cake glistened on Harrison's fork, a last remnant of laughter still lighting his eyes. As he popped it into his mouth, Drake watched his son's face transform in an instant, mirth dissolving into confusion, then panic. The sharp cough that followed pierced the air like a gunshot, shattering the comfortable ambiance.

Linda's voice caught mid-sentence; her fingers frozen around her wine glass. "Harrison?" she breathed, her tone laced with a mother's intuition that something was terribly wrong.

Drake's heart lurched as Harrison's hands flew to his throat, his eyes wide with terror. The boy's wheezing filled the silence, each desperate gasp for air like a knife in Drake's chest.

"Honey, are you—" Linda's words hung unfinished, fear stealing her voice.

Time seemed to slow, stretching like taffy as Drake's mind raced. This can't be happening. We were just laughing. Everything was perfect. His thoughts whirled, a maelstrom of disbelief and horror.

"Harrison!" Drake found himself on his feet, though he had no memory of standing. "Can you breathe? Try to cough!"

But Harrison's face was rapidly turning an alarming shade of red, his movements growing more frantic with each passing second. Drake's legal training, his years of maintaining composure in high-pressure situations, all of it evaporated in the face of his son's distress.

"Linda, get help!" The words tore from his throat, raw and urgent. As Linda scrambled for her phone, Drake moved around the table, his mind a cacophony of half-formed thoughts. I should know what to do. Why can't I remember? God, please, not my boy. Not like this.

39 - 40

Drake reached Harrison's side, his hands trembling as he gripped his son's shoulders. "Harrison! Are you choking?" he demanded, fighting to keep his voice steady despite the panic clawing at his chest.

Harrison's frantic nod sent a wave of dread crashing over Drake. The boy's movements were jerky, panicked, his eyes wide with a fear that mirrored Drake's own.

"Okay, buddy, I'm here. We're going to fix this," Drake said, his words as much for himself as for Harrison. He positioned himself behind his son, wrapping his arms around the boy's middle. As he prepared to perform the Heimlich maneuver, a strange sense of déjà vu washed over him. Have I done this before? In another life, another time?

The thought vanished as quickly as it had come, replaced by a laser focus on the task at hand. "Come on, Harrison," Drake muttered, his voice thick with emotion. "Stay with me."

As he began the upward thrusts, Drake's mind raced. This isn't right. We were supposed to have more time. I was supposed to fix everything. The weight of his failures, both in this world and others he couldn't quite remember, pressed down on him.

"Please," he whispered, his actions growing more desperate with each failed attempt. "I can't lose you. Not again."

41 - 42

"Linda, call 911!" Drake's voice cut through the growing commotion in the restaurant, sharp and commanding. The words tasted bitter on his tongue, a familiar desperation clawing at his throat. He'd uttered these same words before, hadn't he? In another time, another place? The thought flickered and faded, lost in the urgency of the moment.

Linda's face, pale and drawn, swam in his vision as she fumbled for her phone. Her trembling fingers seemed to move in slow motion, each second stretching into eternity. Drake's heart thundered in his chest, a relentless drumbeat of fear and helplessness.

"Hurry," he urged, his voice barely above a whisper. The weight of Harrison's body against him felt both impossibly heavy and terrifyingly fragile. How many times have I held him like this? Drake wondered, a strange sense of déjà vu washing over him once more.

Linda's voice, usually a source of comfort, now quavered with panic as she spoke into the phone. "Yes! My son—he's choking! We're at The Lighthouse on Pier 12. Please hurry!"

The words echoed in Drake's mind, each syllable a hammer blow against his soul. He'd failed to protect his son, failed to prevent this moment. The guilt threatened to overwhelm him, but he pushed it aside, focusing on the rhythmic motions of the Heimlich maneuver.

"Stay with us, Harrison," Drake murmured, his actions growing more desperate with each passing second. "We're not losing you. Not this time." The words slipped out unbidden, carrying a weight he couldn't quite understand.

43 - 44

Drake's arms tightened around Harrison's middle, muscles straining as he thrust upward with practiced precision. The motion felt hauntingly familiar, as if he'd performed it countless times before. "Come on, buddy. Breathe!" he urged, his voice cracking with desperation.

Harrison's body jerked with each thrust, but the obstruction remained stubbornly lodged. Drake's mind raced, fragmented memories of medical training he couldn't recall receiving flashing through his consciousness.

"Harrison, please," Drake whispered, his son's name a prayer on his lips. "You have to fight. You have to stay."

The seconds stretched into what felt like hours, each moment a lifetime of anguish. Drake's arms began to ache, but he refused to relent. He couldn't shake the feeling that this moment was pivotal, that everything hinged on Harrison's survival.

"It's not working," Linda sobbed from somewhere behind him. Her words cut through Drake like a knife, but he couldn't afford to lose focus.

With a heavy heart, Drake realized he needed to change tactics. He lowered Harrison gently to the floor, positioning him on his back. "Stay with me! Stay with me, Harrison!" Drake pleaded, his hands moving to his son's chest to begin CPR.

As he started compressions, Drake's world narrowed to the rhythmic motion of his hands and the silent plea echoing in his mind. Please, not again. Not this time. The thought confused him, but he pushed it aside, focusing solely on keeping his son alive.

45 - 46

Linda's anguished cries pierced the air, her voice cracking as she pleaded into the phone. "Please, hurry! My son... he's not breathing!" The desperation in her tone clawed at Drake's heart, each word a reminder of the precious seconds slipping away.

The restaurant had fallen eerily silent, the usual clatter of dishes and hum of conversation replaced by the suffocating weight of collectively held breath. Drake could feel the eyes of strangers boring into him, their gazes a mix of horror and morbid fascination.

"Come on, Harry," Drake murmured, his hands never ceasing their rhythmic compressions. "You're stronger than this. Fight, damn it!"

Harrison's body lay motionless beneath Drake's palms, his once-animated face now slack and ashen. Those bright brown eyes that had sparkled with mischief just moments ago were now half-lidded and vacant, staring unseeing at the ceiling.

A memory flashed unbidden through Drake's mind - Harrison as a toddler, giggling as he chased bubbles in their backyard. The contrast between that vibrant child and the lifeless form before him was almost too much to bear.

"Linda," Drake called out, his voice strained. "Any word on the ambulance?"

"They... they say five minutes," Linda choked out between sobs. "Drake, please... save our boy!"

Five minutes. An eternity. Drake's arms burned with exertion, but he refused to slow his efforts. "You hear that, Harry?" he said, forcing a note of optimism into his voice. "Help's coming. Just hang on a little longer."

As Harrison's thrashing faded to stillness, a chill ran down Drake's spine. This felt wrong, impossibly wrong, like a nightmare he couldn't shake. He'd experienced loss before, but this... this was different. This felt like a cruel joke, a perversion of the perfect life he'd been living.

"No," Drake whispered, redoubling his efforts. "This isn't how it ends. Not for you, Harry. Not like this."

47 - 48

Drake's whisper crescendo into a desperate plea. "No," he repeated, his voice breaking as a wave of disbelief crashed over him. "No, no, no!"

The words echoed hollowly in the stunned silence of the restaurant. Drake's hands trembled as he continued compressions, each one a futile attempt to breathe life back into his son. His mind raced, grasping at straws, searching for some way to undo this nightmare.

"This can't be real," he thought, a cold sweat beading on his brow. "We were laughing, joking... how did we end up here?"

Linda's anguished cry pierced the air as she collapsed to her knees beside them. Her blonde hair fell forward, obscuring her face as she reached out with shaking hands to touch Harrison's arm.

"My baby," she sobbed, her voice raw with grief. "Please, God, not my baby."

Drake's eyes burned with unshed tears as he watched his wife crumble. The warmth of the evening—the joy, the laughter, the love—shattered like glass around them, leaving behind a hollow, deafening silence.

"Linda," Drake managed, his voice barely above a whisper. "I... I don't know what to do."

For a fleeting moment, as his gaze met Linda's tear-filled eyes, Drake felt a strange sense of displacement. It was as if he'd lived this moment before, in another life, another reality. The feeling vanished as quickly as it had come, leaving behind only the crushing weight of their shared grief.

49 - 49

Drake clutched Harrison's lifeless body, his tears falling onto his son's pale face. The world around him blurred, the once-cozy restaurant fading into a haze of muted colors and distant sounds. His chest heaved with each ragged breath, the pain of loss cutting deeper than any physical wound.

"Harrison," he choked out, cradling his son's head. "I'm sorry. I'm so sorry."

As he held his boy, a memory flickered in Drake's mind—a fleeting image of another tragedy, another loss. It felt both foreign and achingly familiar, like a half-remembered dream.

Linda's hand found his shoulder, her touch trembling. "Drake," she whispered, her voice thick with grief. "What do we do now?"

He looked up at her, his vision swimming. "I don't know," he admitted, the words tasting bitter on his tongue. "This feels... wrong. Like it shouldn't be happening."

A wave of dizziness washed over him, and for a moment, the restaurant seemed to shift and waver, as if reality itself was uncertain. Drake blinked hard, trying to clear his vision.

"Maybe," he thought, a desperate hope kindling in his chest, "this isn't real. Maybe I can fix this."

But as he gazed down at Harrison's still face, the cruel reality of their loss settled over him like a shroud. In that moment, the illusion of perfection—their happy family, their successful lives—dissolved into irreparable loss.

"We need to call someone," Drake said aloud, his lawyer's mind grasping for structure in the chaos. "We need to... to make arrangements."

The words felt hollow, inadequate in the face of their tragedy. Yet even as he spoke them, a part of Drake rebelled against the finality they implied. Something deep within him whispered that this wasn't the end—that there had to be more to the story.

Awakening from a Dream

1 -2 The darkness shattered as Drake's eyes flew open, his heart pounding against his ribs like a caged animal. Sweat clung to his skin, a cold reminder of the nightmare that still lingered at the edges of his consciousness. He gasped for air, the taste of fear bitter on his tongue.

"Linda?" he croaked, his voice hoarse and unfamiliar.

Drake's trembling hand reached out, grasping at the empty space beside him. The sheets were cold, untouched. A wave of panic washed over him as the memories of the previous night crashed through his mind.

Harrison. The restaurant. The choking. The lifeless body in his arms.

"No, no, no," Drake muttered, pushing himself up. His eyes darted around the dim room, searching for any sign of his wife. The silence that greeted him was deafening.

He swung his legs over the side of the bed, his muscles protesting as he stood. The room tilted for a moment, and Drake steadied himself against the nightstand.

How could this be real? he thought, his mind reeling. Just yesterday, we were all together. Happy. Alive.

"Linda?" he called out again, louder this time. His voice echoed through the empty house, mocking him with its hollowness.

Drake stumbled towards the door, his hands shaking as he fumbled with the handle. He had to find her. He had to know if it was all just a terrible dream.

As he stepped into the hallway, the weight of reality pressed down on him. The house felt different, colder somehow. The absence of Harrison's laughter, of Linda's gentle humming, was palpable.

"Please," Drake whispered to the silent walls, "please let them be here."

But deep down, he knew. The grief that coiled in his chest, the emptiness that threatened to swallow him whole – it was all too real. Drake leaned against the wall, his legs suddenly unable to support him.

"I'm sorry," he choked out, tears blurring his vision. "I'm so sorry, Harrison. I should have saved you."

The words hung in the air, unanswered. Drake closed his eyes, willing himself to wake up from this nightmare. But when he opened them again, nothing had changed. The cold, harsh reality remained.

He was alone.

3 - 4

A soft rustle beside him jolted Drake from his spiral of despair. Linda stirred; her golden hair splayed across the pillow like a halo. Her eyes fluttered open, still heavy with sleep.

"Morning, hon," she murmured, her voice husky. "You, okay? You look like you've seen a ghost."

Drake's breath caught in his throat. He stared at Linda, unable to reconcile her presence with the vivid memory of Harrison's lifeless body. His heart raced, torn between overwhelming relief and paralyzing confusion.

"I... you're here," he managed, his voice barely above a whisper. "But Harrison..."

Linda's brow furrowed with concern. "Drake? What about Harrison?"

Before he could respond, the sound of footsteps in the hallway froze him in place. The bedroom door swung open, and there stood Harrison, lanky and tousled, looking every bit the teenager he was.

"You two are slow," Harrison announced, leaning against the doorframe. "I'm starving. Can we please get some breakfast going?"

Drake's mind reeled. How could this be? The choking, the panic, the devastating loss – it had all felt so real. Yet here they were, his family, alive and well. He struggled to form words, caught between the lingering terror of his nightmare and the surreal normalcy of the moment.

"Dad?" Harrison's voice cut through Drake's thoughts. "You look weird. Did you have another one of those crazy dreams or something?"

Drake swallowed hard, forcing a smile. "Yeah, kiddo. Just a dream. Nothing to worry about."

But as he met Linda's concerned gaze, Drake couldn't shake the feeling that something was terribly, inexplicably wrong. The vividness of his "dream" clung to him like a second skin, whispering doubts into his ear. What if this wasn't real? What if he was trapped in some cruel illusion?

"I'll be down in a minute," he said, his voice steadier than he felt. "Go on, start without me."

As Harrison shrugged and headed downstairs, Drake turned to Linda, searching her face for any sign that she understood his turmoil. But all he saw was loving concern, painfully normal and achingly real.

5 - 6

Drake's relief surged through him like a tidal wave, overwhelming his senses. Without a word, he lunged forward, wrapping his arms around Harrison in a fierce embrace. The boy's lanky frame stiffened in surprise, caught off guard by his father's sudden display of emotion.

"Dad?" Harrison's muffled voice came from within the tight hug. "What's going on?"

Drake couldn't speak. He simply held on, breathing in the scent of his son's shampoo, feeling the warmth of his living, breathing body. Tears pricked at the corners of his eyes, and he blinked them back furiously.

Linda sat up in bed, her brow furrowed with concern. "Drake? Honey, is everything alright?"

Finally, Drake found his voice. It came out hoarse and thick with emotion. "I just... I love you, Harrison. Both of you. So much."

He loosened his grip slightly, allowing Harrison to pull back and look at him. The boy's wide brown eyes were filled with confusion and a hint of worry.

"I love you too, Dad," Harrison said slowly, "but you're kind of freaking me out here."

Drake forced a chuckle, trying to lighten the mood. "Sorry, kiddo. I guess I just woke up feeling extra grateful today."

As he spoke, his mind raced. The nightmare felt so real, yet here they were. Safe. Alive. But why did everything feel so... familiar? He pushed the thought aside, focusing on the present moment, on his family's bewildered faces.

"How about we go make that breakfast?" Drake suggested, desperate for normalcy. "I'm thinking pancakes. Extra chocolate chips."

Harrison's face lit up; his earlier confusion forgotten. "Now you're talking! Race you to the kitchen!"

As his son dashed out of the room, Drake turned to Linda, seeing the questions in her eyes. He leaned in, kissing her softly. "I'm okay," he whispered, wishing he believed it himself. "Just a rough night. Let's go feed our boy."

7 - 8

Harrison's footsteps echoed down the hallway, but Drake remained rooted to the spot, his heart still racing. The vivid nightmare clung to him like a shroud, the image of Harrison choking seared into his mind. He inhaled deeply, trying to ground himself in the present moment.

Harrison poked his head back into the room, his unruly blonde hair flopping over his forehead. "Dad, you okay? You're acting... weird."

Drake's throat tightened. The concern in his son's voice was palpable, a stark contrast to the lifeless form he'd held in his dreams. He forced a smile, willing his voice to remain steady.

"I'm fine. Just—just glad to see you, kiddo."

The words felt inadequate, failing to convey the tumult of emotions swirling within him. Relief, fear, confusion—they all battled for dominance. Drake's mind raced, grappling with the surreal sensation of déjà vu that permeated every interaction.

Harrison tilted his head, his brown eyes narrowing slightly. "If you say so," he shrugged, but the doubt in his voice was evident. "You coming for pancakes or what?"

Drake nodded, finally finding the strength to move. As he followed his son out of the room, he couldn't shake the feeling that something was profoundly wrong. The normalcy of the morning felt like a thin veneer, barely concealing a darker truth lurking beneath the surface.

9 - 10

Drake stepped into the kitchen, his senses immediately assaulted by the familiar aroma of coffee and pancakes. Linda stood at the stove, her back to him, spatula in hand. The scene before him was so achingly normal, yet it sent a chill down his spine.

"Morning, sleepyhead," Linda chirped, turning to flash him a smile. "I was beginning to think you'd sleep through breakfast."

Drake's breath caught in his throat. Her words, her tone, even the way she tilted her head—it was all exactly as it had been yesterday. Or had it been yesterday? The line between dream and reality blurred, leaving him disoriented.

"I... yeah, sorry," he managed, lowering himself into a chair at the table. His eyes darted around the kitchen, cataloging every detail. The clock on the wall showed 7:45 AM. The same time as before.

Harrison slid into the seat across from him, already reaching for the syrup. "Mom, can you pick me up at Mike's after school? His car's going in the shop, and we've got that group project to finish."

Drake's head snapped up, a cold dread settling in his stomach. This conversation—they'd had it before. Every word, every inflection was identical. He gripped the edge of the table, his knuckles turning white.

"Drake?" Linda's voice cut through his spiraling thoughts. "You look pale. Are you feeling alright?"

He forced himself to meet her concerned gaze, struggling to keep his voice steady. "I'm fine. Just... didn't sleep well."

As Linda set a plate of pancakes in front of him, Drake's mind raced. How was this possible? Was he losing his grip on reality, or was something far more sinister at play? The weight of his past mistakes pressed down on him, a constant reminder of the price of failure.

"You've been working too hard," Linda said softly, squeezing his shoulder. "Maybe you should take a day off?"

Drake shook his head, attempting a wan smile. "No, I'll be okay. Just need some coffee."

As he mechanically went through the motions of eating breakfast, Drake's thoughts churned. If this truly was a repeat of yesterday, what did it mean? And more importantly, how could he prevent the tragedy that loomed on the horizon?

11 - 12

The kitchen filled with Linda's gentle humming, a melody that twined with the sizzle of bacon and the rich aroma of coffee. Drake's eyes followed her movements, drinking in every detail as if seeing her for the first time. Her blonde hair caught the morning light, creating a soft halo around her face as she swayed to her own tune.

Harrison slouched into the room; his lanky frame still sleep-rumpled. He slumped into a chair, eyeing the stack of pancakes with teenage hunger.

"Morning, Harry," Linda chirped, ruffling his hair as she passed.

Harrison's nose wrinkled in disgust. "Mom, seriously? I've told you a million times, it's Harrison. Harry makes me sound like I'm five."

Drake's breath caught in his throat. The words were identical, down to the exasperated sigh that followed. He gripped his coffee mug tighter, willing his hands not to shake.

"Whatever you say, sweetheart," Linda replied with a fond smile.

Harrison rolled his eyes, then turned to Drake. "Hey, Dad? Can I borrow the car tonight? Mike needs a ride to soccer practice after school. His car's in the shop, and we've got that group project to finish."

The familiar words hit Drake like a physical blow. He stared at his son, mind reeling. How could he respond? Should he change things? What if altering the course of events made everything worse?

"Dad?" Harrison prompted, brow furrowing. "You okay?"

Drake swallowed hard. "I... I'll think about it, Harrison. We'll talk later, alright?"

Harrison shrugged, returning his attention to his breakfast. "Sure, whatever."

As the morning routine continued to unfold with eerie precision, Drake's thoughts raced. Was he trapped in some kind of time loop? Or had yesterday's tragedy simply been a vivid, horrifying dream? The weight of uncertainty pressed down on him, making each breath a conscious effort.

He watched Linda and Harrison, their familiar banter a cruel echo of happiness. How could he protect them from whatever was coming? The possibilities — and the potential consequences — were overwhelming.

13 - 14

The acrid smell of burning toast jolted Drake from his spiraling thoughts. He flinched, anticipating the sound before it even occurred. Right on cue, Linda let out a frustrated groan.

"Oh, for heaven's sake!" she exclaimed, rushing to the toaster. "I can't believe I forgot about it again."

Drake's stomach churned as he watched her wave away the thin wisps of smoke. The scene was playing out exactly as it had before, down to the smallest detail. He gripped the edge of the kitchen counter, his knuckles turning white.

"You okay, Dad?" Harrison asked, eyeing him with concern. "You look like you've seen a ghost."

Drake forced a weak smile. "I'm fine, kiddo. Just... didn't sleep well last night."

Linda turned to him, her brow furrowed. "Another nightmare?"

He nodded, unable to find the words to explain the magnitude of what he was experiencing. How could he possibly convey the bone-deep dread that was settling into his very core?

"Maybe you should take the day off," Linda suggested, placing a comforting hand on his arm. "You've been working too hard lately."

Drake shook his head, his mind racing. "No, I... I'll be fine. It's just déjà vu, that's all."

But even as the words left his mouth, he knew it was more than that. The vivid recollection of Harrison choking, of Linda's panicked screams, felt too real to dismiss. Yet here they were, alive and well, oblivious to the tragedy that had unfolded – or hadn't unfolded – mere hours ago.

"Déjà vu, huh?" Harrison smirked. "Maybe you're psychic now, Dad. Quick, what am I thinking?"

Drake looked at his son, a lump forming in his throat. "That you hope I'll let you borrow the car tonight," he answered quietly.

Harrison's eyes widened. "Whoa, that's crazy! How did you know?"

"Lucky guess," Drake mumbled, his heart pounding. He took a deep breath, trying to center himself. It's just stress, he thought. Just a vivid nightmare and an overactive imagination. Nothing more.

But as he watched his family continue their morning routine, blissfully unaware of his inner turmoil, Drake couldn't shake the feeling that something was terribly, inexplicably wrong. And he had no idea how to fix it.

15 - 16

Drake stepped into the bustling office, the familiar scent of coffee and printer toner assaulting his senses. His colleagues' voices blended into a cacophony of déjà vu, each word and gesture a haunting echo of yesterday – or was it today?

He paused at his desk, fingers grazing the smooth surface. The same stack of files, the same half-empty mug of cold coffee. Even the haphazard arrangement of sticky notes seemed unchanged.

"Morning, Drake," called out Tom from across the room. "Ready for the Hendricks deposition?"

Drake's breath caught in his throat. He knew, with chilling certainty, exactly how Tom would continue.

"It's at two, right?" Drake asked, his voice barely above a whisper.

Tom nodded, eyebrows raised. "Yeah, how'd you... oh, right. I must've mentioned it yesterday."

But you didn't, Drake thought, a cold sweat breaking out on his forehead. I'm living this day again.

He sank into his chair, mind reeling. What if it wasn't a dream? What if Harrison had really...? No. He couldn't bear to finish the thought.

"You okay, man?" Tom asked, concern etching his features. "You look like you've seen a ghost."

Drake forced a wan smile. "Just... didn't sleep well. Strange dreams."

As Tom walked away, Drake's gaze fell on the framed photo of Linda and Harrison on his desk. Their smiling faces mocked him, a reminder of what he'd lost – or hadn't lost. The boundaries of reality seemed to blur with each passing moment.

He reached for his phone, fingers hovering over Linda's number. Should he call? Make sure they were both still...? No. They were fine. They had to be.

"Get it together, Miller," he muttered to himself, running a hand through his disheveled hair. "Focus on work. One step at a time."

But as he opened the first file, the words swam before his eyes, indistinguishable from the ones he'd read yesterday. Or today. He couldn't be sure anymore.

17 - 18

A soft knock at his office door pulled Drake from his spiraling thoughts. Sarah, his assistant, entered with a stack of folders tucked under her arm. Her familiar floral perfume wafted through the air, eerily reminiscent of yesterday's interaction.

"Morning, Mr. Miller," she said, her voice chipper. "I've got the Parker case notes for you. Oh, and Mr. Vega is waiting in the conference room."

Drake's stomach clenched. He'd been dreading this moment, praying it wouldn't unfold as it had before. "Thanks, Sarah," he managed, his voice slightly strained.

As he stood, smoothing his tie, Sarah tilted her head. "Everything alright, sir? You look a bit pale."

"Fine," Drake lied, forcing a smile that didn't reach his eyes. "Just... a long night."

He made his way to the conference room, each step feeling heavier than the last. The polished wood of the door gleamed under the fluorescent lights, and for a moment, Drake hesitated, his hand hovering over the handle. Taking a deep breath, he steeled himself and entered.

Richard Vega sat at the far end of the table; his lean frame hunched over a spread of documents. As Drake entered, Vega glanced up, a smirk playing at the corners of his mouth.

"Well, well," Vega drawled, leaning back in his chair. "Look who finally decided to grace us with his presence. Late night, Drake? Or just losing your touch?"

The words hit Drake like a physical blow. Identical to yesterday. Or today. He swallowed hard, fighting to maintain his composure. "Traffic," he muttered, sliding into a seat across from Vega.

Vega's dark eyes narrowed, studying Drake with an intensity that made him squirm. "You sure you're alright, Miller? You look like you've seen a ghost."

Drake's mind raced. Should he confide in Vega? Tell him about the impossible loop he seemed to be trapped in? No. That way lay madness. Instead, he forced his features into a mask of professional detachment.

"I'm fine," Drake insisted, his voice steadier than he felt. "Let's focus on the case, shall we?"

19 - 20

Drake reached for the case file, his fingers brushing against the cool, glossy surface of the folder. As he opened it, the familiar rustle of papers filled the air, each document seeming to whisper secrets he'd already heard.

"So, the Parker case," Vega began, his voice cutting through Drake's unsettling thoughts. "We've got the witness statements from the neighbors, but there's still the matter of the missing security footage."

Drake nodded mechanically, his mind reeling as Vega's words echoed those from yesterday's meeting with eerie precision. He found himself mouthing along silently, anticipating each point before it was made.

"Drake?" Vega's sharp tone snapped him back to attention. "You with me here?"

"Yeah, sorry," Drake mumbled, rubbing his temples. "Go on."

As Vega continued his analysis, Drake's awareness split. Part of him engaged in the discussion, offering insights and asking questions, while another part observed from a distance, noting with growing unease how each exchange unfolded exactly as before.

"What about the alibi?" Drake heard himself ask, the words leaving his lips before he could stop them. "It seems too convenient."

Vega leaned forward, his eyes glinting with interest. "Funny you should mention that. I was thinking the same thing."

A chill ran down Drake's spine. The sense of déjà vu intensified, transforming from a vague unease into a suffocating certainty. Every word, every gesture, every subtle shift in Vega's expression – it was all a perfect recreation of yesterday's meeting. Yet somehow different.

As the discussion progressed, Drake felt increasingly detached from reality. His responses became automatic, his mind grappling with the impossible situation he found himself in.

"Drake," Vega's voice cut through his thoughts once more, concern etched on his face. "You sure you're okay? You seem... off."

Drake met Vega's gaze, searching for any sign that his colleague sensed the wrongness of their situation. But Vega's expression remained unchanged, showing only mild concern.

"I'm fine," Drake lied, his voice hollow even to his own ears. "Just... didn't sleep well last night."

As Vega nodded and returned to the case details, Drake's mind raced. How could he be the only one aware of this impossible repetition? And more importantly, how could he break free from it?

21 - 22

Drake closed his eyes, inhaling deeply. The scent of stale coffee and paper files filled his nostrils, grounding him in the present moment. He ran a hand through his disheveled hair, willing the fog of confusion to dissipate.

"It's just stress," he muttered under his breath, too low for Vega to hear. "Nothing more than an overactive imagination."

Opening his eyes, Drake forced himself to focus on the case files spread before him. He traced the edge of a photograph with his fingertip, the tactile sensation helping to quiet the cacophony of doubts in his mind.

"Let's take it from the top," Drake said, his voice steadier than he felt. "We might've missed something."

As they delved back into the details, Drake pushed aside the nagging sense of familiarity. He attributed the eerie sensations to burnout, to the vivid nightmare that still clung to the edges of his consciousness. Yet, even as he reasoned with himself, a part of him remained unconvinced.

Hours later, Drake found himself seated at a table in the dimly lit seafood restaurant. The clink of cutlery and the low murmur of conversation surrounded him, but he struggled to focus on the present moment.

"Earth to Dad," Harrison's voice cut through his reverie. "You going to order, or are you planning to photosynthesize?"

Drake blinked, realizing he'd been staring blankly at the menu. "Sorry, kiddo. Just... lost in thought."

Linda reached across the table, her fingers brushing his arm. "Everything okay, honey? You've been distracted all evening."

Drake forced a smile, trying to ignore the way his heart clenched at the sight of her. "I'm fine. Just a long day at work."

As he scanned the menu, Drake couldn't shake the feeling that he'd experienced this moment before. The weight of the menu in his hands, the soft jazz playing in the background – it all felt hauntingly familiar.

"Maybe I'll try something new tonight," Drake mused aloud, his fingers hovering over the seafood options.

"You? Try something new?" Harrison chuckled. "That'll be the day."

Drake's smile felt more genuine this time. "Hey, even old dogs can learn new tricks."

As the waiter approached their table, Drake took a deep breath. Despite his attempts to rationalize away his unease, he couldn't quite silence the whisper of warning in the back of his mind. Something was off, and he couldn't shake the feeling that his choices tonight mattered more than he could possibly understand.

23 - 24

The waiter took their orders, and Drake found himself scrutinizing every word, every gesture of his family. Harrison's fingers drummed an irregular rhythm on the table, a habit Drake had never noticed before. Linda's laugh seemed to echo oddly in the restaurant's ambient noise, as if slightly out of sync with reality.

"So, Harry," Linda began, her voice pulling Drake's attention back to the conversation. "How was school today?"

Harrison's nose wrinkled at the nickname. "Mom, I told you, it's Harrison now. Harry sounds like I'm, like, eight."

The exchange sent a chill down Drake's spine. He'd heard this before, hadn't he? In his dream? Or was it more than a dream?

"Sorry, Harrison," Linda corrected herself, sharing an amused glance with Drake. "How was your day?"

As Harrison launched into a story about his chemistry class, Drake found his gaze drawn to the other diners. A couple by the window, the man in a blue shirt leaning into whisper something to his date. A family of four, the youngest child coloring on her placemat. Everything seemed normal, and yet...

"Dad, are you even listening?" Harrison's voice cut through his thoughts again.

Drake turned back to his son, guilt twisting in his gut. "Of course, buddy. You were saying about the... uh..."

"The whoopee cushion incident," Harrison supplied, rolling his eyes. "Seriously, what's with you tonight?"

Before Drake could respond, their food arrived. The sight of the steaming plates sent a jolt of panic through him. His eyes locked onto Harrison's plate, zeroing in on a particular piece of crab cake nestled among the others.

"That looks delicious," Linda commented, reaching for her fork.

Drake watched, his heart pounding, as Harrison's hand moved towards his plate. Time seemed to slow as his son's fingers closed around the very piece of crab that haunted Drake's nightmares.

"Wait!" Drake blurted out; his voice louder than he'd intended. The restaurant seemed to fall silent around them, all eyes turning to their table.

Harrison froze, the food halfway to his mouth. "Dad?"

Drake's mind raced. How could he explain his irrational fear without sounding crazy? How could he protect his son from a danger he wasn't even sure was real?

25 - 26

Drake's palms were slick with sweat as he gripped the edge of the table. The weight of his family's confused stares bore down on him, but he couldn't shake the overwhelming sense of dread that gripped his chest.

"I just... I think we should say grace first," Drake stammered, the lie tasting bitter on his tongue. He'd never been particularly religious, and Linda's raised eyebrow told him she knew it too.

"Since when do we say grace?" Harrison asked, the crab cake still poised near his mouth.

Drake's mind raced, searching for a way to intervene without raising suspicion. "I've been thinking lately about... gratitude," he said, the words feeling hollow even as he spoke to them. "About how fragile life is, how quickly things can change."

Linda reached across the table, her hand covering his. "Drake, honey, are you feeling alright?"

The concern in her eyes only intensified his internal struggle. How could he explain that in another reality - or was it a dream? - he'd watched their son die at this very table?

"I'm fine," Drake lied, forcing a smile. "Let's just... take a moment, okay? Please?"

Harrison sighed dramatically but lowered his fork back to his plate. "Fine, but make it quick. I'm starving."

As Drake bowed his head, pretending to pray, his mind raced through possibilities. Should he knock the plate away? Create a distraction? The absurdity of the situation wasn't lost on him, but the fear was all too real.

"Amen," he said finally, looking up to find his family watching him with a mix of concern and confusion.

"That was... nice, Dad," Harrison said, clearly humoring him. He reached for the shrimp again, and Drake felt his heart leap into his throat.

"Wait!" he exclaimed again, this time knocking over his water glass in his haste to stop his son.

27 - 28

Drake's hand shot out, fingers closing around Harrison's wrist with an urgency that startled them both. The crab cake, poised at Harrison's lips, trembled in his grasp.

"Dad, what the hell?" Harrison's eyes widened, a mixture of confusion and annoyance flashing across his face.

Drake's heart pounded; each beat a thunderous reminder of the nightmare he was desperately trying to prevent. The restaurant's ambient chatter faded to a dull roar in his ears as he struggled to find words that wouldn't make him sound completely unhinged.

"I just..." Drake began, his voice hoarse with emotion. He loosened his grip on Harrison's wrist but didn't let go entirely. "I thought I saw something. On the shrimp."

Linda leaned forward; her brow furrowed with concern. "Drake, honey, what's going on? You've been acting strange all day."

Drake's mind raced. How could he explain the inexplicable? The vivid memory of Harrison choking, dying in his arms, felt more real than the moment he was currently living. He could still feel the weight of his son's lifeless body, hear the screams that tore from his own throat.

"It's nothing," Drake lied, forcing a smile that felt more like a grimace. "I'm just being overly cautious. You can never be too careful with seafood, right?"

Harrison rolled his eyes, but there was a flicker of worry behind his teenage bravado. "Dad, seriously. You're freaking me out a little."

Drake released Harrison's wrist, his hand trembling slightly as he withdrew it. "I'm sorry, son. I don't mean to... I just want you to be safe."

The words hung in the air, heavy with an urgency that Drake couldn't fully express. He watched as Harrison examined the shrimp, turning it over in his fingers with exaggerated care.

"Well, it looks fine to me," Harrison declared, his tone a mix of exasperation and affection. "But if it'll make you feel better, I'll get something else."

As Harrison signaled the waiter, Drake felt a wave of relief wash over him. He'd averted one disaster, but the night was far from over. The weight of foreknowledge pressed down on him, a burden he couldn't share.

29 - 30

Drake's eyes darted nervously around the table, his heart hammering against his ribcage. The familiar scents of garlic and butter that once brought comfort now seemed cloying, almost suffocating. He watched Linda take a bite of her meal, every chew an eternity.

"Wait—don't eat that!" Drake blurted out; his voice strained with urgency. His hand shot out across the table, nearly knocking over a glass of water.

Harrison froze, the fork halfway to his mouth. "What?" he asked, confusion etched across his face. "It's just shrimp, Dad."

Drake's mind raced, searching for a way to explain his irrational behavior without sounding completely unhinged. The memory of Harrison choking, of his lifeless form, played on a loop in his head. He couldn't shake the feeling that death lurked at this very table, waiting to claim one of them.

"I just... I have a bad feeling about it," Drake said, struggling to keep his voice steady. "Call it lawyer's intuition."

Harrison quirked an eyebrow. "Don't you mean detective's intuition? Dad, you're acting really weird."

"Right, detective," Drake corrected himself, forcing a weak laugh. "Old habits die hard, I guess."

As he spoke, Drake couldn't help but fixate on the word 'die.' It echoed in his mind, a grim reminder of what he was trying to prevent. He watched Harrison set down his fork, relief mingling with a deep-seated dread that this was only the beginning of a long, nightmarish cycle.

31 - 32

Linda's eyes narrowed as she studied Drake's face, concern etched in the delicate lines around her mouth. "What's gotten into you?" she asked, her voice a mix of worry and bewilderment.

Drake's heart raced as he fumbled for an excuse, his mind a whirlwind of fragmented memories and half-formed lies. He forced a smile, hoping it didn't look as strained as it felt. "Oh, you know," he began, his voice unnaturally light, "I just read an article about food safety the other day. Made me a bit paranoid, I guess."

He watched Linda's expression, searching for any sign that she believed him. The weight of his knowledge—of a future that might still come to pass—pressed down on him like a physical force.

"Really?" Linda's eyebrow arched skeptically. "Since when do you read food safety articles?"

Drake shrugged, trying to appear nonchalant. "Just trying to keep us all healthy," he said, reaching for his water glass to hide the tremor in his hands.

As he raised the glass to his lips, a horrible realization struck him. In his desperation to save Harrison, had he inadvertently set something else in motion? The restaurant around them seemed to fade away as a new, terrifying possibility took shape in his mind.

Suddenly, a harsh, choking sound cut through the air.

33 - 34

Drake's head snapped up, his water glass slipping from his fingers and clattering onto the table. The world around him seemed to slow, each second stretching into an eternity as he watched Linda's face contort in panic. Her hands flew to her throat, eyes wide with fear.

"Linda!" Drake cried out, his voice cracking with desperation. He lunged across the table, knocking over dishes in his haste to reach her.

Harrison's voice, high with terror, pierced through the growing commotion. "Mom! What's happening?"

Drake's mind raced, a cacophony of thoughts drowning out everything else. This can't be happening. Not again. Not her. He reached Linda's side, his hands shaking as he grasped her shoulders.

"Breathe, honey. Try to breathe," he urged, his words a frantic mantra. But even as he spoke, a chilling sense of déjà vu washed over him. The scene unfolding before him was a nightmarish mirror of the previous night's events, with Linda now playing the tragic role that had belonged to Harrison.

As Linda's coughing intensified, Drake's world narrowed to a pinpoint focus. He vaguely registered the startled gasps of nearby diners, the scraping of chairs as people stood to get a better view. But all that mattered was Linda, her face growing redder by the second as she struggled for air.

"Someone call an ambulance!" Drake shouted, his voice raw with fear and frustration. He turned back to Linda, cupping her face in his hands. "Hold on, sweetheart. Just hold on."

In that moment, as he stared into Linda's terrified eyes, Drake felt the full weight of his powerlessness. Despite all he knew, despite his desperate attempts to change the course of events, fate seemed determined to extract its cruel price. And as Linda's struggles grew weaker, Drake couldn't shake the haunting thought that in trying to save his son, he might have inadvertently condemned his wife.

35 - 36

Linda's fingers clawed at her throat, her nails leaving angry red marks on her skin as she desperately fought for air. Her eyes, wide with panic, locked onto Drake's, silently pleading for help. The vibrant color drained from her cheeks, replaced by an alarming shade of crimson that spread across her face.

Drake's mind reeled, paralyzed by the horrifying familiarity of the scene. Time seemed to slow, each second stretching into an eternity as he watched his wife struggle. His thoughts raced, a cacophony of disbelief and terror.

"This can't be happening again," he thought, his heart pounding so hard he could feel it in his ears. "I changed it. I saved Harrison. How is this possible?"

For a moment that felt like an age, Drake remained frozen, his body refusing to respond to the urgent commands of his mind. The weight of his guilt, the burden of his knowledge from another timeline, threatened to crush him.

Then, as if a switch had been flipped, Drake snapped into action. He leapt from his chair, nearly knocking it over in his haste. "Linda!" he cried out, his voice cracking with emotion. "I'm here, I've got you!"

He moved behind her, wrapping his arms around her waist. As he positioned himself to perform the Heimlich maneuver, a fleeting thought crossed his mind: "Will this work? Or am I just going through the motions of a predetermined tragedy?"

Pushing aside his doubts, Drake focused on the task at hand. He had to try, had to fight against whatever malevolent force seemed intent on tearing his family apart. With grim determination, he prepared to make his first upward thrust, silently praying that this time, his efforts would be enough to change the course of fate.

37 - 38

Harrison's panicked voice cut through the chaos of the restaurant. "Help! Somebody help my mom!" His lanky frame trembled as he stood, arms outstretched, unsure of what to do.

Drake's muscles tensed as he performed the Heimlich maneuver, each upward thrust more desperate than the last. Linda's body jerked with each attempt, but the obstruction remained stubbornly lodged.

"Come on, Linda," Drake muttered through gritted teeth. "Fight this. Please."

As he continued his efforts, Drake's mind raced. The eerie familiarity of the situation gnawed at him, threatening to overwhelm his focus. He pushed the thoughts aside, channeling all his energy into saving his wife.

Harrison's voice cracked as he cried out, "Dad, why isn't it working? Do something else!"

Drake's heart clenched at his son's plea. "I'm trying, Harry. I'm trying everything I can."

Linda's struggles began to weaken, her face now an alarming shade of purple. Drake felt a cold dread seeping into his bones as he realized his efforts were failing.

"No, no, no," he whispered, his movements becoming frantic. "Linda, stay with me. Don't you dare leave us."

But even as the words left his mouth, Drake felt Linda's body go limp in his arms. Time seemed to slow as he lowered her to the floor, his movements mechanical, disbelieving.

"Linda?" he whispered, cradling her head. Her eyes, once so full of life and love, stared blankly at the ceiling.

The realization hit Drake like a physical blow. He had failed. Again. The weight of two timeline's worth of grief crashed down upon him, threatening to tear him apart.

39 - 40

The restaurant fell into a deathly hush, the air thick with shock and disbelief. The clink of cutlery ceased, conversations died mid-sentence, and all eyes turned to the tragic scene unfolding before them. Drake barely registered the silence, his world narrowing to the lifeless form in his arms.

Linda's body was still warm, her blonde hair splayed across his lap like a golden halo. Drake's hands trembled as he brushed a strand from her face, his touch gentle as if she might shatter beneath his fingers.

"This can't be happening," he whispered, his voice hoarse. "Not again. Not you."

The words caught in his throat, choking him with their bitter irony. He had tried to prevent this, had thought he could outsmart fate. But here he was, cradling his wife's body, just as he had held his son's the night before – or was it a lifetime ago?

Harrison's sobs pierced through Drake's fog of grief. "Mom? Mom, please wake up!"

Drake turned to his son, seeing the raw anguish etched across the boy's face. He wanted to comfort him, to shield him from this nightmare, but how could he when he himself was drowning in despair?

"Harry," Drake managed, his voice barely above a whisper. "I'm so sorry. I tried... I thought..."

His words trailed off, inadequate in the face of their loss. Drake's mind reeled, grappling with the impossibility of their situation. How could this be happening again? What cruel twist of fate had brought them here?

As he held Linda's lifeless form, Drake felt a familiar sense of unreality washing over him. The restaurant, the stunned onlookers, even Harrison's grief-stricken face – it all seemed to fade away, leaving only the crushing weight of his failure.

"I was supposed to save you," Drake murmured, pressing his forehead to Linda's. "Both of you. What am I missing? What am I doing wrong?"

The questions echoed in his mind, unanswered and mocking. As paramedics rushed in, their urgent voices a distant buzz, Drake closed his eyes, wishing desperately for another chance, another reset, anything to undo this moment of devastating loss.

41 - 42

Drake's arms tightened around Linda's still form, his fingers trembling as they traced the contours of her face. The world around him blurred, narrowing to this single, devastating moment.

"Linda," he choked out, his voice raw with anguish. "Please, not you too. I can't lose you both. I can't—"

His words dissolved into a guttural sob that tore from his chest. The weight of two lifetimes of grief crashed over him, threatening to pull him under. How could he have failed so completely, so utterly?

Harrison's hand gripped his shoulder, the boy's touch both an anchor and a reminder of their shared loss. "Dad," he whispered, his voice thick with tears, "what's happening?"

Drake looked up at his son, seeing the confusion and fear etched across his young face. He wanted to offer comfort, to provide answers, but the truth was a tangled mess he couldn't begin to unravel.

"I don't know, Harry," Drake admitted, the words tasting bitter on his tongue. "I thought I could change things, but I—I made it worse."

As he spoke, a chilling realization crept over him. What if this wasn't the end? What if tomorrow brought another reset, another chance to relive this nightmare?

"No," Drake muttered, his grip on Linda tightening. "I won't let this happen again. I can't."

But even as he made this vow, doubt gnawed at him. How many times would he have to watch his family die before he could save them? And at what cost to his own sanity?

43 - 44

The wail of sirens pierced the air, growing louder as the paramedics approached. Drake's heart sank, knowing their arrival was a cruel formality. He cradled Linda's lifeless body, his fingers tracing the contours of her face as if trying to memorize every detail.

"Sir, we need you to step back," a paramedic's voice cut through the haze of Drake's grief.

Reluctantly, he released Linda, watching as the medical team swarmed around her. Their frantic movements, the beeping of machines, the urgent voices—it all blurred into a cacophony of futility.

"Come on, Dad," Harrison tugged at his sleeve, his voice quavering. "Let them work."

Drake stumbled back, his eyes never leaving Linda. "It's too late," he murmured, more to himself than to Harrison. "It's always too late."

As the paramedics continued their efforts, Drake's mind raced. The eerie similarities, the repeated tragedy—it couldn't be coincidence. A chill ran down his spine as he considered the implications.

"Harry," he turned to his son, gripping his shoulders. "Listen to me. If tomorrow—if things seem strange, if you feel like you've lived through the day before, you have to tell me. Promise me."

Harrison's brow furrowed in confusion. "Dad, what are you talking about?"

Drake opened his mouth to explain, but the words died on his lips. How could he possibly make his son understand when he barely comprehended it himself?

"Time of death, 8:47 PM," the paramedic's voice cut through the air like a knife.

The finality of those words hit Drake like a physical blow. He staggered, his vision blurring as the reality of Linda's death crashed over him once more.

"No," he whispered, his voice breaking. "This can't be happening again."

As he stood there, surrounded by the chaos of the restaurant and the suffocating weight of his grief, a terrifying thought took root in Drake's mind. What if he was trapped in some kind of loop, doomed to relive this nightmare over and over?

The world seemed to tilt on its axis, leaving Drake unmoored and adrift in a sea of uncertainty. He clung to Harrison, his last anchor to reality, as the dread of what tomorrow might bring threatened to overwhelm him.

A House Ablaze

1 Drake's eyes snapped open, his chest heaving as if he'd just surfaced from underwater. The room swam into focus—soft golden light filtering through gauzy curtains, casting dancing shadows on the pale walls. His fingers clutched at the tangled sheets, seeking an anchor in this seemingly tranquil morning that felt so at odds with the tumult in his mind.

He turned his head, drinking in the sight of Linda beside him. Her blonde hair fanned out across the pillow, catching the light like spun gold. The gentle rise and fall of her chest as she breathed stirred something deep within him—a mix of relief and an inexplicable, gnawing dread.

Linda shifted, nestling closer to him. Her warmth seeped into his side, a stark contrast to the cold sweat that had broken out across his skin. She let out a soft sigh, her lips curving into a slight smile.

"Morning," she murmured, her voice husky with sleep.

Drake's throat constricted, the simple word carrying a weight he couldn't quite comprehend. He wanted to reach out, to touch her face and reassure himself of her presence, but his limbs felt leaden.

Instead, he lay there, his mind racing. Why did this ordinary morning feel so surreal? Why did Linda's peaceful form beside him fill him with both comfort and an inexplicable sense of loss?

He closed his eyes, trying to shake off the disorientation. The lingering tendrils of a dream—or was it a memory?—tugged at the edges of his consciousness. Something about a car, spinning out of control. The acrid smell of smoke. A figure with a burned face.

Drake's eyes flew open again, his heart hammering against his ribs. He took a deep, shuddering breath, willing the fragments of the nightmare to dissipate in the warm morning light.

"You okay?" Linda's voice was clearer now, tinged with concern. She propped herself up on one elbow, her blue eyes searching his face.

Drake swallowed hard, forcing a smile that didn't quite reach his eyes. "Yeah," he managed, his voice hoarse. "Just... a weird dream."

Linda's brow furrowed slightly, her hand coming to rest on his chest. The gentle pressure of her palm over his racing heart felt like a lifeline. "Want to talk about it?"

He hesitated, the words lodging in his throat. How could he explain the overwhelming sense of wrongness that clung to him? The feeling that this peaceful moment was somehow both a gift and a cruel illusion?

"I... I'm not sure I remember it clearly," he lied, hating the taste of the falsehood on his tongue. "It's fading already."

Linda nodded, her fingers tracing soothing circles on his chest. "Those are always the worst kind," she said softly. "The ones that leave you feeling unsettled without knowing why."

Drake closed his eyes again, leaning into her touch. The weight of unspoken truths pressed down on him, threatening to suffocate him in this sun-drenched bedroom that should have been a sanctuary.

"Linda," he began, his voice barely above a whisper, "do you ever feel like... like something's not quite right? Like we're living in a world that's just slightly off-kilter?"

He felt her pause, her hand stilling on his chest. When he opened his eyes, he found her watching him with a mixture of concern and curiosity.

"What do you mean?" she asked carefully.

Drake struggled to find the words, to articulate the nebulous dread that had taken root in his soul. "I don't know," he admitted, frustration coloring his tone. "It's just a feeling. Like we're... missing something. Or like we've forgotten something important."

Linda's expression softened, a sad smile touching her lips. "Oh, Drake," she murmured, leaning in to press a gentle kiss to his forehead. "Is this about the case you've been working on? You know you can't save everyone, right?"

Her words, meant to comfort, sent a chill down Drake's spine. The case. Of course. That must be it. He latched onto the explanation, even as a part of him rebelled against its simplicity.

"Yeah," he said, forcing a rueful chuckle. "I guess it's getting to me more than I realized."

Linda's smile widened, relief evident in her eyes. "Well, lucky for you, it's Saturday. No cases, no clients. Just us."

Drake nodded, trying to mirror her enthusiasm. But as he lay there, basking in the warmth of Linda's presence and the golden morning light, he couldn't shake the feeling that something fundamental had shifted. That this perfect moment was as fragile as spun glass, ready to shatter at the slightest touch.

3 - 4

Drake's eyes darted around the room, his heart racing as a suffocating wave of dread crept up his spine. The familiar surroundings—the pale blue walls, the framed family photos, the stack of case files on his nightstand—suddenly felt alien and wrong. His breath caught in his throat as vivid, horrifying memories assaulted him.

"Harrison," he whispered, his voice barely audible. "The shrimp... and you—" He turned to Linda, unable to finish the sentence as the image of her lifeless body flashed before his eyes.

Linda propped herself up on one elbow, concern etching her delicate features. "Drake? What's wrong?"

He reached out hesitantly, his calloused fingers brushing against the soft skin of her shoulder. The warmth of her touch sent a jolt through him—relief and fear intertwining in a confusing knot of emotion.

"You're here," Drake murmured, his brown eyes searching her face. "You're alive."

Linda's brow furrowed, a mix of confusion and worry in her striking blue eyes. "Of course I'm alive. Drake, you're scaring me. What's going on?"

Drake swallowed hard, struggling to reconcile the vivid memories of tragedy with the living, breathing woman before him. "I... I don't know," he admitted, running a hand through his disheveled hair. "It felt so real. You and Harrison, both of you were—" He couldn't bring himself to say the word 'dead.'

"It was just a nightmare," Linda soothed, her voice taking on that calming tone she often used with victims' families. "We're fine. Harrison's fine. See?" She gestured towards the door, beyond which they could hear the faint sounds of their son moving about.

Drake nodded, but the gnawing sense of wrongness persisted. "Yeah," he said, not entirely convinced. "Just a nightmare."

Linda studied him for a moment, her gaze penetrating. "There's something else, isn't there? This isn't just about a bad dream."

Drake hesitated, torn between the desire to confide in her and the fear of sounding crazy. "It's... it's like we've done this before," he finally said, his voice low and intense. "Like we're caught in some kind of loop, and I'm the only one who remembers."

5 - 6

A sharp knock shattered the tense silence, and before Drake could gather his thoughts, the door burst open. Harrison strode in, his lanky frame filling the doorway, tie askew and phone clutched in hand like a lifeline.

"Are you guys seriously still in bed? I'm starving," Harrison groaned, his voice a mix of teenage exasperation and genuine hunger.

Drake's breath caught in his throat, his chest constricting painfully as he took in the sight of his son. Alive. Breathing. The last image that had burned itself into Drake's mind was Harrison's lifeless body, limp and cold in his arms. Now, here he stood, full of vibrant energy, rolling his eyes at his apparently lazy parents.

"Harrison," Drake whispered, his voice barely audible. He blinked rapidly, trying to reconcile the two realities warring in his mind. The grieving father and the one who still had everything to lose.

"Uh, yeah, that's me," Harrison quipped, running a hand through his unruly blonde hair. "You okay, Dad? You look like you've seen a ghost."

Drake forced a smile, though it felt brittle on his face. "Just... tired," he managed, his mind racing. How could he explain the overwhelming sense of déjà vu, the bone-deep certainty that he'd lived this moment before – and lost everything?

"Well, wake up already," Harrison insisted, his brown eyes sparkling with impatience. "I've got soccer practice in an hour, and I need fuel."

As Harrison turned to leave, Drake found himself reaching out, an irrational fear gripping him that if his son walked out that door, he might never see him again. "Wait," he called out, his voice strained. "I'll... I'll make breakfast. Just give me a minute."

Harrison paused, surprise flickering across his face. "You? Cook? Are you sure you're feeling alright?"

Drake swung his legs over the side of the bed, fighting the urge to pull Harrison into a crushing embrace. "Never better," he lied, forcing his voice to sound lighter than he felt. "How do pancakes sound?"

As Harrison's face lit up with a grin, Drake's heart ached with a bittersweet mix of love and fear. He'd do anything – everything – to keep that smile on his son's face. To keep him safe. To rewrite the tragic ending that haunted his dreams.

"Awesome," Harrison exclaimed. "I'll go set the table!"

As his son's footsteps retreated down the hallway, Drake closed his eyes, taking a deep breath. He had to find a way to make sense of what was happening. To protect his family from whatever darkness lurked on the horizon. Even if it meant confronting the impossible.

7 - 8

"Harrison," Drake said, his voice cracking with emotion. He stared at his son, drinking in every detail—the familiar crooked smile, the mess of dark hair, the faint freckles dotting his nose. The sight of Harrison, alive and vibrant, sent a wave of conflicting emotions crashing through Drake's chest. Relief, joy, and a gnawing fear all battled for dominance. "You're—"

"Yeah, yeah, I'm amazing," Harrison interrupted with a grin that lit up his entire face. He ran a hand through his unruly hair, a gesture so achingly familiar it made Drake's heart clench. "Now come on. Breakfast isn't going to make itself."

Drake swallowed hard, fighting to keep his voice steady. "Right, of course. I'll be down in a minute."

Harrison raised an eyebrow, his brown eyes sparkling with curiosity. "You okay, Dad? You look like you've seen a ghost."

A ghost. The word hit Drake like a physical blow. Memories of Harrison's lifeless body flashed through his mind, and he had to grip the edge of the bed to steady himself. "I'm fine," he managed, forcing a smile. "Just... had a strange dream."

Harrison tilted his head, his expression softening with concern. "Want to talk about it? I read somewhere that dreams are like, our brain's way of processing stuff. Could be important."

Drake's chest tightened at his son's earnest offer. Even now, facing a reality he couldn't begin to understand, Harrison's innate kindness shone through. "Maybe later," Drake said softly. "Right now, I think we both need some food in our stomachs."

9 - 10

Linda chuckled softly, her eyes still closed. "Pumpkin, give us five minutes."

The gentle sound of her laughter washed over Drake, a balm to his frayed nerves. He turned to look at her, drinking in the sight of her peaceful face, the way the morning light caught in her blonde hair. For a moment, he could almost believe that everything was normal, that the horrors he remembered were nothing more than a terrible nightmare.

"Don't call me pumpkin," Harrison groaned, his voice cracking with teenage indignation. He threw his hands up dramatically, the gesture so quintessentially Harrison that Drake felt a lump form in his throat. "I'm sixteen, Mom. Sixteen! That's way too old for pet names."

Drake watched his son, noting the way his lanky frame seemed to fill the doorway, the subtle signs of the man he was becoming. When had Harrison grown so tall? The question sent a pang of loss through Drake's chest, a reminder of all the moments he feared he'd missed.

"You'll always be our pumpkin," Drake found himself saying, his voice thick with emotion. "No matter how old you get."

Harrison rolled his eyes, but Drake caught the hint of a smile tugging at his son's lips. "Whatever," Harrison muttered, turning to leave. "Just hurry up, okay? I'm starving."

As Harrison's footsteps retreated down the hall, Drake closed his eyes, focusing on the sound. Each step was a reassurance, a confirmation that his son was alive, whole, and blessedly normal. The echo faded, leaving behind a silence that felt both comforting and oddly fragile.

"He's right, you know," Linda murmured beside him. "We should get up."

Drake nodded, unable to find the words to express the turmoil raging inside him. How could he explain the weight of alternate realities, of deaths undone and tragedy averted? Instead, he reached out, gently squeezing Linda's hand. "Yeah," he whispered. "We should."

11 - 12

Drake swung his legs over the side of the bed, his bare feet connecting with the cool hardwood floor. The sensation grounded him, anchoring him to this moment, this reality. He ran a hand through his disheveled hair, feeling the slight tremor in his fingers. "He's here," he whispered, more to himself than to Linda. The words hung in the air, heavy with unspoken relief and lingering disbelief.

Linda stirred beside him, the mattress shifting with her movement. She cracked an eye open, her gaze finding Drake's face in the soft morning light. "Of course he is," she said, her brow furrowing slightly. "What's with you this morning?"

Drake's heart clenched at the normalcy in her voice, the casual acceptance of their son's presence. He struggled to find the right words, to bridge the gap between the horror of his memories and the peaceful reality before him.

"I just..." he began, his voice trailing off. How could he explain the weight of alternate timelines, of deaths undone? "I had a dream," he finally managed, the words feeling inadequate. "It felt so real."

Linda pushed herself up on one elbow, her blonde hair cascading over her shoulder. Her blue eyes, still hazy with sleep, searched his face. "Must have been some dream," she said softly. "You look like you've seen a ghost."

Drake's mind flashed to the image of Harrison choking, of Linda's lifeless body. In a way, he had seen ghosts – specters of a future he was desperate to prevent. "Yeah," he murmured, forcing a weak smile. "Something like that."

He stood, his legs feeling unsteady beneath him. The normalcy of the room – the rumpled sheets, the soft sunlight filtering through the curtains – felt surreal against the backdrop of his tumultuous thoughts. Drake moved to the window, pushing the curtain aside to look out at the quiet street below.

"Drake?" Linda's voice was tinged with concern now. "Are you sure you're okay?"

He turned back to her, drinking in the sight of her – alive, warm, real. The urge to confess everything, to pour out the impossible truth of their situation, rose in his throat. But the words died on his lips. How could he burden her with knowledge that might shatter this fragile peace?

"I'm fine," he said instead, the lie tasting bitter on his tongue. "Just... grateful, I guess. For you. For Harrison. For all of this."

Linda's expression softened, a gentle smile tugging at her lips. "Well, that's sweet," she said, sitting up fully now. "But if you're really grateful, you could start by making some coffee. I have a feeling we're going to need it to keep up with our 'pumpkin' today."

Drake nodded, latching onto the suggestion of normalcy like a lifeline. "Yeah," he said, moving towards the door. "Coffee. I can do that."

As he stepped into the hallway, the scent of brewing coffee already wafting up from the kitchen, Drake paused. The weight of responsibility – of knowing, of remembering – pressed down on him. He glanced back at Linda, still sitting in bed, bathed in the soft morning light.

"I love you," he said suddenly, the words carrying the weight of a thousand unsaid things.

Linda's smile widened, a mix of surprise and affection in her eyes. "I love you too," she replied. "Now go. Before Harrison decides to cook breakfast himself."

Drake nodded, turning away to hide the sudden moisture in his eyes. As he made his way downstairs, each step felt like a choice – a commitment to this reality, this family, this chance to make things right. The future stretched out before him, filled with both promise and peril. But for now, there was coffee to be made, and a family to protect.

13 - 14

Drake hesitated, the words catching in his throat. "Nothing. Just... a bad dream," he finally managed, his voice barely above a whisper. The lie tasted bitter on his tongue, but how could he explain the visceral terror that still clung to him like a second skin?

Linda's brow furrowed, concern etching lines across her forehead. She reached out, her fingers brushing against his arm. "You sure? You look like you've seen a ghost."

He forced a smile, hoping it didn't look as hollow as it felt. "I'm fine, really. Let's just... let's just go have breakfast."

As they made their way downstairs, the scent of freshly brewed coffee and frying bacon enveloped them, a comforting blanket of domesticity. The kitchen was awash in golden morning light, streaming through the windows and casting warm patches on the tiled floor. Harrison sat at his usual spot, his attention wholly consumed by his phone, thumbs tapping away furiously.

Linda moved to the stove with practiced ease, flipping pancakes with a graceful flick of her wrist. "Breakfast's almost ready," she announced, her voice light and carefree.

Drake settled into his chair, his eyes darting between Linda and Harrison. Everything about the scene was perfect – too perfect. A heavy sense of déjà vu settled over him, as oppressive as a wet blanket. He couldn't shake the feeling that he'd lived this moment before, that he knew exactly what would happen next.

"You gonna eat that bacon, Dad, or just stare at it?" Harrison's voice cut through his thoughts, playful but with an undercurrent of concern.

Drake blinked, realizing he'd been lost in his own head. "Sorry, kiddo. Just... thinking."

"Well, don't think too hard," Linda chimed in, sliding a stack of pancakes onto his plate. "You might hurt yourself."

He managed a chuckle, but it felt forced, even to his own ears. As he picked up his fork, Drake couldn't help but wonder: Was this really his family, safe and alive? Or was it all just another cruel trick of fate, destined to be snatched away again?

15 - 16

Drake's hand trembled as he gripped his fork, the metal cool against his clammy palm. He stared at his plate, the golden pancakes and crispy bacon suddenly unappetizing. His gaze flicked between Linda and Harrison, and unbidden, horrific images flashed through his mind.

Harrison's face, contorted in panic, fingers clawing at his throat as he choked. Linda's eyes, wide and glassy, her breath coming in ragged, labored gasps. The memories twisted like a knife in Drake's gut, and he swallowed hard against the surge of nausea.

"Hey, Earth to Dad," Harrison's voice cut through the fog of Drake's thoughts. "You're doing that weird staring thing again."

Drake looked up, meeting his son's concerned frown. Harrison's brow was furrowed, his phone forgotten on the table. The boy's brown eyes, so full of life and curiosity, bore into Drake's own.

"Sorry, I..." Drake trailed off, unsure how to explain the maelstrom of emotions churning within him. How could he tell them about the vivid memories of their deaths, about the overwhelming fear that this moment of domestic bliss was just a cruel illusion?

Linda paused in her cooking, turning to face him. Her blue eyes, usually warm and comforting, now held a hint of worry. "Drake? Is everything alright?"

He opened his mouth to respond, but the words caught in his throat. Instead, he found himself drinking in every detail of their faces, desperately trying to reconcile the living, breathing people before him with the lifeless bodies that haunted his nightmares.

17 - 18

Drake forced a smile, but it didn't reach his eyes. "I'm fine, kiddo. Just thinking." The lie tasted bitter on his tongue, but what else could he say? That he was reliving their deaths over and over in his mind? That he was terrified this reality might shatter at any moment?

Harrison's brow furrowed deeper, unconvinced. He opened his mouth, likely to press further, but Linda intervened.

"Well, think less and eat more," she said, her voice a soothing balm to Drake's frayed nerves. She set a plate of golden pancakes in front of him, the aroma of butter and maple syrup wafting up. As she leaned down to plant a quick kiss on his cheek, Drake inhaled deeply, savoring the familiar scent of her lavender shampoo.

"We've got dinner plans later, remember? The Lighthouse?" Linda's words sent a jolt through Drake's system. The Lighthouse. In his mind's eye, he saw shattered glass, smelled burning rubber and copper. His hands clenched involuntarily beneath the table.

"Right," Drake managed, his voice sounding strained even to his own ears. "The Lighthouse." He picked up his fork, trying to focus on the present moment, on the warmth of the kitchen and the presence of his family. But a nagging voice in the back of his mind whispered that he needed to change their plans, to keep them safe. He just wasn't sure how to do that without sounding completely unhinged.

19 - 20

Drake's fingers tightened around the fork, his knuckles whitening as he struggled to maintain his composure. The weight of his memories pressed down on him, a suffocating blanket of dread that threatened to overwhelm him. He couldn't shake the vivid image of twisted metal and broken bodies, the echo of sirens piercing the night.

"Actually," he began, his voice low and tight, "I was thinking... maybe we should stay in tonight." The words came out hesitantly, each syllable laden with unspoken fears.

Linda paused, the coffee pot hovering over her mug. Her eyebrows knitted together as she studied Drake's face, concern etching lines around her eyes. She set the pot down with a gentle clink and lowered herself into the chair across from him.

"Stay in?" she echoed, her tone a mixture of curiosity and worry. "Why? You've been talking about taking us to The Lighthouse all week."

Drake's gaze dropped to his untouched pancakes, unable to meet Linda's searching eyes. How could he explain the gnawing terror that gripped him at the mere thought of that restaurant? The certainty that stepping foot inside would lead to tragedy?

He swallowed hard, his throat constricting around words he couldn't say. 'Because I've seen you die there,' he thought, the admission echoing in the confines of his mind. 'Because I can't bear to lose you again.'

Instead, he forced himself to look up, meeting Linda's concerned gaze. "I just..." he began, searching for an explanation that wouldn't sound like madness. "I have a bad feeling about it. Can't we just have a quiet night at home?"

21 - 22

Drake's fingers tapped a nervous rhythm on the table as he continued, his voice carefully controlled. "We can cook here. It'll be nice."

The words hung in the air, fragile as spun glass. Drake could feel Linda's questioning gaze boring into him, but he kept his eyes fixed on the sunlight dappling the kitchen counter. His mind raced, searching for a way to make his request sound reasonable, to quell the rising panic without revealing the impossible truth.

Harrison, who had been uncharacteristically quiet, suddenly pushed back from the table. The screech of chair legs against tile made Drake flinch.

"Nice?" Harrison's voice dripped with teenage incredulity. He stood, lanky frame slouched in exaggerated disbelief. "Nice is The Lighthouse's clam chowder. Nice is not eating Dad's spaghetti again."

Drake's heart clenched at his son's words, at the familiar exasperation in his tone. How many times had he heard that voice silenced forever? How many realities had he lived where Harrison's laughter was nothing but a memory?

He wanted to reach out, to pull Harrison close and never let go. Instead, he forced a weak smile. "Hey, my spaghetti's not that bad," he protested, the attempt at levity falling flat even to his own ears.

As Harrison rolled his eyes, Drake's mind raced. How could he keep them safe without sounding like he'd lost his mind? The weight of foreknowledge pressed down on him, suffocating in its intensity.

23 - 24

Linda's smirk was gentle, a mixture of amusement and concern playing across her features. Her blue eyes, always so perceptive, seemed to peer right through Drake's facade. "Drake, what's this really about?" she asked, her tone more curious than teasing.

The question hung in the air, heavy with unspoken implications. Drake's throat constricted, the words he needed to say tangling in a knot of fear and desperation. How could he possibly explain the crushing sense of deja vu, the vivid memories of their deaths that haunted his every waking moment? The image of Linda's lifeless body flashed before his eyes, and he had to grip the edge of the table to steady himself.

"I..." Drake began, his voice barely above a whisper. He cleared his throat, trying again. "I just want us to spend some time together. Here. That's all."

The lie tasted bitter on his tongue, but what choice did he have? To tell them the truth would be to invite skepticism at best, outright disbelief at worst. And yet, as he looked at Linda's worried expression and Harrison's impatient fidgeting, the weight of his secrets threatened to crush him.

Drake's mind raced, grasping for a way to convey the urgency he felt without revealing the impossible. The ticking of the kitchen clock seemed to grow louder with each passing second, a relentless reminder of how little time they might have left.

25 - 26

Linda's blue eyes softened as she studied Drake's face, her brow furrowing slightly. The morning sunlight streaming through the kitchen window caught the golden strands of her hair, creating a halo effect that made Drake's heart ache with a mixture of love and fear.

"Alright," she said finally, her voice gentle but tinged with concern. "If that's what you want." Her hand reached across the table, fingers lightly brushing Drake's knuckles in a gesture of comfort.

Drake felt a rush of relief, quickly followed by a wave of guilt. He didn't deserve her trust, her unwavering support. Not when he was hiding so much from her.

Before he could respond, Harrison's exasperated groan cut through the moment. "Seriously?" The teenager threw his hands up dramatically, nearly knocking over his glass of orange juice. "Fine. But you owe me ice cream."

Drake turned to his son, drinking in the sight of him alive and vibrant. The memory of Harrison's lifeless body flashed unbidden through his mind, and he had to suppress a shudder.

"Deal," Drake managed, forcing a smile that didn't quite reach his eyes. "Double scoop, any flavor you want."

As Harrison's face lit up with a grin, Drake's thoughts raced. How could he protect them? How could he change the course of events he remembered so vividly? The weight of responsibility pressed down on him, threatening to suffocate him with each passing moment.

27 - 28

The morning light filtered through the curtains, casting long shadows across the hardwood floor as Drake moved through the house with leaden steps. Each tick of the clock on the wall seemed to echo his racing heartbeat, a constant reminder of time slipping away. He adjusted his tie mechanically, muscle memory guiding his fingers while his mind churned with suppressed dread.

Linda's presence at his side was both a comfort and a torment. Her familiar scent—a mix of lavender and coffee—enveloped him as she walked him to the door, a steaming mug cradled in her hands. Drake's eyes traced the curve of her cheek, the soft lines around her eyes, committing every detail to memory as if it might be the last time he saw her.

"You know," Linda said softly, her blue eyes searching his face, "I've always been able to read you like a book. But today... it's like you're written in a language I don't understand."

Drake swallowed hard, his throat constricting. "I'm fine," he lied, the words tasting bitter on his tongue. "Just... a lot on my mind with work."

Linda's brow furrowed, unconvinced. "You're sure everything's okay? You've been acting... off."

Drake's hand tightened on the handle of his briefcase, knuckles whitening. How could he explain the inexplicable? The memories of death and loss that haunted him, the weight of foreknowledge that pressed down on his shoulders?

"I—" he began, then faltered. The truth hovered on the tip of his tongue, desperate to be spoken. But the fear of sounding insane, of pushing Linda away when he needed her close, held him back. "It's nothing," he finished lamely, hating himself for the deception.

Linda's eyes softened, a mix of concern and love that made Drake's heart clench. She stepped closer, her free hand coming to rest on his chest, just over his thundering heart. "You know you can tell me anything, right?" she murmured.

Drake nodded, not trusting his voice. He leaned forward, pressing a kiss to her forehead, breathing in the scent of her hair. In that moment, he made a silent vow. Whatever it took, whatever price he had to pay, he would keep her safe. He would rewrite the future, even if it meant tearing apart the fabric of reality itself.

As he pulled away, Drake forced a smile that didn't reach his eyes. "I'll see you tonight," he said, his voice rough with emotion. "I love you."

The words felt inadequate, a pale shadow of the depth of his feelings. But as Linda smiled back, warm and radiant, Drake clung to that image like a lifeline. It would have to be enough. It had to be enough.

With a final, lingering look, Drake stepped out into the morning sun, the weight of the world on his shoulders and the taste of unspoken truths bitter on his tongue.

29 - 30

Drake hesitated, glancing back at the kitchen where Harrison was still glued to his phone. The boy's tousled hair fell over his forehead, his brow furrowed in concentration as his thumbs flew across the screen. A pang of longing struck Drake's heart, sharp and sudden.

"Yeah," he said finally, his voice rough with emotion. "I'm fine. Just... take it easy today, okay? Don't rush around too much."

The words felt heavy on his tongue, laden with unspoken fears. Drake's eyes darted between Linda and Harrison, drinking in their presence, memorizing every detail. The sunlight caught Linda's hair, turning it to spun gold, and for a moment, Drake's breath caught in his throat.

Linda gave him a puzzled smile, her blue eyes searching his face. "Since when do you worry about me rushing around? I'll be fine."

Her tone was light, but Drake could hear the undercurrent of concern. He wanted to tell her everything - about the nightmares, the sense of impending doom, the terrifying feeling that he'd lived this day before. But the words wouldn't come. Instead, he reached out, his hand cupping her cheek gently.

"I just..." Drake paused, swallowing hard. How could he explain the inexplicable? "I have a feeling, that's all. Promise me you'll be careful."

Linda leaned into his touch, her expression softening. "Of course, I promise. But you're starting to worry me, Drake. What's really going on?"

Drake's mind raced, torn between the desire to protect her and the need to unburden himself. The weight of his knowledge pressed down on him, threatening to crush him under its impossible weight.

"It's nothing," he lied, hating the taste of deceit on his tongue. "Just a rough night's sleep. I'll be fine once I get to work."

As the words left his mouth, Drake felt a surge of self-loathing. He was supposed to protect them, to save them, and here he was, lying to their faces. But what choice did he have? How could he explain the unexplainable?

31 - 32

As Drake opened the door, a faint but unmistakable scent assaulted his senses. His nostrils flared, and he inhaled sharply, trying to confirm what his instincts were screaming. Gas. The acrid smell slithered into his lungs, igniting a primal fear that clawed at his chest.

His stomach clenched as his mind raced through a thousand possibilities, each more terrifying than the last. Images of flames devouring their home, of Linda and Harrison trapped inside, flashed before his eyes with sickening clarity.

"Linda," Drake called out, his voice tight with barely contained panic. "Did you turn the oven off after breakfast?"

He turned to face her, his eyes searching her face for any sign of recognition or alarm. Linda frowned, stepping closer to him. The soft padding of her bare feet on the hardwood floor seemed unnaturally loud in the sudden, tense silence.

"I... I don't think I used it," she replied, her brow furrowed in confusion. "Why?"

Drake's heart hammered against his ribs. How could he explain the overwhelming sense of dread that had settled over him? The certainty that something was terribly, irrevocably wrong?

"Can't you smell that?" he asked, fighting to keep his voice steady. "It's gas. There's gas in the house."

Linda's eyes widened, and she sniffed the air tentatively. "I don't smell anything, Drake. Are you sure?"

Her doubt only heightened Drake's anxiety. Was he imagining it? Had the constant fear of losing them again twisted his perceptions so severely? Or was Linda simply unable to detect the danger that seemed so glaringly obvious to him?

"We need to get out," Drake said, his tone brooking no argument. He reached for Linda's hand, his grip perhaps a bit too tight. "Now. Get Harrison."

33 - 34

The world shattered.

A deafening roar ripped through the air, drowning out Drake's desperate cry. The force of the explosion slammed into him like a freight train, lifting him off his feet and hurling him through the open doorway. Time seemed to slow as he flew, his mind struggling to process the chaos erupting around him.

Searing heat licked at his skin, the acrid smell of smoke and chemicals burning his nostrils. Fragments of wood and glass rained down, a deadly hail accompanying his descent. Drake hit the lawn with bone-jarring force, the impact driving the air from his lungs in a painful whoosh.

For a moment, all was silent save for the high-pitched ringing in his ears. Drake lay there, stunned, his body a canvas of pain and shock. Through the ringing, a terrible thought clawed its way to the forefront of his mind.

Linda. Harrison.

He tried to call out, but his voice refused to cooperate, emerging as little more than a ragged gasp. Blinking away the spots dancing in his vision, Drake struggled to focus on the inferno that had once been his home.

"No," he whispered, the word barely audible even to himself. "Not again. Please, not again."

The ringing in his ears began to fade, replaced by the roar of flames and the distant wail of sirens. Drake pushed himself up onto his elbows, every movement sending fresh waves of pain through his battered body. His eyes, stinging from smoke and unshed tears, remained fixed on the blazing ruins before him.

35 - 36

Drake's muscles screamed in protest as he pushed himself to his feet, his legs trembling beneath him. The world tilted and swayed, but he forced himself to focus on the burning house before him. Flames licked at the sky, consuming everything in their path with merciless hunger.

"Linda! Harrison!" he screamed, his voice raw and desperate. The names tore from his throat, carrying with them all the fear and anguish that threatened to overwhelm him.

There was no answer. Only the roar of the fire, an insatiable beast devouring his world.

Drake staggered forward, his mind racing. *They have to be alive. I can't lose them again. Not like this.* The heat intensified with each step, singeing his skin and clothes.

"Dad!" He thought he heard Harrison's voice, faint and terrified, coming from within the inferno. It spurred him on, adrenaline momentarily overriding his pain.

"I'm coming!" Drake shouted, pushing himself closer to the burning structure. "Hold on!"

But as he neared the porch, a blast of scorching air slammed into him like a physical force. Drake stumbled back, shielding his face with his arms. The intensity of the heat was unbearable, an impenetrable wall between him and his family.

"No," he choked out, tears streaking down his ash-covered face. "Linda! Harrison! Can you hear me?"

Silence answered him, broken only by the crackling of flames and the groaning of weakening structures. Drake's heart pounded in his chest, each beat a desperate plea. Not again. Please, not again. I can't fail them again.

37 - 38

As despair threatened to consume him, Drake's gaze swept across the hellish scene. That's when he saw him.

Across the street, beneath the sprawling branches of an ancient oak, stood a figure that seemed to defy reality itself. Drake blinked, certain his mind was playing tricks on him. But the apparition remained, a stark contrast to the chaos unfolding around them.

"What in God's name..." Drake muttered, his voice barely audible over the roar of the flames.

The figure's skin was a grotesque patchwork of charred and disfigured flesh, his face a nightmarish mask that seemed to mock the very concept of humanity. Yet, draped over this horrific form was a pristine white robe, unmarred by the destruction that surrounded them. On the chest of the robe, a symbol caught Drake's eye - a green dragon coiled in a perfect circle.

Drake's mind reeled, struggling to process what he was seeing. Is this real? Am I losing my mind? The questions swirled in his head, competing with the urgent need to save his family.

"Who are you?" Drake called out, his voice cracking with emotion. "What's happening here?"

The figure remained motionless, its very presence an affront to the laws of nature. Drake felt a chill run down his spine, a stark contrast to the inferno at his back. Something about this... thing... felt familiar, yet utterly alien at the same time.

"Answer me!" Drake demanded, taking a step towards the oak tree. "Are you responsible for this?"

As he moved, the figure's head tilted slightly, as if studying Drake with detached curiosity. The simple motion sent waves of revulsion through Drake's body, his instincts screaming at him to run, to get as far away from this abomination as possible.

But he couldn't leave. Not with Linda and Harrison still trapped in the burning house. Drake's fists clenched at his sides, torn between the urge to confront this mysterious figure and the desperate need to save his family.

"I don't know who or what you are," Drake growled, his voice low and dangerous, "but if you've hurt my family, I swear I'll-"

His threat was cut short as a thunderous crack echoed from behind him. Drake whirled around to see a section of the roof collapse, sending a plume of embers into the sky. The sight reignited the urgency of his situation.

"Linda! Harrison!" he screamed once more, his heart shattering with each unanswered call.

When Drake turned back to the oak tree, the figure was gone. He blinked, scanning the area in disbelief. Had it ever really been there? Or was his mind fracturing under the weight of this nightmare?

39 - 40

The figure's grotesque smile widened as it raised a hand, waving with an eerie, deliberate slowness. The motion seemed to mock Drake, a perverse parody of a friendly greeting amidst the chaos and destruction.

Drake's breath caught in his throat, his heart hammering against his ribcage with such force he thought it might burst. Something about this disfigured entity tugged at the edges of his consciousness, a half-forgotten memory struggling to surface.

"Who-" Drake began, but the word died on his lips as a sudden, vivid vision overwhelmed him.

He was in a car, the world outside a dizzying blur of motion. His hands gripped the steering wheel, knuckles white with tension as he fought for control. The sickening screech of metal filled his ears, and then—

The windshield exploded inward, a shower of glass shards raining down. Through the spiderweb of cracks, a face appeared. Charred. Melted. Inhuman. Those same lifeless eyes bored into him, a burnt visage pressed against the fractured glass.

Drake staggered backward, gasping as the vision released him. He blinked rapidly, trying to reconcile the horrific memory with the surreal present.

"It was you," he whispered, his voice hoarse with dawning recognition. "At the accident. But how? Why?"

The figure remained silent, its ruined features frozen in that terrible smile. Drake's mind raced, grasping for explanations, for some thread of logic in this nightmare.

"Is this real?" he demanded, desperation creeping into his tone. "Or am I losing my mind?"

As if in answer, a fresh wave of heat washed over him from the burning house. The acrid smell of smoke filled his nostrils, grounding him in the terrible reality of the moment.

"Linda and Harrison," Drake murmured, torn between confronting this apparition and saving his family. "I have to—"

He turned back toward the inferno that had been his home, anguish twisting in his gut. When he looked to the oak tree again, the figure had vanished, leaving Drake alone with the crackling flames and his fractured memories.

41 - 42

Drake's legs trembled beneath him as he stared at the empty space where the figure had stood. The absence felt more oppressive than its presence, leaving him with a void of unanswered questions.

"Who are you?" Drake whispered, his voice trembling. The words hung in the air, swallowed by the roar of the flames behind him. His mind raced, grasping at the fragments of memory that had surfaced. The car accident, the burned face, the symbol of the green dragon—they swirled together in a dizzying kaleidoscope of horror and confusion.

He took a step toward the tree, his lawyer's instinct pushing him to investigate, to find some tangible evidence of what he'd seen. But as he moved, the vision that had gripped him moments ago began to fade, slipping away like smoke through his fingers.

"No," Drake muttered, pressing his palms against his temples. "Don't go. I need to understand."

But the memory retreated, leaving him standing alone on the lawn, the grass cool beneath his feet. When he looked back at the tree, the figure was gone, as if it had never existed at all. The oak stood silent, its leaves rustling gently in the breeze, oblivious to the chaos unfolding around it.

Drake's shoulders sagged, the weight of his confusion and fear threatening to crush him. "Am I losing my mind?" he wondered aloud, his voice barely audible over the crackling of the flames. "Or is this all part of something bigger?"

He turned back to face the burning house, his heart racing with renewed urgency. "Linda. Harrison," he breathed, torn between the mystery behind him and the crisis before him. "I have to focus. I have to save them."

43 - 43

The inferno roared, an insatiable beast devouring everything Drake held dear. Heat seared his skin as he watched helplessly, the once-comforting structure of his home now a hellish pyre. Acrid smoke stung his eyes, blurring his vision with tears that were as much from grief as they were from the noxious fumes.

"Linda! Harrison!" Drake's voice cracked, raw emotion bleeding through each syllable. His muscular frame, usually a symbol of strength, now trembled with the weight of his failure. He stumbled forward, driven by a desperate, irrational hope. "Please, God, no..."

His knees buckled, and he found himself on the ground, fingers digging into the cool grass. The stark contrast between the lush lawn and the fiery destruction before him was a cruel mockery of the life he'd known mere moments ago.

"I should have known," Drake whispered, his mind racing through the morning's events. "The dreams, the dread... I should have done more."

A guttural scream tore from his throat, primal and agonized. It echoed through the neighborhood, a sound of pure anguish that seemed to make even the flames pause in their relentless advance.

As the scream faded, leaving him breathless, Drake's lawyer's mind kicked in, a defense mechanism against the overwhelming emotion. "Think, Drake," he muttered to himself. "There has to be an explanation. The gas... the figure... it can't all be coincidence."

But logic crumbled in the face of his loss. Images of Linda's smile and Harrison's laughter flashed through his mind, now forever out of reach. The weight of their absence crushed him, a void so vast he felt he might disappear into it.

"I failed them," Drake choked out, his voice barely audible over the crackling flames. "I was supposed to protect them, and I failed."

After the Flames

1 -2
The acrid stench of burning wood and smoke hung heavy in the air, mixing with the distant wail of sirens. Drake sat slumped under the oak tree across the street, his gaze fixed blankly on the smoldering wreckage of his home. Flames had finally given way to charred ruin, leaving behind blackened timbers and collapsing walls. His suit was singed, his hair disheveled, and his face streaked with soot and ash. But none of it registered. His world was gone.

In the hollow emptiness of his mind, echoes of laughter haunted him - Linda's melodic tones, Harrison's gleeful giggles. Gone now, swept away in a maelstrom of fire and smoke. Drake's muscular frame seemed to collapse in on itself, shoulders hunched as if bearing an impossible weight. His fingers dug into the earth, clawing at the grass as if he could somehow anchor himself to this new, desolate reality.

How quickly it had all unraveled, he thought bitterly. One moment, a happy family sleeping peacefully. The next... His mind shied away from the memory, unable to process the horror. Instead, his gaze remained locked on the smoldering ruins before him, seeing not the destruction but the ghosts of what once was. There, where a charred beam jutted from the rubble - that had been Harrison's room. And there, that blackened frame - the kitchen where Linda had danced as she cooked, filling their home with warmth and love.

A sob rose in Drake's throat, choking him. He opened his mouth, desperate to scream, to rail against the cruel twist of fate that had stolen everything from him. But no sound emerged. There were no words for this anguish, this all-consuming grief that threatened to swallow him whole.

"Mr. Miller!"

The voice pierced through the fog of Drake's despair, sharp and urgent. For a moment, hope flared - wild, irrational hope that perhaps it was all a mistake, that his family had somehow escaped. But as quickly as it rose, it was extinguished. Drake knew, with a bone-deep certainty that left him cold, that there was no escaping this nightmare.

His head turned slowly, every movement an effort. Through the smoky veil, a figure approached, but Drake couldn't bring himself to care who it might be. What did it matter now? His world had ended, reduced to ash and memory in the span of a single, terrible night.

3 - 4

The figure materialized through the haze, a young man with a shock of messy dark hair. His wiry frame was taut with tension, eyes wide with panic as he approached. Drake's mind struggled to place him, to connect this apparition to some semblance of reality. A name floated to the surface of his consciousness, a lifeline in the sea of his despair.

"Mike?" Drake mumbled, his voice distant and hoarse. The word scraped against his throat, raw from smoke and unshed tears. He blinked sluggishly, trying to focus on the familiar face before him.

Mike. His sons from school, was stopping by today to pick up Harrison for soccer practice. What was he doing here, amidst the ruins of Drake's life? A part of Drake wanted to laugh at the absurdity of it all, but he couldn't muster the energy. Instead, he stared blankly, his normally sharp mind dulled by shock and grief.

Why is he here? Drake wondered, the thought drifting lazily through his mind. *Does he know? How could he know when I can barely comprehend it myself?*

His gaze drifted back to the smoldering remains of his home, a fresh wave of anguish washing over him. In that moment, Drake longed for the simplicity of his old life, before alternate realities and multiversal anomalies had torn his world apart. Before he'd been granted this cruel second chance, only to watch it crumble to ash before his eyes.

"I failed them," Drake whispered, more to himself than to Mike. "Again."

5 - 6

Mike's eyes widened, panic flashing across his youthful features. He crouched down, his gaze darting between Drake and the charred remnants of the house.

"Mr. Miller, what happened?" Mike asked, his voice cracking with urgency. "Is—are Harrison and Mrs. Miller... where are they?"

The question hung in the air, heavy and suffocating. Drake's chest constricted, each breath a battle against the weight of his grief. He opened his mouth to respond, but the words died on his lips, replaced by a strangled sound that was neither sob nor scream.

How do I tell him? Drake thought, his mind reeling. *How do I put into words the horror I've witnessed, the failure I've endured?*

Images flashed before his eyes—Linda's gentle smile, Harrison's infectious laughter. Both now silenced forever, consumed by flames that had stolen more than just his home. Drake's body began to tremble, the enormity of his loss finally crashing over him like a tidal wave.

"They're..." Drake started, his voice barely above a whisper. But he couldn't finish. Instead, he shook his head violently, as if denying the truth could somehow change it. His hands clenched into fists, nails digging into his palms, the physical pain a welcome distraction from the emotional agony threatening to tear him apart.

I was supposed to protect them, he thought bitterly. *I crossed realities, defied the laws of nature, all to save them. And for what? To watch them die all over again?*

Drake's gaze fixed on the oak tree across the street, its leaves rustling gently in stark contrast to the devastation surrounding them. He remembered standing there earlier, watching a figure wave at him. Had that been real, or just another cruel trick of his fractured reality?

7 - 8

"I—I don't..." Drake stammered, his words dissolving into incoherent murmurs. The acrid taste of smoke lingered on his tongue, each breath a reminder of the inferno that had consumed his world. His thoughts scattered like embers in the wind, each one a searing fragment of memory too painful to grasp.

Linda's eyes, wide with terror. Harrison's small hand reaching out. The roar of flames drowning out their screams.

Drake's fingers dug into the scorched earth beneath him, anchoring himself to the present even as his mind threatened to fracture. He could feel Mike's worried gaze upon him, but couldn't bring himself to meet it. How could he explain the impossible? How could he voice the truth that spanned across realities?

"They're gone," he finally managed, his voice cracking. "I couldn't... I tried to..."

Mike crouched beside him, his face a mask of concern. The young man's proximity was both comforting and suffocating, a reminder of the connections Drake still had in this world—and those he'd lost.

"Mr. Miller, are you okay? You're shaking," Mike said softly, reaching out a tentative hand.

Drake flinched away instinctively, his body betraying his turmoil. *I'm not okay,* he thought. *I'll never be okay again.* But he couldn't form the words, couldn't bridge the chasm between the horrors in his mind and the reality before him.

Instead, he stared at the smoldering ruins of his home, his vision blurring with unshed tears. Somewhere in the ashes lay the remnants of his life, of his family. And somewhere beyond, a disfigured man with a dragon symbol held the answers he desperately needed.

9 - 10

Drake lifted a trembling hand, his gaze fixed upon it as if it were a foreign object. The world around him tilted and swayed, reality itself seeming to bend and warp. His fingers trembled uncontrollably, a physical manifestation of the chaos raging within his mind.

This can't be real, he thought, his inner voice a desperate whisper. *Linda... Harrison... they can't be...*

Determined to prove to himself that this was all some terrible nightmare, Drake attempted to stand. His muscular frame, usually so steady and reliable, betrayed him. His legs buckled beneath him, refusing to support his weight. The ground rushed up to meet him as he collapsed back onto the grass, the impact jarring through his body.

"Mr. Miller!" Mike's shout pierced through the haze of Drake's disorientation. The young man's hand shot out, grabbing Drake's arm with surprising strength. "Easy there, sir. You shouldn't try to move yet."

Drake's eyes met Mike's, seeing the genuine concern etched across the young man's features. For a moment, he was struck by the absurdity of it all - here he was, Drake Miller, successful businessman and family man, sprawled on the grass like a broken doll while his home smoldered behind him.

"I need to..." Drake's voice trailed off, his thoughts scattering like leaves in a storm. What did he need to do? Find Linda and Harrison? Chase down the man with the dragon symbol? Unravel the mystery of the time loop.

Mike's grip on his arm tightened slightly, grounding him. "You need to rest, Mr. Miller. Help is on the way. Just... just try to stay calm, okay?"

Drake nodded numbly, his gaze drifting back to the ruins of his home. *Stay calm,* he thought bitterly. *How can I stay calm when my entire world has just gone up in flames?*

11 - 12

As Drake's mind reeled, a sudden, violent tremor ripped through his body. His muscles seized, limbs jerking uncontrollably as he toppled sideways onto the damp grass. The acrid taste of smoke in his mouth gave way to something more primal - a metallic tang as his teeth clamped down on his tongue.

What's happening to me? The thought flashed through Drake's mind, a pinprick of clarity in a maelstrom of sensation. His vision blurred, the world around him dissolving into a kaleidoscope of fractured images - smoldering timbers, Mike's panic-stricken face, the distant oak tree where he'd seen... something. Someone.

"Mr. Miller!" Mike's voice seemed to come from far away, muffled and distorted. "Oh God, oh God..."

Drake tried to respond, to reassure the young man, but his body refused to obey. He felt a warm, sticky substance at the corners of his mouth - saliva? Blood? - as his eyes rolled back, darkness creeping in at the edges of his vision.

Linda... Harrison... Their names echoed in his mind, a mantra of loss and desperation. *I failed you. I'm sorry. I'm so sorry.*

"Someone help!" Mike's scream pierced through the fog of Drake's fading consciousness, the young man's voice cracking with raw desperation. "Please, anybody! We need help over here!"

As the darkness closed in, Drake's last coherent thought was a grim realization: *This isn't over. Whatever's happening, whatever I've stumbled into... it's only just beginning.*

13 - 14

Drake's consciousness plummeted into an abyss, Mike's frantic cries fading into nothingness. The acrid smell of smoke and ash gave way to a void, devoid of sensation. In this liminal space, suspended between realities, Drake's mind struggled to make sense of his surroundings.

Suddenly, a barrage of images assaulted him. Fragmented memories, distorted and vivid, cascaded through his psyche like shards of broken glass. Each vision more intense than the last, they bombarded him relentlessly.

Linda's laughter, once melodic and soothing, now twisted into a haunting echo. Harrison's cherubic face, usually beaming with innocence, contorted in terror. The visions flickered rapidly, a nightmarish slideshow of his deepest fears and regrets.

What is this? Drake's thoughts echoed in the vastness. *Are these memories? Or something else?*

As if in response, the kaleidoscope of images coalesced into a single, horrifying scene. Drake found himself back in the car, the moment of impact frozen in time. Linda's eyes, wide with fear, locked onto his. Harrison's teenage form, helpless in the backseat, reaching out for his father.

"No!" Drake tried to scream, but no sound emerged. He was trapped, forced to relive the moment that shattered his world.

The visions shifted again, this time to the smoldering ruins of his home. But something was different. A figure stood amidst the flames, untouched by the inferno. As Drake's gaze focused, he recoiled in horror. The man's face was a grotesque mask of burnt flesh, a cruel smile playing on his lips.

Who are you? Drake's mind raced, recognition and confusion warring within him. *What do you want?*

The disfigured man's smile widened, revealing teeth as sharp as razors. He raised a hand, pointing directly at Drake. The gesture carried an unmistakable message: You're next.

15 - 16

The seizure's grip tightened, yanking Drake deeper into the maelstrom of his subconscious. The world around him dissolved, replaced by a vivid memory that felt as real as the day it happened.

He was in the car, the familiar hum of the engine vibrating beneath him. Linda sat beside him, her golden hair catching the last rays of the setting sun. Her laughter, light and melodic, filled the air as she turned to face him.

"Drake, did you hear what Harrison just said?" Linda's blue eyes sparkled with mirth.

Drake's heart clenched. He wanted to reach out, to touch her face one last time, but his body wouldn't respond. He was a prisoner in his own memory.

From the backseat, Harrison's voice bubbled up, full of childish excitement. "Dad, can we get ice cream after dinner? Please?"

"I don't know, buddy," Drake heard himself reply, his voice carrying a lightness he barely recognized. "What do you think, Linda?"

Linda's smile widened. "I think we can manage that. It's a special night, after all."

Special night? Drake's thoughts raced. *What was so special about it?*

As if in response to his unspoken question, his gaze dropped to Linda's left hand. A diamond ring glittered on her finger, catching the golden light of the sunset.

Our anniversary, Drake realized with a jolt of anguish. *This was the night of the accident.*

The car continued its steady journey, oblivious to the impending tragedy. Drake wanted to scream, to warn them, but he was powerless to change the course of events.

17 - 18

The peaceful moment shattered as a piercing screech of tires tore through the air. Drake's hands tightened instinctively on the steering wheel, his knuckles turning white as adrenaline surged through his body.

"Drake!" Linda's cry was drowned out by the cacophony of metal grinding against metal.

The world outside the windows became a dizzying blur of motion and color. Drake's heart hammered in his chest as he fought to regain control of the vehicle. "Hold on!" he shouted, his voice strained with fear and determination.

This can't be happening, his mind screamed. *Not again. Please, not again.*

The car spun wildly, each rotation bringing a fresh wave of terror. Harrison's panicked voice pierced through the chaos. "Dad! Make it stop!"

Drake's thoughts raced. *I have to protect them. I have to save my family.*

A sickening crunch reverberated through the car as it collided with something solid. The windshield exploded inward, showering them with a thousand glittering shards. In that moment, time seemed to slow, each shard catching the fading light like tiny, deadly stars.

"Linda! Harrison!" Drake called out desperately, trying to turn his head to check on them.

Before he could see their faces, his forehead slammed against the steering wheel with brutal force. Pain exploded behind his eyes, momentarily blinding him. As darkness threatened to engulf him, one thought echoed in his mind:

I failed them. Again.

19 - 20

The violent motion ceased abruptly, plunging the world into an eerie stillness. Drake's ears rang, the sudden silence more deafening than the chaos that preceded it. He blinked sluggishly, his vision blurring as warm blood trickled down his face. The metallic tang filled his nostrils, mingling with the acrid scent of burning rubber and twisted metal.

His heart pounded against his ribcage, each beat a painful reminder that he was still alive. Alive, but terrified of what he might find when he turned his head. Drake's fingers trembled as he released his death grip on the steering wheel, leaving behind ghostly white imprints where his knuckles had been.

"Harrison?" he croaked, his voice barely above a whisper. The name caught in his throat, raw with fear and desperation.

Slowly, painfully, Drake turned to face the backseat. His eyes struggled to focus through the haze of shock and injury. *Please*, he thought, a silent prayer to any power that might be listening. *Please let him be okay*.

The silence stretched on, unbearable in its intensity. Drake's breath came in short, ragged gasps as he searched the shadows of the crumpled backseat. "Harrison?" he called again, his voice trembling with a mixture of hope and dread. "Son, can you hear me?"

In the recesses of his mind, a faint memory stirred - another crash, another moment of terrifying silence. But this time had to be different. It had to be.

"Dad?" Harrison's voice, weak but unmistakable, cut through the silence like a beacon of hope.

Relief washed over Drake, so intense it was almost painful. "I'm here, buddy," he managed, his words choked with emotion. "Are you hurt?"

There was a moment of hesitation before Harrison replied, his voice tinged with confusion and fear. "I... I don't know. Everything's fuzzy. Dad, what happened?"

Drake's heart clenched at the uncertainty in his son's voice. "We had an accident, but it's going to be okay," he assured, trying to inject confidence into his words despite his own doubts. "Just stay still for now. I'm going to get us out of here."

As he spoke, Drake's gaze darted to the passenger seat, suddenly aware of the one voice he hadn't heard. "Linda?" he called, dread creeping back into his heart.

21 - 22

Drake's eyes fell upon the backseat, and his world shattered. Harrison lay slumped against the door, his lanky frame unnaturally still. The Spider-Man tie Drake had helped him put on that morning was askew, its vibrant red and blue now spotted with dark, accusing stains.

"No," Drake whispered, his voice barely audible over the ringing in his ears. He reached out, his hand trembling violently as it hovered over his son's motionless form. "No, no, no!"

His fingers brushed against Harrison's arm, cold and unresponsive. Drake recoiled, his mind reeling, unable to process the reality before him.

"This can't be happening," he thought, panic rising in his chest. "Not again. Not like this."

Memories of another crash, another loss, threatened to overwhelm him. But this was different. This was his second chance, his opportunity to make things right.

"Harrison, please," Drake pleaded, his voice cracking with desperation. "Wake up, buddy. You have to wake up."

He fumbled with his seatbelt, ignoring the pain that shot through his body as he twisted to face the backseat fully. His lawyer's mind, always analytical, always searching for solutions, now failed him completely. There were no arguments to be made, no deals to be struck. Only the crushing weight of an unthinkable loss.

"I was supposed to protect you," Drake murmured, tears streaming down his face. "I was supposed to save you this time."

The silence that answered him was deafening, punctuated only by the distant wail of approaching sirens. Drake reached out again, gently brushing a lock of hair from Harrison's forehead. In that moment, the full weight of his failure crashed down upon him, threatening to drag him into an abyss of despair from which he might never emerge.

23 - 24

The scene shifted violently, as if reality itself was tearing at the seams. Drake's vision blurred, the world around him spinning in a dizzying whirl of colors and shapes. When it settled, his heart plummeted to the pit of his stomach.

Linda was there in the passenger seat, her presence a cruel twist of fate. Her face, once radiant with life and love, was now pale and lifeless. Drake's breath caught in his throat, a visceral pain gripping his chest.

"Linda?" he whispered, his voice barely audible over the ringing in his ears.

Her blonde hair, which she always took such pride in styling, lay in tangled disarray across her face. Streaks of crimson marred the golden strands, a stark contrast that made Drake's stomach churn. With trembling fingers, he reached out to her, desperately clinging to a hope he knew was futile.

"This isn't real," Drake thought, even as his fingertips brushed against Linda's cold skin. "It can't be. We were supposed to have more time."

Memories flooded his mind - Linda's laughter echoing through their home, her gentle touch when he'd wake from nightmares of other realities. How could all of that be gone in an instant?

"I'm sorry," he choked out, tears blurring his vision. "I tried to change things, to make it right. But I've failed you both again."

Drake's hand lingered on Linda's cheek, his thumb tracing the curve of her jaw. In that touch, he sought some spark of life, some sign that this was all just another cruel illusion.

But the cold reality remained unyielding. Linda was gone, just as Harrison was gone. And Drake was left alone, trapped in a nightmare he couldn't escape, no matter how many realities he traversed.

25 - 26

"Linda?" Drake's voice cracked, barely a whisper in the eerie silence that had descended upon the wreckage.

His heart pounded against his ribs, each beat a painful reminder that he was alive while she lay motionless. The acrid smell of burning rubber and spilled gasoline filled his nostrils, threatening to overwhelm him.

Suddenly, a chill ran down Drake's spine. The air around him seemed to thicken, pressing against him with an almost tangible weight. He felt a presence, something looming just beyond his peripheral vision.

"No," he thought, panic rising in his chest. "Not here. Not now."

Drake's muscles tensed, every instinct screaming at him to run, to escape. But he couldn't leave Linda. He wouldn't.

With agonizing slowness, he turned his head, his breath hitching in his throat. The world seemed to move in slow motion, each second stretching into an eternity.

"Who's there?" he managed to croak out, his voice hoarse and unfamiliar to his own ears. "Show yourself!"

But only silence answered him, broken only by the distant wail of approaching sirens. Drake's mind raced, fragments of memories from other realities flashing before his eyes. Had he brought some interdimensional horror with him? Was this the price of his meddling with time and space?

As the shadow loomed larger, Drake's hand instinctively tightened around Linda's, a futile gesture of protection. "I won't let you take her," he whispered, more to himself than to the unseen presence. "Not again. Not ever."

27 - 28

Drake's eyes widened in horror as the figure came into view. A man—no, a monstrosity—stood outside the shattered windshield, his face a grotesque mask of burnt flesh and twisted features. The creature's skin was charred and warped, as if he had been pulled from the heart of an inferno and reshaped by malevolent hands.

"Who... what are you?" Drake choked out, his voice barely above a whisper.

The figure didn't respond. Instead, its lips curled into a smile that sent ice through Drake's veins. In that moment, Drake felt a primal fear unlike anything he had ever experienced, even in his journeys across realities.

"Stay back," Drake growled, trying to muster some semblance of strength. "I'm warning you."

The creature's smile only widened, revealing teeth that seemed too sharp, too numerous. It raised a hand, pressing it against the cracked glass of the windshield. Drake's gaze was drawn to the figure's white robe, where a dragon symbol gleamed faintly in the dim light.

"That symbol," Drake thought, his mind racing. "I've seen it before, but where?"

As he struggled to recall, a flood of conflicting memories threatened to overwhelm him. The weight of multiple realities pressed against his consciousness, each vying for dominance.

"What do you want from us?" Drake demanded, his voice cracking with fear and desperation.

The figure remained silent, its burning gaze fixed on Drake with an intensity that seemed to pierce his very soul. In that moment, Drake knew with chilling certainty that this encounter was far from random. This entity, whatever it was, had been waiting for him.

29 - 30

Drake blinked, and the world around him shattered. The car, the disfigured figure, all of it dissolved into a whirlwind of fractured imagery. His stomach lurched as reality shifted, leaving him disoriented and breathless.

Suddenly, an explosion ripped through the air. Drake's eyes widened in shock as a wall of fire and smoke surged towards him, consuming everything in its path. The heat seared his skin, the roar deafening in his ears.

"No!" he shouted, throwing his arms up instinctively. But it was futile. The force of the blast lifted him off his feet, hurling him backward through space. His body felt weightless, suspended in a moment of terrible clarity.

Time seemed to slow as debris rained down around him. Shards of glass glinted like deadly stars, wood splintered into deadly projectiles. Drake's mind raced, grasping for understanding.

"This can't be real," he thought, his lawyer's logic battling against the impossible scenario. "I've seen this before, haven't I? Or is this happening now?"

As he tumbled through the air, memories and realities blurred. He saw flashes of Linda's smile, heard echoes of Harrison's laughter. The weight of his failures, his desperate attempts to save them across multiple worlds, crashed down on him.

"I can't lose them again!" Drake cried out, his voice lost in the chaos. He reached out, grasping at empty air, trying to anchor himself to something, anything.

But there was nothing to hold onto. As the world erupted around him, Drake Miller – once a man of reason and control – found himself utterly powerless against the forces tearing his reality apart.

31 - 32

Amidst the swirling inferno, a face emerged from the flames—Linda's. Her blue eyes, usually so full of warmth, now widened in terror. Her blonde hair whipped wildly around her face, tongues of fire licking at the strands.

"Drake!" she screamed, her voice barely audible above the roar of destruction. "Help us!"

Drake's heart clenched, his body straining against the maelstrom to reach her. "Linda! I'm coming!"

But as he struggled forward, Linda's visage flickered and transformed. Harrison's young face appeared, his brown eyes brimming with tears, his Spider-Man tie askew.

"Dad!" Harrison cried out, his small hands reaching desperately. "Why can't you save us?"

Drake's throat constricted, choking on ash and anguish. "Harrison, I'm trying! I swear I'm trying!"

His mind raced, grappling with the impossibility of the situation. How could they both be here? Was this another cruel illusion, another trap of the fractured reality he'd been fighting against?

Suddenly, the flames parted like a grotesque curtain. There, standing amidst the carnage as if it were a gentle spring day, was the disfigured man. His charred skin gleamed in the firelight, his mouth twisted into a sickeningly wide grin.

Drake felt his blood run cold despite the heat. "You," he growled, memories of past encounters flooding back. "What have you done to my family?"

The figure said nothing. Instead, his grin widened impossibly further as he slowly raised a finger, pointing directly at Drake. The accusation in the gesture was unmistakable.

"No," Drake whispered, his voice breaking. "This isn't my fault. I didn't cause this!"

But even as he protested, doubt gnawed at him. How many realities had he torn through in his desperate quest? How many versions of his family had he failed to save?

The disfigured man's finger remained unwavering, a silent judge amidst the chaos. And as the world continued to burn around them, Drake Miller faced the terrifying possibility that in his attempts to save everything, he might have doomed them all.

33 - 34

"Who are you?" Drake screamed, his voice hoarse and desperate. The inferno roared around him, swallowing his words in its hungry maw. The heat seared his skin, but the pain was nothing compared to the anguish tearing through his soul.

The disfigured man's lips curled into a sneer, his scarred face a grotesque mask of malice. "You know who I am, Drake," he said, his voice eerily calm amidst the chaos. "I'm the consequence of your choices."

Drake's mind reeled, fragments of memories assaulting him with brutal force. A stark hospital room materialized, the beep of monitors a cruel metronome. He saw himself, lying motionless on the bed, tubes snaking from his body. Linda's tear-stained face hovered above him, her whispers lost in the sterile air.

"No," Drake muttered, shaking his head violently. "This isn't real. You're not—"

The scene shifted abruptly. Now he stood before a swirling vortex of darkness, its edges crackling with malevolent energy. The Nexus of Torment. Drake felt the pull of it, threatening to drag him into its depths.

"Remember this place?" the disfigured man taunted, suddenly beside him. "Where it all began to unravel?"

Drake's fists clenched. "I did what I had to do," he growled, even as doubt gnawed at him. "To save them. To save everyone."

Another shift. An ancient tome appeared in his hands, its pages filled with arcane symbols. The Ancient Codex. "The key to everything," Drake whispered, his fingers tracing the worn leather binding.

Sirens wailed in the distance, growing louder. The disfigured man's face contorted, morphing into The disfigured man's features. The sneer remained, but now it was tinged with anger and... was that pain?

"You can't escape this, Drake," The disfigured man snarled, his eyes blazing with an otherworldly fury. "Every choice, every sacrifice—it all leads back to me. To us."

Drake stumbled backward, his mind a maelstrom of conflicting realities. "No," he insisted, more to himself than to The disfigured man. "I'll find a way. I'll save them. I have to."

But as the visions continued to swirl, each more visceral than the last, Drake Miller felt the weight of his quest crushing down upon him. How many more realities would he have to tear through? How many more versions of himself would he have to confront?

And in the end, would any of it be enough to undo the damage he'd already done?

35 - 36

The kaleidoscope of memories imploded, leaving Drake suspended in an inky void. The silence was deafening, pressing against his eardrums like a physical force. He tried to move, to speak, but his body refused to obey. Panic clawed at his throat.

"Linda?" he called out, his voice barely a whisper in the emptiness. "Harrison?"

No response came. Only the oppressive darkness.

Gradually, sensation crept back into his limbs. A heaviness settled over him, as if gravity itself had increased tenfold. Drake's eyelids fluttered, struggling against the weight.

"I can't... I can't lose them again," he thought, his inner voice thick with anguish.

A pinprick of light pierced the darkness, growing steadily brighter. Drake's consciousness swam towards it, desperate for any anchor in this void.

As awareness seeped back, the acrid smell of smoke assaulted his nostrils. The rough texture of grass pressed against his back. His body felt leaden, disconnected, as if he were piloting it from a great distance.

"Mr. Miller?" A voice, muffled and distorted, cut through the haze.

Drake's lips moved, but no sound emerged. His mind raced, trying to piece together the fragments of reality and vision.

"The man... the disfigured man," he thought frantically. "He's the key. But who is he? What does he want?"

37 - 38

Drake's eyes flickered open, the world swimming into focus. The sky above was a hazy grey, obscured by tendrils of smoke that drifted lazily on the breeze. He blinked, struggling to orient himself. The grass beneath him felt damp, its coolness seeping through his singed clothing.

A face hovered over him, features tight with concern. Mike. The young man's usually vibrant eyes were wide with fear, his skin ashen beneath a sheen of sweat.

"Mr. Miller, can you hear me?" Mike's voice trembled, barely above a whisper.

Drake tried to respond, but his throat felt raw, as if he'd swallowed glass. He managed a weak nod, wincing at the effort.

"Thank God," Mike breathed, his shoulders sagging with relief.

As Drake's senses sharpened, the full weight of reality crashed over him. The acrid stench of burnt wood. The distant wail of sirens. The hollow ache in his chest where his family should be.

"Linda... Harrison..." he thought, a fresh wave of anguish threatening to pull him under. The visions of their deaths played on repeat in his mind, each iteration more vivid and painful than the last.

"What happened?" Drake croaked, his voice barely recognizable to his own ears. He struggled to push himself up, arms shaking with the effort.

Mike's hand shot out, steadying him. "Easy, Mr. Miller. You had some kind of seizure. I... I didn't know what to do."

Drake's mind reeled, trying to reconcile the visions with reality. "The man," he muttered, more to himself than to Mike. "Did you see him? The one with the burns?"

Mike's brow furrowed in confusion. "What man? There's been no one here but us, Mr. Miller."

Drake closed his eyes, frustration mixing with his grief. How could he explain what he'd seen? The car crash, the explosion, the figure who seemed to connect it all?

"I need to find him," Drake said, his voice growing stronger with determination. "He has answers. He has to."

39 - 40

Drake's gaze drifted beyond Mike, settling on the ruins of his home. The once-proud structure now stood as a blackened husk against the twilight sky, a grotesque monument to all he had lost. Each charred beam and shattered window felt like a physical blow, driving home the finality of his family's fate.

"They're gone," he murmured, the words tasting like ash in his mouth. Tears welled up, spilling down his soot-stained cheeks as he pushed himself onto his elbows. "They're both gone."

The admission hung heavy in the air, a truth too painful to fully comprehend. Drake's mind raced, grasping for some shred of hope, some alternate explanation that could undo this nightmare. But the visions he'd experienced left no room for doubt.

"Mr. Miller," Mike began, his voice thick with concern, "I don't understand. What happened here?"

Drake turned to face the young man, seeing the fear and confusion etched across his features. How could he possibly explain the inexplicable? The collision of realities, the visions of death and destruction that felt more real than the world around him?

"I couldn't save them," Drake whispered, his voice cracking under the weight of his guilt. "I was supposed to protect them, and I failed. Again."

41 - 42

Mike looked at him, his expression stricken. "I—I'm so sorry," he whispered, his voice trembling with genuine anguish.

Drake barely registered the young man's words, his mind still reeling from the onslaught of visions. He blinked hard, trying to clear the lingering images of flames and twisted metal from his mind's eye. The acrid smell of smoke clung to his nostrils, a constant reminder of the devastation surrounding them.

"Sorry," Drake echoed hollowly, the word tasting bitter on his tongue. "Sorry doesn't bring them back."

His gaze drifted away from Mike, unable to bear the weight of the young man's sympathy. Instead, he found himself staring down the empty street. The oak tree that had stood sentinel through countless peaceful afternoons now loomed like a silent judge, its branches swaying gently in the breeze. Drake's eyes darted from shadow to shadow, searching for... something. Someone.

"I saw him," Drake muttered, more to himself than to Mike. "He was here, watching. Smiling."

But the street remained stubbornly empty. No trace remained of the disfigured man who had haunted his visions, who had pointed at him with such cruel certainty amidst the chaos of his memories. Drake's hands clenched into fists, frustration and confusion warring within him.

"Who was here, Mr. Miller?" Mike asked cautiously, clearly concerned about Drake's state of mind.

Drake shook his head, unable to articulate the fragments of memory and vision swirling through his thoughts. How could he explain a figure that existed somewhere between nightmare and reality? The absence of evidence only deepened his sense of isolation, trapped between worlds he no longer understood.

43 - 44

Drake's brow furrowed, his eyes still scanning the empty street as if the mysterious figure might materialize from thin air. The acrid smell of smoke lingered, a constant reminder of all he had lost. He inhaled deeply, trying to ground himself in the present moment.

"Who was he?" Drake muttered, his voice barely above a whisper. The words felt heavy on his tongue, laden with a significance he couldn't fully grasp. "I've seen him before."

Images flashed through his mind: a grotesquely disfigured face, charred skin, a dragon symbol gleaming on white robes. The memories slipped away like sand through his fingers, leaving him grasping at phantoms.

Mike leaned in closer, his brow furrowing with concern. "Who?" he asked, his voice tinged with a mixture of curiosity and apprehension.

Drake turned to face the young man, seeing his own confusion mirrored in Mike's eyes. He opened his mouth to respond, but found himself at a loss for words. How could he explain something he barely understood himself?

"I don't know," Drake finally admitted, his voice hoarse. "A man... or something that looked like a man. Burned, disfigured. He was here, watching. And in my memories, in the car crash, in the fire..." He trailed off, frustrated by his inability to articulate the swirling chaos in his mind.

Mike's expression shifted from concern to alarm. "Mr. Miller, are you sure? I didn't see anyone else here when I arrived."

Drake's jaw clenched, a flicker of doubt creeping into his thoughts. Was he losing his grip on reality? Or was there something more sinister at play, something beyond the tragedy that had befallen his family?

45 - 46

Drake's gaze drifted back to the empty street, his eyes scanning the shadows between houses and parked cars. The figure was gone, if it had ever been there at all. Yet the feeling of being watched lingered, prickling the back of his neck.

"I'm not sure of anything anymore, Mike," Drake murmured, his voice barely audible above the distant wail of approaching sirens. His mind raced, grasping at fragments of memory and vision. "Everything I thought I knew... it's all slipping away."

He closed his eyes, trying to focus on the elusive threads of thought. The car crash, the explosion, the disfigured man – they swirled together in a dizzying kaleidoscope of horror and loss.

"Mr. Miller," Mike began, hesitation clear in his voice, "maybe we should get you to a hospital. You've been through a lot, and-"

"No," Drake interrupted, his eyes snapping open. The word came out harsher than he intended, and he saw Mike flinch. Softening his tone, he continued, "I'm sorry, but I can't. Not yet. There's something I need to figure out."

As the sirens grew louder, Drake's fists clenched involuntarily. The acrid smell of smoke seemed to intensify, and with it came a fresh wave of grief. Linda's laugh, Harrison's excited chatter – the memories of his family burned anew in his mind, their loss a physical ache in his chest.

"They're gone," he whispered, more to himself than to Mike. "And I don't know why, or how, but I have to find out. I have to make this right."

Ruins of Fire and Memory

1 - 2   The faint strobe of red and blue lights flickered across the blackened ruins of Drake's house, painting the skeletal remains in bursts of color that felt both alive and hauntingly still. Smoke lingered in the air, curling into the early morning sky as the distant chatter of firefighters and paramedics filled the neighborhood. The acrid scent of burnt wood and melted plastic hung heavy, stinging the back of Drake's throat as he sat dazed on the lawn beneath the oak tree.

Drake's muscular frame trembled, his brown hair matted with sweat and soot. His eyes, usually sharp and alert, now gazed unfocused at the devastation before him. In his mind, fractured images played on an endless loop—Linda's smile, Harrison's laughter, the inferno that had consumed it all.

"Sir, can you hear me?" An EMT's voice barely registered, a faint echo in the cacophony of Drake's thoughts.

He wanted to respond, to ask about his family, but his tongue felt leaden in his mouth. Instead, his hand reflexively clenched, searching for Linda's reassuring touch that was no longer there.

"We need to check your vitals," another voice insisted, but Drake barely noticed the hands reaching for him.

His world had narrowed to a pinpoint, replaying the moments before the explosion. Linda's concerned face as she'd asked about his latest project. Harrison's excited chatter about his upcoming soccer game. The sudden, deafening roar that had torn it all apart.

"Linda," Drake finally managed to croak, his voice raw and unfamiliar to his own ears. "Harrison."

The EMT's expression softened with pity, a look Drake couldn't bear to interpret. He turned away, his gaze drawn back to the smoldering remains of his home. Each flicker of the emergency lights felt like a knife twisting in his gut, a cruel reminder of what he'd lost.

In that moment, as the reality of his situation began to sink in, Drake felt a familiar tension coiling within him. The same drive that had pushed him to succeed, to protect, now burned with an intensity that frightened him. He would find answers. He would make this right.

But as the EMTs continued their ministrations, Drake remained outwardly still, a stark contrast to the tempest raging within. His world had been reduced to ashes, and in its place, a singular purpose was taking root—a purpose that would drive him to the very edges of reality itself.

3 - 4

"Mr. Miller?"

The voice pierced through Drake's fog of grief and shock, a lifeline pulling him back from the abyss of his thoughts. He blinked, his eyes struggling to focus as the world slowly sharpened around him. The acrid smell of smoke still burned his nostrils, a constant reminder of the devastation that surrounded him.

Mike's face swam into view, the boy's features etched with worry and fear. Drake noticed the pallor of Mike's skin, the way his eyes darted nervously between him and the charred skeleton of what was once their home. The contrast between Mike's youthful face and the destruction behind him struck Drake as surreal, a cruel juxtaposition of innocence and tragedy.

"Mike," Drake managed, his voice a hoarse whisper. He cleared his throat, tasting ash. "What... what happened?"

Mike's adam's apple bobbed as he swallowed hard. "I don't know, Mr. Miller. I heard the explosion and... and I ran over. I found you here on the lawn."

Drake's mind reeled, grasping for memories that seemed to slip through his fingers like smoke. He remembered Linda's smile, Harrison's laughter, and then... nothing. Just fire and chaos.

"Linda and Harrison," Drake said, his heart rate quickening. "Did you see them? Are they—"

He couldn't finish the sentence, the words sticking in his throat like shards of glass. Mike's expression, a mixture of pity and fear, told him everything he needed to know.

As the reality of his loss crashed over him anew, Drake felt a strange disconnection, as if he were watching himself from afar. Part of him wanted to scream, to rage against the unfairness of it all. But another part, a colder, more calculating part, was already analyzing, searching for answers.

"Mr. Miller," Mike said hesitantly, "before I found you, did you... did you see anyone? Anything strange?"

Drake frowned, a flicker of memory teasing at the edges of his consciousness. A face, terribly scarred, grinning at him from the flames. But as quickly as it appeared, the image vanished, leaving him grasping at shadows.

"I... I'm not sure," Drake replied, his brow furrowed in concentration. "Everything's a blur."

As he spoke, Drake became acutely aware of the weight of his loss, the emptiness that now yawned within him. But beneath the grief, a steely determination was taking root. He would find answers, no matter the cost.

5 - 6

Drake's gaze drifted back to the smoldering remains of his home, the place where his family had lived, laughed, and loved. The weight of finality settled on his shoulders like a leaden cloak, threatening to crush him.

"They're gone," Drake whispered, his voice hollow and raw. The words hung in the air, a terrible truth he couldn't escape. His hands clenched involuntarily, nails digging into his palms as he fought against the tide of despair threatening to engulf him.

Mike shifted uneasily beside him, the young man's face a mask of conflicting emotions. Drake could sense the boy's uncertainty, his struggle to find the right words in the face of such overwhelming loss.

Suddenly, the sound of approaching footsteps drew their attention. Police officers were making their way across the lawn, their faces grim and purposeful. Drake felt a flicker of alarm, his lawyer's instincts kicking in despite his grief-addled state.

Mike hesitated for a moment, his jaw tightening as he glanced between Drake and the officers. Then, with a quick intake of breath, he turned to face the approaching authorities.

"He—he had a seizure," Mike stammered, gesturing toward Drake. His voice quavered slightly, betraying his nervousness. "I don't know what happened. One second he was talking, and the next, he just—collapsed."

As Mike spoke, Drake's mind raced. A seizure? He had no memory of such an event, but then again, his recollections of the past few hours were fragmented at best. Was this another piece of the puzzle, another clue to the mystery surrounding the destruction of his life?

Outwardly, Drake remained silent, his face a mask of grief and shock. But beneath the surface, a familiar determination began to stir. He would unravel this enigma, no matter the cost. For Linda. For Harrison. For the chance at redemption, he'd been inexplicably granted.

7 - 8

The female officer's pen scratched across her notepad; the sound oddly crisp against the backdrop of chaos. Her face remained impassive, a mask of professionalism that betrayed no emotion. Drake's eyes flickered to her badge, then to her partner, who was now crouching beside him.

"Mr. Miller, can you hear me?" The male officer's voice was calm but firm, cutting through the fog in Drake's mind. "We need to get you checked out."

Drake's lips parted, but no words came. Instead, his thoughts splintered, shards of memory piercing through the haze of shock. The roar of the explosion echoed in his ears, the heat of the inferno searing his skin anew. But it was the other image that truly paralyzed him - the burned face of the man in the white robe, grinning at him through charred flesh.

Who was he? The question pounded in Drake's skull, insistent and maddening. He'd seen that face before, he was certain of it. But where? When?

"Sir?" The officer's voice grew more insistent, tinged with concern.

Drake blinked, struggling to focus on the present. He wanted to respond, to assure them he was fine, but the words wouldn't come. His usually sharp mind felt dulled, thoughts slipping away like smoke through his fingers.

Instead, he found himself staring at the smoldering ruins of his home, his heart constricting painfully in his chest. Linda's laugh, Harrison's smile - gone, consumed by flames that seemed to mock him with their destructive dance.

"I... I don't..." Drake finally managed, his voice a hoarse whisper. But even those few words felt like gravel in his throat, and he fell silent once more, lost in the labyrinth of his fractured memories and overwhelming grief.

9 - 10

"Sir, we're taking you to the hospital," the officer said, motioning to the paramedics. His voice cut through Drake's reverie, sharp and insistent.

Drake's gaze finally broke from the ruins, focusing on the officer's face. He wanted to protest, to stay and search for... what? Answers? Remnants of his life? But the words died in his throat, replaced by a hollow ache that seemed to consume him from within.

"I don't need..." he began, but his voice trailed off as he realized the futility of his objection. What did he need now, in this shattered reality?

A paramedic approached, her face a mask of professional concern. "Mr. Miller, please, let us help you," she said softly, reaching for his arm.

Drake felt her hand, firm but gentle, guiding him toward the waiting ambulance. He stumbled slightly, his legs heavy as if the ground were made of quicksand. Each step was a monumental effort, as if his body were rebelling against leaving the scene of his loss.

"Linda... Harrison..." he murmured, his eyes darting back to the house. "I can't leave them."

The paramedic's grip tightened slightly. "Sir, there's nothing more you can do here. Please, let us take care of you now."

As they neared the ambulance, Drake's mind raced. The face of the burned man flashed before him again, a taunting reminder of a mystery he couldn't unravel. "Wait," he said suddenly, his voice stronger. "There was someone else. A man in a white robe. Did anyone see him?"

The paramedic exchanged a worried glance with the officer. "Mr. Miller, you're in shock. Let's get you to the hospital, and we can sort everything out there."

Drake wanted to argue, to make them understand the importance of what he'd seen. But exhaustion washed over him in a relentless wave, and he found himself being guided into the back of the ambulance, the doors closing behind him with a finality that echoed the closing of a chapter in his life.

11 - 12

The sterile odor of disinfectant assaulted Drake's senses as he sat on the gurney, the hospital's fluorescent lights casting harsh shadows across his soot-stained face. The cacophony of beeping monitors and hushed medical jargon seemed a world away from the inferno that had consumed his life mere hours ago.

Drake's hands trembled slightly as he gripped the edge of the gurney, his knuckles white against the stark blue of the hospital gown draped loosely over his shoulders. The weight of loss pressed down on him, threatening to crush what little composure he had left.

"Mr. Miller," a nurse's voice cut through his spiraling thoughts. Her movements were precise as she wrapped a blood pressure cuff around his arm. "We need to run some tests. A CT scan and X-rays."

Drake nodded mechanically; his mind still caught between realities. "My family," he murmured, his voice hoarse from smoke and unshed tears. "They're really gone, aren't they?"

The nurse's eyes softened momentarily, a flicker of compassion breaking through her professional demeanor. "I'm so sorry for your loss, Mr. Miller. We'll take good care of you here."

As she tightened the cuff, Drake's gaze drifted to the traces of soot still clinging to his skin. Each smudge was a painful reminder, a piece of the life he'd lost forever.

"You mentioned tests," Drake said, forcing himself to focus on the present. "What exactly are you looking for?"

The nurse's reply was soft but businesslike. "It's standard procedure after what you've been through. We need to check for any internal injuries or complications from smoke inhalation."

Drake's mind raced, the lawyer in him seeking clarity even as grief threatened to overwhelm him. "And if you find something? What then?"

"Let's not get ahead of ourselves," the nurse advised, her tone gentle but firm. "You may feel disoriented for a while. That's normal after such a traumatic event."

Normal. The word echoed in Drake's mind, a bitter reminder of how far from normal his life had become. He closed his eyes, fighting against the tide of memories threatening to drown him.

"I need to understand what happened," he whispered, more to himself than to the nurse. "There has to be a reason, some explanation for all of this."

The nurse paused in her work, her expression a mix of concern and professional detachment. "Mr. Miller, the best thing you can do right now is rest and let us take care of you. There will be time for questions later."

Drake nodded, but inwardly, he knew he couldn't rest. Not until he uncovered the truth behind the mysterious figure he'd seen, the connection to his past that danced just beyond his grasp. As the nurse finished her preliminary examination, Drake steeled himself for what was to come, determined to find answers no matter the cost.

13 - 14

Drake's mind churned, a maelstrom of fragmented memories and unanswered questions. The disfigured man's face flashed before him again, a grotesque visage that seemed both familiar and utterly alien. His scarred features twisted into a mocking grin, taunting Drake with secrets just beyond his reach.

"Who are you?" Drake muttered; his voice barely audible.

The nurse glanced up; her brow furrowed. "Did you say something, Mr. Miller?"

Drake shook his head, forcing himself to focus on the present. "No, I... it's nothing."

As she wheeled him toward the imaging room, Drake's thoughts raced. Why did this mysterious figure feel so significant? Was he a figment of his trauma-addled mind, or something more sinister?

The imaging room loomed before them, its sterile atmosphere a stark reminder of his current reality. Drake's muscles tensed as he was transferred to the CT scanner's table, the cold surface seeping through the thin hospital gown.

"Try to relax and stay still," the technician instructed, her voice muffled through the intercom.

Drake stared at the machine above him, its circular frame seeming to close in around him. As it whirred to life, the mechanical clicks and hums reverberated through his skull, each sound amplifying the chaos in his mind.

"I've been here before," he thought, a chill running down his spine. "Not this room, but this moment. Why can't I remember?"

The machine's rhythmic noise became a backdrop to his spiraling thoughts. Images flashed before him: the burning house, Linda's smile, Harrison's laughter, all intertwined with the scarred face that haunted him.

"There has to be a connection," Drake whispered to himself, his lawyer's instincts kicking in despite his trauma. "I need to remember. I have to understand."

As the scan continued, Drake clenched his fists, fighting against the rising tide of frustration and grief. He'd unravel this mystery, no matter the cost. For Linda. For Harrison. For the life he'd lost and the truth that lay hidden beneath the ashes of his former existence.

15 - 16

The muted gray walls of the small, windowless room seemed to close in on Drake as he sat, waiting for his test results. The antiseptic smell that permeated the air only intensified his feeling of displacement. He rubbed his temples, his fingers tracing the worry lines that had deepened over the past few hours.

"Come on, Drake," he muttered to himself, closing his eyes. "Remember. There has to be something."

But as he reached for the elusive memories, they slipped away like wisps of smoke, leaving behind only a lingering sense of dread. The disfigured man's face flashed in his mind again, a taunting reminder of a connection he couldn't quite grasp.

Drake's eyes snapped open as the door creaked, breaking the oppressive silence. Two figures stepped inside, their plain clothes belying their authoritative demeanor. Drake straightened, his lawyer's instincts kicking in despite his mental fog.

"Mr. Miller," the woman spoke first, her tone professional but not unkind. "We have some questions for you."

Drake's jaw clenched. "About the fire?" he asked, his voice rougher than he expected.

The man nodded, his weathered face impassive. "Among other things."

As they settled into chairs across from him, Drake's mind raced. What did they know? What had he said during his seizure? The weight of his lost family pressed down on him, mingling with a growing sense of unease.

"I'm not sure how much help I can be," Drake said, struggling to keep his voice steady. "Everything's still... jumbled."

The woman leaned forward slightly. "We understand you've been through a traumatic event, Mr. Miller. But any information you can provide could be crucial."

Drake's hands gripped the arms of his chair. He wanted to help, to find answers, but the truth seemed to dance just out of reach. And beneath it all, a nagging feeling persisted – that there was more to this situation than even these officers realized.

17 - 18

The woman's piercing green eyes studied Drake intently, her gaze both penetrating and oddly reassuring. She extended her hand, her grip firm and professional as she introduced herself. "Detective Holly Kierstead," she said, her voice carrying a note of empathy beneath its authoritative tone.

Drake shook her hand, noting the strength in her grasp. His mind whirled, trying to gauge her intentions. Was she here as an ally or an adversary?

The man beside her moved with a slow, deliberate grace that spoke of years of experience. His weathered face bore the lines of countless investigations, and when he spoke, his baritone voice resonated with a steady confidence. "Detective Franklin Bird," he said, offering Drake a curt nod.

Drake's chest tightened. Two detectives. This was more serious than he'd initially thought. He swallowed hard, his throat dry. "I'm not sure what I can tell you that I haven't already said," he managed, his voice barely above a whisper.

Detective Kierstead's pen hovered over her notepad. "Sometimes, Mr. Miller, details come back to us when we least expect them. Even the smallest recollection could be significant."

As she spoke, Drake's mind flickered to the disfigured man's face, a memory he both longed to grasp and feared to confront. He closed his eyes briefly, willing the image to solidify, but it remained frustratingly elusive.

"I want to help," Drake said, opening his eyes to meet Detective Bird's steady gaze. "But everything's still so... fragmented."

19 - 20

Drake's mind reeled, the sterile hospital room spinning around him as he struggled to process the presence of the two detectives. The acrid smell of smoke still clung to his clothes, a haunting reminder of the inferno that had consumed his life mere hours ago.

"Detectives?" he croaked, his voice hoarse from inhaling the toxic fumes. "What's this about?"

His brown eyes, bloodshot and weary, darted between Detective Kierstead and Detective Bird. The weight of exhaustion pressed down on his broad shoulders, threatening to crush him beneath its burden.

Holly Kierstead lowered herself into the chair across from Drake, her movements deliberate and measured. The soft rustle of her notepad echoed in the quiet room as she flipped it open, her piercing green eyes never leaving Drake's face.

"Mr. Miller," she began, her tone professional yet tinged with a hint of compassion, "first let me say how sorry we are for your loss. What happened this morning was... terrible."

The word 'terrible' hung in the air, woefully inadequate to describe the devastation Drake had witnessed. His mind flashed back to the inferno, the heat searing his skin, the agonizing screams of his family trapped inside. He squeezed his eyes shut, willing the images away, but they persisted, burned into his retinas like cruel, mocking phantoms.

Why are they here? Drake wondered, his heart rate accelerating. Have they discovered something about the fire? About the man with the burned face? The questions swirled in his mind, a dizzying maelstrom of fear and confusion.

He opened his mouth to speak, to ask the detectives about their true intentions, but the words caught in his throat. Instead, he nodded silently, acknowledging Holly's condolences while his fingers gripped the edge of the hospital bed, knuckles turning white with the effort of maintaining his composure.

21 - 22

Drake's stomach tightened at her words, a knot of dread coiling within him. The antiseptic smell of the hospital room suddenly felt oppressive, threatening to choke him. He swallowed hard, tasting the acrid remnants of smoke on his tongue, a bitter reminder of all he had lost. The fluorescent lights overhead seemed to flicker, casting dancing shadows across Holly's face as she leaned forward, her gaze probing.

"We spoke with the young man, Mike, who was at the scene," Holly continued, her voice cutting through the heavy silence. Drake's heart skipped a beat at the mention of Mike. What had the boy seen? What had he told them?

Holly's pen tapped against her notepad, a staccato rhythm that matched Drake's racing pulse. "He told us about your seizure and mentioned that you were rambling before you collapsed."

Drake's mind reeled, fragments of memory flashing before his eyes. The disfigured man's face, the mocking wave, the inexplicable familiarity - all of it swirled in a confusing blur. He opened his mouth to speak, to deny, to explain, but found himself paralyzed by indecision.

What if I say the wrong thing? he thought frantically. What if they think I'm responsible? The weight of suspicion pressed down on him, suffocating in its intensity.

"I... I don't remember much," Drake finally managed, his voice hoarse and uncertain. He ran a hand through his disheveled hair, buying time as he struggled to piece together a coherent response. "Everything happened so fast. The explosion, the fire... it's all a blur."

As he spoke, Drake searched Holly's face for any sign of disbelief or accusation, but her expression remained impassive, professional. The silence stretched between them, pregnant with unasked questions and unspoken fears.

23 - 24

Franklin Bird leaned forward; his weathered face etched with lines of concentration. His gaze, unwavering and penetrating, bore into Drake with the intensity of a seasoned interrogator. "Mike said you were asking about someone—a man. A mysterious figure."

The words hung in the air, heavy and accusatory. Drake's heart hammered against his ribcage; each beat a thunderous reminder of the lies he was about to tell. His hands, trembling slightly, gripped the edges of the chair until his knuckles turned white. The cold metal beneath his fingers grounded him, anchoring him to this moment of deception.

"I don't know what he's talking about," Drake lied, his voice steady despite the turmoil raging within. He could feel Franklin's eyes on him, searching for any flicker of dishonesty. The disfigured man's face flashed in his mind again, a haunting reminder of the truth he was desperately trying to conceal.

Guilt gnawed at Drake's insides, threatening to consume him. How could he explain the inexplicable? The charred face, the mocking grin, the wave that seemed to transcend realities—it all sounded absurd, even to his own ears. And yet, the memory persisted, as vivid and terrifying as the moment he first saw it.

"Are you certain about that, Mr. Miller?" Franklin pressed, his tone measured but tinged with skepticism. "Trauma can affect memory in strange ways. Sometimes, details come back to us in fragments."

Drake swallowed hard, fighting the urge to confess everything. The weight of his family's loss, coupled with the bizarre circumstances surrounding it, threatened to crush him. But he held firm, clinging to his lie like a lifeline.

"I wish I could help you more," Drake said, infusing his voice with a mixture of regret and exhaustion. "But the truth is, I don't remember asking about anyone. It's all just... chaos in my mind."

As the words left his mouth, Drake couldn't help but wonder: how long could he keep up this charade? And at what cost?

25 - 26

Holly's green eyes softened slightly, a flicker of compassion crossing her face. "Drake, may I call you Drake?" she asked, tilting her head. The fluorescent lights cast harsh shadows across her features, accentuating the tension in the room.

Drake gave a small, almost imperceptible nod, his throat too constricted to form words. The acrid smell of smoke still clung to his clothes, a constant reminder of the devastation he'd witnessed.

"We're just trying to understand what happened," Holly continued, her voice steady but gentle. "You've been through a traumatic event. Sometimes, shock can cause the mind to conjure things that aren't real. But Mike seemed pretty convinced you were asking about someone specific."

Drake's jaw clenched involuntarily, the muscles in his face tightening as he fought to maintain composure. The image of the disfigured man's charred face flashed through his mind again, as vivid and terrifying as it had been in the moment. How could he possibly explain this without sounding completely unhinged?

"I..." Drake started, his voice cracking. He cleared his throat and tried again. "I don't remember much," he said finally, the words tasting like ash in his mouth. "The explosion, the fire... it's all a blur."

As he spoke, Drake's hands gripped the arms of his chair, knuckles turning white with the effort. His mind raced, desperately searching for a way to reconcile the impossible reality he'd witnessed with the need to appear sane and cooperative.

"It's like trying to remember a nightmare," he added, his gaze dropping to the floor. "Everything's distorted, fragmented. I can't... I can't make sense of it."

The weight of his lie pressed down on him, threatening to crack his already fragile composure. But how could he tell them the truth? That he'd seen a man who couldn't possibly exist, who seemed to mock him from beyond the veil of reality itself? The thought alone made him question his own sanity.

27 - 28

Franklin's weathered face creased with concern as he exchanged a loaded glance with Holly. The seasoned detective leaned forward, his broad shoulders hunching slightly as if bearing the weight of his next words. "Drake, we need to be honest with you," he said, his deep voice measured and careful. "This isn't just about your seizure or what Mike heard you say."

The words hung in the air, heavy with unspoken implications. Drake's heart quickened, a cold dread seeping into his bones. His mind raced, conjuring a thousand terrible possibilities. What else could there be? What more could they possibly pile onto the mountain of loss and confusion already crushing him?

"What do you mean?" Drake asked, his voice barely above a whisper. He searched Franklin's face for any clue, any hint of what was coming next. The detective's stoic expression revealed nothing, but there was a glimmer of something in his eyes—pity, perhaps, or apprehension.

Drake's fingers drummed restlessly against his thigh, a nervous tic he couldn't control. The sterile hospital room seemed to shrink around him, the walls closing in with each passing second. He could feel Holly's sharp gaze on him, analyzing his every movement, every flicker of emotion that crossed his face.

In the tense silence that followed, Drake's thoughts spiraled. Was this about the disfigured man? Had they somehow discovered something he himself couldn't remember? Or was it something else entirely, some new horror waiting to be unveiled?

As Franklin drew a deep breath, preparing to continue, Drake braced himself for whatever revelation was coming. Whatever it was, he knew with grim certainty that it would change everything—again.

29 - 30

Holly's expression hardened, her piercing green eyes locking onto Drake's. "The fire at your house wasn't an accident," she said, her words falling like lead weights in the sterile air. "The fire department has already completed a preliminary assessment, and it appears the gas line to your stove was tampered with."

The world seemed to tilt on its axis. Drake's vision blurred, the edges of the room growing hazy as he struggled to process Holly's words. Tampered with. Not an accident. The implications crashed over him like a tidal wave, threatening to drag him under.

"Tampered with?" Drake repeated, his voice hoarse and distant to his own ears. He swallowed hard, trying to force moisture into his suddenly parched throat. "You think someone did this intentionally?"

As he spoke, Drake's mind raced through a labyrinth of possibilities. Who would want to harm his family? Why? The faces of clients he'd defended, of people he'd wronged in his past life, flashed before his eyes. But none of it made sense in this reality, where he was just a man with a wife and son, living a quiet life.

Holly leaned forward, her voice low and measured. "We're exploring all possibilities, Drake. That's why we need your full cooperation."

Drake's hands clenched into fists, his nails digging crescents into his palms. The pain was grounding, a sharp counterpoint to the numbness threatening to engulf him. He wanted to scream, to rage against the injustice of it all.

"I don't understand," he said, his words barely audible. "Who would do this? Why?"

The weight of grief and confusion pressed down on him, threatening to crush what remained of his spirit. In that moment, Drake felt more lost than ever before, adrift in a sea of realities he couldn't comprehend, with no anchor to hold him steady.

31 - 32

Franklin shifted his weight, his weathered face etched with a mix of caution and empathy. "It's a possibility," he said carefully, his deep voice resonating in the sterile hospital room. "Right now, we're not ruling anything out."

Drake's heart pounded in his chest, a thunderous rhythm that seemed to echo off the pale walls. The fluorescent lights overhead flickered almost imperceptibly, casting shadows that danced across Franklin's face. In that instant, the image of the disfigured man flooded Drake's mind—his grotesque wave, that mocking grin that seemed to hold dark secrets.

"I... I think I saw someone," Drake muttered, his voice barely above a whisper. He ran a trembling hand through his disheveled hair, the acrid smell of smoke still clinging to his skin. "But it doesn't make sense. I can't place him."

Holly leaned forward; her green eyes sharp with interest. "Can you describe this person, Drake?"

Drake's gaze unfocused, lost in the fractured memories. "His face... it was burned, distorted. But he seemed familiar somehow. Like a ghost from another life."

Franklin exchanged a glance with Holly, his skepticism palpable. "Mr. Miller, trauma can play tricks on the mind. Are you certain about what you saw?"

Drake's jaw clenched, frustration bubbling up inside him. How could he explain the inexplicable? The weight of multiple realities pressed down on him, a burden he alone could bear. "I know how it sounds," he said, his voice strained. "But I'm telling you, he was there. And somehow, I think he's connected to all of this."

As the words left his mouth, Drake felt a chill run down his spine. The pieces were there, just out of reach, like a half-remembered dream slipping away with the dawn.

33 - 34

Drake's eyes snapped up to meet Holly's penetrating gaze. "You're implying I had something to do with this?" he asked, his voice sharp as broken glass. The accusation hung in the air, heavy and suffocating.

Holly's expression remained impassive, but Drake noticed a flicker of something—sympathy, perhaps—in her green eyes. She leaned forward slightly, her posture a mixture of professional detachment and genuine concern. "We're not implying anything," she said evenly, her tone measured and calm. "We're just gathering information. Given the circumstances, we need to bring you in for questioning."

Drake's mind reeled, fragments of memory colliding like shards of a shattered mirror. The disfigured man's face, Linda's smile, Harrison's laughter—all of it swirled together in a dizzying kaleidoscope of grief and confusion. He clenched his fists, feeling the bite of his nails against his palms.

"This can't be happening," he muttered, more to himself than to the detectives. The sterile hospital room seemed to close in around him, the fluorescent lights suddenly too harsh, too revealing. He could feel the weight of Holly's gaze, analyzing his every move, every micro expression.

Franklin shifted his weight, the movement drawing Drake's attention. "Look, Mr. Miller," he began, his voice gruff but not unkind. "We understand you've been through hell. But we need to follow protocol here."

"When can we get this over with?" Drake asked, his voice hollow. He felt drained, as if the fire that had consumed his home had also burned away something vital within him.

Holly stood, her movements fluid and purposeful. "We can head to the station now, if you're feeling up to it," she said, her tone professional but not without compassion.

As Drake rose to follow, he caught a glimpse of his reflection in the window. For a moment, he barely recognized the haggard, soot-stained man staring back at him. He wondered, with a pang of despair, how many other versions of himself were facing similar trials across the multiverse.

35 - 36

Drake's hands trembled, the weight of his grief and disbelief crashing over him like a tidal wave. He clenched his fists, trying to steady himself as he met Holly's gaze. The fluorescent lights overhead seemed to flicker, casting shifting shadows across her face, reminding him of the dancing flames that had consumed his life mere hours ago.

"Questioning?" Drake's voice cracked, raw emotion bleeding through his words. "My wife and son just died, and you think I had something to do with it?" The words tasted like ash in his mouth, each syllable a painful reminder of what he'd lost.

His mind raced, images of Linda's smile and Harrison's laughter intertwining with the horrific sight of their home engulfed in flames. How could they possibly think he was capable of such a monstrous act? The very notion made his stomach churn.

Franklin stepped forward, his weathered face a mask of practiced neutrality. "This is standard procedure," he said, his tone calm but firm. The detective's eyes, however, betrayed a flicker of sympathy. "We're following every lead."

Drake's jaw clenched, a surge of anger momentarily overshadowing his grief. He wanted to lash out, to scream at the injustice of it all. But a small voice in the back of his mind whispered a chilling reminder: in this reality, or perhaps another, had he not been capable of terrible things?

"I understand you have a job to do," Drake said finally, his voice low and strained. "But you have to know how this looks, how it feels. I've lost everything, and now I'm being treated like a suspect?"

He ran a hand through his hair, wincing as his fingers caught on a tangle crusted with dried blood and soot. The physical pain was almost a relief, a momentary distraction from the emotional torment raging inside him.

37 - 38

Drake's gaze flicked between the two detectives, their faces swimming in his vision as exhaustion and grief threatened to overwhelm him. The sterile hospital room seemed to close in, the air growing thick and oppressive. He swallowed hard, his throat raw from smoke and unshed tears.

"I told you, I don't remember what happened," Drake said through gritted teeth, each word a struggle against the maelstrom of emotions roiling within him. His hands, resting on his knees, curled into fists, knuckles whitening with the strain of maintaining control.

In that moment, a fragment of memory flashed through his mind—the disfigured man's grotesque smile, a mocking wave. The image was gone as quickly as it had appeared, leaving Drake feeling disoriented and even more frustrated.

Holly rose from her chair, her movement fluid and purposeful. Her green eyes locked onto Drake's, searching for something—truth, deception, or perhaps just a glimmer of sanity in the chaos.

"Then you'll have a chance to clarify everything at the station," Holly replied, her tone professional but not unkind. She paused, seeming to weigh her next words carefully. "Mr. Miller, I know this is difficult. But the sooner we get to the bottom of this, the better for everyone involved."

Drake's mind reeled. The station. Questioning. The implications hung heavy in the air, a palpable weight pressing down on his already burdened shoulders. How could he explain what he didn't understand himself? The boundaries between realities blurred in his mind, leaving him adrift in a sea of uncertainty.

"And if I refuse?" Drake asked, the words escaping before he could stop them. He immediately regretted the question, knowing it would only cast further suspicion on him.

39 - 40

Drake rose to his feet, his fists clenched at his sides. The hospital gown fluttered around his knees, a stark reminder of his vulnerability. "You're making a mistake," he growled, his voice low and gravelly with emotion.

The fluorescent lights overhead buzzed, casting harsh shadows across the room. Drake's heart pounded in his chest, each beat a painful reminder of all he had lost. How could they suspect him? The very thought made bile rise in his throat.

Holly and Franklin exchanged a glance, a silent conversation passing between them. Drake caught the subtle shift in Franklin's posture, the slight narrowing of his eyes. It was a look he had seen before, in another life, another reality. The look of a decision being made.

Franklin stepped forward, his weathered hands reaching for his belt. The soft clink of metal sent a chill down Drake's spine. "Drake Miller," Franklin began, his deep voice resonating in the small room, "you're not under arrest. But for now, we need you to come with us."

As Franklin pulled out a pair of handcuffs, Drake's mind raced. Images flashed before him—Linda's smile, Harrison's laugh, the burning house. And beneath it all, the constant, nagging presence of the disfigured man. Who was he? What did he want?

"This is insane," Drake muttered, more to himself than to the detectives. His gaze darted between Holly and Franklin, searching for any sign of understanding, any crack in their professional facades. "I didn't do this. I couldn't have."

But even as the words left his mouth, a seed of doubt took root. In a world of shifting realities, how could he be certain of anything?

41 - 42

The cold metal bit into Drake's wrist as Franklin secured the handcuffs, each click echoing in the sterile room like a death knell. Drake's eyes widened, the reality of his situation crashing over him in waves of disbelief and despair. His world, already shattered by the loss of Linda and Harrison, now seemed to crumble further, pieces scattering like ashes in the wind.

"This can't be happening," Drake whispered, his voice hoarse. He flexed his fingers, the restraints a constant, unyielding reminder of his powerlessness. "Franklin, please. You have to believe me."

The older detective's face remained impassive, but something flickered in his eyes—doubt, perhaps, or a hint of sympathy quickly suppressed. "We're just following procedure, Drake. You'll have a chance to explain everything."

As they led him from the room, Drake's mind raced. How could he possibly explain what he didn't understand himself? The disfigured man's face flashed in his memory again, a mocking grin etched into charred flesh. Who was he? Why did he feel so familiar?

The hospital corridors stretched before them, a gauntlet of fluorescent lights and antiseptic air. Drake felt exposed, vulnerable. Patients and staff turned to stare, their curious gazes piercing through him like accusatory daggers.

"Everyone's watching," Drake muttered, hunching his shoulders instinctively. "They think I'm guilty."

Holly's voice was low, meant only for him. "Focus on walking, Drake. Don't make this harder than it needs to be."

But how could he not? With each step, Drake felt the weight of his losses, his confusion, and now this new, crushing suspicion. He thought of Linda and Harrison, their faces already beginning to blur in his mind. Had he failed them? Was he somehow responsible?

"I couldn't have done this," Drake insisted, his words barely audible. "I loved them. I would never—"

Franklin cut him off, his tone gentle but firm. "Save it for the station, Drake. We'll get this sorted out."

As they neared the hospital exit, Drake's heart raced. What awaited him beyond those doors? A world without his family, a reality he didn't understand, and now, the looming specter of guilt—real or imagined. He closed his eyes briefly, trying to center himself.

"I don't belong here," Drake whispered, a truth that ran deeper than even he realized. "This isn't my world."

Holly and Franklin exchanged another glance, concern etching their features. But for Drake, the words resonated with a certainty that cut through his confusion. Whatever was happening, whatever had brought him to this point, he knew one thing for certain: he had to find a way back to the truth, no matter the cost.

43 - 43

The acrid scent of smoke clung to Drake's clothes as he stepped into the crisp morning air, a stark reminder of the inferno that had consumed his life. He glanced back at the hospital doors, their sterile white facade a jarring contrast to the chaos swirling in his mind.

"Watch your head," Franklin said, guiding Drake toward the unmarked sedan parked at the curb.

Drake's muscles tensed as he lowered himself into the back seat, the leather cool against his skin. His eyes darted from the rearview mirror to the tinted windows, searching for answers in a world that suddenly felt alien.

"I don't understand," he murmured, more to himself than to the detectives. "How could this happen?"

Holly turned in the passenger seat, her green eyes softening. "That's what we're trying to figure out, Drake. Can you tell us anything about the hours leading up to the fire?"

Drake closed his eyes, trying to summon memories that seemed to dance just out of reach. "I remember... Linda making breakfast. Harrison talking about soccer practice. But then..." He shook his head, frustration etching lines across his forehead.

As Franklin pulled away from the curb, Drake's gaze was drawn to a figure standing near the hospital entrance. For a fleeting moment, he thought he saw the disfigured man in the white robe, grinning that impossible grin. Drake blinked, and the apparition vanished.

"What is it?" Holly asked, noticing his sudden tension.

"Nothing," Drake lied, his heart racing. "Just... ghosts, I guess."

As they drove through the quiet streets, Drake's mind churned with possibilities. Was he losing his grip on reality? Or was there something more sinister at play, something that tied together the fire, the mysterious figure, and this gnawing sense that he didn't belong?

"I need to see the house," Drake said suddenly, his voice hoarse but determined. "There might be something there, some clue—"

"I'm sorry, Drake," Franklin interrupted, his eyes meeting Drake's in the rearview mirror. "But that's not possible right now. The scene is still being processed."

Drake's fists clenched involuntarily. "You don't understand. I have to go back. I have to fix this."

The words hung in the air, laden with a desperation that surprised even Drake. Fix what, exactly? And how? The questions piled up, each one heavier than the last, as the car carried him further from the ruins of his old life and into an uncertain future.

Shadows of the Dragon

1-2 The disfigured man melted into the inky shadows of the alley, his scarred flesh prickling beneath the tattered robe. The dragon insignia on his chest seemed to writhe in the flickering streetlight. His eyes, cold and calculating, fixed on the police station across the street.

The night air hung thick with anticipation, broken only by the low hum of streetlights and muffled voices from within the building. The disfigured man's lips curled into a twisted smile. Soon, Drake Miller would arrive, and the dance would begin anew.

"Another night, another chance to watch you fall," The disfigured man murmured, his voice a gravelly whisper. He flexed his fingers, feeling the phantom weight of the gun he would soon wield.

The wait gnawed at him, each passing moment an eternity. Yet The disfigured man remained still, a statue carved from shadow and malice. His mind wandered to Drake, imagining the man's fear, his desperation.

"Poor, lost Drake," he mused. "Always searching for answers, never realizing the truth is right in front of you."

A car engine rumbled in the distance. The disfigured man's pulse quickened, his senses sharpening. He peered down the street, watching as headlights pierced the darkness.

"Right on time," he whispered, a thrill of excitement coursing through him. "Let's see how far you'll fall this time, Drake. How much can you lose before you break completely?"

The police cruiser rolled to a stop, and The disfigured man's anticipation peaked. He savored the moment, knowing that soon, chaos would erupt, and Drake's world would shatter once more.

"The game begins again," The disfigured man breathed, stepping from the shadows. "And I always win."

3 - 4

The station door swung open, bathing the sidewalk in a harsh fluorescent glow. Two uniformed officers stepped out, their laughter cutting through the night's stillness. The disfigured man watched them intently, his scarred face hidden in the shadows.

"Did you see Johnson's face when the chief called him out?" one officer chuckled, slapping his partner on the back.

"Priceless," the other replied, wiping tears from his eyes. "I thought he was going to pass out right there."

Their mirth grated on The disfigured man's nerves, a stark contrast to the grim task that lay ahead. He observed silently as they strolled down the street, their voices fading into the distance.

"Enjoy your laughter while you can," The disfigured man muttered, his fingers absently tracing the outline of the dragon insignia on his chest. "Soon enough, there'll be nothing to laugh about."

As the officers disappeared around a corner, The disfigured man adjusted his white robe, wincing as the fabric brushed against his charred skin. The pain was a constant companion, a reminder of the price he'd paid and the burden he carried.

"All for the greater good," he reminded himself, his voice barely above a whisper. "The multiverse demands balance, and I am its instrument."

The disfigured man's gaze drifted back to the police station, his mind racing with possibilities. How would Drake react this time? Would he break sooner or later? The anticipation was intoxicating.

"Soon, Drake," he murmured, a wicked smile playing on his lips. "Soon, you'll understand the futility of your struggle. And when you do, I'll be there to watch you crumble."

5 - 6

Then he saw them.

The black police cruiser materialized out of the night, its headlights cutting through the darkness like twin blades. As it rolled to a stop, the crunch of gravel under its tires echoed in The disfigured man's ears, a harbinger of the chaos to come.

Detective Holly Kierstead emerged first, her long black hair catching the dim streetlight as she scanned the area with piercing eyes. The disfigured man couldn't help but admire her vigilance, even as he plotted her demise.

"Clear on my side," Holly called out, her voice crisp and authoritative.

Detective Franklin Bird followed, his imposing frame unfolding from the driver's seat. His weathered face was a mask of caution as he surveyed the street, one hand resting lightly on his holstered weapon.

"Same here," Franklin responded, his tone measured and low. "But something feels off tonight."

The disfigured man's lips curled into a sardonic smile. If only they knew how right Franklin was.

Holly's brow furrowed as she took a step forward. "You getting one of your hunches again, Bird?"

"Call it what you want, Kierstead," Franklin replied, his eyes never ceasing their vigilant sweep. "But after all these years, I've learned to trust my gut."

The disfigured man leaned forward slightly, drinking in their exchange. The interplay between the detectives always fascinated him—Holly's sharp intuition and Franklin's hard-earned skepticism, a formidable team under normal circumstances.

But these were far from normal circumstances.

"Perhaps," The disfigured man mused silently, "in another reality, we might have been allies." The thought amused him, even as he steeled himself for what came next. The weight of inevitability settled over him like a shroud.

"Ready or not, detectives," he whispered, his charred fingers flexing in anticipation. "It's time to play our parts in this cosmic dance once more."

7 - 8

The passenger door creaked open, its hinges groaning under the weight of anticipation. The disfigured man's breath caught in his throat; his eyes fixated on the figure emerging from the shadows of the cruiser's interior.

Drake Miller stepped out, his movements slow and hesitant. The streetlight cast a harsh glow on his face, accentuating the hollows under his eyes and the tension in his jaw. His disheveled brown hair fell across his forehead, a physical manifestation of the chaos that seemed to swirl around him.

"Easy now, Miller," Holly's voice cut through the night air, a mix of caution and something akin to pity.

Drake's gaze darted around, his eyes wide and unfocused. When he spoke, his words came out fractured, like shards of broken glass. "I... I don't understand. Why am I here? What's happening?"

The disfigured man watched, transfixed, as Drake stumbled slightly. Franklin reached out to steady him, his large hand gripping Drake's arm.

"Take it slow," Franklin advised, his gruff voice softened by concern. "We'll get this sorted out."

Drake's breathing quickened, his chest rising and falling rapidly. "No, you don't... you can't..." He shook his head violently, as if trying to dislodge some invasive thought. "It's all wrong. Everything's wrong."

The disfigured man's fingers twitched, an involuntary response to Drake's distress. He could almost taste the confusion and fear radiating off the man. It was intoxicating, a reminder of the power he held over this unfolding drama.

"Poor, lost Drake," The disfigured man thought, a mix of pity and anticipation coursing through him. "Always searching for answers in a world determined to keep its secrets."

As the detectives began to guide Drake towards the station, The disfigured man's mind raced with possibilities. The pieces were in place, the players assembled. Now, it was time to set the next act in motion.

9 - 10

Drake's cuffed hands trembled, the metal links clinking softly in the night air. His eyes, wild and desperate, scanned the shadows as if searching for a lifeline in the darkness.

"Please," he whispered, his voice hoarse and strained. "There's something... someone... I need to find."

Detective Kierstead's brow furrowed. "Mr. Miller, who are you looking for?"

Drake shook his head, frustration etching deep lines across his pale face. "I don't know. I can't... remember. But it's important. It's everything."

As they moved forward, The disfigured man slipped closer, his white robe ghosting silently over the pavement. The shadows seemed to bend around him, cloaking him in inky darkness.

Drake's gaze swept past The disfigured man's hiding spot, unseeing. A flicker of recognition passed over his features, there and gone in an instant. He stumbled, nearly falling.

"Steady now," Detective Bird murmured, his grip on Drake's arm tightening.

The disfigured man watched a predator observing its prey. His charred skin pulled tight as he smiled, anticipation building in his chest. Soon, he thought. Soon, the real game would begin.

Drake's shoulders slumped, defeat evident in every line of his body. "Why can't I remember?" he asked, his words barely audible. "What's happened to me?"

The question hung in the air, unanswered and heavy with implications. The disfigured man leaned forward, drinking in Drake's despair like a fine wine. The stage was set, the actors in place. All that remained was for him to make his entrance and bring this carefully crafted illusion crashing down around them all.

11 - 12

The trio approached the station's entrance, their footsteps echoing in the quiet night. Detective Kierstead's voice cut through the silence, her tone direct and probing.

"Mr. Miller, we need to discuss your whereabouts during the incident. Your story doesn't add up."

Drake's shoulders tensed, his cuffed hands clenching into fists. "I've told you everything I know. Why won't you believe me?"

Detective Bird's eyes narrowed, his hand hovering near his holster. "Because, son, your story sounds like something out of a sci-fi novel. Time loops? Alternate realities? It's not exactly standard procedure."

As they walked, Drake's mind raced, grasping for memories that seemed to slip through his fingers like smoke. The weight of their disbelief pressed down on him, suffocating.

"You don't understand," he pleaded, his voice cracking. "I'm trying to save them. My family... they're in danger."

Holly's expression softened slightly, but her words remained firm. "We want to help you, Drake. But you need to give us something real to work with."

Drake's gaze darted around, searching for something, anything familiar. His heart pounded in his chest, a desperate rhythm that seemed to echo the ticking of an unseen clock.

"I know it sounds crazy," he whispered, more to himself than to the detectives. "But I've lived this day before. Many times. And each time, it ends in tragedy unless I can figure out how to stop it."

Franklin snorted, his skepticism palpable. "And how many times have you been arrested in these... loops of yours?"

Drake's response was lost in the night air as they neared the station doors. The weight of inevitability settled over him, a familiar cloak of despair.

From the shadows, The disfigured man watched, a wry smile playing on his lips. The scene unfolded before him, each word, each step as predictable as the rise and fall of the sun. He savored the moment, knowing that soon, very soon, he would shatter their illusion of control.

"Predictable," he murmured, his charred fingers tracing the dragon insignia on his chest. The game was set, the pieces in motion. All that remained was for him to make his move and watch as their carefully constructed reality crumbled around them.

13 - 14

The cool pavement pressed against The disfigured man's bare feet as he glided forward, closing the distance between himself and the trio ahead. Each step was measured, silent, a predator's approach. The night air carried the faint sounds of their movement—the crisp shuffle of the detectives' polished shoes, and behind them, the weary drag of Drake's reluctant gait.

Drake's shoulders slumped, his posture a testament to the weight of countless repeated days. His voice, when it came, was barely above a whisper. "You don't understand. This isn't just about me. It's about everyone. The world—"

"Save it for the interrogation room, Miller," Detective Holly cut him off, her tone clipped.

The disfigured man's lips curled into a smirk as he drew nearer. Drake's words hung in the air, unfinished, pregnant with a truth no one else could comprehend. In the silence that followed, The disfigured man could almost taste the desperation radiating from Drake's hunched form.

It's time, The disfigured man thought, his heart quickening with anticipation. The moment stretched, taut as a bowstring, ready to snap.

Drake's mind raced, fragments of memories and possibilities colliding. *There has to be a way out of this loop,* he thought frantically. *Something I haven't tried. Some detail I've missed.* His eyes darted around, searching for anything out of place, any sign that this time might be different.

But as they approached the harsh fluorescent glow of the police station, Drake felt the familiar tendrils of dread coiling in his stomach. He knew what came next. He always knew, and yet he was powerless to stop it.

15 - 16

With a burst of speed, The disfigured man lunged forward, his arm looping around Franklin's neck in a fluid, practiced motion. The detective's body tensed, a startled grunt escaping his lips as his hands instinctively clawed at the unexpected assailant's arm.

"What the—" Franklin's words were cut short as The disfigured man tightened his grip, the chokehold constricting his airway.

The world seemed to slow, each second stretching into an eternity as The disfigured man felt Franklin's weight shift against him, the detective's struggles growing more frantic with each passing moment. The acrid scent of fear mingled with the cool night air, a familiar cocktail that The disfigured man had come to savor.

How many times have we done this dance, Detective Bird? The disfigured man mused silently, his charred skin pulling taut as he maintained his iron grip. *And yet, you never see it coming.*

Holly spun around, her sharp eyes widening with shock as they took in the scene before her. Her hand flew to her holster, muscle memory kicking in even as her mind struggled to process the sudden turn of events.

"Franklin!" Holly's voice cut through the night, a mixture of concern and steely determination. Her gaze locked onto The disfigured man, her analytical mind already cataloging details: the white robe, the dragon insignia, the burns. "Let him go! Now!"

As Holly's fingers closed around the grip of her weapon, The disfigured man felt a thrill of anticipation course through him. *Your move, Detective Kierstead,* he thought, a wicked smile playing at the corners of his lips. *Let's see if you can change the script this time.*

Drake stood frozen, his face a mask of horror and resignation. He'd seen this before, lived it countless times. Yet the dread that filled him was as fresh as ever. *Not again,* he thought, his mind reeling. *Please, not again.*

17 - 18

"Don't," The disfigured man growled, his voice low and guttural. The sound rumbled through his chest, reverberating against Franklin's back.

Holly's hand hovered over her weapon, her fingers twitching with indecision. For a heartbeat, the world seemed to hold its breath.

Come on, Holly, The disfigured man thought, his eyes never leaving her face. *You know how this ends. You've seen it before, even if you don't remember.*

In that moment of hesitation, The disfigured man could almost see the wheels turning in Holly's mind. Her eyes darted between him and Franklin, calculating risks and outcomes. It was a dance they'd performed countless times, yet each iteration held its own unique tension.

Drake, still frozen in place, felt a cold dread seeping into his bones. *She's going to do it,* he thought, his mind racing. *She always does. And then...*

"Let him go," Holly said, her voice steady despite the fear The disfigured man could see flickering in her eyes. "We can talk about this. Whatever you want, we can work it out."

The disfigured man's lips curled into a sardonic smile. *Oh, Detective,* he mused, *if only you knew what I really want.*

That moment of hesitation was all The disfigured man needed. He could feel the familiar rush of adrenaline coursing through his veins, the thrill of what was to come. The game was set, the pieces in motion. And as always, Drake was caught in the middle, a unwitting pawn in a cosmic chess match he couldn't hope to understand.

19 - 20

The disfigured man's fingers closed around Franklin's holstered gun, the cold metal a stark contrast to the heat radiating from his charred skin. In one fluid motion, he aimed it at Holly, his grip steady and sure.

Holly's body went rigid, her eyes locking onto The disfigured man's with a mix of defiance and dawning realization. The weight of her hesitation seemed to pull at her, rooting her to the spot.

She's starting to remember, The disfigured man thought, a flicker of excitement sparking within him. *Good. It makes the game more interesting.*

"Don't do it," Holly said, her voice steady but betrayed by the slight tremor in her hands. Her analytical mind was clearly racing, trying to piece together the fragments of memories that danced just out of reach.

The disfigured man could see the struggle playing out across her face. The seasoned detective was fighting against instincts she didn't fully understand, torn between the reality she knew and the truths she was beginning to suspect.

How far will you go this time, Holly? The disfigured man wondered, his finger resting lightly on the trigger. *Will you be the hero? The victim? Or something else entirely?*

The night air hung heavy around them, thick with tension and unspoken possibilities. In the distance, a siren wailed, a haunting reminder of the world beyond this moment—a world that would soon reset, leaving only The disfigured man to remember the choices made here tonight.

21 - 22

A wicked smile spread across The disfigured man's lips, his charred skin pulling taut. "Too late," he purred, savoring the words like a fine wine.

The shot echoed through the night, sharp and deafening. Holly's body jerked as the bullet tore through her chest, a look of shock and betrayal flashing across her face. Her weapon slipped from her fingers, clattering uselessly to the ground as she crumpled onto the pavement.

The disfigured man watched her fall, a mixture of satisfaction and something akin to regret swirling within him. *How many times have we done this dance, Holly?* he mused silently. *And still, you never see it coming.*

As Holly lay gasping on the cold concrete, her blood pooling around her, The disfigured man knelt beside her. He leaned in close, his voice barely above a whisper. "You were so close this time, Detective. Maybe next reset, you'll remember enough to change the game."

Holly's eyes, once sharp and analytical, now clouded with pain and confusion, searched The disfigured man's face. Her lips moved, forming words that never quite escaped. The disfigured man imagined he could hear them anyway - questions about the nature of their reality, about the endless cycle they seemed trapped in.

"Shh," he soothed, almost tenderly. "It'll all make sense soon. Or maybe it won't. That's the beauty of our little dance, isn't it?"

As the light faded from Holly's eyes, The disfigured man stood, brushing off his white robe. The night suddenly felt emptier, the weight of what he'd done - what he always did - settling over him like a shroud.

Is this what you wanted? a small voice in the back of his mind whispered. *Is this the path to breaking the cycle?*

The disfigured man pushed the thought away, focusing instead on the task at hand. Drake was waiting, after all, and the game was far from over.

23 - 24

Franklin's anguished roar tore through the night, a primal sound of rage and desperation. His struggle intensified, muscles straining against The disfigured man's iron grip. "You bastard!" he bellowed, voice raw with fury and grief.

The disfigured man released his hold, spinning with fluid grace. The gun felt heavy in his hand, its metal still warm from the previous shot. Time seemed to slow as he aimed, Franklin's eyes widening in horrified realization.

The crack of the second shot shattered the air. Franklin staggered, his large frame suddenly unsteady. His hands clutched at his abdomen, fingers spreading as if to stem the crimson tide blooming across his shirt.

"No..." Franklin gasped, his voice barely audible. He stumbled, knees buckling beneath him. As he fell, The disfigured man caught a glimpse of the man's eyes - a maelstrom of emotions swirling in their depths. Fury burned there, hot and bright, but beneath it lay something deeper. Disbelief, yes, but also a glimmer of recognition, as if some part of Franklin understood this wasn't the first time they'd played out this scene.

The disfigured man watched impassively as Franklin's ragged breaths echoed in the still night air. *How many times have we done this dance, old friend?* he mused silently. *How many more before you finally remember?*

25 - 26

"Goodnight, Detective," The disfigured man murmured, his voice a soft contrast to the violence that had preceded it. He pressed the still-warm barrel against Franklin's temple, feeling the faint tremor of the man's pulse beneath the cold metal.

Franklin's eyes locked onto The disfigured man's, a final spark of defiance flaring in their depths. "This... isn't... over," he rasped, each word a struggle against the encroaching darkness.

If only you knew how right you are, The disfigured man thought, a bitter smile tugging at his scarred lips. His finger tightened on the trigger, the weight of inevitability settling over him like a shroud.

The gunshot cracked through the air, sharp and final. Franklin's body jerked once, then slumped forward, all tension draining away in an instant. The silence that followed was deafening, broken only by the soft patter of blood on concrete.

The disfigured man stood motionless; the gun still aimed at the space Franklin's head had occupied moments before. He drew in a deep breath, tasting copper and gunpowder on his tongue. *Another cycle, another death, * he mused. *When will it be enough? *

With a practiced motion, he lowered the weapon. Franklin's lifeless form lay sprawled before him, a testament to the cruel dance they were locked in. The disfigured man's gaze lingered on the detective's face, now slack and empty. *Rest easy, old friend, * he thought. *Until we meet again. *

27 - 28

The world seemed to hold its breath, the only sound the faint crackle of a distant radio from the police cruiser. The disfigured man inhaled deeply, savoring the stillness that followed the chaos. The night air, heavy with the metallic scent of blood, filled his lungs.

He turned slowly, his charred skin pulling uncomfortably beneath his white robe. Drake stood frozen, his eyes wide and uncomprehending. The lawyer's face had drained of all color, his body trembling as he stared at the crimson pool spreading beneath the fallen detectives.

"What have you done?" Drake's voice was barely a whisper, thick with horror and disbelief.

The disfigured man studied him, noting the way Drake's hands shook, the subtle shift of his weight as if he might bolt at any moment. "What needed to be done," he replied, his tone eerily calm. "As always."

Drake's gaze snapped to The disfigured man's face, recognition and fear warring in his eyes. "You... I know you. How is this possible?"

A bitter smile twisted The disfigured man's scarred lips. "Memory's a fickle thing, isn't it, Drake? Always there, just out of reach."

*This can't be happening, * Drake thought, his mind reeling. *I was in the house with Linda and Harrison. I was supposed to attend a work meeting today. How did I get here?* The weight of forgotten memories pressed against his consciousness, elusive and maddening.

"Why?" Drake asked, his voice cracking. "Why are you doing this?"

The disfigured man stepped closer, his movement fluid and predatory. "Because you need to remember, Drake. Because the world needs you to remember."

Drake's hand instinctively reached for a weapon that wasn't there, his lawyer's instincts screaming for self-preservation. "Remember what?" he demanded, anger briefly overriding his fear.

"Everything," The disfigured man whispered, his eyes boring into Drake's. "The choices you made. The lives you destroyed. The world you shattered."

The words hit Drake like physical blows, each one resonating with a truth he couldn't fully grasp. Images flashed through his mind: a car crash, a bomb, a race against time to stop a virus. But as soon as they came the memories vanished.

"I don't understand," Drake said, his voice raw with frustration and growing desperation.

The disfigured man's expression softened, almost imperceptibly. "You will. In time. For now, Drake Miller, you need to run."

29 - 30

"Catch," The disfigured man said casually, tossing the gun toward him.

The word hung in the air, a cruel invitation. Drake's eyes widened, his lawyer's instincts warring with the surreal horror of the moment. Time seemed to slow as the weapon arced through the air, its polished surface gleaming under the harsh streetlights.

No, don't catch it, Drake's mind screamed. But his body betrayed him.

His hands shot out, fingers closing around the cold metal before he could stop himself. The weight of it was shocking, far heavier than he'd imagined. Drake looked down at the gun, horror blooming in his chest as he realized what he'd done. His fingers trembled, threatening to drop the damning evidence.

"I... I didn't mean to," Drake stammered, his voice barely above a whisper. The smell of gunpowder and blood filled his nostrils, making him dizzy. "This isn't right. None of this is right."

His mind raced, desperately trying to make sense of the situation. *How did I get here? Why can't I remember?* The gaps in his memory felt like physical wounds, raw and aching.

"What have you done to me?" Drake demanded, his voice stronger now, fueled by a growing anger. He raised the gun, pointing it at the figure in white, but his hand shook violently. "Who are you? What is this place?"

31 - 32

Drake's throat constricted, his voice cracking as he forced out the words. "W-what—" he stammered, unable to finish the thought. His mind reeled, struggling to process the nightmarish scene before him.

The figure in white stepped closer, the folds of its robe billowing softly in the cool night breeze. Drake fought the urge to step back, his muscles tensing as the acrid smell of smoke and charred flesh invaded his nostrils.

"Relax, Drake," the figure said, its tone mocking and light. The casual familiarity sent a chill down Drake's spine. "They'll be fine. When you wake up again, everything will reset. It always does."

Reset? Wake up? Drake's thoughts raced, fragments of memories flashing through his mind—a car crash, a funhouse, his son's laughter. But nothing cohered, slipping away like sand through his fingers.

The figure leaned in, its charred face mere inches from Drake's. The proximity made his stomach churn, but he stood his ground, gripping the gun tighter.

"The only question is—" the figure's breath was hot against Drake's cheek, "can you survive the rest of the day?"

Drake's heart pounded, the weight of the gun in his hand a constant reminder of his precarious situation. He swallowed hard, fighting to keep his voice steady. "What do you mean, survive? What's happening to me?"

As he spoke, Drake's lawyer's mind kicked in, analyzing the situation, searching for a way out. But the pieces refused to fit together, leaving him adrift in a sea of confusion and fear.

33 - 34

Drake's breath hitched, his eyes darting between the enigmatic figure and the lifeless bodies of the detectives. Blood pooled on the pavement, a stark contrast to the pristine white of his captor's robe. The surreal nature of the scene made his head spin, but he forced himself to focus.

"Who are you?" Drake demanded, his voice wavering despite his attempt at bravado. "Why are you doing this?"

The question hung in the air, heavy with the weight of lives lost and realities shattered. Drake's mind raced, grasping for any semblance of understanding. Had he known this person before? The notion tugged at the edges of his consciousness, like a half-remembered dream.

A soft, hollow chuckle escaped the figure's lips, sending a shiver down Drake's spine. The sound seemed to echo in the still night air, a haunting melody of amusement and malice.

"You already know who I am, even if you don't remember," the figure replied, its tone tinged with a perverse sort of fondness. Drake's brow furrowed, frustration mixing with fear. He should know, shouldn't he? But the knowledge remained just out of reach, taunting him.

The figure's charred hand gestured toward the police station, the movement fluid and graceful despite its grotesque appearance. "And as for why..." A faint smirk played across its lips, a cruel parody of mirth. "Let's just say I enjoy seeing how far you can fall."

Drake's stomach churned at the words, a cocktail of dread and determination swirling within him. *How far I can fall?* he thought, his grip on the gun tightening reflexively. *What does that mean? What game is this monster playing?*

35 - 36

Drake's feet moved of their own accord, carrying him a step backward. The cold metal of the gun pressed against his palm, a stark reminder of the violence he'd just witnessed. His fingers curled tighter around the grip, knuckles whitening with the pressure. The weight of the weapon felt alien in his hands, so different from the familiar heft of a legal brief or the comforting softness of his wife's hand.

"I don't understand," Drake said, his voice barely above a whisper. The words tasted like ash in his mouth, bitter with the realization of how little he truly knew. "What do you want from me?"

The figure's eyes gleamed with an unsettling mixture of amusement and anticipation. "Tick-tock, Drake," it said, the sing-song lilt of its voice a stark contrast to the gravity of the situation. "The clock is always ticking."

Time. It always came back to time, didn't it? Drake's mind raced, grasping at fragments of memory—a car crash, a desperate choice, a world unraveling. But the pieces refused to fit together, slipping away like sand through his fingers.

"What does that mean?" Drake demanded, a note of desperation creeping into his voice. "What clock? What happens when it stops?"

The figure's only response was that infuriating smirk, leaving Drake alone with his questions and the weight of two lives ended at his feet. The gun trembled in his grip as he fought to maintain control, to find a path forward in this nightmare of blood and riddles.

37 - 37

The figure's charred form seemed to melt into the darkness, its white robe the last thing visible before it vanished completely. Drake stood frozen, the gun a leaden weight in his hands, as the reality of his situation crashed over him like a tidal wave.

"Wait!" he called out, his voice cracking. "You can't just leave me here!"

But only silence answered him, punctuated by the distant wail of approaching sirens. Drake's heart hammered in his chest as he looked down at the bodies of Holly and Franklin, their unseeing eyes accusing him from the blood-stained pavement.

"This isn't real," he muttered, squeezing his eyes shut. "It can't be real."

When he opened them again, nothing had changed. The coppery scent of blood filled his nostrils, making his stomach churn. He stumbled backward, his mind reeling.

What am I supposed to do now? he thought frantically. How do I explain this? How do I fix it?

The sirens grew louder, and Drake knew he had to move. But where? Home? What home, after today he had no home to go too. The thought of his wife and son seeing him like this, covered in blood and holding a gun, made him physically ill. Yet how could they, they to were dead.

"Think, Drake," he hissed to himself. "There has to be a way out of this."

But as he stood there, paralyzed by indecision, Drake couldn't shake the feeling that this was just the beginning of something much larger and more terrifying than he could imagine.

The Fugitive

1-2   The cool night air stung Drake's lungs as he ran, his steps uneven on the cracked pavement. The only sounds were his ragged breaths and the faint echo of distant sirens, growing louder with every passing second. He glanced down at his hands, still trembling from the adrenaline. The left hand was shackled, the steel cuff biting into his wrist. The right, however, was free, though the sight of his dislocated thumb made his stomach churn.

"What the hell?" Drake muttered, his voice hoarse. He stumbled to a halt, leaning against a graffiti-covered wall as he examined his misshapen digit. The pain, oddly absent until now, began to throb in time with his racing pulse.

How did that happen? The question echoed in his mind, a haunting refrain amidst the chaos of his thoughts. He closed his eyes, trying to focus, to remember, but the memories slipped away like smoke through his fingers.

"Think, Drake," he growled, frustration evident in his tone. "You're a lawyer, for God's sake. You solve puzzles for a living."

But this puzzle was different. This wasn't a case to be cracked or a legal loophole to exploit. This was his life, fractured and distorted like a funhouse mirror.

The wail of sirens grew closer, jarring him from his introspection. Drake pushed off the wall, wincing as the movement jostled his injured hand. He had to keep moving. Whatever had happened, whatever he had done, he couldn't let them catch him. Not until he understood.

As he resumed his frantic pace, Drake's mind raced. "Linda," he whispered, the name a prayer on his lips. "Harrison." His family, his anchor in this storm of uncertainty. Were they safe? Did they even exist in this reality?

The thought sent a chill down his spine, colder than the night air that whipped past him. He had sacrificed everything once before, leapt into the unknown to save them all. Now, here he was again, running from unseen pursuers in a world that felt both familiar and alien.

"I'll figure this out," Drake promised himself, his determination cutting through the fog of confusion. "I'll find you both, and I'll make this right."

3 - 4

Drake's mind reeled, fragments of memory colliding like shards of glass. The dislocated thumb throbbed, a constant reminder of his desperate escape. But how? When? The details slipped through his grasp like smoke.

"Think, damn it," he muttered, clenching his jaw. "What's the last thing you remember?"

But all that came were flashes: The disfigured man's scarred face, twisted in a sadistic grin; the cold metal of handcuffs; a searing pain in his hand. Nothing cohesive, nothing that made sense.

Drake's fingers brushed against the gun tucked into his waistband, its weight both reassuring and terrifying. He pulled it out, staring at the weapon with a mixture of revulsion and necessity.

"Why?" he whispered, his voice barely audible over his ragged breathing. "Why did you give me this, The disfigured man?"

The memory of The disfigured man's voice, calm and mocking, echoed in his mind: "Oh, Drake. Don't you see? It's not about the gun. It's about the choices you make with it."

Drake shuddered, fighting back the urge to vomit. The gun felt warm, alive almost, as if it carried the essence of the lives it had taken. Lives he couldn't remember ending, but knew, deep in his gut, that he was responsible for.

"I'm not a killer," Drake insisted, his words a desperate plea to the night. But even as he said it, doubt gnawed at him. What if he was? What if this fractured reality was the truth, and everything he thought he knew was a lie?

He tucked the gun away, unable to look at it any longer. The sirens grew louder, more insistent. Drake forced himself to focus, to push past the confusion and fear.

"One step at a time," he told himself, echoing advice he'd given countless clients. "Find somewhere safe. Figure out what happened. Then... then find a way to fix this."

With renewed determination, Drake pushed on into the night, each step carrying him further from the life he knew and deeper into a mystery he couldn't begin to unravel.

5 - 6

The image seared itself into Drake's mind, as vivid as if it were happening before his eyes. Detective Holly Kierstead's face, usually sharp and determined, contorted in shock as she crumpled to the ground. Her black hair splayed out around her head, a stark contrast to the crimson pool spreading beneath her athletic frame.

"No," Drake whispered, his throat constricting. "This can't be real."

But the memory continued its relentless assault. Franklin Bird, his imposing figure suddenly fragile, stumbled forward. His weathered face, lined with years of experience, registered disbelief before he too collapsed, his final breath escaping in a soft wheeze.

Drake's stomach churned. He could almost smell the acrid gunpowder, feel the weight of the weapon in his hand. But how? When? The fragments of his memory refused to align.

"God," Drake muttered under his breath, shaking his head as he pressed forward, his feet pounding against the pavement. Each step felt like a betrayal, carrying him away from a crime he couldn't remember committing.

His mind raced, grasping for explanations. "Holly was observant, intuitive," he thought. "She would have seen this coming, right? And Franklin... he was cautious to a fault. How did I...?"

The sirens wailed in the distance, a mournful cry that seemed to echo his own internal anguish. Drake's muscular frame trembled with each labored breath, his usual strength sapped by the weight of confusion and guilt.

"I'm not a killer," he repeated, the mantra doing little to quell his rising panic. "There has to be an explanation. The disfigured man... he must have done something. Tricked me somehow."

But even as he spoke the words, doubt gnawed at him. The gun at his waist seemed to grow heavier with each step, a grim reminder of the lives it had claimed – lives he had taken, whether he could remember it or not.

7 - 8

The gas station loomed ahead, its fluorescent lights cutting through the darkness like a beacon of hope. Drake's pace slowed as he approached, his brown eyes darting warily across the isolated parking lot. The station stood alone, a solitary outpost in a sea of shadows.

Through the grimy windows, Drake spotted the clerk, a lanky figure hunched over the counter, idly flipping through a magazine. To Drake's weary mind, this mundane sight represented a lifeline – a chance to catch his breath and gather his thoughts.

He hesitated at the door, his hand trembling slightly as he reached for the handle. "Pull yourself together," he muttered, drawing in a deep breath. The cool night air stung his lungs, a sharp reminder of the reality he was desperately trying to escape.

With a determined push, Drake opened the door. A faint chime announced his arrival, the cheerful sound at odds with the turmoil raging within him. The clerk glanced up briefly, his expression a mask of bored indifference, before returning to his magazine.

Drake's heart raced as he stepped inside, the fluorescent lights harsh against his bloodshot eyes. He fought the urge to look over his shoulder, instead forcing himself to walk casually towards the snack aisle.

"Just act normal," he thought, his inner voice tinged with desperation. "Figure out your next move. There has to be a way to prove your innocence."

As he pretended to browse the shelves, Drake's mind whirled with questions. How had he ended up here? What game was the burnt man playing? And most importantly, how could he protect his family from whatever force had thrust him into this nightmare?

9 - 10

Drake's feet felt leaden as he approached the counter, each step a monumental effort to maintain his composure. The clerk's indifference was both a blessing and a curse – it meant he hadn't been recognized, but it also amplified the surreal nature of his situation. Here he was, a man accused of murder, casually asking to use a gas station bathroom.

Swallowing hard, Drake steadied his voice. "Can I use your bathroom?" The words came out huskier than he intended, and he silently cursed his betraying nerves.

The lanky clerk – Keith, according to his name tag – didn't even bother to look up from his magazine. His unkempt hair fell over his eyes as he reached beneath the counter, producing a key attached to a comically large wooden paddle.

"Around the back," Keith drawled, sliding the key across the scratched surface.

As Drake's fingers closed around the paddle, a flood of conflicting emotions washed over him. Relief at this small reprieve warred with the gnawing dread in his gut. He thought of his family, blissfully unaware of the danger they might be in. Of the detectives whose lives had been snuffed out. Of The disfigured man's cryptic words and mocking grin.

"What am I doing?" he wondered, the weight of the key in his hand feeling suddenly oppressive. "Running won't solve this. But what choice do I have?"

11 - 12

"Thanks," Drake mumbled, snatching the key and heading toward the restroom. His footsteps echoed hollowly on the cracked linoleum, each step a reminder of the chasm between his old life and this nightmarish present.

The bathroom door creaked open, revealing a space that seemed to mirror Drake's internal turmoil. Dingy white tiles, stained with years of neglect, stretched across the floor and up the walls. The air hung thick with the acrid scent of industrial cleaner, barely masking an underlying odor of decay.

Drake locked the door behind him, the click of the mechanism sounding unnaturally loud in the confined space. He leaned heavily against the sink, his breath coming in ragged gasps as he tried to center himself.

"Get it together, Miller," he muttered, his voice barely above a whisper. The face that stared back at him from the grimy mirror was a stranger's – haggard, haunted, hunted. "What would you tell a client in this situation?"

The irony wasn't lost on him. Once, he'd been the one offering advice, navigating the intricacies of the law. Now, he was on the other side, a fugitive grasping at straws.

His gaze fell to his dislocated thumb, a stark reminder of his desperate escape. "How did I even do that?" he wondered aloud, the pain finally registering through the haze of adrenaline. "And why can't I remember?"

The questions swirled in his mind, a dizzying maelstrom of confusion and fear. Drake closed his eyes, trying to make sense of the fragmented memories that danced just out of reach. The figures face loomed large in his mind's eye, that knowing smirk taunting him with secrets just beyond his grasp.

"Focus," Drake growled, gripping the edges of the sink until his knuckles turned white. "You're a goddamn lawyer. Think this through logically."

But logic seemed to have abandoned him in this warped reality. How could he apply reason to a situation that defied explanation? His family, alive but oblivious to their shared past. A world both familiar and alien. And now, blood on his hands that he couldn't remember spilling.

Drake's eyes snapped open, meeting his own gaze in the mirror. "One step at a time," he told his reflection, straightening his shoulders. "First, we get out of here. Then we find answers."

With renewed determination, he pushed away from the sink. Whatever twisted game fate was playing, Drake Miller wasn't going down without a fight. He had a family to protect and a mystery to unravel – and somewhere out there, the man in the robe held the key to it all.

13 - 14

Drake turned on the faucet, the sudden rush of icy water over his trembling hands eliciting a sharp hiss. He cupped his palms, splashing the frigid liquid onto his face. The shock of it jolted through him like an electric current, momentarily parting the fog that had settled over his mind.

"Christ," he muttered, blinking rapidly as water dripped from his chin. His fingers curled around the chipped porcelain edges of the sink, knuckles whitening as he leaned in close to the cracked mirror.

The face staring back at him was a stranger's. Gaunt cheeks, sunken eyes rimmed with exhaustion, skin streaked with grime and what looked disturbingly like dried blood. His gaze, bloodshot and wild, held a haunted quality that sent a chill down his spine.

"Is this really me?" Drake whispered, his voice barely audible over the running tap. He ran a trembling hand over his stubbled jaw, wincing at the tenderness there. "What the hell happened?"

His fingers traced the dark smudges marring his skin, and suddenly the acrid scent of smoke filled his nostrils. A flash of memory – flames licking up walls, the crackle of burning wood, his son's terrified scream.

Drake's breath caught in his throat. "The fire," he gasped, gripping the sink tighter as vertigo threatened to overwhelm him. "Our home... it's gone. But how?"

The questions tumbled from his lips, each one spawning a dozen more, none with answers within reach. He stared into his own eyes, searching for some hint of recognition, some flicker of the man he used to be.

"Pull it together, Miller," he growled at his reflection. "You need to figure this out. For Linda. For Harrison."

The mention of his family's names sent another jolt through him, a mixture of longing and fear twisting in his gut. Were they safe? Did they make it out of the explosion? Did they know what had happened to him?

Drake drew in a shaky breath, forcing himself to focus on the immediate problem at hand. "One step at a time," he muttered. "Clean up, then find a way out of here. Then... then we'll figure out the rest."

With renewed determination, he splashed more water on his face, scrubbing at the dirt and soot that clung to his skin. As he worked, he couldn't shake the feeling that with each smudge he removed, he was washing away pieces of a puzzle he desperately needed to solve.

15 - 16

As Drake scrubbed at his face, his mind reeled. "What is happening to me?" he whispered, his voice barely audible over the trickling water. The words hung in the air, heavy with the weight of his confusion and fear.

Suddenly, unbidden and unwelcome, the man's face appeared in his mind's eye. The charred skin, twisted into that infuriatingly smug smile, seemed to mock Drake's confusion. The green dragon insignia on his robe burned bright in his memory, its intricate scales almost seeming to writhe.

Drake's hands trembled as he gripped the sink. "Who are you?" he demanded of the phantom image, his voice a hoarse whisper. "How do you know me?"

The apparition offered no answers, only that same knowing smirk. Drake's frustration mounted. "Why do you seem to know everything about me?" he hissed through clenched teeth. "Even the things I can't remember?"

His mind raced, grasping at fragments of memory that slipped away like smoke. There was something about that disfigured man, something important, but it danced just out of reach. Drake pressed his palms to his temples, willing the answers to come.

"Think, damn it," he muttered. "There has to be a connection. The fire, the detectives, the stalker... it all has to mean something."

But the more he pushed, the more elusive the answers became. Drake's reflection stared back at him, a portrait of desperation and mounting fear. He was a man lost in his own mind, and the way out seemed impossibly far away.

17 - 18

The questions piled atop one another, a crushing weight on Drake's chest. He shut off the faucet with a trembling hand, the sudden silence deafening. Gripping the sink's edge, his knuckles whitened as he fought for control.

"Focus," he muttered, meeting his own gaze in the mirror. The man staring back was a stranger – haggard, haunted. "You have to figure this out. One step at a time."

Drake took a deep breath, steadying himself. The cool air stung his lungs, grounding him in the present. He straightened, smoothing his disheveled hair with a practiced motion that felt like muscle memory from another life.

"Okay," he whispered. "What do I know for certain?"

His mind raced, piecing together the fragments. The fire. The gun. The dead detectives. This evil mans enigmatic presence. Each fact was a puzzle piece, but the picture remained frustratingly unclear.

Resolve steeled his features. Whatever was happening, he'd face it head-on. It was time to move.

Drake unlocked the bathroom door, the key's weight oddly comforting in his palm. As he approached the counter, a prickle of unease crawled up his spine. Keith, the clerk, was no longer engrossed in his magazine. Instead, the young man's posture was rigid, his eyes darting nervously around the store.

"Here's your key," Drake said, his voice carefully neutral as he placed it on the counter.

Keith's hand shot out, snatching the key with uncharacteristic speed. "Thanks," he mumbled, refusing to meet Drake's gaze.

Something about Keith's demeanor made Drake's skin crawl. The air in the store felt charged, as if a storm was brewing just beneath the surface of normalcy.

"Everything alright?" Drake probed, studying the clerk's face.

Keith's eyes flicked to Drake for a split second before darting away. "Fine," he said, his voice an octave too high. "Just fine."

Drake's instincts, honed by years as a lawyer, screamed danger. He needed to leave, now, but curiosity warred with self-preservation.

"You seem... tense," Drake pressed, leaning slightly on the counter. "Did something happen while I was in the bathroom?"

Keith's adam's apple bobbed as he swallowed hard. "N-no," he stammered. "Nothing at all."

The lie hung heavy in the air between them. Drake's mind raced, analyzing every twitch of Keith's face, every nervous glance. What had changed? What did the clerk know?

As Drake opened his mouth to speak again, a distant siren pierced the night. Keith flinched visibly, and Drake's blood ran cold. Somehow, someway, his time had run out.

19 - 20

Drake's gaze swept the store, searching for the source of Keith's unease. Then he saw it.

The TV mounted on the wall behind the counter flickered with life, its glow casting an eerie blue light across Keith's pale face. Drake's breath caught in his throat as he recognized the grainy image on the screen: a police station parking lot, eerily familiar.

His own figure stood there, frozen in time, the gun the robed man had tossed him clutched in his trembling hand. The sight of himself, looking lost and dangerous, sent a chill down Drake's spine.

"Is that...?" Keith's voice trailed off, his eyes darting between Drake and the TV.

Drake swallowed hard, his mind racing. "It's not what it looks like," he said, the words sounding hollow even to his own ears.

How could he explain something he barely understood himself? The weight of the disfigured man's manipulations, the confusion of lost memories, the desperation that had driven him to this point – it all swirled in his mind, a maelstrom of guilt and fear.

"I didn't..." Drake began, but the words died on his lips as he watched bold red letters crawl across the bottom of the screen. His heart pounded, each beat a thunderous reminder of how quickly his world was unraveling.

"They're saying you killed those detectives," Keith whispered, his voice barely audible over the hum of the refrigerators. "Is it true?"

Drake's hands clenched into fists, his nails digging into his palms. The pain grounded him, a sharp counterpoint to the surreal horror of the moment. "I don't know," he admitted, the truth of it burning in his chest. "I can't remember."

The sirens grew louder, their wail a harbinger of the reckoning to come. Drake's mind raced, searching for a way out, for some explanation that could make sense of the nightmare he found himself in.

"I need to go," he said, more to himself than to Keith. But as he turned to leave, he caught sight of his reflection in the store's window – a man on the edge, haunted by deeds he couldn't recall, pursued by forces he didn't understand.

In that moment, Drake Miller, once a pillar of the legal community, now a fugitive, realized the true weight of the disfigured man's machinations. He was a pawn in a game that spanned realities, and the consequences were spiraling far beyond his control.

21 - 22

The bold red letters on the screen burned into Drake's retinas, each word a dagger twisting in his gut. ARMED AND DANGEROUS—COP KILLER ON THE LOOSE. His own face stared back at him from the grainy footage, a stranger wearing his skin.

"This can't be happening," Drake muttered, his voice hoarse. He ran a trembling hand through his disheveled hair, feeling the weight of every sleepless night in the gesture.

Keith's eyes darted between Drake and the TV. "You're him, aren't you? The one they're looking for?"

Drake's mind raced, fragments of memories colliding like shards of broken glass. Holly's sharp insights during their last conversation, Franklin's skeptical frown as Drake tried to explain the impossible. Now, their names scrolled beneath his picture, victims of a crime he couldn't remember committing.

"I didn't... I couldn't have..." Drake's words trailed off, uncertainty gnawing at him. He turned to Keith, desperation etched in every line of his face. "You have to believe me, I'm not a killer."

But even as he spoke, doubt crept in. The gun at his waist felt heavier, a silent accusation. What if the disfigured man's manipulations ran deeper than he realized? What if the multiverse had twisted him into something unrecognizable?

"I don't know what to believe, man," Keith replied, his voice wavering. "But those cops... they were good people. Detective Kierstead helped my sister once."

The words hit Drake like a physical blow. He stumbled back, his broad frame suddenly seeming small and vulnerable. "I need to figure this out," he said, more to himself than to Keith. "There has to be an explanation."

But as sirens began to wail in the distance, Drake knew his time was running out. The world was closing in, and the truth—whatever it might be—seemed further away than ever.

23 - 24

Drake's heart pounded in his chest, each beat a painful reminder of his predicament. "Shit," he hissed under his breath, instinctively stepping back. His muscles tensed, ready to flee, but there was nowhere to go.

The fluorescent lights buzzed overhead, casting harsh shadows across the linoleum floor. Drake's eyes darted around the small convenience store, searching for an escape route that didn't exist. That's when he noticed the phone. It was off the receiver, resting haphazardly on the counter. Faintly, he could hear the voice of a 911 operator on the other end.

Time seemed to slow as realization dawned. Keith had called the police. Drake's mind raced, memories of Linda and Harrison flashing before him. How could he protect them if he couldn't even protect himself?

"Why?" Drake asked, his voice barely above a whisper. "Why did you call them?"

Keith's eyes widened, fear evident in his trembling hands. "I... I had to, man. You're all over the news. They said you killed those detectives."

Drake closed his eyes, fighting against the wave of despair threatening to overwhelm him. "You don't understand," he said, opening his eyes to meet Keith's gaze. "Nothing is what it seems. There's more going on here than you could possibly imagine."

As he spoke, Drake's thoughts drifted to the complexities of the multiverse, to the disfigured man's cryptic words and mocking grin. How could he explain something he barely understood himself?

25 - 26

The 911 operator's voice crackled through the phone's speaker, piercing the tense silence. "Hello? Are you there? Is everything alright?"

Drake's jaw clenched, his fingers curling into fists at his sides. The weight of the gun pressed against his lower back, a grim reminder of the chaos that had led him to this moment. He watched as Keith's hand slowly moved beneath the counter, the clerk's eyes darting between Drake and the hidden space.

"Don't," Drake warned, his voice low and gravelly. The word hung in the air, heavy with unspoken threat.

Keith's movement halted, but his hand remained out of sight. Drake's mind raced, calculating the odds. Was there a weapon beneath the counter? A silent alarm? Or was Keith simply reaching for something innocuous, driven by fear and nervous energy?

"I'm not the person they're saying I am," Drake said, his tone softening. He took a step closer to the counter, hands raised in a placating gesture. "I know how this looks, but I swear to you, I'm trying to save lives, not take them."

As he spoke, Drake's thoughts drifted to Linda and Harrison, to the alternate versions of his family that existed in this twisted reality. How could he protect them if he couldn't even protect himself? The weight of his mission pressed down on him, threatening to crush him beneath its enormity.

"Please," Drake continued, his voice barely above a whisper. "I need your help. Just... just give me a chance to explain."

27 - 28

Drake's heart pounded in his chest, each beat a thunderous reminder of the precarious situation he found himself in. The fluorescent lights flickered overhead, casting an eerie glow across the gas station's interior, transforming familiar objects into sinister shadows.

"What are you doing?" Drake asked, his voice low and threatening. The words slipped from his lips like a coiled serpent, ready to strike at the slightest provocation.

Keith froze, his eyes wide with fear. "I—uh—nothing, man. Just... just ringing you up."

Drake's gaze bore into Keith, searching for any hint of deception. The clerk's Adam's apple bobbed nervously as he swallowed, his fingers twitching beneath the counter. In that moment, Drake felt the weight of his choices pressing down on him, each decision a step further into a labyrinth of consequences he couldn't begin to fathom.

"Look," Drake said, his tone softening slightly, "I know this looks bad. But I'm not who they say I am. I'm trying to fix something... something bigger than all of this."

As he spoke, images of Linda and Harrison flashed through his mind. Their faces, so familiar yet distant in this warped reality, served as both anchor and torment. How could he protect them when he could barely protect himself?

Keith's eyes darted between Drake and the TV screen, which still displayed the damning footage. "Man, I don't know what's going on, but those cops... they're dead. And you're here."

Drake closed his eyes for a moment, the weight of guilt threatening to suffocate him. When he opened them again, his gaze was steely with resolve. "I didn't kill them. But I need time to prove it. Can you help me?"

29 - 30

Drake's hand moved instinctively to his waistband, fingers wrapping around the cold metal of the gun. The weight of it felt both foreign and familiar, a grim reminder of the path he now trod. In one fluid motion, born more of desperation than skill, he drew the weapon and aimed it at Keith's chest.

The clerk's eyes widened, his face draining of color as he stared down the barrel. Drake's hands trembled, betraying the turmoil raging within him. This wasn't who he was—or who he wanted to be. But the stakes were too high, the consequences too dire to falter now.

"Don't," Drake warned, his voice low and gravelly. He struggled to keep it steady, to project a confidence he didn't feel. "Whatever you're reaching for, don't."

As he held the gun, Drake's mind raced. How had it come to this? One moment he was a successful lawyer, the next a fugitive in a world that felt increasingly alien. The faces of Linda and Harrison haunted him, driving him forward even as guilt threatened to drag him under.

"Listen," Drake said, trying to inject calm into his voice, "I don't want to hurt anyone. I just need time to figure this out. To set things right."

Keith's hands slowly rose, palms out in a gesture of surrender. "Okay, man. Okay. Just... just take it easy."

Drake nodded, a small part of him relieved at the clerk's compliance. But the larger part knew this was just another step down a dangerous path, one that might lead him further from the truth—and from his family—than ever before.

31 - 32

Keith's hands shot up, his face pale as moonlight. "Hey, man, I don't want any trouble. I was just... I wasn't doing anything, I swear." His voice quivered, a tremolo of fear that resonated through the small space.

Drake's heart pounded, each beat a thunderous reminder of his predicament. The gun felt heavy in his hand, an anchor tethering him to this moment of crisis. He glanced back at the TV, the flickering image a cruel mirror. His own face stared back at him like a ghost, a stranger wearing his skin.

"Bullshit," Drake snapped, his voice rising with a mixture of fear and frustration. The words tasted bitter on his tongue. "You already called the cops, didn't you?"

As he spoke, Drake's mind raced. How had he become this person? A man holding a gun on an innocent clerk, accused of murders he couldn't remember committing. The weight of his actions, both known and unknown, pressed down on him like a physical force.

He thought of Linda and Harrison, their faces swimming in his mind's eye. Were they safe? Did they even exist in this twisted version of reality? The questions gnawed at him, fueling his desperation.

"Look," Drake said, trying to soften his tone, "I'm not who they say I am. There's been a mistake, a terrible mistake." He struggled to keep his voice steady, to convey the sincerity he felt. "I need to figure this out, to protect my family. You understand that, don't you?"

Keith nodded nervously, his eyes darting between Drake and the gun. The tension in the room was palpable, a living thing that seemed to pulse with each passing second.

33 - 34

Keith's silence hung heavy in the air, a damning confirmation that chilled Drake to his core. The young clerk's eyes, wide with fear, darted towards the phone on the counter.

Drake's grip on the gun tightened, his knuckles turning white. "Dammit," he muttered, a mixture of resignation and desperation in his voice. He ran his free hand through his disheveled hair, his mind racing to formulate a plan.

The faint wail of sirens pierced the night, growing louder with each passing moment. Drake's chest constricted, his breath coming in short, ragged gasps as the reality of his situation crashed down upon him.

"I never wanted this," Drake said, more to himself than to Keith. His voice was barely above a whisper, thick with regret. "I was trying to save them all, to fix everything. How did it come to this?"

The sirens grew closer, their urgent cry a stark reminder of Drake's dwindling options. He glanced towards the store's entrance, his heart pounding in his ears. Time was slipping away, like sand through an hourglass.

"They won't understand," Drake said, turning back to Keith. "Nobody understands. I'm not a killer. I'm a father, a husband. I had a life, a purpose." His voice cracked, the weight of his words hanging in the air between them.

As the sirens reached a fever pitch outside, Drake's mind raced through fragmented memories – Linda's smile, Harrison's laughter, the weight of responsibility he'd carried across realities. He was running out of time, out of choices, out of hope.

35 - 36

The gas station erupted in a cacophony of flashing lights, bathing the interior in an eerie, pulsating glow. Drake's heart hammered against his ribs as he watched the scene unfold through the grimy windows. Police cruisers screeched to a halt, surrounding the building in a suffocating ring of authority.

"This can't be happening," Drake muttered, his voice barely audible over the chaos outside. He pressed his back against the counter, feeling the cold metal of the gun dig into his spine. The weight of it was a grim reminder of how quickly his world had unraveled.

"Holly," he whispered, a surge of conflicting emotions washing over him. "If only you could have remembered..."

His thoughts were cut short by a booming voice over a megaphone. "Come out with your hands up! We know you're armed!"

"They don't understand," Drake thought, his mind racing. "How can I explain something I barely comprehend myself?"

He closed his eyes, trying to center himself amidst the chaos. The faces of Linda and Harrison flashed before him, a stark reminder of what he was fighting for.

"I can't give up now," Drake muttered, steeling his resolve. "There's too much at stake."

37 - 38

Drake's fingers tightened around the grip of the gun, his knuckles turning white. He paced the length of the counter, each step deliberate and heavy, as if the weight of his predicament was a physical burden. His mind raced, desperately seeking an escape route, but every potential plan crumbled before it could fully form.

"Think, Drake," he muttered to himself, running a hand through his disheveled hair. "There has to be a way out of this."

But the more he searched for a solution, the more his thoughts seemed to slam against an impenetrable wall. The faces of Linda and Harrison swam before his eyes, a painful reminder of what he stood to lose.

Behind the counter, Keith let out a whimper, his hands trembling in the air. "Please, man," he pleaded, his voice barely above a whisper. "Don't shoot me. I didn't mean—"

Drake's gaze snapped to the clerk, seeing the fear etched across the young man's face. For a moment, he saw himself reflected in Keith's terrified eyes – a man pushed to the brink, desperate and dangerous.

"I'm not going to hurt you," Drake said, his voice low and strained. He struggled to keep his tone even, to project a calm he didn't feel. "I just need time to think."

As he spoke, Drake's mind raced back to his life as a lawyer, to the countless times he'd talked his way out of impossible situations. But this was different. This was life and death, with the added complication of a reality he barely understood.

"If I could just make them understand," he thought, his free hand clenching into a fist. "But how can I explain something I can't even comprehend myself?"

39 - 40

"Shut up!" Drake barked, his voice cracking under the pressure. The sound of his own desperation echoed in his ears, a harsh reminder of how far he'd fallen. His hand trembled, the gun's weight suddenly unbearable.

Outside, the night air crackled with tension. Flashing lights painted the gas station's grimy windows in alternating hues of red and blue, a surreal backdrop to the unfolding drama. Drake's breath came in short, sharp gasps, each inhalation carrying the acrid scent of fear and uncertainty.

The megaphone voice spoke again, firm and unyielding. "Put the weapon down and exit the building with your hands above your head! We can work this out."

Drake's mind reeled. Work this out? How could they possibly understand? He thought of Linda and Harrison, of the life he'd glimpsed in this alternate reality. It felt both achingly familiar and impossibly distant.

"I can't go back," he muttered, more to himself than to Keith or the unseen officers outside. "Not when I'm so close to understanding."

His gaze darted around the small store, searching for an escape that didn't exist. The fluorescent lights buzzed overhead, their harsh glare seeming to mock his predicament. Drake's fingers flexed around the gun's grip, a cold sweat breaking out across his brow.

"There has to be another way," he thought desperately. "I didn't sacrifice everything just to end up here, trapped and alone."

41 - 42

Drake's eyes darted toward the glass doors, the shadowy figures of officers barely visible behind their vehicles. His thoughts were a chaotic whirlwind, each fragment vying for dominance in his fractured mind.

"The disfigured man," he whispered, the name tasting like ash on his tongue. The image of the scarred man's mocking grin flashed before him, as vivid as the fire that had consumed his home. "What game are you playing?"

The detectives' faces swam into view next—Holly Kierstead's shocked expression as she fell, Franklin Bird's last, rattling breath. Drake's stomach churned with guilt and confusion.

"Linda," he breathed, his voice catching. "Harrison." Their names were a lifeline in the stormy sea of his thoughts. He could almost feel Linda's gentle touch, hear Harrison's carefree laughter. But they seemed to belong to another life, another Drake.

"None of it makes sense," he muttered, running a trembling hand through his disheveled hair. "And now I'm trapped."

A metallic clink snapped him back to reality. Drake's head whipped around, his muscles tensing as he searched for the source of the sound.

43 - 44

The tear gas canister rolled across the linoleum floor, its metallic body gleaming under the harsh fluorescent lights. A hiss filled the air as noxious fumes began to spew forth, quickly engulfing the small space.

Drake's eyes widened in horror. "No," he gasped, the word barely escaping his lips before the acrid gas invaded his lungs. His throat constricted violently, each breath a struggle against the burning sensation that spread through his chest.

Stumbling backward, Drake's broad shoulders collided with a rack of snacks, sending packages clattering to the floor. His vision blurred, tears streaming down his face as he fought to keep his eyes open.

"Linda," he choked out, his mind grasping for an anchor amid the chaos. "I'm sorry. I never meant for any of this."

The room filled with a thick, oppressive smoke, obscuring everything beyond arm's reach. Drake's coughs echoed in the confined space, each one wracking his muscular frame.

"Get down!" an officer's voice boomed from outside, barely audible over the pounding in Drake's ears.

His legs trembled, threatening to give way. "Is this how it ends?" he thought, a bitter laugh bubbling up through the coughs. "After everything I've done, all the worlds I've seen... taken down by a can of gas in a convenience store?"

As the smoke thickened and his consciousness began to fade, Drake's thoughts turned to the family he'd lost and found again. "I'll find a way back to you," he promised silently. "Somehow, I'll make this right."

A Fragmented Memory Recap

1-2   Drake's consciousness swirled in a maelstrom of fragmented memories; each vision more vivid than the last. The world around him blurred into a kaleidoscope of faces, places, and moments that felt both foreign and achingly familiar.

"What's happening to me?" he whispered, his voice barely audible in the cacophony of his mind.

Suddenly, the kaleidoscope settled on a single, crystal-clear image. Drake found himself gripping the steering wheel of his car, knuckles white with tension. The road ahead stretched like a ribbon of shadows, winding through the night. He glanced at the rearview mirror, catching sight of Linda's warm smile and Harrison's excited chatter in the backseat.

"We're almost there, buddy," Drake heard himself say, the words echoing strangely in his ears. "The best crab cakes in town, remember?"

Harrison's gleeful response was cut short by a flash of headlights in the side mirror. Drake's heart raced as he saw a car approaching at breakneck speed, weaving erratically across the lanes.

"Hold on!" he shouted, desperately trying to maintain control of the vehicle.

The world tilted sideways as the approaching car slammed into them. Metal screamed against metal, and Drake felt the sickening lurch as their car careened off the road. Time seemed to slow as they plummeted towards the inky darkness of the river below.

Linda's terrified scream pierced through the chaos, intertwining with Harrison's panicked cries. Drake's mind reeled, grasping for a way to save them, to change the outcome he knew was coming.

"No, not again," he thought, his chest constricting with a mixture of fear and guilt. "I can't lose them. I can't fail them again."

As the car hit the water, the cold shock jolted Drake back to a fragmented reality. The montage of memories continued to assault his senses, each one carrying the weight of choices made and unmade, of lives lived and lost across countless realities.

Drake's voice, hoarse with emotion, broke through the swirling visions. "I'll find a way to fix this. I have to. For them. For all of us."

The memories faded, leaving Drake adrift in a sea of possibilities, each one holding the potential for redemption or further tragedy. The burden of his past mistakes pressed down on him, but beneath it all, a spark of determination refused to be extinguished.

3 - 4

The sterile scent of disinfectant assaulted Drake's nostrils as he blinked awake, the harsh fluorescent lights of the hospital room searing his vision. His body ached, a dull throb pulsing through every limb. Confusion clouded his mind as he tried to piece together fragmented memories.

A doctor approached, his face a mask of professional sympathy. "Mr. Miller, you're awake. I'm so sorry, but I have some difficult news."

Drake's heart clenched, a cold dread seeping through his veins. "What... what happened?" he croaked, his voice barely above a whisper.

"There was an accident," the Dr. Lee began, his words echoing strangely in Drake's ears. "Your wife... she didn't make it."

The world seemed to tilt on its axis, and Drake felt himself falling into an abyss of grief. But something wasn't right. This wasn't how it happened. Was it?

Suddenly, the scene shifted, blurring and reforming. The same hospital room, but different. A different doctor, a different moment in time.

"Mr. Miller," this doctor said, his voice tinged with sorrow, "I'm afraid your son Harrison didn't survive the crash."

Drake's mind reeled, struggling to reconcile these conflicting realities. "No," he thought, his inner voice a mixture of desperation and disbelief. "This can't be happening. Not both of them. Not in different... timelines?"

As he grappled with these devastating revelations, another memory surfaced, sharp and clear amidst the chaos. He saw himself, not just as a grieving husband and father, but as a detective, standing in a precinct bustling with activity.

Holly Kierstead stood beside him, her presence steady and reassuring. Her dark eyes were fixed on a case file, brow furrowed in concentration. "Drake," she said, her voice cutting through his tumultuous thoughts, "what do you make of this?"

He remembered the weight of the badge on his hip, the responsibility that came with it. Working alongside Holly felt right, natural, as if they'd been partners for years.

"We're missing something," Drake heard himself say, the words feeling both familiar and foreign on his tongue. "There's a connection here we're not seeing."

Holly nodded, a small smile playing at the corners of her mouth. "That's why we make a good team, Miller. You see the patterns others miss."

As the memory faded, Drake found himself adrift once more, torn between realities. The grief of losing his family warred with the satisfaction of his work as a detective. Which was real? Which was the life he was meant to live?

"I don't understand," he whispered to the empty hospital room, his voice thick with confusion and anguish. "How can all of this be true? How can I fix what's broken when I don't even know what's real anymore?"

5 - 6

The hospital room dissolved, replaced by a vivid, haunting memory that gripped Drake's consciousness with icy fingers. He found himself standing in the doorway of his own home, heart pounding, as the scene unfolded before him.

Linda's terrified scream pierced the air. "Drake! Help us!" Her voice was raw with panic, her eyes wide with fear as she struggled against the disfigured mans iron grip. The same disfigured man haunting Drake now. Who was he?

"Dad!" Harrison cried out, his hand reaching towards darkness of the abandoned funhouse.

Drake lunged forward, his fingers grazing Harrison's outstretched hand. "No!" he roared, desperation clawing at his insides. "Let them go, the monster!"

Evils scarred face twisted into a cruel smile. "You can't save them, Drake. They're mine now." His voice was calm, almost soothing, a stark contrast to the violence of his actions.

As they vanished through a shimmering portal of his memories, Drake fell to his knees, the weight of his failure crushing him. "I'll find you," he whispered, tears streaming down his face. "I swear, I'll bring you both home."

The memory shifted, and Drake found himself standing before an abandoned funhouse, its faded exterior adorned with a garish green dragon logo. The air was thick with tension and the scent of decay.

"Harrison?" Drake called out, his voice echoing in the eerie silence. "I'm here, son. Where are you?"

As he stepped inside, the funhouse came alive with distorted carnival music and flickering lights. Mirrors reflected fractured versions of himself, each one a reminder of the different lives he'd lived.

"You're too late, Drake," the man's voice resonated from everywhere and nowhere. "You've already lost."

Drake's hand instinctively reached for his weapon. "Show yourself, you coward!" he shouted, eyes darting from one warped reflection to another.

Suddenly, Harrison appeared at the end of a long corridor. "Dad!" he cried out, his face a mixture of relief and terror.

Drake sprinted towards his son, heart pounding. "I'm coming, Harrison! Just hold on!"

But as he reached out to grab Harrison's hand, a searing pain tore through his hip. Drake looked down to see blood blossoming across his shirt, the kidnappers triumphant laughter ringing in his ears.

As darkness closed in, Drake's last thought was of his family. "I'm sorry," he whispered, collapsing to the funhouse floor. "I failed you both."

7 - 8

Drake's consciousness swirled, and suddenly he found himself standing amidst the ruins of a once-thriving city. The air was thick with ash, and the sky bore an ominous reddish hue. Crumbling skyscrapers loomed like ancient monoliths, their shattered windows staring blindly at the desolation below.

"What is this place?" Drake muttered; his voice barely audible over the howling wind. He stumbled forward, feet crunching on debris-strewn ground.

A figure emerged from the haze, and Drake's heart leapt as he recognized his son Harrison. His coat was tattered, his hair dulled by the perpetual dust storm.

"Harrison? What are you doing here?" Drake asked, his eyes scanning the ravaged landscape.

Then he remembered. "This is what becomes of our world if we fail, Drake. The future you're fighting to prevent."

Drake's fists clenched at his sides. "No. I won't let this happen. There has to be a way to stop it."

Harrisons laugh was bitter. "You've said that in every timeline, Drake. Yet here we are."

As Drake opened his mouth to respond, the scene shifted abruptly. He found himself standing in a sterile hospital corridor, the smell of antiseptic sharp in his nostrils. A sense of urgency gripped him as he recognized the familiar surroundings.

"The bomb," he whispered, memories flooding back. "I have to find it."

Drake raced down the hallway, his heart pounding. He could hear the muffled sounds of patients and staff, blissfully unaware of the danger that lurked.

"Where is it?" he muttered, frantically searching each room. Time seemed to slow as panic set in.

Then he saw it – a nondescript package tucked away in a supply closet. The timer blinked ominously: 00:30.

Drake's mind raced. There wasn't enough time to evacuate everyone. He thought of Harrison, of Linda, of all the lives that hung in the balance.

"I'm sorry," he whispered, gathering the bomb in his arms. "I hope you understand someday, son."

With a deep breath, Drake ran towards the nearest exit, determination etched on his face. He had to get far enough away to minimize the damage. As the timer ticked down, he realized with grim certainty that this was always meant to be his fate.

"At least this time," Drake thought, sprinting into the parking lot, "I can save them."

The world exploded in a blinding flash of light, and Drake's sacrifice echoed across timelines.

9 - 10

Drake's consciousness plummeted through a kaleidoscope of shattered realities, each fragment a reminder of lives lived and lost. As the maelstrom subsided, he found himself in a stark, unfamiliar room. The air felt heavy, oppressive with unspoken grief.

He blinked, disoriented, as a stern-faced doctor approached his bedside. "Mr. Miller, I'm sorry, but there's no easy way to say this," the man began, his voice a somber drone. "The accident was... severe. Your wife and son... they didn't make it."

Drake's world imploded. "No," he choked out, memories of Linda's laugh and Harrison's smile flashing through his mind. "That's impossible. I just saw them. I..." He trailed off, realizing with mounting horror that in this reality, he had no connection with his family.

The doctor's words faded into background noise as Drake's mind reeled. He searched desperately for a connection, a thread to pull that might unravel this nightmare. But there was nothing – no alternate timelines, no parallel worlds where Linda and Harrison lived. In this cruel twist of fate, they were simply... gone.

"How long have I been here?" Drake managed to ask, his voice barely above a whisper.

"Three days," the doctor replied, sympathy etched on his face. "You've been in and out of consciousness."

Drake closed his eyes, overwhelmed by a tidal wave of grief and confusion. "This can't be real," he thought, clenching his fists. "There has to be a way to fix this, to get back to them."

But as the hours crawled by, the harsh reality of this new world settled in. Drake found himself trapped in a life devoid of the very people he had fought so desperately to save across countless realities.

Just as despair threatened to consume him, the world began to blur and shift once more. Colors swirled, time seemed to bend, and suddenly...

Drake's eyes snapped open. He found himself lying in his familiar bed, the soft warmth of Linda's body next to him. Sunlight filtered through the curtains, casting a golden glow across the room. For a moment, he lay perfectly still, afraid that any movement might shatter this fragile reality.

"Linda?" he whispered, his voice trembling.

She stirred beside him, turning to face him with a sleepy smile. "Good morning, honey. Did you have another bad dream?"

Drake's heart raced as he took in her face, alive and vibrant. He reached out, gently touching her cheek, reassuring himself of her presence. "I... yeah. It was... intense."

Linda's brow furrowed with concern. "Do you want to talk about it?"

Drake hesitated, the weight of countless alternate realities pressing down on him. How could he possibly explain? "I... I lost you," he finally said, his voice thick with emotion. "You and Harrison. And I couldn't find my way back."

Linda pulled him close, her embrace a lifeline in the storm of his thoughts. "We're right here, Drake. We're not going anywhere."

As he held her, Drake's mind raced. His day had restarted again, offering both relief and a gnawing uncertainty. What cruel twist awaited him this time? How many more cycles must he endure?

"I love you," he murmured into Linda's hair, clinging to this moment of peace. "Both of you. More than you could ever know."

The Barricaded House

1-2   Drake's eyes snapped open, his heart thundering against his ribs like a caged animal desperate for escape. Soft amber light filtered through the curtains, painting abstract patterns on the walls that seemed to mock the chaos swirling in his mind. For a fleeting moment, hope fluttered in his chest—had the nightmare finally ended?

He flexed his fingers instinctively, a habit born from countless mornings of uncertainty. Sharp, searing pain lanced through his hand, reality crashing down upon him with merciless force. His thumb jutted at an unnatural angle, angry and swollen.

"No," he whispered, the word barely audible as it escaped his lips. "Not again."

Drake pushed himself up, wincing as he cradled his injured hand against his chest. The dislocated thumb felt like a cruel reminder, a physical manifestation of his failures etched into his flesh. He glanced around the familiar bedroom, searching for any sign that this time might be different.

But everything was exactly as it had been before—the framed family photo on the nightstand, Linda's robe draped over a chair, the faint scent of her lavender shampoo lingering in the air. It was all achingly normal, a facade of domestic tranquility that concealed the horrors he knew were coming.

"I can't keep doing this," Drake muttered, running his good hand through his disheveled hair. "There has to be a way to break the cycle."

He closed his eyes, trying to focus his thoughts. The weight of responsibility pressed down on him, threatening to crush his resolve. How many times had he failed to save them? How many more times would he have to watch his family die?

"Dad?" Harrison's voice drifted through the closed door, innocent and unaware of the danger that loomed. "Are you okay? I heard you talking."

Drake's breath caught in his throat. Every fiber of his being longed to rush to his son, to hold him close and never let go. But he knew that any deviation from the pattern could have unforeseen consequences.

"I'm fine, buddy," he called back, forcing a steady tone. "Just... just stubbed my toe. Go on down for breakfast, I'll be there in a minute."

As Harrison's footsteps faded away, Drake's mind raced. He had to find a way to protect them, to outsmart whatever malevolent force kept resetting the day. But first, he needed to deal with his injury.

With gritted teeth, he gripped his dislocated thumb. The pain that shot through his hand as he wrenched it back into place was almost a relief—a reminder that he was still alive, still fighting.

"This time," Drake vowed, his voice low and determined, "I won't let you down. I'll save you both, no matter what it takes."

3-4

Drake rose from the bed, his movements careful and deliberate as he tested his newly relocated thumb. The joint throbbed, a constant reminder of the chaos that had unfolded—or would unfold—at the gas station. He flexed his fingers, wincing at the lingering pain.

"Gas station," he muttered, shaking his head. "No, that's not right."

Fragments of memories assaulted him: the acrid smell of gunpowder, Holly's wide eyes filled with terror, Franklin's body crumpling to the ground. And that face—that horribly disfigured face, grinning as it tossed him the gun.

Drake pressed his palms against his temples, trying to sort through the jumbled timeline. "Focus," he commanded himself. "What's real? What matters?"

He glanced at his thumb again, the swelling already visible. "This," he said softly. "This is real. This carries over."

The realization hit him like a physical blow. If injuries persisted through the loops, what else might? Could he use this to his advantage somehow?

"Drake?" Linda's voice called from downstairs. "Breakfast is ready!"

He closed his eyes, savoring the normalcy of her tone. How long before that normalcy shattered again?

"Coming!" he replied, his voice steadier than he felt.

As he dressed, Drake's mind raced with possibilities. This loop would be different. It had to be. He'd make sure of it.

5 - 6

The amber light of early morning filtered through the curtains, casting long shadows across the rumpled bed sheets. Drake's breath caught in his throat as Linda's voice, soft and groggy, broke the silence.

"Drake? Are you alright?"

He turned, his heart clenching at the sight of her. Linda's blonde hair fell across her face as she propped herself up on an elbow, her blue eyes clouded with sleep but filled with concern. For a moment, Drake was frozen, drinking in the sight of her alive and whole.

She doesn't know, he thought, a wave of relief and despair washing over him. *She has no idea what's coming.*

"I'm fine," he managed, his voice rough with emotion. "Just... didn't sleep well."

Linda stirred beside him, her movements slow and languid. "Another nightmare?" she asked, reaching out to touch his arm gently.

Drake nodded, not trusting himself to speak. How could he explain the truth? That her death—their son's death—played on repeat in his mind, a cruel loop he couldn't escape?

"Do you want to talk about it?" Linda's voice was tender, filled with a compassion that made Drake's chest ache.

He closed his eyes, wrestling with the urge to spill everything. To warn her, to beg her to help him figure out how to break this cycle. But the words caught in his throat, held back by the fear of sounding insane, of pushing her away when he needed her most.

"It's... complicated," he finally said, meeting her gaze. "I just need to keep you and Harrison safe. That's all that matters."

Linda's brow furrowed, concern deepening in her eyes. "Drake, you're scaring me a little. What's going on?"

He reached out, cupping her face in his hand, his thumb—the one that was dislocated across reality—brushing her cheek. "Trust me, Linda. Please. I promise I'll explain everything, but for now... just trust me."

The weight of unspoken truths hung heavy between them as Linda searched his face, her expression a mix of worry and love. Drake held his breath, silently pleading for her to understand, to believe in him even when he couldn't fully explain why.

7 - 8

Drake swallowed hard, the lie tasting bitter on his tongue. "It's fine," he said, though the sharp throbbing told a different story. "I must've hit it on something."

Linda's eyes narrowed, her wifely nurse's intuition clearly not buying his feeble explanation. She turned his hand in hers, her touch gentle yet purposeful as she examined the injury. Drake winced, the pain flaring as she probed the swollen joint.

"Drake," Linda said softly, her voice a mixture of concern and exasperation, "this isn't just a bump. It's dislocated." She paused, meeting his gaze with a look that spoke volumes about her worry. "I can set it, but it's going to hurt."

He nodded, a lump forming in his throat. The physical pain was nothing compared to the emotional turmoil churning inside him. How many times had he seen Linda die? How many times had he failed to protect her and Harrison? The weight of those memories pressed down on him, threatening to crush his resolve.

"Do it," Drake whispered, his voice barely audible. He closed his eyes, bracing himself not just for the physical pain, but for the day ahead. Whatever happened, he couldn't let history repeat itself. Not again. Not ever.

9 - 10

Drake clenched his jaw, the muscles in his neck tightening as he steeled himself. "Just do it," he said through gritted teeth, his voice a low growl of determination. The pain in his thumb was a constant throb, a reminder of the nightmarish loops he'd endured. But it was also proof that something had changed, that this time might be different.

Linda's eyes softened, a mixture of concern and resolve flickering across her face. She nodded, her movements slow and deliberate as she positioned herself. "Alright," she murmured, her tone gentle yet firm. She braced his hand with one of hers, her touch warm and familiar against his skin. With her other hand, she gripped his thumb firmly, her fingers steady and sure.

"Ready?" Linda asked, her gaze locked on Drake's face.

Drake's mind raced, memories of past failures and future possibilities colliding in a dizzying whirlwind. He thought of Harrison, of the countless times he'd failed to save their son. This time had to be different. This time, he would protect them both, no matter the cost.

He drew in a deep breath, the scent of Linda's lavender shampoo filling his nostrils. It was a smell that had always brought him comfort, but now it only intensified the ache in his chest. How many more mornings would he wake up to that scent, only to lose her again?

"Drake?" Linda's voice cut through his spiraling thoughts, concern etching deeper lines around her eyes. "Are you okay?"

He blinked, forcing himself back to the present moment. "Yeah," he rasped, his throat dry. "I'm ready."

11 - 12

Drake barely had time to nod before Linda yanked. A searing, white-hot pain shot through his hand, radiating up his arm like lightning. The joint popped back into place with a sickening crunch, and Drake hissed through clenched teeth, his entire body tensing as if electrified. His free hand gripped the table, knuckles turning white as he fought against the urge to cry out.

The throbbing in his thumb intensified, a pulsing reminder of the strange reality he found himself trapped in. Drake's eyes squeezed shut, his breaths coming in short, sharp gasps as he rode out the waves of pain.

"There," Linda said, her voice a soothing balm amidst the storm of his agony. Her tone was calm, but Drake could hear the undercurrent of concern. "You'll need to ice it."

He forced his eyes open, meeting Linda's worried gaze. The softness in her blue eyes threatened to undo him. How many times had he seen that look? How many times had she cared for him, unaware of the horrors that awaited them?

"Thanks," Drake managed to grunt, his voice hoarse. He flexed his fingers experimentally, wincing at the lingering ache. "I'll be fine."

Linda's brow furrowed, her hand still gently cradling his. "Drake, what's really going on? This isn't like you."

For a moment, Drake considered telling her everything – the loops, the deaths, the overwhelming fear that gripped him every time he woke up. But the words caught in his throat. How could he burden her with that knowledge?

Instead, he forced a weak smile. "Just clumsy, I guess. Don't worry about it."

13 - 14

Drake's mind raced, the realization hitting him like a freight train. The injury had carried over. His thumb, dislocated in one loop, remained injured in the next. This was new, unprecedented. The implications sent a chill down his spine.

"Drake?" Linda's voice cut through his thoughts. "You look pale. Are you sure you're alright?"

He blinked, focusing on her face. The concern in her eyes was almost too much to bear. "Yeah, I'm... I'm fine," he lied, his voice tight.

But he wasn't fine. Not even close. The robed man's words echoed in his mind, a sinister mantra that refused to be silenced: "Survive the day, Drake. Let's see if you can make it."

Drake's jaw clenched. He could almost see his scarred face, that twisted sneer mocking him. The bastard knew something about these loops, about why injuries were now persisting. But what did it mean?

"I think I need some air," Drake muttered, standing abruptly. The room seemed to spin for a moment, his perception skewed by the weight of this new development.

Linda reached out, her fingers brushing his arm. "Drake, please. Talk to me."

He paused, torn between the desperate need to protect her and the longing to share his burden. But how could he explain the unexplainable? How could he make her understand that their lives were on repeat, that danger lurked around every corner?

"I just..." Drake started, then stopped, running a hand through his disheveled hair. "I need to figure something out. I promise I'll explain later."

As he turned to leave, the weight of his responsibility pressed down on him. Survive the day. Save his family. Unravel the mystery. The task seemed insurmountable, but failure wasn't an option. Not when Linda and Harrison's lives hung in the balance.

15 - 16

Drake's fists clenched involuntarily, his newly-aligned thumb protesting with a dull throb. The pain grounded him, a stark reminder of the stakes. He closed his eyes, and unbidden, the memories flooded in—Linda's lifeless body sprawled across the kitchen floor, Harrison's wide, terrified eyes as the car crashed. Each death, each failure, etched into his mind with cruel precision.

"No," he whispered, his voice barely audible. "Not again. Never again."

Linda's soft touch on his shoulder startled him. "Drake? What's wrong?"

He turned to face her, drinking in the sight of her alive, whole. The concern in her blue eyes was almost more than he could bear. How many times had he seen that look, only to watch it fade into nothingness?

"I need to tell you something," Drake said, his voice rough with emotion. "And I need you to believe me, even if it sounds impossible."

Linda's brow furrowed, but she nodded. "Of course. You're scaring me a little, but... I'm listening."

Drake took a deep breath, steeling himself. "We're in danger. All of us. And I think I know how to save us, but I need your help."

As he spoke, laying out the bizarre truth of their situation, Drake's mind raced. The plan was forming, nebulous but urgent. They needed to stay together, to fortify their home against unseen threats. But more than that, they needed to break the cycle.

"I know it sounds crazy," Drake finished, watching Linda's face carefully.

She was silent for a long moment, her expression unreadable. Then, to his surprise, she reached out and took his hand. "I don't understand everything," she said slowly, "but I trust you, Drake. What do we need to do?"

Relief washed over him, tinged with a fierce determination. This time would be different. This time, he would keep them safe.

"First," Drake said, his voice steadier now, "we need to talk to Harrison. And then... we prepare."

17 - 18

The sizzle of bacon filled the kitchen, a mundane soundtrack to the turmoil churning in Drake's gut. He stood, arms crossed tightly over his chest, watching Linda's practiced movements at the stove. Her blonde hair caught the morning light, a halo of normalcy that felt like a cruel taunt.

Harrison hunched over his phone at the table, thumbs tapping rapidly. The tinny sounds of his game drifted up, mingling with the cooking sounds. It was all so achingly familiar, so deceptively ordinary.

Drake's thumb throbbed, a constant reminder of the truth. His eyes darted from Linda to Harrison, drinking in their presence, memorizing every detail. How many more mornings would he have like this?

"Dad, you're doing that thing again," Harrison said without looking up.

Drake blinked. "What thing?"

"The creepy staring thing," Harrison replied, finally glancing up with a half-smile. "You okay?"

Linda turned, spatula in hand, her brow furrowed with concern. "Drake?"

He forced a smile, uncrossing his arms with effort. "Yeah, just... thinking."

"About what?" Linda asked, her voice gentle.

Drake hesitated, weighing his words carefully. "About how lucky I am," he said finally. "To have you both."

Linda's expression softened, but concern still lingered in her eyes. "That's sweet, hon. But you've been acting strange lately. Is everything alright?"

The lie rose automatically to Drake's lips, but he swallowed it back. "No," he admitted quietly. "It's not. But I'm working on it. I promise."

Harrison set his phone down, suddenly alert. "Dad? What's wrong?"

Drake looked between them, his family, his whole world. The weight of what he knew, what he'd seen, pressed down on him. But he couldn't burden them, not yet. Not until he had a plan.

"Nothing we can't handle together," he said, injecting confidence into his voice. "Now, how about those eggs?"

19 - 20

Drake's heart raced as he watched Linda turn back to the stove, her blonde hair catching the morning light. The sizzle of bacon filled the kitchen, a mundane sound that now seemed painfully precious. He cleared his throat, fighting to keep his voice steady.

"Hey, Linda?"

She glanced over her shoulder, spatula poised mid-flip. "Hmm?"

Drake's mind raced. He wanted to tell her everything—about the other realities he remembered, the danger, the desperate need to keep them safe. But the words stuck in his throat. How could he explain without sounding insane? How could he protect them without terrifying them? She trusted him about his explanation about the loops, but did she fully understand the enormity of the situation?

"I was thinking," he began, then faltered. His injured thumb throbbed, a stark reminder of the stakes. He flexed his hand, trying to ignore the pain. "Maybe we could... do something different today?"

Linda turned fully now, her blue eyes searching his face. "Different how?" she asked, her voice tinged with curiosity and a hint of concern.

Drake opened his mouth to respond, but Harrison's voice cut in. "If you're going to suggest we skip soccer practice again, Dad, I'm all for it."

"Harrison," Linda admonished gently, but her gaze remained fixed on Drake. "What did you have in mind, hon?"

Drake's mind raced. He needed to keep them close, keep them safe, but without raising suspicion. The weight of responsibility pressed down on him, threatening to crush his resolve. But as he looked at Linda—patient, loving Linda—he found a flicker of strength.

"I was thinking," he said slowly, carefully choosing each word, "maybe we could have a family day. Just the three of us."

21 - 22

Drake's heart raced as he watched Linda's expression shift, her brow furrowing slightly. The sizzle of bacon in the pan filled the momentary silence, a mundane sound that felt jarringly out of place amidst the turmoil in his mind.

"Let's stay home today," he said, the words tumbling out before he could second-guess himself.

Linda's hand stilled, the spatula hovering over the pan. She turned to face him fully, her eyes widening with surprise. "Stay home? What do you mean?"

Drake swallowed hard; his throat suddenly dry. The weight of his decision pressed down on him, each second feeling like an eternity. He could see the concern etching itself into the lines of Linda's face, the same worry that had haunted her eyes in countless iterations of this day.

"I just..." he began, struggling to find the right words. How could he convey the urgency without revealing the impossible truth? "I have this feeling. Like we need to be together today. All of us."

Linda's gaze softened, a mix of confusion and affection in her eyes. "Drake, is everything okay? You've been... different lately."

The irony of her words wasn't lost on him. Different. If only she knew how many times he'd lived this day, how desperately he was trying to change its outcome. He flexed his injured thumb, the dull ache a constant reminder of the stakes.

"I'm fine," he lied, forcing a smile that didn't quite reach his eyes. "I just want to spend time with you and Harrison. Is that so strange?"

As Linda opened her mouth to respond, Drake silently prayed that this time, just this once, fate would be on his side.

23 - 24

Drake took a deep breath, his gaze drifting to the kitchen window where sunlight streamed in, painting golden patterns on the tile floor. The normalcy of the scene felt like a cruel joke against the weight of his knowledge.

"I mean..." he said, his voice low and urgent, "let's not go anywhere. No practice, no work, no errands. Just us. Here."

The words hung in the air, heavy with unspoken implications. Drake's heart raced as he watched Linda's expression shift, her brow furrowing in concern. He longed to tell her everything, to share the burden of his impossible reality, but he knew she wouldn't understand. Couldn't understand.

From the corner of his eye, Drake saw movement. Harrison had looked up from his phone, his lanky frame straightening in the chair. The teenager's brown eyes, were wide with a mix of curiosity and confusion.

"Why?" Harrison asked, his voice cracking slightly in the way it had started to do recently. "What's going on?"

Drake's chest tightened at the sound of his son's voice. How many times had he heard that same question, seen that same look of bewilderment on Harrison's face? The memory of his son's broken body beneath the collapsed barricade flashed through his mind, and he had to grip the edge of the counter to steady himself.

"Nothing's going on," Drake lied, hating the taste of deceit on his tongue. "I just thought... we could spend a day together. As a family."

He watched as Harrison and Linda exchanged glances, saw the unspoken communication between them. It struck him then, how close they were, how in tune with each other's thoughts and feelings. He felt a pang of jealousy, of isolation. How could he bridge this gap when he was carrying the weight of multiple realities on his shoulders?

Drake hesitated, searching for the right words. The kitchen suddenly felt too small, the air heavy with unspoken tension. He ran a hand through his disheveled hair, buying time as he tried to articulate the nameless dread coiling in his gut.

"I just... have a bad feeling," he finally said, his voice low and strained. "Like something's going to happen." He looked at Linda, then Harrison, his eyes pleading. "I'd feel better if we all stayed together."

The words hung in the air, fragile and desperate. Drake could see the doubt creeping into Harrison's expression, the furrow deepening between Linda's brows. He wanted to shake them, to make them understand the urgency that thrummed through his veins like an electric current.

Linda exchanged another glance with Harrison, her blue eyes clouded with concern. She turned back to Drake, her blonde hair catching the morning light as she moved. "Drake," she said softly, her tone a mixture of worry and confusion, "are you feeling okay? You've been on edge lately."

The gentleness in her voice was almost his undoing. Drake swallowed hard, fighting back the urge to confess everything—the loops, the deaths, the maddening repetition of tragedy. Instead, he clenched his fists, feeling the dull ache in his recently reset thumb.

"I'm fine," he insisted, though even to his own ears, the words sounded hollow. "I just... I need you both to trust me on this. Please."

25 - 26

Linda's eyes searched his face, her expression a tapestry of concern, love, and growing unease. Drake held her gaze, silently willing her to understand, to sense the desperation that he couldn't fully explain. The kitchen fell silent, save for the soft ticking of the clock on the wall, each second a reminder of the precious time slipping away.

Finally, Linda sighed, her shoulders dropping slightly. "Alright," she said, her voice tinged with resignation. "If it'll make you feel better, we'll stay home today."

Relief washed over Drake, momentarily drowning out the persistent anxiety. He reached out, gently grasping Linda's hand. "Thank you," he murmured, his voice thick with emotion.

As Linda squeezed his hand in return, Drake's mind raced. He had bought them time, but what now? How could he protect them from a threat he couldn't name, couldn't even fully understand? The weight of responsibility settled on his shoulders like a physical burden.

He glanced at Harrison, noting the teen's poorly concealed frustration. This was just the beginning, Drake realized. Keeping them safe meant more than just staying home—it meant navigating the minefield of their questions, their doubts, their growing suspicions. And all the while, the clock would keep ticking, bringing them closer to... what?

Drake took a deep breath, steeling himself for the day ahead. One step at a time, he thought. We're together. We're safe. For now, that has to be enough.

27 - 28

Harrison's face contorted in disbelief, his brown eyes widening as he processed his father's words. The teen's lanky frame tensed, his fingers gripping the edge of the kitchen table until his knuckles whitened.

"You can't be serious," Harrison groaned, his voice cracking with a mixture of frustration and desperation. "I've got soccer practice tryouts today! And Mike's waiting to give me a ride."

Drake's heart clenched at the sight of his son's distress. He longed to explain, to make Harrison understand the invisible danger that loomed over them. But how could he convey the weight of repeated tragedy, the suffocating dread of watching his family die over and over?

Instead, Drake squared his shoulders, his jaw set in determination. "You're staying home," he said firmly, his tone leaving no room for argument. "That's final."

The words hung in the air, heavy and unyielding. Drake watched as a flicker of hurt crossed Harrison's face, quickly replaced by teenage defiance. He braced himself for the inevitable pushback, his mind racing to find a way to make this easier, to soften the blow without compromising their safety.

But how do you protect someone from a threat they can't see, can't understand? Drake wondered, his previously dislocated thumb throbbing as if in response. The pain was a constant reminder of the stakes, of the cruel reality that bled through each loop.

"Dad, come on," Harrison pleaded, his voice softer now, tinged with confusion. "This isn't like you. What's really going on?"

Drake swallowed hard, the weight of unspoken truths pressing against his chest. He met his son's gaze, seeing not just the stubborn teenager before him, but echoes of past Harrisons—laughing, crying, dying. The memories threatened to overwhelm him, but he pushed them back, clinging to the present moment.

"I know it doesn't make sense," Drake said, his voice low and intense. "But I need you to trust me on this, Harrison. Please. It's important—more important than you can imagine."

29 - 30

Harrison's brow furrowed, a mix of concern and frustration etched across his features. He opened his mouth to protest again, but Drake cut him off with a raised hand.

"I promise I'll explain everything later," Drake said, the lie tasting bitter on his tongue. "For now, I need to make sure we're safe."

Without waiting for a response, Drake turned and strode towards the garage, his movements purposeful and tense. The cool darkness of the space enveloped him as he flicked on the light, illuminating shelves lined with tools and forgotten projects.

His eyes scanned the cluttered workbench, searching. There—a hammer, its wooden handle smooth from years of use. Drake grabbed it, testing its weight in his hand. It felt solid, reassuring. A tool for building, for fixing things. But today, it would be a tool for protection.

As he gathered nails and planks of wood, Drake's mind raced. How much time did they have? Would this be enough? The uncertainty gnawed at him, threatening to paralyze him with indecision.

"No," he muttered to himself, shaking off the doubt. "Focus, Drake. One step at a time."

He emerged from the garage, arms laden with supplies. Linda stood in the kitchen doorway, her expression a mixture of concern and confusion.

"Drake," she began, her voice soft but firm. "What's going on? You're scaring me."

Drake paused, meeting her gaze. The love and worry in her eyes threatened to undo him. How many times had he seen that look, just before losing her? The memory of her lifeless body, sprawled across countless iterations of this very floor, flashed through his mind.

"I'm trying to keep us safe," he said, his voice hoarse with emotion. "Please, Linda. I need you to trust me."

31 - 32

Drake moved to the nearest window, setting down his supplies with a dull thud. The sound echoed through the quiet house, a stark reminder of the tension that hung in the air. He began hammering wooden boards across the window frame, each strike resonating with desperate determination.

Linda approached; her footsteps hesitant. "Safe from what again, exactly?" she asked, her arms crossed tightly over her chest.

Drake paused mid-swing; the weight of unspeakable truths heavy on his tongue. How could he explain the loops, the deaths, the constant resets? The words caught in his throat, tangled with fear and frustration.

Instead, he resumed his work, speaking between hammer blows. "I can't... I can't explain it all right now. But something's coming, Linda. Something bad."

He felt her eyes on him, studying his tense shoulders, his white-knuckled grip on the hammer. In his peripheral vision, he saw her reach out, then hesitate, her hand hovering uncertainly in the air between them.

"Drake," she said softly, "you're not making any sense. We can't just barricade ourselves in here without—"

"We can," he interrupted, turning to face her. The desperation in his eyes must have been evident, for Linda took a small step back. "We have to. Please, just... help me with this. I promise I'll explain everything later."

As he spoke, Drake moved to the kitchen, unplugging the stove with swift, practiced movements. His hands shook slightly as he reached for the gas valve, memories of past explosions flashing through his mind.

"No chances," he muttered to himself. "Not this time."

Linda watched him, her brow furrowed with worry. "Drake, you're really starting to scare me. Maybe we should call someone, get you some help—"

"No!" Drake's voice came out sharper than he intended, making Linda flinch. He took a deep breath, trying to soften his tone. "No calls. No one in or out. Just us, safe inside. That's all that matters right now."

He returned to the windows, resuming his methodical barricading. With each board nailed into place, a small part of him hoped that this time, finally, it would be enough to keep the horrors at bay.

33 - 34

The rhythmic thud of the hammer echoed through the house as Drake worked, each nail a testament to his determination. Linda's presence lingered behind him; her concern palpable in the tense silence.

"Making sure we're safe," he replied without looking up, his voice tight with barely contained anxiety. The weight of repeated failures pressed down on him, driving each strike of the hammer with renewed urgency.

Linda's soft intake of breath was audible even over the pounding. "Drake please talk to me. Safe from what?" she asked, her voice trembling slightly.

Drake's hand stilled mid-swing, the hammer suspended in the air as he wrestled with how to answer. How could he explain the nightmarish loop he was trapped in? The constant threat of losing everything he loved, over and over again?

He turned to face her, his eyes haunted by memories of horrors she couldn't begin to comprehend. "From everything," he whispered, his voice hoarse. "From the world outside these walls. From... from fate itself."

Linda's face contorted with a mixture of confusion and growing alarm. Drake could see the questions forming on her lips, but he couldn't bear to hear them. Not now, when every second counted.

"Please," he said, cutting off her unspoken words. "I need you to trust me. Can you do that?"

As he awaited her response, Drake's mind raced with contingencies, desperate to find the one path that would keep his family alive this time.

35 - 36

Drake's grip tightened on the hammer, his knuckles turning white as he struggled to maintain his composure. The weight of unsaid words hung heavy between them, a chasm of unspoken truths and impossible explanations.

"I don't know," he finally admitted, his voice barely above a whisper. He turned to face Linda fully, the hammer hovering forgotten in his hand. "But something's coming. I can feel it."

The admission felt like a defeat, a crack in the armor of certainty he'd been trying so hard to maintain. In the depths of his being, Drake knew the danger was real, but how could he explain the inexplicable?

Linda's frown deepened, etching lines of worry across her forehead. She took a hesitant step closer, her eyes searching his face for answers he couldn't provide. "Drake, this isn't like you," she said, her voice tinged with a mixture of concern and fear. "You're scaring me."

The words hit Drake like a physical blow. He'd faced death, destruction, and the unraveling of reality itself, but somehow, the fear in Linda's eyes cut deeper than any of it. He wanted to reach out, to hold her, to promise that everything would be alright. But the lies stuck in his throat, choking him with their hollowness.

Instead, he turned back to the window, his eyes scanning the seemingly peaceful neighborhood beyond. How long before the illusion shattered? How long before death came knocking at their door once again?

"I'm sorry," he murmured, more to himself than to Linda. "I just need to keep you safe. Both of you."

37 - 38

Drake's hand clenched around the hammer, his knuckles whitening with the force of his grip. The weight of unseen dangers pressed down on him, making each breath a struggle. He turned back to Linda, his eyes pleading for understanding.

"I'm trying to protect you," he said, his voice rising slightly, edged with desperation. "You and Harrison. That's all that matters."

The words hung in the air between them, heavy with unspoken fears. Drake watched as emotions flickered across Linda's face - confusion, concern, and something deeper, a flicker of recognition that perhaps there was more to his actions than mere paranoia.

Linda hesitated, her blue eyes searching his face. In that moment, Drake saw the strength that had always been her hallmark, the quiet resilience that had weathered so many storms. She took a deep breath, seeming to come to a decision.

"Alright," she nodded, her voice soft but firm. "But you need to tell me what's going on. The truth."

From upstairs, the sound of Harrison's video game drifted down, a cheerful melody at odds with the tension in the room. It was a stark reminder of what was at stake - the innocence he was desperately trying to preserve.

"Linda," he began, his voice barely above a whisper, "you wouldn't believe me if I told you."

39 - 40

Drake's gaze drifted to the window, where the late morning sun cast long shadows across the yard. He could see the faint outline of his own reflection, a man haunted by unseen specters.

"I will," he promised, turning back to Linda. "Just... let me finish this first."

His fingers flexed involuntarily, the lingering ache in his thumb a stark reminder of the reality he was trying to prevent. Drake picked up the hammer once more, its weight both reassuring and ominous in his grip.

Linda's brow furrowed, concern etching deeper lines around her eyes. "Drake, I—"

"Please," he interrupted, his voice soft but firm. "I need to do this."

As he resumed his work, methodically nailing boards across the windows, Drake's mind raced. How could he possibly explain the inexplicable? The loops, the deaths, the cosmic game he seemed to be trapped in - it all sounded like the ravings of a madman.

The rhythmic thud of hammer on nail filled the air, each impact driving home not just wood, but Drake's determination. He worked tirelessly, sweat beading on his brow, his muscles aching with the effort. But he couldn't stop. Not when every moment could be the difference between life and death.

Time seemed to stretch and warp as the day unfolded. Shadows lengthened across the floor, creeping inch by inch as the sun traversed the sky. Drake's vigilance never wavered, his eyes constantly scanning for any sign of the impending danger he felt in his bones.

From the kitchen, he could hear Linda's muffled voice, likely trying to explain their impromptu "staycation" to Harrison. The guilt gnawed at Drake's insides. He was robbing them of normalcy, of peace. But the alternative was unthinkable.

As afternoon bled into evening, the silence in the house grew oppressive. Drake's nerves were frayed, every creak of the house setting his teeth on edge. He paced from room to room, checking and rechecking his fortifications.

"Dad?" Harrison's voice startled him. "Can we at least order pizza or something? This is getting weird."

Drake turned, seeing the mixture of confusion and annoyance on his son's face. For a moment, he was overwhelmed by a wave of love and fear so intense it nearly brought him to his knees.

"Yeah," he managed, forcing a smile. "Pizza sounds good."

As Harrison retreated, Drake leaned against the wall, closing his eyes. How long could he keep this up? How long before the other shoe dropped?

The day continued to unfold, each passing minute both a victory and a torment. Drake knew that somewhere out there, the clock was ticking. And he was running out of time.

41 - 42

Linda's gentle laughter drifted from the living room, a stark contrast to the tension coiled tight within Drake's chest. He peered through a gap in the curtains, his eyes tracing the familiar contours of their suburban street. Everything looked normal, painfully so.

"Your turn, Mom," Harrison called out, his voice tinged with excitement.

Drake's thumb throbbed, a constant reminder of the stakes. He flexed his hand, wincing at the lingering pain. How many more times would he have to relive this day? How many more ways could it go wrong?

"Drake?" Linda's voice pulled him from his spiraling thoughts. "Come join us. Please?"

He turned, catching sight of his wife and son hunched over a board game. The normalcy of the scene felt like a knife twisting in his gut.

"I... I can't," he muttered, his voice hoarse. "I need to keep watch."

Linda's smile faltered, concern etching lines around her eyes. "Watch for what, exactly?"

Drake opened his mouth, then closed it. How could he explain the inexplicable? The words caught in his throat, choking him with their impossibility.

"It's just a feeling," he finally managed, hating how weak it sounded.

The silence that followed was deafening. Drake could feel the weight of Linda's gaze, could sense Harrison's growing unease. The atmosphere in the house grew heavier with each passing moment, thick with unasked questions and unspoken fears.

As the afternoon light began to fade, casting long shadows across the room, Drake felt a familiar dread settling in his stomach. Time was running out, and he was no closer to understanding how to break this cruel cycle.

43 - 44

Harrison's chair scraped against the floor as he stood abruptly, breaking the oppressive silence that had fallen over the room. Drake's muscles tensed instinctively, his eyes darting to his son's lanky frame.

"Dad," Harrison said, his voice a mixture of frustration and pleading. "This is stupid. Nothing's happening. Can I at least go out back?"

The words hung in the air, heavy with the weight of normalcy that Drake desperately wished he could grant. For a fleeting moment, he saw his son as he used to be – carefree, unburdened by the horrors that haunted Drake's every waking moment. The urge to say yes, to let Harrison escape the suffocating tension of the house, was almost overwhelming.

But then the memory of Harrison's broken body flashed before his eyes, and Drake's resolve hardened.

"No," he said quickly, his voice sharp enough to cut through steel. The word left his lips before he could soften it, carrying all the fear and desperation he'd been holding back.

Drake watched as disappointment and confusion warred on Harrison's face. He longed to explain, to make his son understand the danger that lurked just beyond their walls. But how could he describe the endless loop of tragedy he'd been forced to witness? How could he convey the bone-deep certainty that stepping outside would lead to disaster?

As Harrison's shoulders slumped in resignation, Drake felt the familiar ache of guilt gnawing at his insides. He was pushing them away, he knew, but the alternative was unthinkable. He'd rather have them alive and resentful than...

Drake swallowed hard, forcing the thought away. He had to focus, had to find a way to break this cycle before it broke him instead.

45 - 46

Harrison's frustration boiled over, his lanky frame tensing as he threw his hands up in exasperation. The afternoon light caught the unruly strands of his dirty blonde hair, casting shadows across his expressive brown eyes.

"Come on! This is ridiculous!" Harrison's voice cracked with a mix of anger and desperation, the words echoing in the oppressive silence of the living room.

Drake's heart clenched at the sight of his son's distress. He wanted nothing more than to relent, to give Harrison the freedom he craved. But the weight of unseen dangers pressed down on him, invisible chains binding him to this course of action.

Linda's weary sigh cut through the tension. "Harrison, listen to your father," she said, her tone a blend of resignation and subtle support.

Drake caught her eye, seeing the conflicted emotions swirling in their blue depths. She didn't understand – couldn't understand – but she was trying to hold their family together in the face of his inexplicable behavior.

As Harrison slumped back onto the couch, muttering under his breath, Drake's mind raced. How could he protect them when the very act of protection was tearing them apart? The dislocated thumb throbbed, a constant reminder of the stakes at play in this twisted game of survival.

He turned back to the window, scanning the quiet street beyond. Somewhere out there, the threads of fate were being woven, and Drake was determined to unravel them before they could strangle his family once again.

47 - 48

Harrison's fingers drummed restlessly against the arm of the couch, each tap a muffled accusation. Drake's gaze flickered between his son's sullen form and the deceptively peaceful street outside, his mind a battlefield of conflicting impulses.

"Dad," Harrison's voice broke the tense silence, laced with a mix of frustration and genuine concern. "Can you at least tell us what you're so afraid of?"

Drake's throat tightened. How could he explain the inexplicable? The loops, the deaths, the suffocating weight of foreknowledge?

"It's... complicated, Harrison," he managed, turning to face his family. Linda's worried eyes met his, silently pleading for answers.

"But we're safe here, right?" Harrison pressed, a flicker of his usual optimism breaking through. "I mean, you've practically turned the house into Fort Knox."

A humorless chuckle escaped Drake's lips. "I hope so, buddy. I really hope so."

The air in the room seemed to grow thicker, charged with unspoken fears and mounting tension. Drake's fingers twitched, longing for action, for some tangible way to fight the invisible threat looming over them.

As the afternoon light began to fade, casting long shadows across the living room, Drake felt a shift. A tipping point approached, silent and inexorable as the turning of the Earth.

49 - 50

Drake's thumb throbbed, a persistent reminder of the stakes at hand. He flexed his fingers, wincing at the dull ache that radiated up his arm. The pain grounded him, a tangible link to the reality of his situation amidst the surreal nature of his predicament.

"I need some air," he muttered, more to himself than to his family. Linda's concerned gaze followed him as he moved to the window, pressing his forehead against the cool glass.

Outside, the world carried on, oblivious to the turmoil within these walls. Neighbors chatted on porches; kids rode bikes down the sidewalk. The normalcy of it all felt like a cruel joke.

"How much longer are we going to do this, Drake?" Linda's voice was soft, but it carried an undercurrent of steel. "The kids are scared. I'm scared."

Drake turned, his expression a mask of determination and fear. "As long as it takes to keep you safe. All of you."

The words hung in the air, heavy with unspoken truths. Drake's mind raced, grappling with the impossible task before him. How could he protect them from a threat he barely understood?

As twilight deepened, casting long shadows across the room, Drake felt a chill run down his spine. Something was different. Wrong.

Then he heard it: the faint creak of floorboards upstairs.

His body tensed, every nerve on high alert. "Did you hear that?" he whispered, eyes darting to the ceiling.

51 - 52

Drake's heart pounded in his chest as he scanned the room, his gaze settling on the hammer lying on the kitchen counter. In one fluid motion, he crossed the space and snatched it up, the weight of the tool reassuring in his grip.

"Stay here," he said, his voice low and urgent. The hammer hung at his side, a makeshift weapon against an unseen threat.

Linda's brow furrowed, her blue eyes searching his face. "What is it?" she asked, concern etching lines around her mouth. Her hand reached out, almost touching his arm before falling away.

Drake hesitated, torn between the desire to protect her from the truth and the need for her to understand the gravity of their situation. The memory of her repeated deaths flashed through his mind, each one a fresh wound on his soul.

"I'm not sure," he finally admitted, his voice barely above a whisper. "But something's not right. I need to check it out."

Linda's expression softened, a mix of worry and resignation. "Drake, please," she pleaded, her tone gentle but firm. "Talk to me. What's really going on?"

The weight of his knowledge pressed down on him, threatening to crush him under its burden. How could he explain the loops, the deaths, the impossible choices he'd been forced to make? The words caught in his throat, choking him with their intensity.

53 - 54

"Just... stay here," he repeated, the words heavy with unspoken fears. His gaze lingered on Linda for a moment, memorizing the concern in her eyes, before he turned toward the stairs.

Each step creaked under his weight as Drake climbed slowly, his heart thundering in his chest. The sound echoed in the eerie silence of the house, a rhythmic counterpoint to his ragged breathing. He gripped the hammer tighter, his injured thumb throbbing in protest.

As he reached the landing, the hallway stretched before him, a corridor of shadows and whispered dangers. The dim light filtering through the boarded windows cast strange, elongated shapes on the walls. Drake's eyes darted from corner to corner, searching for any sign of movement.

A chill ran down his spine as he moved toward Harrison's room, the door slightly ajar. The wood grain beneath his fingers felt rough, almost alive, as he placed his hand on the door frame.

"Harrison?" he called softly, his voice barely audible even to himself. "Are you in there, buddy?"

Silence answered him, broken only by the rapid beating of his own heart. Drake's mind raced, memories of past loops blending with the present moment. How many times had he climbed these stairs, only to find tragedy waiting?

"I can't lose you again," he whispered, more to himself than to his absent son. "Not this time. Not ever."

With a deep breath, Drake steeled himself for whatever lay beyond the door, his grip on the hammer white-knuckled and resolute.

55 - 56

He pushed it open cautiously, his breath catching in his throat. The window was open, the wooden boards ripped away, leaving jagged splinters framing the gaping hole like broken teeth.

Drake's heart plummeted, a cold dread seeping into his bones. "No," he whispered, rushing to the window. The cool evening air rushed in, carrying with it the scent of freshly cut grass and the faint echoes of distant laughter.

His eyes frantically scanned the yard below, searching for any sign of Harrison. "This can't be happening," he muttered, his voice thick with desperation. "Not again. Not when I was so careful."

The hammer slipped from his grasp, clattering to the floor. Drake barely noticed, his fingers gripping the windowsill so tightly his knuckles turned white.

"Harrison!" he called out, his voice cracking with emotion. "Harrison, where are you?"

Only silence answered him. Drake's mind raced, replaying every moment of the day, searching for the mistake, the oversight that had led to this. Had he not been vigilant enough? Had his attempts to protect his family only pushed them away?

"I should have told them everything," he thought, regret washing over him. "Maybe if they understood, if they knew what was at stake..."

But there was no time for self-recrimination now. Drake turned from the window, his eyes wild with determination. "Linda!" he shouted, already moving towards the door. "Linda, Harrison's gone!"

As he rushed from the room, a small part of him clung to hope. Maybe it wasn't too late. Maybe this time, he could change the outcome. But the larger part of him, the part that had lived through this nightmare countless times before, braced for the tragedy he feared was inevitable.

57 - 58

Drake thundered down the stairs, his heart pounding in his ears. The living room was empty, Linda nowhere in sight. He burst through the front door, the cool evening air hitting his face like a slap.

And there, on the lawn, stood Harrison.

Relief flooded Drake for a split second before dread seized him anew. Harrison wasn't alone. Mike's car idled at the curb, its headlights cutting through the gathering dusk. Drake's son leaned against the passenger door, deep in animated conversation with his friend.

"Harrison!" Drake shouted, his voice filled with panic. He sprinted across the yard, grass crunching under his feet. "Get away from the car!"

Harrison turned, his brow furrowed in confusion. "Dad? What's wrong?"

Drake's mind raced. How could he explain? How could he make his son understand the danger without sounding completely unhinged?

"Just... come inside. Now," Drake pleaded, reaching for Harrison's arm. His eyes darted between his son and Mike, searching for any sign of the impending disaster he felt in his bones was about to unfold.

"Whoa, Mr. Miller," Mike said, holding up his hands. "We were just talking. Is everything okay?"

Drake swallowed hard, fighting the urge to physically drag Harrison away. "Everything's fine," he lied, his voice strained. "Harrison needs to come inside. Family emergency."

Harrison's eyes narrowed. "Dad, what's going on? You've been acting weird all day."

The weight of unspoken truths pressed down on Drake. How could he possibly explain the loops, the repeated tragedies, the desperate attempts to change fate? He opened his mouth, searching for words that would make his son understand, that would keep him safe.

But before he could speak, a sound caught his attention. A faint creaking, barely audible over the idling car engine. Drake's blood ran cold as he realized what it meant.

"Harrison, move!" he yelled, lunging forward to push his son out of harm's way.

59 - 60

Time seemed to slow as Drake's feet pounded against the grass, each step echoing in his ears like a thunderclap. The distance between him and Harrison stretched impossibly, a chasm of fate he desperately needed to cross.

"Dad, you're freaking me out!" Harrison called, his voice tinged with a mix of confusion and growing alarm.

Drake's heart hammered against his ribs, a frantic drumbeat of fear and desperation. His mind raced through a kaleidoscope of memories—Harrison's first steps, his gap-toothed grin on the first day of school, the proud smile when he made the soccer team. All of it threatened to slip away in an instant.

"Please, son," Drake gasped, his voice raw with emotion. "Just trust me. Come here now!"

He was so close. Just a few more steps. Drake's fingers stretched out, reaching for Harrison's sleeve. He could almost feel the fabric beneath his fingertips. The he was there, he had ahold of Harrison and was dragging him back towards the house. Everything was fine again, and Drake and Harrison were under the awning of the house that Drake Barricaded.

As they lunged forward, time snapped back into its merciless march. The creaking grew to a deafening roar, and Drake's eyes widened in horror as he realized he was too late. Again.

"Harrison!" The name tore from his throat, a primal cry of anguish and futile warning.

In that moment, suspended between hope and devastation, Drake's mind screamed a silent plea to whatever force governed this cruel cycle: Not again. Please, not again.

61 - 62

The air shattered with a thunderous crack, wood splintering and groaning as the makeshift barricade gave way. Drake's world narrowed to a single, horrifying image: Harrison's eyes, wide with surprise and fear, locked onto his father's for one eternal instant before disappearing beneath the cascade of falling debris.

"No!" Drake's scream ripped through the evening air, raw and primal. He lunged forward, his hands clawing at the wreckage, splinters digging into his palms as he frantically tore at the wooden planks.

"Harrison! Harrison, can you hear me?" His voice cracked, desperation seeping through every syllable.

From beneath the rubble came a muffled groan, weak but unmistakable. Drake's heart leapt, a flicker of hope amidst the chaos.

"Dad?" Harrison's voice was faint, laced with pain and confusion. "What... what happened?"

Drake redoubled his efforts, muscles straining as he lifted a heavy beam. "It's okay, son. I'm here. Just hold on, I'll get you out."

As he worked, Drake's mind raced. This wasn't supposed to happen. He'd tried to change things, to keep them safe. But the universe, or the robed man, or whatever cruel force was behind this, had found a way to strike regardless. The realization was a cold weight in his stomach: no matter what he did, tragedy seemed inevitable.

"Dad," Harrison's voice wavered, "I can't... I can't feel my legs."

The words hit Drake like a physical blow. He paused, just for a moment, his chest tight with a suffocating mix of fear and guilt. Then, with renewed determination, he attacked the debris pile.

"It's going to be okay," he said, as much to himself as to Harrison. "We'll figure this out. We always do."

But even as the words left his mouth, Drake couldn't shake the sinking feeling that this time, perhaps, they wouldn't.

63 - 64

Drake's hands trembled as he cleared away more debris, revealing Harrison's pale face. Blood trickled from a gash on his forehead, and his eyes were wide with fear.

"Linda!" Drake called out; his voice hoarse. "Call an ambulance!"

He turned back to Harrison, trying to keep his voice steady. "Just stay still, buddy. Help's coming."

Linda's scream pierced the air, shattering the eerie calm that had settled over the scene. She came running, her blonde hair whipping behind her as she fell to her knees beside them.

"Oh God, Harrison!" she cried, reaching out to touch their son's face with trembling fingers. "My baby..."

Drake watched as Linda's nurse's instincts kicked in, her hands moving quickly to assess Harrison's injuries. But he could see the barely contained panic in her eyes, the way her lower lip quivered as she worked.

"Drake," Linda said, her voice low and urgent. "We need to get this off him. Now."

He nodded, muscles tensing as he prepared to lift again. As he strained against the weight, Drake's mind raced. How many times had he seen his family die? How many times had he failed to save them? The weight of those memories pressed down on him, heavier than any debris.

"Dad?" Harrison's voice was weak, barely above a whisper. "I'm scared."

Drake's heart clenched. He wanted to reassure his son, to promise him everything would be okay. But the words stuck in his throat, choked by the bitter taste of uncertainty and fear.

65 - 66

Drake's legs trembled as he staggered forward, each step feeling like an eternity. The world around him seemed to blur, his focus narrowing to the broken form of his son beneath the splintered wood. His mind raced, a torrent of regret and desperation crashing against the walls of his consciousness.

"I did everything," Drake whispered, his voice hoarse with anguish. "Everything I could think of to keep you safe."

Linda looked up at him, her eyes glistening with tears. "Drake, what are you talking about? This... this was an accident."

But Drake knew better. This was no accident. This was failure—his failure—playing out in cruel, agonizing detail before his eyes. He had barricaded them in, tried to change the course of events, and still...

A faint, mocking laughter echoed in the recesses of his mind, sending a chill down his spine. The man's voice, cold and taunting, seemed to whisper directly into his thoughts.

"Did you really think you could outsmart fate, Drake?" the disembodied voice sneered. "How many more times will you watch them die before you understand?"

Drake clenched his fists, his once dislocated thumb throbbing in protest. "Shut up," he growled through gritted teeth.

"Drake?" Linda's concerned voice cut through his inner turmoil. "Who are you talking to?"

He shook his head, trying to focus on the present moment. "No one. I just... we need to get Harrison help. Now."

As they worked to free their son, Drake's mind raced with possibilities. If injuries carried over between loops, what else might? Could he find a way to break this cycle, to truly save his family? Or was he doomed to relive this nightmare, again and again, with the evil man's laughter as his constant, mocking companion?

67 - 67

The world around Drake began to blur, colors melding into a hazy, indistinct swirl. His vision tunneled, narrowing to a pinpoint focused on Harrison's still form. The cacophony of sirens in the distance, Linda's anguished sobs, and the frantic shouts of neighbors all faded into a distant, muffled roar.

"No," Drake whispered, his voice hoarse and barely audible. "Not again. Please, not again."

He reached out with trembling fingers, grasping Harrison's limp hand. The boy's skin felt cool to the touch, a stark contrast to the warmth that had always radiated from his vibrant son.

Linda's voice cut through the haze. "Harrison, stay with me. The ambulance is coming."

But Drake could feel himself slipping away, darkness encroaching at the edges of his consciousness. His body swayed, no longer able to support his weight.

"I'm sorry," he murmured, his words slurring. "I thought I could... I thought this time..."

As he collapsed beside Harrison, Drake's last conscious thought was a desperate plea to whatever force controlled this twisted cycle:

"Let me save them. Just once. Please."

Then the world faded to black, and Drake surrendered to the void, knowing that when he opened his eyes again, the nightmare would begin anew.

Despair on Repeat

1 -2   A kaleidoscope of horrors flickered before Drake's eyes. Linda's golden hair matted with blood as she crumpled beneath a falling beam. Harrison's small body twisted at impossible angles, crushed by an oncoming truck. Their faces contorted in agony, mouths frozen in silent screams.

Drake jolted awake, heart pounding against his ribcage. Sweat-soaked sheets clung to his trembling form as he gasped for air, the lingering images of death burning behind his eyelids.

"No, no, no," he muttered, fingers clawing at his scalp. "Not again. Please, not again."

The familiar weight of dread settled in his stomach as Drake's eyes darted around the dimly lit bedroom. Everything was as it should be—the antique dresser Linda had insisted on keeping, Harrison's Little League trophy perched proudly on the nightstand. Yet an insidious wrongness permeated the air.

Drake swung his legs over the side of the bed, wincing as his bare feet met the cold hardwood floor. The chill grounded him, a stark reminder that he was awake—truly awake this time.

"Linda?" he called out, voice hoarse. "Harrison?"

Silence answered him, heavy and oppressive. Drake's heart rate quickened, memories of countless mornings just like this one flooding his mind. How many times had he woken to find them gone, only to relive their deaths in increasingly horrific ways?

He stumbled to his feet, legs unsteady beneath him. "I can't do this again," Drake whispered, despair threatening to overwhelm him. "I can't watch them die. Not again."

As he reached for the bedroom door, a flicker of movement caught his eye. Drake froze, breath catching in his throat as he turned towards the full-length mirror on the closet door. For a moment, he swore he saw evil's smirking face reflected back at him, eyes gleaming with malicious glee.

Drake blinked, and the image vanished, leaving only his own haggard reflection staring back. He ran a trembling hand through his disheveled hair, a habit born of stress and sleepless nights.

"Pull yourself together," he growled, meeting his own gaze in the mirror. "They need you. You have to save them this time."

With renewed determination, Drake squared his shoulders and reached for the doorknob. Whatever horrors awaited him beyond this room, he would face them. He had to—for Linda, for Harrison, for the family he refused to lose again.

3 - 4

The acrid smell of smoke assaulted Drake's senses as he flung open the bedroom door. Thick, black plumes billowed through the hallway, obscuring his vision and stinging his eyes. The heat was oppressive, sweat already beading on his brow as he stumbled forward.

"Harrison! Linda!" Drake's voice was hoarse, barely audible above the roar of the flames. His heart pounded in his chest, a frantic rhythm that matched the crackling of the fire consuming their home.

He heard a muffled cry from down the hall. "Dad! Help!"

Drake surged forward, adrenaline coursing through his veins. He found Harrison huddled in the corner of his room; eyes wide with terror.

"I've got you, son," Drake said, scooping Harrison into his arms. "We're getting out of here."

As they made their way through the smoke-filled corridor, Drake's mind raced. Where was Linda? He hadn't seen her, hadn't heard her voice. The familiar dread settled in his stomach, a leaden weight he'd felt too many times before.

"Mom!" Harrison cried out, coughing violently. "We have to find Mom!"

Drake's jaw clenched. "We will, buddy. We will."

They reached the top of the stairs, and Drake's heart sank. Through the haze, he could see Linda trapped beneath a fallen beam, her face contorted in pain.

"Linda!" Drake shouted, setting Harrison down. "Hold on, I'm coming!"

He took a step forward, but a sickening groan from above stopped him in his tracks. The ceiling was buckling, ready to collapse at any moment.

"Drake," Linda's voice was weak, but resolute. "Get Harrison out. Please."

Time seemed to slow as Drake stood frozen, torn between the two people he loved most in the world. Harrison tugged at his sleeve, tears streaming down his soot-stained face.

"Dad, we can't leave her!"

The ceiling gave another ominous creak. Drake made his choice, scooping Harrison back around his shoulders and bolting for the stairs.

"No!" Harrison screamed, struggling against his father's grip. "Mom!"

They burst through the front door just as a deafening crash echoed behind them. Drake turned; horror etched on his face as he watched the second floor of their home cave in.

"Linda," he whispered, his voice breaking.

As the flames consumed what remained of their life together, Drake held Harrison close, the boy's sobs muffled against his chest. The weight of his failure pressed down on him, suffocating as the smoke that still clung to their clothes.

"I'm sorry," Drake murmured, more to himself than to Harrison. "I'm so sorry."

The world began to blur, fading at the edges. Drake closed his eyes, knowing what was coming next. When he opened them again, he found himself back in bed, sheets tangled around his legs, the phantom smell of smoke still lingering in his nostrils.

5 - 6

The morning sun filtered through the curtains, casting a deceptively cheerful glow across the bedroom. Drake's heart raced as he listened intently, relief washing over him at the sound of Harrison's footsteps padding down the hallway. He was alive. They both were. For now.

Drake dragged himself out of bed, his muscles aching with the memory of a fire that hadn't happened. Not in this version of reality, at least. He made his way to the kitchen, drawn by the mundane sounds of domestic life.

Harrison stood at the sink; his lanky frame hunched over as he reached for something. "Morning, Dad," he called over his shoulder. "I think the disposal's jammed again."

"Don't-" Drake started, but it was too late. Harrison flicked the switch, and a sickening grinding noise filled the air, followed by a bloodcurdling scream.

"Harrison!" Drake lunged forward, yanking his son's arm free. Blood gushed from Harrison's mangled hand, spattering across the pristine countertop.

"Oh God, oh God," Harrison whimpered, his face pale with shock. "Dad, it hurts so much."

Drake's mind raced, desperately trying to process the situation. "We need to get you to the hospital," he said, grabbing a clean dish towel and wrapping it tightly around Harrison's hand. "Can you walk?"

As he guided Harrison towards the door, a familiar dizziness swept over him. No, Drake thought frantically. Not now. Not like this. He fought against the encroaching darkness, willing himself to stay present, to save his son.

"Dad?" Harrison's voice sounded distant, fading. "What's happening?"

Drake's vision blurred, the world tilting on its axis. "I'm sorry," he whispered, his words swallowed by the void as consciousness slipped away.

He woke with a start, sheets once again tangled around his legs. The bedroom was bathed in the soft light of early morning, unchanged from moments before. Drake pressed his palms against his eyes, willing away the image of Harrison's blood-soaked hand.

"How many times?" he muttered to himself, despair clawing at his chest. "How many more ways can I fail them?"

7 - 8

Drake stumbled out of bed, his heart pounding with a familiar dread. The house was quiet, too quiet. He rushed to Harrison's room, finding it empty, the bed neatly made. Panic rising, he sprinted downstairs, calling out desperately.

"Linda? Harrison?"

The kitchen was pristine, no sign of the gruesome scene that had haunted his dreams. On the counter, a hastily scrawled note caught his eye. Drake's hands trembled as he read:

"We can't do this anymore. We're leaving. Please don't try to find us. -L"

"No," Drake whispered, his voice cracking. He fumbled for his phone, dialing Linda's number with shaking fingers. It went straight to voicemail.

"Linda, please," he pleaded, "Whatever you're thinking, it's not safe out there. You have to come back. We can figure this out together."

As he spoke, a sickening screech of tires pierced the air, followed by the deafening crash of metal on metal. Drake's blood ran cold. He bolted out the front door, barefoot and still in his pajamas.

The scene that greeted him was one of carnage. Two cars were mangled beyond recognition at the intersection, smoke billowing from their crumpled hoods. And there, trapped in the wreckage, he saw a flash of blonde hair.

"Linda!" Drake screamed, sprinting towards the crash. "Harrison!"

He clawed at the twisted metal, ignoring the searing pain as jagged edges sliced into his hands. Through the shattered window, he could see Linda's lifeless eyes staring back at him, Harrison's broken body cradled in her arms.

"No, no, no," Drake sobbed, his vision blurring with tears. "Not like this. Please, not like this."

As sirens wailed in the distance, Drake felt the familiar pull of consciousness slipping away. He fought against it with every fiber of his being, desperate to stay, to save them somehow.

"I'm sorry," he choked out, darkness encroaching. "I'm so sorry..."

Drake's eyes snapped open, his chest heaving as he gasped for air. Sunlight streamed through the bedroom window, mockingly cheerful. The clock on the nightstand read 7:15 AM, just as it had countless times before.

He lay there, paralyzed by grief and the crushing weight of failure. How many more times would he be forced to watch his family die? How many more ways could his heart be shattered?

"I can't keep doing this," Drake whispered to the empty room, his voice hoarse with unshed tears. "I can't lose them again."

9 - 10

Drake's heart hammered in his chest as he and Harrison walked along the bustling sidewalk towards his law office. Every step felt like a tightrope walk over an abyss of potential tragedy.

"Dad, you're squeezing my arm too tight," Harrison complained, trying to wriggle free.

Drake loosened his grip slightly, but his eyes never stopped scanning their surroundings. "Sorry, buddy. I just... I need you to stay close, okay?"

Harrison sighed, his lanky frame slouching with teenage exasperation. "You've been acting weird all morning. What's going on?"

"Nothing," Drake lied, his throat tight. How could he explain the nightmare loop they were trapped in? "I just want us to be careful, that's all."

As they approached the crosswalk, Drake's gaze locked onto a familiar, menacing figure standing next to him. The scarred man stood there; his scarred face twisted into a cruel smirk.

Time seemed to slow as Drake watched his muscular arm shoot out, shoving Harrison with shocking force. "No!" Drake screamed, lunging for his son.

But it was too late. Harrison stumbled, wide-eyed and confused, directly into the path of an oncoming bus. The sickening thud of impact echoed through Drake's skull as he collapsed to his knees, howling in anguish.

"Why?" he sobbed, looking up at the killers retreating form. "Why are you doing this?"

As the world began to fade, Drake's mind raced. How many more times would he be forced to witness this horror? How many more ways could his family be torn from him?

The cycle repeated, an endless parade of nightmarish scenarios. Linda attacked by a dog at the beach. Harrison drowning in a freak accident. Both of them clawing at their throats from a poison ingested in their drinks as Drake watched helplessly.

With each reset, Drake's desperation grew. He tried different routes, different warnings, but evil always seemed one step ahead, finding new and horrific ways to shatter Drake's world.

"I can't keep losing them," Drake whispered to himself in the quiet moments before each new awakening. "There has to be a way to break this cycle. There has to be..."

The Day I Gave Up

1-2 The golden stripes on the ceiling blurred as Drake's eyes struggled to focus. Each ray of sunlight felt like a dagger, piercing through the numbness that had settled over him during the night. He blinked slowly, his body heavy with the familiar weight of dread.

"Not again," he whispered, the words barely audible even to himself.

Drake turned his head, wincing at the slight movement. Linda lay beside him, her face serene in sleep. Her blonde hair cascaded across the pillow, catching the morning light like spun gold. A faint crease furrowed her brow, then smoothed as she sighed contentedly.

He reached out, his fingers hovering just above her cheek. How many times had he woken to this same scene? How many more times would he have to endure it?

"Linda," Drake murmured, his voice thick with emotion.

She stirred, her blue eyes fluttering open. "Mmm? Drake? What's wrong?"

He swallowed hard, forcing a smile. "Nothing. Just... admiring you."

Linda's lips curved into a sleepy smile. "That's sweet. But you look troubled. Another bad dream?"

Drake's heart clenched. If only it were that simple. "Something like that," he replied, running a hand through his disheveled hair. "It's nothing to worry about."

She propped herself up on one elbow, her gaze searching his face. "You know you can talk to me about anything, right?"

The concern in her voice was almost too much to bear. Drake sat up, swinging his legs over the side of the bed. His muscles protested, as if they too remembered the horrors that lay ahead.

"I know," he said softly. "I just... I need a minute."

Linda's hand brushed his back, a gentle touch that sent a shiver through him. "Take all the time you need. I'll start the coffee."

As she padded out of the room, Drake buried his face in his hands. How could he explain the impossible? How could he tell her that every day ended in tragedy, no matter what he did?

He stood, his movements mechanical as he dressed. The routine was ingrained now, a cruel dance he was forced to perform over and over. But beneath the resignation, a spark of determination still flickered.

"This time," Drake muttered to himself, clenching his fists. "This time, I'll find a way to save them both."

3 - 4

Drake made his way downstairs, the familiar scent of coffee mingling with the aroma of Linda's blueberry pancakes. As he entered the kitchen, Harrison looked up from his phone, his brown eyes wide with excitement.

"Dad! You're up early. Are you coming to my soccer tryouts today?"

The innocence in Harrison's voice was a knife twisting in Drake's gut. He forced a smile, ruffling his son's unruly blonde hair. "Wouldn't miss it for the world, buddy."

Linda turned from the stove, spatula in hand. "That's a surprise. I thought you had that big case today?"

Drake's throat tightened. He'd cancelled that meeting in a hundred different timelines, each ending in disaster. "It can wait," he managed. "Some things are more important."

Harrison beamed, but Linda's brow furrowed with concern. "Are you feeling alright, Drake? You've seemed... off lately."

He'd seen that look before—worry etched into her features, moments before flames engulfed her, before a car swerved into their lane, before a thousand other horrors. Drake's hands trembled as he poured his coffee.

"I'm fine," he lied, the words bitter on his tongue. "Just haven't been sleeping well."

"Is it nightmares again?" Harrison asked, his voice dropping to a near-whisper. "Like the ones you used to have about Mom?"

Drake's cup clattered against the counter. "It's nothing like that," he said quickly, perhaps too sharply. He softened his tone. "Don't worry about me, Harrison. Today's your big day."

As Harrison launched into an excited description of the drills he'd practiced, Drake's mind raced. He'd tried warning them, tried keeping them home, tried a thousand variations. But death always found a way, as inexorable as the tide.

"Earth to Drake," Linda's voice cut through his spiraling thoughts. "Where'd you go just now?"

He blinked, realizing he'd been staring blankly at his untouched coffee. "Sorry, I was just... thinking about how proud I am of you both."

The words felt hollow, knowing what lay ahead. But the smiles they brought to Linda and Harrison's faces—those were real. For a moment, Drake allowed himself to bask in their warmth, even as the weight of inevitability pressed down upon him.

5 - 6

Drake swallowed hard, the lump in his throat threatening to choke him. He blinked rapidly, willing away the moisture gathering in his eyes. The kitchen suddenly felt too small, too suffocating. He gripped the edge of the countertop, his knuckles turning white.

"This time, I won't fight it," he whispered, so softly that neither Linda nor Harrison could hear.

"Did you say something, honey?" Linda asked, her brow furrowing with concern.

Drake forced a smile, shaking his head. "Just talking to myself. Old habit."

He moved to the table, sliding into his usual seat. The normalcy of it all—Linda humming as she flipped pancakes, Harrison engrossed in his phone—felt like a cruel joke. How many times had he lived this moment? How many times had he tried to change it?

"So, Harrison," Drake began, his voice steadier than he felt, "are you nervous about the tryouts?"

Harrison looked up, his eyes bright with excitement. "A little, but I've been practicing that new move Coach showed us. I think I've got it down."

Drake nodded, fighting to keep his expression neutral. "That's great, buddy. I'm sure you'll do amazing."

Linda set a plate of pancakes in front of him, the sweet aroma mingling with the bitter scent of coffee. "You're being awfully quiet this morning," she observed, sliding into the chair across from him.

Drake shrugged, cutting into his pancakes with mechanical precision. "Just thinking about how fast time flies. Seems like yesterday Harrison was learning to walk, and now he's trying out for the soccer team."

As Linda and Harrison chatted about the upcoming day, Drake retreated into his thoughts. He'd made his decision. This time, he wouldn't try to change anything. He'd let the day unfold as it was meant to, no matter how much it tore him apart inside. Maybe then, finally, the loop would end.

But as he watched his family—Linda's gentle laugh, Harrison's animated gestures—Drake wondered if he had the strength to follow through. Could he really stand by and watch them die, even if it meant potentially breaking the cycle?

The weight of that choice pressed down on him, heavier than any burden he'd ever carried.

7 - 8

Drake's fork scraped against the ceramic plate, the sound grating in his ears. He forced himself to take another bite, the pancakes tasting like ash in his mouth. Linda's humming drifted from the stove, a haunting melody that seemed to underscore the inevitable tragedy lurking on the horizon.

"Dad, are you coming to my tryouts today?" Harrison asked, looking up from his phone with hopeful eyes.

Drake's chest constricted, but he managed to smile. "Of course, buddy. Wouldn't miss it for the world."

Linda turned, spatula in hand, her brow furrowed with concern. "Drake, are you sure you can get away from work? I know you've been swamped lately."

He met her gaze, drinking in the warmth of her blue eyes. "Some things are more important than work," he said softly, his voice thick with emotion.

Harrison grinned, oblivious to the undercurrent of tension. "Awesome! I've been working on this new move—"

As Harrison launched into an enthusiastic explanation, Drake found himself torn between savoring every moment and bracing for the pain to come. His son's excitement was infectious, a stark reminder of the vibrant life that would be snuffed out all too soon.

"Sounds like you've been putting in the work," Drake said, his words barely audible over the roaring in his ears. He clenched his fist under the table, nails digging into his palm. "I can't wait to see it."

Linda rested a hand on his shoulder as she passed, the gentle touch sending a jolt through him. "Are you feeling alright, honey? You look a little pale."

Drake covered her hand with his own, relishing the warmth of her skin. "I'm fine," he lied, the words tasting bitter on his tongue. "Just a little tired. Nothing to worry about."

9 - 10

Drake cut into his pancake, the syrup pooling around the golden edges. "I've just been tired," he lied, the words tasting bitter on his tongue. He paused, steeling himself for what he was about to say. "But I'm taking the day off today."

The fork Linda had been raising to her lips froze midway. Her eyebrows shot up, surprise etched across her features. "You? Taking a day off?" she asked, her voice a mixture of disbelief and amusement. "Did hell freeze over?"

Drake's chest tightened at her reaction. How many times had he prioritized work over family, believing there would always be more time? The weight of missed opportunities pressed down on him, threatening to crush his resolve.

He forced a chuckle, the sound hollow to his own ears. "Is it really so hard to believe?" he asked, watching Linda's face carefully. The sunlight streaming through the kitchen window caught her hair, turning it to spun gold. He wanted to reach out and touch it, to memorize the silky texture beneath his fingers.

Linda tilted her head, studying him with those perceptive blue eyes. "It's just... not like you," she said softly. "You've always been so driven, so focused on your career."

Drake's mind raced, grappling with the desire to confess everything and the need to protect her from the horrifying truth. He settled for a half-truth. "Maybe I'm realizing there are more important things," he said, his voice thick with emotion.

11 - 12

Drake cleared his throat, attempting to lighten the mood. "Funny," he said dryly, though his eyes betrayed a deeper emotion. "I just... want to spend some time with you two." He paused, his gaze shifting to Harrison, who was scrolling through his phone with one hand while shoveling cereal with the other. "Harrison's tryouts are today, right?"

The mention of his name caused Harrison to look up, his brown eyes widening with surprise and excitement. The spoon clattered against the bowl as he set it down, his full attention now on his father. "Yeah!" he exclaimed, a grin spreading across his face. "You're coming, right?"

Drake's heart clenched at the unbridled hope in his son's voice. He remembered countless times he'd missed these moments, always with the promise of 'next time.' But there wouldn't always be a next time, he knew that now with a certainty that weighed heavily on his soul.

"Of course," Drake replied, forcing a smile that didn't quite reach his eyes. He watched as Harrison's face lit up, the boy practically vibrating with excitement. The innocence and joy radiating from his son was almost painful to witness, knowing what lay ahead.

Linda reached across the table, her fingers brushing against Drake's hand. The touch sent a jolt through him, a bittersweet reminder of all he stood to lose. "This means a lot to him," she said softly, her eyes searching his face. "To both of us."

Drake nodded, unable to trust his voice. He turned his hand over, interlacing his fingers with Linda's, savoring the warmth of her skin against his. The kitchen suddenly felt too small, too fragile, as if the slightest movement might shatter this precious moment.

13 - 14

"Wouldn't miss it," Drake said, his chest tightening. The words caught in his throat, each syllable a struggle against the rising tide of emotions threatening to overwhelm him. He swallowed hard, forcing back the bitter taste of foreknowledge.

Harrison beamed, oblivious to his father's inner turmoil. "I've been practicing my corner kicks all week," he announced, pantomiming the motion with enthusiasm. "Coach says I might even start this game!"

Drake nodded, a ghost of a smile flitting across his face. "That's great, buddy," he managed, his voice barely above a whisper. He cleared his throat, trying to infuse some normalcy into his tone. "Why don't you go get your gear ready? We'll head out soon."

As Harrison bounded up the stairs, his footsteps echoing with youthful energy, Drake's gaze lingered on the empty doorway. The weight of inevitability pressed down on him, each tick of the kitchen clock a countdown to heartbreak.

Linda's hand on his arm startled him from his reverie. "You, okay?" she asked, concern etching lines around her eyes. "You seem... distant."

Drake turned to her, drinking in the sight of her face, committing every detail to memory. "I'm fine," he lied, the words tasting like ash on his tongue. "Just... thinking about how fast he's growing up."

The drive to the soccer field was a blur of suburban landscapes and internal anguish. Drake's knuckles were white on the steering wheel, his mind racing through possibilities, searching for a way to change the outcome he knew was coming. But each scenario ended the same way, a cruel loop of loss and despair.

As they pulled into the parking lot, the vibrant green of the soccer field stretched out before them, a stark contrast to the darkness swirling in Drake's mind. Parents and children milled about, their excited chatter a discordant symphony against the backdrop of his silent dread.

"Dad, come on!" Harrison called, already halfway across the lot, his cleats dangling from his hand. "I don't want to be late!"

Drake forced himself to move, each step feeling like he was wading through molasses. He plastered on a smile, determined to give his son this moment of normalcy, this last precious memory unmarred by tragedy.

As they approached the field, the scent of freshly cut grass filled the air, mingling with the acrid tang of anticipation that clung to Drake's senses. He watched Harrison join his teammates, the boy's face alight with excitement and promise.

"He looks so happy," Linda murmured, leaning into Drake's side.

Drake nodded, unable to speak past the lump in his throat. He wrapped an arm around Linda's waist, pulling her close, savoring her warmth even as his mind raced with the knowledge of what was to come. The tryouts were about to begin, and with them, the inexorable march towards a future he was powerless to change.

15 - 16

The field stretched out before them, a patchwork of green and brown, its uneven surface bearing silent testimony to countless games and practices. Drake's eyes swept across the worn grass, each patch a reminder of fleeting moments of joy and triumph that had unfolded here. Parents lined the sidelines, their folding chairs creating a makeshift barrier between spectators and players.

Drake settled between Linda and another parent, his hands coming to rest on his knees. The warm sun beat down on his face, but its gentle caress did little to thaw the icy dread pooling in his stomach. He drew in a deep breath, the scent of grass and earth filling his lungs.

"Beautiful day for tryouts, isn't it?" Linda remarked, her voice carrying a lightness that Drake envied.

He turned to her, drinking in the sight of her smile, the way the sunlight caught in her blonde hair. "Yeah," he managed, his voice rougher than he intended. "Perfect."

Linda's brow furrowed slightly. "Are you alright, Drake? You seem... tense."

Drake forced his features into what he hoped was a reassuring expression. "Just nervous for Harrison, I guess. You know how much this means to him."

As he spoke, his gaze drifted back to the field where Harrison stood with his teammates, listening intently to the coach's instructions. The boy's enthusiasm was palpable, even from a distance, and it twisted something deep inside Drake's chest.

"He'll do great," Linda said, reaching over to squeeze his hand. "He always does."

Drake nodded, unable to voice the dark thoughts swirling in his mind. Instead, he watched as the drills began, each movement of his son on the field both a joy and a torment. How many more moments like this would they have? How many had already been lost to the cruel cycle he found himself trapped in?

As the warm breeze rustled through the nearby trees, Drake closed his eyes for a moment, trying to commit every sensation to memory. The sound of cleats on grass, the murmur of conversation around him, the feel of Linda's hand in his – all of it precious, all of it fleeting.

"I love you," he said suddenly, turning to Linda. "Both of you. So much."

Surprise flickered across her face, followed by a softer smile. "We love you too, Drake. Is everything okay?"

He swallowed hard, fighting back the urge to confess everything, to shatter this moment of peace with the weight of his knowledge. Instead, he simply nodded, his grip on her hand tightening ever so slightly.

"Everything's fine," he lied, his gaze drifting back to the field where their son ran, blissfully unaware of the shadows looming on the horizon. "Let's just... enjoy this moment."

17 - 18

Harrison's lanky form darted across the field, a blur of motion as he weaved between orange cones with effortless grace. His dirty blonde hair bounced with each step; a perpetual grin plastered across his face. The sheer joy radiating from him was palpable, infectious even, drawing cheers and applause from the other parents lining the sidelines.

Drake's heart swelled with a bittersweet mix of pride and anguish. He watched his son's every move, drinking in the sight of Harrison's unbridled enthusiasm, knowing all too well how fleeting these moments could be. The cold pit in his stomach twisted, a stark contrast to the warmth of the sun on his face.

"You've got a good one there," the man beside Drake remarked, his voice tinged with admiration.

Drake turned, meeting the stranger's gaze. He forced a smile, though it didn't quite reach his eyes. "Thanks," he replied, his voice barely above a whisper. "He's... everything to me."

As Harrison completed another flawless run through the drill, Drake's mind raced. How many times had he witnessed this scene? How many variations of this moment had played out across the fractured timelines of his existence? The weight of his knowledge pressed down on him, threatening to crush the fragile illusion of normalcy he clung to.

"He's got real talent," the man continued, oblivious to Drake's inner turmoil. "Been playing long?"

Drake hesitated, memories of countless soccer practices from different timelines blurring together. "It feels like forever," he answered truthfully, his gaze never leaving Harrison. "But every game still feels like the first."

19 - 20

The shrill blast of the referee's whistle cut through the air, signaling the start of the game. Drake's posture straightened; his eyes fixed on Harrison as his son jogged into position on the field. For a moment, a flicker of hope kindled in Drake's chest, warm and fragile as a candle flame in a storm.

"Come on, Harrison!" Linda cheered from beside him, her voice filled with maternal pride.

Drake watched as Harrison received a pass, his movements fluid and confident. The boy's dirty blonde hair, so like his mother's, flopped across his forehead as he deftly maneuvered around an opposing player. Drake's breath caught in his throat, his hands gripping his knees tightly.

"He's gotten so fast," Drake murmured, more to himself than anyone else. In his mind, he saw flashes of Harrison at different ages, in different timelines – always running, always full of life. The contrast with the charred, motionless body he'd held in his arms countless times before was almost too much to bear.

Harrison passed the ball to a teammate, then sprinted forward, positioning himself for a potential shot. Drake leaned forward, his heart racing. For a split second, he allowed himself to imagine a future where this moment wasn't overshadowed by impending tragedy – where Harrison would grow up, play more games, live a full life.

"You okay, honey?" Linda asked, placing a hand on his arm. "You look pale."

Drake turned to her, forcing a smile. "I'm fine," he lied, his voice strained. "Just... caught up in the game."

As he looked back to the field, Drake's mind raced. How could he savor this moment of hope while knowing what lay ahead? How many more times would he have to watch his son's life cut short?

21 - 22

The ball arced through the air, spinning as it descended towards Harrison. Time seemed to slow as Drake watched his son's eyes lock onto the approaching sphere, his body coiling like a spring. In that instant, Harrison's face was a mirror of Linda's determined focus, a trait Drake had always admired in both of them.

Without hesitation, Harrison's leg swung in a graceful arc. The resounding thwack of foot meeting leather echoed across the field, and the ball soared towards the goal. Drake held his breath, his heart pounding in his ears as he watched its trajectory.

The net bulged as the ball sailed past the goalkeeper's outstretched fingers. A perfect shot.

"Yes!" Linda's voice erupted beside him, full of unbridled joy. She leapt to her feet, her blonde hair catching the sunlight as she pumped her fist in the air. "That's our boy!"

Drake's chest swelled with bittersweet pride. He wanted to join in Linda's celebration, to lose himself in the moment of triumph. But the weight of foreknowledge pressed down on him, suffocating his elation.

"Did you see that, Dad?" Harrison called from the field, his face beaming with excitement.

"I saw it, buddy," Drake managed to reply, his voice thick with emotion. "Great shot."

As Harrison turned back to his cheering teammates, Drake's mind raced. How much longer did they have? How many more moments of joy before everything came crashing down? He longed to freeze time, to preserve this perfect instant of happiness and pride.

"Drake?" Linda's voice cut through his spiraling thoughts. She had sat back down, her eyes now filled with concern. "Are you sure you're alright?"

He swallowed hard, forcing down the lump in his throat. "Yeah, I'm just... overwhelmed. It's a big day for him."

Linda squeezed his hand, her touch both comforting and agonizing. "It sure is. But he's got this. And we're here for him, together."

Together. The word echoed in Drake's mind as he looked from Linda to Harrison on the field. How many more times would he have to lose them? How many more times would he fail to save them?

As the game resumed, Drake wrestled with the urge to grab them both and run, to try and outpace the inevitable. But he knew, deep down, that there was no escaping what was to come. All he could do was cherish these fleeting moments of joy, even as the shadow of impending tragedy loomed ever closer.

23 - 24

The air crackled with excitement as parents and children alike celebrated Harrison's goal. Drake's hands moved mechanically, clapping along with the crowd, but his eyes never left his son. Harrison's face was alight with pure, unbridled joy, his grin stretching from ear to ear as his teammates swarmed around him, patting his back and ruffling his hair.

"Did you see that, Dad?" Harrison called out, his voice carrying across the field. "Did you see?"

Drake's throat tightened, a bittersweet mixture of pride and dread washing over him. "I saw, buddy," he managed to reply, his smile genuine for the first time in what felt like an eternity. "You were amazing."

As Harrison turned back to his teammates, Drake's mind raced. How much longer did they have? How many more moments of joy before everything came crashing down? He longed to freeze time, to preserve this perfect instant of happiness and pride.

"Drake?" Linda's voice cut through his spiraling thoughts. "You look... different. Happy, but also worried. What's going on in that head of yours?"

He swallowed hard, struggling to find the right words. "I'm just... savoring the moment. You never know when everything might change."

Linda's brow furrowed, concern etching lines across her forehead. "Change? Drake, what are you-"

Her words were cut off by a deafening roar. The world around them erupted in chaos, a blinding flash searing Drake's retina as the explosion ripped through the air. In that split second, as debris rained down and screams filled the air, Drake's heart shattered. He knew, with sickening certainty, that his fleeting moment of happiness had come to a violent, inevitable end.

25 - 26

The acrid scent of charred meat mingled with the sweetness of grilled onions, wafting through the air as Drake leaned against a gnarled oak tree. His eyes never left Harrison, who bounded from one end of the picnic table to the other, piling his plate impossibly high with burgers, hot dogs, and an assortment of sides.

"Slow down, champ," Drake called out, his voice a mixture of amusement and underlying tension. "The food's not going anywhere."

Harrison grinned back, a smear of ketchup already adorning his cheek. "But Dad, I'm starving! All that running really works up an appetite."

Drake's lips curved into a sad smile, his heart aching at the innocence in his son's voice. He wanted to freeze this moment, to hold onto it forever. But the weight of what was to come pressed down on him, suffocating in its inevitability.

Nearby, Linda's laughter drifted over, light and carefree as she chatted with another mother. "Oh, you should have seen Harrison out there," she was saying, pride evident in her tone. "He's got his father's determination, that's for sure."

Drake's fingers dug into the rough bark of the tree, anchoring himself to the present. His mind raced, searching for a way out, a way to change the course of events. But deep down, he knew it was futile. How many times had he tried? How many times had he failed?

"Hey, Earth to Drake!" Linda's voice cut through his spiraling thoughts. She approached, concern etched on her face. "You okay? You look like you're a million miles away."

He forced a smile, reaching out to squeeze her hand. "Just thinking about how lucky we are," he lied, the words tasting bitter on his tongue. "How perfect this moment is."

Linda's eyes softened, but before she could respond, Harrison's excited shout drew their attention. "Mom! Dad! Come on, you've got to try these burgers!"

As they made their way to the picnic table, Drake's steps felt leaden. Each moment that ticked by was one moment closer to the inevitable. He wanted to scream, to warn everyone, to grab his family and run. But he remained silent, trapped in a nightmare of his own making, powerless to stop the tragedy that loomed on the horizon.

27 - 28

Drake's heart swelled as he watched Harrison enthusiastically devour his burger, ketchup smeared across his cheek. Linda sat beside their son, her melodious laughter harmonizing with the ambient chatter of the picnic. For a fleeting instant, Drake allowed himself to be swept up in the illusion of normalcy.

"You've outdone yourself, Coach," Drake called out, his voice steadier than he felt. "Best post-game meal we've had yet."

The coach grinned, flipping another patty on the grill. "Glad you're enjoying it, Drake. Your boy's got a bright future ahead of him."

Drake's smile faltered for a moment, but he caught himself. "He sure does," he replied, his words heavy with unspoken meaning.

Linda leaned into him, her warmth a stark contrast to the chill creeping up his spine. "This is nice," she murmured. "We should do this more often."

"Yeah," Drake agreed, his throat tight. "We should."

As he gazed at his family, time seemed to slow. The sunlight dappled through the leaves, casting a golden glow on Linda's hair. Harrison's eyes sparkled with joy, his laughter echoing across the field. The scent of grilled meat and fresh-cut grass mingled in the air, creating a sensory snapshot of perfection.

For a brief moment, everything felt perfect.

Then the air changed.

It was subtle at first – a shift in the breeze, a sudden hush falling over the crowd. Drake's muscles tensed instinctively, his senses on high alert. He scanned the area, searching for the telltale signs he had come to dread.

"Drake?" Linda's voice was laced with concern. "What's wrong?"

He opened his mouth to respond, but the words died on his lips as he caught sight of the grill. His heart plummeted, a cold sweat breaking out across his skin.

"No," he whispered, his body already in motion. "Not again."

29 - 30

Drake's attention snapped to the grill, where one of the coaches was struggling with the propane tank. A faint hiss reached his ears, and his heart dropped into his stomach. Time seemed to slow as his mind raced through countless iterations of this moment, each ending in tragedy.

"No," he whispered, taking a step forward. His legs felt leaden, every movement a battle against the weight of his foreknowledge.

Linda's hand caught his arm. "Drake, what is it?" Her voice was tinged with worry, but to him, it sounded distant, muffled by the roaring in his ears.

He turned to her, his eyes wide with panic. "We need to get everyone away from here. Now." The urgency in his tone was palpable, his words clipped and sharp.

"What? Why?" Linda's brow furrowed in confusion.

Drake's gaze darted between Linda and the grill, his mind racing. How could he explain without sounding insane? How could he save them this time?

"Trust me," he pleaded, his voice cracking. "Please, just trust me."

As he spoke, his eyes locked onto Harrison, laughing with his teammates near the grill. The sight of his son, so alive and unaware of the danger, sent a jolt of terror through Drake's body.

"Harrison!" he called out, his voice carrying across the field. "Come here, buddy. Right now!"

The boy looked up, surprise evident on his face. Drake's heart pounded in his chest, each beat a reminder of how little time they had left.

31 - 32

Before Drake could utter another word, the world erupted into chaos. The propane tank exploded with a deafening roar, unleashing a fireball that ripped through the air like a vengeful beast. The picnic table splintered into a thousand deadly projectiles, debris flying in every direction as if propelled by an unseen force.

"Get down!" Drake bellowed, his muscular frame moving instinctively to shield Linda and Harrison. The heat from the blast seared his back, but he barely registered the pain. His eyes, sharp and focused despite the pandemonium, scanned frantically for his son.

Linda's scream pierced through the cacophony of destruction. "Harrison! Where's Harrison?"

Drake's heart hammered against his ribs as he shouted, "Stay here!" He pushed Linda down behind an overturned table, his detective instincts kicking in even as fear threatened to overwhelm him.

As he turned to search for Harrison, Drake's mind raced. 'Not again,' he thought, desperation clawing at his insides. 'I can't lose him again. I can't fail them both.'

Through the smoke and chaos, he caught a glimpse of dirty blonde hair. "Harrison!" he called out, his voice hoarse from the acrid air. "Son, can you hear me?"

The boy's faint reply came from somewhere to his left, barely audible above the screams of terrified parents and children. Drake surged forward, dodging flaming debris and panicked bystanders.

'This time will be different,' he told himself, even as the familiar weight of failure pressed down on him. 'It has to be.'

33 - 34

Drake's eyes locked on Harrison, who stood frozen mere feet from the epicenter of the blast. Time seemed to slow as Drake watched in horror, his son's wide brown eyes reflecting the approaching inferno. Flames licked at Harrison's shirt, hungry tendrils reaching out to claim him.

"No!" Drake's mind screamed, even as his body propelled him forward. 'Not again. Not this time.'

In an instant, Harrison was engulfed, the fire wrapping around him like a malevolent embrace. The sight ignited something primal in Drake, a surge of adrenaline that pushed him beyond his limits.

"Harrison!" Drake screamed; his voice raw with desperation. He sprinted toward his son, dodging debris and fallen picnic tables. The heat intensified with each step, singeing his clothes and hair, but he barely noticed.

As he ran, memories flashed through Drake's mind: Harrison's first steps, his infectious laughter, the pride in his eyes after scoring his first goal. Each recollection fueled Drake's determination.

"Hold on, buddy!" he shouted, hoping his voice could reach Harrison through the roar of the flames. "Dad's coming!"

Drake's heart pounded in his ears, a frantic rhythm matching his footsteps. He was vaguely aware of Linda's screams behind him, of other parents calling out for their children. But his world had narrowed to a single point: his son, wreathed in fire, needing him.

'I won't let you down,' Drake vowed silently, pushing himself harder. 'Not this time. Not ever again.'

35 - 36

Harrison's screams pierced the air, a sound so raw and primal it shattered Drake's heart. The boy's frail body writhed in agony, flames devouring him like a ravenous beast. Drake dropped to his knees beside his son, his hands hovering uselessly, afraid to touch and cause more pain.

"Harrison!" Drake choked out; his voice thick with anguish. "I'm here, buddy. I'm here."

The heat seared Drake's skin, but he barely felt it. His mind raced, searching desperately for a way to save his son. 'Water. Blanket. Anything!' But there was nothing within reach.

Harrison's eyes, wide with terror, locked onto Drake's. "Dad," he whimpered, his voice barely audible over the crackling flames. "It hurts..."

Drake's composure crumbled. "I know, son. I know," he sobbed, tears streaming down his face. "Just hold on. Please, hold on."

As he watched his son burn, Drake's thoughts spiraled into despair. 'I've failed him again. No matter what I do, I can't change this. I can't save him.'

The acrid smell of burning flesh filled the air, making Drake gag. He could hear Linda's anguished cries growing closer, but he couldn't tear his eyes away from Harrison.

"I'm sorry," Drake whispered, his voice breaking. "I'm so sorry, Harrison. I love you. I love you so much."

37 - 38

Drake's hands trembled as he tore off his jacket, the fabric catching on his watch. "Hold still! Hold still!" he yelled, his voice cracking with desperation. The flames danced malevolently, mocking his efforts as he draped the jacket over Harrison's writhing form.

The heat was unbearable, an inferno that seared Drake's flesh and scorched his lungs with every ragged breath. He patted frantically at the fire, ignoring the blistering pain that bloomed across his arms. His own screams melded with Harrison's, a horrific duet that pierced the chaos around them.

'I can't lose him again,' Drake thought, gritting his teeth against the agony. 'Not like this. Not ever.' The memory of countless resets flashed through his mind, each one ending in tragedy. But this time felt different, more visceral, more final.

"Dad," Harrison gasped between sobs, his voice barely audible beneath the crackling flames. "I'm scared."

Drake's heart shattered anew at his son's words. "I know, buddy," he choked out, still fighting the relentless fire. "I'm here. I won't leave you."

As he battled the flames, Drake's mind raced. 'Why can't I change this? What am I missing?' The question that had plagued him through countless loops echoed in his head, unanswered and mocking.

39 - 40

Linda's anguished cries cut through the pandemonium, her voice raw with terror. "Drake! Harrison!" She sprinted towards them, her blonde hair whipping wildly behind her, eyes wide with horror.

Drake's heart clenched at the sound of his wife's voice. He wanted to call out to her, to reassure her, but his focus remained on Harrison. 'I can't let her see him like this,' he thought, his stomach churning. 'God, please, not again.'

As Linda drew closer, the flames finally began to subside, leaving behind a devastating aftermath. Harrison lay motionless in Drake's arms, his once vibrant skin now a patchwork of blisters and char. His eyes remained closed, shallow breaths rattling in his chest like a grim metronome.

"Harrison?" Drake whispered; his voice barely audible over the surrounding chaos. He gently brushed a lock of singed hair from his son's forehead, his touch feather-light. "Can you hear me, buddy?"

No response came from the boy's lips. Drake felt a familiar despair creeping in, threatening to overwhelm him. 'This can't be happening,' he thought, his mind reeling. 'I was supposed to protect him. I was supposed to change things this time.'

Linda fell to her knees beside them, her hands hovering uncertainly over Harrison's burned form. "Oh God," she choked out, her voice thick with tears. "Drake, is he...?"

Drake swallowed hard, unable to meet his wife's gaze. "He's breathing," he managed, the words tasting like ash in his mouth. "But we need help. Now."

41 - 42

Drake collapsed beside Harrison, his muscular frame giving way under the weight of grief and pain. He clutched his son's burned body close, the acrid smell of scorched flesh assaulting his nostrils. His own arms throbbed with searing agony, the skin blistered and raw, but the physical pain paled in comparison to the anguish tearing through his heart.

"Harrison," he whispered, his voice hoarse and broken. "I'm so sorry, buddy. I'm so sorry."

Linda dropped to her knees beside them, her slender body wracked with violent sobs. Her trembling hands reached out, hesitating for a moment before gently touching Harrison's cheek.

"My baby," she wailed, her voice cracking. "Oh God, my baby boy."

Drake looked up at his wife, meeting her tear-filled eyes. The depth of her pain mirrored his own, and for a moment, he felt the crushing weight of his failure anew. 'I was supposed to prevent this,' he thought, his mind reeling. 'How many times will I have to watch them suffer?'

"Linda," he choked out, "I... I couldn't..."

She shook her head, cutting him off. "We need to get him help," she said, her voice trembling but determined. "Drake, we have to move him."

The thought of jostling Harrison's broken body made Drake's stomach lurch. "I don't know if we should," he said, his eyes darting frantically between his wife and son. "What if we make it worse?"

Linda's hand found his, squeezing tightly despite the burns. "We can't just sit here," she insisted, her voice thick with desperation. "Please, Drake. We have to try."

As Drake looked down at Harrison's blistered face, a familiar sense of futility washed over him. 'It won't matter,' a voice in his head whispered. 'Nothing we do will change the outcome.' But he pushed the thought away, forcing himself to nod.

"Okay," he said, his voice barely above a whisper. "Okay, let's... let's try to get him to the car."

43 - 44

"Do something!" Linda screamed at Drake, her voice raw with desperation. "Save him!"

The words hit Drake like a physical blow, each syllable amplifying the crushing weight of his failure. He wanted to move, to act, to be the hero his family needed. But his body betrayed him, refusing to respond to his frantic mental commands.

"I can't," he whispered, the admission tearing at his throat. "Linda, I... I can't move."

The world around him began to blur, edges softening as his vision swam. The acrid smell of burned flesh gave way to a dizzying nothingness. Drake's arms, still wrapped around Harrison's motionless form, throbbed with an intensity that threatened to consume him.

'This is how it always ends,' he thought, a bitter taste rising in his mouth. 'No matter what I do, no matter how hard I try, I can't save them.'

Linda's sobs faded into the background as Drake's consciousness began to slip away. The pain in his arms, a cruel reminder of his futile efforts, overwhelmed his senses. As darkness crept in at the edges of his vision, a final, agonizing thought flashed through his mind:

'I'm sorry. I'm so sorry I couldn't protect you both.'

And then, mercifully, everything went black.

45 - 46

The darkness enveloped Drake, a void both familiar and terrifying. He felt himself falling, tumbling through an endless abyss. The screams that had filled the air moments ago faded away, replaced by a suffocating silence that pressed in on him from all sides.

'Not again,' Drake thought, his inner voice echoing in the emptiness. 'Please, not again.'

But the pull was inexorable, dragging him through the fabric of reality itself. Time seemed to stretch and compress simultaneously, a nauseating sensation that left Drake disoriented and gasping for breath he couldn't find.

Memories flashed before him in rapid succession: Harrison's smile as he kicked the winning goal, Linda's laughter as she flipped pancakes, the warmth of their family breakfast. Each image was a dagger to his heart, a reminder of the happiness that always slipped through his fingers.

"I can't keep doing this," Drake whispered into the void, his words swallowed by the silence. "How many more times do I have to watch them die?"

The darkness offered no response, no comfort. It simply continued to pull him along, indifferent to his anguish. Drake felt the last vestiges of his strength ebbing away, replaced by a bone-deep weariness that threatened to consume him entirely.

As he drifted through the nothingness, a single, desperate thought crystallized in his mind: 'This time, I have to find a way to break the cycle. No matter what it takes.'

47 - 48

Drake's eyes snapped open, his heart pounding as he found himself once again in the familiar confines of his bedroom. Sunlight filtered through the blinds, casting warm stripes across the bedspread. He turned his head, his gaze settling on Linda's sleeping form beside him.

She lay on her side, facing him, her blonde hair splayed across the pillow. Her chest rose and fell with each steady breath, a peaceful rhythm that belied the turmoil raging within Drake. He resisted the urge to reach out and touch her, fearing that even the slightest contact might shatter this fragile moment of calm.

The faint aroma of freshly brewed coffee drifted up from downstairs, accompanied by the soft clink of dishes. Harrison, Drake realized, already up and about, likely preparing his usual bowl of cereal before school.

Drake closed his eyes, inhaling deeply. "I can't do this again," he whispered, his voice barely audible.

Linda stirred beside him, her eyes fluttering open. She smiled softly, still half-asleep. "Did you say something, honey?"

Drake forced a smile, his chest tightening with the effort. "Just thinking out loud," he replied, his voice strained. "How did you sleep?"

"Like a rock," Linda said, stretching languidly. She propped herself up on one elbow, studying his face with concern. "You look tired. Another rough night?"

Drake nodded, unable to meet her gaze. How could he explain the weight of countless resets, the agony of watching his family die over and over again? The words caught in his throat, threatening to choke him.

"I'm fine," he managed, sitting up and swinging his legs over the side of the bed. "Just... a lot on my mind."

Linda's hand on his shoulder was warm, comforting. It took every ounce of willpower not to flinch away from her touch. "You know you can talk to me about anything, right?" she said softly.

Drake turned to face her, drinking in the sight of her concerned blue eyes, the gentle curve of her lips. He wanted to memorize every detail, to hold onto this moment forever. But he knew it was futile. It always was.

"I know," he said, his voice thick with emotion. "I just... I need to figure some things out on my own."

49 - 50

Linda nodded, her brow furrowed with worry. "Alright," she said, squeezing his shoulder gently. "But don't shut me out completely, okay?"

Drake's heart clenched. If only she knew how desperately he wanted to let her in, to share the burden of his knowledge. But he couldn't. He wouldn't risk her sanity, her happiness, even if it was all an illusion.

"I won't," he promised, the lie bitter on his tongue.

He stood, muscles aching with phantom pains from injuries long healed. The scent of coffee wafted up from downstairs, a cruel reminder of the normalcy he could never truly have.

"Harrison's tryouts are today," Linda said, her voice brightening. "Are you coming?"

Drake closed his eyes, fighting back the wave of nausea that threatened to overwhelm him. Images of flames, of Harrison's screams, flashed through his mind.

"Of course," he said, forcing a smile. "Wouldn't miss it for the world."

As Linda bustled out of the room, chattering about breakfast and schedules, Drake remained rooted to the spot. His gaze drifted to the window, where golden sunlight streamed in, painting the world in deceptively cheerful hues.

"How many more times?" he whispered to himself, his voice barely audible. "How many more times do I have to watch them die?"

A Spark of Truth

1 ^{- 2} Drake Miller's eyes snapped open, his consciousness yanked from the depths of a fitful sleep. The familiar ache in his bones greeted him like an old friend, a constant companion in this endless loop of days. Golden sunlight filtered through the blinds, painting stripes across the rumpled bedsheets and casting long shadows on the far wall. He drew in a sharp breath, the air tasting of stale coffee and regret.

"Another day," he muttered, his voice rough with exhaustion. "Another chance to fail."

As he pushed himself upright, Drake's gaze fell upon his arms. Something was different, wrong in a way he couldn't immediately place. He flexed his fingers experimentally, wincing at the twinge of pain that shot through his hand—a souvenir from yesterday's futile attempts to change fate. But it was his arms that truly caught his attention, a nagging sense of unease settling in his gut.

"What the hell?" he whispered, brow furrowing as he examined his skin more closely.

His mind raced, fragments of memory flashing behind his eyes: flames, screams, the acrid stench of burning flesh. Drake's breath hitched in his throat, a cold sweat breaking out across his forehead. How could this be possible? How could the physical evidence of yesterday's tragedy persist into this new cycle? Then he remembered his thumb from earlier, how he had dislocated it only to have it carry over to the new days loop.

"Drake?" Linda's voice, soft and sleepy, broke through his spiraling thoughts. "Are you okay? You've been tossing and turning all night."

He hesitated, torn between the instinct to protect her from the truth and the overwhelming desire to finally unburden himself. In the end, self-preservation won out.

"I'm fine," he lied, the words tasting bitter on his tongue. "Just a bad dream."

As he swung his legs over the side of the bed, Drake's mind whirled with possibilities. Was this a sign? A crack in the fabric of this twisted reality? Or merely another cruel trick of fate, designed to torment him further?

"It has to mean something," he murmured to himself, running a hand through his disheveled hair. "But what?"

The weight of countless repeated days pressed down upon him, threatening to crush his resolve. Yet beneath the exhaustion and despair, a tiny spark of hope flickered to life. If this day was already different, perhaps there was still a chance to break the cycle, to save his family from the inevitable tragedy that loomed on the horizon.

Drake stood, squaring his shoulders as he prepared to face yet another iteration of this cursed day. But this time, armed with new evidence and a renewed determination, he allowed himself to believe that maybe, just maybe, he could finally change the outcome.

"I won't let you down," he whispered, a promise to his sleeping wife and the son who waited downstairs, blissfully unaware of the danger that threatened to tear their world apart. "Not again. Not this time."

3 - 4

Drake's eyes fell to his arms, and his breath caught in his throat. The skin was a tapestry of pain, blistered and raw, angry red patches running from wrists to elbows. He traced a finger along one of the blisters, wincing as sharp, searing pain shot through his nerves.

"God," he muttered, the memories flooding back with visceral intensity. The explosion. Harrison's screams. Flames licking at his skin as he desperately tried to save his son.

The acrid stench of scorched flesh filled his nostrils, so vivid he could almost taste it. Drake swallowed hard, fighting the wave of nausea that threatened to overwhelm him.

"Dad?" Harrison's voice drifted up from downstairs, tinged with its usual mix of curiosity and concern. "You okay up there?"

Drake closed his eyes, steadying himself. "Yeah, buddy. I'll be down in a minute."

He couldn't let Harrison see the burns. Not yet. The boy's innocence, his unwavering belief that his father could fix anything, was both a blessing and a curse. How could he explain the inexplicable?

"What am I going to do?" Drake whispered to himself, gingerly touching the damaged skin. "How do I stop this from happening again?"

The weight of responsibility pressed down on him, heavier than ever. He had to find a way to break this cycle, to save his family. But with each reset, the task seemed more impossible.

Drake took a deep breath, steeling himself for the day ahead. "One step at a time," he murmured. "Just... one step at a time."

5 - 6

Drake stared at his blistered arms, a cold dread settling in his stomach. The injuries were fresh, angry and raw as if he'd just pulled his hands from the flames moments ago. Time should have dulled the pain, allowed the wounds to begin healing. But here they were, a vivid reminder of his failure, mocking him with their persistence.

"Drake?" Linda's voice drifted from the other side of the bed, soft and groggy with sleep.

His heart lurched. In one fluid motion, born from the instinct of countless repetitions, Drake yanked the blanket over his arms. The rough fabric scraped against his burns, sending a jolt of pain through his body. He bit back a hiss, forcing his features into a mask of normalcy.

"Morning," he managed, his voice strained despite his best efforts.

Linda shifted, the mattress dipping slightly as she rolled to face him. "You're up early," she murmured, concern lacing her tone.

Drake's mind raced. How many times had he lied to her in these endless loops? How many half-truths and evasions? The weight of it all pressed down on him, threatening to crush what remained of his resolve.

"Just... couldn't sleep," he replied, the words tasting bitter on his tongue.

He wanted to tell her everything. To pour out the madness of his reality, the desperation that clawed at his insides. But the memory of her skeptical eyes, the hurt and confusion that always followed his revelations, held him back.

"Bad dreams again?" Linda asked, reaching out to touch his shoulder.

Drake flinched involuntarily, his burned arms screaming in protest beneath the covers. "Something like that," he muttered, guilt gnawing at him.

How long could he keep this charade up? How many more mornings would he wake to fresh wounds and the crushing knowledge of what lay ahead? The questions swirled in his mind, a relentless torment with no clear answers.

7 - 8

Drake's gaze fixed on a patch of sunlight creeping across the bedroom floor, its golden warmth a stark contrast to the cold dread settling in his stomach. He swallowed hard, his throat dry and constricted.

"Yeah?" he managed, the single syllable heavy with unspoken turmoil.

Linda's hand found his shoulder again, her touch gentle but insistent. "Are you okay? You've been restless all night."

The concern in her voice was a double-edged sword, both comforting and agonizing. Drake closed his eyes, fighting against the urge to spill everything, to burden her with the impossible truth of their fractured reality.

"I'm..." he began, the lie dying on his lips. How could he be 'fine' when he carried the weight of countless deaths, countless failures?

Instead, he exhaled slowly, buying time as he wrestled with what to say. The burns on his arms throbbed, a physical reminder of the stakes at play.

"Just a lot on my mind," he finally offered, the understatement of the century. He turned to face Linda, drinking in the sight of her - alive, whole, unknowing of the horrors that awaited them.

The urge to protect her, to shield her from the nightmare he lived, warred with his desperate need for understanding, for an ally in this impossible fight. But as he met her worried gaze, Drake knew he couldn't bring himself to shatter her world. Not yet. Not again.

"Work stuff," he added lamely, hating himself for the deception even as he uttered the words.

9 - 10

"I'm fine," he muttered, swinging his legs over the side of the bed and standing. The floorboards creaked beneath his feet, a sound that seemed to echo the fragility of his world.

Drake's muscles tensed as he rose, his body a coiled spring of anxiety and unspent energy. He clenched and unclenched his fists, fighting the urge to punch something, anything, to release the maelstrom of emotions churning within him.

He wasn't fine. Nothing was fine.

The morning light filtering through the curtains felt like a cruel joke, its golden warmth at odds with the darkness that threatened to consume him. Drake stared at his reflection in the mirror across the room, barely recognizing the haggard man staring back at him.

"Are you sure you're alright?" Linda's voice floated from behind him, laced with concern.

Drake swallowed hard, his throat constricting around the words he couldn't say. "Yeah," he managed, the lie tasting bitter on his tongue. "Just need some coffee."

As he moved towards the door, his mind raced through the possibilities of the day ahead. Would this be the cycle where he finally broke through? Or would he be forced to watch his loved ones die once more, helpless to change their fate?

The weight of his knowledge pressed down on him, threatening to crush his spirit entirely. But beneath the despair, a tiny spark of determination still flickered. He had to keep trying. For Linda. For Harrison. For the chance to reclaim the life that had been stolen from him.

Drake paused at the threshold, his hand resting on the doorknob. He turned back to Linda, drinking in the sight of her one last time before facing whatever horrors awaited him beyond.

"I love you," he said softly, the words carrying the weight of a thousand unspoken truths.

Then, squaring his shoulders, Drake stepped out into the hallway, ready to face another day that wasn't fine at all.

11 - 12

The aroma of pancakes wafted through the air, a bittersweet reminder of normalcy that Drake knew was anything but. He shuffled into the kitchen, his burned arms throbbing beneath the sleeves of his shirt. Linda took over at the stove, her blonde hair catching the morning light as she hummed a soft tune. The sight of her, alive and whole, made Drake's heart clench.

"Morning, honey," Linda said, glancing over her shoulder with a warm smile. "Pancakes?"

Drake forced a nod, his throat tight. "Sounds great," he managed.

As he moved to the coffee pot, his eyes fell on Harrison, hunched over his phone at the table. The boy's brow was furrowed in concentration, his thumbs tapping rapidly on the screen. Drake's mind flashed to the image of his son engulfed in flames, and he gripped the counter to steady himself.

"You okay, Dad?" Harrison asked, looking up from his device. "You look kind of pale."

Drake's thoughts raced. Should he tell them? Would they even believe him? He poured coffee with shaking hands, buying time.

"I... I need to talk to you both," he said finally, his voice barely above a whisper. "It's important."

Linda turned off the stove, her expression shifting to concern. "What is it, Drake?"

He took a deep breath, steeling himself. "You're going to think I'm crazy, but I swear it's true. I've been living this same day over and over again. And... and in every version, something terrible happens to you both."

The kitchen fell silent, save for the soft sizzle of the cooling pan. Harrison's phone slipped from his fingers, clattering onto the table.

"Dad..." Harrison started, his voice uncertain.

"I know how it sounds," Drake interrupted, rolling up his sleeves to reveal the angry burns. "But these... I got these trying to save you yesterday. Or in the last cycle. I don't even know anymore."

Linda gasped, her hand flying to her mouth. "Drake, what happened? We need to get you to a hospital!"

"No," Drake said firmly. "What I need is for you to listen. To believe me. Because if we don't figure this out together, I'm afraid I'll lose you both. Again."

13 - 14

Linda exchanged a worried glance with Harrison, her blue eyes filled with a mix of concern and confusion. She set the spatula down on the table with a soft clatter, the sound echoing in the suddenly tense kitchen. Harrison scooted his chair closer, his lanky frame hunched forward, his expression a blend of curiosity and apprehension.

Drake's chest tightened as he watched them, his family, unknowingly perched on the precipice of a truth that would shatter their reality. He took a deep breath, the air feeling thick and heavy in his lungs. The words he needed to say danced on the tip of his tongue, threatening to choke him.

"You're not going to believe me, but..." Drake began, his voice barely above a whisper. He clenched his fists, feeling the pull of his burned skin, a physical reminder of the countless cycles he'd endured. "I've been living this same day over and over again."

The words hung in the air, heavy and surreal. Drake watched as confusion bloomed across Linda's face, her brow furrowing deeper. Harrison's eyes widened, a flicker of disbelief mixed with fascination dancing in their depths.

How many times had he imagined this moment? Drake wondered. How many cycles had he spent rehearsing these words in his mind, only to hold them back at the last second? Now that they were out, he felt both relieved and terrified. There was no going back now.

"What do you mean, Drake?" Linda asked, her voice soft and cautious. She reached out, her hand hovering over his arm, as if afraid to touch him.

Drake swallowed hard, his throat constricting. "I mean exactly that. Every morning, I wake up, and it's the same day. The same conversations, the same events. And no matter what I do, it always ends in tragedy."

15 - 16

Harrison blinked, his lanky form leaning forward in his chair. His unruly hair fell across his forehead as he tilted his head, a mixture of confusion and curiosity etched on his youthful features. "What?" he breathed, the single word laden with disbelief and a hint of the wonder that often colored his voice.

Drake's gaze flickered between his son and wife, his heart hammering against his ribcage. The weight of countless repeated days pressed down on him, threatening to crush the fragile hope that had blossomed with his confession. He opened his mouth to elaborate, but Linda's voice cut through the tense silence.

"Drake," she said, her tone a delicate balance of skepticism and concern. Her blue eyes, usually a source of comfort, now held a wariness that made Drake's stomach clench. "What are you talking about?"

The question hung in the air, heavy with unspoken implications. Drake ran a hand through his disheveled hair, wincing as the movement pulled at his burned skin. How could he make them understand? The enormity of his experience seemed impossible to convey in mere words.

"I know it sounds crazy," he started, his voice rough with emotion. "But I've lived this day so many times. I've seen..." He trailed off, the memories of their repeated deaths flashing before his eyes. He couldn't bring himself to voice those horrors, not yet.

17 - 18

Drake's fingers curled around the edge of the kitchen table, his knuckles whitening with the intensity of his grip. The familiar scent of pancakes, once comforting, now seemed to mock him with its normalcy.

"I mean it," he insisted, his voice rising slightly as desperation clawed at his throat. "Every day, I wake up, and it's the same. It always starts the same: I wake up next to you, Linda. I come down here, and you're cooking pancakes, Harrison's on his phone, and everything feels... normal."

He paused, his gaze darting between Linda's skeptical expression and Harrison's wide-eyed stare. The weight of their disbelief pressed against him, threatening to suffocate the truth he'd kept buried for so long.

With a shaky exhale, Drake lifted his arms, the angry red burns a stark contrast to his pale skin. "But the day always ends in tragedy," he continued, his voice hoarse. "You both die. Sometimes it's Harrison, sometimes it's you, Linda, and sometimes it's both of you. I've tried everything to stop it, but no matter what I do, it keeps happening."

The words hung in the air, heavy and oppressive. Drake's heart thundered in his chest as he watched comprehension slowly dawn on their faces. Would they believe him this time? Or would he be forced to watch them die again, helpless to change their fate?

Linda's hand trembled as she reached across the table, her fingers ghosting over the blistered skin of his forearm. "Drake," she whispered, her voice a mixture of horror and concern, "how did this happen?"

Drake closed his eyes, the memory of flames and screams threatening to overwhelm him. "I wish I knew how to make it stop," he thought, a wave of exhaustion washing over him. "I wish I could save you both, just once."

19 - 20

Linda's face softened with concern, though her eyes still held doubt. "Drake... that's not possible. You must have hurt yourself somehow and—"

The words hit Drake like a physical blow, igniting a fire in his chest that blazed hotter than the burns on his arms. His hand came down on the table with a resounding crack, dishes rattling in its wake. "No!" he snapped, his voice raw with frustration and desperation.

The sudden outburst startled Linda, her blue eyes widening as she instinctively leaned back. Drake felt a pang of regret, but the urgency of his situation propelled him forward. He thrust his arms out, the angry red welts on full display.

"I'm not imagining this," he insisted, his voice trembling with barely contained emotion. "These burns—" He rotated his arms, letting the morning light catch every blister and raw patch of skin. "I got them yesterday. Or... in the last cycle."

The memory of heat and chaos flooded his senses. He could almost smell the acrid stench of burning propane, hear the panicked screams echoing across the soccer field. Drake swallowed hard, forcing the words past the lump in his throat.

"I tried to save Harrison when the propane tank at the soccer tryouts exploded," he explained, his eyes locked on Linda's face, searching desperately for a flicker of belief. "He caught fire, and I burned my arms trying to put it out."

As he spoke, Drake's mind raced. Would this be the time they finally understood? Or was he doomed to repeat this confession, over and over, always met with disbelief and concern? The weight of countless failed attempts pressed down on him, threatening to crush what little hope remained.

21 - 22

Harrison leaned back in his chair, his lanky frame seeming to shrink as he processed his father's words. His wide brown eyes darted between Drake and Linda, a mixture of confusion and disbelief etched across his youthful features. The boy's fingers twitched nervously, reaching for the phone he'd set aside, as if seeking an anchor in the familiar device.

"That doesn't make any sense, Dad," Harrison said, his voice cracking slightly. "You were probably dreaming or something. Maybe you burned yourself and just don't remember—"

Drake felt a surge of frustration rising within him, threatening to spill over. He clenched his jaw, willing himself to remain calm. The kitchen suddenly felt stifling, the scent of pancakes now cloying and oppressive.

"I remember everything," Drake interrupted, his tone sharp enough to make Harrison flinch. He immediately regretted his harshness but pressed on. "And it's not just these cycles. I'm remembering... other things too. Other lives."

He paused, running a hand through his disheveled hair. How could he possibly explain the fragmented memories that haunted him? The weight of multiple realities pressed against his consciousness, each vying for attention.

"I remember a car accident," Drake continued, his voice softening. "I was stranded in two different worlds. In one, I was still a lawyer, just like now. In the other, I was a detective." He looked at Harrison, seeing not just his son, but echoes of the boy in other timelines, other realities. "I had to stop bombs in both of them."

Drake's throat constricted as he recalled the frantic race against time, the lives hanging in the balance. And always, lurking in the shadows, that haunting presence. "And the man responsible—"

He faltered, the words catching in his throat. How could he describe the disfigured face that plagued his nightmares? The malevolent force that seemed to follow him across realities? Drake's hands trembled as he struggled to continue, the weight of his experiences threatening to overwhelm him.

23 - 24

Drake's throat tightened, his breath catching as he tried to force out the words. The kitchen suddenly felt claustrophobic, the warm scent of pancakes now cloying and oppressive. He loosened his collar, desperate for air.

Linda leaned forward, her blue eyes filled with a mix of concern and skepticism. Her voice was soft but carried an undercurrent of urgency. "What man, Drake?" she pressed, reaching out to place a comforting hand on his arm.

The gentle touch sent a jolt through Drake's system. For a moment, he was transported back to another time, another place—Linda's hand on his arm as they stood before a gravestone, mourning a life that never was. He blinked hard, forcing himself back to the present.

"I—" Drake began, his voice hoarse. He cleared his throat, trying again. "He's... not like anyone I've ever seen before." The words came slowly, each one carefully chosen. "His face... it's like looking at a nightmare made flesh."

Harrison shifted uncomfortably in his chair, the legs scraping against the tile floor. The sound grated on Drake's nerves, reminding him of screeching metal and shattering glass. He shook his head, trying to dispel the intrusive memory.

"Dad," Harrison said, his voice small and uncertain. "You're scaring us."

Drake looked at his son, seeing the fear and confusion in the boy's eyes. It mirrored the turmoil he felt inside, threatening to consume him. How could he protect them when he could barely make sense of what was happening himself?

"I'm sorry," Drake whispered, more to himself than to his family. "I never wanted to bring this darkness into our home. But I can't keep pretending everything's normal. Not when I know what's coming."

25 - 26

Drake leaned forward, his voice lowering to a hushed, urgent tone. "A disfigured man. His face is burned, like he's been through hell and back." His fingers tightened around his coffee mug, knuckles whitening as he struggled to maintain composure. "He's been haunting me in these loops. He was there during the accident. I remember seeing him through the windshield, his eyes... God, his eyes were so cold."

A shiver ran down Drake's spine, and he swallowed hard before continuing. "He's the one who keeps showing up, taunting me. And he's responsible for some of your deaths."

The words hung in the air, heavy and oppressive. Drake's gaze darted between Linda and Harrison, searching their faces for any sign of understanding, of belief. But all he saw was shock and confusion.

The kitchen, once warm and inviting with the scent of pancakes, now felt suffocating. The silence stretched on, broken only by the soft ticking of the clock on the wall. Drake could hear his own heartbeat thundering in his ears, each second feeling like an eternity.

He wanted to say more, to make them understand the gravity of the situation. But how could he explain the weight of countless deaths, of watching his family perish over and over again? The words caught in his throat, choking him with their intensity.

Linda's hand trembled as she reached for her water glass, the soft clink of ice cubes shattering the stillness. Harrison's eyes were wide, his phone forgotten on the table as he stared at his father with a mixture of fear and disbelief.

Drake's mind raced, grasping for something, anything to break this unbearable tension. But for once, the man who had lived countless versions of this day found himself at a loss, trapped in a moment he had never experienced before.

27 - 28

Linda reached across the table, placing a hand on his. The warmth of her touch sent a jolt through Drake's body, grounding him in this fragile moment. Her blue eyes, usually so full of comfort, now swirled with a mix of concern and uncertainty.

"Drake, listen to yourself," she said softly, her voice barely above a whisper. "You're not making sense." Her fingers tightened around his, a gesture that once brought solace, now feeling like an anchor dragging him back to a reality he no longer recognized. "Maybe... maybe these burns are causing you to hallucinate. You could be in shock—"

The words hit Drake like a physical blow. He pulled his hand away, the sudden absence of her touch leaving him cold. His heart raced, pounding against his ribcage as if trying to break free. How many times had he heard similar words, in different variations, across countless loops? The familiar sting of disbelief threatened to overwhelm him.

"I'm not hallucinating," Drake interrupted, his voice hoarse with emotion. He leaned forward, eyes locked on Linda's, wishing her to see the truth behind his words. "And I'm not in shock." The burns on his arms throbbed, a painful reminder of the reality he alone seemed to remember. "I've never fully told you the truth in any of the loops before. This is the first time."

As the words left his mouth, Drake felt a strange mix of relief and terror. He had finally broken the cycle of secrecy, but what would it cost him? Would this be the key to saving them, or would it push them further away, leaving him more alone than ever in his desperate quest?

29 - 30

Harrison's brow furrowed, his youthful features creased with a mix of confusion and concern. "Why now?" he asked, his voice cautious, tinged with the innocence that Drake had fought so hard to protect across countless iterations of this day.

Drake's gaze shifted to his son, taking in the familiar unruly dirty blonde hair and wide, questioning eyes. A lump formed in his throat as he considered how to answer. The weight of countless failures pressed down on him, threatening to crush the fragile hope that had bloomed with his confession.

"Because I'm tired of lying," Drake admitted, his voice barely above a whisper. The words hung in the air, heavy with the accumulated guilt of a hundred lifetimes. He ran a hand through his disheveled hair, wincing as the movement pulled at his burned skin. "And because I need you both to trust me."

His eyes darted between Linda and Harrison, searching for any sign of understanding, any flicker of belief. The kitchen, once a bastion of normalcy, now felt alien and oppressive. The scent of pancakes, usually comforting, turned his stomach.

"This is new territory for me, too," Drake continued, his words picking up speed as if racing against an invisible clock. "I've never told you what's happening before. Maybe this time..." He paused, swallowing hard against the emotion threatening to choke him. "Maybe this time, we can figure it out together."

As he spoke, Drake's mind raced through the possibilities. Could this be the key? Had his silence in previous loops been the very thing trapping them in this endless cycle of tragedy? The hope was almost painful in its intensity, a sharp contrast to the dull ache of resignation he'd grown accustomed to.

31 - 32

Linda's blue eyes bored into Drake, her lips pressed into a thin line. The silence stretched between them, taut as a wire. Drake could almost see the gears turning in her mind, weighing his impossible story against years of shared trust and love.

Harrison, usually so quick with a quip or question, remained uncharacteristically quiet. His fingers danced nervously over his phone screen; eyes fixed downward. The soft tapping of his thumbs filled the silence, a nervous metronome counting the seconds.

Drake's heart hammered in his chest. He'd never made it this far before, never laid bare the truth of their twisted reality. The possibility of rejection, of being labeled insane by the two people he loved most, threatened to overwhelm him.

Finally, Linda sighed, her shoulders sagging slightly. "I don't know what to think," she admitted, her voice a mixture of concern and cautious belief. Her hand reached across the table, fingers intertwining with Drake's. The touch was electric, grounding him in the moment. "But... you're my husband. If you say this is real, then I'll listen."

Relief flooded through Drake, threatening to buckle his knees. He tightened his grip on Linda's hand, anchoring himself to her unwavering support. It wasn't full belief, not yet, but it was a start – a crack in the impenetrable wall of disbelief he'd faced in every previous cycle.

23 - 24

Harrison's eyes flickered up from his phone, meeting Drake's gaze for the first time since the revelation. The boy's brow furrowed, a mixture of confusion and reluctant acceptance etched across his youthful features. His fingers, usually so nimble on the device's screen, now lay still.

"Yeah," Harrison said, his voice barely above a whisper. He swallowed hard, Adam's apple bobbing in his throat. "Me too. But it's crazy, Dad. You know that, right?"

The words hung in the air, heavy with the weight of a reality too bizarre to fully comprehend. Drake felt a surge of pride for his son's willingness to even consider such an outlandish claim. He remembered the countless times he'd watched Harrison die, the searing pain of loss etched into his very soul. Now, here was his boy, alive and grappling with an impossible truth.

Drake allowed himself a small, weary smile. The corners of his mouth lifted, but the expression didn't quite reach his eyes. Those remained shadowed, haunted by memories of cycles past and the ever-present fear of failure.

"Believe me, kid," Drake said, his voice rough with emotion. "I know."

He leaned back in his chair, the weight of countless repeated days pressing down on his shoulders. The burns on his arms throbbed, a physical reminder of the stakes at play. Drake's mind raced, calculating the potential consequences of this new development. Would sharing the truth change anything? Or had he simply added a new burden to his family's shoulders?

"I never wanted to drag you both into this," Drake thought, his chest tight with a mixture of relief and apprehension. "But maybe, just maybe, together we can find a way out of this nightmare."

35 - 36

Drake stood, his chair scraping against the kitchen floor. The sound echoed in the stillness, a stark reminder of the ordinary world that continued to spin around him despite the extraordinary circumstances.

"I need to clean up," he muttered, more to himself than to Linda or Harrison.

As he trudged up the stairs, each step felt heavier than the last. The bathroom door clicked shut behind him, and Drake leaned against it, exhaling slowly. His reflection in the mirror caught his eye – a man worn down by an impossible burden, the weight of countless repeated days etched into the lines of his face.

He turned the shower on, letting steam fill the room. As he stepped under the hot spray, Drake hissed through clenched teeth. The water stung his burned arms, but he welcomed the pain. It was real, tangible – unlike the shifting sands of reality he found himself trapped in.

"How many times have I done this?" Drake wondered, closing his eyes as water cascaded over his face. "How many showers, how many mornings, how many deaths?"

The burns throbbed relentlessly, each pulse a stark reminder of his latest failure. He could still smell the acrid stench of burning flesh, could still hear Harrison's agonized screams. Drake's hands clenched into fists, his nails digging into his palms.

"I won't let it happen again," he vowed, his voice barely audible over the rush of water. "Not this time. Not ever again."

But even as the words left his lips, doubt crept in. How many times had he made that same promise, only to watch helplessly as tragedy unfolded once more?

Drake leaned his forehead against the cool tile, letting the water sluice over his battered body. "What if telling them changes nothing?" he murmured. "What if I've only given them a burden they can't possibly shoulder?"

The water began to cool, jolting Drake from his introspection. He shut it off, the sudden silence deafening. As he reached for a towel, his gaze fell once more on his burned arms – angry, red, a physical manifestation of his failures.

"One step at a time," Drake told himself, wrapping the towel around his waist. "Figure out what's different. Find the disfigured man. Break the cycle."

But as he stared at his reflection, Drake couldn't shake the nagging feeling that he was missing something crucial – a piece of the puzzle that had been right in front of him all along.

37 - 38

Steam billowed out as Drake opened the bathroom door, his skin still flushed from the shower's heat. Linda stood waiting, her blonde hair tucked behind her ears, a first aid kit clutched in her hands. Her blue eyes, usually bright with warmth, now held a shadow of concern that made Drake's chest tighten.

"Let me take care of those burns," Linda said softly, gesturing to his arms.

Drake nodded, sinking onto the edge of the bed. As Linda began to carefully wrap his arms in gauze, he found himself studying her face, searching for any sign that she truly believed his impossible story. Her touch was gentle, almost tentative, as if she feared he might shatter beneath her fingers.

"You're still going to work?" she asked, her voice barely above a whisper as she fastened the bandages.

Drake swallowed hard, his mind racing. Should he stay? Try a different approach? But no, he had to see if anything had changed, if his confession had altered the course of events.

"Yeah," he replied, his voice rougher than he intended. "I need to see if there's anything I can do differently." He paused, the weight of responsibility settling heavily on his shoulders. "But I want you both to stay home. Don't go anywhere. Stay safe."

Linda's hands stilled, her eyes meeting his. "Drake," she began, hesitation clear in her tone, "I know you believe what you told us, but-"

"Please," Drake interrupted, reaching out to clasp her hands in his. "I know it sounds crazy. I know you probably think I've lost my mind. But I can't... I can't lose you again. Either of you. Just promise me you'll stay here today."

He searched her face, desperate for understanding, for belief. Linda's expression softened, a mix of love and worry etched in the lines around her eyes.

"Okay," she said finally, squeezing his hands. "We'll stay. But promise me you'll be careful out there."

Drake nodded, relief washing over him. As he stood to get dressed, a thought nagged at him: What if keeping them home wasn't enough? What if the danger found its way to them regardless? He pushed the fear aside, focusing instead on the task ahead. One step at a time, he reminded himself. Find what's different. Break the cycle. Save them all.

39 - 40

Linda's words hung in the air, the uncertainty in her voice a stark reminder of the fragility of their situation. Drake nodded; his throat tight with unspoken fears. He turned away, unable to meet her gaze any longer, and headed upstairs to change.

In the bedroom, Drake reached for his suit, the familiar fabric a stark contrast to the chaos swirling in his mind. As he dressed, his fingers moved with practiced precision, tucking his tie into place with a perfection born of habit. Each motion felt charged with significance, as if this simple act of normalcy could somehow anchor him in the tumultuous sea of repeated days.

Descending the stairs, Drake's heart clenched at the sight of Harrison waiting at the bottom. His son's face was a mixture of concern and something else—a glimmer of hope, perhaps, or the last vestiges of childlike faith in his father's ability to fix anything.

Harrison raised his hand, giving Drake a hesitant thumbs-up. "Good luck, Dad," he said, his voice wavering slightly. "Try not to... you know, reset the day again or whatever."

The casual way Harrison referenced the impossible situation they found themselves in sent a jolt through Drake. He forced a smile, though it felt more like a grimace. "I'll do my best, kiddo," he replied, his voice rougher than he intended.

As he stood there, looking at his son, Drake's mind raced. How many times had he said goodbye like this, only to wake up and do it all over again? How many times had he failed to protect them? The weight of countless repeated tragedies pressed down on him, threatening to crush his resolve.

But he couldn't falter. Not now. Not when they finally knew the truth.

"Harrison," Drake began, struggling to find the right words. "I know this is all... a lot. But I need you to trust me. To believe me. Can you do that?"

41 - 42

Harrison chuckled dryly, the sound hollow in his throat. "I'll do my best," he repeated, more to himself than to his father. The words felt like ash on his tongue, a promise he'd made and will break.

Drake turned to Linda, her blue eyes filled with a mixture of concern and love that made his chest ache. Drake leaned in, pressing a gentle kiss to her cheek. The familiar scent of her lavender shampoo enveloped him, a bittersweet reminder of the normalcy they'd lost.

"Be safe," Linda whispered, her hand lingering on his arm. "We'll be here when you get back."

Drake nodded, unable to voice the fear that gripped him—the possibility that he might not return, that this cycle could end in tragedy once more.

Turning to Harrison, he ruffled the boy's unruly hair, a gesture that felt both comforting and painfully inadequate. "Keep an eye on your mom for me, okay?" Drake said, forcing a smile.

As he stepped out the door, the weight of responsibility settled heavily on Drake's shoulders. The crisp morning air filled his lungs, carrying with it the scent of freshly cut grass and possibility. He walked to his car, each step deliberate, his mind churning with potential scenarios and outcomes.

"What if..." Drake muttered to himself, unlocking the car door. "What if I took a different route to work? Or called in sick?" The possibilities seemed endless, yet each one carried the risk of failure, of losing everything all over again.

He slid into the driver's seat, his hands gripping the steering wheel tightly. The leather creaked under his fingers, grounding him in the present moment. As he started the engine, Drake cast one last glance at the house—at the life he was desperately trying to save.

"This time," he whispered, determination hardening his resolve, "this time, I'll find a way to keep them safe."

43 - 43

Drake eased the car out of the driveway, his eyes scanning the familiar neighborhood with newfound intensity. Every detail—the swaying branches of the old oak tree, the jogger rounding the corner, the stray cat slinking across the road—seemed loaded with potential significance.

"It's all connected," he murmured, his brow furrowing. "But how?"

As he navigated the morning traffic, Drake's mind raced through the events of previous cycles. The burns on his arms throbbed, a visceral reminder of his failures. He flexed his fingers on the steering wheel, wincing at the pain.

"There has to be something I'm missing," he thought, frustration mounting. "A clue, a pattern, anything."

At a red light, Drake closed his eyes briefly, trying to center himself. When he opened them, he caught sight of a newspaper stand on the corner. The headline screamed about a local amusement park closing down.

"The amusement park," he whispered, a spark of recognition igniting. "It was there in one of the cycles. Or was it the other realities? But what happened?"

As the light turned green, Drake made an impulsive decision. Instead of heading to his law office, he steered the car towards the industrial district.

"I'm sorry, Linda," he said aloud, as if she could hear him. "I know I promised to go to work, but this might be the key."

The car wound through increasingly desolate streets, factories looming on either side like silent sentinels. Drake's heart raced as he approached the shuttered gate to the park he recognized from his fragmented memories.

Pulling into the empty parking lot, he killed the engine and sat for a moment, staring at the dilapidated structure. "What am I even looking for?" he wondered aloud, doubt creeping in.

But as he stepped out of the car, a figure caught his eye—a man limping through the open gate, his face obscured by a heavy hood.

Drake's breath caught in his throat. "It's him," he realized, his pulse quickening. "The disfigured man."

Without hesitation, Drake broke into a run, determined to confront the figure that had haunted his nightmares and his waking hours. This time, he vowed silently, this time he would get answers.

The Green Dragon

1 ⁻² The sun hung high over the abandoned amusement park, the parks structures casting eerie shadows across the cracked asphalt. A faint wind whistled through the empty fairgrounds, carrying with it the metallic creak of a carousel that swayed slowly in the breeze. Drake's footsteps crunched against the cracked pavement; his eyes locked on the disfigured man in the distance.

Drake's heart pounded as he pursued the figure through the derelict park. Each step felt heavy with the weight of his past mistakes, the guilt that had driven him to this moment. The wind whipped his disheveled hair, a physical reminder of the restless nights that had led him here.

"Is this what it's come to?" Drake muttered to himself; his voice barely audible over the whistling breeze. "Chasing ghosts through abandoned relics?"

He paused, scanning the eerie landscape. The looming silhouettes of defunct roller coasters stretched toward the sky like skeletal fingers, a stark reminder of happier times long past. Drake couldn't shake the feeling that he'd been here before, in another life, another reality.

His eyes narrowed as he caught a flicker of movement near a dilapidated ticket booth. "I know you're there," he called out, his voice echoing in the emptiness. "No more games. It's time we talked."

Silence answered him, broken only by the persistent creaking of the carousel. Drake's jaw clenched, frustration building within him. He took a deep breath, trying to center himself.

"What am I doing here?" he wondered aloud, running a hand through his hair. "Am I chasing answers or just running from the truth?"

The question hung in the air, unanswered. Drake's mind raced, grappling with the surreal nature of his reality. Was this all just an illusion? A test? Or something far more sinister?

He pressed forward, each step a conscious choice to confront the specter of his former self. The crunch of gravel under his feet seemed to echo the fractures in his own psyche.

"I won't let you win," Drake declared to the shadows, his voice carrying the weight of his determination. "Whatever game you're playing, whatever reality this is, I'll find a way to save them. To save everyone."

As he moved deeper into the park, the sunlight caught the edge of something metallic near an overturned garbage can. Drake approached cautiously, his heart rate quickening. He reached down, fingers closing around a cold, familiar object.

His old watch. The one he'd been wearing the night of the accident.

Drake's breath caught in his throat as he turned the timepiece over in his hands. "How is this possible?" he whispered, his voice trembling.

The watch's face was cracked, its hands frozen at 11:59. One minute to midnight. One minute before everything had changed.

Drake looked up, scanning the shadows with renewed intensity. "Is this what you wanted me to find?" he called out, his voice echoing across the abandoned park. "What does it mean?"

Only the wind answered, whistling through the empty rides like a mournful song. Drake clutched the watch tightly, its weight a tangible link to his past, to the mistakes that had led him here.

"I'll figure this out," he promised himself, his voice low and determined. "For my family. For everyone I've lost. I'll make it right."

With renewed purpose, Drake pocketed the watch and pressed on into the heart of the abandoned amusement park, chasing answers that seemed to dance just beyond his reach.

3 - 4

The man's white robe, tattered and singed, glowed faintly under the moonlight. The green dragon emblem on his chest seemed almost alive, twisting in the dim light as he moved deeper into the park. Drake's eyes narrowed, focusing on the intricate design that seemed to ripple with each step the disfigured man took.

A memory flashed through Drake's mind—a similar emblem, etched into the leather-bound cover of an ancient tome he'd once held. The connection sent a chill down his spine, and he felt the weight of his past decisions pressing down on him.

"Hey!" Drake called, his voice echoing in the stillness. The word hung in the air, charged with desperation and a hint of fear. He swallowed hard, his throat dry from the dust and decay that permeated the abandoned park.

As the sound of his voice faded, Drake's thoughts raced. What if this man held the key to saving his family? To breaking the cycle of death that haunted him. The possibility both thrilled and terrified him.

"I need answers," Drake muttered to himself, clenching his fists. "I can't let him slip away. Not again."

He took a step forward, the crunch of gravel under his feet seeming unnaturally loud in the eerie quiet. The disfigured man continued his steady pace, moving with an unsettling grace that belied his twisted appearance.

Drake's heart pounded in his chest; each beat a reminder of the urgency that drove him. He couldn't shake the feeling that time was running out—for him, for his family, for everything he held dear.

"Wait!" he shouted, his voice cracking with emotion. "Please, I just want to talk!"

5 - 6

The disfigured man paused, his silhouette stark against the cloudy sky. For a fleeting moment, Drake's breath caught in his throat, hope surging through him. But as quickly as it had come, the moment passed. The figure turned slightly, just enough for Drake to catch a glimpse of his scarred profile, before slipping around the corner of a battered ticket booth.

"No," Drake whispered, his voice barely audible. "Not this time."

He broke into a jog, his footsteps echoing off the decrepit structures surrounding him. The cool air stung his lungs as he ran, but he pushed through the discomfort. His heart pounded, not just from exertion, but from the weight of everything at stake.

As he ran, memories flashed through his mind— he recounted time spent in therapy sessions after the car accident, the warmth of his Harrisons and Lindas embrace, the sound of metal tearing as the car rolled down over an embankment. Then, darker images: their lifeless bodies, the cycle of death repeating endlessly. The juxtaposition tore at his soul, fueling his determination.

"I won't let you take them again," Drake growled, his words lost in the wind. He rounded the corner, scanning the shadows for any sign of movement. "I deserve answers. They deserve a chance."

The cycle of death, the fractured memories, the sense of a world askew—it all led to this enigmatic figure. Drake knew, with a certainty that ran bone-deep, that this man held the key to unraveling the mystery that had consumed his life.

"Who are you?" he called out, his voice echoing in the empty park. "What do you know about what's happening to me... to my family?"

7 - 8

Drake's pace quickened, his eyes darting from shadow to shadow, searching for any sign of the disfigured man. The abandoned amusement park seemed to close in around him, its once-cheerful attractions now twisted into grotesque mockeries of themselves in the moonlight.

Suddenly, a sharp vibration against his thigh jarred Drake from his focused pursuit. His phone buzzed insistently in his pocket, the sensation feeling alien and intrusive in this otherworldly setting.

"Damn it," Drake muttered, his stride faltering. He considered ignoring it, his hand hovering over his pocket. The weight of his quest pressed down on him, urging him forward. But what if it was Linda? What if something had happened?

Not now, he thought, gritting his teeth. The timing couldn't be worse, but the nagging possibility that his family needed him gnawed at his resolve.

Drake's fingers twitched, caught between the urge to answer and the desperate need to continue his chase. The phone buzzed again, more insistent this time, as if sensing his indecision.

"I can't lose him," Drake whispered, his voice hoarse with frustration. "But I can't lose them either."

The conflict tore at him, each second of hesitation potentially widening the gap between him and the answers he sought. Yet the thought of missing a crucial call, of failing his family once again, was equally unbearable.

Drake's pace slowed to a walk, his breath coming in ragged gasps as he wrestled with the decision. The phone fell silent, leaving him in the eerie quiet of the abandoned park, the weight of his choice hanging heavy in the air.

9 - 10

The silence was fleeting. The phone erupted again, vibrating against Drake's thigh with renewed vigor. A string of profanities escaped his lips, echoing in the desolate amusement park. With a swift, agitated motion, he plunged his hand into his pocket and withdrew the device.

The screen illuminated his face in the dim light, casting harsh shadows across his furrowed brow. Richard Vega's name glared back at him, a harbinger of unwelcome interruption.

Drake's thumb hovered over the screen, his mind racing. Why was Richard calling now? Was it about work, or something more sinister? The memory of Richard's betrayal in another reality flashed through his mind, igniting a spark of suspicion.

"I don't have time for this," Drake muttered, his voice tight with frustration. But even as he considered rejecting the call, a nagging doubt crept in. What if Richard knew something? What if this call held a crucial piece of the puzzle?

The phone continued its relentless buzzing, each vibration sending a jolt of urgency through Drake's arm. He closed his eyes briefly, torn between the pursuit of the disfigured man and the potential information Richard might possess.

"Damn you, Vega," Drake growled, his finger poised over the answer button. "This better be worth it."

11 - 12

Drake's jaw clenched as he made his decision. With a swift motion, he silenced the call and shoved the phone deep into his pocket. The weight of it felt like an anchor, pulling him back to a world he was desperately trying to escape. But he couldn't afford distractions, not now.

His feet pounded against the cracked pavement as he quickened his pace, each step echoing in the eerie stillness of the abandoned park. The cool autumn air bit at his skin, his breath forming misty clouds that dissipated as quickly as they appeared. Drake's heart raced, not just from exertion, but from the growing sense of urgency that threatened to overwhelm him.

"I can't lose him," Drake muttered to himself, his voice barely above a whisper. "Not when I'm this close."

He rounded the corner, his eyes darting frantically from shadow to shadow, searching for any sign of movement. But as he scanned the area, the bitter realization set in. The fairground stretched out before him, empty and lifeless.

The disfigured man was gone.

Drake's fists clenched at his sides, frustration and despair washing over him in equal measure. "No," he breathed, his voice cracking. "No, no, no!"

He spun in a circle, desperately hoping to catch a glimpse of the white robe, the twisted face, anything. But there was nothing. Just the wind whistling through the decaying rides and the distant creaking of rusted metal.

"Where are you?" Drake shouted into the void, his voice echoing off the abandoned structures. "You can't just disappear! I need answers!"

As the echo of his voice faded, the weight of his failure settled on his shoulders. He had been so close, mere steps away from unraveling the mystery that had consumed his life. And now, in the blink of an eye, it had slipped through his fingers.

Drake sank to his knees, the rough pavement digging into his skin. He buried his face in his hands, his mind racing. "What am I missing?" he murmured, his voice muffled. "What am I not seeing?"

The cool air swirled around him, carrying with it the faint scent of decay and forgotten dreams. In that moment, surrounded by the remnants of joy and laughter long past, Drake felt more alone than ever before.

13 - 14

The sudden vibration against his thigh jarred Drake from his spiraling thoughts. His phone buzzed insistently; the sound amplified in the eerie stillness of the abandoned park. For a moment, he considered ignoring it again, unwilling to break his tenuous connection to this place, to the answers that seemed to hover just out of reach.

But as the device continued its relentless demand for attention, Drake's resolve crumbled. With a heavy sigh, he reached into his pocket and withdrew the phone, its screen illuminating his face with a harsh, blue glow. Richard Vega's name flashed across the display, a reminder of the life he was supposed to be living, the responsibilities he was neglecting.

Drake's jaw tightened, muscles working beneath his skin as he fought against the urge to hurl the phone into the darkness. Instead, he took a deep breath, steeling himself for the conversation to come. His thumb hovered over the screen for a heartbeat before he finally answered, his voice rough with frustration and barely contained anger.

"What is it, Richard?"

As he awaited Vega's response, Drake's eyes scanned the shadowy landscape around him, part of him still hoping to catch a glimpse of the elusive figure in white. His free hand clenched and unclenched at his side, a physical manifestation of the tension coiling within him.

How could he explain this to Richard? How could he make his colleague understand that the world they knew, the reality they took for granted, was nothing but an illusion? The weight of his knowledge, of the responsibility thrust upon him, felt crushing in that moment. Drake closed his eyes, bracing himself for the mundane concerns that Richard was about to voice, all while the fate of existence itself hung in the balance.

15 - 16

"Finally," Vega said, his tone clipped. "Where the hell are you, Drake? We're supposed to be preparing for the Parker deposition today. You've been dodging my calls all morning."

The words sliced through the eerie silence of the abandoned amusement park; a jarring reminder of the life Drake was supposed to be living. He felt the weight of his dual existence pressing down on him, threatening to crush him beneath its impossible burden.

"I'm home sick," Drake lied, his eyes scanning the darkened booths and decaying rides around him. The rusted metal gleamed dully in the sunlight, a graveyard of forgotten joy. He swallowed hard, tasting the bitterness of the falsehood on his tongue.

As he spoke, Drake's gaze lingered on a tattered banner fluttering in the night breeze. The faded image of a grinning clown seemed to mock him, its painted smile a stark contrast to the desolation surrounding it. He wondered, not for the first time, how he could bridge the gap between these two realities – the mundane world of legal depositions and the terrifying truth of his mission.

"Sick?" Richard's voice dripped with skepticism. "You sound fine to me, Miller."

Drake closed his eyes, pinching the bridge of his nose. The temptation to confide in Richard, to unburden himself of this crushing secret, was almost overwhelming. But he knew the consequences of such an action could be catastrophic.

"It's just a migraine," he muttered, the lie feeling hollow even to his own ears. "I'll be back on my feet tomorrow, I promise."

As he spoke, Drake's free hand traced the outline of the metal rod in his pocket, a tangible reminder of the danger that lurked in the shadows. The weight of it grounded him, anchoring him to this surreal moment caught between worlds.

17 - 18

Richard's sharp intake of breath crackled through the phone line. "Home sick?" Vega's voice was sharp with disbelief. "Drake, you've been missing too much time lately. Your cases are slipping. If you don't get your act together, the partners are going to notice."

The words struck Drake like a physical blow. He gritted his teeth, clenching his free hand into a fist so tight he could feel his nails digging into his palm. The pain was a welcome distraction from the maelstrom of emotions threatening to overwhelm him.

How could he explain that the fate of his family – of the entire world – hung in the balance? That every moment spent on legal minutiae felt like a betrayal of his true purpose?

"I'll be fine," Drake managed, his voice strained. He watched his breath form small clouds in the cool september air, dissipating like the fragments of his former life. "Look, let's meet later. I'll fill you in over dinner."

As he spoke, Drake's eyes darted to a nearby carousel. Its once-vibrant horses now stood frozen in eternal stillness, their painted eyes seeming to follow him accusingly. He wondered if, like these abandoned rides, he too was trapped in an endless, futile cycle.

The silence on the other end of the line stretched on, heavy with unspoken tension. Drake could almost see Richard's furrowed brow, the way his former colleague would be pacing in his office, tie loosened in frustration.

"Dinner," Drake repeated, desperation creeping into his voice. He needed this connection to his old life, this tenuous thread of normalcy. Even as he spoke, he knew it was a selfish request, pulling Richard into a world he couldn't possibly understand.

19 - 20

"Dinner?" Vega's voice dripped with incredulity, cutting through the eerie silence of the abandoned park. "You're blowing off work, but you want to meet for seafood? You've got a strange way of handling stress, Miller."

Drake's jaw clenched, his free hand curling into a tight fist. The absurdity of the situation wasn't lost on him – here he stood, surrounded by the decaying remnants of joy, chasing ghosts and impossible truths, while his old life crumbled around him. He could almost taste the salt of the sea on his tongue, a phantom reminder of simpler times when dinner with a colleague was just that – dinner.

His eyes traced the silhouette of the defunct roller coaster looming against the night sky, its skeletal frame a stark reminder of how quickly things could fall apart. How many lives had been lived and lost in the endless cycles he was trapped in? The weight of it all pressed down on him, threatening to crush what little resolve he had left.

"Are you coming or not?" Drake snapped, his patience wearing thin. The words came out harsher than he intended, laced with desperation he couldn't quite mask. He needed this connection to his old life, this fleeting moment of normalcy, even as he knew it was a selfish indulgence.

As he waited for Vega's response, Drake's mind raced with the implications of his request. How could he possibly explain the inexplicable? The disfigured man, the cycles of death, the memories that haunted him – they would sound like the ravings of a madman to anyone else. Yet, he yearned for someone, anyone, to understand the burden he carried.

21 - 22

There was a pause on the other end of the line, heavy with unspoken tension. Drake's heart thudded in his chest; each beat a reminder of the precious seconds ticking away. Finally, Vega's voice crackled through the phone, tinged with resignation.

"Fine. I'll meet you at The Lighthouse tonight. Eight sharp. But you better have something worth discussing, because this is getting old."

Relief washed over Drake, mingling with a swell of guilt. He was dragging Vega into a world he couldn't possibly understand, risking not just their professional relationship but potentially Vega's safety. Yet, the selfish part of him clung to this lifeline, this last thread connecting him to a life that felt increasingly distant.

"See you then," Drake said curtly, ending the call before he could second-guess himself.

As he lowered the phone, the weight of his decision settled over him like a shroud. The abandoned amusement park seemed to close in around him, its empty attractions mocking the emptiness he felt inside. He ran a hand through his disheveled hair, his mind already racing ahead to the impending meeting.

What could he possibly say to Vega? How could he convey the urgency of his situation without sounding completely unhinged? The truth was a burden he longed to share yet feared to voice aloud. As he stood there, surrounded by the remnants of forgotten joy, Drake couldn't shake the feeling that he was running out of time – not just for himself, but for everyone he held dear.

23 - 24

Drake slid the phone back into his pocket, his fingers lingering on the cool metal as if reluctant to break this final connection to normalcy. He exhaled slowly, the sound mingling with the eerie creaks and groans of the decaying park around him. The distraction of Vega's call had momentarily pulled him from his purpose, but now the weight of his mission settled back onto his shoulders with crushing force.

"Focus," he muttered to himself, his voice barely audible over the whisper of wind through rusted rides. "Linda, Harrison... they're counting on me."

His eyes scanned the darkened landscape, searching for any sign of the disfigured man's white robe or the telltale green dragon emblem. The hunt wasn't over - it couldn't be. Every second that ticked by was another moment his family remained in danger, trapped in a cycle he barely understood.

As Drake's gaze swept across the abandoned fairgrounds, it caught on a structure looming in the distance. The Funhouse. Even from here, its dilapidated form seemed to beckon to him, promising answers and secrets within its twisted corridors.

"Why there?" Drake wondered aloud, his brow furrowing. "What are you trying to tell me, you bastard?"

He took a tentative step forward, then another, drawn inexorably towards the Funhouse. With each step, a nagging sense of familiarity grew in the back of his mind, like an itch he couldn't quite scratch.

"I've been here before," he realized, the words catching in his throat. "But when? How?"

The questions swirled in his mind, mixing with the ever-present fear for his family's safety. As he approached the Funhouse, Drake couldn't shake the feeling that he was walking into a trap - but also that he had no choice but to spring it.

25 - 26

Drake's pace slowed as he neared the Funhouse, its decrepit facade looming before him like a specter from a forgotten nightmare. What had once been a vibrant attraction now stood as a monument to decay, its once-cheerful colors faded to ghostly echoes of their former vibrancy. Peeling paint flaked off in the gentle afternoon breeze, scattering remnants of lost laughter across the cracked pavement.

"Christ," Drake muttered, his eyes trailing upward. "What the hell happened to this place?"

Above the entrance, a massive green dragon statue perched precariously, its jaws frozen in an eternal roar. The beast's eyes, though dulled by time and neglect, seemed to follow Drake's every move. He couldn't shake the unsettling feeling that the statue was more than just weathered fiberglass and paint.

"Is this where you're hiding, asshole?" Drake called out, his voice echoing hollowly across the empty park. "Or is this just another one of your sick games?"

The dragon offered no response, its stone gaze as inscrutable as ever. Drake took another step forward, then froze. Something about the sight before him sent a jolt of recognition through his body, stopping him dead in his tracks.

"I know this place," he whispered, a cold sweat breaking out across his forehead. "But how? When?"

Fragments of memory danced at the edges of his consciousness, tantalizingly close yet frustratingly out of reach. Drake closed his eyes, willing the pieces to fall into place, but they remained stubbornly scattered.

"Dammit!" he hissed, slamming his fist against his thigh in frustration. "What aren't you telling me, Drake? What can't you remember?"

The Funhouse loomed before him, a silent sentinel holding the keys to a past he couldn't recall. Drake knew that stepping inside might bring him closer to the truth – or closer to his doom. But with his family's lives hanging in the balance, what choice did he really have?

27 - 28

Drake's eyes fixed on the dragon statue, its emerald scales catching the moonlight. The realization hit him like a physical blow.

"The robe," he muttered, his voice hoarse. "It's the same symbol."

The green dragon emblem that had adorned the disfigured man's chest now stared back at him, larger than life and impossibly familiar. Drake's heart raced as he tried to piece together the connection.

Suddenly, the world around him shifted. The decrepit funhouse facade melted away, replaced by a vibrant, pulsing version of itself. Neon lights danced across polished mirrors, and the air thrummed with the excited chatter of long-gone patrons.

"What the hell?" Drake whispered; his eyes wide with disbelief.

He found himself moving through the funhouse, but not of his own volition. It was as if he were watching a movie played out through his own eyes. The kaleidoscope of lights reflected off the mirrors, creating a dizzying array of colors and shapes.

Then, the sound of footsteps behind him. Heavy, purposeful, closing in fast.

Drake's heart pounded in his chest, a primal fear gripping him. He wanted to turn, to face whatever was coming, but his body wouldn't respond.

The sickening crack of a gunshot shattered the carnival atmosphere. Pain exploded in Drake's hip, white-hot and all-consuming. He gasped, the taste of copper filling his mouth as he collapsed to the ground.

"No," Drake choked out, snapping back to the present. He stumbled backward, his hand instinctively clutching at his side where phantom pain still lingered. "What was that? A memory? Or something else?"

The questions swirled in his mind; each one leading to a dozen more. But one thing was clear – the answers he sought lay within the twisted confines of the funhouse before him.

29 - 30

Drake gasped, his hand flying to his side as the vivid memory faded. The phantom pain lingered, a ghostly echo of the gunshot that had torn through him in that haunting vision. His breath came in ragged pants, visible in the cool air.

"I've been here before," he muttered, his voice barely audible over the wind's mournful whistle. The realization settled over him like a heavy shroud, bringing with it a surge of conflicting emotions.

Drake's eyes darted around the dilapidated funhouse entrance, searching for something—anything—familiar beyond the unsettling déjà vu. The peeling paint, the rusted metal, the shattered windows – they all seemed to mock him with their decay, hiding the vibrant past he'd glimpsed in his vision.

"But how?" he wondered aloud, his brow furrowing. "I don't remember ever coming to this place, and yet..."

He trailed off, the unfinished thought hanging in the air. Drake's hand absently traced the spot where he'd felt the imaginary bullet's impact. There was no wound, no scar, but the memory of pain felt as real as the chill seeping into his bones.

"Is this what he meant?" Drake mused, thinking back to the disfigured man's cryptic words. "The mistake I made, the loop I need to break – is it all connected to this place?"

The wind picked up, carrying with it the faint echo of carnival music. Drake tensed, unsure if it was real or just another trick of his increasingly unreliable mind. He took a hesitant step towards the funhouse entrance; drawn by an inexorable pull he couldn't explain.

"I need answers," he said firmly, steeling himself against the fear threatening to paralyze him. "And if they're in there, then that's where I have to go."

With one last deep breath, Drake squared his shoulders and prepared to enter the funhouse, determined to unravel the mystery that seemed to hold his fate—and his family's—in its twisted grasp.

31 - 32

Drake's fingers closed around the rusted metal rod, its cold weight a stark reminder of the danger he faced. He hefted it, testing its balance, a grim smile tugging at the corners of his mouth. "Not exactly my usual courtroom weapon," he muttered, "but it'll have to do."

With measured steps, Drake crossed the threshold into the funhouse. The change in atmosphere was immediate and oppressive. The musty air clung to his skin, carrying with it the acrid scent of decay and lost memories. His eyes strained to adjust to the dim interior, the shadows seeming to writhe and dance in his peripheral vision.

"Christ," Drake whispered, his voice unnaturally loud in the stillness. He flinched at the sound, his grip on the rod tightening reflexively.

His footsteps echoed with an eerie resonance; each step amplified as if the funhouse itself were mocking his intrusion. Drake's gaze darted from mirror to mirror, their tarnished surfaces offering distorted reflections of a man he barely recognized.

Is this what I've become? he wondered, studying the haggard face that stared back at him. The successful lawyer was gone, replaced by a man haunted by secrets he couldn't remember and burdened by a mission he didn't understand.

"Focus, Drake," he chided himself aloud, the sound of his own voice oddly comforting in the oppressive silence. "The answers are here. They have to be."

As he ventured deeper into the labyrinth of mirrors, Drake couldn't shake the feeling that he was being watched. Every reflection seemed to hold a secret; every shadow concealed a potential threat. The weight of his family's fate pressed down on him, spurring him forward despite the growing dread in the pit of his stomach.

"I won't let you down," he vowed, his words barely more than a whisper. "Not again. Whatever it takes, I'll break this cycle. I'll save you all."

33 - 34

Drake's jaw clenched, his resolve hardening as he stared into the endless reflections surrounding him. The funhouse seemed to stretch on infinitely, a twisted maze of his own fractured psyche.

"Alright," Drake called into the darkness, his voice steady despite the tremor in his hands. "I'm here. Let's talk."

The words hung in the air for a moment before bouncing back to him in distorted fragments, each echo warping his voice until it was unrecognizable. Drake shivered, the sound of his own distorted voice unsettling him more than he cared to admit.

Is this what it feels like to lose yourself? he wondered, his eyes scanning the shadows for any sign of movement. The thought sent a chill down his spine, reminding him of the stakes at hand.

"I know you're here," Drake continued, forcing confidence into his tone. "You wanted me to follow you. Well, here I am. No more games."

As he spoke, Drake's mind raced, grappling with the weight of his situation. His family's lives hung in the balance; their fates intertwined with a cosmic mistake he couldn't even remember making. The irony wasn't lost on him – a lawyer who had built his career on facts and evidence, now chasing ghosts and battling unseen forces.

"I need answers," he said, his voice dropping to a near-whisper. "My family... they don't deserve this. Whatever I did, whatever mistake I made, let me fix it. Just... just tell me how."

The silence that followed was deafening, broken only by the sound of Drake's ragged breathing. He waited, every muscle tense, for a response that didn't come.

35 - 36

The silence stretched on, oppressive and thick, until Drake's own words began to mock him, echoing back in a distorted chorus.

"Let's talk... let's talk... let's..."

His fragmented voice bounced off the warped mirrors, creating a disorienting cacophony that made Drake's head spin. He squeezed his eyes shut, trying to center himself, but the echoes seemed to seep into his very bones.

Just as the echoes began to fade, a low chuckle cut through the silence, chilling and guttural. It reverberated through the funhouse, seeming to come from everywhere and nowhere at once.

"Still chasing answers, Drake? You're more stubborn than I gave you credit for."

Drake's heart raced, a mix of fear and determination coursing through his veins. He clenched his fists, willing his voice to remain steady as he responded.

"Stubbornness is all I have left," he said, his words laced with a bitter resolve. "When the world stops making sense, when everything you love is at stake, what else is there?"

As he spoke, Drake's mind whirled with possibilities. Was this mysterious figure the key to unraveling the cosmic mistake he'd made? Or just another dead end in an increasingly maddening maze?

"You know what I did," Drake continued, his voice dropping to a near-whisper. "You know how to fix this. My family's lives are on the line. If there's any humanity left in you, help me save them."

37 - 38

Drake's knuckles turned white as he tightened his grip on the metal rod, the cool rust biting into his palm. His heart thundered in his chest; each beat a reminder of the precious seconds ticking away. The funhouse's oppressive silence seemed to close in around him, broken only by his ragged breathing.

"Show yourself!" Drake demanded, his voice echoing off the distorted mirrors. The desperation in his tone betrayed the façade of control he desperately tried to maintain.

For a moment, only silence answered him. Then, the chuckle returned, growing louder, morphing into a bone-chilling cackle that seemed to emanate from the very walls themselves.

"Why would I make it that easy?" the disembodied voice taunted, its amusement palpable. "Where's the fun in that?"

Drake's jaw clenched, frustration and fear warring within him. He thought of his family, of the countless iterations of their deaths he'd witnessed. The weight of his unknown mistake pressed down on him, threatening to crush what little resolve he had left.

'I can't fail them again,' he thought, his grip on the rod tightening further. 'Not this time. Not ever again.'

39 - 40

Drake turned the corner, his breath catching in his throat as he faced a corridor lined with mirrors. His reflection multiplied endlessly, each version of himself distorted by the imperfections in the glass. The sight was disorienting, unsettling. In every warped image, Drake saw the toll of his journey etched into his features—the desperation in his eyes, the tight set of his jaw, the weight of guilt bowing his shoulders.

'Is this how the universe sees me?' he wondered, a cold dread settling in his stomach. 'Fractured, flawed, endlessly repeating my mistakes?'

His gaze darted from mirror to mirror, searching for any sign of the disfigured man among the sea of his own twisted reflections. The metal rod felt heavier in his hand, a useless anchor in this maze of illusions.

"You think breaking the glass will help you?" The disfigured man's voice echoed from everywhere and nowhere, each syllable dripping with mockery. "As if shattering these mirrors could shatter the reality you've created."

Drake's fingers twitched around the rod. "This isn't about breaking things," he retorted, his voice low and strained. "It's about fixing what I've done. Tell me how to save them. Please."

A mirthless laugh reverberated through the corridor. "Always the noble hero, aren't you, Drake? Even when you don't remember why."

Drake closed his eyes, fighting against the surge of frustration. When he opened them, he locked gazes with one of his reflections—the only one that seemed clear, undistorted. "I may not remember everything," he said, addressing both the reflection and the hidden figure, "but I know who I am. I know what matters. My family needs me, and I won't let them down again."

41 - 42

With a guttural cry, Drake swung the rod at the nearest mirror, unleashing a cacophony of shattering glass. Jagged shards rained down, reflecting fractured light across the darkened funhouse corridor. The impact reverberated through his arms, a physical manifestation of his inner turmoil.

"Is this what you want?" Drake shouted; his voice raw with desperation. He pivoted, bringing the rod down on another mirror. The crash echoed his frustration, each broken reflection a testament to his fractured reality. "You can't hide forever!"

As he turned to the next mirror, Drake caught a glimpse of his own face—haggard, eyes wild with a mix of determination and fear. 'What am I becoming?' he thought, hesitating for a split second before smashing through the glass barrier.

"Where are you?" he yelled, his voice hoarse from exertion and emotion. The words bounced off the remaining mirrors, a chorus of his own desperation. "Face me! If you know so much about my mistakes, then help me fix them!"

Drake's breaths came in ragged gasps as he surveyed the destruction around him. Shattered glass crunched beneath his feet, a grim reminder of the path he'd chosen. 'Is this how I save them?' he wondered, doubt creeping into his mind. 'By destroying everything in my way?'

43 - 44

Drake's heart pounded as he scanned the remaining mirrors, his eyes darting from one reflective surface to another. Suddenly, a flicker of movement caught his attention. In the cracked glass, a distorted image appeared—evil's burned visage, his scarred lips curled into a sneer. Drake lunged forward, but the image vanished as quickly as it had appeared.

"What the—" Drake muttered, spinning around. In another mirror, the burned mans face materialized, his eyes gleaming with malevolent amusement. Drake reached out, his fingers brushing against cold glass before the apparition disappeared once more.

"Stop playing games!" Drake shouted, his voice echoing through the funhouse. He clenched his fists, frustration building within him. 'Is this real, or am I losing my mind?'

The mans chilling laughter filled the air, seeming to come from everywhere at once. "You're wasting your time," he said, his voice dripping with amusement. "Breaking mirrors won't bring you any closer to the truth, Drake."

Drake's jaw tightened, his eyes scanning the room frantically. "Then tell me the truth! What mistake did I make? How do I fix this?"

"Oh, Drake," the disfigured man's voice taunted, "if only it were that simple. But where's the fun in spoon-feeding you answers?"

'He's toying with me,' Drake realized, a cold dread settling in his stomach. 'But I can't give up. My family's lives depend on this.'

"I won't stop," Drake declared, his voice low and determined. "No matter how many mirrors I have to break, no matter how long it takes, I'll figure this out."

Evils laughter echoed once more, fading into an eerie silence that left Drake alone with his thoughts and the shattered remnants of his reflection.

45 - 46

Drake's heart pounded in his chest as he gripped the metal rod tighter, his knuckles turning white. The funhouse's distorted mirrors reflected a kaleidoscope of his determined face, each fractured image a reminder of the fragmented reality he now inhabited. With a guttural cry, he swung the rod at another mirror, the sound of shattering glass piercing the air.

"Enough games!" Drake shouted; his voice hoarse with desperation. "Face me, you coward!"

As if in answer to his challenge, Drake's next swing connected with something solid. Time seemed to slow as he found himself staring into the burned, twisted visage of the disfigured man. His charred lips curled into a sneer, his grip on the rod unbreakable.

"Still so angry, Drake," he taunted, his voice a raspy whisper. "Always lashing out, never stopping to think."

With a sudden jerk, the man wrenched the rod from Drake's hands. The metallic clang of the weapon hitting the floor echoed through the funhouse, a stark counterpoint to Drake's ragged breathing.

Drake stumbled backward, his mind reeling. 'This is real. He's here. But how? Why?'

"What's the matter, Drake?" he asked, advancing slowly. "Isn't this what you wanted? To confront me face to face?"

Drake's back hit a cracked mirror, shards digging into his shirt. He swallowed hard, his throat dry. "I want answers. My family—"

"Your family?" the man interrupted, his tone mocking. "The ones you've failed so many times? In how many realities, Drake?"

The words hit Drake like a physical blow. He clenched his fists, fighting back the wave of guilt threatening to overwhelm him. "I'll save them this time. I have to."

The disfigured man's laugh was cold and mirthless. "You don't even know what you're saving them from. Or why."

Drake's mind raced, searching for a response, a plan, anything. But as he stared into his twisted face, he realized with growing dread that he was utterly unprepared for this confrontation.

47 - 48

The disfigured man's scarred face contorted into a cruel smile, his eyes glinting in the dim light of the funhouse. "Almost killed you here once," he said, his voice low and menacing. "I could do it again without breaking a sweat."

Drake's heart pounded in his chest, each beat echoing in his ears. The funhouse mirrors reflected distorted versions of himself, fractured and broken, much like the fragments of his memory. He could feel the cold sweat beading on his forehead, his lawyer's composure crumbling in the face of this nightmarish encounter.

'Think, Drake,' he urged himself silently. 'There has to be a way out of this.'

His breathing shallow, Drake's mind raced for something—anything—to say. The weight of his family's fate pressed down on him, driving him to push through his fear. "Why are you doing this?" he managed, his voice hoarse. "What do you want from me?"

As the words left his mouth, Drake's thoughts turned to his wife and son, their faces clear in his mind despite the confusion surrounding his current reality. 'I have to protect them,' he thought desperately. 'Whatever the cost.'

The disfigured man took a step closer, his presence suffocating in the cramped, mirror-lined corridor. Drake instinctively pressed himself against the wall, feeling the sharp edges of broken glass through his shirt.

"Want?" the man repeated, his tone mocking. "You assume this is about desire, Drake. Always the lawyer, looking for motives, for reasons."

Drake's fists clenched at his sides, his nails digging into his palms. The pain helped him focus, pushing back against the rising tide of panic threatening to overwhelm him.

49 - 50

The disfigured man tilted his head, his charred lips curling into a cruel smile. The movement caused the shadows to dance across his ruined face, making it appear even more grotesque. "It's not about what I want, Drake. The universe is trying to fix itself. You made a mistake, and now it's my job to make sure you never remember what it was."

Drake's mind reeled at the implications. The universe? A mistake? His heart pounded in his chest; each beat a reminder of how fragile his grasp on this reality truly was. He could feel the weight of countless lives—his family's lives—pressing down on him.

"What mistake?" Drake's voice cracked, betraying the fear and desperation he was trying so hard to contain. His legal training kicked in, urging him to probe further, to find a weakness in this cryptic explanation. "What did I do?"

As he spoke, Drake's eyes darted around the funhouse, searching for an escape route, anything that might give him an advantage. But the distorted reflections in the cracked mirrors only served to disorient him further, echoing the fractured state of his memories.

'There has to be more to this,' Drake thought, his mind racing. 'If I could just remember...' But the harder he tried to grasp the missing pieces of his past, the more they seemed to slip away, like smoke through his fingers.

The disfigured man's silence stretched on, heavy with unspoken accusations. Drake could feel the pressure building, the need for answers warring with his instinct for self-preservation. Whatever this mistake was, it had cost him everything—and might cost him everything again.

51 - 52

The disfigured man leaned in, his charred face mere inches from Drake's. The acrid smell of burnt flesh assaulted Drake's nostrils, making him recoil involuntarily. But there was nowhere to go; his back pressed against the cold, cracked mirror behind him.

"You'll figure it out eventually," the man rasped, his voice a grating whisper. "But until then, your family is destined to die. Over and over. Until you find a way to break the loop."

The words hit Drake like a physical blow. Images flashed through his mind: his wife's smile, his son's laughter, the warmth of their embraces. All of it threatened, all of it ephemeral. The weight of this revelation crashed down on him, constricting his chest until he could barely breathe.

'No,' Drake thought, his inner voice a desperate plea. 'Not them. Not again.' He tried to speak, to deny this cruel fate, but his throat closed up, choking on unshed tears and unvoiced anguish.

The man's burned lips twisted into what might have been a smile, a grotesque parody of empathy. "The universe demands balance, Drake. Your actions tipped the scales. Now, it's correcting itself."

Drake's eyes filled with tears, blurring his vision. The funhouse around him seemed to waver and distort, mirroring the turmoil in his soul. His fists clenched at his sides, nails digging into his palms, the pain a sharp counterpoint to the emotional agony tearing through him.

"You bastard," Drake finally managed to spit out, his voice thick with rage and sorrow. The words echoed off the walls, a pitiful challenge against the cosmic cruelty laid before him.

53 - 54

The disfigured man rose to his full height, looming over Drake like a twisted specter of fate. Shadows danced across his scarred visage, lending an otherworldly quality to his already unsettling appearance. Drake felt small, insignificant in the face of this harbinger of doom.

"Midnight, Drake," the man intoned, his voice reverberating through the decaying funhouse. "That's all you've got. Let's see if you can even get them that far."

The words hung in the air, heavy with implication. Drake's mind raced, grasping at the fragments of memory that had been eluding him. Midnight. His family. The cycle of death. It was all connected, but the pieces refused to fit together.

'I need more time,' Drake thought desperately. 'I can't lose them again. Not when I've just found them.'

He opened his mouth to speak, to demand more answers, to plead for mercy—anything to buy himself more time. But before a single word could escape his lips, he saw a flash of movement.

The rusted metal rod, forgotten in the intensity of their exchange, arced through the air. Drake's eyes widened in shock and realization, his body tensing to dodge, but it was too late.

A sickening crack echoed through the funhouse as the rod connected with Drake's temple. Pain exploded behind his eyes, a supernova of agony that threatened to consume him. As darkness crept in at the edges of his vision, one thought burned bright in his fading consciousness:

'I must save them. No matter the cost.'

55 - 56

The world went black.

In that endless void, Drake floated, untethered from time and space. The pain in his skull receded, replaced by a numbing emptiness that threatened to swallow him whole. Fragments of memories flickered like dying stars in the darkness—his wife's laughter, his son's first steps, the weight of a law book in his hand.

"Wake up," a distant voice urged. Was it his own? Or someone else's?

Drake struggled against the encroaching oblivion, clawing his way back to consciousness. He couldn't give up now. Not when so much was at stake.

"I can't... I can't lose them again," he mumbled, his words slurred and barely audible.

Slowly, agonizingly, the sensation returned. The cold, damp floor of the funhouse pressed against his cheek. The taste of copper filled his mouth. Drake's eyelids fluttered open, his vision blurry and unfocused.

'How long was I out?' he wondered, panic rising in his chest. 'What time is it?'

With a groan, Drake pushed himself up onto his elbows, the world spinning around him. He fumbled for his phone, squinting at the bright screen.

8:47 PM.

"No," he whispered, his voice hoarse. "No, no, no."

Drake staggered to his feet, using the cracked mirrors for support. His reflection stared back at him—a man battered and desperate, blood matting his hair and trickling down his temple.

'I have to get to them,' he thought, his determination cutting through the fog of pain. 'I have to warn them, protect them. Before it's too late.'

As Drake stumbled out of the funhouse and into the cool night air, one thought echoed in his mind, driving him forward:

Midnight. That was all he had.

Crab Cakes at The Lighthouse

1 -2

The world blurred at the edges, a kaleidoscope of darkness and neon streaks. Drake's head pounded, each throb a reminder of the disfigured man's assault. He squinted against the pain, willing his vision to focus on the road ahead.

"Get it together, Miller," he muttered, his voice barely audible over the roar of the engine. His knuckles whitened as he gripped the steering wheel, anchoring himself to reality.

The highway stretched before him, an endless ribbon of asphalt disappearing into the night. Streetlights flashed by their harsh glow reflecting in his rearview mirror like silent sentinels. Drake's eyes darted between the road and the mirror, searching for signs of pursuit.

His thoughts raced, fragmented and chaotic. Memories of his past life as a successful lawyer collided with the surreal present. The weight of his mission—to unravel the mystery of the multiversal anomaly—pressed down on him, threatening to crush his resolve.

"I can't fail them again," he whispered, thinking of Linda and Harrison. His family, yet not his family. Strangers wearing familiar faces, unaware of the bond they once shared.

The dashboard clock caught his eye: 9:12 PM. Drake's breath hitched. Time was slipping away, each passing second a potential harbinger of disaster.

He pressed harder on the accelerator, the car's engine growling in response. The landscape outside became a smear of darkness, punctuated only by the occasional flash of light.

"What if I'm too late?" The question burned in his mind, fueling his growing desperation. "What if this time, I can't save them?"

Drake shook his head, immediately regretting the action as pain danced through his skull. He blinked rapidly, fighting to clear his vision.

"Focus, damn it," he growled, his jaw clenched. "You've got one shot at this. One chance to make it right."

The memory of his sacrifice in another reality flooded his senses—the searing pain, the overwhelming guilt, the desperate hope that his actions would be enough. Now, granted a second chance in this unfamiliar world, Drake felt the weight of that sacrifice pressing down on him.

"I won't let it be for nothing," he vowed, his voice low and determined. "I'll find the answers. I'll save them all."

As he sped through the night, Drake couldn't shake the feeling that he was racing against more than just time. He was battling against fate itself, against the very fabric of reality that seemed determined to unravel around him.

The neon lights continued to flash in his rearview mirror, a silent countdown to a moment of reckoning he couldn't fully comprehend. Drake Miller, once a man of logic and reason, now found himself adrift in a sea of uncertainty, clinging to the hope that somehow, this time, he would make the right choice.

3 - 4

Drake's knuckles whitened as he gripped the steering wheel, his eyes darting between the road and the dashboard clock. 9:13 PM. The realization hit him like a physical blow.

"Damn it," he muttered, his foot pressing even harder on the accelerator. "Linda, Harrison... I'm coming."

The wind howled against the windows, a cacophony that couldn't drown out the chaos in Drake's mind. The burned man's taunting voice echoed through his memories, each word a dagger of doubt.

"Midnight, Drake. That's all you've got."

He shook his head, trying to dispel the haunting voice. "No, I won't let it end like before. Not this time."

The car swerved slightly as Drake's vision blurred, the pain in his head intensifying. He blinked rapidly, forcing himself to focus on the road ahead.

"Richard's probably already there with them," Drake thought, his jaw clenching. "Waiting. But for what?"

The image of Linda's worried face flashed before him, followed by Harrison's trusting eyes. The weight of their fate pressed down on Drake's chest, making it hard to breathe.

"I should have told them everything," he whispered, regret coloring his words. "Maybe then they'd understand. Maybe then they'd believe me. If only I remembered."

The crunch of shattered mirrors beneath his feet echoed in his mind, a grim reminder of the reality he was desperately trying to change. Drake's fingers tapped nervously on the steering wheel, a physical manifestation of his inner turmoil.

"What if I'm too late?" The question slipped out, unbidden and terrifying. "What if I can't save them this time either?"

Drake shook his head, immediately regretting the action as pain danced through his skull. He blinked rapidly, fighting to clear his vision.

"Focus, damn it," he growled, his jaw clenched. "You've got one shot at this. One chance to make it right."

5 - 6

The Lighthouse Seafood Restaurant loomed before him, its windows like warm beacons cutting through the night's darkness. Drake's tires screamed in protest as he jerked the wheel, the car lurching to an abrupt stop in the parking lot. The sudden halt sent a fresh wave of agony through his head, and he couldn't suppress a groan of pain.

With trembling hands, Drake fumbled with the door handle, nearly falling out of the car as he emerged. The cool night air hit his face, offering a momentary respite from the throbbing in his temple. He swayed slightly, steadying himself against the car's frame.

"Get it together," he muttered, blinking hard as he felt something warm trickle down the side of his face. Drake raised a hand to his temple, his fingers coming away sticky with blood. He stared at the crimson stain, a stark reminder of his encounter with the disfigured man.

"Damn it," Drake hissed, hastily wiping his hand across his cheek. He knew he must look a mess, but there was no time to worry about appearances. Every second counted.

As he stumbled towards the restaurant's entrance, Drake's mind raced. "What if they see me like this and panic? What if Vega tries to stop me from taking Linda and Harrison?" The questions swirled in his mind, each one adding to the weight of urgency pressing down on him.

He paused at the door, catching a glimpse of his reflection in the glass. Blood smeared across his cheek, his eyes wild with fear and determination. For a moment, he hardly recognized himself.

"This is it," Drake thought, his heart pounding. "Whatever happens in there, I can't let them down. Not again."

With a deep breath, he reached for the door handle, steeling himself for what lay ahead. The warm glow of the restaurant beckoned, but Drake knew the real challenge awaited inside. Time was running out, and he was their only hope.

7 - 8

Drake pushed through the door, and the cacophony of the restaurant enveloped him. The soft strains of jazz mingled with the clinking of silverware and the low hum of conversation, creating a discordant symphony that grated against his frayed nerves. The warm, golden light from crystal chandeliers cast a deceptive glow of normalcy over the scene.

As he moved through the dining room, the aroma of seafood and butter wafted past, turning his stomach. Families laughed, couples leaned in close, all blissfully unaware of the impending doom that hung over them like a shroud. Drake's eyes darted from table to table, searching.

"How can they all be so happy?" he thought, his chest tightening. "Don't they know? Can't they feel it?"

Near the back, he spotted them. Linda's blonde hair caught the light, her worried expression a stark contrast to the carefree diners around her. Harrison slouched in his chair, the blue glow of his phone illuminating his face. And there was Vega, his suit impeccable, his posture radiating an air of control that made Drake's skin crawl.

Drake's hands clenched into fists at his sides. "They look so normal," he mused, his thoughts racing. "But everything's about to change. I have to make them understand."

He took a step forward, then hesitated. The weight of what he had to do, what he had to convince them of, suddenly felt insurmountable. But the image of Harrison choking, of Linda's lifeless eyes, flashed through his mind. He couldn't let that happen. Not again.

With renewed determination, Drake strode towards the table, ignoring the curious glances from nearby diners. He had to focus. He had to save them. And he was running out of time.

9 - 10

Drake took a deep breath, steeling himself as he approached the table. The familiar scent of Linda's perfume reached him first, a bittersweet reminder of a life that felt increasingly distant with each passing moment.

"Drake," Linda said, rising to her feet. Her blue eyes, usually so warm and comforting, widened in shock as they took in his disheveled appearance. "What happened to you? Are you okay?"

The concern in her voice pierced through Drake's resolve, threatening to unravel the fragile composure he'd managed to muster. He opened his mouth to respond, but the words caught in his throat. How could he possibly explain the weight of countless realities, the burden of foreknowledge that pressed down upon him?

Instead, he reached out, his fingers hovering just inches from Linda's arm, afraid that if he touched her, she might dissolve like a mirage. "Linda," he breathed, his voice barely above a whisper. "I... I need you to listen to me. All of you."

Drake's gaze swept across the table, taking in Harrison's confused expression and Vega's raised eyebrow. The urgency of the situation clawed at him, each passing second feeling like sand slipping through an hourglass.

"We don't have much time," he continued, his words tumbling out in a rush. "I know this sounds crazy, but you have to believe me. We're in danger. All of us. And if we don't leave now something terrible is going to happen."

Linda's hand reached out, hovering near the cut on his temple. "Drake, you're bleeding. We need to get you to a hospital."

"No!" Drake exclaimed, perhaps too forcefully. He softened his tone, aware of the stares from nearby tables. "No hospitals. Please, Linda. Trust me. We need to go. Now."

As he spoke, Drake's mind raced, replaying the countless iterations of this moment he'd lived through. How many times had he failed? How many times had he watched his family slip away, powerless to save them? The weight of it all threatened to crush him, but he pushed back against despair. This time would be different. It had to be.

11 - 12

Drake's chest tightened as he fought to control his breathing, the familiar panic threatening to overwhelm him. He forced a weak smile, hoping to reassure Linda and Harrison, but the strain was evident in his voice.

"I'm fine," Drake said quickly, though his tone was anything but reassuring. His eyes darted between her and Harrison, his chest tightening. The sight of his son, alive and unharmed, sent a wave of relief through him, quickly followed by a surge of dread. How long could he keep Harrison safe this time?

Vega's sharp voice cut through Drake's spiraling thoughts. "You're late," he said, leaning back in his chair. His voice was calm but edged with irritation. "And you look like hell. What's going on?"

Drake's mind raced, searching for the right words to convey the urgency of their situation without sounding completely unhinged. He'd hadn't been down this road before, but like each time, his warnings had fallen on deaf ears. The memory of past failures weighed heavily on him, each one a scar on his psyche.

"Richard," Drake began, his voice low and intense, "I know this is going to sound impossible, but we're caught in some kind of loop. A time loop, or... I don't know. But I've lived this night before. Many times. And each time, something terrible happens."

He paused, noting the concern in Linda's eyes, the skepticism in Vega's, and the growing unease in Harrison's posture. Drake's heart ached, knowing the burden he was about to place on his family. But what choice did he have?

"I know it's hard to believe," he continued, his words tinged with desperation, "but please, I need you to trust me. We must leave. Now. Before it's too late."

13 - 14

Drake's gaze locked onto Linda and Harrison, his eyes burning with an intensity that made them both flinch. The ambient chatter of the restaurant faded away, leaving only the pounding of his own heart in his ears. He leaned forward, his voice dropping to an urgent whisper.

"We need to leave. Right now."

The words hung in the air, heavy with unspoken dread. Drake's fingers twitched, itching to grab their hands and pull them to safety. But he knew better. He had to make them understand, to choose to follow him.

Linda's brow furrowed, her eyes searching Drake's face for some explanation. The lines around her mouth deepened with worry, and Drake felt a pang of guilt for the fear he was causing her. But it was nothing compared to the horror that awaited if they stayed.

"What? Why?" Linda asked, her voice tinged with confusion and growing alarm.

Drake's mind raced, weighing how much to reveal. The disfigured man's warnings echoed in his head, reminding him of the consequences of saying too much. He glanced at Harrison, noting the boy's wide-eyed concern, and decided.

"There's danger here," Drake said, his voice low and urgent. "I can't explain everything now, but I promise I will. We just... we need to get somewhere safe first."

He reached out, gently taking Linda's hand in his own. The warmth of her skin grounded him, reminding him of all he stood to lose. "Please," he whispered, his eyes never leaving hers. "Trust me."

15 - 16

Richard Vega's smooth voice cut through the tension like a knife, startling Drake from his intense focus on Linda. "You just got here," Vega said, his tone deceptively casual as he glanced at his watch. The slight furrow in his brow betrayed a hint of irritation beneath his composed exterior. "And we still need to discuss the Parker deposition. What's so urgent?"

Drake's heart raced, the throbbing in his temple intensifying. He could feel time slipping away, each second bringing them closer to an unseen catastrophe. The weight of his knowledge pressed down on him, threatening to crush him under its burden.

"You don't understand," Drake said, his voice rising despite his efforts to remain calm. The words tumbled out, urgent and desperate. "Something's going to happen. I need to keep you safe—to get you to midnight."

As soon as the words left his mouth, Drake regretted them. He saw the shift in Vega's eyes, the subtle narrowing that spoke of suspicion and disbelief. Linda's grip on his hand tightened, a mixture of concern and fear evident in her touch.

Drake's mind whirled, searching for a way to convince them without revealing too much. The disfigured man's warnings echoed in his thoughts, a constant reminder of the delicate balance he had to maintain. He couldn't risk altering events too drastically, but he couldn't stand by and watch his family suffer again.

"Listen," he said, leaning in close to the table, his voice dropping to an urgent whisper. "I know this sounds crazy, but I've seen something—something that's going to happen tonight. And if we don't leave now my son or wife or both will die and ill have to repeat this day tomorrow."

The words hung in the air, heavy with implication. Drake's eyes darted between Linda, Harrison, and Vega, searching for any sign of understanding or belief. His heart pounded in his chest; each beat a reminder of the precious time ticking away.

17 - 18

"Midnight?" Linda echoed, her brow furrowing with deepening concern. She reached out to touch Drake's arm, her fingers trembling slightly as they neared his skin. But Drake flinched away, the memory of her touch in countless other iterations of this night burning like a brand.

The hurt in Linda's eyes was palpable, a sharp pang that twisted in Drake's chest. He wanted nothing more than to embrace her, to feel the warmth and comfort of her presence. But he couldn't. Not now. Not when every second counted.

"Linda, please," Drake begged, his voice cracking under the weight of his desperation. The words felt raw in his throat, scraping against the lump of emotion that threatened to choke him. "I've seen this before. This place—this night—it always ends the same. One of you dies. I can't... I can't let that happen again."

His gaze swept across the table, taking in the familiar faces of his family and Vega. How many times had he sat here, watching the horror unfold? How many times had he failed to save them? The memories blurred together, a kaleidoscope of terror and loss that threatened to overwhelm him.

Drake's hands clenched into fists, his nails digging into his palms. The pain grounded him, a sharp counterpoint to the chaos of his thoughts. He could feel the eyes of nearby diners on him, their curious glances burning into his skin. But none of that mattered. All that mattered was getting his family out of here, away from the impending doom that hung over them like a shroud.

19 - 20

Harrison's lanky frame shifted uncomfortably in his seat, his unruly blonde hair falling across his forehead as he set his phone down on the table. The soft clatter seemed to echo in the tense silence that had fallen over their corner of the restaurant. His wide brown eyes, usually filled with teenage mischief, now reflected a growing unease.

"Dad, you're scaring me," Harrison said, his voice cracking slightly. The words hung in the air, heavy with the weight of a child's shattered innocence.

Drake's heart constricted at the fear in his son's voice. He wanted to reach out, to offer comfort, but his body felt frozen, trapped between the urgency of his mission and the crushing guilt of frightening his own child.

Linda's gaze darted to Vega, her blue eyes clouded with a mix of concern and resignation. She tucked a strand of blonde hair behind her ear, a nervous gesture that Drake had seen countless times before. When she spoke, her voice was soft, barely above a whisper.

"I told him about the visions," she admitted, her words carrying a hint of apology. "About the... things he's been saying. The repeating days, the disfigured man."

Drake's mind reeled at Linda's confession. She had told Vega? The man who had betrayed them, who had orchestrated her kidnapping in another timeline? Anger and betrayal warred with the desperate need to protect his family.

"Why?" Drake asked, his voice hoarse. "Why would you tell him?"

Linda's eyes met his, filled with a quiet determination that both frustrated and awed him. "Because you need help, Drake. You can't keep doing this alone."

The weight of her words settled over Drake like a heavy blanket. He understood her reasoning, but the risk... God, the risk was too great. His gaze flickered to Vega, searching for any sign of the man's true intentions. But Vega's face remained impassive, a mask of professional concern that revealed nothing of the turmoil Drake knew lurked beneath.

"We don't have time for this," Drake said, his words clipped and urgent. "We need to leave. Now."

The ticking of his watch seemed to grow louder, each second a reminder of the approaching midnight deadline. How much time had they wasted already? How close were they to the moment when everything would fall apart again?

21 - 22

Vega leaned forward; his brow furrowed. He pinched the bridge of his nose, a gesture that seemed to Drake both calculated and condescending. "Drake," Vega said, his tone steady but firm, "you need help. This isn't real. You've been under a lot of stress. Maybe it's time to talk to someone."

The words hit Drake like a physical blow. His chest tightened, breath catching in his throat. How could Vega dismiss everything so easily? The burns on his arms throbbed, a painful reminder of the reality he'd endured.

Rage bubbled up inside him, hot and fierce. Without thinking, Drake slammed his hand on the table. The sharp crack echoed through the restaurant, silverware rattling and glasses wobbling precariously. "It is real!" he snapped, his voice raw with emotion.

The other diners turned to look, their hushed murmurs filling the air like an accusatory buzz. Drake could feel their eyes on him, judging, questioning his sanity. But he couldn't back down now. Not when so much was at stake.

"You don't understand," Drake continued, struggling to keep his voice level. "I've lived this night over and over. I've watched you all die, in ways you can't even imagine. And if we don't leave now, it's going to happen again."

His gaze darted between Linda and Harrison, desperation clawing at his insides. How could he make them see? How could he save them when they refused to believe in the danger they were in?

23 - 24

With trembling hands, Drake grasped the cuffs of his shirt. The fabric felt rough against his skin, a stark contrast to the smooth scar tissue beneath. He took a deep breath, steeling himself for what he was about to reveal.

"You want proof?" he asked, his voice barely above a whisper. "I'll give you proof."

In one fluid motion, Drake rolled up his sleeves, exposing the network of burns that ran along his arms. The angry red marks stood out starkly against his pale skin, a testament to the horrors he'd endured.

"Look at this!" he exclaimed, thrusting his arms forward. The scars seemed to pulse in the dim light of the restaurant, each one a painful memory etched into his flesh. "These are from the last cycle. I got them trying to save Harrison from a propane explosion at his soccer tryouts."

Drake's eyes locked onto Vega's, challenging him. "Do you think I made that up? Do these burns look fake to you?"

The weight of his words hung in the air, heavy and suffocating. Drake's heart raced, pounding so loudly he was sure everyone could hear it. Time seemed to stretch, each second an eternity as he waited for a response.

Linda's sharp intake of breath cut through the silence. "Drake..." she gasped, her hand flying to her mouth. Her eyes, wide with shock and horror, were fixed on the scars that marred his skin.

Drake's stomach churned with a mix of guilt and desperation. He hated causing Linda pain, hated seeing the fear in her eyes. But if this was what it took to make them understand, to keep them safe, then he had no choice.

"I'm sorry," he whispered, more to himself than anyone else. "I'm so sorry."

25 - 26

Vega's face hardened, his brow furrowing as he studied Drake with a mixture of concern and suspicion. The warmth of the restaurant seemed to dissipate, replaced by a chill that crept up Drake's spine. He watched as Vega's eyes darted to a nearby waiter, his hand rising in a subtle gesture.

"Call 911," Vega said quietly, his voice barely above a whisper.

The words hit Drake like a physical blow. Panic surged through him, his vision narrowing to a tunnel. No, no, no. This couldn't happen. Not now. Not when he was so close to saving them.

"Richard, no!" Drake shouted; his voice raw with desperation. He lunged forward, gripping the edge of the table. The silverware rattled, water glasses teetering precariously. "You don't understand what's happening."

Drake's mind raced, images of the disfigured man flashing before his eyes. The twisted smile, the cold touch, the whispered threats. His heart pounded so hard he thought it might burst from his chest.

"There's a man—a disfigured man," he continued, the words tumbling out in a frantic rush. "He's been haunting me, taunting me. He says I made a mistake, something that broke the universe."

Drake's eyes darted between Vega, Linda, and Harrison, searching for any sign of understanding, any flicker of belief. The restaurant's ambient noise faded away, leaving only the sound of his own ragged breathing.

"And now it's punishing me, punishing us—" he choked out, his voice cracking under the weight of his fear and guilt.

27 - 28

Vega's eyes narrowed, his jaw clenching as he leaned forward. The soft light from the table's candle cast deep shadows across his face, accentuating the lines of tension etched around his mouth.

"Drake," Vega said, his tone sharp enough to cut glass. "Calm down. You're not making any sense."

The words sliced through Drake's panic, igniting a spark of anger deep in his chest. How could Vega be so blind? So dismissive? Drake's hands clenched into fists, his nails digging crescents into his palms.

"Of course, I'm not making sense!" Drake shot back, his voice rising. He could feel the stares of nearby diners boring into him, but he didn't care. All that mattered was making them understand. "None of this makes sense! But it's happening, and if I don't figure out how to stop it, my family is going to die!"

The last word echoed in Drake's mind, a grim reminder of what was at stake. His gaze flicked to Linda and Harrison, their faces were a mix of concern and fear. The sight twisted something inside him, a cold dread seeping into his bones.

I can't lose them, Drake thought, his heart racing. Not again. Not ever. He took a shaky breath, trying to steady himself. But how can I save them when no one believes me?

29 - 30

Harrison's fork clattered against his plate, the sudden sound piercing through the tense silence. Drake watched as his son's shoulders hunched inward, making the boy seem smaller, more vulnerable.

"Dad, stop," Harrison said, his voice barely above a whisper. He looked down at his plate, pushing it away slightly. "You're scaring mom."

The words hit Drake like a physical blow, stealing the air from his lungs. He'd seen that look in Harrison's eyes before, in countless iterations of this night. Fear. Confusion. A child grappling with the realization that his father might not be the infallible protector he'd always believed him to be.

Drake's throat tightened. I'm supposed to keep him safe, not terrify him, he thought, shame and frustration warring within him. But how can I protect him if I can't make them understand?

Linda's hand reached out, her fingers brushing against Drake's arm. The gentle touch sent a jolt through him, a bittersweet reminder of the connection they once shared, now strained by the weight of his impossible truth.

"Drake, please," Linda said, her blue eyes shimmering with unshed tears. "Let's go to the hospital. We'll figure this out together."

Drake's heart clenched at the concern in her voice, but it was tinged with something else. Doubt. Disbelief. The unspoken implication that he was losing his grip on reality.

"Linda, I-" Drake began, his voice cracking. He wanted to explain, to make her see. But the words died on his tongue as he looked at Harrison's downcast face, at Linda's pleading eyes. The realization hit him like a thunderbolt: his desperation to save them was pushing them away.

He ran a hand through his disheveled hair, feeling the weight of every repeated day, every failed attempt pressing down on him. "I just... I need you to believe me," he whispered, more to himself than to them.

31 - 32

The cacophony of clinking glasses and murmured conversations faded to a distant hum as a sudden, harsh sound sliced through the air. Drake's world narrowed to a single, horrifying focus: Harrison's desperate gasps for air.

Drake's head snapped toward his son, his heart plummeting into an abyss of dread. Harrison's eyes, wide with panic, locked onto his father's. His hands clawed at his throat, fingers scrabbling against skin that was rapidly flushing an alarming shade of crimson.

"Harrison!" Drake's voice cracked, terror coursing through his veins like ice water. He lunged forward, nearly upending the table in his haste to reach his son.

Time seemed to slow, each second stretching into an eternity as Drake watched Harrison struggle. This can't be happening, not again, his mind screamed. The burns on his arms throbbed, a painful reminder of his past failures.

"Someone help!" Linda's frantic cry pierced through Drake's momentary paralysis. He reached Harrison's side, his hands hovering uselessly over his son's convulsing form.

"Breathe, buddy," Drake pleaded, his voice a hoarse whisper. "Please, just breathe." His mind raced, searching desperately for a solution. How many times had he watched this scene unfold? How many times had he failed?

As Harrison's face began to take on a bluish tinge, Drake felt a surge of determination cut through his panic. Not this time, he vowed silently. I won't lose you again.

33 - 34

Drake's hands trembled as he reached for Harrison, his mind a whirlwind of fragmented memories and desperate prayers. The restaurant's ambient noise faded away, replaced by the thunder of his own heartbeat in his ears.

"No," Drake whispered, his body frozen in place, muscles locked with the weight of his recurring nightmare. "Not again."

The words escaped his lips like a plea to an unseen force, a desperate bargain with the universe that had trapped him in this endless cycle of loss. He could feel the eyes of the other diners on them, their curious glances morphing into looks of horror as the scene unfolded.

"Harrison!" Linda cried; her voice laced with raw anguish as she rushed to her son's side. Her blonde hair whipped around her face as she moved, blue eyes wide with terror.

Drake watched as if from a great distance, his consciousness splitting between the urgent present and the haunting echoes of past failures. How many times had he heard Linda's voice break like that? How many times had he seen the light fade from Harrison's eyes?

"We need to do something," Drake muttered, his voice barely audible. He took a faltering step forward, his mind racing through potential solutions. CPR? The Heimlich maneuver? What if those made it worse?

Linda's hands fluttered over Harrison, her maternal instinct warring with her fear of causing further harm. "Drake, help him!" she pleaded, her gaze locking onto her husband's paralyzed form.

The weight of responsibility crashed down on Drake's shoulders. He had to act, had to change the outcome this time. But the fear of failure, of watching Harrison slip away once more, threatened to overwhelm him.

"I... I don't know what to do," Drake admitted, his voice breaking. The admission tasted like ash in his mouth, bitter with the knowledge of his own limitations.

35 - 36

Drake's paralysis shattered. With a surge of desperate energy, he lunged forward, his hands grasping Harrison's shoulders. The boy's skin felt clammy under his touch, a stark reminder of the life slipping away.

"It's okay, buddy," Drake said, his voice trembling as he carefully lowered Harrison to the ground. "I've got you."

The cool hardwood floor creaked beneath them, the sound jarring against the backdrop of panicked breaths and murmured concerns from nearby diners. Drake's heart hammered in his chest; each beat a countdown to a future he refused to accept.

As he positioned Harrison's lifeless form, memories flooded Drake's mind—teaching his son to ride a bike, cheering at soccer games, late-night talks about the mysteries of the universe. The weight of those moments pressed down on him, fueling his determination.

"Come on, Harrison," Drake whispered, interlacing his fingers and placing his hands on his son's chest. "Stay with me."

He began compressions, the rhythm matching the frantic tempo of his own racing pulse. Each press sent a jolt through Drake's arms, a physical manifestation of his desperation.

"Breathe, Harrison. Please, breathe!" Drake's voice cracked, raw emotion bleeding through his words.

As he worked, Drake's mind raced. How many times had he been here before? How many iterations of this moment had he lived through, each ending in tragedy? The disfigured man's taunts echoed in his ears, a cruel reminder of the stakes.

"I can't lose you again," Drake muttered between compressions, his words meant for Harrison but also a defiant challenge to the universe itself. "Not this time. Not ever."

37 - 38

Linda's anguished cry pierced through Drake's concentration. "It's not working!" she sobbed, clutching at Drake's arm with trembling fingers. Her touch was both a lifeline and an anchor, tethering him to this horrific moment.

Drake's vision blurred, a mix of sweat and unshed tears stinging his eyes. The weight of his failure—not just in this moment, but in all the moments that had led to this—crashed over him like a tidal wave. His chest constricted, each breath a battle against the crushing despair.

"I told you!" Drake shouted at Linda, his voice breaking. The words tasted bitter on his tongue, laced with frustration and helplessness. "I told you this would happen! Why didn't you believe me?"

As soon as the words left his mouth, Drake regretted them. He saw the hurt flash across Linda's face, her blue eyes wide with shock and pain. It wasn't her fault—how could it be? In this reality, she had no memory of the cycles, no understanding of the torment he'd endured.

Drake's hands never stopped moving, pressing against Harrison's chest with a desperate rhythm. Each compression felt like a plea to whatever forces governed this twisted multiverse.

Please, he thought, his inner voice a ragged whisper. *Let this time be different. Let me save him.*

The sounds of the restaurant faded away, leaving only the thunderous beating of Drake's own heart and the ragged gasps of his breath. Time seemed to stretch and warp around him, each second an eternity of hope and dread.

"I'm sorry," Drake choked out, his eyes locked on Harrison's pale face. "I'm so sorry, Linda. I just... I can't lose him. Not again."

39 - 40

Suddenly, a firm hand gripped Drake's shoulder, jolting him from his desperate reverie.

"Move!" Vega barked, shoving Drake aside with unexpected force.

The world tilted as Drake lost his balance, his palms slapping against the cold tile floor. For a moment, he was disoriented, the restaurant's dim lighting swirling around him like a kaleidoscope of shadows and muted colors.

"What are you doing?" Drake yelled, scrambling to his feet. His heart hammered against his ribs, a frantic drumbeat of fear and confusion. He watched in stunned disbelief as Vega took his place beside Harrison's motionless form.

This isn't how it's supposed to go, Drake thought, his mind reeling. In all the cycles, in all the iterations of this moment, no one had ever intervened like this. Was this a new twist in the universe's cruel game? Or could it be...hope?

Drake's eyes darted between Vega's determined face and Harrison's pale features. The restaurant's ambient noise faded to a dull roar in his ears, every fiber of his being focused on this unexpected turn of events.

"Richard," Drake said, his voice hoarse with emotion, "please... save him." The words felt strange on his tongue, a plea to a man he both trusted and doubted in equal measure.

As Vega worked, Drake clenched his fists at his sides, fighting the urge to push him away and take control again. But something in Vega's confident movements held him back. Was this the key? Had his own desperation been the very thing holding him back from saving Harrison all along?

The seconds ticked by like hours, each one carrying the weight of a lifetime. Drake held his breath, silently praying to whatever forces might be listening in this fractured reality.

Please, he thought, his inner voice a desperate whisper. *Let this be the change we need. Let this be the moment that breaks the cycle.*

41 - 42

Vega's hands moved with practiced precision, each compression precise and measured. The stark contrast between his calm efficiency and Drake's earlier frantic attempts was painfully apparent. Drake's stomach churned with a mixture of hope and bitter self-recrimination.

"Come on, Harrison," Drake whispered, his voice barely audible. He watched his son's still face, searching for any sign of life. The boy's usually vibrant features were ashen, his unruly blonde hair matted with sweat against his forehead.

Vega's cold demeanor seemed to crack for a moment as he spoke without looking up. "Drake, get me that tablecloth. We need to elevate his head."

Drake snapped into action, grateful for something to do. As he reached for the cloth, his mind raced. *Why is Vega helping? What does he know that I don't?* The questions swirled, threatening to overwhelm him.

"How... how do you know what to do?" Drake asked, his voice trembling as he handed over the makeshift pillow.

Vega's eyes flickered up for a split second, his expression unreadable. "You're not the only one with secrets, Drake," he replied cryptically, returning his focus to Harrison.

The words sent a chill down Drake's spine. He watched Vega's hands, moving with such surety, and felt a pang of inadequacy. *All this time, all these cycles, and I've been doing it wrong, * he thought, the realization settling like lead in his gut.

"Is he... will he..." Drake couldn't finish the question, fear constricting his throat.

Vega didn't respond, his concentration unwavering. The silence stretched, punctuated only by the rhythmic sound of compressions and the distant murmur of shocked onlookers.

Drake's world narrowed to this moment, to his son's pale face and Vega's determined efforts. Everything else - the disfigured man, the fractured timelines, even his own confusion - faded into the background. All that mattered was Harrison's next breath.

43 - 44

Vega's jaw clenched, a bead of sweat trickling down his temple. "Come on, kid," he muttered, his voice barely audible. "Don't give up on me."

The words hung in the air, heavy with desperation. Drake's heart pounded; each beat a silent prayer. *Please, Harrison. Please fight. *

Suddenly, Harrison's body convulsed violently. A harsh, guttural sound erupted from his throat as he vomited onto the floor. The acrid smell filled the air, but Drake had never been so relieved to smell something so foul.

Harrison gasped, his chest heaving as he struggled to breathe. His hands clutched at his shirt, twisting the fabric. Tears streamed down his face, mingling with the remnants of vomit on his chin.

Drake's instinct was to rush forward, to gather his son in his arms. But he hesitated, paralyzed by the fear that any movement might shatter this fragile moment of life.

"Dad?" Harrison's voice was weak, barely more than a whisper. His brown eyes, usually so full of curiosity and wonder, now reflected confusion and fear.

"I'm here, buddy," Drake managed, his own voice thick with emotion. He inched closer, carefully, as if approaching a wounded animal. "You're okay. You're going to be okay."

*But will he? * The thought intruded, unbidden. *How many more times will I have to watch him suffer? *

Vega sat back on his heels; his expression inscrutable. "He needs a hospital," he said flatly, wiping his hands on a napkin. "This isn't over."

Drake nodded numbly, unable to tear his gaze from Harrison's trembling form. The relief of the moment was already giving way to a fresh wave of dread. *What comes next? * he wondered. *What new horror awaits us at midnight? *

45 - 46

"Harrison!" Linda cried, her voice cracking with relief and anguish. She reached for their son, pulling him into her arms with a desperate urgency. Her fingers trembled as they stroked his hair, matted with sweat and tears.

Drake watched, his heart constricting painfully in his chest. The sight of his wife and son, alive and together, sent a surge of conflicting emotions through him. Joy warred with exhaustion; relief tangled with a gnawing fear of what might still come.

*We're not safe yet, * he thought, the weight of unseen futures pressing down on him. *This moment... it's just a reprieve. *

His legs gave way beneath him, and Drake sank to his knees. The world tilted and swam before his eyes, the cacophony of the restaurant fading to a dull roar. He could hear Linda's soft murmurs of comfort to Harrison, could see the way she cradled him protectively.

"It's okay, baby," Linda whispered, her voice carrying to Drake despite the chaos around them. "Mommy's here. You're going to be alright."

Drake's vision blurred, whether from tears or fatigue, he couldn't tell. His mind raced, replaying the endless iterations of this moment, each one ending in tragedy. But not this time. Not yet.

"Linda," he croaked, his voice hoarse. "We need to go. Now."

She looked up at him, her eyes wide with a mixture of fear and determination. "Drake, what's happening? What aren't you telling us?"

He shook his head, unable to find the words to explain the impossible. How could he make them understand the weight of time itself bearing down on them?

"Please," was all he could manage. "Trust me."

47 - 48

Linda's gaze shifted from Drake to Vega, her blue eyes shimmering with unshed tears. The tension in her slender frame was palpable, a mother's protective instinct warring with the gratitude she felt towards the man who had just saved her son's life.

"Thank you," Linda whispered to Vega, her voice thick with emotion. The words hung in the air, fragile and weighted with unspoken complexities.

Drake watched the exchange, his heart hammering in his chest. He knew the tenuous nature of their alliance with Vega, the hidden currents of distrust that flowed beneath the surface. Yet in that moment, he couldn't deny the debt they owed him.

Vega stood, his movements deliberate and controlled as he wiped his hands on a napkin. The stark white fabric came away smeared with traces of Harrison's ordeal, a visceral reminder of how close they'd come to tragedy. Drake's stomach churned at the sight.

Turning his attention to Drake, Vega's expression hardened, his dark eyes glinting with a mixture of concern and something colder, more calculating. "Good thing you invited me to dinner," he said, his tone clipped and matter of fact. "Otherwise, your manic episode might have killed him."

The words struck Drake like a physical blow. He flinched, shame and anger roiling within him. *He doesn't understand, * Drake thought desperately. *None of them do. How can I make them see? *

"Richard," Drake began, his voice trembling with the effort to remain calm. "This isn't... it's not what you think. There's so much more at stake here."

Vega's eyebrow arched skeptically, but before he could respond, Linda interjected, her voice soft but firm. "Drake, please. We need to focus on getting Harrison help. Whatever's going on... we can figure it out later."

Drake's gaze darted between them, the weight of unspoken truths pressing down on him. He knew they saw him as unstable, possibly dangerous. But how could he convince them of the danger that still loomed, invisible but no less real?

49 - 50

Drake opened his mouth to respond, but the world tilted violently. A searing pain exploded behind his eyes, radiating outward in pulsing waves. He staggered, gripping the edge of the table for support.

"Drake?" Linda's voice seemed to come from far away, muffled and distorted.

The elegant dining room blurred, its warm lights smearing into a nauseating kaleidoscope. Drake blinked hard, trying to focus, but the darkness crept in from the edges of his vision like encroaching shadows.

*No, not now, * he thought desperately. *I have to make them understand. I have to keep them safe. *

"Linda," he gasped, reaching out blindly. "The disfigured man... he's coming. You have to believe me. You have to—"

His legs gave way beneath him, and Drake felt himself falling. The last thing he registered was Linda's panicked cry, piercing through the fog that enveloped his mind.

"Drake!"

Then darkness swallowed him whole, and he knew no more.

Fractured Memories

1 - 2   The darkness engulfed Drake, an oppressive void that pressed against his consciousness. Suspended in nothingness, he felt untethered from reality, adrift in a sea of emptiness. Then, without warning, a torrent of memories crashed over him, each fragment a shard of his fractured existence.

Flashes of light and sound assaulted his senses. The acrid smell of gunpowder. The metallic taste of blood. The sickening crunch of metal on metal. Each sensation more vivid than the last, threatening to overwhelm him completely.

"Linda," he whispered into the void, his voice hoarse with desperation. "Harrison."

Their faces flickered before him, tantalizingly close yet impossibly distant. Drake reached out, trying to grasp onto something, anything solid. But his fingers closed on empty air.

As the barrage of memories continued, one image began to coalesce, rising above the chaotic swirl of sensations. The funhouse. Even in this formless void, the very thought of it sent a chill down Drake's spine.

"No," he muttered, squeezing his eyes shut as if that could block out the unwanted vision. "Not there. Anywhere but there."

But the memory persisted, dragging him inexorably towards that fateful night. The garish colors of the carnival rides. The discordant calliope music. And looming above it all, the dilapidated funhouse, its once-cheerful facade now a grotesque parody of joy.

Drake's heart raced, his breath coming in short, sharp gasps. He could feel the rough texture of the funhouse's warped floorboards beneath his feet, smell the musty air thick with decay.

"I can't go back," he pleaded, though to whom, he wasn't sure. "I can't face it again."

But even as the words left his lips, Drake knew the truth. He had to confront this memory, had to unravel its secrets if he ever hoped to save his family and set things right.

With a deep, shuddering breath, Drake steeled himself. "Alright," he said, his voice steadier now, tinged with grim determination. "Show me. Show me what I need to see."

And with that, the darkness receded, replaced by the nightmarish interior of the funhouse. Drake stood at the entrance, poised on the threshold of memory and nightmare, ready to face whatever horrors awaited him within.

3 - 4

Drake's footsteps echoed hollowly as he entered the funhouse, each step sending vibrations through the rotting floorboards. The stench of mildew and decay assaulted his nostrils, a putrid reminder of the building's decay. Distorted mirrors lined the walls, reflecting grotesque versions of himself as he pressed forward.

"I know you're here," Drake called out, his voice steady despite the fear coiling in his gut. "Show yourself."

A low chuckle reverberated through the air, sending chills down Drake's spine. From the shadows, a figure emerged – the disfigured man, his charred face twisting into a mockery of a smile.

"Welcome back, Drake," the man sneered, his voice grating like sandpaper. "I've been expecting you."

Drake's fists clenched at his sides. "Why am I here? What do you want from me?"

The disfigured man's grin widened, revealing blackened teeth. "Oh, it's not about what I want. It's about what you need to remember."

A sharp pain suddenly lanced through Drake's hip, causing him to stumble. He looked down, horror blooming in his chest as he saw blood spreading across his shirt.

"What have you done?" Drake gasped, pressing a hand to the wound.

The disfigured man raised a smoking gun, his eyes gleaming with malice. "Sometimes, Drake, pain is the key to unlocking the truth."

As Drake's vision began to blur, he couldn't shake the feeling that this moment was pivotal – a turning point in the labyrinth of memories and realities he'd been navigating. But what did it mean? And how could he use this knowledge to save his family?

5 - 6

"Choices, Drake," the man sneered, his voice dripping with contempt. "Always choices."

The words echoed through the funhouse, reverberating off the warped mirrors surrounding them. Drake's mind raced, desperately trying to make sense of the situation. Was this another test? Another layer of the twisted reality he found himself trapped in?

"What choices?" Drake managed to choke out, his voice strained with pain and confusion. "I never wanted any of this!"

The disfigured man's laughter cut through the air like a knife. "Oh, but you did. Every decision, every path taken or not taken – they've all led you here, to this moment."

Drake staggered backward, his vision swimming as the loss of blood began to take its toll. The floor beneath him seemed to tilt and shift, reality bending at the edges. He thought of Linda, of Harrison – were they real? Were they waiting for him somewhere beyond this nightmarish carnival of horrors?

"My family," Drake gasped, fighting to stay conscious. "They're innocent in all this. Whatever game you're playing, leave them out of it!"

As he spoke, Drake's heel caught on a loose floorboard. He felt himself falling, the world tilting on its axis. The mirrors surrounding him exploded in a cacophony of shattering glass, each fragment reflecting his face contorted in agony.

In that fractured moment, suspended between standing and falling, Drake saw countless versions of himself – the lawyer, the detective, the father, the husband. Which one was real? Which life was truly his?

"Remember, Drake," the disfigured man's voice echoed as Drake plummeted towards the glass-strewn floor. "The truth lies in the fragments. Put them together, and you might just save them all."

Then darkness claimed him, leaving only the lingering question: What if every choice, every version of himself, was equally real and equally false?

7 - 8

The pain didn't fade. It carried over, following Drake like a phantom, a constant reminder of the choices that had led him to this point. He found himself in a dimly lit street, the air heavy with the scent of rain and exhaust. A black sedan sat idle nearby, its engine ticking as it cooled.

Drake's hand instinctively went to his side, where the phantom pain throbbed in time with his racing heart. "Linda," he whispered, his voice hoarse. "Harrison. I have to find them."

He stumbled towards the car, each step sending shockwaves of agony through his body. As he drew closer, he noticed something off about the driver's silhouette.

"Hey," Drake called out, rapping his knuckles against the window. "You alive?"

No response.

Drake's detective instincts, honed through years of experience he couldn't quite remember living, kicked in. He peered closer, his breath fogging the glass.

The driver sat motionless; head slumped forward unnaturally. A chill ran down Drake's spine as he recognized the telltale signs of death.

"No," he muttered, fumbling for the door handle. "Not again. Not like this."

As he wrenched the door open, the cab's interior light flickered to life, revealing the grisly scene within. The driver's lifeless eyes stared blankly ahead, a trickle of blood trailing from his temple.

Drake's mind raced, fragments of memories and alternate realities colliding. Was this the same cab that had caused his accident? Was this driver another pawn in the disfigured man's twisted game?

"I'm sorry," Drake whispered to the dead man, his voice thick with emotion. "I'll find out who did this to you. To us."

As sirens wailed in the distance, Drake stepped back from the cab, his head spinning with questions. He had to piece together the truth before it was too late, before he lost Linda and Harrison forever.

"Whatever it takes," he vowed, clenching his fists as the pain in his side flared anew. "I'll make this right."

9 - 10

The rain intensified, pelting Drake's face as he turned away from the grim scene. His hand instinctively moved to his side, pressing against the phantom pain that seemed to transcend realities. Through the downpour, he caught sight of his partner, Detective Holly Kierstead, striding towards him with purposeful steps.

"Miller," Holly called out, her voice cutting through the cacophony of sirens and radio chatter. "What've we got?"

Drake's jaw clenched, the weight of his conflicting memories bearing down on him. "Cab driver. Neck snapped. Looks like an execution."

Holly's sharp eyes narrowed as she surveyed the scene. "Any signs of struggle?"

"None that I can see," Drake replied, fighting to keep his voice steady. He couldn't shake the feeling that this was more than just another case. It was a piece of a larger puzzle, one that stretched across realities he couldn't fully comprehend.

As Holly ducked her head into the cab for a closer look, Drake's mind raced. How could he explain the significance of this scene to her when he barely understood it himself? The urge to confide in her warred with the fear of sounding utterly insane.

"Holly," he began, his voice low and urgent. "There's something about this that feels... familiar. Like we've been here before."

She turned to him, one eyebrow raised. "Déjà vu, Miller? Or is there something you're not telling me?"

Drake hesitated; the words caught in his throat. How could he possibly explain the fragmented memories, the sense of a world out of joint? He opened his mouth to respond but was cut short by a flash of lightning that illuminated the alley, casting eerie shadows across the crime scene.

11 - 12

In that instant, as the thunder rumbled overhead, a sudden realization struck Drake with the force of a physical blow. His breath caught in his throat, and he staggered back a step, steadying himself against the rain-slicked wall of the alley.

"This isn't just an accident," he muttered, his voice barely audible over the patter of rain. The words echoed in his mind, tinged with a certainty that seemed to come from somewhere beyond his current self. "This was the vehicle that caused my accident. The driver was just a casualty."

Holly turned to him; concern etched across her face. "Drake? What are you talking about?"

But Drake was no longer fully present in the alley. His vision swam, and suddenly he was elsewhere—tumbling, falling, the world spinning around him in a sickening kaleidoscope of metal and glass. The memory hit him with such force that he could almost feel the impact, hear the screech of tires and the crunch of his car as it careened down the embankment.

"Jesus," he gasped, pressing a hand to his temple. "I remember. The hit-and-run. It wasn't random. This taxi—"

He broke off, struggling to piece together the fragments of memory that were flooding back. The sharp jolt as everything went black, the searing pain that followed. It all led back here, to this rain-soaked alley and the dead man slumped over the steering wheel.

"Drake," Holly's voice cut through his thoughts, grounding him. "Talk to me. What's going on?"

He met her gaze, seeing the mixture of concern and suspicion in her eyes. How could he explain something he barely understood himself? But he had to try. This wasn't just about solving a case anymore. It was about unraveling a mystery that seemed to stretch across realities.

"The taxi driver's death," Drake began, his voice low and urgent. "It's connected to the hit-and-run that nearly killed me. But it's more than that. It's... it's the catalyst. The beginning of something bigger than we can imagine."

13 - 14

Drake's throat tightened as the realization washed over him. The rain pattered against the pavement; each drop a ticking clock in his mind. He turned to face the alley, his eyes fixed on the abandoned car.

"This is where it began," Drake whispered to himself, his voice barely audible above the distant wail of sirens. "This is what set everything in motion."

The world around him blurred, colors bleeding into one another like a watercolor painting left out in the rain. Drake blinked, and suddenly he was no longer standing in the alley. The acrid smell of wet asphalt gave way to the sharp scent of antiseptic.

A rhythmic beeping filled the air, steady and insistent. Drake found himself lying in a hospital bed, the starched sheets rough against his skin. An IV snaked its way into his arm, the clear tube a lifeline tethering him to consciousness. His body felt leaden, every breath a struggle against the weight of his injuries.

"Linda," he croaked, his voice barely above a whisper. "Harrison."

But there was no response. The room remained empty, save for the steady beep of the heart monitor and the soft hum of medical equipment.

Drake's mind raced, trying to reconcile the fragments of memory that swirled within him. The car crash, the funhouse, the disfigured man – it all seemed both distant and immediate, like a half-remembered nightmare.

"What's happening to me?" he thought, clenching his fists against the sheets. "Am I losing my mind, or is there something more at play here?"

The silence of the room pressed in on him, offering no answers. Only the persistent beep of the monitor reminded him that he was still alive, still fighting against a tide of confusion and fear that threatened to overwhelm him.

15 - 16

As Drake's eyes adjusted to the dim light, a shadow detached itself from the corner of the room. His heart rate spiked, the monitor's beeping accelerating in tandem with his rising panic. The figure approached, and Drake's breath caught in his throat as he recognized the disfigured face, partially obscured by shadows but unmistakable in its grotesque features.

The man's charred skin glistened in the dim light, a cruel parody of a smile twisting his ruined lips. In his hand, he held a syringe filled with a dark red liquid that seemed to pulse with an otherworldly energy.

Drake's mind raced, searching for an explanation, an escape. He tried to move, but his body refused to respond, still weak from the crash. "Who are you?" he managed to croak, his voice hoarse and unfamiliar to his own ears. "What do you want from me?"

The disfigured man leaned in close, his breath hot against Drake's ear. "You're special, Drake," he said, his voice low and menacing, each word dripping with malevolent intent. "Your blood... it's unique. A gift, really. But gifts come with a price."

Drake's thoughts whirled, a maelstrom of confusion and fear. Unique blood? A gift? None of it made sense, yet a part of him resonated with the words, as if some buried truth was struggling to surface.

"I don't understand," Drake whispered, his eyes fixed on the syringe. "What price? What are you talking about?"

The man's laugh was a harsh, grating sound that sent shivers down Drake's spine. "Oh, you will," he promised, raising the syringe. "You'll understand everything soon enough."

17 - 18

Drake's muscles tensed, a primal instinct to flee overwhelming him. But his body betrayed him, paralyzed by weakness and fear. He could only watch in horror as the disfigured man plunged the syringe into his arm, the thick liquid burning like molten lava as it entered his veins.

"No!" Drake gasped, his voice barely a whisper. The pain was immediate and all-consuming, radiating from the injection site and spreading through his body like wildfire.

His vision blurred, the hospital room dissolving into a kaleidoscope of fractured images. Drake's body convulsed violently, his back arching off the bed as he fought against the invasive substance coursing through him.

"What's... happening to me?" he choked out, his words lost in a sea of agony.

As the world spun around him, Drake found himself standing in two distinct realities simultaneously. In one, he wore a crisp suit, surrounded by the trappings of a high-powered law office. In the other, he donned a detective's badge, the weight of a gun at his hip unfamiliar yet somehow right.

"Impossible," Drake muttered, his mind reeling as he tried to process the dual existences. "How can I be in two places at once?"

But in both realities, a constant remained: the throbbing pain in his hip, a phantom wound from the funhouse encounter. Drake clutched at it instinctively, feeling the warmth of blood seeping through his clothes.

"The choices you make," the disfigured man's voice echoed from everywhere and nowhere, "shape more than just your own destiny, Drake. They ripple across realities."

Drake struggled to make sense of it all, his lawyer's analytical mind battling against the detective's instincts. "Why me?" he demanded, his voice a mix of desperation and defiance. "What makes my blood so special?"

The only answer was the man's mocking laughter, fading away as Drake's consciousness teetered on the edge of oblivion.

19 - 20

The kaleidoscope of memories dissolved, and Drake found himself sitting cross-legged on the living room floor. The plush carpet beneath him grounded him in this new reality, a stark contrast to the disorienting visions he'd just experienced. Beside him, Harrison hunched over a sheet of paper, his small hands moving with surprising dexterity as he sketched.

Drake watched his son, a bittersweet ache filling his chest. Harrison's brow furrowed in concentration, his tongue poking out slightly as he worked. The boy's dirty blonde hair fell across his forehead, and Drake resisted the urge to brush it back, not wanting to break his son's focus.

"What are you drawing there, buddy?" Drake asked softly, his voice slightly hoarse from the lingering emotions of his recent vision.

Harrison looked up, his brown eyes bright with excitement. "It's for my story," he explained, holding up the paper. "Sir Mordred and the Green Dragon."

Drake leaned in, studying the intricate drawing. A fierce dragon coiled around a gleaming sword; its scales rendered in meticulous detail. The image stirred something in Drake's memory, a faint echo of significance he couldn't quite grasp.

"That's incredible, Harrison," Drake said, genuine awe in his voice. "You've got a real talent for this."

As Harrison beamed at the praise, Drake's mind raced. How many times had he sat here, in this moment? How many iterations of this scene had played out across different realities? The weight of his mission pressed down on him, but here, watching his son create, Drake felt a flicker of hope.

"Tell me about the story," Drake prompted, desperate to hold onto this moment of normalcy. "What adventures does Sir Mordred have?"

21 - 22

Drake smiled, ruffling his son's hair. "You've got a real talent, kiddo. What does the dragon mean?"

Harrison's eyes lit up, a spark of imagination dancing within them. He held up the drawing, his small hands trembling slightly with excitement. "It's a protector," he explained, his voice carrying a wisdom beyond his years. "It guards the Codex of Camelot. Only the worthy can read it."

Drake's breath caught in his throat, a chill running down his spine. The Codex. Why did that word resonate so deeply within him? He struggled to keep his expression neutral, not wanting to alarm Harrison.

"That's fascinating," Drake managed, his mind racing. "Tell me more about this Codex."

As Harrison launched into a detailed explanation, Drake found himself torn between two realities. Part of him was the proud father, hanging on every word of his son's imaginative tale. But another part – the part that had lived countless iterations of this day – recognized the potential significance of Harrison's story.

"It's like a really old book," Harrison was saying, "with all these secrets about magic and different worlds."

Drake nodded; his throat tight. "And only the worthy can read it, huh?" he asked, thinking of the strange, angular letters he'd seen in his visions. "That's quite a story you've come up with."

Harrison grinned, oblivious to his father's internal struggle. "Maybe we can write it together sometime, Dad!"

"I'd like that," Drake replied softly, fighting back the urge to pull Harrison into a tight embrace. Instead, he forced a smile, keenly aware that this moment – like so many others – might slip away at any second.

23 - 24

The memory blurred, shifting like smoke in the wind. Drake found himself standing in a cavernous stone chamber, the air thick with the scent of ancient dust and forgotten secrets. Flickering torchlight danced across rough-hewn walls, casting long shadows that seemed to writhe with a life of their own.

In the center of the room, atop a weathered pedestal, sat an ancient codex. Drake's heart thundered in his chest as he approached, his eyes fixed on the cover. There, emblazoned in tarnished gold, was the same green dragon symbol from Harrison's drawing.

With trembling hands, Drake reached out to touch the tome. The leather binding felt warm beneath his fingers, as if pulsing with an inner energy. He opened it carefully, the brittle pages crackling softly.

Strange, angular letters covered the yellowed parchment, unlike any language Drake had ever seen. Yet, there was an unsettling familiarity to them, as if he should be able to decipher their meaning.

"What are you?" Drake whispered, tracing a finger along the incomprehensible script.

As if in answer, Harrison's voice echoed faintly through the chamber: "It's the language of the worthy. You have to believe in the story to understand it."

Drake's head snapped up, searching for his son. But he was alone in the vast, torch-lit room. Still, Harrison's words resonated within him, stirring something deep in his subconscious.

"Believe in the story," Drake murmured, his brow furrowed in concentration. He stared intently at the strange letters, willing them to make sense. "What story am I supposed to believe in, Harrison? Our story? The one where I keep reliving this nightmare?"

He closed his eyes, taking a deep breath. When he opened them again, the letters seemed to shimmer, as if on the verge of revealing their secrets. But true comprehension remained frustratingly out of reach.

25 - 26

The Codex pulsed with an ethereal light, casting eerie shadows across the chamber walls. Drake's eyes widened as the strange letters began to shift and rearrange themselves, flowing like liquid across the page.

"My God," he breathed, his voice barely above a whisper. "It's... responding."

The angular script morphed into familiar shapes, but before Drake could grasp their meaning, they dissolved back into obscurity. He pressed his palms against his temples, frustration mounting.

"What are you trying to tell me?" he demanded, his voice echoing in the cavernous space. "I need to understand. For Harrison. For Linda."

As if triggered by the mention of his family, Drake's mind erupted in a maelstrom of memories. Images flashed before his eyes, each more vivid than the last:

Linda's smile on their wedding day, radiant and full of promise.

Harrison's first steps, tiny hands reaching for him.

The acrid smell of smoke, panic rising in his throat as flames engulfed their home.

"No," Drake gasped, staggering back from the Codex. "Not again. I can't—"

But the flood of memories was relentless, fragments of his past colliding and intertwining:

The weight of his briefcase as he left for work, guilt gnawing at him for missing another of Harrison's soccer games.

The cold metal of a gun pressed against his hip, the badge heavy in his pocket — a life he both remembered and didn't.

"What's happening to me?" Drake whispered, his voice breaking. He looked down at his hands, expecting to see the smooth palms of a lawyer, but finding instead the callused grip of a detective. "Who am I really?"

The chamber began to spin, the flickering torchlight blurring into streaks of orange and red. Drake fell to his knees, overwhelmed by the assault on his senses and the fracturing of his identity.

27 - 28

Drake's head snapped up as a shadow fell over him. The disfigured man loomed above; his charred features twisted into a sardonic grin. In his hands, he held the Codex, its ancient pages glowing with an otherworldly light.

"You're finally beginning to see, aren't you, Drake?" the man's raspy voice echoed off the stone walls. "The truth of your fractured existence."

Drake's fists clenched, his jaw tightening as he struggled to his feet. "What have you done to me? To my family?"

The man's laugh was a harsh, grating sound. "I've merely shown you the possibilities. The paths not taken."

As Drake lunged forward, desperate to snatch the Codex, the air around them began to crackle with energy. The disfigured man raised the book high, its pages fluttering wildly.

"You can't stop what's already in motion," he sneered.

A blinding light erupted from the Codex, engulfing them both. Drake felt a sickening lurch in his stomach, as if the very fabric of reality was tearing apart.

Through the chaos, Drake's mind raced. 'Harrison, Linda,' he thought desperately. 'I have to find a way back to them. To make this right.'

The light intensified, and Drake saw impossible things: skyscrapers melting into medieval castles, smartphones transforming into smoke signals. Two worlds, two timelines, colliding and merging in a cacophony of impossibility.

"What's happening?" Drake shouted over the deafening roar of collapsing realities.

The disfigured man's voice seemed to come from everywhere and nowhere. "The universe is correcting itself, Drake. The question is: which version of you will survive?"

As the light engulfed him completely, Drake's last coherent thought was of Harrison's drawing – the green dragon coiled protectively around a sword. 'I have to be worthy,' he realized. 'For them.'

Then everything went white.

29 - 30

The white light faded, replaced by a suffocating darkness that pressed against Drake's consciousness. In this void, the disfigured man's laughter echoed, a cruel, mocking sound that seemed to reverberate through Drake's very bones.

"You thought you could change the story, Drake?" The man's voice dripped with disdain. "You're nothing but a pawn in a game you can't even comprehend."

Drake's fists clenched; his jaw tight with frustration. "This isn't a game," he growled, his voice hoarse. "These are people's lives. My family's lives."

The laughter intensified, seeming to come from all directions at once. Drake spun around, trying to locate its source, but the darkness was impenetrable.

Suddenly, a flash of emerald light caught his eye. Drake turned, his heart pounding, to see a colossal green dragon materializing out of the shadows. Its scales shimmered with an otherworldly iridescence, each movement causing ripples of light to dance across its serpentine body.

The dragon's eyes fixed on Drake, glowing with an intense, alien intelligence. As it coiled its massive body, Drake felt a strange sense of recognition.

"Harrison's drawing," he whispered, his mind racing. "The protector of the Codex."

The dragon's gaze seemed to pierce through Drake, as if judging his very soul. Its eyes pulsed with an eerie light, and Drake felt a sudden, overwhelming urge to reach out and touch it.

"What are you trying to tell me?" Drake asked, his voice barely audible over the fading echoes of the disfigured man's laughter.

As if in response, the dragon's form began to shift and writhe, its body elongating and contracting in impossible ways. Drake watched, mesmerized, as images flickered across its scales – fleeting glimpses of his life, both lived and unlived.

"The paths not taken," Drake murmured, understanding dawning. "It's showing me the possibilities."

31 - 32

Gabriel's voice sliced through the dreamscape, cold and mocking. "The universe is trying to correct itself, Drake. It's up to you to remember the mistake."

The words reverberated through Drake's consciousness, carrying with them a weight that seemed to drag him down into the depths of reality. His eyes snapped open, body jerking as if he'd been struck by lightning. The sterile smell of disinfectant assaulted his nostrils, a stark contrast to the otherworldly scents of his fading dream.

Drake's heart raced, matching the frantic beeping of the monitor beside his bed. He gasped for air, each breath feeling like sandpaper against his dry throat. The dim hospital room swam into focus, the shadows in the corners seeming to pulse with lingering traces of his vision.

"Remember the mistake," he rasped, his voice barely audible. Drake's mind reeled, grasping at the fragments of his dream. The green dragon, evil's sneering face, the fleeting images of paths not taken – they all swirled together in a dizzying kaleidoscope.

He clenched his fists, feeling the pull of the IV in his arm. "What mistake?" Drake whispered to the empty room. "What am I supposed to remember?"

The silence offered no answers, only the steady rhythm of the heart monitor. Drake closed his eyes, trying to steady his breathing. When he opened them again, he half-expected to see the disfigured man looming over him, that twisted grin mocking his confusion. But there was only the stark white ceiling, unyielding and indifferent to his inner turmoil.

"I have to figure this out," Drake muttered, his determination rising even as exhaustion threatened to pull him back under. "For Linda. For Harrison. For all the realities I've seen torn apart."

He turned his head, wincing at the stiffness in his neck, and stared out the darkened window. Somewhere beyond that glass, the world continued on, oblivious to the cosmic chess game being played with their lives as pawns. Drake felt the weight of responsibility settle onto his shoulders, heavier than ever before.

"I won't let you win," he vowed, his voice growing stronger. "Whatever game you're playing, whatever mistake I made – I'll set it right. I have to."

33 - 34

Drake's head felt heavy, like it was filled with lead, as he slowly turned it to the side. The room swam before his eyes, a blurry kaleidoscope of shadows and muted colors. He blinked hard, willing his vision to clear, focusing all his energy on the simple task of seeing.

Gradually, the world came into focus. The stark white walls of the hospital room, the dull glint of medical equipment, and there – on the far wall – a round clock face emerged from the haze.

"Twelve... fifteen," Drake mumbled, his voice hoarse and unfamiliar to his own ears. He squinted, making sure he'd read it correctly. "AM."

The time seemed to mock him, its glowing digits a silent challenge. Drake's mind raced, trying to piece together the significance of this moment. Why did 12:15 AM feel so monumental?

"I've... I've never made it this far before," he whispered, a mix of wonder and trepidation in his voice. "But why now? What's changed?"

He attempted to sit up, but his body protested, muscles screaming in revolt. Drake fell back against the pillows, frustration bubbling up inside him.

"Think, Drake," he urged himself, closing his eyes tight. "What does he want? What mistake am I supposed to remember?"

The silence of the room pressed in on him, broken only by the steady beep of the heart monitor. Drake opened his eyes again, staring at the clock as if it might hold the answers he so desperately sought.

"Linda... Harrison," he breathed, their names a talisman against the confusion threatening to overwhelm him. "I have to find a way back to them. No matter what it takes."

35 - 36

Drake's gaze darted around the dimly lit hospital room, the unfamiliar surroundings amplifying his sense of isolation. The realization that he had broken through the midnight barrier crashed over him like a tidal wave, leaving him breathless and disoriented.

"I did it," he whispered, his voice trembling with a mixture of awe and trepidation. "But at what cost?"

He tried to push himself up, his muscles protesting with each movement. The IV in his arm tugged painfully, a stark reminder of his physical limitations. Drake gritted his teeth, determination etched across his face.

"Come on, get it together," he muttered to himself. "They need you."

As he settled back against the pillows, the emptiness of the room seemed to close in around him. The absence of Linda's comforting presence and Harrison's infectious laughter felt like a physical ache in his chest.

Drake's mind raced, trying to piece together the fragments of his fractured memories. "What changed?" he wondered aloud. "Why now, after all those resets?"

The steady beep of the heart monitor seemed to mock him, each pulse a reminder of the seconds ticking by in this unfamiliar timeline. Drake closed his eyes, fighting against the wave of despair threatening to engulf him.

"I'm alone," he whispered, the words hanging heavy in the air. "But I can't give up. Not when I'm finally making progress."

37 - 38

Drake's parched lips parted, his voice barely audible as he croaked, "Linda... Harrison..." The names hung in the sterile air, fragile as wisps of smoke. He blinked hard, willing their faces to materialize before him, but the room remained stubbornly empty.

A kaleidoscope of memories crashed through his mind, each fragment more vivid and disorienting than the last. The funhouse loomed large, its warped mirrors reflecting a thousand versions of himself, each wearing an expression of abject terror. The disfigured man's laughter echoed in his ears, a cruel counterpoint to the steady beep of the heart monitor.

"No," Drake growled, pressing his palms against his temples. "Focus, damn it."

He squeezed his eyes shut, trying to latch onto something concrete. The Codex. Its pages seemed to flutter behind his eyelids, the strange angular script dancing and rearranging itself.

"Harrison's drawing," he muttered. "The green dragon... it means something. It has to."

Drake's fingers clutched at the thin hospital blanket; his knuckles white with strain. The pain in his head crescendo, threatening to split his skull.

"What am I missing?" he gritted out, his jaw clenched so tight he could hear his teeth grinding. "Linda would know. She always knows."

He pictured Linda's face, her blue eyes filled with that mix of sorrow and hope he'd come to know so well. In his mind, she reached out to him, her voice a soothing balm.

"You can do this, Drake," he imagined her saying. "You've come so far. Don't give up now."

Drake nodded, swallowing hard against the lump in his throat. "I won't," he whispered to the phantom Linda. "I promise. I'll find you both. Whatever it takes."

39 - 40

Drake's eyes snapped open, his gaze darting around the dimly lit hospital room. The faint glow of the monitors cast an eerie blue light across the sterile surfaces, creating shadows that seemed to dance at the edges of his vision.

"What changed?" he whispered, his voice hoarse. "Why now?"

He flexed his fingers, feeling the pull of the IV in his arm. The sensation was oddly grounding, a reminder that this was real. That he had finally broken through the endless loop of repeating days.

Drake's mind raced, trying to piece together the fragments of memory that swirled like a tempest in his head. "The funhouse," he muttered. "The taxi driver. The Codex. They're all connected, but how?"

He closed his eyes, concentrating on the image of the green dragon from Harrison's drawing. It seemed to come alive in his mind's eye, coiling and uncoiling around a gleaming sword.

"It guards the Codex," Drake murmured, recalling Harrison's words. "Only the worthy can read it."

A sudden thought struck him, causing his eyes to fly open. "Am I... worthy now? Is that what's changed?"

The question hung in the air, unanswered. Drake felt a surge of frustration rise within him, threatening to overwhelm the fragile hope that had begun to take root.

"Damn it," he growled, slamming his fist against the bed rail. "I'm so close. I can feel it. But it's still just out of reach."

He took a deep breath, trying to calm the storm of emotions raging within him. The answers were there, he was sure of it. Hidden in the depths of his fractured memories, waiting to be uncovered.

"I'll figure it out," Drake vowed, his voice barely above a whisper. "For Linda. For Harrison. For all of us."

As he spoke, the shadows in the room seemed to deepen, as if responding to the weight of his words. Drake shivered, suddenly acutely aware of how alone he was in this strange, altered reality.

41 - 41

Drake's fingers curled into tight fists, the skin of his burnt arms stretching painfully as he clenched his jaw. The sterile hospital room seemed to close in around him, the beeping of the heart monitor a relentless reminder of his isolation.

"Linda," he whispered, his voice hoarse with emotion. "Harrison. I swear I'll find you."

He closed his eyes, conjuring the image of his wife's warm smile, his son's infectious laughter. The memories were a balm to his battered soul, but also a sharp reminder of all he had lost.

"I don't care what it takes," Drake muttered, his eyes snapping open with renewed determination. "I'll face that disfigured bastard again if I have to. I'll decipher the Codex. I'll unravel this whole damn multiverse if that's what it takes to bring you back."

He shifted in the bed, wincing as pain shot through his body. The physical discomfort was nothing compared to the ache in his heart, the gnawing emptiness of where his family should be.

"I've made so many mistakes," Drake said softly, addressing the empty room as if his loved ones could hear him. "But this... this I'll get right. Whatever the cost."

His gaze fell on his burnt arms, a visceral reminder of the trials he'd already endured. Each scar told a story of survival, of perseverance in the face of impossible odds.

"I'm not giving up," he declared, his voice gaining strength. "Not now. Not ever. Whatever it takes, I'll find them. I'll fix this."

As the words left his lips, Drake felt a surge of energy course through him. It was more than just determination - it was a primal, unshakeable resolve. He would rewrite reality itself if that's what it took to reunite his family and set things right.

Finally Seeing Tomorrow

1-2   The sterile white ceiling loomed above Drake, a blank canvas for his racing thoughts. The rhythmic beep of the heart monitor punctuated the silence, each pulse a reminder that time was moving forward. Drake's eyes flicked to the digital clock on the nightstand: 3:17 AM. He had survived the night.

"I made it," he whispered, his voice hoarse and unfamiliar in the quiet room. The words hung in the air, tentative and fragile.

Drake's mind whirled with possibilities. Had he finally broken free of the relentless loop? Or was this simply another cruel twist in the cosmic game he seemed trapped in? He clenched his fists, feeling the pull of the IV in his arm.

"Focus," he muttered to himself. "You're here. Now. That's what matters."

He tried to sit up, wincing at the dull ache in his head. The room swam for a moment before settling into focus. Drake's gaze landed on a vase of flowers on the windowsill, their vibrant colors a stark contrast to the clinical white of the room.

"Linda," he breathed, a lump forming in his throat. Had she brought them? Was she safe?

The questions threatened to overwhelm him, but Drake forced them back. He couldn't afford to lose himself in speculation. Not now, when he might finally have a chance to set things right.

A small, cautious smile tugged at his lips. It felt foreign, almost painful after so many cycles of despair. But it was there – a flicker of hope in the darkness.

"One step at a time," Drake told himself, his voice gaining strength. "You've made it this far. Now you just have to figure out what comes next."

He closed his eyes, letting out a long, shaky breath. The weight of his past mistakes pressed down on him, but for the first time in what felt like an eternity, Drake felt a glimmer of possibility. He had broken the cycle. Now, he had to find a way to save his family – and perhaps, in doing so, save himself.

3 - 4

Drake's arms throbbed beneath the bandages, a constant reminder of the ordeal he'd endured. The sharp, raw pain seemed to pulse in time with his heartbeat, each throb echoing the tick of the clock on the wall. He shifted slightly, wincing as the movement sent a fresh wave of discomfort through his body.

"At least I'm feeling something," he thought grimly, his eyes tracing the slow rotation of the clock's hands. The steady march of time felt almost surreal after countless resets. "Proof that this is real. That I've finally broken through."

The painkillers dulled the edge of his injuries, wrapping his thoughts in a hazy cocoon. Drake struggled against the fog, forcing himself to stay alert. He couldn't afford to let his guard down, not when he'd finally made progress.

A soft creak broke the room's stillness. Drake's muscles tensed instinctively as the door swung open, revealing a middle-aged man in a crisp white coat. The doctor's warm smile and easy manner should have been reassuring, but Drake felt his hackles rise.

"Good morning," the man said, his voice gentle. "How are we feeling today?"

Drake studied him warily, searching for any hint of threat or deception. "I've been better," he replied cautiously, his tone guarded. "But I suppose I've been worse, too."

The doctor nodded sympathetically, moving closer to the bed. "That's understandable. You've been through quite an ordeal."

"You have no idea," Drake thought, but kept the words to himself. Instead, he asked, "When can I leave? I need to see my family."

A flicker of concern crossed the doctor's face. "Let's not get ahead of ourselves. We need to make sure you're stable first."

Drake's jaw clenched. He couldn't afford to be trapped here, not when Linda and Harrison might be in danger. "I appreciate your concern, doctor, but I really need to go."

As the doctor opened his mouth to respond, Drake's mind raced. How much could he reveal without sounding completely insane? How could he convince them to let him leave when he barely understood what was happening himself?

The weight of his mission pressed down on him, heavier than any physical pain. Drake took a deep breath, steeling himself for the battle ahead. One way or another, he would find a way out of this room and back to his family. He had to. The fate of more than just his world might depend on it.

5 - 6

The doctor's eyes met Drake's, a hint of curiosity mingling with his professional demeanor. "Mr. Miller," the man said, pulling a rolling stool closer to the bed. "I'm Dr. Charles Lee. I've been assigned to your case."

Drake's heart skipped a beat. The name stirred something in his mind—fragments of a memory. He had seen this man before, though not in this hospital, not in this reality. His fingers tightened imperceptibly on the thin hospital blanket, knuckles whitening as he fought to keep his expression neutral.

"Dr. Lee," Drake echoed, his voice hoarse. He swallowed hard, his throat suddenly dry. "Have we... met before?"

The doctor's brow furrowed slightly, a flash of confusion crossing his features. "I don't believe so, Mr. Miller. This is our first encounter."

Drake's mind raced, images flickering through his consciousness like a damaged film reel. Dr. Lee in a different hospital, wearing a different coat. Dr. Lee, his face grave, delivering news that made Drake's world crumble.

"Right," Drake managed, forcing a weak smile. "Of course. I must be confused from the medication."

Dr. Lee nodded; his pen poised over a clipboard. "That's not uncommon. How are you feeling this morning?"

Drake hesitated, weighing his words carefully. How much could he reveal? How much did he dare? The weight of unseen worlds pressed down on him, countless realities hanging in the balance of his next words.

"I'm... adjusting," he said finally, his gaze fixed on the doctor's familiar-yet-unfamiliar face. "It's been a long night."

7 - 8

Dr. Lee flipped through a chart, his brow furrowing slightly as he skimmed the notes. The soft rustle of paper seemed amplified in the sterile room, each turn of the page causing Drake's pulse to quicken. He fought the urge to peek at the contents, to see what this reality's version of himself had endured.

"You've had quite a night, I hear," Dr. Lee said, his tone carefully neutral. "A head injury and severe burns on both arms."

Drake's gaze flickered to his bandaged forearms, a dull throb pulsing beneath the gauze. How many times had he seen these same wounds, felt this same pain? The memories blurred together, a kaleidoscope of agony and desperation.

"We've treated the burns, but they'll take some time to heal properly," the doctor continued. "As for the head injury, I'd like to ask a few questions to assess your cognitive function. Routine stuff."

Drake nodded; his throat tight. "Of course," he managed, his mind racing. What if he slipped up? What if he revealed too much about the loops, about the other realities? The weight of countless worlds pressed down on him, threatening to crush him under their collective mass.

"Just take your time," Dr. Lee said, his pen hovering over the chart. "There's no rush."

But there was, Drake thought, a familiar urgency clawing at his insides. Time was always running out, always resetting, always slipping through his fingers like sand. He drew a deep breath, steeling himself for the questions to come, praying he could navigate this minefield without detonating the fragile peace he'd found in this new reality.

9 - 10

Dr. Lee leaned forward, his eyes searching Drake's face. "Can you tell me what happened last night?"

Drake's heart hammered against his ribs; each beat a reminder of the precarious nature of his situation. He swallowed hard, his mind a maelstrom of conflicting memories and realities. How could he possibly explain the truth without sounding completely insane?

"I..." Drake began, his voice hoarse. He cleared his throat, buying precious seconds to compose his thoughts. "It's all a bit hazy, to be honest."

Dr. Lee nodded encouragingly, his pen scratching softly against the chart. "That's not uncommon with head injuries. Just tell me what you can remember."

Drake's gaze drifted to the window, where the first light of dawn was beginning to paint the sky. How many sunrises had he witnessed, only to have them erased by the cruel cycle of the loops? He clenched his fists, ignoring the sharp sting of pain from his burns.

"I remember being at the restaurant," Drake said carefully, each word feeling like a tightrope walk over a chasm of impossibility. "There was... confusion. People were panicking."

He paused, searching Dr. Lee's face for any sign of disbelief or suspicion. But the doctor's expression remained neutral, professional. Drake pressed on, threading his way through the minefield of his memories.

"I think there was a fire," he continued, the lie tasting bitter on his tongue. But it was safer than the truth, safer than trying to explain the inexplicable. "I must have tried to help, and that's how I got the burns."

Dr. Lee jotted something down, his brow furrowing slightly. "And the head injury?"

Drake closed his eyes, feeling the weight of countless realities pressing down on him. How could he possibly keep all of this straight? How could he protect his family, save the world, when he could barely keep his own mind intact?

"I don't know," he admitted, opening his eyes to meet the doctor's gaze. "Everything after that is just... darkness."

11 - 12

Drake's fingers traced the edge of the hospital blanket, the rough texture a stark reminder of his current reality. He felt the weight of Dr. Lee's gaze upon him, probing for answers that Drake couldn't—wouldn't—provide.

"I passed out," Drake said simply, his voice low and tinged with exhaustion. "It's... been a stressful week. I haven't been sleeping well."

The admission wasn't entirely false. How could he sleep, knowing that each time he closed his eyes, he might wake to find his world reset, his loved ones in danger once again? The memory of countless failed attempts to break the loop haunted him, a relentless specter lurking at the edges of his consciousness.

Dr. Lee glanced up, his expression neutral. "And the burns? How did those happen?"

Drake's heart raced, his mind scrambling for a plausible explanation. The truth—that these wounds were physical manifestations of his desperate attempts to save his family across multiple realities—was too fantastical, too dangerous to reveal. He needed to protect his family, to shield them from the horrors he had witnessed.

As he opened his mouth to respond, Drake's gaze drifted to the window, where the first rays of dawn were beginning to paint the sky. How many sunrises had he witnessed, only to have them erased by the cruel cycle of the loops? He clenched his fists, ignoring the sharp sting of pain from his burns.

13 - 14

Drake hesitated; his eyes still fixed on the horizon beyond the window. The weight of his experiences pressed down on him; each loop etched into his psyche like scars. He turned back to Dr. Lee, his voice rough with emotion.

"I—uh, got them trying to put out a fire. At the restaurant."

The half-truth tasted bitter on his tongue. In his mind's eye, he saw the flames again—not from the restaurant, but from countless other disasters he'd faced in his attempts to break the loop. The searing heat, the acrid smoke, the desperate cries of those he couldn't save—all of it threatened to overwhelm him.

Dr. Lee's pen scratched against the chart; the sound amplified in the sterile quiet of the hospital room. Drake watched the doctor's hand move, wondering what conclusions this man was drawing about him. Would he see through the lie? Would he somehow discern the impossible truth?

"Understandable," Dr. Lee said at last, his tone professional yet tinged with sympathy. "Burns of this severity can be quite painful. It's important to stay hydrated and keep the bandages clean. If you notice any unusual swelling or redness, let the nurse know immediately."

Drake nodded, his throat constricting. The doctor's mundane advice felt surreal against the backdrop of his extraordinary experiences. How could he explain that these burns were the least of his concerns? That they were merely physical reminders of the cosmic battle he was waging.

As Dr. Lee continued to speak about treatment and recovery, Drake's mind drifted. He thought of Linda and Harrison, of the countless times he had failed to save them. Now, with the loop seemingly broken, a new fear gripped him. What if this reality, too, was just another illusion? What if he was still trapped, and this apparent escape was merely a cruel form of torment?

15 - 16

Drake's parched throat constricted as he nodded once more, his mind a whirlpool of conflicting thoughts and emotions. The weight of his recent experiences pressed down on him, making even this simple gesture feel monumental.

Dr. Lee rose from his seat, the legs of the stool scraping softly against the linoleum floor. He offered Drake a polite smile, though it did little to assuage the turmoil churning within the patient's chest.

"I'll let you rest for now," the doctor said, his voice carrying a practiced bedside manner. "If you need anything, press the call button."

As Dr. Lee turned to leave, Drake's heart raced. He wanted to call out, to confess everything – the loops, the multiverse, the disfigured man. But the words died in his throat, held back by the fear of being labeled insane.

Instead, he watched silently as the doctor's white coat disappeared through the doorway, leaving him alone with his thoughts. The steady beep of the heart monitor seemed to mock him, a constant reminder of the passage of time that had eluded him for so long.

"What now?" Drake whispered to himself; his eyes fixed on the ceiling. The bandages on his arms itched, a physical manifestation of the restlessness that consumed him. He had escaped the loop, yes, but at what cost? And what dangers still lurked in this new reality?

The weight of his choices, past and future, pressed down on him like a physical force. Drake closed his eyes, allowing himself a moment of vulnerability in the solitude of his hospital room. Tomorrow would bring new challenges, new mysteries to unravel. But for now, he would rest, gathering strength for the battles that lay ahead.

17 - 18

As Dr. Lee's footsteps faded down the hallway, Drake's ears pricked at the sound of a familiar voice just outside his door. His heart leapt, a mixture of hope and anxiety coursing through his veins.

"Is he okay? Can I see him?" The words, muffled but unmistakable, carried a note of concern that made Drake's throat tighten with emotion.

He pushed himself up on his elbows, wincing as the movement pulled at his bandaged arms. The voice outside – was it real, or just another cruel trick of his mind? After countless loops of loss and heartbreak, Drake hardly dared to hope.

"Please," he whispered, his voice barely audible even to himself. "Let it be her."

Drake's eyes remained fixed on the door; his breath held in anticipation. The possibility of seeing a loved one – alive and well – after so many iterations of tragedy left him simultaneously elated and terrified. What if this, too, was just another illusion?

As he waited, tense and expectant, Drake's mind raced with questions. How much did they know? How much could he reveal without sounding completely unhinged? The weight of his experiences pressed down on him, a secret burden he longed to share but feared might destroy the very reality he had fought so hard to reach.

19 - 20

The door creaked open, and Linda stepped inside, her blonde hair catching the harsh fluorescent light. Drake's breath caught in his throat. She was here, alive, her blue eyes filled with a mixture of concern and relief.

"Drake," she breathed, rushing to his bedside. Her hand reached out, hovering uncertainly over his bandaged arm before gently settling on his shoulder. "What happened? Are you alright?"

Drake swallowed hard, fighting back the flood of emotions threatening to overwhelm him. "I'm okay," he managed, his voice hoarse. "Linda, I... I'm so glad you're here."

She smiled softly, but her brow remained furrowed with worry. "Of course I'm here. Where else would I be?"

The simple question hit Drake like a punch to the gut. In how many realities had she been absent, lost to the cruel machinations of the loops? He struggled to find the right words, to bridge the gap between his experiences and her reality.

"I just... I've missed you," he said finally, reaching out to grasp her hand. The warmth of her skin against his was an anchor, grounding him in this moment.

Linda's expression softened, a hint of confusion flickering across her face. "Drake, it's only been a few hours since..."

"I know," he interrupted, not wanting to hear about a timeline he had already relived. "It just feels like longer."

As Linda settled into the chair beside his bed, Drake's mind raced. How much could he tell her? How much would she believe? The weight of his experiences pressed down on him, a secret burden he longed to share but feared might shatter this fragile peace.

"Harrison?" he asked, unable to keep the note of urgency from his voice.

"He's fine," Linda assured him quickly. "He's just outside with Richard. We were all so worried when you collapsed at the restaurant."

Drake nodded, relief washing over him. They were both safe. For now, at least, the nightmare had ended. But as he looked into Linda's concerned eyes, he knew that the journey was far from over. The truth of what he had experienced – of the multiverse and the loops – still lay between them, an unspoken chasm he would eventually have to bridge.

For now, though, he simply held onto her hand, savoring the feeling of being reunited with his family, whole and unharmed. Whatever challenges lay ahead, they would face them together.

21 - 22

"Dad!" Harrison exclaimed, his lanky frame propelling him across the room. The teenager's unruly dirty blonde hair bounced as he rushed to Drake's bedside, eyes wide with a mixture of relief and concern.

Drake instinctively reached out, ignoring the sharp sting that shot through his bandaged arms as he pulled Harrison into a fierce embrace. The familiar weight of his son against his chest sent a surge of conflicting emotions through him – gratitude, fear, and an overwhelming sense of protectiveness.

"It's okay, Dad," Harrison murmured, his voice muffled against Drake's hospital gown. "We're here now."

Drake closed his eyes, savoring the moment, his mind racing. How many times had he lost them? How many iterations of this day had ended in tragedy? The memories threatened to overwhelm him, but he pushed them back, focusing on the solid presence of his son in his arms.

"I know, buddy," he whispered, his voice hoarse. "I know."

As he held Harrison, Drake's gaze drifted to Linda, still lingering by the door. Her arms were crossed, a defensive posture he recognized from countless arguments and tense moments. But her expression was soft, blue eyes brimming with an emotion he couldn't quite name.

"Linda," he said, his throat tight. "I... I'm so glad you're both here."

She nodded, taking a hesitant step forward. "Of course we are, Drake. Where else would we be?"

The simple question hit him like a punch to the gut. Where else? In a hundred different nightmares, that's where. Dead in a car crash, consumed by fire, victims of a madman's plot. Drake swallowed hard, pushing back the flood of horrific memories.

"I just... I was worried," he managed, his grip on Harrison tightening slightly. "These past few days have been... difficult."

Linda's brow furrowed, concern deepening the lines around her eyes. "Drake, what's really going on? You're not making sense."

23 - 24

Drake's gaze darted between Linda and Harrison, his heart racing. The weight of his experiences pressed down on him, threatening to crush the fragile moment of reunion.

"You're here," Drake whispered, his voice cracking. "You're okay."

The words felt inadequate, a pale shadow of the relief flooding through him. He drank in the sight of them, alive and whole, committing every detail to memory. Harrison's warmth against his chest, the worried crease between Linda's brows, the antiseptic smell of the hospital room mingling with her familiar perfume.

Linda's expression softened further, and she took another step closer to the bed. "Of course we're here," she said, reaching out to touch Drake's arm gently. "Why wouldn't we be?"

The simple question sent a tremor through Drake. Images flashed through his mind: Linda's lifeless body in a wrecked car, Harrison disappearing in a blinding flash of light. He squeezed his eyes shut, trying to banish the memories.

When he opened them again, Linda was studying him intently, her blue eyes searching his face. Drake struggled to find words that wouldn't sound completely unhinged.

"I just... I had a feeling," he said finally, his voice low. "Like something terrible was going to happen. To both of you."

It wasn't a lie, not exactly. But it felt hollow, a pale imitation of the truth he couldn't bring himself to voice.

25 - 26

Drake leaned back, his hands resting on Harrison's shoulders. The boy's lanky frame felt solid beneath his palms, grounding him in this reality. He took a deep breath, steeling himself for what he knew would sound impossible.

"You don't understand," he began, his voice barely above a whisper. "I... I made it past midnight. The loops—they're over."

The words hung in the air, heavy with unspoken implications. Drake's heart raced, anticipating their reactions. He searched their faces, hoping against hope for a flicker of recognition, of shared understanding.

Linda's brow furrowed, her blonde hair catching the harsh fluorescent light as she tilted her head. "Drake, you're not making sense again," she said, her tone a mixture of concern and exasperation. "What loops?"

The question struck Drake like a physical blow. Of course they didn't remember. How could they? He alone had carried the burden of those endless, horrifying repetitions.

"I—" Drake began, then faltered. How could he possibly explain? The words caught in his throat, threatening to choke him. He glanced up at Harrison, whose wide brown eyes were fixed on him, filled with a mix of confusion and worry.

'They think I'm losing it,' Drake realized, a cold dread settling in his stomach. 'Maybe I am.'

He swallowed hard, trying to organize his thoughts. "It's... complicated," he said finally, knowing how inadequate the explanation was. "I've been through something... something you can't imagine."

Linda's expression softened slightly, but the worry in her eyes only intensified. "Drake, honey," she said gently, "you've been through a traumatic experience. It's natural to feel disoriented."

Drake shook his head, frustration building within him. "No, you don't—" he started, then cut himself off. How could he make them understand without sounding completely insane?

27 - 28

Drake took a deep breath, his chest expanding painfully against his bruised ribs. The antiseptic smell of the hospital room seemed to intensify, making his head swim. He could feel the weight of Linda's gaze, heavy with concern and skepticism.

"I've been living the same day over and over," he blurted out, the words tumbling from his lips in a frantic rush. "Every time, one of you dies. Sometimes both of you. I've tried everything to stop it, but it always resets."

Linda's blue eyes widened, her lips parting in shock. Drake pressed on, desperate to get it all out before she could interrupt.

"And then there's this man—this disfigured man. He told me I made a mistake, something that broke the universe." Drake's hands trembled as he gestured, his heart pounding. "I think it has something to do with the multiverse, with Harrison's story about Sir Mordred and the green dragon."

The silence that followed was deafening. Drake could hear the rapid beeping of his heart monitor, betraying his agitation. He searched Linda's face, hoping against hope to see a glimmer of belief, of understanding.

Linda stared at him, her face a complex tapestry of emotions—concern, skepticism, and something deeper, more painful. "Drake..." she began, her voice barely above a whisper.

'She doesn't believe me,' Drake thought, a wave of despair washing over him. 'How can I make her understand when I barely understand it myself?'

29 - 30

Drake's desperation mounted, his chest tight with the need to make them understand. He gripped the edges of his hospital gown, the thin fabric bunching under his fingers.

"I'm serious," he insisted, his voice raw with emotion. With trembling hands, he pulled up his sleeves, revealing the angry red burns that snaked up his forearms. The bandages had shifted, exposing patches of blistered skin. "These—these are from the loops. They carry over every time. This is real."

The sight of his wounds sent a shudder through Drake's body, memories of searing pain and acrid smoke flooding his senses. He swallowed hard, fighting back the bile rising in his throat.

Linda gasped, her hand flying to her mouth. Her eyes, wide with shock, darted between Drake's face and his injured arms. Drake could see the conflict in her expression—the desire to believe him warring with the impossibility of his claims.

Harrison leaned in closer, his brow furrowed as he examined the burns. Drake watched his son's face, searching for any sign of recognition, any hint that the boy's innate curiosity might lead him to believe. But as Harrison's gaze flicked between Drake and Linda, doubt clouded his young features.

"Dad, are you sure?" Harrison asked, his voice small and uncertain. "I mean, it sounds... pretty crazy."

The words hit Drake like a physical blow. He'd expected skepticism from Linda, but hearing doubt in Harrison's voice—Harrison, who had always believed in the impossible, who had sparked this whole journey with his story—felt like a betrayal.

'How can I make them see?' Drake thought, panic rising in his chest. 'If they don't believe me, how can I protect them? How can I stop this from happening again?'

31 - 32

Drake's chest tightened, desperation clawing at his insides. He leaned forward, his eyes darting between Linda and Harrison, silently pleading for them to understand.

"I know how it sounds," Drake said, his voice hoarse and urgent. "But I've seen it. I've lived it." He ran a trembling hand through his disheveled hair, wincing as his fingers brushed against the bandage on his head. "Every day, the same nightmare. Watching you both—" His voice cracked, and he swallowed hard, unable to finish the thought.

Linda's expression softened, a mix of concern and confusion etched across her delicate features. She reached out, her touch gentle as she placed her hand on Drake's arm, careful to avoid the bandages. The warmth of her skin against his was both comforting and agonizing—a reminder of what he'd fought so hard to preserve.

"Drake," she said, her voice low and soothing, "you've been through a lot." Her blue eyes searched his face, as if trying to decipher a complex puzzle. "Richard Vega, Harrison and I saw you pass out at the restaurant last night. He brought us here."

Drake's mind reeled at the mention of Richard Vega. Images flashed through his mind—Vega's smug smile, his calculated words, the way he always seemed to be one step ahead. A chill ran down Drake's spine as he realized the implications of Vega's presence.

'What game is he playing now?' Drake thought, his jaw clenching. 'Is this another trick? Another loop?'

Linda continued, unaware of the storm brewing in Drake's mind. "He's been in the hallway talking to the police about what happened."

Drake's heart raced, his palms growing slick with sweat. The police. Vega. It was all happening again, but differently. He couldn't shake the feeling that he was missing something crucial, that the truth was dancing just beyond his grasp.

"The police?" he whispered, more to himself than to Linda. "What could they want?"

As the words left his mouth, Drake realized he'd made a mistake. Linda's brow furrowed, her hand withdrawing slightly from his arm. He'd revealed too much, shown too clearly that his mind was somewhere else entirely.

'Focus,' he told himself, taking a deep breath. 'You have to make them understand. You have to keep them safe.'

33 - 34

Drake's eyes darted to Linda's face, searching for any sign of understanding, any flicker of recognition. But all he saw was concern tinged with a growing wariness. He swallowed hard, his throat dry and constricted.

"The police?" he repeated, forcing his voice to remain steady. "What do they want?"

Linda's fingers tightened on his arm, her touch a conflicting mix of comfort and restraint. Her blue eyes, usually so full of warmth, now held a guarded look that made Drake's heart ache.

"I don't know," she said softly, her words measured. "But they said they need to talk to you."

Drake's mind raced, memories of countless iterations flashing through his consciousness. How many times had he faced questioning, each loop bringing new variations of the same torment? He closed his eyes briefly, wishing the room to stop spinning.

'This is different,' he reminded himself. 'You made it past midnight. This isn't a loop. It's real.'

When he opened his eyes again, Linda was watching him closely, her expression a mixture of love and worry that threatened to unravel him completely.

"Drake," she whispered, leaning in closer, "what's really going on? You can tell me."

He wanted to. God, how he wanted to pour out everything—the loops, the disfigured man, the weight of a thousand lifetimes pressing down on his soul. But the words caught in his throat, tangled in a web of fear and doubt.

35 - 36

Before Drake could formulate a response, the door swung open with a soft creak. The sound sent a jolt through his body, every muscle tensing as if preparing for a fight. Two figures stepped into the sterile hospital room, their presence immediately filling the space with an air of authority.

Drake's eyes darted between them, his mind frantically searching for any hint of recognition. Had he seen these detectives before, in another loop, another life? The familiar yet foreign faces blurred in his vision, memories and reality colliding in a dizzying whirl.

"Mr. Miller," the woman said, her voice crisp and professional. "We'd like to ask you a few questions about last night's incident."

Drake's fingers clutched at the thin hospital blanket, seeking an anchor in this suddenly unstable world. He forced a deep breath, willing his racing heart to slow.

'Stay calm,' he told himself. 'You've done this before. Just... not quite like this.'

"Of course," he managed, his voice rougher than he'd intended. "What do you need to know?"

As the detectives approached his bedside, Drake's gaze flicked to Linda and Harrison. Their faces were etched with concern, and he felt a surge of protectiveness wash over him. Whatever came next, he had to shield them from the truth—the impossible, unbelievable truth that threatened to shatter their reality as surely as it had shattered his.

'I made it past midnight,' he reminded himself again, clinging to that fact like a lifeline. 'Whatever happens now, at least they're safe. At least we're all still here.'

37 - 38

Detective Kierstead's sharp eyes scanned Drake's face, her expression unreadable. "Can you walk us through what happened at the restaurant last night?"

Drake swallowed hard, his throat suddenly dry. The weight of her gaze seemed to press down on him, demanding truths he couldn't possibly share.

"I... I'm not sure," he began, his voice faltering. "Everything's a bit hazy."

Detective Bird, his imposing frame filling the space at the foot of the bed, grunted softly. "Understandable, given your injuries. But anything you can remember would be helpful."

Drake's mind raced, fragments of memories from countless loops swirling together. Which version was real this time? What had actually happened in this reality?

"I remember... smoke," he said slowly, buying time. "And heat. There was a fire in the kitchen, I think."

Linda stepped forward; her brow furrowed. "Drake, you weren't in the kitchen. You collapsed at our table, remember?"

'No,' Drake thought, panic rising in his chest. 'I don't remember. I don't know which version is real anymore.'

"Right," he said aloud, forcing a weak smile. "Sorry, I'm still a bit... confused."

Detective Kierstead's eyes narrowed slightly. "Mr. Miller, we have reports of a disturbance. Witnesses say you were acting erratically, shouting about... loops and danger. Can you explain that?"

Drake's heart hammered against his ribs. How could he possibly explain without sounding completely insane?

"I've been... under a lot of stress lately," he said, the half-truth tasting bitter on his tongue. "I think I might have had some kind of... episode."

39 - 40

Drake's gaze darted between the detectives, his fingers twisting the thin hospital blanket. The familiar weight of guilt settled in his chest, a constant companion through countless iterations of this day.

"An episode," Detective Kierstead repeated, her tone neutral but her eyes sharp. "Can you elaborate on that?"

Drake swallowed hard; his throat dry. "I've been having... nightmares. Vivid ones. Sometimes it's hard to tell what's real and what's not."

As he spoke, a memory flickered in his mind—Detective Bird, sprawled on the ground, his unseeing eyes staring at the sky as blood licked at his clothes. Drake shuddered, forcing the image away.

"These nightmares," Detective Bird interjected, his voice gruff but not unkind. "They related to these so called loops somehow?"

Drake hesitated, weighing his words carefully. "In a way, yes. I keep seeing... bad things happening. To my family, to others. I guess I got caught up in it last night."

Linda's hand found his, squeezing gently. The touch anchored him, a reminder that this moment, at least, was real.

Detective Kierstead leaned forward, her piercing gaze never wavering. "Mr. Miller, we're trying to understand what happened. Your episode caused quiet a disturbance, with someone of your stature its... how do you say.... suspicious."

Aloud, he said, "I wish I could tell you more. Everything's just... jumbled."

The weight of unspoken truths hung heavy in the air. How could he possibly explain the disfigured man, the disfigured puppet master pulling strings across realities? Or the crushing responsibility of trying to save everyone, only to fail time and time again?

Detective Bird sighed, his pen tapping against his notepad. "Alright, Mr. Miller. We'll give you some time to rest. But we'll need to speak again soon."

As the detectives turned to leave, Detective Kierstead stood fast and without hesitation said "Wait," she called out, her voice firm. "There's something else. You're not telling us the whole truth. Lets talk about the Parker Deposition."

Interrogation in Bandages

1⁻² The antiseptic scent of bleach and disinfectant assaulted Drake's nostrils, a stark reminder of his precarious situation. He shifted uncomfortably in the hospital bed, the crinkle of starched sheets beneath him like sandpaper against his raw nerves. His bandaged arms felt heavy, useless appendages resting atop the thin blanket.

Linda's hand found his, her touch warm and familiar. Drake's gaze flickered to her face, etched with worry lines that seemed to have deepened overnight. Harrison sat beside her, his young features a mix of curiosity and apprehension. The boy's eyes darted between his father and the two detectives looming at the foot of the bed, as if trying to piece together a puzzle beyond his years.

Detective Kierstead's piercing green eyes bore into Drake, dissecting him with clinical precision. Her tall frame cast a shadow across the room, her presence alone seeming to suck the air from Drake's lungs. Beside her, Detective Bird's stocky build and calm demeanor provided a stark contrast, though Drake found little comfort in the man's placid expression.

"Mr. Miller," Kierstead began, her voice cutting through the tension like a scalpel, "we need to discuss the events of last night."

Drake swallowed hard, his throat suddenly dry. The pain in his head pulsed, a dull throb that threatened to crescendo into a roar. He glanced at Linda, seeing the silent plea in her eyes. Tell them everything, they seemed to say. But how could he? How could he explain the inexplicable?

"I'm not sure what I can tell you," Drake said, his voice hoarse. "It's all... jumbled."

Detective Bird leaned forward slightly, his brow furrowed. "Start from the beginning, sir. What do you remember about the restaurant?"

Drake closed his eyes, fragments of memories flashing behind his eyelids like a broken film reel. The clink of glasses, the murmur of conversation, the sudden, heart-stopping moment when Harrison began to choke. And beneath it all, the suffocating sense of déjà vu, of having lived this nightmare before.

"We were at dinner," Drake began slowly, each word feeling like gravel in his mouth. "Everything was fine, and then... it wasn't."

He opened his eyes, meeting Kierstead's unwavering gaze. "I know how this sounds, but I've been through this before. Multiple times. It's like... like I'm stuck in a loop, and I can't break free."

The detectives exchanged a glance, a silent conversation passing between them. Drake's heart sank. They didn't believe him. Of course they didn't. How could they?

"Mr. Miller," Kierstead said, her tone carefully neutral, "are you aware of any threats made against you or your family recently? Any connection to your work, perhaps?"

Drake frowned, a chill running down his spine. "Threats? No, I... what are you implying, Detective?"

As Kierstead opened her mouth to respond, Drake's mind raced. What weren't they telling him? What did they know that he didn't? The weight of unseen forces pressed down on him, suffocating in its intensity. He gripped Linda's hand tighter, anchoring himself to the present even as the edges of reality seemed to blur.

3 - 4

Detective Kierstead's piercing green eyes bore into Drake, her gaze a scalpel dissecting his every reaction. The tension in the room thickened, palpable as the antiseptic scent that clung to the air.

"Mr. Miller," Kierstead began, her voice steady but edged with suspicion, "thank you for speaking with us. We understand you've had a... difficult night."

Drake's jaw clenched, the pain in his head pulsing in time with his racing heart. Difficult night? The understatement of the century. He glanced at Linda and Harrison, their worried faces a stark reminder of what was at stake. The weight of countless iterations, countless failures, pressed down on him like a physical force.

"I suppose you could say that," Drake nodded cautiously, his words measured. He fought to keep his voice level, to not betray the storm of emotions roiling beneath the surface. How could he possibly explain the inexplicable? The time loops, the mysterious figure, the constant dance with death that seemed to shadow his every move?

As he spoke, Drake's mind raced, analyzing Kierstead's tone, her choice of words. There was something lurking beneath her professional demeanor, a hint of knowledge or suspicion that set his nerves on edge. What did she know? What pieces of this impossible puzzle did she hold?

The bandages on his arms itched, a constant reminder of the physical toll this ordeal had taken. But it was nothing compared to the mental exhaustion, the bone-deep weariness that came from fighting against the very fabric of reality itself.

5 - 6

Kierstead's piercing green eyes flicked briefly to Linda and Harrison, their presence a tangible weight in the sterile hospital room. Drake felt a surge of protectiveness, his hand tightening imperceptibly on the blanket covering his legs. When the detective's gaze returned to him, he saw a glimmer of something—curiosity? Suspicion?—in her sharp features.

"Before we get into the details," Kierstead said, her voice a careful blend of professionalism and probing inquiry, "let me ask: How are you feeling?"

The question hung in the air, deceptively simple yet loaded with implications. Drake's mind raced, weighing his response. How was he feeling? Exhausted beyond measure. Terrified of losing his family again. Desperate for answers. Angry at the universe for its cruel game.

Instead, he settled for a single word, his tone guarded and tinged with a weariness that went beyond physical fatigue. "Alive," Drake said, the word tasting bitter on his tongue. He paused, memories of countless failed loops flashing through his mind like a macabre slideshow. "Which is more than I can say for how I've felt these past few days."

As he spoke, Drake's gaze drifted to the window, where golden afternoon light filtered through the blinds. It was a cruel irony—the world outside continued on, oblivious to the temporal nightmare he'd been living. He wondered, not for the first time, if this moment too would dissolve, leaving him once again at the beginning of this twisted cycle.

7 - 8

Kierstead's eyebrow arched, a subtle movement that spoke volumes. Her penetrating green eyes studied Drake, as if trying to dissect the layers of meaning behind his cryptic response. The silence stretched, pregnant with unasked questions.

Drake's heart hammered against his ribs as Kierstead reached into her jacket, extracting a small, worn notepad. The soft whisper of pages turning seemed unnaturally loud in the sterile hospital room. He watched her fingers, noting the slight calluses on her trigger finger—a detail that hadn't registered in previous iterations.

"We're here to talk about your behavior at The Lighthouse Seafood Restaurant last night," Kierstead said, her tone measured but tinged with an undercurrent of urgency. The mention of the restaurant sent a jolt through Drake's system, memories of choking sounds and panic flooding back.

She continued, "From what we've gathered, you were erratic, shouting about 'loops,' making claims about someone dying."

Drake's fingers tightened on the blanket, his knuckles whitening. How much did they know? How could he possibly explain the inexplicable?

"You passed out shortly after your son choked but, fortunately, survived."

Relief washed over Drake at the mention of Harrison's survival, even as a new wave of anxiety crashed through him. He'd saved his son this time, but for how long? Would the universe find another way to snatch him away?

"I know how it sounds," Drake said, his voice hoarse. He glanced at Linda and Harrison, their worried faces a painful reminder of what was at stake. "But there's more to this than you could possibly understand."

9 - 10

Drake shifted uncomfortably, the hospital gown rustling against the coarse sheets. The movement sent a sharp pain through his bandaged arms, a physical reminder of the ordeal he'd endured across countless iterations of this day. "What's your point, Detective?" he asked, his voice tight with barely contained frustration.

Detective Bird stepped forward, his imposing frame casting a shadow over the foot of the bed. Despite his size, there was a gentleness in his demeanor that Drake hadn't noticed before. "We're trying to understand why someone in your position—a respected lawyer—would have such an episode," Bird said, his tone calm but firm. His eyes, weathered by years of seeing the worst of humanity, held a glimmer of genuine concern. "And whether it has anything to do with the Parker case."

The mention of the case sent a chill down Drake's spine. How could they possibly know about that? In his mind, he saw flashes of documents, of whispered conversations in darkened parking garages, of a money hungry man's taunting smile. He swallowed hard, his throat suddenly dry.

"The Parker case?" Drake repeated, buying time as his mind raced. He could feel Linda's eyes on him, her worry palpable in the air between them. "I don't see how that's relevant to what happened at the restaurant."

But even as the words left his mouth, a nagging doubt gnawed at him. Was there a connection he'd missed? Some thread linking his temporal predicament to the case that had consumed so much of his professional life? The possibility made his head spin, adding another layer of complexity to an already impossible situation.

11 - 12

Linda's chair creaked as she leaned forward, her brow furrowing in a mix of confusion and protective instinct. The sunlight streaming through the hospital window caught the golden strands of her hair, creating a halo effect that reminded Drake of happier times. "What does his work have to do with last night?" she asked, her voice steady but tinged with an undercurrent of worry. "He's been under a lot of stress, yes, but—"

Drake reached out, his bandaged hand gently grasping Linda's. The warmth of her skin against his was an anchor, grounding him in this reality that still felt so fragile. His mind raced, trying to connect the dots between the case, his temporal loops, and the detectives' suspicions.

"Linda," he began, his voice hoarse with fatigue and uncertainty. "I don't know what they're implying, but—" He paused, the weight of his experiences pressing down on him. How could he explain the inexplicable? How could he make them understand the impossible journey he'd been on?

Detective Kierstead's sharp gaze flicked between them, her pen poised over her notepad like a predator ready to strike. The tension in the room was palpable, thick enough to cut with a knife. Drake's heart pounded in his chest, each beat a reminder of the precarious nature of his situation.

I've lived and watch those I love die a thousand times, he thought, *and yet I've never felt more trapped than I do right now.*

13 - 14

Detective Kierstead's voice cut through the tense silence, her words precise and measured. "Mrs. Miller," she interjected smoothly, her green eyes fixed on Linda with an intensity that made Drake's skin prickle, "your husband is involved in one of the most high-profile cases currently unfolding. Parker vs. NovaTech Industries."

The detective's words hung in the air, heavy with implication. Drake's fingers tightened around Linda's hand, seeking comfort in her touch as his mind reeled. *How deep does this go?* he wondered, a chill creeping up his spine.

Kierstead continued, her tone unwavering. "A case that has already seen key witnesses disappear, others intimidated, and allegations of illegal activity escalate into criminal territory."

The room seemed to shrink around Drake, the sterile white walls closing in. He could feel Linda's gaze on him, questioning, worried. The weight of responsibility, of lives potentially at stake, pressed down on his chest.

"I..." Drake began, then faltered. He frowned, confusion etching deep lines across his forehead. "I'm aware of the case," he said, his voice low and tinged with bewilderment. The memories of his work on Parker vs. NovaTech felt distant, as if from another lifetime – or perhaps another loop. "But we were close to settling it outside of court. NovaTech made an offer. The clients were considering it."

As he spoke, Drake's mind raced. *What am I missing? What happened in the time I've been... away?* The discrepancy between his recollection and the detective's implications sent a surge of unease through him, mingling with the constant undercurrent of fear for his family's safety.

15 - 16

Detective Bird's eyes narrowed, his weathered face a mask of skepticism. "That's not what we've heard," he said, his deep voice resonating through the small hospital room.

Drake's heart skipped a beat. The beeping of the heart monitor quickened imperceptibly, matching the sudden surge of adrenaline coursing through his veins. *What have they heard?* he wondered, a cold sweat breaking out on his forehead. The bandages on his arms suddenly felt too tight, a physical reminder of the surreal nightmare he'd been living.

Kierstead leaned forward slightly, her pen poised over her notepad. The fluorescent lights caught the sharp angles of her face, casting dramatic shadows that only intensified her piercing gaze. "Mr. Miller," she began, her voice low and measured, "were you aware that several key witnesses for Parker have gone missing in recent weeks?"

The question hung in the air, heavy and ominous. Drake's mind reeled, grasping for an explanation that could bridge the gap between his fragmented memories and this new, disturbing reality. He glanced at Linda, seeing the worry etched deep in her features. *How much more can she take?* he wondered, guilt gnawing at his insides.

"Missing?" Drake repeated, his voice barely above a whisper. The word tasted bitter on his tongue, laden with implications he couldn't begin to fathom. He closed his eyes for a moment, trying to reconcile this information with the loops he'd experienced. *Could this be connected? Or am I losing my grip on reality entirely?*

17 - 18

Drake's mouth opened, then closed, his thoughts a whirlwind of confusion and disbelief. The sterile hospital air seemed to thicken around him, making it harder to breathe. "Missing? No. I—what are you talking about?" he finally managed, his voice hoarse with uncertainty.

Detective Kierstead's green eyes narrowed, her pen tapping rhythmically against the notepad. The sound echoed in Drake's ears, each tap like a hammer driving home the gravity of the situation. She leaned in closer, her presence suddenly looming larger than her physical frame.

"Jane Crawford," Kierstead said, her tone sharp enough to cut through the fog of Drake's bewilderment. "Former NovaTech employee turned whistleblower. She was set to testify about witness tampering and the use of proprietary data in training NeuraLex. She vanished two weeks ago."

The words hit Drake like a physical blow. He felt the color drain from his face, his hands gripping the hospital blanket until his knuckles turned white. *Jane Crawford.* The name stirred something in the recesses of his mind, a fleeting memory that slipped away before he could grasp it.

How could I not know about this? Drake wondered, his thoughts racing. *Have I been so caught up in these loops that I've lost touch with reality? Or is this some new, twisted version of events I haven't experienced before?*

He glanced at Linda, seeing the mixture of confusion and concern in her eyes. The weight of her gaze, coupled with the intensity of Kierstead's scrutiny, made Drake feel trapped, cornered by circumstances he couldn't begin to understand.

19 - 20

Drake swallowed hard, his throat dry and constricted. The sterile hospital air seemed to grow thicker, pressing in on him from all sides. He shook his head, the motion causing a dull throb behind his eyes.

"I didn't know that. I swear," he said, his voice barely above a whisper. The words felt hollow, inadequate in the face of such a revelation. Drake's mind raced, trying to reconcile this new information with the fragmented reality he'd been living.

Detective Bird shifted his weight, his imposing frame casting a shadow across the foot of the bed. His eyes, normally sharp and discerning, held a hint of something else—concern, perhaps, or a flicker of doubt.

"What about Alan Shore?" Bird added, his deep voice rumbling through the room. "Another whistleblower. His car was found abandoned in a parking lot just outside the city. No one's seen him since."

The name struck Drake like a physical blow. Alan Shore. Another piece of a puzzle he didn't even know existed. His heart hammered against his ribs, each beat a reminder of how little control he had over his own life—over any life.

Shore. Crawford. Missing witnesses. What's happening? Drake's thoughts whirled, a maelstrom of confusion and fear. *Is this connected to the loops? To the man in the white robe? Or is this some cruel new twist of fate?*

He looked at his bandaged arms, the physical evidence of his ordeal. But now, in light of these revelations, even his own memories felt suspect. Drake's gaze darted between the two detectives, searching their faces for any hint of understanding, any sign that they could see the impossible situation he found himself in.

21 - 22

Drake's chest tightened, his pulse quickening. The sterile hospital air suddenly felt thick, oppressive. He swallowed hard, his throat dry. "I don't know anything about that," he managed, the words tasting like ash in his mouth.

Detective Kierstead's piercing green eyes narrowed, scrutinizing Drake's face for any tell, any flicker of deception. She exchanged a meaningful glance with Bird, a silent communication born of years of partnership. Drake felt exposed, vulnerable under their combined scrutiny.

They don't believe me, he realized, a cold dread settling in his stomach. *How could they? The truth is too bizarre, too impossible.*

Kierstead leaned forward slightly, her voice low and measured. "We've also been informed by your colleague, Richard Vega, that you've been acting... erratically. Missing time at work. Unfocused on your cases."

The mention of Richard's name hit Drake like a punch to the gut. His mind reeled, trying to reconcile the friend he thought he knew with this apparent betrayal.

Richard. Of course. But how much does he know? How much has he seen?

Drake's fingers clenched the thin hospital blanket, his knuckles white. He struggled to keep his expression neutral, even as a storm of emotions raged within him. Confusion, anger, fear—they swirled together, threatening to overwhelm him.

"I've been... under a lot of stress," Drake said carefully, each word chosen with deliberate caution. He looked at Linda, seeing the worry etched in her face, then back to the detectives. "The Parker case, it's... complicated. High stakes."

But even as he spoke, Drake knew his explanation rang hollow. How could he possibly convey the true nature of his stress, the nightmarish loop he'd been trapped in? The weight of countless deaths, the desperate struggle to save his family—it was a burden he carried alone, invisible to the world around him.

23 - 24

Drake stiffened, his shoulders tensing as if bracing for a blow. "Richard said that?" The words escaped him in a hoarse whisper, betrayal etching itself across his features.

Detective Bird's steady gaze met Drake's, his expression a mixture of concern and professional detachment. "He said you've been distant since Miller & Co. took on the Parker case," Bird confirmed, his deep voice resonating in the sterile hospital room. "Your performance has been slipping, and you've been difficult to reach. He's worried about you."

The fluorescent lights seemed to flicker, casting strange shadows across the room. Drake's mind raced, fragments of memories from countless iterations of the same day colliding with the stark reality before him. His fingers twitched, unconsciously reaching for Linda's hand before curling into a fist at his side.

Richard, you bastard, Drake thought, a surge of anger rising within him. *You have no idea what I've been through, what I'm trying to prevent.* But beneath the anger lurked a gnawing fear. How much did Richard actually know? Had he somehow glimpsed the truth of Drake's impossible situation?

"I've been... preoccupied," Drake finally managed, his voice strained. He met Bird's gaze, searching for any hint of understanding or belief. "The Parker case is more complex than we initially thought. There are... implications I couldn't have foreseen."

The weight of unspoken truths hung heavy in the air. Drake longed to explain, to make them understand the cosmic tangle he found himself caught in. But the words caught in his throat, held back by the certainty that the truth would only make him appear more unstable, more suspect.

25 - 26

Linda shifted in her chair, the plastic creaking softly. Her eyes, pools of concern, met Drake's. "It's true," she said softly, her voice barely above a whisper. "You haven't been yourself lately. You've had restless nights, nightmares. You wake up in a sweat, muttering things I don't understand."

Drake's heart clenched. The pain in Linda's voice was palpable, a reminder of the toll his ordeal had taken not just on him, but on his family. He remembered countless nights of waking up, gasping for air, the images of Linda and Harrison dying in various horrific ways still seared into his mind.

"Linda," he began, his voice hoarse with emotion. Hurt flashed in his eyes, a complex mixture of guilt, frustration, and desperation. "You know why. I told you everything."

The words hung in the air, heavy with unspoken implications. Drake's mind raced, torn between the need to protect his family and the desperate desire to make them understand. He'd shared his impossible story with Linda, poured out his heart about the time loops, the deaths, the mysterious figure haunting him. But now, with the detectives present, he felt the walls closing in.

How much can I say? Drake wondered, his gaze darting between Linda and the detectives. *Will they believe me, or will it just make everything worse?* The weight of his knowledge, of the cosmic stakes at play, pressed down on him like a physical force.

27 - 28

Detective Kierstead's pen hovered over the page, her sharp green eyes fixed on Drake with an intensity that seemed to pierce through his defenses. "What exactly did you tell her, Mr. Miller?" she asked, her voice steady but laced with a hint of skepticism.

Drake's fingers tightened on the hospital blanket, the rough texture grounding him in this moment of reality. He hesitated, his mind racing through the potential consequences of revealing the truth. The sterile hospital air felt thick in his lungs as he struggled to find the right words.

They'll think I'm crazy, he thought, his heart pounding against his ribcage. *But if I don't tell them, how can I ever hope to stop this?*

Taking a deep breath, Drake steeled himself. The weight of countless repeated days, of watching his family die over and over, pressed down on him. He could feel Linda's worried gaze and Harrison's confused stare, adding to the pressure.

"That I've been living the same day over and over again," Drake finally said, his voice barely above a whisper. He paused, watching Kierstead's expression for any sign of disbelief or judgment. Finding none, he continued, his words gaining strength. "That every time, my wife or my son—or both of them—die. I've tried everything to stop it, but it keeps resetting. Until last night."

The confession hung in the air, heavy with implications. Drake's heart raced as he awaited their reaction, wondering if he'd just sealed his fate or taken the first step towards salvation.

29 - 30

Kierstead's pen hovered above her notepad, motionless. The silence in the room was palpable, broken only by the steady beep of the heart monitor. Drake's gaze flickered between the detective's impassive face and her unmoving hand, his anxiety mounting with each passing second.

Finally, Kierstead's eyes narrowed, her piercing green gaze locking onto Drake's bandaged arms and the gauze wrapped around his head. "And these injuries?" she asked, her voice a mix of skepticism and curiosity. "Are they from these supposed 'loops'?"

Drake swallowed hard, his throat suddenly dry. The memory of searing heat and blinding pain flashed through his mind, causing him to wince involuntarily. He could almost smell the acrid scent of burning flesh, hear Harrison's terrified screams.

"Yes," he managed, his voice hoarse. Drake's fingers tightened on the blanket, anchoring himself to the present. "I got the burns trying to save Harrison from a propane explosion."

He paused, the throbbing in his head intensifying as he recalled the funhouse mirror maze, the shadows dancing and distorting around him. The disfigured man's laughter echoed in his ears, a chilling reminder of the danger that still lurked.

"The head injury is from..." Drake hesitated, the words catching in his throat. How could he explain the inexplicable? "...an attack."

As soon as the words left his mouth, Drake knew how it sounded. He could see the doubt creeping into Kierstead's eyes, the slight furrow of her brow as she processed his explanation.

She doesn't believe me, he thought, a wave of despair washing over him. *None of them do. How can I make them understand when I barely understand it myself?*

31 - 32

Kierstead leaned forward, her green eyes narrowing with intense focus. The fluorescent lights cast harsh shadows across her face, accentuating the sharpness of her features. "An attack? By who?" Her voice was a mixture of professional curiosity and barely concealed skepticism.

Drake's heart raced, pounding against his ribs like a caged animal desperate for escape. He could feel Linda and Harrison's eyes on him, their concern palpable in the sterile hospital air. How could he possibly explain the nightmare that had become his reality?

"A disfigured man," Drake finally said, the words tumbling out in a rush. He closed his eyes, trying to steady his breathing as the image of his tormentor flashed vividly in his mind. "He wears a white robe with a green dragon emblem on it."

The memory of the man's twisted face, the cruel gleam in his eyes, sent a shiver down Drake's spine. He opened his eyes, meeting Kierstead's penetrating gaze. "He's been haunting me, taunting me. He attacked me at an abandoned amusement park, in the funhouse."

As he spoke, Drake could almost smell the musty air of the dilapidated funhouse, hear the creaking of rusty machinery. The surreal quality of the memory made him question his own sanity for a moment.

Am I losing my mind? he wondered, a flicker of doubt creeping into his thoughts. *Or is this nightmare really happening?*

33 - 34

Kierstead's expression hardened, her green eyes narrowing as she studied Drake with an intensity that made him feel like a specimen under a microscope. The sharp angles of her face seemed to cut through the haze of his confusion, demanding clarity where there was none to be found.

"Do you understand how that sounds, Mr. Miller?" Her voice was cool, professional, but Drake could hear the underlying skepticism, the unspoken accusation of delusion or deception.

Drake's jaw clenched, a surge of frustration rising within him like a tidal wave. He gripped the hospital blanket tightly, his knuckles turning white with the effort of maintaining his composure. The weight of disbelief from everyone around him – the detectives, his wife, even his own son – pressed down on his chest, threatening to suffocate him.

"I know how it sounds," Drake shot back, his voice carrying a sharp edge of desperation. He leaned forward, ignoring the twinge of pain from his injuries. "But it's the truth."

His mind raced, grappling with the enormity of what he was about to reveal. The words of the disfigured man echoed in his ears, a haunting refrain that had pursued him through countless iterations of this cursed day.

"He said..." Drake paused, swallowing hard against the lump in his throat. "He said I made a mistake. That the universe is trying to correct itself, and my family is caught in the middle of it."

The memory of the attack flashed before his eyes – the funhouse mirrors distorting reality, the sickening crack as his head hit the floor. Drake's voice dropped to a near-whisper, heavy with the weight of his revelation.

"He attacked me to make sure I don't remember what the mistake is."

As the words left his mouth, Drake felt a chill run down his spine. He searched Kierstead's face for any sign of understanding, any flicker of belief. But all he saw was the hardened mask of a detective who had heard one too many far-fetched stories.

They don't believe me, he thought, a wave of hopelessness washing over him. *How can I protect my family if no one believes the truth?*

35 - 36

Detective Bird sighed heavily, his large frame shifting as he rubbed the back of his neck. The gesture, so mundane and human, struck Drake as oddly incongruous with the surreal nature of their conversation. Bird's weathered face creased with a mixture of concern and skepticism.

"Look, Mr. Miller," Bird began, his voice low and measured, "we're not here to argue the metaphysical. But this story you're spinning—it sounds like someone trying to cover up a traumatic event. Something like being tortured."

The word hung in the air, heavy and ominous. Drake felt his heart rate quicken, the steady beep of the heart monitor betraying his rising anxiety. His mind reeled, struggling to process the implication.

"Tortured?" Drake repeated, his voice rising. The word tasted bitter on his tongue, a cruel mockery of the hell he'd been living through. He clenched his fists, ignoring the sharp pain from his burned arms.

Tortured? As if reliving the deaths of my family over and over wasn't torture enough? The thought blazed through his mind, a mixture of indignation and despair.

Drake's gaze darted between Bird and Kierstead, searching their faces for any sign of understanding. But all he saw was the cool, analytical stare of investigators who thought they'd cracked a case.

"You think I made this up?" Drake asked, his voice trembling with barely contained emotion. "That I—what? Burned myself? Bashed my own head in?" He gestured to his injuries, wincing at the movement.

The absurdity of it all threatened to overwhelm him. How could he make them understand? The loops, the deaths, the mysterious figure—it all seemed to slip further away with each passing moment, like trying to hold onto the fragments of a fading dream.

37 - 38

Kierstead leaned closer, her piercing green eyes locked onto Drake's. The scent of her crisp, no-nonsense perfume mingled with the antiseptic hospital air. "Mr. Miller," she said, her voice low and intense, "we believe NovaTech may have tried to silence you. Maybe you got too close to the truth. The burns, the head injury—they could be from someone trying to make sure you stay quiet. And this 'loop' story could be your way of protecting your family. Of keeping yourself from snitching."

Drake's mind reeled, the words hitting him like a physical blow. *NovaTech? Silencing me?* The thought was almost laughable, if not for the deadly seriousness in Kierstead's eyes. He felt a surge of frustration, bordering on panic, rising in his chest.

"That's insane!" Drake shouted, his voice echoing off the sterile hospital walls. He struggled to sit up straighter, ignoring the pain that flared through his body. "I don't know anything about missing witnesses or intimidation. And I'm not covering for NovaTech!"

His heart raced, the monitor beside him beeping more rapidly. Drake's gaze darted between Kierstead and Bird, searching for any sign of belief, of understanding. But their faces remained impassive, professional masks that revealed nothing.

How can I make them understand? Drake thought desperately. *The loops, the deaths, the disfigured man—it's all real. It has to be.* But even as the thought formed, a flicker of doubt crept in. Could it all have been some sort of elaborate delusion? A way for his mind to cope with something too terrible to face?

39 - 40

Kierstead's eyes narrowed, her piercing green gaze boring into Drake. The tension in the room thickened, almost palpable. "Are you sure about that? Because from where I'm sitting, it looks like you're deeply tangled in this case—whether you know it or not."

Drake's breath caught in his throat. The certainty in her voice sent a chill down his spine. He opened his mouth to protest, but the words died on his lips. *What if she's right?* The thought slithered through his mind, unwelcome and terrifying. *What if there's more to this than I realize?*

His gaze drifted to the bandages on his arms, stark white against his skin. The burns beneath them throbbed, a constant reminder of a reality he couldn't fully grasp. The memory of flames, of Harrison's screams, flashed through his mind. It had felt so real, so visceral. But now, under Kierstead's scrutiny, even those memories began to waver.

Linda's hand found his, her touch warm and grounding. Drake turned to meet her eyes, seeing the worry etched deeply in her features. "Drake, please," she said softly, her voice trembling slightly. "Just tell them everything. Maybe they can help."

The gentle plea in her words tore at Drake's heart. He wanted to reassure her, to tell her everything would be alright. But the truth was, he wasn't sure of anything anymore. The world he thought he knew—with its loops and impossible choices—was crumbling around him. And in its place, a new, equally terrifying reality was taking shape.

"I—" Drake started, his voice hoarse. He swallowed hard, trying to organize his thoughts. "I don't know what to tell them, Linda. I've already said everything I know."

41 - 42

Drake's voice trembled as he spoke, the words barely audible above the steady beep of the hospital machinery. "I already have," he said, his eyes darting between Linda and Detective Kierstead. The weight of their expectations pressed down on him, suffocating in its intensity.

He could feel his pulse quickening, the rhythm matching the frantic pace of his thoughts. *What more do they want from me?* he wondered, a wave of desperation washing over him. *How can I make them understand when I barely understand it myself?*

Kierstead's piercing gaze locked onto Drake, her expression a mix of skepticism and something else—was it pity? She closed her notepad with a deliberate snap, the sound echoing in the sterile room like a final judgment. As she stood, her posture straightened, radiating an air of authority that seemed to fill the space.

"We appreciate your time, Mr. Miller," Kierstead said, her tone neutral but tinged with an undercurrent of disappointment. "We'll be in touch."

Drake watched her, his mind racing. He wanted to say more, to make her understand the impossible situation he found himself in. But the words stuck in his throat, trapped behind a wall of fear and uncertainty. *What if she's right?* The thought slithered through his mind, unwelcome and terrifying. *What if there's more to this than I realize?*

43 - 44

Detective Bird shifted his weight, drawing Drake's attention. The stocky man's calm demeanor seemed at odds with the tension in the room. His eyes, weathered by years of service, held a flicker of something Drake couldn't quite place—sympathy, perhaps, or resignation.

"Mrs. Miller, Harrison, take care," Bird said, offering a polite smile that didn't quite reach his eyes. His voice was gruff yet gentle, a stark contrast to Kierstead's sharp tones.

Linda's hand tightened around Drake's, her touch a lifeline in the storm of his thoughts. Harrison, perched on the edge of his chair, looked between his parents and the detectives, his young face a canvas of confusion and worry.

As the detectives turned to leave, their footsteps echoing in the hallway beyond, Drake felt the last of his strength ebb away. He slumped back against the pillows, the starched fabric rough against his skin. His mind spun, a kaleidoscope of fragmented memories and half-formed theories.

What have I done? he thought, closing his eyes against the harsh fluorescent lights. *How deep does this go?* The weight of the multiverse pressed down on him, each possibility a new thread in an ever-expanding tapestry of confusion.

"Drake?" Linda's voice was soft, tentative. "Are you alright?"

He opened his eyes, meeting her concerned gaze. "I don't know," he admitted, his voice barely above a whisper. "I just... I don't know anymore."

45 - 46

Drake's eyes darted around the sterile hospital room, his gaze flitting from the beeping monitors to the wilting flowers on the bedside table. The scent of antiseptic mingled with the faint aroma of day-old lilies, creating a jarring contrast that mirrored the chaos in his mind.

"What just happened?" he muttered, his voice hoarse and tinged with disbelief. The weight of the detectives' accusations pressed down on him, each word a brick in a wall of confusion and fear that threatened to entomb him.

Linda leaned forward, her blonde hair catching the harsh fluorescent light. Her blue eyes, usually a source of comfort, now swirled with a maelstrom of emotions. She squeezed his hand, her touch both familiar and foreign in this surreal moment.

"I don't know," she whispered, her voice trembling slightly. "But whatever this is, we'll get through it together." The words hung in the air, a fragile promise in a world that seemed to be unraveling at the seams.

Drake's mind raced, replaying the detectives' words. Missing witnesses. Erratic behavior. Torture. Each accusation felt like a dagger, piercing through the fragile construct of reality he'd been clinging to.

"Linda," he began, his voice barely audible, "I swear I don't know anything about those missing people. I'm not... I wouldn't..." He trailed off, unable to articulate the swirling storm of thoughts and emotions.

She nodded, her expression a battlefield of worry and unwavering support. "I believe you, Drake. But these accusations, the case... it's all so much bigger than we realized."

Drake closed his eyes, feeling the weight of multiple realities pressing down on him. The loops, the disfigured man, the constant deaths of his family - how could he explain any of it without sounding completely insane?

"I feel like I'm losing my mind," he confessed, opening his eyes to meet Linda's gaze. "Everything I've experienced, everything I've told you... it's real to me. But hearing it laid out like that, by the detectives... God, Linda, what if I am going crazy?"

47 - 47

Drake's fingers tightened around Linda's hand, seeking an anchor in the churning sea of his thoughts. The sterile hospital air seemed to thicken, pressing against his skin like an invisible weight.

"I don't know what's real anymore," he whispered, his voice hoarse. "The loops, the deaths, that... that man. They feel as vivid as this moment right now. But how can that be?"

Linda leaned closer, her free hand brushing a stray lock of hair from his forehead. "Drake, you've been under immense stress. Maybe—"

"No," he interrupted, shaking his head. The movement sent a sharp pain through his skull, a reminder of the wound he couldn't explain. "It's more than stress. It's like... like I'm living in two worlds at once."

He glanced at Harrison, who sat silently, eyes wide with a mixture of concern and confusion. Drake's heart clenched. How many times had he watched his son die? The memory of Harrison choking at the restaurant flashed vividly in his mind.

"I can't lose you both again," Drake murmured, his gaze shifting between Linda and Harrison. "But I don't know how to stop it. And now, with these accusations... Linda, what if I've done something terrible and can't remember?"

The weight of uncertainty pressed down on him, suffocating in its intensity. Drake wasn't sure of anything anymore – not his sanity, not his innocence, not even the reality of the world around him.

Following the Threads

1⁻² The crisp autumn air nipped at Holly Kierstead's cheeks as she stepped out of the hospital, her eyes squinting against the harsh glare of streetlights reflecting off the damp pavement. She pulled her coat tighter, the chill seeping through despite her layers. Behind her, Franklin Bird's heavy footsteps echoed, his hulking frame casting a long shadow as the automatic doors hissed shut.

Holly's mind raced, replaying the interview they'd just conducted. The victim's words echoed in her head, each outlandish claim more perplexing than the last. She glanced at Bird, noting the deep furrow in his brow, the tightness around his eyes. He was troubled too, she realized, though he'd never admit it outright.

They walked in silence for a moment, the weight of unspoken questions hanging between them. Holly's fingers twitched, itching to reach for her notebook, to start piecing together the puzzle that had just been dumped in their laps. But she held back, knowing Bird needed time to process.

Finally, Bird broke the silence, his gravelly voice cutting through the quiet night. "Hell of a story he gave us." The words were laced with his trademark skepticism, but Holly caught the undercurrent of curiosity beneath.

She nodded, her own thoughts a tangled mess of possibilities. "It's certainly... unique," she offered, carefully neutral. Her analytical mind was already dissecting each claim, searching for inconsistencies, for threads to pull.

Bird grunted, shoving his hands deeper into his pockets. "Unique's one word for it. I was thinking more along the lines of 'batshit crazy.'"

Holly couldn't help the small smile that tugged at her lips. Despite his gruff exterior, Bird's dry humor often surfaced at the most unexpected moments. "Maybe," she conceded, "but you have to admit, there's something compelling about it."

She watched as Bird's expression shifted, the hint of a frown deepening the lines around his mouth. He was conflicted, she realized. His years of experience screamed that this was nonsense, but that same instinct that had made him such an effective detective was telling him there was more to the story.

"I don't know, Kierstead," he said finally, his voice low. "It feels like we're chasing shadows here. Alternate realities? Time loops? It's the stuff of bad sci-fi novels, not real police work."

Holly nodded, understanding his reservations. But something nagged at her, a feeling she couldn't quite shake. "I hear you, Frank. But what if... what if there's even a grain of truth to it? We can't just dismiss it outright, can we?"

Bird sighed, his breath visible in the cold air. "No," he admitted reluctantly. "We can't. But where the hell do we even start with something like this?"

Holly's mind was already racing, piecing together a plan of action. "We start where we always do," she said, her voice gaining confidence. "We follow the evidence, no matter where it leads us."

As they reached their car, Holly caught Bird's eye. In that moment, she saw a flicker of the same determination she felt burning in her chest. Whatever they were facing, whatever strange twists this case might take, they would face it together.

3 - 4

Holly's gaze drifted to the horizon, her sharp eyes scanning the cityscape as if searching for answers among the distant skyscrapers. The fading sunlight cast long shadows across her face, accentuating the determined set of her jaw.

"Yeah," Kierstead replied, her voice low and measured. "But people don't burn their arms and crack their heads open over a story, Frank."

She turned to face her partner, noting the way his brow furrowed in contemplation. The weight of their shared experience hung between them, a silent acknowledgment of the bizarre turns their investigation had taken.

Bird nodded, his breath forming a misty cloud in the chilly air. "Still, loops? A disfigured man in a robe? Feels like he's borrowing from bad sci-fi to cover up something worse."

Holly's mind raced, piecing together the fragments of their witness's account. The injuries were real, undeniable. Yet the explanation strained credulity. She found herself caught in the liminal space between skepticism and the nagging sense that they were on the cusp of something far beyond their usual fare.

"I know it sounds far-fetched," she conceded, her fingers absently tracing the outline of her badge. "But we've seen stranger things, haven't we? Remember the Holloway case?"

Bird's expression softened slightly at the memory. "That was different, Holly. Weird, sure, but explainable. This... this is something else entirely."

As they stood there, the distant wail of a siren pierced the air, a stark reminder of the very real dangers that lurked in their city. Holly couldn't shake the feeling that they were standing on the precipice of something monumental, something that would challenge everything they thought they knew about the nature of reality itself.

5 - 6

Holly's fingers traced the cool metal of the cruiser's roof, her eyes distant as she processed the implications of their witness's story. The chill of the autumn air seeped through her coat, mirroring the unease that had settled in her chest.

"Maybe," she conceded, her voice low and thoughtful. "But the guy's clearly been through hell, and I don't think he's faking his fear. He believes what he's saying."

She turned to face Bird, noting the deep furrows in his brow. His skepticism was palpable, but there was something else there too—a flicker of uncertainty that resonated with her own conflicted feelings.

Bird's hand rested on the driver's side door, but he made no move to open it. His gaze met hers, searching. "You think he's connected to the missing Parker witnesses?"

The question hung in the air between them, heavy with possibility. Holly's mind raced, weighing the improbable against the impossible. The burn marks, the head injury—they were tangible, undeniable. But could they truly be evidence of something beyond their understanding?

She inhaled deeply, the crisp air filling her lungs. "I don't know, Frank. But there's got to be a reason he's so terrified. And if there's even a chance it's linked to Parker..." She trailed off, leaving the implications unspoken.

Bird's jaw tightened, his years of experience warring with the bizarre nature of their current situation. "It's a hell of a leap, Holly. From missing witnesses to... what? Time loops and disfigured assailants?"

"I know how it sounds," Holly admitted, her voice barely above a whisper. "But we owe it to those witnesses—and to Drake—to follow every lead, no matter how strange."

As they stood there, the weight of their responsibility settled over them like a shroud. The city hummed around them, oblivious to the potential threads of an impossible mystery unraveling in their midst.

7 - 8

Holly hesitated, her jaw tightening as she contemplated the implications. The streetlight cast long shadows across her face, accentuating the furrow in her brow. "It's possible," she said finally, her voice low and measured. "The timing lines up—his erratic behavior started after the case heated up."

She ran a hand through her hair, a rare gesture of uncertainty. "Vega said he's been distracted, missing time at work. Something's weighing on him."

The words hung in the air, heavy with possibility. Holly's mind raced, piecing together fragments of a puzzle she wasn't sure she wanted to solve. The city sounds faded into the background as she focused on the connections forming in her mind.

Bird shifted his weight, the car door creaking slightly under his grip. His expression was thoughtful, lines deepening around his eyes as he considered her words. "And you think this 'disfigured man' angle has legs?" he asked, his tone a mix of skepticism and curiosity.

Holly's gaze drifted to the hospital entrance, recalling Drake's wild-eyed fear. The image of his burns, angry and raw, flashed in her mind. She suppressed a shudder.

"I don't know, Frank," she admitted, turning back to her partner. "But those injuries were real. And the fear in his eyes..." She trailed off, searching for the right words. "It wasn't the kind of fear you can fake."

The weight of the unknown pressed down on her, a familiar discomfort she'd learned to embrace in her years as a detective. But this case felt different, as if they were standing on the edge of something vast and incomprehensible.

9 - 10

Holly's eyes met Bird's, her gaze resolute. "It's worth looking into," she said firmly, her voice cutting through the chill night air. "If it's just a delusion, fine. But if it's something more? If someone's actually been threatening him—or worse—then we need to figure out who."

She felt a familiar tightness in her chest, the mix of anticipation and dread that came with every new case. But this time, it was tinged with something else—a sense that they were treading into uncharted territory.

Bird's eyes narrowed slightly, his years of experience evident in the way he weighed her words. He gave a slight nod, his weathered features softening. "Alright," he conceded, his voice gruff but not unkind. "What's the plan?"

Holly's mind raced, considering their options. The abandoned amusement park loomed large in her thoughts, a decaying monument to forgotten dreams. She imagined its rusted gates, the eerie silence that must blanket the grounds after dark. A shiver ran down her spine that had nothing to do with the cold.

"We need to check out that amusement park," she said, her voice low and determined. "If Drake's story is true, there might be evidence there. Something he missed, or couldn't see in the dark."

Bird's brow furrowed, concern etching deeper lines into his face. "That's risky, Holly. If someone really is after Drake, they could still be hanging around."

Holly felt a surge of stubbornness, tempered by the knowledge that Bird's caution came from a place of experience. "I know," she admitted. "But we can't ignore this. Something's happening, Frank. I can feel it."

11 - 12

Holly's sharp eyes met Bird's, her gaze unwavering. The streetlights cast a pallid glow across her face, accentuating the determination etched in her features. She drew in a deep breath, the crisp autumn air filling her lungs as she formulated their next move.

"You head back to the precinct," Kierstead said, her voice steady and authoritative. "Pull any security footage we can get from the area around that abandoned amusement park. See if there's anything that backs up his story about being there—or someone else being there with him."

As she spoke, Holly's mind raced through the possibilities. Grainy CCTV footage of a figure in a white robe, perhaps? Or maybe just Drake himself, wandering alone and disoriented? Either way, it was a lead they couldn't ignore.

Bird nodded, his expression a mix of concern and resignation. "And you?" he asked, though there was a hint in his tone that suggested he already knew the answer.

Holly hesitated, her fingers unconsciously tracing the outline of her badge through her coat. The weight of it felt heavier than usual, a reminder of the responsibility she carried. She thought of Drake, his haunted eyes and trembling hands as he recounted his bizarre tale. Something in his fear had struck a chord within her, awakening an instinct she couldn't ignore.

"I'll follow up on some other leads," she replied, carefully omitting her true intentions. It wasn't a lie, not exactly, but the omission left a bitter taste in her mouth. Still, she knew Bird would try to stop her if she revealed her plan to investigate the amusement park alone.

As Bird's gaze lingered on her, Holly fought the urge to fidget. She could almost see the gears turning in his mind, likely piecing together what she'd left unsaid. The silence stretched between them, filled with unspoken concerns and a shared understanding of the risks that came with their profession.

13 - 14

Holly took a deep breath, the crisp autumn air filling her lungs as she steeled herself for what was to come. The weight of her decision pressed upon her, but there was no turning back now.

"I'm going to the amusement park," Kierstead said, a determined edge in her voice. She met Bird's gaze unflinchingly, her dark eyes reflecting the muted glow of the streetlights. "If he was attacked there, maybe there's something he missed. Blood, footprints, hell—even signs of a struggle."

The words hung in the air between them, heavy with implication. Holly could almost see the memories of past cases flickering behind Bird's eyes—times when seemingly innocuous leads had unraveled into something far more sinister.

Bird's brow furrowed, deep lines etching themselves across his weathered face. "You sure that's a good idea?" he asked, his normally gruff voice softened by genuine concern. "If someone was stalking him there, they could still be around."

Holly's hand instinctively moved to rest on her holstered weapon, a gesture of reassurance more for Bird's benefit than her own. She understood his worry; it mirrored her own buried apprehensions. But the pull of the mystery, the need to uncover the truth, was far stronger than her fear.

"I have to check it out, Frank," she said quietly, her voice barely above a whisper. "Something about Drake's story... it doesn't add up, but it doesn't feel like a lie either. I can't shake the feeling we're missing something crucial."

As she spoke, Holly's mind raced through the possibilities. What if the abandoned park held the key to unlocking not just Drake's mysterious injuries, but the larger puzzle surrounding the missing Parker witnesses? The connection seemed tenuous, yet her instincts screamed that there was more to this than met the eye.

Bird's shoulders sagged slightly, a silent acknowledgment of her determination. "Just... be careful," he said, his tone a mixture of resignation and fatherly concern. "And keep your radio on. First sign of trouble—"

"I'll call for backup," Holly finished, offering him a small, reassuring smile. "I promise."

With a final nod to her partner, Holly turned and walked towards her car, each step feeling heavier than the last. As she reached for the door handle, a chill ran down her spine that had nothing to do with the autumn air. Whatever awaited her at that abandoned amusement park, she couldn't shake the feeling that it would change everything.

15 - 16

Holly's fingers tightened around her car keys, the cold metal biting into her palm. The weight of Bird's concern hung in the air, mingling with the damp chill of the evening. She paused, her gaze fixed on the horizon where the city's glow faded into the encroaching darkness.

"I'll be careful," she said, her voice steady despite the flutter of apprehension in her chest. "Besides, it's better if I go alone. Less chance of spooking anyone who might still be hanging around."

The words rang hollow even to her own ears, but Holly couldn't shake the feeling that this was a path she needed to walk alone. Her mind flickered to the countless realities she'd glimpsed, each version of herself driven by the same relentless curiosity. It was both a blessing and a curse, this need to unravel the mysteries that others would rather leave buried.

Bird's sigh cut through her thoughts, heavy with resignation. "Fine," he conceded, his weathered face etched with worry. "But call me if you find anything. And don't do anything stupid, alright?"

Holly turned to face her partner, struck by the genuine concern in his eyes. In that moment, she saw not just the skeptical veteran detective, but a man who'd seen too many good cops fall victim to their own bravado. The temptation to reassure him battled with her innate honesty.

"I'll do my best," she offered instead, a wry smile tugging at her lips. "But you know me, Frank. Sometimes stupid is the only way forward."

As she slid into her car, Holly couldn't help but wonder which version of herself she was channeling – the rookie detective eager to prove herself, or the interdimensional traveler who'd seen the consequences of playing it safe. Either way, she knew that the abandoned amusement park held answers she couldn't ignore, no matter the risk.

The engine roared to life, dispelling the eerie silence that had settled around them. With one last nod to Bird, Holly pulled away, her headlights cutting a path through the encroaching night. The mystery of Drake's encounter loomed before her, a tangled web of realities waiting to be unraveled.

17 - 18

Holly's gaze flicked to the rearview mirror, watching Bird's cruiser recede into the distance. The fading red and blue lights seemed to pulse in sync with her quickening heartbeat. She exhaled slowly, her fingers drumming a restless rhythm on the steering wheel.

"Alright, Drake," she murmured to the empty car, "let's see what kind of trouble you've really gotten yourself into this time."

Her mind raced, cataloging the possibilities that lay ahead. Was Drake truly experiencing a mental break, or had he stumbled upon something far more sinister? The image of a disfigured man in a white robe flickered through her thoughts, sending an involuntary shiver down her spine.

Holly's eyes narrowed as she focused on the road ahead, her analytical mind already piecing together a strategy. "First, sweep the perimeter," she said to herself, her voice barely above a whisper. "Then work my way inward. Look for any signs of recent activity, disturbances in the dust..."

She trailed off, a nagging sense of déjà vu tugging at the edges of her consciousness. Had she done this before? In another life, another reality? Holly shook her head, pushing the unsettling thought aside. Now wasn't the time for existential crises. She had a job to do, a mystery to unravel.

As the city lights faded behind her, Holly steeled herself for whatever awaited her at the abandoned amusement park. Whether it was a mundane explanation or something far more extraordinary, she was determined to find the truth – no matter where it might lead her.

19 - 20

The road stretched before Holly like a dark ribbon, unspooling into the night. Streetlights grew sparse, their glow fading to pinpricks in her rearview mirror. The asphalt beneath her tires crackled, pockmarked with age and neglect.

"What am I really walking into here?" Holly murmured, her fingers tapping a restless rhythm on the steering wheel. The question hung in the air, unanswered.

As she drove, the landscape transformed. Manicured lawns gave way to overgrown fields, weeds encroaching onto the shoulder of the road like grasping fingers. Holly's eyes darted from the road to the shadows beyond, ever-vigilant.

"Drake's story... it doesn't add up," she said aloud, her voice cutting through the eerie silence. "But fear like that? You can't fake it."

A memory surfaced – Drake's wild eyes, the tremor in his hands as he recounted his experience. Holly frowned, her analytical mind dissecting every detail.

"If someone's threatening him, why go to these lengths? Why not just..." She trailed off, unwilling to voice the darker possibilities.

The car jostled as it hit a particularly deep pothole, jarring Holly from her thoughts. She gripped the wheel tighter, refocusing on the treacherous road ahead.

"Stay sharp, Kierstead," she chided herself. "You're walking into unknown territory. Can't afford distractions."

As the miles ticked by, a growing sense of unease settled over Holly. The world outside her car windows seemed to retreat, leaving her isolated in a bubble of dim dashboard lights and the steady hum of the engine.

"Whatever I find," she said softly, her resolve hardening, "I'm getting to the bottom of this. For Drake's sake... and for the truth."

21 - 22

Holly's thoughts drifted back to Drake's haunting words, the memory as vivid as if he were sitting beside her in the passenger seat.

"A disfigured man in a white robe with a green dragon emblem," she murmured, her brow furrowing. "He attacked me in the funhouse."

The absurdity of the statement hung in the air, mingling with the growing tension. Holly shook her head, her analytical mind struggling to reconcile the fantastical elements with the very real fear she'd witnessed in Drake's eyes.

"It's ridiculous," she said aloud, her voice tight with frustration. "A man in a robe? At an abandoned amusement park? It sounds like something out of a bad horror movie."

And yet, as she replayed Drake's account in her mind, she couldn't shake the nagging feeling that there was more to his story. The details were too specific, too visceral to be mere fabrication.

"The way he described the emblem," Holly mused, her fingers tapping a restless rhythm on the steering wheel. "The texture of the robe, the smell of decay in the funhouse... You don't invent details like that out of thin air."

She exhaled slowly, her keen detective's instincts warring with her logical mind. "What are you missing, Kierstead? What's the piece that makes this all make sense?"

As the abandoned amusement park loomed ahead, a silhouette against the darkening sky, Holly steeled herself for whatever she might find. Drake's story may have been absurd, but the fear in his eyes had been all too real. Something had happened in that funhouse, and she was determined to uncover the truth, no matter how strange or unsettling it might be.

23 - 24

The rusted gate of Dreamland Fairgrounds materialized in Holly's headlights, a decrepit sentinel guarding forgotten memories. She eased her car to a stop, the gravel crunching softly beneath the tires. For a moment, she sat motionless, studying the weathered sign that clung precariously to a single hinge.

"What secrets are you hiding?" Holly murmured, her eyes tracing the faded lettering.

With a deep breath, she killed the engine and stepped out into the biting night air. The silence was oppressive, broken only by the whisper of wind through skeletal trees. Holly zipped her jacket higher, suppressing a shiver that had little to do with the cold.

"Alright, Drake," she said softly, "let's see if your story holds water."

Her hand instinctively brushed her holstered weapon as she approached the gate. Years of police work had honed her instincts, and something about this place set every nerve on edge. The gate's hinges groaned in protest as she pushed it open, the sound unnaturally loud in the stillness.

Holly paused at the threshold, her analytical mind cataloging details. Broken glass glinted dully in the moonlight, mingling with discarded trash and nature's slow reclamation. The air carried a musty scent of decay, tinged with something acrid she couldn't quite place.

"This is insane," she muttered, shaking her head. "I'm chasing ghosts based on a tale that belongs in a psych ward."

And yet, she couldn't deny the pull of the mystery. Drake's fear had been genuine, his injuries real. Whatever had happened here, it went beyond simple delusion.

Holly took a steadying breath and stepped into the park proper, her footfalls crunching softly on gravel and dead leaves. The abandoned rides loomed around her, once-cheerful facades now grotesque in their dilapidation.

"If I were a man in a white robe," she mused aloud, her voice barely above a whisper, "where would I be lurking?"

Her eyes scanned the shadows, searching for any sign of recent disturbance. Part of her hoped to find nothing, to write this off as a wild goose chase. But a deeper instinct, the same one that had made her an exceptional detective, told her there was more to this story than met the eye.

"Drake," she said softly, her words carried away by the chill wind, "what really happened to you here?"

25 - 26

Holly's flashlight beam cut through the darkness, illuminating the derelict remains of what was once a bustling amusement park. The stillness was oppressive, broken only by the occasional whisper of wind through rusted metal and rotting wood.

"Christ," she muttered, her keen eyes taking in every detail. "This place is a tetanus shot waiting to happen."

As she moved deeper into the park, her boots crunched against loose gravel, the sound unnaturally loud in the eerie silence. To her right, a carousel stood frozen in time, its once-majestic horses now chipped and peeling, their painted eyes seeming to follow her as she passed.

"Creepy bastards," Holly murmured, suppressing a shiver. She paused, sweeping her flashlight across the carousel's base. "No signs of a struggle here. Where were you, Drake?"

Her gaze drifted upward, settling on the looming silhouette of a Ferris wheel against the night sky. Its skeletal frame creaked faintly in the wind, a mournful sound that set Holly's nerves on edge.

"This whole place is like a graveyard," she thought, her analytical mind racing. "Perfect spot for an ambush. But why here? What's the connection?"

Holly's hand instinctively brushed against her holstered weapon, a gesture of reassurance in the face of the unknown. She took a deep breath, steeling herself against the growing unease in her gut.

"Alright, Holly," she said aloud, her voice steady despite her inner turmoil. "Time to earn that detective badge. If there's something to find here, you're damn well going to find it."

With renewed determination, she pressed on into the heart of the abandoned park, her senses on high alert for any sign of the truth behind Drake's bizarre tale.

27 - 28

The beam of Holly's flashlight caught a glint of shattered glass near a dilapidated food stand, its weathered awning sagging under years of neglect. She paused, her boots crunching softly on gravel as she approached.

"Well, well," she murmured, crouching to examine the scattered shards. "What have we here?"

Her gloved fingers sifted through the debris, a frown creasing her brow. The glass sparkled innocently in the harsh light, revealing nothing but the passage of time and careless vandals.

"Just more ghosts," Holly sighed, standing and brushing off her coat. The chill air nipped at her exposed skin, a stark reminder of the encroaching autumn night.

Her mind drifted to Drake Miller, his haunted eyes and trembling hands vivid in her memory. What had driven a successful lawyer to such a state of desperation? What horrors lurked behind his fragmented tale?

"Alright, Drake," she muttered, her voice barely above a whisper. "Where did you get into trouble?"

Holly's gaze swept across the desolate landscape, searching for any sign of recent disturbance. The weight of Drake's story pressed heavily upon her, a mix of skepticism and curiosity warring within.

"A disfigured man in a white robe," she mused, her tone laced with doubt. "Sounds like something out of a bad dream. But those burns were real enough."

She took a step forward, her resolve strengthening. "If there's any truth to your story, Drake, I'll find it. For your sake, and for the sake of those missing witnesses."

The abandoned park seemed to hold its breath, waiting to reveal its secrets as Holly ventured deeper into its shadowy embrace.

29 - 30

The funhouse loomed before her, a grotesque sentinel in the gloom. Holly's flashlight beam caught the faded façade, revealing peeling paint and weathered wood. Above the entrance, a large green dragon statue perched, its once-vibrant scales now dulled and cracked.

"Well, aren't you a charming welcome committee," Holly muttered, her voice tight with tension.

She traced the dragon's outline with her light, noting the intricate details that had somehow survived years of neglect. Its emerald eyes, though tarnished, seemed to follow her movements. A chill ran down her spine that had nothing to do with the autumn air.

"Focus, Kierstead," she chided herself. "It's just a statue."

Yet as she approached the entrance, her hand instinctively moved to rest on her holstered weapon. The funhouse exuded an aura of menace that set her nerves on edge.

"If Drake's story has any merit," Holly thought, "this is where it all went down."

She paused at the threshold, her analytical mind cataloging every detail. The door hung slightly ajar, its hinges groaning softly in the breeze. Cobwebs adorned the corners, undisturbed.

"No signs of recent entry," she observed aloud, her voice steady despite her growing unease. "But that doesn't mean much in a place like this."

Taking a deep breath, Holly steeled herself for what lay ahead. "Alright, funhouse. Let's see what secrets you're hiding."

With one last glance at the dragon statue, its emerald eyes seeming to gleam with an otherworldly light, Holly pushed open the door and stepped into the waiting darkness.

31 - 32

The green dragon's emerald eyes seemed to follow Holly as she stood before the funhouse entrance, her heart pounding in her chest. Its scales, though faded and chipped, held an eerie vibrancy in the beam of her flashlight.

"Christ," Holly muttered, her voice barely above a whisper. "Drake wasn't kidding about the dragon."

She recalled Drake's words, his voice trembling as he described the disfigured man's robe. The green dragon emblem, he'd said, had been unmistakable. Holly's stomach tightened, a cold dread seeping into her bones.

"Could it really be connected?" she wondered aloud, her gaze fixed on the statue. "Or am I grasping at straws here?"

The wind picked up, rustling through the abandoned park. Holly shivered, pulling her coat tighter around herself.

"Coincidence or not," she said firmly, steeling her resolve, "there's only one way to find out."

With a deep breath, Holly approached the funhouse entrance, her hand hovering near her holster. The dragon's emerald eyes seemed to watch her every move, a silent sentinel guarding whatever secrets lay within.

"Alright, Drake," she murmured, her voice tinged with determination. "Let's see if your story holds water."

33 - 34

Holly drew her sidearm, the weight of the weapon familiar and reassuring in her hand. Her eyes narrowed, scanning the entrance for any signs of recent disturbance. The door hung slightly ajar, its rusted hinges groaning softly in the night breeze.

"Bridgewater PD," she called out, her voice firm despite the unease churning in her gut. "Anyone in there, come out now."

Silence answered her, broken only by the distant creak of metal somewhere in the abandoned park. Holly's jaw tightened as she approached the door, her muscles taut with anticipation.

"Last chance," she warned, though she knew the likelihood of a response was slim.

With a deep breath, Holly pushed the door open, wincing at the ear-splitting screech of metal on metal. The smell hit her immediately – a nauseating cocktail of mildew, decay, and something else she couldn't quite place. Her flashlight beam cut through the darkness, revealing warped mirrors lining the walls.

"Jesus," Holly muttered, her reflection fracturing and multiplying in the funhouse mirrors. Each distorted version of herself seemed to stare back with accusing eyes, as if questioning her decision to enter this forsaken place.

The floorboards creaked beneath her feet as she took a tentative step forward. Holly's mind raced, analyzing every shadow, every sound. "What happened to you in here, Drake?" she whispered, her words swallowed by the oppressive silence.

As she moved deeper into the funhouse, Holly couldn't shake the feeling that she was being watched. The mirrors seemed to twist and warp with each step, creating a disorienting kaleidoscope of reflections. She swallowed hard, fighting back the rising tide of claustrophobia.

"Focus, Kierstead," she chided herself. "There's got to be something here. Some proof of what Drake experienced."

But as her flashlight beam danced across the decaying interior, Holly couldn't help but wonder if she was chasing ghosts. Had she let Drake's fantastical story cloud her judgment? Or was there truly something sinister lurking in the shadows of this forgotten place?

35 - 36

Holly's pulse quickened as she ventured further into the funhouse's maze-like interior. The floorboards groaned beneath her weight, each step sending echoes bouncing off the warped walls. She paused, listening intently for any sign of movement, but only the faint whisper of wind through rotting timbers answered her.

"Come on, Drake," she murmured, her voice barely audible. "Show me what you saw."

The beam of her flashlight danced across peeling paint and shattered mirrors, creating a dizzying array of fractured light. Holly's trained eye scanned for any anomaly, any trace of the struggle Drake had described. Her fingers tightened around her sidearm, a reflex born of years on the force.

Halfway down the corridor, something caught her attention. A glint, small and metallic, reflecting her flashlight's beam from the floor ahead. Holly's breath caught in her throat.

"What have we here?" she whispered, crouching down to examine the object more closely. Her mind raced with possibilities. Could this be the evidence she needed to corroborate Drake's story? Or was it just another piece of discarded trash, a red herring in this house of illusions?

As she reached out to investigate, a sudden chill ran down her spine. The funhouse seemed to close in around her, the mirrors reflecting countless versions of herself, each one vulnerable and exposed. For a moment, Holly understood the terror Drake must have felt in this place.

"Get it together, Kierstead," she muttered, steeling herself against the growing unease. "Whatever happened here, you're going to figure it out."

37 - 38

Holly's fingers closed around the object, its cool metal surface a stark contrast to the gritty dust coating the floor. She lifted it, her flashlight revealing a spent shell casing. The sight sent her pulse racing, adrenaline flooding her system as the implications sank in.

"Drake," she murmured, her voice heavy with a mix of concern and vindication.

She turned the casing over in her palm, her detective's mind already piecing together a potential sequence of events. The weight of it felt significant, like a key unlocking a door to a deeper mystery.

"What happened to you here?" Holly whispered, her words echoing softly in the eerie stillness of the funhouse. She glanced around, half-expecting to see the disfigured man Drake had described lurking in the shadows.

The creaking of the old structure seemed to intensify, as if responding to her unspoken fears. Holly stood, her grip tightening on both the shell casing and her weapon.

"Alright, let's think this through," she said to herself, her analytical nature asserting itself. "A shell casing means a gun was fired. But no blood, no body... What am I missing?"

She swept her flashlight across the area again, searching for any signs she might have overlooked. The distorted reflections in the funhouse mirrors seemed to mock her efforts, multiplying her lone figure into an army of investigators, each as perplexed as she was.

"Drake's story is starting to look a lot less like delusion," Holly muttered, her skepticism giving way to a growing certainty that something sinister had indeed occurred in this forgotten place of entertainment.

39 - 40

The beam of Holly's flashlight caught a glint of red, drawing her attention to the warped floorboards. Her breath caught as she knelt down, the wood creaking ominously beneath her weight. Smears of crimson, unmistakably blood, stood out starkly against the faded paint.

"Damn it," she whispered, her fingers hovering just above the stains. "This is real. This happened."

The sight of blood transformed the funhouse from an eerie relic into a crime scene. Holly's mind raced, piecing together the evidence before her. She thought of Drake's haunted eyes, the fear that had radiated from him as he recounted his story.

"Okay, think," she muttered, standing up and scanning the room once more. "If Drake was attacked here, where did his assailant go? And why come to an abandoned amusement park in the first place?"

The mirrors surrounding her offered no answers, only distorted reflections of her troubled expression. Holly took a deep breath, trying to center herself amidst the growing sense of unease.

"Frank's not going to believe this," she said, reaching for her phone. Her finger hovered over the call button as a new thought struck her. "But what if this goes beyond Drake? What if this is connected to the Parker witnesses?"

The possibility sent a chill down her spine. If there was a connection, it meant they were dealing with something far more dangerous than they'd initially believed. Holly's grip tightened on her phone as she weighed her next move.

"I need more," she decided, lowering the device. "More evidence, more answers before I bring anyone else into this mess."

With renewed determination, Holly turned her attention back to the blood-stained floor, her keen eyes searching for any additional clues that might shed light on the growing mystery surrounding Drake Miller and the abandoned Dreamland Fairgrounds.

41 - 42

Holly's fingers traced the outline of the shell casing in her pocket as her mind raced, piecing together the fragments of evidence before her. The metallic tang of blood hung in the air, mingling with the musty scent of decay that permeated the funhouse.

"Dammit, Drake," she whispered, her voice barely audible over the creaking of weathered wood. "What have you gotten yourself into?"

The distorted mirrors lining the walls seemed to watch her, their warped reflections a fitting metaphor for the twisted reality she found herself navigating. Holly's eyes darted from one surface to another, half-expecting to catch a glimpse of the disfigured man Drake had described.

"This doesn't add up," she muttered, running a hand through her hair. "A man in a robe with a dragon emblem? It sounds like something out of a fever dream."

As if in response, the funhouse groaned, the sound reverberating through the empty corridors. Holly's hand instinctively moved to her holster, her breath catching in her throat.

"Get a grip, Kierstead," she chided herself. "You've faced worse than a creaky old funhouse."

But even as she spoke the words, a nagging doubt gnawed at the edges of her mind. This case was different. It reeked of something beyond the usual crimes she investigated – something that defied rational explanation.

Holly took a tentative step backward, her eyes still scanning the shadows. "If Drake was telling the truth," she reasoned aloud, "then there's more to this place than meets the eye. And if he wasn't..."

She left the thought unfinished, unwilling to voice the alternative. The implications of Drake fabricating such an elaborate story were almost as unsettling as the possibility of it being true.

As she neared the entrance, Holly felt a sudden, inexplicable urge to flee. The darkness seemed to press in around her, the beam of her flashlight cutting through it like a lifeline.

"Time to regroup," she decided, her voice steadier than she felt. "Whatever happened here, I'm not going to solve it alone in the dark."

With one final glance over her shoulder, Holly retreated toward the exit, her mind already formulating the next steps in unraveling the mystery that had brought Drake Miller to this forsaken place.

43 - 43

Holly emerged from the funhouse, the cold night air biting at her cheeks. She inhaled deeply, grateful for the crisp freshness after the musty confines of the decrepit structure. Her fingers tightened around the shell casing, its weight a tangible reminder of the violence that had occurred within.

"Let's see what you're hiding," she muttered, raising the casing to eye level. The moonlight caught its brass surface, revealing smudges and scratches that spoke of its recent discharge.

Holly's mind raced, piecing together the puzzle before her. "If Drake's story is true, then this could be evidence of self-defense," she mused aloud, her voice barely above a whisper. "But against what? A disfigured man in a robe? It sounds absurd."

She pocketed the casing, her practiced movements betraying years of investigative experience. As she scanned the abandoned park, the looming silhouettes of derelict rides seemed to mock her efforts at rationality.

"What am I missing?" Holly questioned, frustration creeping into her tone. "There's got to be more here than just a shell casing and some blood."

Her gaze settled on the dragon statue atop the funhouse, its emerald scales dulled by time and neglect. A chill ran down her spine as she recalled Drake's description of the emblem on his attacker's robe.

"Too many coincidences," she muttered, shaking her head. "Drake might be unstable, but he's no liar. Something happened here, something he can barely comprehend."

Holly's hand instinctively moved to her holster, the familiar weight of her sidearm offering little comfort against the growing unease in her gut. She took a step back, her eyes darting between shadows, suddenly acutely aware of how alone she was in this forsaken place.

"Time to call for backup," she decided, reaching for her radio. "Whatever's going on here, I'm not equipped to handle it solo."

As she keyed the mic, a flicker of movement caught her eye, there and gone in an instant. Holly froze, her heart pounding in her chest.

"Who's there?" she called out, her voice steady despite the adrenaline surging through her veins. Silence answered, broken only by the distant rustle of leaves in the autumn wind.

I Remember, You Remember

1 -2 The antiseptic scent of the hospital room stung Drake's nostrils, a constant reminder of his confinement. Through the half-open blinds, slivers of street light cast long shadows across the linoleum floor, creating a patchwork of light and dark that mirrored the turmoil in Drake's mind.

Dr. Charles Lee's pristine white coat seemed to glow in the dim room as he approached Drake's bedside. The soft rustle of papers on his clipboard punctuated the muted bustle beyond the door, where nurses moved with quiet efficiency between rooms.

Drake's gaze fixed on Dr. Lee's face, searching for any hint of what was to come. The doctor's expression was a carefully crafted mask of professionalism, but Drake detected a flicker of sympathy in his eyes.

"You're free to leave, Mr. Miller," Lee said, flipping a page on his clipboard. "But there are conditions."

Drake's heart leapt at the prospect of freedom, even as dread coiled in his stomach at the doctor's ominous tone. He longed to tear off the hospital bracelet that chafed against his wrist, to escape the sterile walls that seemed to close in around him with each passing moment.

"What kind of conditions?" Drake asked, his voice raspier than he'd expected. He cleared his throat, acutely aware of how vulnerable he felt in the thin hospital gown.

As Dr. Lee began to explain, Drake's mind raced. Would these conditions interfere with his mission? How could he protect his family and unravel the mystery of the colliding worlds if he was tethered to medical appointments and medication schedules?

The weight of responsibility pressed down on Drake's shoulders, threatening to crush him. But beneath the fear and uncertainty, a fierce determination burned. He would find a way. He had to. The fate of not just his family, but entire worlds, hung in the balance.

3 - 4

Drake sat on the edge of the bed, his bandaged arms resting on his knees. The rough texture of the gauze against his skin served as a constant reminder of his recent ordeal. He flexed his fingers, wincing at the dull ache that radiated up his forearms.

Linda and Harrison stood nearby, their postures a mix of relief and lingering concern. Drake's gaze flicked between them, drinking in the sight of his family—whole, safe, here. For now.

"What kind of conditions?" Drake asked, his voice cautious. The words tasted bitter on his tongue, like admitting defeat. But he knew he had to play along, at least for the moment.

Linda's hand tightened on Harrison's shoulder, and Drake caught the silent exchange of glances between them. His son's eyes were wide, brimming with a mixture of fear and hope that made Drake's chest ache.

"We just want you home, Dad," Harrison said softly, his voice cracking slightly.

Drake nodded, swallowing hard against the lump in his throat. "I know, buddy. I want that too." But even as he spoke the words, images of the codex and the fractured worlds flashed through his mind. How could he focus on recovery when the fate of the multiverse hung in the balance?

He turned his attention back to Dr. Lee, bracing himself for the restrictions that were sure to come. Whatever the conditions, Drake knew he'd have to find a way around them. The stakes were too high for anything else.

5 - 6

Dr. Lee adjusted his glasses, the fluorescent light glinting off the lenses. Drake found himself fixating on that small reflection, a pinprick of clarity in the haze of uncertainty that shrouded his mind.

"I want you to follow a strict regimen," Lee began, his tone measured and clinical. "Plenty of rest, avoid stress, and take the prescribed medications to manage any lingering effects from your... episode."

Drake's jaw clenched at the word 'episode.' It felt dismissive, reducing the weight of his experiences—the visions of collapsing worlds, the urgent need to find Rachel Summers—to mere delusions. He forced himself to nod, though his thoughts raced. How could he rest when the fate of multiple realities might hang in the balance?

Lee looked up from the clipboard, his gaze steady and piercing. "I also recommend seeing a psychiatrist. The visions, the paranoia—they're signs of something deeper that needs addressing."

A cold dread settled in Drake's stomach. He could feel Linda and Harrison's eyes on him, their concern palpable in the sterile hospital air. He knew what they must be thinking—that he was losing his grip on reality. But the truth was far more complex, far more terrifying.

"I'll follow the rules, Doctor. Promise," Drake said, his voice low and measured. The lie tasted acrid on his tongue, but he forced a wan smile. As he spoke, his mind was already formulating plans—how to find Rachel, how to decode the ancient text, how to save not just this world, but all of them.

The weight of his responsibility pressed down on him, threatening to crush him beneath its enormity. But as he glanced at Linda and Harrison, their faces etched with worry and love, Drake felt a surge of determination. He would protect them, no matter the cost. And somehow, he would find a way to unravel the mystery that bound him to this fractured reality.

7 - 8

Dr. Lee's eyes narrowed, scrutinizing Drake with the practiced gaze of a man who had seen countless patients try to conceal their true intentions. The fluorescent lights cast harsh shadows across his face, accentuating the lines of concern etched into his brow.

"Alright," Lee said, his voice tinged with a mix of professional detachment and genuine worry. "But if anything changes—any worsening of symptoms—you come back here immediately. Understood?"

Drake's fingers tightened imperceptibly on the edge of the hospital bed, the coarse fabric of the sheets grounding him in this moment even as his mind raced with possibilities. He could feel the weight of the codex in his memories, its pages whispering secrets that threatened to tear reality apart.

"Understood," Drake replied, his voice steady despite the tempest of emotions roiling within him. He met Lee's gaze unflinchingly, knowing that behind his calm exterior, a war was raging—a battle between the man he appeared to be in this world and the one who carried the burden of universes on his shoulders.

As Lee's footsteps receded, echoing softly in the hospital corridor, Drake's thoughts turned inward. How could he possibly explain to Linda and Harrison the magnitude of what they faced? How could he protect them from a threat they couldn't even comprehend? The answers eluded him, slipping through his grasp like wisps of smoke, leaving behind only the bitter taste of uncertainty and the gnawing fear of what was to come.

9 - 10

The automatic doors of the hospital hissed open, releasing Drake, Linda, and Harrison into the crisp morning air. Drake inhaled deeply, the sharp scent of autumn leaves and antiseptic mingling in his nostrils. The parking lot stretched before them, a sea of gleaming metal under the pale sun.

"It feels good to be out," Drake murmured, his eyes scanning the horizon. The weight of the past few days seemed to lift slightly, but a nagging unease lingered in the pit of his stomach.

Linda's hand found his, her fingers intertwining with his own. "We're here with you, Drake," she said softly, her blue eyes searching his face. "Whatever comes next, we face it together."

Harrison bounced on the balls of his feet, his youthful energy a stark contrast to the somber mood. "Yeah, Dad. We've got your back."

Drake managed a small smile, though his mind raced with the implications of their shared visions. The codex, the virus, the colliding worlds—it all seemed so far removed from this mundane parking lot. Yet he knew the threat was real, lurking just beneath the surface of their fragile reality.

"I appreciate that," Drake replied, giving Linda's hand a gentle squeeze. "But I can't shake the feeling that we're standing on the edge of something... monumental."

As they walked, the cool breeze ruffled Drake's disheveled hair, carrying with it the promise of change. He found himself hyper-aware of every detail: the crunch of gravel under their feet, the distant hum of traffic, the way the sunlight glinted off nearby windshields.

Harrison's voice cut through his thoughts. "Dad, do you think we'll ever understand what's really happening? With the visions and everything?"

Drake paused, choosing his words carefully. "I hope so, son. But right now, there's so much we don't know. We need to be cautious, keep our eyes open for anything unusual."

Linda's grip on his hand tightened. "Drake, you're not planning on doing anything... rash, are you?"

He met her gaze, seeing the mixture of love and concern in her eyes. "No, Linda. But we can't ignore what I've seen, what I've experienced. There's more at stake here than just us."

As they neared their car, Drake couldn't shake the feeling that every step was taking them closer to an inevitable confrontation with forces beyond their understanding. The weight of responsibility settled heavily on his shoulders, a burden he knew he couldn't share fully with his family, no matter how much he wanted to protect them.

11 - 12

Linda unlocked the car with a soft click, the familiar sound anchoring Drake momentarily in the present. Harrison's backpack sailed through the air, landing with a thud in the backseat.

"Shotgun!" Harrison called out, a fleeting moment of teenage normalcy that made Drake's heart ache.

But as Linda and Harrison moved to get in, Drake found himself rooted to the spot. His gaze drifted past the parking lot, past the sprawling hospital complex, to the distant horizon where the sky met the earth in a hazy line.

"Drake?" Linda's voice seemed to come from far away. "Aren't you getting in?"

He couldn't respond. Something tugged at the edges of his consciousness, a feeling of déjà vu so strong it made his head spin. The world around him seemed to flicker, like a faulty lightbulb struggling to stay lit.

"Dad?" Harrison's concern cut through the haze. "What's wrong?"

Drake's mouth went dry. He knew, with a certainty that chilled him to his core, that something was about to happen. Something that would change everything.

"I..." he began, but the words died in his throat as the feeling intensified.

And then it hit him.

13 - 14

A searing pain shot through Drake's skull, blinding in its intensity. He stumbled, his knees buckling as the world around him blurred into a kaleidoscope of fractured light and shadow. The concrete beneath his feet seemed to shift and warp, no longer solid.

"Drake!" Linda's panicked cry sounded muffled, as if coming from underwater.

He tried to reach out, to anchor himself to something real, but his limbs felt leaden and unresponsive. The parking lot, the car, his family—all of it faded away, replaced by a cascade of fragmented images that assaulted his senses.

"What's happening?" Drake thought, his inner voice echoing in the chaos of his mind. "Is this another episode? Or something more?"

Flashes of unfamiliar landscapes flickered through his consciousness: a world engulfed in flames, another lush with impossible greenery, a third cold and mechanical. Each vision lasted only a fraction of a second, but left an indelible imprint on his psyche.

"Dad! Dad, can you hear me?" Harrison's voice penetrated the maelstrom, a lifeline Drake desperately wanted to grasp.

But the visions pulled him deeper. A face appeared, unfamiliar yet somehow known, speaking words he couldn't quite catch. A book, its pages filled with symbols that seemed to writhe and change as he looked at them.

"This isn't just in my head," Drake realized, a cold certainty settling in his gut. "These are memories. But from where? From when?"

The pain intensified, threatening to split his skull. Drake gritted his teeth, fighting against the torrent of images, struggling to make sense of what he was seeing. He had to remember. He had to understand.

Because somehow, he knew that everything—his family, his world, perhaps even reality itself—depended on it.

15 - 16

The ancient codex materialized in Drake's mind, its presence both alluring and menacing. The green dragon on its cover seemed to breathe, scales shimmering with an otherworldly light. Drake's fingers trembled as he reached out, not physically, but within the vision, to touch the book's weathered surface.

"What secrets do you hold?" he whispered, his voice lost in the void of his consciousness.

As if in response, the codex sprung open. Pages fluttered by, each filled with intricate, angular script that defied comprehension. Drake squinted, desperately trying to decipher the text, but it shifted and rearranged itself before his eyes, tantalizing glimpses of meaning evaporating like mist.

"It's trying to tell me something," Drake thought, frustration mounting. "But what?"

A voice cut through the confusion, calm and steady, yet tinged with urgency. "The codex is more than just a book, Drake. It's a key to understanding the multiverse."

Rachel Summers' face flickered into view, her sharp eyes fixed on him with an intensity that made him want to look away. Her graying red hair was pulled back tightly, emphasizing the lines of determination etched into her features.

"Rachel?" Drake's mind reeled. "I know you. But... how?"

She continued as if she hadn't heard him. "Each symbol, each line of text, represents a different reality. The connections between them, the points where they intersect—that's where the true power lies."

Drake struggled to process her words, his thoughts a whirlwind of confusion and half-formed memories. "Intersections? Different realities? What does that mean for me? For my family?"

Rachel's image wavered, her voice growing fainter. "You've seen them, Drake. The other worlds. They're all connected, all part of a greater whole. And you... you're the lynchpin."

As she spoke, the codex's pages began to glow, emitting a soft, pulsating light that seemed to reach out to Drake. He felt a pull, an inexorable draw towards something both terrifying and essential.

"I don't understand," Drake pleaded, reaching out to Rachel's fading form. "What am I supposed to do?"

But Rachel was gone, leaving Drake alone with the enigmatic codex and a growing sense that the fate of not just one world, but many, rested on his shoulders.

17 - 18

Rachel's voice resonated with urgency, cutting through Drake's confusion. "You don't understand what you're holding," she said, her words carrying the weight of countless worlds.

Before Drake could respond, the vision violently shifted. The codex and Rachel vanished, replaced by a nightmarish landscape that assaulted his senses. Intense heat seared his skin as he found himself standing in the midst of a chaotic, burning cityscape.

Buildings crumbled around him, their structures groaning and collapsing in showers of sparks and debris. The sky above churned with angry crimson clouds, casting an eerie, blood-red glow over everything. Screams of terror and anguish echoed from all directions, piercing Drake's heart.

He began to run, his feet pounding against cracked pavement. "What am I looking for?" he thought desperately, his eyes darting from one destroyed structure to another. The acrid smell of smoke filled his lungs, making it hard to breathe.

As he sprinted down a desolate street, Drake's mind raced. "Is this the Black World? One of the realities Rachel mentioned? God, it's like hell itself."

A woman's scream cut through the cacophony, eerily familiar. Drake's heart clenched. "Linda?" he called out, his voice hoarse from the smoke. He changed direction, heading towards the sound.

"I have to find them," he muttered, pushing himself harder. "Linda, Harrison... they have to be here somewhere. I can't lose them again."

The ground shook beneath his feet, nearly throwing him off balance. As he regained his footing, Drake caught a glimpse of a figure in the distance, obscured by smoke and falling ash.

"Rachel?" he called out, hope and desperation mingling in his voice. "Tell me what I need to do! How do I stop this?"

But the figure remained silent, fading into the inferno as Drake raced towards it, driven by an overwhelming need to understand, to save, to redeem himself from the mistakes of his past.

19 - 20

The vision shifted abruptly, and Drake found himself enveloped in a world of vibrant green. Towering trees stretched towards a cerulean sky, their leaves rustling in a gentle breeze. For a moment, the serenity washed over him, a stark contrast to the chaos he'd just witnessed.

"This... this is beautiful," Drake whispered, his eyes wide with wonder. He reached out to touch a nearby fern, its delicate fronds cool against his fingertips. "Is this what we're trying to save?"

But even as the thought formed, the tranquility began to unravel. The lush foliage around him started to wither, leaves curling and browning before his eyes. Drake's heart sank, a wave of despair washing over him.

"No, no, no," he muttered, spinning around as the forest crumbled to ash. "This can't be happening. There has to be a way to stop it!"

The ground beneath his feet trembled, fissures spreading like spiderwebs. Glowing energy pulsed from the cracks, bathing the dying world in an otherworldly light.

Drake stumbled backwards, his mind reeling. "Is this the virus Rachel mentioned? Or something else entirely?" he wondered, his thoughts a jumble of fragmented memories and urgent questions.

As the last tree disintegrated into dust, the scene morphed once more. Cold, sterile air hit Drake's lungs as he found himself standing in the midst of a futuristic cityscape. Sleek metallic structures loomed overhead, their surfaces reflecting a faint blue glow that seemed to emanate from everywhere and nowhere at once.

"The Blue World," Drake breathed, his voice barely audible over the hum of advanced machinery. He watched in growing horror as the machines around him began to falter, their lights flickering and dying.

"It's happening here too," he realized, a chill running down his spine. "The virus, it's consuming everything, across all realities."

As the last of the machines fell silent, Drake clenched his fists, determination setting his jaw. "I have to find Rachel," he thought fiercely. "She's the key to understanding all of this. And I swear, I'll find a way to save them all – Linda, Harrison, and every soul across these worlds. No matter the cost."

21 - 22

Drake's heart raced as fragmented memories flooded his mind. He could almost feel the urgency of his past self, sprinting through unfamiliar landscapes, desperately trying to outpace an invisible enemy.

"The virus," he muttered, his voice thick with frustration. "I remember chasing it, but why? How?"

He pressed his palms against his temples, willing the memories to sharpen. Flashes of code scrolled behind his eyelids, a digital plague devouring reality itself. But the specifics remained maddeningly out of reach, like trying to grasp smoke.

"Dammit!" Drake cursed, slamming his fist against his thigh. The pain grounded him, bringing his surroundings back into focus.

And there she was again. Rachel Summers, her face etched with determination, her graying hair escaping a messy bun. Drake's breath caught in his throat.

"Rachel," he whispered, reaching out as if he could touch the memory. "You were there. You showed me something... the codex?"

In his mind's eye, he saw Rachel's hands, steady despite the chaos around them, holding an ancient book. The green dragon on its cover seemed to writhe, almost alive.

"Why?" Drake demanded of the apparition. "Why was it so important?"

But Rachel's image faded, leaving him with more questions than answers. Drake clenched his jaw, a mix of frustration and resolve coursing through him.

"I'll find you," he vowed, his voice barely above a whisper. "Whatever it takes, I'll piece this together. For Linda, for Harrison... for all of us."

23 - 24

The world tilted violently as Drake's knees buckled beneath him. His vision swam, reality blurring into a kaleidoscope of fragmented memories. He collapsed onto the cold, unforgiving pavement of the hospital parking lot, his hands instinctively clutching at his head as if he could physically contain the onslaught of images.

"No, not again," Drake gasped, his breath coming in ragged bursts. The visions assaulted him with merciless intensity – the codex pulsing with otherworldly energy, Rachel's urgent warnings, worlds burning and freezing and shattering all at once.

Through the haze of pain, a part of Drake's mind clung desperately to coherence. "Focus," he commanded himself, his voice a hoarse whisper. "There has to be a pattern, a reason..."

But the memories slipped away like water through his fingers, leaving behind only tantalizing fragments. Drake's shoulders heaved as he fought to regain control, his fingers digging into his scalp.

"Dad? Drake?" The concerned voices of Harrison and Linda pierced through his mental fog, but Drake couldn't respond. He was lost in the maelstrom of his own fractured psyche, grappling with the weight of worlds he couldn't fully remember.

As the intensity of the vision began to ebb, Drake found himself adrift in a sea of confusion and half-formed recollections. "What am I missing?" he muttered, more to himself than to his worried family. "There's a key here, something I'm not seeing..."

He raised his head, meeting the anxious gazes of Linda and Harrison. The depth of their concern only heightened his resolve. "I won't let you down," Drake vowed silently. "Whatever it takes, I'll unravel this mystery and keep you safe."

25 - 26

"Dad!" Harrison shouted, rushing to his side. The teenager's lanky form moved with surprising agility, his unruly dirty blonde hair bouncing as he dropped to his knees beside Drake.

"Drake!" Linda cried, kneeling beside him. Her slender fingers reached out, hesitating just short of touching her husband's trembling form.

Drake's vision swam, the world around him blurring into a kaleidoscope of colors. He could feel the rough asphalt of the parking lot beneath his palms, grounding him in this reality even as his mind reeled from the onslaught of fragmented memories.

"I'm... I'm alright," he managed to croak, though the words felt hollow even to his own ears. Drake's gaze flickered between Linda and Harrison, noting the fear etched across their faces. A pang of guilt stabbed through him. "How much have I put them through?" he wondered silently.

Linda's voice was steady, belying the worry in her blue eyes. "Can you stand, love? We should get you back inside, have Dr. Lee take another look."

Drake shook his head, wincing at the motion. "No," he insisted, his voice growing stronger. "No more hospitals. We need to..." He trailed off, the urgency of their situation warring with his instinct to protect his family from the truth.

Harrison leaned in, his youthful face a mask of determination. "We need to what, Dad? Whatever it is, we're in this together."

The sincerity in his son's voice nearly broke Drake. He looked to Linda, seeing the same unwavering support in her eyes. In that moment, he made a decision.

"We need to find Rachel Summers," Drake said, his voice low and intense. "She's the key to understanding what's happening to us, to... to everything."

As the words left his mouth, Drake felt a shift in the air around them. The weight of their shared destiny settled over the family like a shroud, binding them together in ways they had yet to fully comprehend.

27 - 28

As Drake's words hung in the air, Linda's hand brushed against his arm, her fingers seeking comfort and reassurance. In that instant, the world around them seemed to shatter.

Linda's eyes widened, her pupils dilating as if trying to absorb the torrent of images flooding her mind. Her lips parted in a silent gasp, and her hand flew to her mouth, trembling against her skin. The visions cascaded through her consciousness—worlds aflame, forests withering, cities of cold steel and blue light—each fragment a piece of a puzzle she hadn't known existed.

Harrison stumbled backward, his lanky frame wavering as if buffeted by an unseen force. Tears welled in his eyes, spilling over as he clutched at his head. The onslaught of memories—memories that felt both foreign and achingly familiar—threatened to overwhelm him.

Drake watched in horror as his family experienced the same psychic assault that had plagued him. His heart raced, torn between the need to comfort them and the fear of what this shared vision might mean.

"Linda? Harrison?" His voice cracked with concern. "What... what did you see?"

Linda lowered her hand, her blue eyes now haunted by the weight of newfound knowledge. "I saw... everything," she whispered, her normally soothing voice trembling. "The codex, the worlds... Drake, how is this possible?"

Harrison blinked rapidly, struggling to process the flood of information. "Dad," he said, his voice small and frightened, "I remember Rachel Summers. She showed me the codex. She said... she said it was important. That we needed to find it."

Drake's mind reeled. The fragments of his own memories were suddenly thrown into sharp relief, pieces of the puzzle snapping into place. "You both saw it too," he breathed, a mixture of relief and dread washing over him. "We're connected to this somehow, all of us."

29 - 30

The parking lot faded into a hazy backdrop as the three of them huddled together, their shared experience creating an invisible bubble of isolation. Drake's fingers trembled as he reached out, gently touching Linda's shoulder, then Harrison's arm, as if to reassure himself of their physical presence.

Silence stretched between them, heavy with unspoken questions and the weight of revelations too vast to immediately comprehend. Drake's mind raced, grappling with the implications of this shared vision. Had he inadvertently dragged his family into the dangerous reality he'd been desperately trying to shield them from?

Finally, unable to bear the quiet any longer, Drake broke the silence. His voice was hoarse, barely above a whisper, as he asked, "You... you saw it?"

The words hung in the air, laden with fear, hope, and a desperate need for confirmation. Drake's gaze darted between Linda and Harrison, searching their faces for any sign of understanding, any indication that he wasn't alone in this madness anymore.

As he waited for their response, a thought echoed in his mind: 'What have I done? I wanted to protect them, and now...' He swallowed hard, steeling himself for whatever came next, knowing that their answer would irrevocably change everything.

31 - 32

Linda's blue eyes met Drake's, brimming with tears that threatened to spill over. Her slender frame shook as she nodded, her blonde hair swaying with the motion. "The codex," she whispered, her voice trembling like a leaf in a storm. "The virus. The worlds..." Her words trailed off, as if speaking them aloud made the visions more real, more terrifying.

Drake's heart constricted, a mixture of relief and dread washing over him. He wasn't alone anymore, but at what cost? His gaze shifted to Harrison, noting the way his son's unruly hair fell across his forehead, partially obscuring eyes that now held a haunted look far beyond his years.

Harrison stared back at his father, his young face a canvas of conflicting emotions. Fear etched lines around his mouth, but determination burned in his brown eyes. "It's all real," he said, his voice stronger than Linda's but still tinged with disbelief. "I remember... I remember talking to Rachel Summers. She showed me the codex. She said it was the key to everything."

As Harrison spoke, fragments of memory flashed through Drake's mind—Rachel's sharp eyes, her graying hair tied back, the weight of the codex in his hands. He wanted to reach out, to comfort his son, but uncertainty held him back. Instead, he asked softly, "What else do you remember about Rachel, Harrison?"

The question hung in the air, heavy with implications. Drake's mind raced, trying to piece together the fragments of their shared vision. 'Rachel Summers,' he thought. 'The connection we've been missing. But how deep does this go? And what does it mean for us now?'

33 - 34

Drake's heart raced, pounding against his ribs like a caged animal seeking escape. The name echoed in his mind, a beacon cutting through the fog of fractured memories. "Rachel Summers," he breathed, his voice barely above a whisper. "I knew her name sounded familiar. She's the connection."

His hands trembled slightly as he ran them through his disheveled hair, the weight of realization settling upon him like a heavy cloak. The parking lot around them seemed to fade away, leaving only the three of them in a bubble of shared understanding.

Linda's cool hand found its way to his shoulder, her touch both grounding and electrifying. "Drake," she said, her voice soft but steady, "this reality—it's... it's different." Her blue eyes, usually so calm, now held a storm of emotions. "It's like the worlds colliding created something new. That's why we couldn't remember."

Drake nodded slowly, his mind reeling with the implications. He gazed at Linda, taking in the worry lines etched around her eyes, the slight tremble in her lower lip. How many times had they lived through this? How many versions of themselves had been lost in the collision of worlds?

"A new reality," he mused, his voice thick with contemplation. "But if that's true, then what does that mean for us? For who we were before?" The questions tumbled from his lips, each one carrying the weight of countless lives lived and forgotten.

He turned to Harrison, studying his son's face. The boy looked back at him, fear and determination warring in his eyes. Drake felt a surge of protective instinct, mingled with a deep, aching guilt. 'I've dragged them into this,' he thought. 'But maybe, just maybe, they're the key to finding our way out.'

35 - 36

Drake's gaze hardened, his jaw clenching as the pieces began to fall into place. The weight of their shared vision pressed down on him, fueling a newfound resolve. "Then Rachel might know how to fix it," he said, his voice low and determined. "We need to find her."

The parking lot seemed to shrink around them, the world beyond fading into insignificance as the enormity of their task loomed. Drake's mind raced, mapping out possibilities, potential leads that could guide them to Rachel. His fingers twitched, itching to take action, to start the search immediately.

Linda's voice cut through his thoughts, fragile and trembling. "But what about us?" she asked, her eyes glistening with unshed tears. The fear in her voice was palpable, a living thing that wrapped around them all. "What if this... this starts again? The loops, the deaths?"

Her words hung in the air, heavy with the weight of countless iterations, countless losses they could no longer fully remember. Drake felt a surge of protectiveness, mixed with a gnawing guilt. He had brought this upon them, hadn't he? In his relentless pursuit of answers, he had exposed them to horrors beyond imagination.

He reached out, his calloused hand finding Linda's. The warmth of her skin against his was an anchor, a reminder of what he was fighting for. "I don't know," he admitted, his voice barely above a whisper. "But we can't stay here, paralyzed by fear. Finding Rachel... it's our best shot at understanding what's happening, at fixing this mess."

As he spoke, Drake's eyes darted between Linda and Harrison, taking in their expressions of mingled hope and apprehension. The responsibility he felt was overwhelming, threatening to crush him under its weight. But beneath that, a spark of determination flickered, growing stronger with each passing moment.

37 - 38

Drake squeezed Linda's hand, his thumb tracing small circles on her skin. "I won't let that happen again," he vowed, his voice low and intense. The memories of countless loops, of watching his family die over and over, flashed through his mind. He pushed them away, focusing on the present. "I'll keep you safe. Both of you."

The parking lot suddenly felt too exposed, the morning sunlight harsh and unforgiving. Drake's eyes darted around, searching for unseen threats. His muscles tensed, ready to spring into action at a moment's notice.

Harrison shifted his weight, drawing Drake's attention. The boy's face was a canvas of conflicting emotions – fear, hope, and a flicker of the unwavering trust that had always been there, even when Drake felt least deserving of it.

"How?" Harrison asked, his voice small and uncertain. The word hung in the air, laden with all the doubts and fears that Drake himself wrestled with daily.

Drake's mind raced, searching for an answer that would reassure his son without making promises he couldn't keep. The weight of responsibility pressed down on him, threatening to crush his resolve. But as he looked at Harrison's expectant face, he felt a surge of determination.

"I don't have all the answers," Drake admitted, his voice rough with emotion. "But I know we're stronger together. We'll figure this out, step by step. And I swear to you, I won't let anything tear us apart again."

As he spoke, Drake's free hand reached out to rest on Harrison's shoulder, forming a physical connection between the three of them. In that moment, despite the uncertainty that loomed ahead, Drake felt a flicker of hope. They were a family, united against the chaos of the multiverse. And somehow, someway, they would find a way through this together.

39 - 40

Drake's gaze drifted to the horizon, the weight of his next words heavy on his tongue. The hospital parking lot seemed to stretch endlessly, a concrete sea reflecting the uncertainty of their future. He drew a deep breath, the crisp morning air filling his lungs with resolve.

"I'll call someone I trust," Drake finally said, his voice low and measured. "A friend who's gotten me this far. They'll ensure you're protected while I search for Rachel."

As he spoke, Drake's mind raced with images of his mysterious ally, fragments of memories from other worlds flickering like static. Who were they? How had they helped him before? The answers danced just out of reach, maddeningly close yet impossible to grasp.

Linda's grip on his hand tightened, drawing Drake back to the present. He turned to meet her gaze, finding a mixture of fear and determination in her blue eyes. The gentle pressure of her fingers against his palm grounded him, a lifeline in the storm of uncertainty.

"We trust you, Drake," Linda said softly, her voice carrying the weight of their shared experiences across realities.

The simple statement hit Drake like a physical force, threatening to buckle his knees. Trust. After everything they'd been through – the loops, the deaths, the shattered worlds – they still believed in him. The enormity of that faith was both terrifying and empowering.

"I won't let you down," Drake whispered, as much to himself as to Linda and Harrison. "Not this time. Not ever again."

41 - 42

Harrison wiped his eyes with the back of his hand, smearing tears across his cheek. For a moment, Drake saw not the lanky teenager before him, but the young boy from another life, wide-eyed and full of wonder. The contrast made his heart ache.

"Me too," Harrison said, his voice cracking slightly. He managed a small smile, a fragile thing that seemed to flicker like a candle in the wind. "I trust you, Dad."

The words 'Dad' hung in the air, heavy with meaning. Drake felt a surge of warmth in his chest, mixed with a sharp pang of guilt. How many times had he failed this boy across countless realities? How many promises had he broken?

Drake exhaled slowly, feeling the weight of the moment settle on his shoulders like a physical burden. He looked from Linda to Harrison, taking in their faces - scared, hopeful, determined. For the first time in what felt like an eternity, he wasn't alone in this fight. The knowledge was both comforting and terrifying.

"We're in this together now," Drake said, his voice low and intense. "No more secrets, no more half-truths. Whatever comes next, we face it as a family."

As he spoke the words, Drake felt something shift inside him. The relentless guilt that had been his constant companion began to loosen its grip, replaced by a fierce resolve. He would protect them. He would find Rachel Summers. He would set things right.

"So," Harrison said, a hint of his old curiosity creeping into his voice, "what's our next move?"

Drake allowed himself a small, grim smile. "We start by making that call. Then, we prepare for whatever comes next."

43 - 43

Drake reached into his pocket, his fingers brushing against the cool metal of his phone. As he pulled it out, the weight of their shared memories pressed down on him, each fragment a reminder of the impossible task ahead.

"Who are you calling?" Linda asked, her voice barely above a whisper.

Drake hesitated, his thumb hovering over the screen. "Someone who's been there from the beginning. Someone who might be able to help us make sense of all this."

As he dialed the number, Drake's mind raced with possibilities. Would Holly remember? Would she believe him if she didn't? The line rang once, twice, three times before a familiar voice answered.

"Vega."

Drake closed his eyes, relief washing over him. "Richard, it's Drake. I need your help."

There was a pause on the other end, filled with unspoken tension. When Richard spoke again, his voice was cautious. "Drake? What's going on?"

He took a deep breath, glancing at Linda and Harrison. "It's happening again, Richard. The visions, the worlds... it's all real. And this time, I'm not the only one who remembers."

The silence that followed was deafening. Drake could almost see Vega's furrowed brow, his sharp eyes narrowing as he processed his words. Finally, he spoke.

"Meet me at the Lexington Hotel in an hour. And Drake? Be careful."

As the call ended, Drake felt a mix of hope and apprehension. He turned to his family, their faces mirroring his own conflicted emotions.

"Let's go," he said softly. "It's time to face this head-on."

A Promise to Keep

1^{-2} The Lexington Hotel loomed over the quiet city street, its art deco façade illuminated by warm golden lights that softened the edges of the night. Drake parked the car across the street, his hands gripping the steering wheel tightly as he stared at the building. Inside, Richard Vega waited for them—a colleague Drake trusted more out of necessity than choice.

Drake's knuckles whitened as he clenched the wheel, his jaw tightening as he fought the urge to drive away. The weight of what he was about to do pressed down on him, threatening to crush his resolve. He could feel Linda's eyes on him, her concern radiating through the tense silence of the car.

"Are you sure about this?" Linda asked, her voice breaking the silence.

Drake turned to face her, taking in the worry etched across her delicate features. Her blue eyes, usually so full of warmth, now held a storm of emotions—fear, uncertainty, and a flickering hope that tore at his heart.

He wanted to reassure her, to promise that everything would be alright, but the words caught in his throat. How could he offer comfort when he himself was drowning in doubt?

Instead, he reached out and gently took her hand, his calloused fingers intertwining with hers. The simple gesture spoke volumes, conveying what he couldn't bring himself to say aloud.

"I wish there was another way," Drake said softly, his voice rough with emotion. "But Vega... he's our best shot at keeping you safe while I figure this out."

Linda's grip tightened on his hand, her touch anchoring him in the present moment. "I know," she whispered, her voice barely audible over the hum of the car's engine. "I just can't shake this feeling that something's going to go wrong."

Drake closed his eyes briefly, the weight of their shared fear pressing down on him. When he opened them again, he met Linda's gaze with a determination he didn't entirely feel. "We've come too far to turn back now," he said, his words carrying the weight of all they'd been through. "Whatever happens, we face it together."

As he spoke, Drake's mind raced with the possibilities that lay ahead. The risks were immense, but the alternative—losing Linda and Harrison to the twisted machinations of the multiverse—was unthinkable. He had to believe that this gamble would pay off, that trusting Vega was the right move.

With a deep breath, Drake released Linda's hand and reached for the door handle. "It's time," he said, his voice steady despite the turmoil within. As he stepped out into the cool night air, the weight of their future settled heavily on his shoulders.

3 - 4

Drake turned back to face Linda, the worry in her eyes mirroring his own. He reached over, taking her hand in his. The warmth of her skin against his calloused palm was a stark reminder of everything at stake. "I don't have a better option right now," he said softly, his voice barely above a whisper. The words felt heavy on his tongue, laden with the weight of their predicament. "Vega has connections, resources. He'll keep you and Harrison safe while I figure this out."

As he spoke, Drake's mind raced with doubts. Could he truly trust Vega? The man was an enigma, his motives as shadowy as the night that enveloped them. But in this moment, with the safety of his family hanging by a thread, Drake had no choice but to place his faith in his former colleague.

Linda's fingers tightened around his, her touch both a comfort and a silent plea. Before she could respond, Harrison's voice cut through the tense silence from the back seat. "Dad, are you sure you should be doing this alone?" The tremor in his son's voice sent a pang through Drake's heart. "What if—what if that guy with the dragon robe comes after you again?"

Drake's breath caught in his throat. The image of the man in the dragon robe flashed through his mind, a vivid reminder of the danger that lurked in the shadows of reality. He turned to face Harrison, forcing a reassuring smile that didn't quite reach his eyes. "I'll be careful, buddy. I promise." The words felt hollow, even as he spoke them.

5 - 6

Drake's forced smile wavered, his eyes shadowed with the weight of their predicament. "That's exactly why I need to do this," he said, his voice low and tinged with determination. "To stop him, to stop this... loop we're trapped in." The words hung heavy in the car's confined space, each syllable a reminder of the surreal nightmare they found themselves in.

He gazed out at the Lexington Hotel, its art deco facade a stark contrast to the chaos swirling in his mind. The warm golden lights that bathed the building seemed to mock the darkness of their situation. Drake's fingers tightened on the steering wheel, his knuckles turning white with the strain.

Linda's grip on his hand intensified, her touch both a comfort and a desperate plea. "Just promise me you'll come back, Drake," she whispered, her voice breaking. "Don't leave us like this." The anguish in her blue eyes, usually so full of warmth and hope, tore at Drake's heart.

He turned to face her, drinking in the sight of her face, committing every detail to memory. The gentle curve of her cheek, the worried crease between her brows, the slight tremble of her lower lip. Drake's throat constricted with emotion. How many times had he left her behind in other realities? How many versions of Linda had he failed?

"I..." Drake started, his voice hoarse. He wanted to reassure her, to make promises he wasn't sure he could keep. But the weight of their altered reality pressed down on him, reminding him of the fragility of such vows. Instead, he leaned in, pressing his forehead against hers. "I'll do everything in my power to return to you both," he murmured, his breath mingling with hers.

As he pulled back, Drake caught sight of Harrison in the rearview mirror. The boy's face was a mixture of fear and resignation, a look no child should ever wear. The sight steeled Drake's resolve. He had to end this, had to find a way to give his family the life they deserved, free from the specter of alternate realities and temporal loops.

With a deep breath, Drake reached for the car door handle. It was time to face whatever lay ahead, no matter the cost.

7 - 8

Drake swallowed hard, nodding. "I'll come back. I swear." The words felt heavy on his tongue, laden with the weight of countless promises made and broken across realities he could barely remember. He squeezed Linda's hand one last time, trying to convey everything he couldn't say aloud – his love, his fear, his determination.

As he stepped out of the car, the cool night air hit Drake's face, a stark contrast to the warmth of the vehicle's interior. The Lexington Hotel loomed before him, its art deco façade a testament to a bygone era. Drake's eyes scanned the entrance, searching for any sign of Richard Vega.

His heart raced as he approached the revolving doors, each step feeling like a betrayal of the family he was leaving behind. What if this was another trap? What if Vega was working with Gabriel, the man in the dragon robe? Drake's mind reeled with possibilities, each more dire than the last.

"Focus," he muttered to himself, clenching his fists at his sides. "You have to do this. For them."

As he entered the lobby, the opulent surroundings seemed to mock the gravity of his situation. Crystal chandeliers cast a soft glow over marble floors, creating an illusion of normalcy that felt painfully out of place. And there, standing near a pillar with his hands clasped behind his back, was Richard Vega.

Drake approached cautiously, studying the man's face for any sign of deception. Vega's expression was unreadable, a mask of professional courtesy that revealed nothing of his true intentions.

"Richard," Drake said, his voice low and controlled. "I appreciate you meeting us here."

Vega nodded, his eyes darting briefly to the doors behind Drake. "I assume your family is...?"

"Safe," Drake finished, unwilling to divulge more information than necessary. "For now, at least. But we need to talk."

9 - 10

The opulent lobby seemed to shrink around Drake as Vega's piercing gaze met his own. Polished marble reflected the warm glow of ornate chandeliers, casting dancing shadows across Vega's impeccably tailored suit. The air felt thick with unspoken tension, a stark contrast to the quiet luxury surrounding them.

Vega's lips curved into a practiced smile as he strode forward, his footsteps eerily muffled by the plush carpeting. "Drake," he said, extending a hand. "I wasn't sure if you'd come."

Drake hesitated for a fraction of a second before grasping Vega's hand, his grip firm but guarded. The weight of his decision to trust this man pressed down on him like a physical force. He searched Vega's face for any hint of deceit, any flicker that might betray ulterior motives.

"I didn't have much choice," Drake replied, his voice low and tinged with resignation. He glanced around the lobby, hyper-aware of potential eavesdroppers. "This situation... it's spiraling out of control."

Vega's brow furrowed slightly, concern seeping through his composed facade. "I gathered as much from your cryptic message. What exactly are we dealing with here, Drake?"

Drake's mind raced, torn between the need for help and the fear of revealing too much. How could he explain the impossible without sounding completely unhinged? The memory of the man in the dragon robe flashed through his thoughts, sending a chill down his spine.

"It's complicated," Drake finally managed, running a hand through his disheveled hair. "And you probably won't believe half of it. But I need your resources, your connections. My family's safety depends on it."

Vega studied him for a long moment, his expression inscrutable. Drake could almost see the calculations happening behind those sharp eyes, weighing risks and potential benefits.

"You know I've always respected you, Drake," Vega said carefully. "But I need to understand what I'm getting myself into. This isn't just about calling in a favor, is it?"

Drake shook his head, feeling the weight of worlds on his shoulders. "No," he admitted. "It's about saving everything we know... and some things we don't."

11 - 12

Vega's eyes narrowed imperceptibly, a flicker of curiosity—or perhaps wariness—crossing his face. He glanced at Linda and Harrison, his gaze lingering for a moment before returning to Drake. With a slight nod, he spoke, his voice low and measured.

"Of course. I've reserved a suite under an alias. It's secure, and I've got a couple of trusted contacts watching the place. No one will bother you here."

Drake felt a momentary surge of relief, quickly tempered by the knowledge that this was only the beginning. He studied Vega's face, searching for any hint of deception. The man's words seemed genuine, but years of experience had taught Drake that appearances could be deceiving.

"Thank you," Drake muttered, the words feeling inadequate given the magnitude of what he was asking. His hand unconsciously moved to his pocket, fingers brushing against the cold metal of the strange device he'd acquired. Its presence was a constant reminder of the impossible task ahead.

As Vega continued explaining the security measures, Drake's mind wandered. He pictured the suite—a temporary sanctuary in the storm. But would it be enough? The image of the dragon-robed figure loomed in his thoughts, a spectral threat that no locked door could keep at bay.

"Drake?" Vega's voice cut through his reverie. "Are you alright?"

Drake blinked, forcing himself back to the present. "Yeah," he lied, aware of Linda's concerned gaze. "Just... processing everything."

The weight of his next steps pressed down on him. Finding Rachel Summers, unraveling the mystery of the codex—it all seemed insurmountable. But as he looked at his family, Drake knew he had no choice but to try.

13 - 14

Linda stepped forward, her blue eyes reflecting the soft glow of the lobby's chandeliers. "Thank you," she said, her voice a blend of sincerity and barely concealed worry. Her slender fingers intertwined with Drake's, seeking comfort in the familiar touch.

Drake felt the gentle pressure of her hand, a bittersweet reminder of all they stood to lose. He watched as Linda's gaze swept across the opulent lobby, no doubt cataloging potential escape routes—a habit born from their tumultuous recent past.

Harrison, however, wasn't so easily placated. His lanky frame taut with tension, he fixed Vega with a skeptical stare. "How do we know we can trust you?" he demanded, his adolescent voice cracking slightly with the strain of recent events.

Drake winced inwardly at his son's bluntness, even as a surge of pride welled up within him. Harrison's curiosity and keen instincts had served them well in navigating this fractured reality. But now, those same traits threatened to unravel the fragile alliance they so desperately needed.

"Harrison," Drake began, his tone gentle but firm. He paused, weighing his next words carefully. How could he explain the complexities of trust and necessity to a boy who'd seen his world shattered time and again?

As the silence stretched, Drake found himself acutely aware of the hotel's ambient sounds—the soft hum of the air conditioning, the distant ding of the elevator, the muffled conversations of late-night guests. Each noise seemed to underscore the precariousness of their situation.

15 - 16

Vega's response surprised Drake. Instead of bristling at Harrison's challenge, the man crouched down, his tailored suit creasing as he met the boy's gaze. The gesture seemed to strip away some of Vega's usual guarded demeanor, revealing a flicker of genuine concern.

"Your dad and I may not always see eye to eye," Vega began, his voice low and measured, "but I've got no reason to betray him—or you. Keeping you safe is the least I can do."

Drake studied Vega's face, searching for any hint of deception. The man's words rang true, yet a nagging doubt lingered. In this fractured reality, trust was a luxury they could ill afford.

Harrison's brow furrowed, his expressive brown eyes darting between Vega and his father. Drake recognized the internal struggle playing out on his son's face—the desire to believe warring with hard-learned caution.

After a moment that seemed to stretch into eternity, Harrison crossed his arms, his lean frame still radiating tension. He gave a reluctant nod, the gesture small but significant.

Drake released a breath he hadn't realized he'd been holding. The fragile alliance had held, at least for now. But as he watched his son's guarded posture, he couldn't shake the feeling that they were balanced on a knife's edge, with the fate of multiple realities hanging in the balance.

17 - 18

Vega straightened, his lean frame casting a long shadow across the polished marble floor. The warm glow of the chandeliers caught the sharp angles of his face, accentuating the exhaustion etched into his features. He turned to Drake, his dark eyes probing.

"Drake," Vega said, his voice low and tinged with a mixture of curiosity and concern. "I assume this is about more than just hiding your family. What's your next move?"

The question hung in the air, heavy with unspoken implications. Drake's gaze flickered to Linda and Harrison, taking in their worried expressions. A pang of guilt twisted in his chest, threatening to unravel his resolve. He had to protect them, but at what cost?

Swallowing hard, Drake reached out, gently grasping Vega's elbow. "A word," he murmured, guiding them a few steps away from his family. The familiar scent of Vega's cologne - sandalwood and something distinctly expensive - brought back a flood of memories from their shared past, both the triumphs and the betrayals.

Drake's mind raced, weighing the risks of trusting Vega with this information. But time was a luxury they no longer possessed. He leaned in close, his voice barely above a whisper. "I need to find someone. Rachel Summers." The name felt foreign on his tongue, loaded with both hope and danger. "She knows about the codex, the multiverse, and everything that's been happening. If anyone has answers, it's her."

As the words left his mouth, Drake studied Vega's face intently, searching for any flicker of recognition or deceit. His heart pounded in his chest, each beat a reminder of the precious seconds ticking away. Would this gamble pay off, or had he just sealed their fate?

19 - 20

Vega's eyebrow arched, his expression a mixture of surprise and skepticism. The dim hotel lobby lighting cast shadows across his face, accentuating the lines of worry etched there. "Summers?" he echoed, his voice low and tinged with disbelief. "Isn't she the one who went underground after that multiverse theory of hers went wrong?"

Drake felt his stomach tighten. Of course Vega would know about Rachel's disappearance. The man's network of connections seemed to stretch across every reality they'd encountered.

"She's a ghost, Drake," Vega continued, his eyes darting around the lobby as if Rachel might materialize at any moment. "Finding her won't be easy."

The weight of the task ahead pressed down on Drake's shoulders, threatening to crush him. He clenched his jaw, steeling himself against the doubt that threatened to creep in. The image of Linda and Harrison, vulnerable and scared, flashed through his mind, fueling his determination.

"I don't have a choice," Drake said firmly, meeting Vega's gaze with unwavering intensity. His hands curled into fists at his sides, nails digging into his palms. "She's the key to ending this. I just need time."

As he spoke the words, Drake realized how hollow they sounded. Time. It was the one thing they never seemed to have enough of, slipping through their fingers like grains of sand. But he had to believe it was possible. For Linda. For Harrison. For all of them trapped in this nightmarish loop.

21 - 22

Vega's dark eyes bore into Drake, searching for something—weakness, perhaps, or a flicker of doubt. The opulent lobby seemed to fade away, leaving just the two men locked in a silent battle of wills. Drake fought the urge to look away, to break under the weight of Vega's scrutiny.

After what felt like an eternity, Vega's shoulders relaxed slightly. He gave a slow, deliberate nod. "Alright," he said, his voice low and tinged with resignation. "I'll keep your family safe."

Relief flooded through Drake, but it was short-lived. Vega wasn't finished.

"But, Drake—" Vega's brow furrowed, a hint of genuine concern creeping into his usually guarded expression. "Be careful. You're not exactly in the best shape right now."

Drake couldn't help the wry smirk that tugged at the corner of his mouth. It was true; he felt like he'd been run over by a truck, then thrown into a blender for good measure. Every muscle ached, a constant reminder of the battles he'd fought across countless realities.

"When am I ever?" Drake quipped, his voice rough with exhaustion.

Internally, Drake wondered if Vega's concern was truly for his well-being, or if it was just another calculated move in whatever game the man was playing. Trust was a luxury he couldn't afford, not when the stakes were this high. And yet, a small part of him desperately wanted to believe that somewhere, beneath the layers of secrets and self-preservation, there was still a shred of the colleague he'd once known.

23 - 24

The elevator doors slid shut with a soft hiss, sealing Drake, Linda, and Harrison into the confined space. Drake's heart felt as heavy as lead, each beat a painful reminder of the impossible choice he was about to make. The tension in the air was thick enough to cut with a knife, suffocating in its intensity.

Linda leaned against the mirrored wall, her arms crossed tightly over her chest. Drake caught her reflection, watching as she studied him from the corner of her eye. The worry etched into her features made his chest constrict.

"Linda," he began, his voice barely above a whisper.

She turned her head slightly, acknowledging him without meeting his gaze. "Don't," she said, her tone a mixture of resignation and barely contained anguish. "Just... don't."

Drake swallowed hard, his throat tight. He wanted to reach out, to pull her close and promise that everything would be alright. But the words died on his lips. How could he make promises he wasn't sure he could keep?

The elevator continued its ascent, each floor passing in agonizing silence. Drake's mind raced, replaying every moment that had led them here. The weight of his decisions, of the lives hanging in the balance, threatened to crush him.

Harrison shifted uncomfortably, his young face a mask of confusion and fear. "Dad?" he asked, his voice small and uncertain. "We're going to be okay, right?"

Drake crouched down, placing a hand on his son's shoulder. He forced a smile, hoping it looked more convincing than it felt. "Of course, buddy. I'm going to fix this. I promise."

As the words left his mouth, Drake caught Linda's reflection once more. The pain in her eyes was unmistakable, a silent accusation that cut him to his core. He knew what she was thinking – how many more promises would he have to break before this was over?

25 - 26

The elevator chimed softly as it reached their floor, the doors sliding open to reveal a plush hallway. Drake stepped out first, his shoulders tense as he scanned the area out of habit. Linda followed, her arms still crossed tightly against her chest.

"You're really going to leave us here?" she asked, her voice quiet but heavy with emotion. The words hung in the air, each syllable laden with unspoken fears and accusations.

Drake turned to face her, his brown eyes clouded with a mixture of guilt and determination. He ran a hand through his disheveled hair, a gesture that betrayed his inner turmoil. "I don't want to," he admitted, his voice barely above a whisper. "But I don't have a choice. If I don't find Summers, this will keep happening. I can't lose you both again. Not like this."

As he spoke, memories of past iterations flashed through his mind – Linda's lifeless body, Harrison's terrified screams. The weight of those moments pressed down on him, threatening to crush his resolve. But beneath the fear, a spark of hope flickered. Rachel Summers held the key to unraveling this nightmare, and he would move heaven and earth to find her.

Linda's eyes softened slightly, a glimmer of understanding breaking through her anger. She reached out, her fingers brushing against Drake's arm. "I know you're trying to protect us," she said softly. "But leaving us behind... it feels like you're giving up on us."

Drake's heart clenched at her words. He wanted to explain everything – the loops, the multiverse, the impossible choices he'd had to make. But how could he burden them with that knowledge? Instead, he gently took her hand in his, his thumb tracing small circles on her skin.

"I could never give up on you," he said, his voice thick with emotion. "You and Harrison are everything to me. That's why I have to do this. To give us a chance at a real future, without fear, without constantly looking over our shoulders."

27 - 28

Harrison's frown deepened, his young face etched with a mixture of worry and determination that seemed far beyond his years. "You better come back, Dad. You promised," he said, his voice wavering slightly despite his attempt to sound tough.

Drake felt a sharp pang in his chest at his son's words. He knelt down, placing a hand on Harrison's shoulder, feeling the slight tremor beneath his palm. The boy's brown eyes, so like his own, were wide with a mix of fear and hope that threatened to unravel Drake's composure.

"I will," Drake assured him, his voice low and steady. He searched for the right words, ones that could bridge the gap between the harsh reality he knew and the innocence he desperately wanted to preserve in his son. "And when I do, this will all be over. No more loops. No more fear."

As he spoke, Drake's mind raced with the weight of his promise. How many times had he made similar vows, only to find himself trapped in another iteration of this nightmare? The thought of failing again, of leaving Harrison and Linda vulnerable, sent a chill down his spine.

But looking into Harrison's eyes, seeing that unwavering trust, Drake felt a surge of determination. This time would be different. It had to be. He pulled his son into a tight embrace, inhaling the familiar scent of his hair, committing this moment to memory.

"I love you, buddy," Drake whispered, his voice thick with emotion. "Stay strong for me, okay?"

29 - 30

Harrison nodded reluctantly, though his eyes betrayed his uncertainty. The boy's lanky frame tensed, his fingers fidgeting with the hem of his shirt. Drake felt a pang of guilt, recognizing the weight of responsibility he'd placed on his son's young shoulders.

"Come on," Drake said softly, guiding Harrison towards the elevator with a gentle hand on his back. "Let's get you and your mom settled."

The elevator whispered open, revealing a plush interior that seemed at odds with the gravity of their situation. As they ascended, Drake's mind raced, cataloging potential threats and escape routes. The silence hung heavy between them, broken only by the soft hum of machinery.

When they reached the suite, Drake's trained eyes immediately swept the space. The room was bathed in warm, golden light that did little to dispel the shadows lurking in his heart. He moved with purpose, checking locks and windows, his movements precise and practiced.

"Linda," he called, his voice low but urgent. "Over here." He gestured to a sleek phone mounted on the wall near the kitchenette. "This is the emergency line. Direct connection to Vega's security team."

Linda nodded, her blonde hair catching the light as she moved. "And if we need to leave?" she asked, her calm tone belying the fear Drake could see in her eyes.

Drake's jaw tightened. "Multiple exits," he explained, pointing out each one. "Fire escape, service elevator, and a concealed passage behind the wardrobe. Vega's thorough, I'll give him that."

As he spoke, Drake's gaze drifted to Harrison, who stood by the floor-to-ceiling windows, his silhouette stark against the city lights below. The boy's reflection in the glass seemed ghostly, fragile. Drake swallowed hard, fighting back a wave of emotion.

"It's a lot to take in," he murmured, more to himself than to Linda. "I never wanted this for you both."

Linda's hand found his, her touch anchoring him to the present. "We'll manage," she assured him, her voice steady. "Just... come back to us, Drake. Whatever it takes."

Drake nodded, unable to trust his voice. The weight of their faith in him was both a burden and a blessing, fueling his resolve even as it threatened to crush him. As he turned to leave, he allowed himself one last look at his family, etching their faces into his memory. Whatever lay ahead, this moment—this love—would be his guiding light in the darkness to come.

31 - 32

The city sprawled beneath them, a tapestry of twinkling lights and shadowed streets. Linda stood motionless by the window, her slender frame silhouetted against the nocturnal panorama. Drake paused in his preparations, struck by the vulnerable set of her shoulders.

"You know, I keep thinking this is just some nightmare I'm going to wake up from," Linda said softly, her words barely above a whisper.

Drake's heart clenched. He crossed the room, each step heavy with the weight of their shared uncertainty. His hand found her shoulder, a gentle touch meant to comfort, to anchor them both in this surreal moment.

"I've thought the same thing," he admitted, his voice rough with emotion. The confession hung in the air between them, a shared vulnerability. "But this is real. And we're going to get through it. I promise."

As he spoke, Drake's mind raced. How could he make her understand the gravity of their situation without crushing her hope? The memory of alternate realities, of losses endured and sacrifices made, threatened to overwhelm him. He pushed them back, focusing on the warmth of Linda's presence beside him.

Linda turned, her blue eyes searching his face. "How can you be so sure?" she asked, her tone a mixture of doubt and desperate hope.

Drake's jaw tightened. He wanted to tell her everything – about the other worlds, the dangers they'd faced, the love that had transcended reality itself. But he couldn't burden her with that knowledge, not now.

Instead, he gently squeezed her shoulder. "Because I have to be," he said, infusing his words with a confidence he didn't entirely feel. "For you, for Harrison. For all of us."

The city lights flickered, casting dancing shadows across Linda's face. In that moment, Drake saw flashes of the woman he'd known across countless realities – strong, resilient, always by his side. It strengthened his resolve.

"Whatever happens," he continued, his voice low and intense, "remember that I love you both more than anything. That's the one constant in all of this madness."

Linda nodded, a small smile tugging at her lips despite the worry in her eyes. "We love you too, Drake. Just... be careful out there."

As Drake turned to leave, the weight of his mission pressing down on him, he held onto that moment – the warmth of Linda's presence, the love in her eyes. It would be his talisman against the darkness he was about to face.

33 - 34

Linda turned to face him, her eyes glassy with unshed tears that caught the city's distant glow. The soft light accentuated the worry lines etched around her eyes, a stark reminder of the toll this ordeal had taken on her. She reached out, her fingers tracing the stubble on Drake's jaw, a familiar gesture that spoke volumes of their shared history.

"You always were stubborn," she whispered, her voice wavering slightly. "Just... don't get yourself killed out there, okay?"

Drake's heart clenched at the raw emotion in her words. He wanted to reassure her, to promise her the impossible, but the weight of their reality hung heavy between them. Instead, he leaned in, closing his eyes as he pressed a gentle kiss to her forehead. The scent of her shampoo – lavender and chamomile – enveloped him, a bittersweet reminder of quieter times.

"I'll be back before you know it," he murmured against her skin, willing his words to be true.

As he pulled away, Drake's mind raced with all the things left unsaid. The alternate realities, the dangers they'd faced, the love that had survived across dimensions – it all bubbled just beneath the surface, threatening to spill out. But he swallowed hard, forcing himself to maintain composure. Linda didn't need that burden, not now.

He gazed into her eyes, blue as a summer sky, and saw the strength that had drawn him to her in every reality. It fortified him, steeling his resolve for the task ahead. Whatever came next, he would face it with the memory of this moment, of Linda's unwavering love, etched into his very being.

35 - 36

The city's nighttime silence enveloped Drake as he stepped out of the Lexington Hotel, each footfall echoing softly against the polished sidewalk. The weight of his promise to Linda and Harrison pressed down on his shoulders, heavier than any physical burden he'd ever carried.

As he approached his car, the streetlights cast long shadows, transforming familiar objects into ominous silhouettes. Drake paused, his hand on the door handle, and surveyed the eerily quiet street. The usual bustle of the city had faded away, leaving an unsettling stillness in its wake.

"This isn't right," he muttered to himself, his voice barely above a whisper. "It's too damn quiet."

Drake slid into the driver's seat, the leather cool against his back. He gripped the steering wheel tightly, his knuckles turning white as he battled the urge to turn back, to rush upstairs and gather his family in his arms.

Instead, he closed his eyes, took a deep breath, and started the engine. As the car hummed to life, Drake's mind raced with possibilities and fears.

"I'm doing this for them," he reminded himself, his voice thick with emotion. "To keep them safe, to end this madness once and for all."

The car pulled away from the curb, headlights cutting through the darkness. As Drake navigated the empty streets, his gaze flicked constantly between the road and the rearview mirror, searching for any sign of pursuit.

"What if I'm wrong?" he wondered aloud, the question hanging in the air unanswered. "What if leaving them is exactly what *he* wants?"

The image of the man in the dragon robe flashed through Drake's mind, sending a chill down his spine. He pressed harder on the accelerator, as if he could outrun his doubts and the looming threat that seemed to shadow his every move.

37 - 38

Rachel Summers. The name pulsed through Drake's mind like a beacon in the darkness, each repetition a reminder of the fragile hope he clung to. His fingers drummed an erratic rhythm on the steering wheel as he drove, the soft tapping a counterpoint to the engine's steady hum.

"Where are you, Rachel?" he murmured, his eyes scanning the shadowy streets. "What happened to you after everything went sideways?"

The cityscape blurred past his windows, a kaleidoscope of muted lights and looming buildings. Drake's jaw clenched as he remembered the last time he'd seen Rachel – disheveled, eyes wild with a mixture of fear and determination, clutching her research notes like a lifeline.

"I should have listened to you then," he admitted to the empty car, his voice barely audible. "Maybe if I had, we wouldn't be in this mess."

As he approached a red light, Drake's gaze drifted to the rearview mirror. For a moment, he could almost see Linda and Harrison's reflections, their faces etched with worry and confusion. The light turned green, but he hesitated, lost in the phantom image.

A car horn blared behind him, jolting Drake back to reality. He accelerated, his heart racing as guilt washed over him anew.

"I'm sorry," he whispered, though they couldn't hear him. "I know I promised to protect you, to keep us together. But this... this is the only way I know how."

The city gave way to suburbs, then to open highway. Drake's mind wandered to Richard Vega, the uneasy alliance they'd forged. He gripped the steering wheel tighter, knuckles white with tension.

"Can I really trust him?" Drake asked himself, frowning. "Or am I just trading one danger for another?"

The questions hung in the air, unanswered and heavy with implications. Drake shook his head, trying to focus on the task at hand. Finding Rachel was the key – he had to believe that. It was the only thread of hope he had left to follow.

39 - 39

The highway stretched before him, an endless ribbon of asphalt cutting through the night. Drake's eyes scanned the horizon, searching for any sign, any clue that might lead him to Rachel Summers. The weight of his decision pressed down on him, suffocating in its intensity.

"Rachel," he murmured, her name a talisman against the encroaching darkness. "Where are you?"

His mind conjured an image of her: brilliant, determined, a woman who had faced societal rejection yet remained undaunted. He remembered her vibrant red hair, now probably dulled by years in hiding. What would she look like now? What secrets did she hold?

A sign for a rest stop appeared, and Drake pulled over, needing a moment to gather his thoughts. As he stepped out of the car, the cool night air hit him, carrying with it the scent of pine and distant rain.

"I can't go back," he said to himself, leaning against the car. "Not until I have answers."

He closed his eyes, picturing Linda and Harrison safe in the hotel suite. Were they sleeping? Or were they as restless as he was, plagued by uncertainties?

"Dad?" Harrison's voice echoed in his memory. "You promised you'd come back."

Drake's eyes snapped open, his resolve strengthening. "I will, son. I swear it."

He took a deep breath, steeling himself for the journey ahead. Rachel Summers was out there, holding the key to unraveling this twisted reality. And Drake would find her, no matter the cost.

"Time to end this cycle," he muttered, climbing back into the car. "For all of us."

As he pulled back onto the highway, a sense of purpose filled him. The road ahead was uncertain, fraught with danger, but Drake knew one thing for certain: Rachel Summers held the answers he sought, and he would not rest until he found her.

A Fractured Reflection

1 -2
The muted television flickered, casting ghostly shadows across Linda's face as she sat motionless on the hotel suite's plush couch. Her fingers intertwined tightly, knuckles white with tension. The news anchor's lips moved in a silent dance, words lost to the oppressive quiet that blanketed the room like a heavy fog.

Linda's thoughts swirled, a maelstrom of worry and uncertainty. How had they ended up here, in this unfamiliar world where everything felt slightly off-kilter? Her gaze drifted to Harrison, her son's lanky frame pacing back and forth across the carpeted floor.

Harrison's footsteps seemed to echo in the stillness, each one a stark reminder of the passage of time. His unruly hair fell across his forehead, partially obscuring the furrow of his brow. Linda ached to reach out, to smooth away the lines of concern etched on his young face.

"Mom?" Harrison's voice cut through the silence, tinged with a hint of desperation. "Do you think Dad's really going to fix this?"

Linda's heart clenched. How could she answer when doubt gnawed at her own resolve? She forced a small smile, hoping it conveyed more confidence than she felt. "Your father has always found a way, Harrison. We have to believe in him."

Harrison nodded, but his restless pacing continued. Linda could almost see the gears turning in his mind, processing the impossible situation they found themselves in. She longed for the carefree boy he had once been, before the weight of alternate realities and fractured timelines had settled on his shoulders.

"I'm gonna use the bathroom," Harrison suddenly announced, his words shattering the fragile quiet.

As he disappeared into the adjoining room, Linda's gaze returned to the television. The anchor's lips continued their silent monologue, oblivious to the turmoil churning within her. She wondered what news this world deemed important, what trivial concerns occupied the minds of those who had never glimpsed the terrifying vastness of the multiverse.

A soft sigh escaped her lips. How long could they maintain this facade of normalcy? The urge to act, to do something—anything—to set their fractured reality right clawed at her insides. But for now, all she could do was wait, a sentinel in the quiet hotel room, guarding against the encroaching darkness that threatened to swallow them whole.

3 - 4

"Alright," Linda murmured, her blue eyes flickering briefly towards Harrison before returning to the muted television. The words left her lips mechanically, a reflex born from years of motherhood rather than genuine attention.

Harrison's footsteps receded, followed by the soft click of the bathroom door closing. Linda's shoulders sagged imperceptibly, the weight of their situation pressing down on her once more. She ran a hand through her blonde hair, her mind drifting to the countless alternate realities where this moment might be playing out differently.

"How did we end up here?" she whispered to herself, her voice barely audible above the city's distant hum. The question hung in the air, unanswered and perhaps unanswerable.

Her gaze fell to her hands, noting the slight tremor in her fingers. Linda clenched them tightly, willing herself to be strong. For Harrison. For Drake. For the countless versions of themselves scattered across the multiverse.

"We'll find a way," she affirmed, her words a quiet mantra against the encroaching despair. "We have to."

The silence of the room seemed to amplify her thoughts, each possibility and fear echoing louder in the absence of distraction. Linda found herself straining to hear any sound from the bathroom, suddenly anxious for Harrison's return, for any break in the oppressive quiet.

5 - 6

The fluorescent light flickered to life with a faint buzz, casting a harsh glow over Harrison's features as he stood before the mirror. His reflection stared back at him, wide-eyed and pale, a stark contrast to the boy who once explored the woods of Bridgewater with carefree abandon.

Harrison leaned closer, his breath fogging the glass as he examined the dark circles under his eyes. "You look like crap, Miller," he muttered, a weak attempt at humor that fell flat in the empty bathroom.

Cupping his hands under the faucet, he splashed cold water on his face, hoping to wash away the lingering unease that had settled over him since their arrival at the Lexington Hotel. The chill shocked his system, but did little to dispel the fog of anxiety clouding his mind.

As he reached for a towel, Harrison's gaze caught on the dragon emblem embroidered on the hotel's linens. For a moment, he could have sworn it pulsed with an eerie green light. He blinked hard, and the illusion vanished.

"Get it together," he whispered to himself, gripping the edges of the sink. "Dad's counting on you. Mom's counting on you."

His thoughts drifted to his father, the man who was both familiar and a stranger in this fractured reality. "He'll fix this," Harrison said, his voice wavering slightly. "He has to."

The unspoken question hung in the air: But what if he can't?

Harrison shook his head, dispelling the traitorous thought. He stared at his reflection, willing himself to see the strength his parents seemed to find in him. Instead, he saw only a scared kid way out of his depth.

"Come on, Harrison," he urged his reflection. "You can do this. You have to."

With a deep breath, he straightened his shoulders, trying to project a confidence he didn't feel. The mirror seemed to mock his efforts, reflecting back a boy playing at being a hero in a world that had long since outgrown such simple narratives.

7 - 8

As Harrison looked up, his reflection wavered, like ripples in a pond. He squinted, leaning closer to the mirror, his breath creating a fine mist on the cool surface. Something wasn't right.

"What the hell?" he muttered, his heart rate quickening.

The fluorescent light flickered, casting eerie shadows across his face. For a split second, Harrison could have sworn his eyes glowed an unnatural green. He blinked rapidly, trying to clear his vision.

"Mom?" he called out instinctively, his voice cracking. No response came from beyond the bathroom door.

Harrison's gaze darted to the corners of the mirror, searching for something—anything—to explain the unsettling sensation creeping up his spine. That's when he saw it: a faint shadow, barely perceptible, moving across the room behind him.

He spun around, pulse pounding in his ears. "Who's there?" he demanded, his voice a mixture of fear and defiance.

The bathroom was empty.

Harrison's mind raced. Was he losing it? The stress of their situation, the weight of expectations—were they finally taking their toll?

"Keep it together," he whispered to himself, clenching his fists. "For Mom and Dad. For everyone counting on us."

But as he turned back to face the mirror, the doubt lingered. In this fractured reality, could he trust even his own reflection?

9 - 10

Harrison's trembling fingers gripped the edge of the sink as he forced himself to look back into the mirror. His heart, already racing, skipped a beat and then plummeted into his stomach. The face staring back at him wasn't his own.

"No," he whispered, his voice barely audible over the sudden roaring in his ears. "It can't be."

But it was. Gabriel's scarred visage filled the mirror, those cold, calculating eyes boring into Harrison's soul. The boy's mind reeled, desperately trying to make sense of the impossible.

"You're not real," Harrison said, his words a mix of defiance and terror. "You can't be here."

Gabriel's lips curled into a cruel smile. "Oh, but I am, Harrison. I'm always here, in every reflection, every shadow."

Harrison's hands shook as he ran them through his hair, squeezing his eyes shut. "This isn't happening. It's just stress. It's not real."

"Open your eyes, boy," Gabriel's voice taunted. "Face the truth you've been running from."

Against his better judgment, Harrison looked. Gabriel's image remained, unwavering.

"What do you want?" Harrison demanded, his voice cracking. "Why won't you leave us alone?"

Gabriel's laughter echoed in Harrison's mind. "Because you carry the key, Harrison. The language, the memories—they're all part of a greater design."

Harrison's thoughts raced. The strange symbols he sometimes saw, the fragments of memories that didn't quite fit—could they really be connected to all of this?

"I don't understand," he admitted, hating how small and scared he sounded.

"You will," Gabriel promised, his tone chilling. "In time, you'll see the role you play in unraveling—or preserving—reality itself."

As Gabriel's image began to fade, Harrison felt a surge of desperate curiosity. "Wait!" he called out. "What do you mean? What role?"

But the mirror showed only his own pale, frightened face once more, leaving Harrison with more questions than answers and a growing sense that the fate of everything might rest on his shoulders.

11 - 12

The figure's disfigured face stared at Harrison from within the glass, its burnt and twisted features partially obscured by the hood of a white robe. A green dragon emblem on the chest of the robe glowed faintly, pulsing like a heartbeat. Harrison's breath caught in his throat, his wide brown eyes reflecting terror in the mirror's surface.

"No," Harrison whispered, backing away. His legs trembled beneath him, threatening to give way. "This can't be happening again."

He blinked hard, hoping the apparition would vanish. But Gabriel's haunting visage remained, those cold eyes boring into him. Harrison's mind raced, fragments of memories flashing through his consciousness—symbols he couldn't quite grasp, whispers of a language only he seemed to understand.

"Why are you here?" Harrison's voice quavered, a mix of fear and defiance. "What do you want from me?"

The pulsing dragon emblem seemed to grow brighter, casting an eerie green glow across the bathroom tiles. Harrison's gaze was drawn to it, mesmerized despite his terror. He found himself wondering if it held some hidden meaning, some clue to the fractured reality he now inhabited.

"I'm just a kid," he muttered, more to himself than to the specter in the mirror. "I can't be responsible for... for whatever this is."

But even as the words left his lips, Harrison felt the weight of uncertainty. The virus, the multiverse, his father's transformation from lawyer to detective—it all seemed impossibly tangled, with him at the center of the knot.

13 - 14

Gabriel's voice echoed in Harrison's mind, low and taunting. "You can't escape it, boy. The bloodline carries the truth, and the truth will break you."

The words reverberated through Harrison's skull, each syllable a hammer blow against his fragile sense of reality. He stumbled backward, his lower back hitting the cold porcelain of the sink. The fluorescent light above flickered, casting dancing shadows across Gabriel's disfigured face.

"What truth?" Harrison demanded, his voice cracking. "What do you mean by bloodline?" His thoughts raced, grasping for understanding in a sea of confusion. Was this connected to his father's mysterious past? To the strange symbols that sometimes danced at the edges of his vision?

Gabriel's lips curled into a cruel smirk, but he offered no further explanation. The pulsing of the green dragon emblem intensified, its rhythmic glow matching the frantic beating of Harrison's heart.

Harrison clutched his head, squeezing his eyes shut. "You're not real. You're not real!" he chanted, willing the apparition to disappear. But behind his closed lids, he could still see the afterimage of Gabriel's scarred face, feel the weight of his ominous words.

"I'm just a kid," Harrison thought desperately. "I'm supposed to be worrying about homework and first crushes, not... not this." Tears pricked at the corners of his eyes, a mix of frustration and fear threatening to overwhelm him.

15 - 16

When Harrison finally summoned the courage to open his eyes, Gabriel was gone. The bathroom mirror reflected only his own pale, sweating face. He let out a shaky breath, relief flooding through him.

"It was just my imagination," he whispered, trying to convince himself. "Just stress playing tricks on me."

But as he reached for the faucet, intending to splash some cold water on his face, a searing pain erupted in his abdomen. It felt as if someone had plunged a white-hot knife into his gut and was slowly twisting it. Harrison doubled over, a strangled gasp escaping his lips.

"What's... happening?" he thought, panic rising in his chest. The pain intensified, radiating outward from his stomach in waves of agony. His vision blurred, the edges of the world growing dark and fuzzy.

Harrison's knees buckled, and he slid down to the cold tile floor. He wanted to call out for his mom, but his voice failed him. All he could manage was a weak whimper as another spasm of pain wracked his body.

"Is this... real?" he wondered, his thoughts growing sluggish. "Or is Gabriel still here, somehow doing this to me?" The line between reality and nightmare began to blur, leaving Harrison adrift in a sea of confusion and agony.

17 - 18

The pain in Harrison's nose erupted like a lightning strike, sudden and searing. He cried out, the sound echoing off the bathroom tiles. His hands flew to his face, fingers trembling as they brushed against something warm and wet. Blood. The metallic scent filled his nostrils, making his stomach churn.

Harrison stumbled forward, his legs unsteady beneath him. The edge of the sink was cold against his palms as he gripped it, knuckles turning white with the effort to keep himself upright. He stared at his reflection in the mirror, hardly recognizing the pale, terrified face that looked back at him.

"What's happening to me?" he thought, his mind reeling. The pain pulsed in time with his racing heartbeat, each throb sending a fresh trickle of blood down his chin. It dripped onto the pristine white porcelain, stark crimson against the sterile surface.

His body felt alien, as if it were rebelling against him. Was this some twisted effect of the multiverse? Or was Gabriel's ghostly presence still lingering, tormenting him from beyond the mirror?

With trembling lips, Harrison managed to call out, his voice barely above a whisper, "Mom?"

He waited, straining to hear any response from beyond the bathroom door. The silence that followed was deafening, broken only by the sound of his ragged breathing and the steady drip of blood into the sink.

"Please," he thought desperately, "I need you, Mom. I don't understand what's happening. I'm scared."

19 - 20

Another wave of pain crashed over Harrison, this time emanating from deep within his stomach. It was as if a white-hot knife was twisting in his gut, stealing the breath from his lungs. His knees buckled, no longer able to support his weight.

"No, no, no," he gasped, his fingertips sliding uselessly against the smooth porcelain as he collapsed to the cold tiles below.

The bathroom floor pressed against his cheek, its chill a stark contrast to the fire burning inside him. Harrison's vision swam, the room tilting and swaying like a ship caught in a storm. He blinked rapidly, trying to focus on something, anything, to anchor himself to reality.

"Mom," he croaked, his voice barely audible even to his own ears. "Help me."

His breathing came in short, sharp bursts, each inhale feeling like sandpaper against his throat. The pain in his stomach intensified, spreading outward like tendrils of lightning across his entire body.

As Harrison lay there, curled into himself, a new sensation began to creep over him. A sickening twist in his gut, a roiling nausea that threatened to overwhelm him. He swallowed hard, fighting against the rising bile.

"What's happening to me?" he thought desperately, tears stinging his eyes. "Is this because of what we saw? Because of Gabriel?"

The memory of the disfigured face in the mirror flashed through his mind, sending a fresh wave of terror coursing through him. Was this some sort of punishment? A consequence of meddling with forces beyond their understanding?

As the nausea intensified, Harrison closed his eyes tightly, wishing with all his might that when he opened them again, he'd be back home in Bridgewater, safe in his bed, with his mom and dad just down the hall. But the cold bathroom floor beneath him was an unrelenting reminder of his grim reality.

21 - 22

Harrison gagged, the metallic taste of blood flooding his mouth. His body convulsed violently, muscles contracting as he vomited, the sound harsh and guttural in the small space. Each heave sent shockwaves of pain through his lanky frame, tears streaming down his face.

"Dad," he whimpered between retches, his voice cracking. "Dad, where are you? I need you to fix this."

His mind raced, grasping for explanations. Was this tied to the virus that had fractured reality? Or was it something more sinister, connected to the cryptic warnings Gabriel had hissed at him from the mirror?

When the spasms finally subsided, Harrison's hands trembled uncontrollably as he wiped his mouth. His breathing came in ragged gasps, the taste of copper lingering on his tongue.

"Maybe... maybe it's over now," he whispered to himself, clinging to a shred of hope. "Maybe everything will go back to normal."

Slowly, hesitantly, he glanced down at the mess on the floor and froze. His brown eyes, usually so full of wonder and curiosity, widened in horror at what he saw.

"Oh God," he breathed, his voice barely audible. "What's happening to me?"

23 - 24

Amid the blood and bile, a single tooth lay stark white against the crimson-stained tile. Harrison's stomach lurched again, but there was nothing left to expel. His mind reeled, struggling to process the horrifying reality before him.

"This can't be real," he murmured, his voice trembling. "It's just another nightmare, like the ones about Mom."

But the sharp, throbbing pain in his jaw told a different story. Harrison's chest heaved as panic clawed its way up his throat, threatening to choke him. He scrambled backward, his lanky limbs tangling as he pressed himself against the cold bathroom wall.

With shaking fingers, he reached up to his mouth, dreading what he might find. His tongue probed gingerly, exploring the familiar landscape of his teeth until it encountered an unexpected void. The gap where his tooth had been felt impossibly large, a cavern of absence that seemed to mock his desperate hope for normalcy.

"Dad always says there's an explanation for everything," Harrison whispered to himself, clinging to the comforting memory of his father's reassuring words. "But what could possibly explain this?"

As he sat there, trembling and alone, Harrison couldn't help but wonder if this was somehow connected to the fractured reality he'd found himself in. Was this physical transformation another symptom of the world gone wrong? Or was it something more personal, a manifestation of the chaos that had upended his life?

25 - 26

Tears welled in Harrison's eyes, blurring his vision as he stared at the bloodied tile floor. "No," he whispered, his voice barely audible over the hum of the fluorescent lights. "What's happening to me?"

The question hung in the air, unanswered and terrifying. Harrison's mind raced, grasping for any logical explanation, but finding none. He felt adrift, untethered from the reality he thought he knew.

"Dad," he called out weakly, longing for Drake's steady presence. "Dad, I need you."

But the words caught in his throat, choked by fear and confusion. Harrison wrapped his arms around himself, seeking comfort in the gesture. The fabric of his shirt felt rough against his skin, every sensation heightened by his growing panic.

"Think, Harrison," he muttered, trying to channel his father's analytical approach. "There has to be a reason. Maybe it's... maybe it's part of growing up?"

Even as he voiced the thought, he knew it was absurd. Teeth didn't just fall out without warning, not at his age. The metallic taste of blood lingered on his tongue, a constant reminder of the inexplicable horror he'd just experienced.

Harrison's gaze drifted to the mirror, half-expecting to see Gabriel's twisted visage staring back at him. Instead, he saw only his own reflection, pale and frightened. The contrast between his normal appearance and the trauma he'd just endured felt jarring.

"Mom and Dad will know what to do," he said, his voice steadier now as he clung to this lifeline of hope. "They always figure things out."

With trembling legs, Harrison pushed himself to his feet, using the sink for support. He took a deep breath, steeling himself to face whatever came next. As he reached for the doorknob, a final thought flickered through his mind:

"What if this is just the beginning?"

27 - 28

Linda's voice, tinged with concern, filtered through the bathroom door. "Harrison? Are you okay?"

The words hung in the air, heavy with maternal worry. Harrison's mouth opened, but no sound emerged. His throat felt constricted, as if the weight of his experience had physically manifested, choking off any attempt at response.

He slumped against the cool tile wall, his legs no longer able to support him. The vision of Gabriel's disfigured face danced at the edges of his consciousness, a nightmarish reminder of the inexplicable events unfolding around him. Harrison's mind reeled, desperately grasping for some semblance of rationality in a world that seemed to be unraveling at the seams.

"It's not real," he whispered to himself, his voice barely audible. "It can't be real."

But the dull ache in his jaw and the lingering taste of blood argued otherwise. Harrison's fingers absently probed the gap where his tooth had been, each touch sending a jolt of pain and disbelief through his system.

Linda's voice came again, more urgent now. "Harrison, please answer me. What's going on in there?"

He wanted to reassure her, to tell her everything was fine, but the words wouldn't come. Instead, silent tears traced paths down his cheeks, a physical manifestation of the fear and confusion swirling within him.

"Mom," he finally managed to croak, his voice breaking. "I... I don't know what's happening to me."

29 - 30

The bathroom door rattled violently, the sound jarring Harrison from his stupor. Linda's voice, tinged with panic, cut through the haze of his thoughts.

"Harrison!" She called, her tone sharp with worry. "Open the door!"

Harrison's heart raced, the rapid thudding echoing in his ears. He knew he had to move, had to let her in, but his limbs felt leaden, unresponsive.

'What if she sees?' The thought flashed through his mind. 'What if this makes it real?'

Gritting his teeth against the pain, Harrison forced himself to crawl towards the door. The tile floor was cold against his palms, grounding him in this surreal moment. Each movement sent waves of nausea through him, but he pressed on.

"I'm... coming," he managed to call out, his voice weak and trembling.

As he reached the door, Harrison's hand shook violently as he stretched up towards the lock. The simple action felt monumental, as if he were reaching across worlds rather than mere inches.

'Please,' he thought desperately, 'let this all be a dream.'

The lock clicked, and before Harrison could retreat, the door burst open. Linda stood there, her blue eyes wide with shock as they took in the scene before her. Harrison watched as her expression shifted from concern to horror, and he felt a pang of guilt for causing her such distress.

"Mom," he whispered, his voice cracking. "I'm sorry. I don't... I don't understand what's happening."

31 - 32

Linda's face paled as she dropped to her knees beside Harrison, her hands hovering over him, unsure where to touch without causing more harm. "Harrison!" she cried, her voice thick with fear and concern. "Oh my God, what happened?"

The anguish in her voice pierced Harrison's heart. He opened his mouth to explain, but the words caught in his throat. How could he describe the inexplicable? The vision of Gabriel, the searing pain, the... He shuddered, unable to complete the thought.

Instead, Harrison pointed towards the bloodied mess on the floor, his hand trembling uncontrollably. Linda's gaze followed, and he watched as comprehension dawned on her face. Her eyes widened, horror twisting her features as she saw the tooth amid the blood.

"No," Linda whispered, her voice barely audible. "This can't be happening."

Harrison felt tears welling up in his eyes. "Mom, I'm scared," he admitted, his voice small and vulnerable. "What's wrong with me?"

Linda's arms encircled him, careful yet protective. "We'll figure this out," she murmured, but Harrison could hear the tremor in her voice. As she held him, he couldn't shake the feeling that their world was unraveling, thread by impossible thread.

33 - 34

Linda's arms tightened around Harrison, her fingers threading through his damp hair. "It's okay," she said, her voice wavering despite her attempt at reassurance. "We'll figure this out."

Harrison buried his face in the crook of her neck, his body wracked with sobs. The metallic taste of blood lingered in his mouth, a stark reminder of the inexplicable horror he'd just experienced. "How?" he choked out between ragged breaths. "How can this be okay?"

Linda's hand moved in soothing circles on his back, but Harrison could feel the slight tremor in her touch. "I don't know," she admitted softly, her words barely audible above his crying. "But we're together, and that's what matters."

As Harrison clung to his mother, his mind raced with fragmented thoughts. Gabriel's twisted face in the mirror, the searing pain, the tooth... It all seemed like a nightmare, but the evidence was there on the bathroom floor, impossible to ignore.

Linda pulled back slightly, cupping Harrison's face in her hands. Her blue eyes, usually so calm and reassuring, now swam with unshed tears. "We've faced challenges before," she said, her thumb gently wiping away a tear from his cheek. "We'll face this one too."

Harrison nodded weakly, wanting desperately to believe her. But as he leaned into her embrace once more, he couldn't shake the feeling that this was only the beginning of something far beyond their understanding.

In the quiet of the bathroom, broken only by Harrison's muffled sobs, Linda's mind raced. What have we gotten ourselves into? The thought echoed loudly in her head, a stark contrast to the comforting words she whispered to her son.

Beneath the Funhouse

1-2 The dilapidated funhouse loomed before Holly Kierstead, its once-vibrant façade now a grotesque mask of peeling paint and rusty metal. She inhaled sharply, the cold night air biting at her lungs as she stepped through the creaking entrance.

Broken glass crunched beneath her boots, the sound echoing off crumbling walls like whispered secrets. Holly's eyes darted from shadowy corner to shadowy corner, her detective's instincts on high alert. Something about this place felt... off. Like a discordant note in an otherwise familiar melody.

"Get a grip, Kierstead," she muttered to herself, her voice barely audible above the wind whistling through cracks in the walls. "You've seen stranger things."

But had she really? Drake Miller's words echoed in her mind, a cacophony of improbable truths. A disfigured man. Temporal loops. A multiverse teetering on the brink of collapse. It all seemed too fantastical, too far-fetched to be real.

And yet...

Holly's flashlight beam cut through the darkness, illuminating a twisted corridor of warped mirrors. Her own reflection stared back at her, distorted and fragmented. For a moment, she could almost believe she was looking at versions of herself from other realities, each one a path not taken.

"Focus," she chided herself, shaking off the unsettling thought. "There has to be something here. Some piece of evidence that ties it all together."

As she ventured deeper into the funhouse, Holly couldn't shake the feeling that she was being watched. Every creak of the floorboards, every rustle of torn fabric set her nerves on edge. But it wasn't just the decrepit surroundings that unsettled her. It was the growing certainty that Drake Miller's wild tales weren't so wild after all.

"If I'm right about this," Holly whispered, her words barely audible even to herself, "then everything we thought we knew about reality is wrong. And if I'm wrong..." She let the thought trail off, unwilling to contemplate the alternative.

3 - 4

Holly's breath caught in her throat as she adjusted her flashlight, the beam cutting through the darkness like a knife. The funhouse's warped mirrors reflected distorted versions of herself, each one a haunting reminder of the multiverse theory Drake had shared. Her footsteps echoed softly as she ventured deeper into the labyrinth of decaying attractions.

"Focus, Kierstead," she whispered to herself, her voice barely audible. "There's got to be something here..."

Suddenly, a faint sound ahead made her freeze. Her trained ears picked up the unmistakable rustle of movement. Holly's heart raced as her flashlight beam caught a glimpse of white fabric disappearing around a corner.

A figure. In white. Again

Holly's analytical mind kicked into overdrive. "Who the hell would be here at this hour?" she thought, her eyes narrowing as she quickened her pace. The figure seemed unaware of her presence, moving swiftly through the funhouse as if on a predetermined path.

"Bridgewater PD! Stop right there!" Holly called out, her voice echoing off the walls. But the figure showed no sign of slowing down.

As she rounded another corner, Holly caught a clearer view of the mysterious individual. It was definitely human-shaped, but something about its movements seemed... off. Unnatural. A chill ran down her spine as she remembered Drake's words about beings from other realities.

"This can't be happening," Holly muttered, her breath coming in short gasps as she pursued the figure. "But if it is... if Drake was right about everything..."

The implications were staggering. Holly's mind raced with possibilities as she chased the enigmatic figure deeper into the heart of the funhouse, each step taking her further from the world she thought she knew and closer to a truth that threatened to shatter reality itself.

5 - 6

The figure rounded a corner, vanishing from Holly's sight like a ghost dissipating into the night. Her flashlight beam swept across the now-empty corridor, illuminating peeling wallpaper and shattered mirrors that fragmented her reflection into a thousand distorted pieces.

"Damn it," Holly hissed through gritted teeth, her chest heaving as she paused to catch her breath. The musty air of the funhouse filled her lungs, tinged with the acrid scent of decay. She had to catch up, had to unravel this mystery before it slipped through her fingers like smoke.

Her mind raced, piecing together the puzzle. "If this figure is connected to Drake's story," she mused aloud, her voice barely above a whisper, "then everything we thought we knew about reality..."

Holly shook her head, forcing herself to focus. Now wasn't the time for existential crises. She had a job to do.

"Hello?" she called out, her voice echoing off the walls. "I'm not here to hurt you. I just want to talk."

Silence answered her, broken only by the faint drip of water from a leaking pipe somewhere in the distance. Holly's hand instinctively moved to her holster, fingers brushing against the cool metal of her service weapon. She hoped she wouldn't need it, but in this twisted funhouse of mirrors and secrets, anything seemed possible.

"Focus, Kierstead," she muttered to herself, eyes darting from shadow to shadow. "You've come too far to lose the trail now."

With renewed determination, Holly pressed forward, her footsteps echoing in the eerie silence. Whatever answers lay ahead, she was determined to find them, no matter where they might lead.

7 - 8

Holly's heart pounded as she raced down the narrow hallway, her flashlight beam dancing wildly across warped mirrors and peeling paint. The funhouse's distorted reflections seemed to mock her, multiplying her image into a dizzying array of Hollys, each one as determined and breathless as the last.

"Stop!" she shouted, her voice bouncing off the walls. "I just want to talk!"

No response came, save for the faint echo of footsteps ahead. Holly pushed herself harder, her muscles burning with exertion. She couldn't lose this lead, not when she was so close to unraveling the truth.

As she rounded another bend, her flashlight caught a glimpse of white fabric disappearing around the corner. "Gotcha," she murmured, a grim smile playing at her lips.

But the triumph was short-lived. The next corridor opened into a circular room filled with funhouse mirrors, each one reflecting a different version of reality. Holly's breath caught in her throat as she saw herself reflected a hundred times over, some tall and stretched, others squat and compressed.

"What is this place?" she wondered aloud, her analytical mind struggling to make sense of the disorienting scene. "Is this what Drake meant by multiple realities?"

For a moment, Holly lost her bearings, unsure which reflection was real, and which was illusion. Her training kicked in, steadying her racing thoughts. "Focus on the facts," she reminded herself. "One step at a time."

She scanned the room, searching for any sign of movement among the countless reflections. There – a flash of white, real this time, not a reflection. Holly's instincts surged, propelling her forward once more.

9 - 10

Holly lunged forward, her heart pounding in her ears as she pushed through the dizzying maze of mirrors. "Stop!" she called out, her voice echoing off the warped surfaces. "BWPD! I just want to talk!"

No response came, save for the faint echo of footsteps ahead. Holly pushed herself harder, her muscles burning with exertion. She couldn't lose this lead, not when she was so close to unraveling the truth.

"Damn it," she muttered under her breath, rounding another corner at full speed. "Who are you? What are you hiding?"

Her mind raced with possibilities as she ran. Could this be connected to the Parker deposition? To NovaTech? Or was it something even bigger, something that tied into Drake's wild theories about multiple realities?

Holly's ponytail whipped behind her as she sprinted down the narrow corridor, her flashlight beam bouncing erratically off the walls. She was so close now; she could feel it. This time, she'd get answers.

But as she burst around the final corner, her momentum carrying her forward, Holly skidded to a halt. The figure was gone. Vanished, as if into thin air.

"No," she whispered, her chest heaving as she tried to catch her breath. "No, no, no. This isn't possible."

Holly spun in a slow circle, her flashlight illuminating every corner of the dead-end corridor. There were no doors, no hidden passages that she could see. Just blank walls and her own frustrated reflection staring back at her.

"Where did you go?" she demanded of the empty air, her voice tinged with a mix of anger and disbelief. "How did you just... disappear?"

11 - 12

Holly stood motionless, her ragged breaths echoing in the eerie silence of the abandoned funhouse. Her keen eyes scanned every inch of the space, searching for any clue, any indication of where her quarry had vanished. The stale air hung heavy with dust and decay, a stark reminder of the park's long-forgotten glory.

"Think, Kierstead," she murmured to herself, her analytical mind kicking into overdrive. "There has to be something you're missing."

As her breathing steadied, Holly became acutely aware of the oppressive quiet. No footsteps, no shuffling, not even the scurry of vermin that one might expect in such a dilapidated structure. The stillness was unnatural, almost suffocating.

She took a cautious step forward, her boots crunching softly on the debris-strewn floor. "If I were trying to hide something in this godforsaken place, where would I—"

Her words caught in her throat as a flicker of movement caught her peripheral vision. Holly's head snapped to the side, her flashlight beam following suit. There, partially obscured by a tattered cloth, was an old cellar door. Its rusted hinges creaked softly in the silence, as if beckoning her closer.

"Well, well," Holly breathed, a mixture of trepidation and excitement coursing through her veins. "What secrets are you hiding down there?"

She approached the door cautiously, her free hand instinctively moving to rest on her holstered weapon. Years of detective work had honed her instincts, and right now, every fiber of her being screamed that she was on the precipice of something big. Something that could tie together all the disparate threads of this bizarre case.

As Holly reached for the cloth, preparing to pull it aside, she hesitated. Drake's words echoed in her mind, reminders of alternate realities and the dangers that lurked between worlds. Was she truly ready for what lay beyond this threshold?

With a deep breath, Holly steeled herself. "No turning back now," she whispered, her resolve hardening. "Whatever's down there, I'm going to find it. And I'm going to get to the bottom of this madness, once and for all."

13 - 14

Holly gripped the rusted handle, her knuckles whitening as she pulled the cellar door open with a low, ominous groan. A gust of frigid air rushed up from the darkness below, carrying with it the pungent odor of mildew and something far more unsettling. She recoiled instinctively, her nose wrinkling at the assault on her senses.

"Christ," she muttered, shining her flashlight into the inky blackness. The beam barely penetrated the gloom, revealing only the first few steps of a steep, narrow staircase. "What the hell happened down there?"

Her analytical mind raced, piecing together possibilities. This smell, this cold - it wasn't natural for a simple cellar. It reminded her of crime scenes, of places where time seemed to stand still, preserving the echoes of past horrors.

Holly's instincts screamed at her to retreat, to call for backup before venturing further. But the same drive that had propelled her through multiple realities, that had led her to sacrifice everything for the greater good, pushed her forward now.

"Come on, Kierstead," she whispered to herself, taking the first tentative step down. "You've faced worse than this. Whatever's down there, you can handle it."

The wood creaked beneath her weight, and Holly paused, listening intently for any sign of movement below. Nothing but silence greeted her, punctuated only by the faint drip of water somewhere in the darkness.

"I have to know," she said softly, steeling herself against the growing unease. "For Drake, for all of us caught in this mess. Whatever the truth is, it's down there. And I'm going to find it."

With each step, Holly descended further into the unknown, her flashlight beam cutting through the darkness like a lifeline. The air grew thicker, heavier with each breath, as if the very atmosphere was trying to push her back. But Holly Kierstead had never been one to back down from a challenge, especially when the stakes were this high.

15 - 16

As Holly reached the bottom of the stairs, her flashlight beam swept across the basement, revealing a space that seemed to breathe with untold secrets. The contrast to the gaudy funhouse above was stark, like stepping from a child's nightmare into an adult's cold reality.

"Jesus," she muttered, her voice barely above a whisper. "What happened down here?"

The beam of light danced across damp walls, illuminating patches of mold and decay. Broken furniture lay scattered about, remnants of a past long forgotten. Holly's trained eye caught sight of something else - dark stains on the concrete floor, their pattern all too familiar.

"Blood," she thought, her heart rate quickening. "Old, but unmistakable."

She moved cautiously, each step calculated. The dripping sound grew louder, a steady rhythm that seemed to mock the tension building within her.

"Focus, Holly," she coached herself silently. "What does this place tell you?"

Her gaze fell upon a large wooden crate pushed against one wall. It seemed out of place, too new compared to the rest of the decrepit surroundings.

"Now, what are you hiding?" Holly mused aloud, approaching the crate.

As she neared it, a chill ran down her spine that had nothing to do with the damp air. Something about this basement felt wrong, felt like a piece of a larger puzzle she'd been trying to solve across multiple cases.

"Drake," she whispered, thinking of her partner. "I hope you're onto something too. Because whatever this is, it's bigger than both of us."

With a deep breath, Holly reached out to examine the crate, her detective instincts on high alert. Whatever secrets this basement held, she was determined to uncover them, no matter the cost.

17 - 18

The beam of Holly's flashlight danced across the room, casting long, eerie shadows that seemed to reach out with ghostly fingers. Her breath caught in her throat as the light settled on a sight that made her blood run cold.

"Oh God," she whispered, her voice barely audible over the thundering of her heart.

There, in the far corner of the basement, lay a cluster of bodies. The flickering light revealed pale, lifeless faces frozen in expressions of terror. Holly's mind raced, struggling to process the horrific scene before her.

"This can't be happening," she thought, her grip on the flashlight tightening. "How many? Who are they?"

She took a tentative step forward, her police training kicking in despite the shock. Her eyes scanned the bodies, trying to count, to identify, to make sense of this nightmare.

Her free hand moved instinctively to her holster, fingers brushing against the cool metal of her weapon. The basement suddenly felt smaller, more oppressive, as if the walls were closing in around her.

"Stay calm, Kierstead," she coached herself silently. "You've seen worse. You can handle this."

But even as she tried to reassure herself, Holly knew this was unlike anything she'd encountered before. The bodies, the funhouse, the echoes of Drake's warnings – it all pointed to something far beyond her usual cases.

"I need to call this in," she said aloud, her voice sounding strangely hollow in the damp air. "But first..."

Holly steeled herself and moved closer to the bodies, determined to gather as much information as possible. Whatever dark secrets this basement held, she was resolved to uncover them, no matter the cost to her own peace of mind.

19 - 20

Holly's stomach lurched as the full horror of the scene unfolded before her. At least half a dozen bodies lay sprawled across the concrete floor, their limbs contorted in unnatural angles. The stench of decay hit her like a physical force, and she fought the urge to gag.

"Focus," she whispered to herself, her analytical mind kicking into overdrive. "Some recent, some... not so recent."

She approached the nearest body, a man whose skin had taken on a sickly green hue. His unseeing eyes stared up at her, accusatory in their eternal silence.

"I'm sorry," Holly murmured, her voice barely audible. "I'll find who did this to you."

As she moved her flashlight beam across the faces, recognition dawned. These weren't random victims. These were the missing Parker deposition witnesses she'd been searching for.

"Oh God," she breathed, bile rising in her throat. She swallowed hard, forcing herself to remain professional. "It's them. All of them."

Holly's mind raced, connecting dots she'd previously thought unrelated. The multiverse theory, Drake's ravings about loops and alternate realities - suddenly, it all seemed horrifyingly implausible.

"What if..." she started, then shook her head. "No, focus on the facts, Kierstead. What do you see?"

She knelt beside one of the bodies, careful not to disturb anything. "Multiple victims, various stages of decomposition. Obvious signs of struggle. This wasn't random. This was planned, meticulous."

As she stood, a wave of dizziness washed over her. The weight of what she'd discovered pressed down on her shoulders like a physical burden.

"I need to call this in," Holly said, reaching for her radio. "But first, I need to make sure I'm not missing anything. These people deserve justice, and I'll be damned if I let whoever did this get away with it."

21 - 22

Holly's flashlight beam trembled slightly as she forced herself to examine each victim, her analytical mind pushing through the horror.

"Jane Crawford," she whispered, recognizing the woman's once-vibrant red hair, now matted and lifeless. "And Alan Shore." The man's distinctive glasses lay askew on his face, lenses cracked and clouded.

She continued, naming each victim in turn, her voice growing hoarser with each identification. These weren't just case files anymore. They were people - people she'd failed to protect.

"All of you," Holly said, her voice barely above a whisper. "You were supposed to be safe. Alive and well, ready to testify." She clenched her jaw, anger mixing with her grief. "Who could have done this? And why?"

Her mind raced through possibilities. NovaTech had the motive, certainly, but this level of brutality seemed beyond even their reach. And what about Drake's warnings about alternate realities? Could there be a connection?

Holly's fingers tightened around her flashlight. "Focus," she chided herself. "Deal with what's in front of you."

She took a deep, steadying breath, the musty air of the basement filling her lungs. As she exhaled, two words escaped her lips, laden with the weight of her discovery:

"Jesus Christ."

The curse hung in the air, a prayer and a lament for the lives lost and the magnitude of what she'd uncovered. Holly knew, in that moment, that nothing would ever be the same. The case, her career, perhaps even her understanding of reality itself - it had all shifted on this gruesome axis.

23 - 24

Holly took an involuntary step backward, her boot heel catching on the uneven concrete floor. The beam of her flashlight danced erratically across the grim tableau before her, casting grotesque shadows that seemed to writhe in the darkness. Her mind, usually a bastion of analytical calm, now raced with fragmented thoughts and half-formed theories.

"NovaTech," she muttered, her voice tight with a mixture of anger and disbelief. "Or someone else. This isn't just silencing witnesses. This is... extermination."

The realization hit her like a physical blow. These people hadn't simply disappeared; they'd been systematically eliminated and discarded like refuse in this forsaken place. The funhouse, once a symbol of joy and innocence, had been perverted into a mass grave.

Holly's stomach roiled, acid burning the back of her throat. She swallowed hard, forcing herself to maintain composure. Her hand, usually steady as a rock, trembled as she reached for the radio clipped to her belt.

"Bird needs to see this," she thought, her fingers fumbling with the device. "We're in way over our heads."

As she raised the radio, a chilling thought stopped her cold. What if the killer was still here, lurking in the shadows? What if making this call would alert them to her presence?

"Get it together, Kierstead," she chided herself. "You can't handle this alone. Bird needs to know."

Her thumb hovered over the transmit button, hesitation warring with necessity. The weight of the moment pressed down on her, as suffocating as the dank air of the basement. With a deep breath, she steeled herself to make the call that would irrevocably change the course of the investigation – and perhaps her entire understanding of the world.

25 - 26

"Franklin," she said, her voice tight as she spoke into the device. "I need backup. You won't believe what I've found."

The words hung in the stale air of the basement, echoing off the damp walls. Holly's heart pounded in her ears as she waited for a response, her eyes darting between the bodies and the shadows that seemed to writhe at the edges of her flashlight beam.

After what felt like an eternity, the radio crackled to life. Franklin Bird's gravelly voice came through, tinged with a mix of concern and his ever-present skepticism.

"Holly? What's your location? Are you alright?"

She could almost picture him, brow furrowed, his imposing frame tensed and ready for action. Despite their occasional disagreements, Bird's unwavering dedication to the job always shone through in moments like these.

"I'm in the basement of the old funhouse at Dreamland Fairgrounds," Holly replied, struggling to keep her voice steady. "Franklin, it's... it's worse than we imagined. The missing witnesses—they're all here. Dead."

There was a pause, and Holly could almost hear the gears turning in Bird's mind, his natural caution warring with the gravity of her words.

"Jesus," he finally muttered. "Stay put, Holly. Don't touch anything. I'm on my way."

As the radio fell silent, Holly felt a mix of relief and dread wash over her. Help was coming, but now she had to wait in this makeshift morgue, alone with the victims and her racing thoughts.

"What have we stumbled into?" she wondered, her gaze sweeping across the grim scene once more. "And how deep does this rabbit hole go?"

27 - 28

Holly's flashlight beam swept across the basement, revealing more horrific details with each pass. The bodies lay in unnatural poses, their limbs twisted like broken marionettes. Blood stains, long since dried to a rusty brown, painted macabre patterns on the concrete floor.

"God," she whispered, her voice barely audible even to herself. "What kind of monster could do this?"

Her eyes caught on a large wooden crate shoved hastily against the far wall. Its position seemed deliberate, as if it had been moved to conceal something. Holly's instincts screamed at her to investigate, but Bird's warning echoed in her mind.

Don't touch anything.

Instead, she forced herself to catalog every detail, her detective's mind working overtime despite the revulsion churning in her gut. A shattered chair lay on its side, one leg missing. Scratch marks marred the walls near one of the bodies. Each new observation painted a more disturbing picture.

"Multiple victims, signs of struggle," Holly muttered, her analytical nature providing a thin veneer of professional detachment. "This wasn't just an execution. They fought back."

A sickening thought crept into her mind, unbidden and unwelcome. How many more bodies might be hidden here? In other parts of the park? The scale of this cover-up was staggering, and Holly felt the weight of it pressing down on her chest.

She closed her eyes for a moment, taking a deep breath to steady herself. When she opened them again, her gaze fell on the face of one of the victims – Jane Crawford, she realized with a jolt. The woman's eyes were open, unseeing, a final moment of terror frozen on her features.

"I'm sorry," Holly whispered, fighting back the sting of tears. "We should have found you sooner. But I promise, we'll get justice for you. For all of you."

The silence of the basement seemed to press in around her, broken only by the faint drip of water from somewhere in the darkness. Holly had never felt more alone, or more determined to uncover the truth behind this twisted mystery.

29 - 30

The crackling static of the radio shattered the oppressive silence, causing Holly to flinch. Her heart raced as Franklin Bird's gravelly voice cut through the gloom.

"Talk to me, Holly. What did you find?"

She exhaled slowly, her breath visible in the cold, damp air. How could she possibly convey the horror of what she'd discovered? Holly's eyes darted from one lifeless form to another, her mind racing to piece together the gruesome puzzle before her.

"It's... it's worse than we thought, Frank," she finally managed, her voice barely above a whisper. "There are bodies. Multiple victims. And evidence... God, there's so much evidence."

Her free hand trembled slightly as she swept her flashlight across the basement once more, illuminating the grim tableau. The beam caught a glint of metal near one of the corpses – a watch, its face shattered, frozen at 3:47.

Time of death? she wondered. Or something more significant?

"I need more details, Kierstead," Bird pressed, his tone a mixture of concern and impatience. "What kind of evidence are we talking about?"

Holly swallowed hard, forcing herself to focus. "Blood spatter patterns, signs of struggle. This wasn't just an execution, Frank. They fought back. And there's more – documents, personal effects. It's like... like someone wanted us to find this. But why now?"

As she spoke, her gaze landed on a crumpled piece of paper near one of the bodies. Something about it nagged at her, demanding her attention. She crouched down, careful not to disturb the scene, and leaned in for a closer look.

"Hold on," she murmured into the radio. "I think I've found something that might explain..."

31 - 32

Holly's words trailed off as she studied the paper, her mind racing to decipher its significance. The silence stretched, heavy with unspoken dread.

"These are your missing witnesses," she said, her voice low, almost a whisper. "All of them. Dead. In the basement of the funhouse."

The words hung in the air, their weight crushing. Holly's chest tightened as the full implications sank in. These weren't just bodies; they were people – witnesses who had been silenced; lives snuffed out to protect... what? The scope of this conspiracy suddenly felt vast and terrifying.

There was a brief pause on the line, and Kierstead could practically hear Bird's disbelief. She imagined him at his desk, running a hand over his bald head as he often did when processing difficult information.

"Shit... Holly, I'll be there in ten. Don't touch anything. Wait for me."

Bird's voice was gruff, but Holly detected a tremor beneath his usual stoicism. This case had just escalated beyond anything they'd anticipated.

"Understood," she replied, her eyes still roving over the grim scene before her. As she ended the call, a chill ran down her spine that had nothing to do with the damp basement air. The funhouse mirrors that had seemed so whimsical earlier now felt sinister, as if they were watching her, waiting to reveal some terrible secret.

Holly took a deep breath, steeling herself. Ten minutes. She had ten minutes to observe to piece together what she could before Bird arrived. Her analytical mind kicked into overdrive, cataloging details even as a part of her recoiled from the horror surrounding her.

33 - 34

Holly's flashlight beam swept across the basement, casting eerie shadows that seemed to dance among the bodies. The stench of decay hung heavy in the air; a constant reminder of the lives lost. She swallowed hard, pushing down the nausea that threatened to overwhelm her.

"I'm not going anywhere," Kierstead said, her voice barely above a whisper. Her eyes darted back to the bodies, each one a testament to the depths of this conspiracy. "This... this is bigger than we thought. Someone's been cleaning up their mess, Frank. And it's not just NovaTech. We need to figure out who else is involved."

The silence on the other end of the line was palpable. Holly could almost see Franklin Bird's furrowed brow, his mind racing to connect the dots just as hers was. When he finally spoke, his voice was heavy with concern.

"Just hold tight, okay? I'm on my way."

As the connection clicked off, Holly felt a wave of isolation wash over her. The weight of what she'd discovered pressed down on her shoulders, threatening to crush her resolve. But she steeled herself, years of detective work kicking in.

Who could have orchestrated this? she wondered, her keen eyes scanning the room for any clues she might have missed. The precision of it all spoke of resources, of power. This wasn't just some random act of violence. This was calculated, cold-blooded murder on a scale that made her head spin.

Holly's hand unconsciously moved to her holster, seeking reassurance in the solid presence of her weapon. The shadows seemed to lengthen, and for a moment, she could have sworn she saw movement out of the corner of her eye. But when she whirled around, flashlight beam cutting through the darkness, there was nothing but stillness and death.

35 - 36

Holly's breath caught in her throat as her gaze settled on one of the bodies—a man, his face partially obscured by a black cap. There was something about his posture, even in death, that drew her attention. His arm was outstretched, fingers frozen in a desperate reach towards a crumpled piece of paper on the floor.

"What were you trying to tell us?" Holly murmured, her analytical mind already piecing together possibilities.

Crouching down, she pulled on a latex glove and carefully retrieved the paper. The chill of the basement seemed to seep into her bones as she unfolded it, revealing a letter marred by age and grime.

"Come on, give me something," she whispered, squinting at the smudged text.

Her heart raced as she made out fragmented phrases, each one a potential key to unraveling this twisted mystery. The words danced before her eyes, their implications sending a shiver down her spine. Symbols she couldn't understand were scrawled on the paper, and one name that stood out. Could it be? Drake Miller – Miller and Co. was scrawled across the paper.

Holly's mind whirled with connections. "This isn't just about silencing witnesses," she realized, her voice barely audible in the oppressive silence. "It's about protecting something bigger. But what?"

She stood, letter clutched tightly in her gloved hand, her sharp eyes darting between the bodies and the shadows. The weight of lives lost, of truths buried, settled heavily on her shoulders.

"I'll figure this out," she promised the silent room, her determination cutting through the gloom. "Whatever it takes, I'll bring this to light."

37 - 38

The fragmented phrases on the crumpled letter burned into Holly's mind: "... make sure the truth never gets out... the code is the key... cannot let Kierstead or Miller figure it out."

Her breath caught in her throat, the implications of these words crashing over her like a tidal wave. The chill of the basement seemed to intensify, seeping into her very bones as the realization dawned.

"This wasn't just a cover-up," she whispered to herself, her voice barely audible over the thundering of her heart. "This was planned. Meticulously. But why me?"

Holly's eyes darted around the room, seeing the bodies in a new light. Each victim wasn't just a silenced witness; they were pieces of a larger, more sinister puzzle.

"But what's the connection to Drake Miller?" she mused, her brow furrowing. "And why me?"

She paced the damp floor, her footsteps echoing in the oppressive silence. The weight of discovery pressed down on her, a mix of exhilaration and dread coursing through her veins.

"If Miller's involved," Holly reasoned aloud, her words a lifeline in the darkness, "then this goes deeper than we ever imagined. But how does it all fit together?"

She paused, her gaze falling once more on the letter in her hand. The mention of a code niggled at the back of her mind, a tantalizing thread she longed to unravel.

"Whatever this code is," she muttered, determination hardening her voice, "it's the key to everything. And someone was willing to kill to keep it hidden."

The Missing Truth

1 $^{-2}$ The flickering fluorescent light cast a sickly pallor over Detective Franklin Bird's weathered face as he hunched over the computer monitor. The grainy security footage from Dreamland Fairgrounds danced before his tired eyes, its timestamp a constant reminder of the night that had brought Drake Miller's fantastical tale to his desk.

"Come on, give me something," Bird muttered, adjusting his headphones. The tinny audio crackled in his ears, a cacophony of white noise and distorted fairground music.

His gaze flicked to the timestamp. 5:42 PM. The exact moment Miller claimed his encounter with the disfigured man in white began. Bird's jaw clenched, the muscles working beneath his stubbled cheek.

What am I missing? he wondered, his eyes scanning the grainy entrance to the park. The shadows seemed to writhe and twist, playing tricks on his weary mind.

Bird leaned back, his chair creaking in protest. He rubbed his eyes, feeling the weight of sleepless nights pressing down on him. This case was getting under his skin, gnawing at his usual skepticism.

"Miller," he sighed, the name heavy on his tongue. "What kind of game are you playing?"

He hit play again, watching as the empty fairground entrance remained stubbornly devoid of life. No disfigured man. No white robe. Just the eerie stillness of an abandoned amusement park.

Bird's fingers drummed against the desk, a staccato rhythm matching the growing unease in his gut. Something wasn't adding up, and he couldn't shake the feeling that he was missing a crucial piece of the puzzle.

"If you're lying, Miller," he spoke to the empty room, his voice low and gravelly, "I'll find out. But if you're not..." The thought trailed off, leaving a chill in its wake.

Bird squared his shoulders, his resolve hardening. He'd seen his fair share of liars and lunatics in his years on the force, but something about Drake Miller's desperation rang true. And that, more than anything, unsettled him.

3 - 4

Bird leaned closer, his nose nearly touching the screen. The faint glow of Drake's flashlight cut through the darkness like a knife, casting eerie shadows across the abandoned fairground. He tapped his pen against the desk, its rhythm matching the erratic beat of his heart.

"Come on, Miller," he muttered, eyes narrowing. "Show me something."

As if on cue, Drake appeared on screen, his movements frantic and disjointed. Bird's grip tightened on his pen, knuckles whitening as he watched the man stumble deeper into the park.

"What are you running from?" Bird whispered, the question hanging in the air unanswered.

Drake's figure disappeared for a moment, swallowed by the shadows. Bird's breath caught in his throat, anticipation building. When Drake reappeared near the funhouse, Bird leaned in even closer, scrutinizing every pixel.

The man on the screen looked over his shoulder, eyes wide with fear. Bird couldn't shake the feeling that Drake was expecting to be followed, hunted even. But by what?

"Dammit, Miller," Bird growled, frustration seeping into his voice. "Where's this disfigured man you keep talking about?"

He rewound the footage, watching it again with growing unease. Drake's terror seemed genuine, but the emptiness of the park was undeniable. Bird's skepticism warred with his instincts, leaving him feeling off-balance.

"If you're not lying," he mused, running a hand over his balding head, "then what the hell is really going on here?"

5 - 6

The silence of the precinct office pressed in on Bird as he stared at the grainy footage, the weight of unanswered questions settling heavily on his shoulders. Drake's solitary figure loomed large on the screen, a stark contrast to the man's wild claims of a mysterious attacker.

"But there was no one else," Bird murmured, his voice barely above a whisper. The words tasted bitter, laced with disappointment and a growing suspicion.

He leaned back in his chair, the leather creaking in protest. His eyes never left the screen as he reached for the remote, rewinding the footage once more. The familiar scene played out again: Drake's frantic movements, the erratic sweep of his flashlight, the paranoid glances over his shoulder. But no matter how many times Bird watched, the result remained unchanged.

"What am I missing?" he wondered aloud, frustration coloring his tone. "There has to be something..."

Bird's fingers danced over the controls, switching between camera angles, slowing down the footage, zooming in on areas of interest. Each new perspective only served to deepen the mystery.

"If you're not crazy, Drake," Bird muttered, "then you're one hell of an actor."

He paused the video on a frame of Drake emerging from the funhouse, blood trickling down his temple. The image gnawed at Bird's detective instincts. Something wasn't adding up.

"Alright, let's break this down," he said to himself, reaching for his notepad. "Either you're lying, or..." He trailed off, pen hovering over the paper as a chilling thought took root. "Or there's something here we can't see."

The implications of that possibility sent a shiver down Bird's spine. He shook his head, trying to clear away the creeping unease. "Focus, Franklin," he chided himself. "Stick to the facts."

As he jotted down his observations, Bird couldn't shake the feeling that he was standing on the edge of something far bigger and stranger than a simple case of assault. The security footage held the truth, he was certain. He just had to figure out how to see it.

7 - 8

Bird leaned back in his chair, the creak of worn leather punctuating the silence of the dimly lit office. His eyes, weary from hours of scrutiny, remained fixed on the grainy monitor before him. With a deep sigh, he reached for the controls once more.

"One last time," he muttered, his gravelly voice barely above a whisper.

The footage rewound with a soft whir, scenes flickering backward until Drake's figure reappeared at the entrance of the funhouse. Bird's brow furrowed as he tapped the play button, setting the video to half speed.

On screen, Drake's movements became eerily deliberate, each step drawn out in the slowed playback. The beam of his flashlight danced erratically across the faded façade, casting long, distorted shadows that seemed to writhe in the darkness.

"Come on, Drake," Bird murmured, leaning closer to the screen. "Show me what you saw."

But as the seconds ticked by, the detective's hope dwindled. The footage remained stubbornly unchanged, revealing nothing but Drake's solitary figure moving through the abandoned park.

"No sign of anyone else," Bird finally conceded, slumping back in his chair. The weight of disappointment settled heavily on his shoulders.

His mind raced, grappling with the implications. Was Drake Miller, the man who spoke of multiverses and time loops, simply delusional? Or was there something more sinister at play, something that defied conventional explanation?

"What aren't you telling me, Drake?" Bird asked the frozen image on the screen, his voice tinged with a mixture of frustration and curiosity. The case was far from closed, but the path forward remained shrouded in mystery.

9 - 10

Bird's fingers hovered over the keyboard, hesitating for a moment before pressing the fast-forward button. The footage accelerated, blurring Drake's movements into a frantic dance of light and shadow. His eyes, sharp and discerning despite the late hour, scanned every pixel for a hint of another presence.

"Where are you, you disfigured bastard?" Bird muttered, his voice gravelly with fatigue and growing frustration.

Minutes of footage flew by, the timestamp in the corner ticking away relentlessly. Bird's heart sank with each passing second, the absence of evidence weighing heavily on his conscience. Then, suddenly, movement caught his eye.

"Wait, what's this?" He leaned in, fingers fumbling to slow the playback.

Drake stumbled out of the funhouse, his formerly steady gait now uneven and erratic. Blood glistened darkly on his temple, catching the dim light of the park's sparse illumination.

Bird's breath caught in his throat. "Jesus, Drake. What happened in there?"

He replayed the segment, searching desperately for any sign of an assailant, but found nothing. The park remained as empty and desolate as before, offering no explanation for Drake's apparent injury.

A heavy sigh escaped Bird's lips as he ran a weathered hand down his face, feeling every line and wrinkle etched by years of similar cases. But this one... this one was different. It nagged at him, defying easy categorization.

"What am I missing?" he wondered aloud, his voice barely above a whisper. "What aren't you showing me, you damned cameras?"

11 - 12

Bird's fingers danced across the keyboard, switching to another camera angle. The new view captured the park's main thoroughfare, its once-cheerful façade now ominous in the nighttime gloom. The image was clearer here, but the story it told remained frustratingly incomplete.

Drake stumbled into frame, his silhouette a lone figure against the abandoned attractions. His steps were unsteady, each movement a battle against some unseen force. Bird leaned closer, his nose nearly touching the screen.

"Come on, Drake," he muttered. "Show me something. Anything."

But as Drake moved haltingly towards the park's exit, Bird's hope dwindled. No mysterious attacker materialized from the shadows. No disfigured man in a white robe appeared to corroborate Drake's fantastic tale.

Bird's pen tapped an anxious rhythm against his desk. "This doesn't add up," he said to the empty room. "A man like Drake Miller doesn't just... lose it."

He thought back to Drake's reputation as a brilliant lawyer, known for his sharp mind and unwavering determination. How could such a man fabricate such an elaborate story? And yet, the evidence before him told a different tale.

"What are you hiding, Miller?" Bird whispered, his voice tinged with a mix of curiosity and growing suspicion. "Or what's hiding from you?"

As Drake's figure finally disappeared from view, Bird felt the first tendrils of doubt creeping into his mind. The case that had seemed so straightforward was rapidly unraveling, leaving him with more questions than answers.

13 - 14

Bird removed his headphones with a weary sigh, the weight of his growing suspicions settling over him like a heavy cloak. He sat back, his weathered frame sinking into the creaky office chair as he stared at the frozen image of Drake on the screen. The man's disheveled appearance and wild eyes seemed to mock Bird's earlier convictions.

"No disfigured man," he said aloud, the words hanging in the stale precinct air. The realization hit him with the force of a physical blow, and he felt his carefully constructed theories begin to crumble.

Bird's mind raced, recalling Drake's impassioned pleas and frantic descriptions of alternate realities. He'd wanted to believe him, to see the brilliant lawyer he'd once known shine through the apparent madness. But the evidence before him told a different story.

"Dammit, Miller," Bird muttered, running a hand over his balding head. "What's really going on in that head of yours?"

He leaned forward, squinting at Drake's frozen form on the screen. The man's eyes seemed to bore into him, challenging him to unravel the mystery.

"If you're not lying," Bird said to the image, "then what the hell am I missing?"

The detective's gut churned with unease. Years of experience told him there was more to this case than met the eye, but for once, he found himself at a loss. The multiversal anomaly Drake spoke of seemed impossible, yet the desperation in the man's voice had been undeniably real.

Bird's fingers drummed restlessly on the desk. "One thing's for sure," he mused, "this case is far from closed."

15 - 16

Bird sighed heavily, the weight of his doubts pressing down on him like a physical force. He reached for the lukewarm coffee on his desk, grimacing as he took a sip. The bitter taste matched his mood perfectly.

"I wanted to believe you, Drake," he muttered, his eyes fixed on the screen. "God knows, I wanted to."

He stood up, stretching his stiff muscles, and began to pace the small office. Each step felt like a battle against his own skepticism.

"But this..." Bird gestured at the monitor, frustration evident in his voice. "This doesn't add up."

He stopped, leaning against the wall, his mind churning with conflicting thoughts. Drake's earnest face flashed in his memory, contrasting sharply with the erratic figure on the security footage.

"Multiverse anomalies? Time loops?" Bird scoffed, shaking his head. "It's the stuff of science fiction, not real police work."

Yet, a nagging doubt persisted. Something about Drake's desperation, the raw fear in his eyes when he spoke of his experiences, had struck a chord with Bird. It wasn't the typical behavior of a liar or a lunatic.

"But the facts," Bird murmured, his brow furrowing. "The cold, hard facts are staring me in the face."

He returned to his desk, rewinding the footage once more. As he watched Drake's solitary figure move through the abandoned amusement park, Bird felt his patience finally snap.

"What am I missing, Miller?" he growled at the screen. "What piece of this puzzle am I not seeing?"

17 - 18

Bird tapped his pen against the desk, the rhythmic sound echoing in the quiet office. His eyes narrowed, scrutinizing every pixel of the grainy footage.

"If you were attacked, Drake," he murmured, his voice tinged with a mix of frustration and curiosity, "where's your assailant?"

He leaned back in his chair, the leather creaking beneath him. The weight of the case pressed down on his shoulders, heavier than ever.

"No sign of struggle, no mysterious figure," Bird muttered, running a hand over his balding head. "Just you, talking to thin air."

He stood up abruptly, pacing the small confines of his office. Each step was measured, deliberate, as if he could walk his way to a solution.

"You're either the best liar I've ever met," Bird said to the empty room, "or..."

He trailed off, his mind recoiling from the alternative. The possibility that Drake's far-fetched tale of multiverses and time loops might hold a grain of truth was almost too much to bear.

"Or I'm losing my damn mind right along with you," he finished, a wry smile twisting his lips.

Bird returned to his desk, his pen tapping a staccato beat against the wood. He stared at the frozen image of Drake on the screen, willing it to reveal its secrets.

"What are you hiding, Miller?" he asked softly. "What's really going on in that head of yours?"

As the questions hung in the air, unanswered, Bird felt the case slipping further from his grasp. Either Drake was lying, or something far stranger was at play. And for the first time in his long career, Franklin Bird wasn't sure which option he feared more.

19 - 20

Bird leaned back in his chair, the leather creaking under his weight. His eyes, weary from hours of scrutiny, flickered between the monitor and his notepad. The pen in his hand hovered, poised to capture any revelation that might surface from the murky depths of this case.

"One more time," he murmured, hitting the replay button with a sense of grim determination.

As the footage rolled, Bird's gaze sharpened, searching for any detail he might have missed. The grainy image of Drake stumbling through the amusement park played out before him, a silent testimony to a night shrouded in mystery.

"No footprints but your own," Bird observed, jotting down a note. "No shadows, no movement in the periphery."

He paused the video, zooming in on Drake's face. The man's eyes were wide, darting frantically from side to side. Bird's brow furrowed.

"You're reacting to something, Miller," he said softly. "But what?"

A thought struck him, causing his pen to pause mid-stroke. "What if... what if you're not lying? What if you're seeing something we can't?"

The implications of that possibility sent a chill down Bird's spine. He'd spent his career dealing in facts, in the tangible world of evidence and logical deductions. But this case was pushing him into uncharted territory, challenging everything he thought he knew about reality itself.

"Multiverses," Bird muttered, shaking his head. "Time loops. Christ, what am I even considering here?"

He scribbled another note, his handwriting growing more erratic as his mind raced with possibilities. The weight of the case, of its potential to upend everything he understood about the world, pressed down on him like a physical force.

"If I'm right about this," Bird said to the empty room, "nothing will ever be the same again."

21 - 22

Bird leaned closer to the screen, his eyes narrowing as he studied Drake's erratic movements. The man's gestures were wild, his body jerking and twisting as if dodging invisible obstacles.

"What are you running from, Miller?" Bird murmured, his fingers hovering over the keyboard.

He rewound the footage, playing it back at half speed. Drake's mouth moved, forming words that the silent video couldn't capture. Bird's brow furrowed as he tried to read the man's lips.

"It's like he's having a conversation," Bird mused, scribbling another note. "But with who? Or... what?"

The detective's mind raced, recalling Drake's desperate pleas about alternate realities and time loops. He'd dismissed them as the ravings of a troubled mind, but now...

"Could it be?" Bird whispered, a mixture of fear and fascination creeping into his voice. "Are you really seeing something we can't, Drake?"

He paused the video on a frame where Drake's face was clearly visible. The man's eyes were wide with terror, his features contorted in a silent scream. It was the look of someone facing an unspeakable horror.

Bird leaned back in his chair, running a hand through his thinning hair. "If you're not crazy, and you're not lying," he said to the frozen image of Drake, "then God help us all."

23 - 24

Bird's gaze shifted to the area outside the funhouse, scrutinizing every pixel for signs of conflict. The worn pavement remained undisturbed, no scuff marks or debris to indicate a physical altercation. Even the garish, peeling paint of the funhouse facade bore no fresh scratches or impact marks.

"Nothing," Bird muttered, his voice thick with frustration. He leaned forward, the glow of the monitor casting deep shadows across his weathered face. "Not a damn thing out of place."

The detective's pen hovered over his notepad, tapping an erratic rhythm as he wrestled with the implications. His eyes drifted to the word "alone" scrawled in his untidy hand. With a swift, decisive motion, he circled it, the ink bleeding into the paper.

"What am I missing, Drake?" Bird whispered, his gaze fixed on the frozen image of the man stumbling out of the funhouse. "What did you see that we can't?"

He rolled his shoulders, feeling the weight of sleepless nights and unanswered questions. The case had burrowed under his skin, gnawing at his instincts. Bird prided himself on his ability to read people, to discern truth from lies, but Drake Miller... he was an enigma wrapped in a riddle.

"If you're not crazy," Bird murmured, his voice barely audible, "then we're in deeper trouble than I thought."

25 - 26

Bird leaned back in his chair, the leather creaking under his weight. The fluorescent lights hummed overhead, casting a sickly pallor over the cramped office. He rubbed his temples, feeling the beginnings of a headache forming.

"If he's making this up," Bird muttered, his voice a low growl in the quiet room, "why go to all this trouble? What's he trying to hide?"

The question hung in the air, unanswered. Bird's mind raced, piecing together fragments of evidence like a jigsaw puzzle with half the pieces missing. Drake Miller, successful lawyer turned enigmatic figure, had upended everything Bird thought he knew about reality.

A sudden thought struck him, jolting him upright. Bird's hand moved swiftly, flipping back through pages of notes from earlier conversations with Drake. His eyes scanned the hastily scribbled words, searching for something he might have overlooked.

"The burns on his arms," Bird mumbled, tracing the words with his finger. "The head injury, those bizarre visions he described..."

He paused, his brow furrowing deeper. "Could it all be a cover for something else?"

Bird's mind whirred with possibilities. Was Drake protecting someone? Himself? Or was there a deeper, more sinister explanation lurking beneath the surface?

"Dammit, Miller," he growled, frustration edging his voice. "What aren't you telling me?"

The detective stared at the security footage once more, willing it to reveal its secrets. But the grainy images remained stubbornly silent, offering no answers to the questions that plagued him.

27 - 28

Bird's pen hovered over the paper, its tip barely grazing the surface as he hesitated. The weight of his suspicions pressed down on him, urging him to commit his thoughts to paper. With a deep breath, he finally scrawled another note:

"Drake's behavior at the restaurant."

The memory of that night flooded back, vivid and unsettling. Bird closed his eyes, recalling the scene in stark detail.

"He was... off," Bird muttered to himself, his voice barely above a whisper. "Jumpy. Like he was seeing things that weren't there."

The detective's mind replayed Drake's erratic movements, the way his eyes had darted around the room, focusing on empty spaces as if they held invisible threats. Bird's pen tapped rhythmically against the desk as he pondered.

"It wasn't just nerves," he mused aloud, his voice tinged with a mix of concern and suspicion. "There was something... more."

Bird leaned back in his chair, the old wood creaking under his weight. He rubbed his temples, trying to make sense of it all.

"What if..." he started, then hesitated, almost afraid to voice his theory. "What if Drake's not lying? What if he's genuinely experiencing something we can't see?"

The possibility sent a chill down Bird's spine. He'd seen his fair share of strange cases, but this... this was something entirely different.

"Or," he countered himself, playing devil's advocate, "what if it's all an elaborate act? A smokescreen to cover up something worse?"

Bird's eyes drifted back to the security footage, still paused on Drake's lone figure. The man's isolation in the frame seemed to mirror the isolation of Bird's own understanding.

"One thing's for sure," Bird muttered, his jaw set with determination. "Drake Miller is at the center of something big. And I'll be damned if I don't figure out what it is."

29 - 30

Bird's weathered hands clasped together, his knuckles whitening as he recalled Vega's report. The words seemed to echo in his mind, painting a vivid picture of Drake's descent into apparent madness.

"Erratic behavior," he murmured, his brow furrowing deeply. "Talking to thin air, eyes darting about..."

The detective's gaze drifted to the window, where the city lights flickered like distant stars. He could almost see Drake there, wild-eyed and frantic, gesticulating at invisible entities.

"And then, the collapse," Bird continued, his voice barely above a whisper. "Right there in the middle of the restaurant."

He turned back to his desk, fingers drumming an anxious rhythm on the worn wood. The pieces were there, but they refused to fit together in any logical way.

"What if..." Bird began, then paused, the weight of his suspicion heavy on his tongue. "What if he's losing it?"

The words hung in the air, charged with possibility and dread. Bird's mind raced through the implications, each more troubling than the last.

"If Drake's mind is fracturing," he mused, "then everything he's told us... the loops, the multiverse... it could all be a delusion."

But even as the thought formed, doubt crept in. Bird had seen the fear in Drake's eyes, felt the urgency in his words. Could a man fabricate such conviction?

"Or," Bird countered himself, "what if his apparent madness is a symptom of something real? Something beyond our understanding?"

The detective leaned back, his chair creaking in protest. The case had seemed straightforward at first, but now it twisted and turned like a labyrinth in his mind.

"One thing's for certain," Bird muttered, his resolve hardening. "Whether Drake's losing his grip on reality or tapping into something beyond it, we need to find out. And fast."

31 - 32

Bird's gaze drifted to the clock on the wall, its relentless ticking a stark reminder of time's passage. The hour was late, shadows lengthening across the precinct floor like grasping fingers. He pictured Holly at the amusement park, her keen eyes scanning the derelict attractions for clues.

"Whatever she's found," Bird mused, his brow furrowing, "it must be significant."

He could almost see Holly there, her long black hair pulled back tightly, her athletic frame taut with concentration as she pieced together the puzzle. The image of her steadfast determination stirred something in Bird - a mix of admiration and unease.

"She's always been quick to adapt," he murmured, recalling how swiftly Holly had embraced Drake's outlandish theories. "But this... this is different."

Bird's fingers tapped an irregular rhythm on his desk, mirroring the chaotic thoughts swirling in his mind. The weight of his earlier realization - Drake's solitary presence in the security footage - pressed heavily upon him.

"If Holly's found something to corroborate Drake's story," he pondered, his voice barely above a whisper, "then we're dealing with something far beyond our usual jurisdiction."

The detective's eyes drifted to the phone on his desk. He knew he should call her, share his findings about the security footage. But a part of him hesitated, reluctant to shatter whatever fragile leads Holly might be pursuing.

"What if I'm wrong?" Bird asked the empty room. "What if there's more to this than meets the eye?"

33 - 34

Bird's hand hovered over the phone, hesitation etched in the lines of his face. The precinct's dim lighting cast long shadows across his desk, mirroring the doubts that stretched across his mind. With a deep breath, he steeled himself and reached for the receiver.

He picked up his phone and dialed her number, each tone echoing in the quiet office like a countdown to an uncertain revelation. Bird's free hand drummed nervously on his thigh as he waited, his mind racing through potential scenarios.

"What if she's found proof?" he thought, a mixture of anticipation and dread churning in his stomach. "Or worse, what if she's in danger?"

The line crackled to life, interrupting his spiraling thoughts.

"Kierstead," she answered after a moment, her voice clipped.

Bird recognized the tension in Holly's tone immediately. It was the voice she used when she was onto something big, when her analytical mind was working overtime to piece together a complex puzzle. He could almost see her standing amidst the decaying amusement park rides, her sharp eyes darting from clue to clue, her body coiled with the energy of a breakthrough on the horizon.

"Holly," he began, his own voice thick with the weight of his recent discoveries. He opened his mouth to continue, but found himself suddenly at a loss for words. How could he convey the gravity of what he'd seen - or rather, hadn't seen - in the security footage?

35 - 36

Bird cleared his throat, pushing past his hesitation. "It's Bird," he said, his voice low and grave. "I've been going through the security footage from Dreamland. You're not gonna like this."

He paused, giving Holly a moment to brace herself. The silence on the other end of the line felt heavy, pregnant with unspoken questions and mounting tension. Bird's eyes drifted back to the grainy footage frozen on his monitor, Drake's lone figure a stark reminder of the inconsistencies in their case.

Holly's voice cut through his thoughts, sharp as a knife. "Spit it out," she replied, her tone impatient. Bird could almost see her furrowed brow, the way she'd be pinching the bridge of her nose in frustration.

He took a deep breath, weighing his words carefully. How much should he reveal over the phone? How would Holly react to the possibility that their key witness might be delusional - or worse, lying? The weight of their investigation, of the strange events unfolding around them, seemed to press down on his shoulders.

"Holly," he began again, his voice barely above a whisper, "I think we might be dealing with something far more complex than we initially thought. The footage... it's not what we expected. Not at all."

37 - 38

Bird's fingers tightened around the phone, his knuckles whitening as he steeled himself for Holly's reaction. The soft hum of the precinct faded into the background, leaving only the sound of his own heartbeat thudding in his ears.

"I've got nothing," Bird said bluntly, the words tasting bitter on his tongue. "No disfigured man, no white robe, no one else at the park that night but Drake. He's completely alone in every frame."

The confession hung in the air, heavy and unyielding. Bird's eyes darted back to the monitor, where Drake's solitary figure stood frozen in time, a stark testament to the unraveling mystery. He found himself wondering, not for the first time, what demons truly haunted the man at the center of their investigation.

There was a pause on the other end, the silence stretching thin like a wire about to snap. Bird could almost see Holly's face in his mind's eye - the slight narrowing of her eyes, the tightening of her jaw as she processed this new information. He braced himself for the barrage of questions that was sure to follow, his mind already racing to formulate answers he didn't have.

As the silence persisted, Bird's thoughts drifted to Drake Miller. The man's haunted eyes and desperate pleas for understanding flashed through his memory. Was Drake truly losing his grip on reality, or was there something more sinister at play? The weight of uncertainty pressed down on Bird's shoulders, a familiar companion in his line of work, but rarely so heavy as it felt now.

39 - 40

"What are you saying?" Kierstead's voice finally crackled through the line, her tone a mixture of disbelief and thinly veiled frustration.

Bird inhaled deeply, his fingers drumming an anxious rhythm on the desk. The dim light of his office seemed to close in around him, mirroring the tightening of his thoughts. He chose his words carefully, aware of the implications they carried.

"I'm saying Drake might be lying," Bird said, the words tasting bitter on his tongue. "Or he's delusional. Either way, this story about the loops and the multiverse—it's looking more like a cover for something."

As he spoke, Bird's mind raced through the possibilities. Was Drake Miller a master manipulator, weaving an intricate web of deceit? Or was he a man trapped in the labyrinth of his own fractured psyche? The detective's instincts, honed over years of service, screamed that there was more to this case than met the eye.

He pictured Drake's imposing frame, the shadows under his eyes, the desperation that seemed to cling to him like a second skin. Something didn't add up, and Bird felt the familiar surge of determination to uncover the truth, no matter how ugly it might be.

"Damn it," Kierstead muttered, her frustration palpable even through the phone. "This complicates things."

Bird nodded, though she couldn't see him. "I know. But we can't ignore the evidence, Holly. Something's not right here, and we need to figure out what it is before anyone else gets hurt."

41 - 42

The static-laced silence stretched between them, heavy with unspoken concerns. Bird could almost see Kierstead's furrowed brow, her sharp eyes narrowing as she processed this new information.

Kierstead exhaled sharply, the sound harsh in Bird's ear. "Great. Just what we need."

Her words dripped with sarcasm, but Bird detected a hint of genuine worry beneath. He leaned forward in his chair, the leather creaking softly. His free hand drummed an anxious rhythm on the desk, betraying his growing unease.

"What's going on over there?" Bird asked, his voice low and measured. He fought to keep his tone neutral, but curiosity and concern seeped through despite his best efforts.

As he waited for Kierstead's response, Bird's gaze drifted to the frozen image of Drake on his monitor. The man's haunted expression seemed to mock him, a silent challenge to unravel the truth. Bird's mind raced, piecing together fragments of evidence, searching for the elusive thread that would tie it all together.

Whatever Kierstead was dealing with at the amusement park, Bird sensed it was about to throw their investigation into uncharted territory. He steeled himself for her answer, knowing that every new piece of information could potentially reshape their understanding of this increasingly complex case.

43 - 44

Kierstead's voice crackled through the phone, tinged with a mix of frustration and urgency. "Let's just say I've got bigger problems than his story," she replied cryptically. Bird could almost see her glancing over her shoulder, eyes darting to unseen threats. "I'll fill you in when you get here."

The weight of her words settled in Bird's gut like a stone. His mind raced through possibilities, each more unsettling than the last. What could be worse than a potentially delusional witness and a case built on shifting sand?

Bird's frown deepened, etching new lines into his weathered face. His free hand tightened around the pen he'd been fidgeting with, knuckles whitening. "On my way," he said, curiosity and concern warring in his tone.

As he hung up, Bird's gaze lingered on the grainy image of Drake frozen on his monitor. The man's haunted eyes seemed to follow him, silently pleading or perhaps accusing. Bird shook off the unsettling feeling, reminding himself that evidence, not intuition, would solve this case.

Rising from his chair, Bird's joints protested with a series of soft pops. He paused, suddenly aware of the late hour and the weight of fatigue settling over him. But Kierstead's cryptic words echoed in his mind, spurring him into action. Whatever was waiting for him at Dreamland Fairgrounds, it wouldn't wait until morning.

45 - 46

Bird snatched his notepad from the desk, fingers brushing against the rough edges of torn pages. His coat, a well-worn leather jacket that had seen better days, hung heavy on his shoulders as he shrugged it on. The precinct's fluorescent lights cast long shadows as he made his way toward the exit, each step echoing in the near-empty bullpen.

His mind churned with questions, a relentless tide of doubt and speculation. The security footage replayed in his mind's eye, Drake's solitary figure moving through the abandoned park like a ghost. Bird muttered to himself, "What aren't you telling us, Drake?"

As he pushed through the precinct doors, the cool night air hit him like a slap, jolting him from his reverie. Bird paused on the steps, his breath misting in the air before him. The city stretched out below, a tapestry of twinkling lights and shadowed alleys. Somewhere out there, answers awaited.

"Liar or victim?" Bird mused aloud, his voice barely above a whisper. The wind caught his words, carrying them away into the darkness. He frowned, a new, more troubling thought taking root. "Or something far worse?"

With a shake of his head, Bird descended the steps, each footfall heavy with the weight of uncertainty. The case, once seemingly straightforward, had twisted into something unrecognizable. As he reached for his car door, a chill ran down his spine that had nothing to do with the night air.

Whatever awaited him at Dreamland Fairgrounds, Bird couldn't shake the feeling that it would change everything.

A Visitor in the Night

1 The dishwasher's gentle hum filled the kitchen, a rhythmic heartbeat in the quiet house. Emily Vega ran a damp cloth over the granite countertop, wiping away the last traces of dinner. Upstairs, muffled giggles floated down—Maya and Liam lost in their own world of imagination.

Emily paused, a faint smile tugging at her lips as she listened to her children's laughter. How different their lives were from the one she'd known growing up. Safe. Secure. Protected from the harsh realities that had shaped her own childhood.

The under-cabinet lights cast a warm glow, transforming the kitchen into a cozy sanctuary. Emily's gaze drifted to the family photos adorning the fridge—snapshots of happier times, of beach trips and birthday parties. Her eyes lingered on Richard's face, his smile easy and carefree. When was the last time she'd seen him look that relaxed?

She sighed, her brow furrowing. Something had changed in Richard over the past few months. A shadow had fallen over him, darkening his eyes and tightening the set of his jaw. He'd grown distant, secretive. Emily had tried to bridge the growing chasm between them, but Richard had retreated further into himself with each attempt.

The back door creaked open, shattering the tranquil atmosphere. Emily's hand froze mid-wipe, her heart lurching painfully in her chest. She turned, expecting—hoping—to see Richard's familiar silhouette in the doorway.

But the kitchen remained empty, the open door revealing only the inky blackness of the night beyond. A chill wind swept in, carrying with it the scent of rain and something else—something acrid and unsettling. Emily's fingers tightened around the cloth, her knuckles whitening as she stared at the yawning darkness.

"Richard?" she whispered, her voice barely audible over the sudden pounding of her heart.

Silence answered her, broken only by the faint laughter of her children upstairs oblivious to the encroaching danger. Emily's mind raced, torn between the instinct to flee upstairs and gather her children close, and the desperate hope that it was Richard returning home early.

She took a hesitant step forward, her bare feet silent on the cool tile. "Richard, is that you?"

3 - 4

Emily's voice wavered, uncertainty and fear lacing her words. The dish towel twisted in her grip, a flimsy shield against the unknown. She strained her ears, listening for any sign of movement, any hint of Richard's familiar footsteps.

The silence stretched, oppressive and thick. Emily's chest tightened, her breaths coming in short, shallow gasps. Her eyes darted to the knife block on the counter, calculating the distance. Would she be fast enough if it wasn't Richard?

"Honey?" she called again, forcing a lightness into her tone that she didn't feel. "If that's you, this isn't funny."

Her mind raced, recalling Richard's increasingly erratic behavior. The hushed phone calls, the late nights at the office, the haunted look in his eyes when he thought she wasn't watching. What had he gotten himself into?

Emily took another tentative step forward, her heart hammering against her ribs. The open door seemed to mock her, a gaping maw of uncertainty. She swallowed hard, her throat dry.

"Richard, please," she whispered, her voice barely audible even to herself. "If it's you, just say something."

The silence that followed was deafening, broken only by the distant rumble of thunder. Emily's fingers tightened on the dish towel; her knuckles white with tension. Whatever—or whoever—had opened that door, she knew with a sinking certainty that her world was about to change irrevocably.

5 - 6

As the door creaked wider, Emily's breath caught in her throat. A figure emerged from the shadows, and her world tilted on its axis. The man who stepped into her kitchen was not Richard, but a nightmare made flesh.

"Oh God," Emily whispered, her voice barely audible over the thundering of her heart.

The intruder's tattered white robe billowed slightly in the draft from the open door. Emily's eyes were drawn to the dragon emblem on his chest, its faint glow seeming to pulse with an otherworldly energy. She blinked rapidly, wondering if her fear-addled mind was playing tricks on her.

The man's face, what little she could see beneath the hood, made her stomach lurch. Twisted, scarred flesh spoke of unimaginable agony, and Emily found herself backing away involuntarily.

Who is he? What does he want? The questions ricocheted through her mind as she gripped the edge of the counter for support. Her thoughts raced to Maya and Liam upstairs, blissfully unaware of the danger that had invaded their home.

"Stay calm," Emily told herself, fighting to keep her voice steady. "Think of the children."

She forced herself to take a deep breath, drawing on reserves of strength she didn't know she possessed. The dish towel fell from her trembling fingers as she squared her shoulders, determined to face whatever threat this grotesque figure posed.

"Who are you?" Emily demanded, surprised by the steel in her own voice. "What do you want?"

The silence that followed her questions was oppressive, filled with unspoken menace. Emily's gaze darted to the knife block again, gauging the distance. Could she reach it before he closed the gap between them?

7 - 8

The intruder's low, menacing voice shattered the tense silence. "Good evening, Mrs. Vega," he said, each word dripping with a chilling calm that made Emily's skin crawl.

Emily's heart hammered against her ribs as she took another step back, her fingers gripping the counter's edge so tightly her knuckles turned white. The cool granite beneath her palms was an anchor to reality, even as her world tilted on its axis.

"Who are you?" she repeated, her voice barely above a whisper. "What do you want?"

As she spoke, Emily's mind raced through possibilities. Was this a robbery gone wrong? A case of mistaken identity? Or something far more sinister? The man's intimate use of her name suggested the latter, and a cold dread settled in the pit of her stomach.

She glanced toward the stairs, straining to hear any sound from Maya and Liam. The silence from above was both a relief and a torment. Safe for now, but for how long?

The scarred intruder took a deliberate step forward, his movements predatory and calculated. Emily tensed, ready to bolt or fight if necessary. But where could she go? How could she protect her children from this nightmare made flesh?

9 - 10

Gabriel tilted his head slightly, his charred lips curling into a cruel smile. The expression transformed his already grotesque features into something truly nightmarish, and Emily felt her breath catch in her throat.

"Your husband," he said simply, his voice a low purr that sent shivers down Emily's spine.

Emily blinked, momentarily thrown off balance by the unexpected response. "Richard?" she whispered, her mind reeling. What could this terrifying man possibly want with her husband?

Gabriel's eyes glinted with malicious amusement, clearly savoring her confusion and fear. He took another step closer, his tattered white robe brushing against the kitchen island. The dragon emblem on his chest seemed to pulse with an eerie light, drawing Emily's gaze despite her terror.

"What do you want with Richard?" Emily managed to ask, her voice trembling. She pressed herself further against the counter, desperately wishing she could melt into the cabinets behind her.

Gabriel didn't answer immediately. Instead, he reached into his robe, the movement slow and deliberate. Emily tensed; her heart pounding so hard she could hear the blood rushing in her ears. Was he reaching for a weapon?

To her surprise, he pulled out a sleek black phone. The ordinary object looked jarringly out of place in his scarred hand. Gabriel's lips twisted into what might have been a smile on a less disfigured face.

"You're going to help me deliver a message," he said softly, his tone deceptively gentle. But there was no mistaking the underlying threat in his words.

11 - 12

Emily's breath hitched as she backed further away, her eyes darting toward the doorway to the living room. The warm glow of the kitchen lights suddenly felt oppressive, casting long shadows that seemed to reach for her like grasping fingers. Her heart raced, thoughts of her children's safety warring with her instinct for self-preservation.

Maybe if I'm quick enough, I can make it to the stairs, she thought, muscles tensing in anticipation. The living room was only a few steps away, and beyond that, freedom. Or at least a chance to warn Maya and Liam.

But before she could act on her desperate plan, Gabriel's voice sliced through the air, freezing her in place.

"I wouldn't," he said, his tone calm but laced with menace. The burns on his face twisted grotesquely as he spoke, lending an otherworldly quality to his words. "If you care about those two little ones upstairs, you'll stay right where you are."

Emily's blood turned to ice. How did he know about her children? The thought of this monster anywhere near Maya and Liam made her want to scream, but terror kept her silent.

"Please," she whispered, hating how weak her voice sounded. "They're just children. They have nothing to do with... whatever this is."

Gabriel's lips curled into a cruel smile. "Oh, but they have everything to do with it, Emily. Your family is the key to all of this."

Emily's mind raced, trying to make sense of his words. What could he possibly mean? And how was she going to protect her babies from this nightmare that had invaded their home?

13 - 14

Emily's throat constricted, her voice barely a whisper as she forced out the words. "What do you want with Richard?" The question hung in the air, heavy with dread and the acrid scent of fear that now permeated the once-cozy kitchen.

Gabriel stepped closer, his movements deliberate and predatory. The floorboards creaked beneath his weight, each sound amplifying Emily's racing heartbeat. His scarred face loomed in the dim light, a grotesque mask of malevolence that sent shivers down her spine.

"Richard and I have unfinished business," he drawled, his voice a low, menacing purr. "And since he's not here, I thought I'd have a little chat with you instead."

Emily's mind whirled, desperately trying to piece together the fragments of information. What business could Richard possibly have with this terrifying figure? Her husband, always so reserved about his work, now seemed a stranger to her. Had he been hiding something all along?

She swallowed hard, her mouth dry as sandpaper. "I don't understand," she managed, her eyes darting between Gabriel's disfigured face and the staircase behind him. Maya and Liam were up there, blissfully unaware of the danger that had invaded their home. The urge to rush to them, to shield them from this nightmare, was almost overwhelming.

Gabriel's lips twisted into a cruel facsimile of a smile. "Understanding isn't necessary, my dear," he said, his words dripping with false sweetness. "Your role is much simpler than that."

15 - 16

Emily's fingers dug into the counter's edge, her knuckles blanching white with the intensity of her grip. The cool surface anchored her to reality as her world tilted on its axis. She inhaled sharply, the scent of dish soap and lingering dinner aromas a stark contrast to the acrid fear that now coated her tongue.

"I don't know what you're talking about," she whispered, her voice trembling like a leaf in a storm. "Please, just leave us alone." The words felt hollow even as they left her lips, a futile plea against the darkness that had invaded her home.

Gabriel's response was a soft chuckle, the sound slithering through the air like a venomous serpent. Emily's skin prickled, goosebumps rising along her arms as that eerie laughter wormed its way into her very bones. Her mind raced, frantically searching for an escape route, a way to protect her children from this nightmare made flesh.

"Oh, Emily," Gabriel purred, his voice a sickening blend of amusement and menace. "You don't need to understand." He took another step forward, his scarred visage now fully illuminated by the under-cabinet lights. "You just need to follow instructions."

Emily's heart hammered against her ribcage, a frantic drumbeat of terror. What instructions? What could this monster possibly want from her? And where was Richard? The questions swirled in her mind, a dizzying maelstrom of fear and confusion. She glanced again at the staircase, her maternal instincts screaming at her to run, to grab her children and flee. But Gabriel's presence, looming and malevolent, held her rooted to the spot.

17 - 18

Gabriel's hand disappeared into the folds of his tattered white robe, the movement slow and deliberate. Emily's breath caught in her throat, her muscles tensing as she braced for the worst. But instead of a weapon, he withdrew again a sleek black phone, its screen glowing faintly in the dim kitchen light.

With a casual flick of his wrist, Gabriel slid the device across the granite countertop. It came to rest just inches from Emily's trembling fingers, a silent harbinger of dread.

"Call him," Gabriel commanded, his voice low and insistent. The dragon emblem on his chest seemed to pulse with an otherworldly light, matching the intensity of his gaze. "Tell him he needs to come home. Now."

Emily's mind reeled. Richard. He wanted Richard. But why? What could her husband have possibly done to attract the attention of this nightmarish figure? Her fingers hovered over the phone, indecision paralyzing her.

"What if I don't?" The words tumbled from her lips before she could stop them, a desperate act of defiance born from fear and maternal instinct. As soon as they left her mouth, she regretted them, terror clawing at her insides.

Gabriel's eyes narrowed, the burn scars on his face twisting into a grotesque mask of cruel amusement. "Are you sure you want to find out, Emily?" he asked, his tone deceptively light. "Consider carefully. Your choices now will echo through more realities than you can imagine."

Emily's hand closed around the phone; her decision made. Whatever game this was, she couldn't risk her children's safety. With shaking fingers, she began to dial.

19 - 20

Gabriel leaned in closer, his disfigured face now fully visible beneath the hood. The sight made Emily's stomach churn. His skin was a patchwork of angry red scars and mottled flesh, a testament to some horrific ordeal. The acrid scent of burnt fabric and something else—something chemical and alien—wafted from his robes.

"My appearance unsettles you," Gabriel observed, his lips curling into a mirthless smile. "Good. Let it serve as a reminder of the consequences of defiance."

Emily's mind raced, searching for an escape, a way to protect her children upstairs. Their laughter, once a source of joy, now felt like a ticking clock counting down to potential tragedy. She opened her mouth to speak, but Gabriel cut her off.

"If you don't," he said softly, his words barely above a whisper, "I'll go upstairs and make sure your children understand the price of your defiance."

The threat hung in the air, heavy and suffocating. Emily's heart hammered against her ribcage; each beat a desperate plea for her babies' safety. She thought of Maya's gap-toothed smile, of Liam's infectious giggles. The idea of this monster touching them made her blood run cold.

"You wouldn't," Emily managed to choke out, her voice hoarse with fear. "They're innocent children."

Gabriel's eyes glinted with a cold, otherworldly light. "Innocence," he mused, "is such a fragile thing. So easily shattered across the multiverse. Don't test me, Emily. Make the call."

Her fingers tightened around the phone, the decision weighing on her like a physical force. With a shuddering breath, she began to dial, praying that whatever Richard had done, he could fix it before their world came crashing down around them.

21 - 22

Emily's breath caught in her throat, a strangled sob threatening to escape. Tears welled in her eyes, blurring her vision as she clutched the phone tightly, her knuckles turning white. The cold plastic against her palm felt like a lifeline and a death sentence all at once.

She nodded shakily, unable to form words. Her mind raced with possibilities, each more terrifying than the last. What had Richard done to bring this nightmare into their home? How could she protect her children from a threat she didn't understand?

"Good girl," Gabriel murmured, stepping back. His voice carried a twisted warmth, as if praising a pet for performing a trick. The sound made Emily's skin crawl.

As Gabriel retreated, Emily's fingers hovered over the keypad. She hesitated, her heart pounding so loudly she was sure Gabriel could hear it. "What do I tell him?" she whispered, her voice barely audible.

Gabriel's scarred lips curled into a cruel smile. "The truth, of course. That an old friend is waiting for him. That the fate of realities hangs in the balance." He paused, his eyes glinting with malice. "And that his family's safety depends on his prompt return."

Emily swallowed hard; her throat dry as sandpaper. As she began to dial, she silently prayed that wherever Richard was, whatever he was doing, he would find a way to save them all from this nightmare that had invaded their home.

A Voice from the Past

1^{- 2} The soft hum of fluorescent lights cast a pallid glow over the Lexington Hotel's hallway, painting Richard Vega's face in harsh shadows as he stood sentry outside the Millers' suite. He glanced at his watch for the umpteenth time, the weight of each passing second pressing down on his shoulders like an invisible burden.

Leaning against the wall, Vega crossed his arms, his fingers digging into the fabric of his jacket. The muffled sound of Harrison's animated voice filtered through the door, followed by Linda's melodic laughter. The juxtaposition struck him like a discordant note in an otherwise harmonious symphony.

How can they sound so... normal? Vega wondered, a bitter taste rising in his throat. The thought of normalcy seemed like a cruel joke now, a relic of a past life that no longer existed.

"Hey, Mom, remember that time when Dad tried to make pancakes and set off the smoke alarm?" Harrison's voice rang out, clearer now.

Linda's laughter swelled again. "Oh, goodness, yes! The look on his face when he realized he'd forgotten to grease the pan..."

Vega's jaw clenched, his chest tightening with a mixture of envy and guilt. They don't know, he reminded himself. They can't know how precarious their situation truly is.

He found himself straining to hear more, desperate for a glimpse into the warmth and love that seemed to radiate from within the suite. It was a stark contrast to the cold, calculating world he now inhabited, where every decision carried the weight of life and death.

"I wish Dad was here," Harrison's voice softened, a hint of melancholy creeping in. "He'd know what to do next."

There was a pause, and Vega could almost picture Linda's comforting smile as she responded. "He'll find us, sweetheart. Your father always finds a way."

If only they knew, Vega thought, his heart heavy with the secrets he carried. There is no such thing as normal anymore. Not for them, not for Drake, and certainly not for me.

He pushed himself off the wall, pacing the length of the hallway as his mind raced. The laughter from within the suite now felt like a cruel reminder of everything he stood to lose, of the impossible choice that loomed before him.

Protect the Millers and condemn his own family? Or betray the very people he had sworn to keep safe?

Vega's steps faltered as the weight of his predicament threatened to crush him. He leaned against the wall once more, closing his eyes and taking a deep breath. The cheerful voices from within the suite continued, oblivious to the storm raging just outside their door.

For now, at least, they were safe. But Vega knew all too well that in this fractured reality, safety was nothing more than an illusion – as fragile and fleeting as the laughter that echoed through the walls.

3 - 4

The sudden vibration against his thigh shattered the tense quiet. Vega's hand moved swiftly, retrieving the phone from his pocket. His brow furrowed as Emily's name illuminated the screen, a knot of dread tightening in his stomach.

"What now?" he muttered, his voice barely above a whisper. His thumb hovered over the answer button for a fraction of a second before he pressed it, bringing the device to his ear. "Emily? Everything alright?"

As he waited for a response, Vega's free hand clenched into a fist, his nails digging into his palm. Why was she calling now? Had something happened to the kids? Or worse, had Gabriel already—

No. He couldn't let his mind wander down that treacherous path. Not yet. Not until he knew for certain.

The silence on the other end of the line stretched on, each passing second feeling like an eternity. Vega's heart raced, the sound of his own pulse thundering in his ears. He glanced back at the door to the Millers' suite, acutely aware of how quickly his carefully constructed facade of normalcy could come crashing down.

"Emily?" he repeated, struggling to keep the rising panic out of his voice. "Are you there? Talk to me, please."

In that moment, as he stood in the hushed hallway awaiting his wife's response, Richard Vega felt the full weight of his choices bearing down upon him. The laughter from within the suite now seemed a distant echo, drowned out by the deafening silence of his phone call and the crushing pressure of the decision that loomed before him.

5 - 6

The silence shattered, but not with Emily's familiar timbre. Instead, a voice that haunted Vega's darkest nightmares slithered through the receiver.

"Richard," the disfigured man said, his tone low and mocking.

A cold shiver raced down Vega's spine, his muscles tensing as if preparing for a physical blow. He swallowed hard, his throat suddenly dry as sandpaper.

"You," Vega whispered, barely audible even to himself. His mind raced, memories of their last encounter flooding back - the desperation, the deal, the weight of his betrayal.

The man chuckled, a sound devoid of warmth. "Surprised to hear from me so soon? I do hope I'm not interrupting anything... important."

Vega's gaze darted to the Millers' door, his heart pounding. He took a step away, lowering his voice. "How did you get Emily's phone?"

"Oh, Richard," the man sighed, feigning disappointment. "Always asking the wrong questions. It's not about how I got it, but rather, what I'm willing to do with it... and with her."

Vega's free hand clenched into a fist, his nails biting into his palm. He fought to keep his voice steady, aware of how thin the hotel walls could be. "What do you want?"

As he awaited the man's response, Vega's mind whirled with possibilities, each more horrifying than the last. How had it come to this? He'd tried so hard to protect his family, to break free from this cycle of betrayal, but here he was again, caught in the disfigured man's web.

The sound of laughter drifted from the Millers' suite, a cruel reminder of the normalcy he was struggling to maintain. Vega closed his eyes, steeling himself for whatever demand was about to be made, knowing that no matter what, someone would suffer for his choices.

7 - 8

Vega's blood ran cold, his throat constricting as if an invisible hand had seized it. The hallway seemed to narrow, the faint hum of the overhead lights now a deafening roar in his ears. He swallowed hard, forcing the words out through gritted teeth.

"Who is this? Where's my wife?"

His voice trembled, betraying the facade of calm he desperately tried to maintain. In his mind's eye, he saw Emily's face, her warm smile now twisted with fear. The weight of his past decisions pressed down on him, threatening to crush what little resolve he had left.

A soft, menacing chuckle echoed through the receiver, sending icy tendrils of dread crawling up Vega's spine. The sound was achingly familiar, a haunting reminder of promises made in desperation and regretted ever since.

"She's safe. For now." The voice oozed false reassurance, each word dripping with veiled threat. "But you and I need to have a conversation."

Vega's free hand found the wall, steadying himself as the world seemed to tilt beneath his feet. He glanced at the Millers' door, acutely aware of how close they were, how fragile this moment of peace was. His mind raced, searching for a way out, a solution that wouldn't end in tragedy. But deep down, he knew – there was no escaping the consequences of his choices.

9 - 10

Vega's jaw tightened, the muscle in his cheek twitching as he fought to control the surge of anger and fear that threatened to overwhelm him. His free hand balled into a fist, knuckles turning white as he pressed it against the wall. The cool surface anchored him, a stark contrast to the fire burning in his veins.

"If you hurt her or my kids—" he began, his voice low and dangerous, each word laced with the promise of retribution.

But the disfigured man cut him off, his tone dripping with false reassurance that only served to heighten Vega's anxiety. "Calm yourself," he purred, the words slithering through the phone like a venomous snake. "I made you a promise once before, Richard. Don't make me keep it."

Vega's breath caught in his throat, memories of that fateful day rushing back with brutal clarity. He closed his eyes, willing the images away, but they persisted – the desperate deal, the weight of betrayal, the cost of his family's safety.

"You bastard," he whispered, more to himself than the man on the phone. His gaze darted to the Millers' door again, guilt gnawing at his insides. How could he protect them when he couldn't even safeguard his own family?

The disfigured man's words echoed in his mind, a cruel reminder of the precarious balance he'd been maintaining. Vega's thoughts raced, searching for a way out, a loophole in this twisted game. But deep down, he knew – he was trapped, cornered by his own past actions.

"What do you want?" he finally managed, his voice barely above a whisper, heavy with the weight of impending doom.

11 - 12

Vega froze, his fingers tightening around the phone as if it were a lifeline. The hallway suddenly felt too narrow, the air too thick. His free hand brushed against the textured wallpaper, seeking something solid to ground him in this nightmare.

"You... I know you," he said, his voice barely audible even to himself. The words hung in the air, heavy with the weight of recognition and dread.

Memories he'd tried so desperately to bury clawed their way to the surface. The dimly lit parking garage, the acrid smell of fear, the sound of his own heartbeat drowning out reason. A deal struck in desperation, a moment of weakness that had haunted his every step since.

Vega's eyes darted to the Millers' door again, guilt twisting like a knife in his gut. How many times had he stood guard, playing protector while carrying the seeds of their destruction?

"Ah," the man on the phone purred, his voice a silken caress that made Vega's skin crawl. "There it is. Recognition. Good. That will make this much easier."

Vega's jaw clenched, fighting back the urge to hurl the phone against the wall. Instead, he forced out a question, dreading the answer. "Easier for what?"

His mind raced, searching for an escape, a way to shield both his family and the Millers from the approaching storm. But deep down, he knew the truth – he was caught in a web of his own making, with no clean way out.

13 - 14

The hallway seemed to constrict around Vega, the faint hum of the overhead lights now a deafening roar in his ears. His free hand pressed against the wall, seeking stability as the world tilted beneath his feet.

"What do you want?" Vega demanded, his voice sharp now, a desperate attempt to mask the tremor of fear coursing through him.

The disfigured man's chuckle slithered through the phone, cold and hollow. "Oh, Richard. Always so direct. It's not about what I want. It's about what you owe."

Vega's stomach churned, bile rising in his throat. He swallowed hard, fighting to maintain composure. Inside the suite, he heard Harrison's muffled voice, followed by Linda's soft reply. The normalcy of their interaction felt like a mockery of the nightmare unfolding around him.

"I don't owe you anything," Vega hissed, even as his mind raced through the implications. His eyes darted up and down the empty hallway, half-expecting to see shadowy figures materializing from the corners.

"Tsk, tsk," the man chided. "Denial doesn't suit you, Richard. Remember our little arrangement? The clock is ticking, and it's time to pay up."

Vega's breath caught in his chest, a vice grip of panic squeezing his lungs. He thought of Emily, of his children, their faces flashing before his eyes. Then Linda and Harrison, trusting and unaware behind that closed door. The weight of their lives pressed down on him, an impossible burden to bear.

"Whatever it is," Vega said, his voice low and strained, "there has to be another way."

15 - 16

The disfigured man's voice dripped with false sympathy as he replied, "Simple. Dispose of the Miller family. Make it look clean, like an accident. Do that, and your precious Emily and those darling children of yours will remain safe and sound."

Vega's entire body went rigid, his free hand clenching into a tight fist. The fluorescent lights overhead seemed to flicker, casting dancing shadows across the faded wallpaper. Inside his chest, his heart hammered a frantic rhythm against his ribs.

"You're insane," Vega hissed, his voice barely above a whisper. The words tasted like ash in his mouth. "I'm not going to kill anyone, especially not Drake's family."

As he spoke, memories of Drake flooded his mind – their shared past, the trust that had once existed between them. Trust that Vega had already betrayed once. The guilt gnawed at him, a constant, merciless presence.

From inside the suite, Linda's laughter drifted through the door, light and carefree. The sound cut through Vega like a knife, a stark reminder of the innocence at stake. He closed his eyes, fighting against the wave of nausea that threatened to overwhelm him.

"Think carefully, Richard," the disfigured man purred, his tone laced with menace. "Your family or theirs. It's a simple choice, really."

Vega's mind raced, searching desperately for a way out, a solution that wouldn't end in bloodshed. But with each passing second, the walls of his predicament seemed to close in tighter, leaving him trapped and suffocating under the weight of an impossible decision.

17 - 18

A chuckle, cold and hollow as a winter wind, slithered through the phone's receiver. Vega felt it crawl up his spine, each vertebra freezing in its wake. The disfigured man's voice dripped with malice, coating every word like poison.

"Richard, you misunderstand. This isn't a negotiation. If you refuse, I'll dispose of your family instead. Slowly. Painfully. And I'll make sure you get to hear every scream."

The threat hung in the air, heavy and oppressive. Vega's breath quickened, his lungs constricting as if he were drowning. His grip on the phone tightened until his knuckles turned white, the plastic creaking under the pressure. The hallway seemed to spin around him, the gaudy hotel carpet swirling in dizzying patterns.

"Why?" Vega choked out, his voice raw with desperation. "Why the Millers? What do they have to do with you?"

As he spoke, his mind raced through a labyrinth of possibilities. Had Drake uncovered something during their time at the firm? Was Linda somehow involved? Or was this simply another cruel twist in the nightmare that had become his life?

Inside the suite, he heard Harrison's muffled voice, followed by Linda's soft response. The normalcy of their interaction was a stark contrast to the storm raging within Vega. He closed his eyes, trying to steady himself, to find some anchor in the chaos.

"Oh, Richard," the man on the phone purred, his tone almost pitying. "Always asking the wrong questions."

19 - 20

The man's voice dripped with false amusement, each word a dagger aimed at Vega's core. "It's not about what they have to do with me. It's about what you have to do for me."

Vega's jaw clenched, a muscle twitching beneath his skin. The implications of those words hit him like a physical blow, forcing the air from his lungs. He leaned against the wall, its coolness seeping through his shirt, a stark reminder of his own mortality.

"I'll protect them," Vega growled, his voice low and dangerous. The words tasted like ash in his mouth, bitter with the knowledge of his own powerlessness. His free hand curled into a fist, nails digging into his palm. "I'll tell them—"

As he spoke, his mind raced, searching for a way out of this impossible situation. How could he warn the Millers without endangering his own family? What could he possibly say that wouldn't lead to more bloodshed?

The laughter from inside the suite cut through his thoughts like a knife, a cruel reminder of the innocence he was tasked with destroying. Vega closed his eyes, the weight of his choices pressing down on him like a physical force.

21 - 22

"You'll tell them what?" the man snapped, his voice suddenly sharp and menacing. The abrupt shift in tone sent a chill down Vega's spine, his skin prickling with cold sweat. "That you're a coward who made a deal you couldn't keep? That you sold out everyone who trusted you to save your own miserable skin?"

Vega's breath caught in his throat, the truth of those words hitting him like a physical blow. His mind raced, memories of that fateful decision flooding back – the desperation, the fear, the moment of weakness that had led him to this point.

"No, Richard," the man continued, his voice a low, dangerous purr. "You won't tell them anything."

The hallway seemed to close in around Vega, the faint hum of the overhead lights now a deafening roar in his ears. He could feel the weight of his choices pressing down on him, each breath a struggle against the crushing guilt and fear.

Inside the suite, he heard Harrison's muffled voice, followed by Linda's soft reply. The normalcy of their interaction was a stark contrast to the turmoil raging within him.

Vega's mind raced, searching for a solution, a way out of this impossible situation. But every path seemed to lead to tragedy – either for the Millers or for his own family. He thought of Emily, of his children, their faces swimming before his eyes. Then he saw Linda and Harrison, trusting and unaware of the danger that lurked just outside their door.

"I can't," he whispered, his voice barely audible even to himself. "I can't do this."

But even as the words left his lips, Vega knew he had no choice. The decision loomed before him, inescapable and devastating. Whatever he chose, lives would be shattered, trust broken beyond repair. And he would be the one to wield the hammer.

23 - 24

Vega's chest heaved as he struggled to keep his composure, each breath a battle against the panic threatening to overwhelm him. The sound of Linda's laughter drifted through the door, a cruel reminder of the impossible choice before him. It was a sound so carefree, so unburdened – everything he wasn't in this moment.

His fingers trembled as they gripped the phone, knuckles white with tension. The disfigured man's words echoed in his mind, a sinister mantra he couldn't shake. Vega's eyes darted to the suite door, imagining the unsuspecting faces of Linda and Harrison on the other side.

"You can't make me do this," Vega said, his voice cracking under the weight of his desperation. The words felt hollow even as he spoke them, a futile protest against the inevitable. "There has to be another way."

He ran a hand through his disheveled hair, mind racing for alternatives, for some miraculous solution that would spare everyone. But each possibility crumbled as quickly as it formed, leaving only the cold reality of his predicament.

Inside the suite, Harrison's voice rose in excitement about something on the television. The normalcy of it all was a knife twisting in Vega's gut. How could he even contemplate destroying that? And yet, how could he not, when his own family's lives hung in the balance?

Vega leaned heavily against the wall, closing his eyes as he fought to steady his breathing. He had navigated impossible situations before, had made deals and compromises that haunted his conscience. But this – this felt like a point of no return.

"Think, Richard," he muttered to himself, desperation clawing at his insides. "There's got to be a way out of this. There's always a way."

But as the laughter from inside the suite faded into concerned murmurs, Vega felt the suffocating weight of reality settling over him. Time was running out, and with it, his chances of finding that elusive third option.

25 - 26

The disfigured man's voice slithered through the phone, a serpent coiling around Vega's heart. "There's always another way," he said, his tone dripping with false sympathy that made Vega's skin crawl. "But none that spare your family. So, what will it be, Richard? Their lives... or yours?"

Vega's throat constricted, his breath catching as the full weight of the choice bore down on him. He leaned heavily against the wall, its cool surface the only thing keeping him upright as his world tilted on its axis. Inside the suite, Linda's soft laughter floated through the air, a cruel reminder of the lives hanging in the balance.

"I can't," Vega whispered, more to himself than to the voice on the phone. His mind raced, desperately seeking an escape route that didn't exist. "Linda and Harrison... they've been through so much already. And Emily, the kids..."

He closed his eyes, seeing his wife's smile, hearing his children's laughter. Then, unbidden, came the image of Linda's tear-stained face when he had betrayed her trust before. The guilt of that moment mixed with the terror of his current predicament, creating a toxic brew in his chest.

"Time's running out, Richard," the disfigured man purred. "Make your choice."

Vega's fist clenched at his side, nails digging into his palm. "There has to be another way," he said, voice hoarse with desperation. "Something I can offer you instead."

But even as the words left his mouth, he knew it was futile. The man on the phone held all the cards, and Vega was left with an impossible decision that would haunt him regardless of his choice.

27 - 28

"Tick-tock, Richard," the man added, his voice dripping with malicious glee. "Don't keep me waiting."

The words hung in the air, each syllable a blade against Vega's throat. His pulse thundered in his ears, drowning out the faint sounds of the Millers' domesticity behind the suite door. He opened his mouth to respond, to plead, to bargain—but before he could utter a sound, the line went dead.

The sudden silence was deafening. Vega's hand trembled as he lowered the phone, its smooth surface now slick with sweat. He stared at the dark screen, half-expecting—hoping—it would light up again, that this had all been some cruel joke. But the seconds ticked by, each one carrying the weight of lives in the balance.

"God," he whispered, the word escaping his lips like a prayer and a curse rolled into one. His mind raced, replaying the conversation, searching for a loophole, an escape. But there was none. The disfigured man's ultimatum echoed in his thoughts, a relentless, tormenting refrain.

Vega's gaze drifted to the suite door. Behind it, Linda and Harrison lived in blissful ignorance of the sword now dangling over their heads. He could warn them, but then what? Run? Hide? The disfigured man would find them—find his family. There was no escape, no clever solution that would save everyone.

His legs threatened to give way, and he slumped against the wall, feeling the rough texture of the wallpaper against his back. It grounded him, a harsh reminder that this wasn't some nightmare he could wake from. This was real, and he had to make a choice.

29 - 30

Vega's fingers tightened around the phone, his knuckles whitening. He closed his eyes, trying to steady his ragged breathing. The weight of the decision pressed down on him, threatening to crush his very soul.

"I can't," he muttered, barely audible. "I can't do this."

But even as the words left his lips, a part of him knew it was a lie. He could do it. He had done worse before, hadn't he? The memory of his past betrayals rose unbidden, taunting him with the knowledge that he was capable of far more than he wanted to admit.

Vega's eyes snapped open, darting left and right down the empty hallway. Paranoia gripped him. Was he being watched? Had the disfigured man planted cameras, waiting to see his next move?

"Get it together, Richard," he hissed to himself, straightening up. He ran a hand through his disheveled hair, forcing his features into a mask of calm. The Millers couldn't suspect anything was amiss. Not yet. Not until he figured out a way to save everyone—or at least, save those he could.

His hand hovered over the suite's doorknob. One choice could save his family but doom the Millers. The other... Vega's throat tightened. The other didn't bear thinking about.

31 - 32

Inside the suite, Linda's melodious laughter faded, replaced by Harrison's eager voice. "Mom, come quick! You've got to see this!"

Vega's hand froze on the doorknob, his breath catching in his throat. Through the wood, he could hear the rustling of Linda's movements, the soft pad of her feet as she crossed the room to join her son.

"What is it, sweetheart?" Linda's voice carried a hint of concern beneath its warmth.

Vega leaned his forehead against the door, closing his eyes. The disfigured man's threat echoed in his mind, a sinister whisper that seemed to seep into the very walls around him.

"You'll dispose of them, or I'll dispose of your family. Slowly. Painfully."

His stomach churned, bile rising in his throat. The hallway seemed to narrow, the air growing thick and oppressive. Vega's chest heaved as he struggled to draw breath, the weight of his impossible choice crushing down upon him.

"Oh my god," Linda's gasp filtered through the door. "Harrison, turn it up."

Vega's eyes snapped open. What were they seeing? Had news of Emily's abduction already hit the airwaves? His hand trembled as he reached for the doorknob again, torn between the need to know and the fear of facing the Millers.

"I can't do this," he whispered, his voice hoarse. "But I have to. For Emily. For the kids."

The sound of the TV grew louder, an announcer's voice carrying through the door. Vega strained to hear, his heart pounding in his ears.

"...multiple reports of strange phenomena across the city..."

Vega's brow furrowed. This wasn't about Emily. But then, what...?

He took a deep breath, steeling himself. Whatever was happening, he had to maintain his facade. He had to protect the Millers, even as he plotted... what? Their demise? Their salvation?

With a trembling hand, Vega turned the doorknob and stepped into the suite, the weight of lives hanging in the balance with every step he took.

33 - 34

Vega's fingers gripped the cool metal of the doorknob, his knuckles white with tension. He forced his face into a mask of calm, though his insides roiled with turmoil. The door swung open with a soft creak, revealing the warm glow of the suite's interior.

Linda stood by the television, her slender figure silhouetted against the flickering screen. Her blonde hair caught the light, creating a halo effect that seemed cruelly ironic given the circumstances. She turned at the sound of Vega's entrance, her blue eyes wide with concern.

"Richard," she said, her voice a mixture of relief and worry. "Did you hear what's happening?"

Vega swallowed hard, his throat dry. "I... no. What's going on?"

He moved further into the room, his steps measured and careful. Every movement felt like a betrayal, a step closer to a decision he couldn't bear to make.

Linda gestured to the TV, where images of chaos flashed across the screen. "They're saying there are... anomalies appearing all over the city. Strange distortions, objects disappearing and reappearing. It's like..." She paused, her voice dropping to a whisper. "It's like what Drake described. About the other realities."

Vega's heart skipped a beat. This was unexpected, a wild card in an already impossible game. His mind raced, calculating how this new development might affect the disfigured man's plans... and his own desperate attempts to find a way out.

"That's... concerning," he managed, his voice carefully neutral. "But I'm sure there's a logical explanation. We should stay calm and—"

"Calm?" Harrison's voice cut in from across the room. "Richard, look at this. How can we stay calm?"

Vega turned, watching as Harrison pointed to the window. Outside, the night sky rippled like water, stars blinking in and out of existence. The sight sent a chill down Vega's spine, a visceral reminder of the fragility of their reality.

"We need to contact Drake," Linda said firmly. "He'll know what to do. He always does."

The irony of her trust wasn't lost on Vega. Here she was, relying on him to protect them, unaware of the Sword of Damocles hanging over their heads—with him holding the thread.

"Let's... let's not be hasty," Vega said, fighting to keep his voice steady. "We don't know what's causing this. It could be dangerous to move right now."

Linda's brow furrowed, a flicker of suspicion crossing her face. "Richard, what's really going on? You seem... off."

Vega's heart raced. He had to deflect, to buy time. But as he opened his mouth to speak, a deafening crack split the air, and the world outside the window began to fracture like breaking glass.

35 - 36

Vega took a deep breath, forcing himself to steady. "Yeah," he called back, his voice barely betraying the turmoil inside. "Everything's fine."

But it wasn't. The weight of the disfigured man's threat pressed down on Vega's chest, each breath a struggle against the crushing reality of his situation. He ran a hand through his disheveled hair, once meticulously styled, now a reflection of his inner turmoil.

"Are you sure?" Linda's voice carried a note of concern. "You've been out there for a while."

Vega's mind raced, searching for the right words. "Just... checking the perimeter," he lied smoothly, years of practice allowing him to maintain his facade. "Can't be too careful these days."

He heard footsteps approaching the door and quickly straightened his posture, schooling his features into a mask of calm professionalism. The door opened, revealing Linda's worried face.

"Richard, you look pale," she said, her brow furrowing. "Come inside, please. Harrison's found something on the news you need to see."

As Vega followed her into the suite, his thoughts whirled. How could he protect them when he was the very threat they needed protection from? The irony of his position wasn't lost on him, a bitter taste in his mouth as he contemplated the impossible choice before him.

"What's going on?" he asked, his voice carefully modulated to hide the storm raging within.

Harrison turned from the television, his face grim. "It's happening again, Richard. The fabric of reality... it's unraveling."

Vega's heart sank. He knew, deep down, that this was only the beginning. And as he stood there, surrounded by the people he was meant to betray, he realized that "fine" was the furthest thing from the truth.

37 - 37

Vega's gaze drifted to the television, where a news anchor's voice droned on about unexplained phenomena occurring across the city. His stomach churned as he recognized the telltale signs of reality fracturing. The weight of his impossible choice pressed down on him, threatening to crush his resolve.

"It's not just isolated incidents anymore," Harrison said, his young voice tinged with a wisdom beyond his years. "Look at the pattern, Richard. It's spreading faster than before."

Linda's hand found Vega's arm, her touch both comforting and accusatory. "What do we do now?" she asked, her blue eyes searching his face for answers he couldn't provide.

Vega swallowed hard, his throat constricting. "We... we need to stay calm," he managed, the words tasting like ash in his mouth. "Drake and Rachel are working on a solution. We just need to hold out a little longer."

As he spoke, his mind raced through possibilities, desperately seeking a way out of this nightmare. Could he warn them without revealing his own betrayal? Could he find a way to save both families?

Harrison's gaze bore into him, as if the boy could sense the turmoil beneath Vega's carefully constructed facade. "But what if they can't fix it in time?" he asked, his voice small and afraid.

Vega knelt before Harrison, placing a hand on the boy's shoulder. "Then we'll face it together," he said, the lie burning in his throat. "I promise, I'll do everything in my power to keep you safe."

As the words left his lips, Vega felt the weight of his deception settle over him like a shroud. He was trapped, caught between impossible choices, and the fate of two families hung in the balance. Not even close to fine, indeed.

Visions of Wrath

1 -2 Richard Vega's fingers trembled as he pressed them against the cool, textured wallpaper of the Lexington Hotel's hallway. The ornate patterns blurred before his eyes, swirling into a dizzying kaleidoscope of muted golds and burgundies. His chest constricted, each breath a labored gasp that barely filled his lungs.

"Dispose of the Miller family, or I'll dispose of yours."

The disfigured man's gravelly voice reverberated through Vega's mind, a sinister echo that refused to fade. He glanced at his watch—a nervous habit that had intensified since this nightmare began—and saw his own haunted reflection in its face.

"I can't do this," he whispered, the words barely audible even to himself. "I can't betray them again."

But even as he spoke, images of his own family flashed before him: Emily's warm smile, Maya's infectious laughter, Liam's curious eyes. The thought of losing them twisted like a knife in his gut.

Vega squeezed his eyes shut, willing the world to disappear. The warmth of the hallway seemed to leech away, replaced by a bone-deep chill that made him shiver. The soft hum of the overhead lights, once a comforting white noise, faded into an oppressive silence.

In that moment of sensory deprivation, Vega's mind raced. How had it come to this? He'd once been Drake Miller's trusted colleague, and now he was contemplating the unthinkable. The weight of his choices—past and future—pressed down on him like a physical force.

"I'm sorry, Drake," he murmured, his voice cracking. "I never wanted any of this."

But apologies wouldn't save his family. And they certainly wouldn't save the Millers. Vega's hand drifted to his pocket, where the cold metal of his gun pressed against his thigh. It was a grim reminder of what Gabriel expected him to do.

He thought of Linda Miller, her graceful resilience in the face of unimaginable circumstances. And Harrison, the boy whose innocence and optimism seemed to defy the horrors they'd all endured. Could he really be the one to snuff out that light?

"There has to be another way," Vega muttered, his fingers clenching into fists. "Some way to outsmart Gabriel, to protect everyone."

But even as he spoke the words, doubt gnawed at him. Gabriel's reach seemed infinite, his cruelty boundless. And Vega was just one man, trapped in a web of impossible choices.

The silence of the hallway pressed in on him, suffocating in its intensity. In that moment, Richard Vega felt more alone than he ever had in his life.

3 - 4

Then it hit him—a sharp, visceral sensation, like hands closing around his throat. Vega's eyes widened in panic, his fingers scrabbling at his neck, finding nothing but his own clammy skin. The hallway blurred, colors melting together like a twisted watercolor.

"What's... happening?" he gasped, his voice barely a whisper.

The world spun, reality folding in on itself. Vega stumbled, his back hitting the wall with a dull thud. His vision swam, dark spots dancing at the edges. He blinked rapidly, trying to clear his sight, but the darkness only grew.

"Emily," he choked out, thinking of his wife. "Maya, Liam..."

Their faces flashed before him, a cruel reminder of what he stood to lose. The pressure on his throat increased, invisible fingers tightening their grip. Vega's knees buckled, and he slid down the wall, his chest heaving as he fought for air.

As consciousness began to slip away, a new sensation washed over him. It was as if he were falling, plummeting into an endless void. The hotel hallway faded entirely, replaced by a swirling darkness that seemed to pulse with malevolent energy.

"No," Vega whispered, terror gripping his heart. "This can't be real."

But as the last vestiges of reality slipped away, he knew with chilling certainty that whatever was happening, it was far from over. The vision was only beginning.

5 - 6

The darkness enveloped Vega, a suffocating blanket that seemed to steal the very air from his lungs. He gasped, each breath a laborious effort that left him dizzy and disoriented. The void stretched endlessly around him, a vast expanse of nothingness that threatened to swallow him whole.

"Where am I?" Vega's voice echoed strangely, swallowed by the oppressive silence. His heart thundered in his chest, each beat a painful reminder of his own vulnerability.

As if in response to his question, a figure materialized before him. Gabriel's scarred visage emerged from the shadows, his lips curled into a cruel smile that sent shivers down Vega's spine. The tattered white robe hung loosely from his broad shoulders, the green dragon emblem on his chest pulsing with an eerie, otherworldly light.

Vega instinctively took a step back, his mind reeling. "This isn't real," he muttered, more to himself than to Gabriel. "It can't be."

Gabriel's laugh was a cold, brittle sound that seemed to cut through the thick air. "Oh, Richard," he said, his voice dripping with malice. "Your reality is whatever I decide it to be."

The disfigured man took a step forward, his limp barely noticeable in the featureless void. Vega found himself rooted to the spot, unable to move as Gabriel's presence seemed to fill the entire space.

"What do you want from me?" Vega asked, hating the tremor in his voice. He thought of his family, of the Millers, of the impossible choice before him. "Why are you doing this?"

Gabriel's eyes glinted with a predatory gleam. "Want? I want nothing more than to watch you squirm, Richard. To see you writhe under the weight of your own choices."

Vega's fists clenched at his sides, a mixture of fear and anger coursing through him. "You're a monster," he spat, even as his mind raced, searching for a way out of this nightmare.

7 - 8

Gabriel's scarred face contorted into a grotesque smile, his eyes boring into Vega with an intensity that seemed to pierce through flesh and bone. "Richard," he said, his voice a chilling blend of amusement and contempt, "You thought you could choose to defy me?"

The words hung in the air, heavy and oppressive. Vega felt his throat constrict, his breath coming in short, ragged gasps. The void around them seemed to pulse with malevolent energy, mirroring the glowing dragon emblem on Gabriel's chest.

"I didn't do anything!" Vega shouted, his voice echoing in the emptiness. "I didn't—" He cut himself off, realizing the futility of his protest. In his mind, he saw Linda Miller walking out of the hotel suite, blissfully unaware of the danger that lurked in the shadows. He had let her go, hadn't he? Was that act of mercy truly a defiance?

Gabriel's laughter filled the void, a sound devoid of warmth or humanity. "Oh, but you did, Richard. You made a choice. And now, you'll face the consequences."

Vega's heart raced, pounding against his ribcage like a trapped animal. He thought of his wife, Emily, of his children, Maya and Liam. Their faces flashed before his eyes, a reminder of everything he stood to lose. The weight of his decision pressed down on him, threatening to crush him under its enormity.

"There has to be another way," Vega whispered, more to himself than to Gabriel. But even as the words left his lips, he knew the truth. In this twisted game of Gabriel's making, there were no easy choices, no clean escapes. Only the sickening knowledge that whatever he decided, someone would suffer.

9 - 10

Before Vega could react, Gabriel moved with a speed that defied human limitations. His scarred hand lashed out, fingers curling around Vega's throat with crushing force. The world tilted as Vega's feet left the ground, his body suspended in the oppressive void.

Panic surged through Vega's veins as he clawed desperately at Gabriel's iron grip. His legs kicked uselessly in the air, searching for purchase where none existed. Each attempt to draw breath became a desperate struggle, his lungs burning for air that wouldn't come.

"You let her go," Gabriel snarled, his disfigured face mere inches from Vega's. His breath was hot and foul, carrying the stench of decay. "You thought mercy would save you. But mercy only makes you weak."

Vega's vision began to blur, dark spots dancing at the edges. In his fading consciousness, a single thought crystallized: I was trying to do the right thing. But as Gabriel's words sank in, doubt gnawed at him. Had his attempt at mercy doomed not only the Millers but his own family as well?

"Please," Vega managed to rasp, the word barely audible as it squeezed past Gabriel's grip. "My family... they're innocent."

Gabriel's lips twisted into a cruel smirk, the scars on his face contorting with the movement. "Innocence," he spat, "is a luxury you can't afford, Richard. Not in this game."

As the darkness encroached, Vega's thoughts turned to Emily, to Maya and Liam. He had promised to protect them, to keep them safe. Now, with each fading heartbeat, that promise seemed to slip further from his grasp.

11 - 12

Suddenly, the void around Vega shimmered and fractured. Gabriel's grip vanished, and Vega stumbled forward, gasping for air. The oppressive darkness dissolved, replaced by the muted elegance of the Lexington suite. His heart pounded in his chest as he struggled to orient himself.

"Are you sure you don't want to join us for dinner, Richard?" Linda Miller's melodic voice cut through his disorientation.

Vega blinked, his mind reeling. Linda stood before him, her blonde hair catching the warm light of the suite, her blue eyes filled with genuine concern. Behind her, Harrison fidgeted with the strap of his backpack, his youthful face a mixture of curiosity and impatience.

"I... I'm fine," Vega managed, his throat raw. He forced a smile, desperately trying to mask the terror that still gripped him. "You two enjoy yourselves."

Linda tilted her head, her brow furrowing slightly. "If you change your mind, we'll be at the hotel restaurant."

As they moved towards the door, Vega's mind raced. This was the moment - the pivotal decision he had made before. The choice that had set everything in motion. He opened his mouth, words of warning on the tip of his tongue, but they died before he could utter them.

What if this was another of Gabriel's tricks? What if speaking out now would only hasten the fate he was trying to avoid?

Harrison paused at the threshold, glancing back at Vega. "You sure you're okay, Mr. Vega? You look like you've seen a ghost."

Vega's laugh was hollow, brittle. "Just tired, Harrison. Nothing to worry about."

As the door clicked shut behind them, Vega's legs gave out. He sank to the floor, his back against the wall, and buried his face in his hands. The weight of his choices - past, present, and future - pressed down on him like a physical force.

"What have I done?" he whispered to the empty room, his words heavy with the knowledge of what was to come.

13 - 14

Gabriel's voice slithered into Vega's ear, cold and insidious. "This is the moment you chose wrong."

The world around Vega warped and twisted, reality bending like a funhouse mirror. When it settled, he found himself on his knees, the taste of copper flooding his mouth. His face throbbed, a constellation of pain blooming across his cheeks and jaw.

Emily stood before him, but this wasn't the woman he knew. Her eyes, once warm and full of life, were now vacant pools of nothingness. She gazed down at him, her expression a mask of indifference.

"Emily," Vega croaked, his voice raw and desperate. "What's happening? Where are the kids?"

His wife didn't respond, didn't even blink. It was as if she were looking through him rather than at him. A chill ran down Vega's spine as he noticed what lay behind her.

Maya and Liam, their small bodies contorted at unnatural angles, lay motionless on the floor. The sight sent a surge of primal terror through Vega's heart.

"No," he whispered, trying to crawl towards them. "This can't be real. It can't be."

Gabriel's laughter echoed in his mind. "Oh, but it is, Richard. This is the price of your defiance, the cost of your misplaced mercy."

Vega's thoughts raced, a torrent of guilt and horror. Had his attempt to save the Millers led to this? Was this the future that awaited him if he didn't comply with Gabriel's demands?

"Why?" he choked out, tears mingling with the blood on his face. "Why show me this?"

The air around him seemed to thicken, Gabriel's presence oppressive and all-encompassing. "To remind you of what's at stake, Richard. Your family or theirs. The choice is yours."

15 - 16

"No!" Vega screamed, his voice cracking under the weight of his anguish. The word tore from his throat, raw and primal, echoing in the surreal nightmare that surrounded him. His hands clawed at the floor, desperate to reach his children, to prove that this horrific vision wasn't real.

But before he could move, Gabriel materialized before him, a twisted apparition of malevolence. The scarred man's presence filled the room with an oppressive chill, his tattered white robe billowing as if caught in an otherworldly breeze.

"Did you think your defiance would go unpunished, Richard?" Gabriel's voice dripped with cold amusement as his hand shot out, fingers wrapping around Vega's throat with inhuman strength.

Vega gasped, his eyes widening as he felt the air being squeezed from his lungs. He clawed at Gabriel's arm, but his fingers seemed to pass through smoke, unable to find purchase.

Gabriel leaned in close, his burned face inches from Vega's. "This is what happens when you disobey me, Richard. This is the cost of defiance."

As spots danced in his vision, Vega's mind raced. How had he ended up here? He'd only wanted to protect everyone – the Millers, his own family. But now, trapped in Gabriel's grip, he realized the cruel irony of his situation. In trying to save them all, he might lose everything.

"Please," Vega managed to choke out, "my family... they're innocent."

Gabriel's lips curled into a sneer. "Innocence means nothing in the grand scheme, Richard. You made your choice. Now live with the consequences."

17 - 18

Vega's lungs burned, desperate for air. He thrashed wildly, his legs kicking out, seeking purchase against any surface. But there was nothing—only the void and Gabriel's iron grip.

"You can't—" Vega gasped, his words barely a whisper. The edges of his vision began to darken, the world narrowing to a pinpoint.

Gabriel's scarred face loomed larger, filling Vega's fading sight. "I can do whatever I please, Richard. Across realities, across time. You're nothing but a pawn in a game you can't comprehend."

As consciousness slipped away, Vega's thoughts turned to Emily, to Maya and Liam. Their faces flickered in his mind, a bittersweet reminder of what he stood to lose. He'd made so many mistakes, crossed so many lines. But it had all been for them.

With the last of his strength, Vega raised his hand, not to claw at Gabriel's arm, but to reach for the fading image of his family. His fingers trembled in the air, grasping at ghosts.

"I'm... sorry," he mouthed, unsure if the words even left his lips.

The darkness closed in, inexorable and absolute. Vega's last coherent thought was a desperate plea to a universe that seemed indifferent to his suffering: Let them be safe. Let this nightmare end.

But as the last glimmer of awareness faded, he knew—deep in his bones—that this was only the beginning.

19 - 20

As the void threatened to consume him, Vega summoned the last reserves of his strength. His lungs burned, desperate for air, and his vision swam with dark spots. With trembling lips, he forced out words that were barely more than a whisper.

"You don't have to do this," Vega rasped, his voice barely audible.

The words hung in the oppressive silence, a fragile plea against the crushing weight of Gabriel's grip. For a fleeting moment, Vega allowed himself to hope—hope that somewhere beneath the scarred exterior and cruel demeanor, a shred of humanity remained in his tormentor.

Gabriel's response shattered that illusion. A laugh escaped his charred lips, cold and hollow, devoid of any warmth or mercy. It echoed in the featureless void, a chilling reminder of the futility of Vega's appeal.

"Oh, Richard," Gabriel sneered, his disfigured face twisting into a grotesque parody of amusement. "You're mistaken. I don't have to do anything. But I enjoy watching you squirm."

As Gabriel's words sank in, Vega felt a wave of despair wash over him. His mind raced, grasping for options, for some way out of this nightmare. But with each passing second, as his body weakened and his thoughts grew sluggish, the reality of his situation became painfully clear.

He was at the mercy of a man—if Gabriel could even be called that anymore—who reveled in suffering. A being who traversed realities and manipulated time itself, all for the sake of his twisted games. And Vega, for all his cunning and desperation, was nothing more than a pawn on Gabriel's cosmic chessboard.

21 - 22

Gabriel's face loomed closer, the acrid stench of burnt flesh assaulting Vega's nostrils. The scarred lips curled into a sneer, revealing teeth stained with malice. "You made a promise once, remember?" Gabriel's words slithered into Vega's mind, coiling around his thoughts like a venomous serpent. "A promise to protect your family at all costs."

Vega's heart clenched, memories of Emily's gentle smile and the children's laughter flashing before his eyes. He had made that vow, hadn't he? On their wedding day, with hope in his heart and love in his eyes. Now, that sacred oath hung like a noose around his neck.

"Are you ready to break that promise, Richard?" Gabriel's voice dripped with false concern. "Or will you do as I say?"

The weight of the choice pressed down on Vega, threatening to crush him. His mind raced, searching for an escape, a loophole, anything to avoid the impossible decision before him. But Gabriel's grip was unyielding, both physically and metaphorically.

"I... I can't," Vega choked out, his voice barely a whisper. "There has to be another way."

Gabriel's laugh was a harsh, grating sound. "There is no other way, Richard. There never was."

As the words sank in, something shifted within Vega. A spark of defiance, long dormant, flickered to life. With a surge of desperate strength, he grasped Gabriel's wrist, his fingernails digging into the scarred flesh.

"No," Vega growled, his vision blurring at the edges. "I won't be your puppet anymore."

23 - 24

The world around Vega shattered like a broken mirror, fragments of the nightmarish void dissolving into nothingness. He gasped, his lungs burning as they desperately gulped in air. The plush carpet of the Lexington Hotel's hallway rushed up to meet him as he stumbled backward, his hand instinctively flying to his throat.

"Christ," he rasped, his voice hoarse and unfamiliar to his own ears. The phantom sensation of Gabriel's iron grip lingered, a ghostly pressure that made him want to claw at his own skin.

Vega's legs trembled, threatening to give way beneath him. He leaned heavily against the wall, the cool surface a stark contrast to the feverish heat radiating from his body. His breath came in ragged gasps, each inhale a reminder of how close he'd come to suffocation—real or imagined.

"Was it real?" he whispered to the empty hallway, his eyes darting nervously from side to side. "Or am I losing my goddamn mind?"

The memory of Gabriel's disfigured face, twisted in malicious glee, flashed before his eyes. Vega squeezed them shut, willing the image away, but it seemed seared into his retinas.

"Get it together, Richard," he muttered to himself, running a shaky hand through his disheveled hair. "You can't afford to fall apart now."

But even as he tried to steady himself, Vega couldn't shake the lingering dread that coiled in his gut. Gabriel's words echoed in his mind, a sinister promise that sent chills down his spine.

"I made a choice," Vega realized, his voice barely audible. "But at what cost?"

25 - 26

Vega pressed a trembling hand to his chest, feeling the erratic pounding of his heart beneath his palm. Each beat seemed to echo Gabriel's threat, a relentless reminder of the impossible choice before him. His gaze drifted to the suite door, its polished surface now a barrier between two worlds—one of temporary safety, and another of looming danger.

"Linda," he whispered, her name a mixture of regret and resolve on his lips. "Harrison."

He took a hesitant step towards the door, then faltered. Through the wood, he could almost imagine their voices—Linda's gentle tone, Harrison's youthful energy. For now, they were oblivious to the storm gathering around them.

Vega's hand hovered over the doorknob, trembling. "How long can I keep them safe?" he murmured, his voice thick with doubt. "How long before Gabriel..."

He couldn't finish the thought. The weight of his past decisions pressed down on him, each betrayal and compromise leading to this moment. Vega leaned his forehead against the cool surface of the door, closing his eyes.

"I'm sorry," he breathed, though whether to Linda and Harrison or to his own family, he wasn't sure. "I never meant for any of this to happen."

But intentions, Vega realized with a sinking feeling, counted for little in the face of Gabriel's ruthless determination. The disfigured man's threat hung in the air like a toxic cloud, poisoning every breath, every moment of reprieve.

Vega's fingers curled into a fist against the door. "How long?" he asked again, this time to the empty hallway, to the uncaring universe. "How long before I have to choose?"

27 - 28

Gabriel's mocking voice slithered through Vega's mind, each syllable dripping with venom. "You thought mercy would save you." The words coiled around his thoughts, constricting like a serpent.

Vega's eyes snapped open, his vision blurring as he stared at the intricate patterns on the hotel's wallpaper. The once-elegant design now seemed to twist and writhe, morphing into grotesque shapes that mirrored the turmoil in his soul.

"Mercy," he whispered, tasting the bitterness of the word on his tongue. "What mercy is there in this?"

His hands clenched involuntarily, nails digging into his palms. The sharp pain grounded him, pulling him back from the precipice of despair. Vega's jaw tightened, muscles straining as he fought to regain control.

"I can't," he muttered, his voice hoarse. "I can't do this again."

But even as the words left his lips, Vega knew the lie they carried. He could. He would. Because the alternative was unthinkable.

The choice loomed before him, a yawning chasm with no bridge in sight. On one side stood the Millers, innocent and unaware. On the other, his own family, their faces etched with fear and betrayal from the vision Gabriel had thrust upon him.

"Emily," Vega breathed, his wife's name a prayer and a curse. "Maya. Liam."

He straightened, shoulders squaring as if bracing against an unseen weight. The hallway seemed to stretch endlessly in both directions, offering no escape, no reprieve from the decision that would haunt him for eternity.

"What kind of man am I?" Vega asked the empty corridor, his words echoing softly. "What kind of man will I become?"

The silence that answered was deafening.

Fragments of the Past

1 The bathroom mirror reflected a stranger. Linda Miller barely recognized the woman staring back at her, blonde hair limp and lifeless, blue eyes dulled by exhaustion and worry. She traced the dark circles under her eyes, evidence of sleepless nights filled with unanswered questions.

"What are we doing here?" she whispered to her reflection, her voice barely audible over the hum of the hotel air conditioning.

The weight of recent events pressed down on her shoulders like a physical burden. Memories of shattered realities and impossible choices swirled in her mind, a dizzying kaleidoscope of "what-ifs" and "should-haves."

Linda's gaze drifted to the closed bathroom door. Beyond it, she knew Harrison paced the hotel suite, his restless energy a constant reminder of the stakes they faced. His determination had been her anchor in this storm of uncertainty, but even that felt tenuous now.

"We're going to fix this," Drake's voice echoed in her memory, firm and unwavering. "We have to."

She wanted to believe him. God, how she wanted to believe. But as the days stretched on and the answers remained elusive, doubt crept in like a shadow.

Linda splashed cold water on her face, hoping to wash away the gnawing unease. As she patted her skin dry, she caught sight of her wedding ring glinting in the harsh bathroom light. It was a reminder of simpler times, of promises made before the world turned upside down.

"Harrison?" she called out, suddenly needing to hear his voice, to ground herself in the present.

"Yeah?" His response came quickly, tinged with concern.

Linda opened the bathroom door, stepping out into the dimly lit suite. Her son stood by the window, his broad shoulders tense as he gazed out at the city below. He turned to face her, and the lines of worry etched on his face mirrored her own.

"Are we doing the right thing?" she asked, voicing the fear that had been growing in her heart.

Harrison's expression softened, and he crossed the room to take her hands in his. "Dad's trying to save our family, our world. How can that not be right?"

Linda squeezed his hands, drawing strength from his touch. "I know, but... what if the truth is worse than not knowing? What if we can't handle what we find?"

Harrison's jaw tightened, a flicker of doubt crossing his features before he masked it with determination. "We have to try, mom. For us, for everyone caught in this mess."

She nodded, wanting to believe, needing to believe. But as she looked into harrison's eyes, she saw the same fear reflected back at her – the terrifying possibility that their quest for answers might lead them down a path from which there was no return.

3 - 4

Linda turned back to the bathroom sink, her hands trembling as she reached for the faucet. The cool water flowed over her fingers, a momentary respite from the relentless pounding in her head. She cupped her palms, gathering the liquid before splashing it onto her face.

The shock of cold against her skin was instant, droplets cascading down her cheeks and chin. For a fleeting moment, the ache in her temples subsided, replaced by a crisp clarity. But as she straightened, reaching for a towel, a sharp, searing pain lanced through her head.

"Ah!" she gasped, her knuckles turning white as she gripped the edge of the sink. The world tilted, the bathroom fixtures blurring in her vision.

Harrison's voice came from the other room, laced with worry. "Mom? You okay in there?"

She wanted to respond, to reassure him, but the words caught in her throat. The pain intensified, a pressure building behind her eyes that threatened to split her skull. Linda squeezed her eyes shut, willing the agony to pass.

When she opened them again, the world had changed. The familiar bathroom vanished, replaced by a swirling vortex of images and sensations. Linda's heart raced, her breath coming in short, panicked gasps.

"What's happening to me?" she whispered, her voice barely audible over the rushing in her ears.

As the visions began to take shape, a distant part of Linda's mind registered the oddity of the situation. She was experiencing something beyond the realm of normal perception, yet a strange calmness settled over her, as if she were merely an observer in her own mind.

5 - 6

The bathroom light flickered, casting eerie shadows that danced across Linda's face. Her reflection in the mirror warped and distorted, stretching and twisting like a carnival funhouse. She blinked hard, trying to clear her vision, but the distortions only intensified.

"This can't be real," Linda murmured, her voice trembling. She reached out to touch the mirror, but her fingers met only empty air. The solid surfaces of the bathroom seemed to melt away, leaving her suspended in a void of swirling darkness.

Panic clawed at her throat. "Drake!" she called out, but no sound escaped her lips. The darkness pressed in, suffocating and oppressive.

Then, as suddenly as it began, the void vanished. Linda found herself in a dimly lit room, her wrists and ankles bound tightly to a cold metal chair. The air hung heavy with the acrid smell of chemicals and the faint hum of machinery filled her ears, sending chills down her spine.

"Where am I?" she whispered, her eyes darting around the unfamiliar space. The room was sparse, industrial, with concrete walls and a single flickering light overhead. Linda's nurturing instincts, usually so strong, were overwhelmed by a rising tide of fear.

She tested her restraints, wincing as they bit into her skin. "This isn't possible," she thought, her mind racing. "I was just in the hotel bathroom. How did I get here?"

The hum of machinery grew louder, more insistent. Linda's heart pounded in her chest, each beat echoing in the oppressive silence of the room. Despite her terror, a part of her remained oddly detached, observing the situation with a strange clarity.

"Drake always said there were other realities," she mused, her thoughts a lifeline in the sea of confusion. "Is this what he meant? Am I seeing another world?"

7 - 8

As Linda's eyes adjusted to the dim light, a figure emerged from the shadows. Her breath caught in her throat as she recognized the disfigured face of Gabriel, partially obscured by the hood of his tattered white robe. The glowing green dragon emblem on his chest pulsed faintly, casting an eerie, sickly light across the room.

Linda's stomach churned at the sight of him. She'd heard Drake's descriptions, but nothing could have prepared her for the reality of Gabriel's presence. His scarred visage seemed to twist into a cruel sneer, and the air around him felt charged with malevolence.

"Welcome, Linda," Gabriel's voice slithered through the air, unnervingly calm. "I trust you're finding your accommodations... suitable?"

She wanted to respond, to demand answers, but fear paralyzed her vocal cords. Instead, her gaze darted to the figure standing beside Gabriel. Richard Vega. His familiar face was a shock in this alien environment, but the guilt etched in his features and his averted eyes spoke volumes.

"Richard?" Linda's mind raced. "What's he doing here? Is he working with Gabriel?"

The tension in Vega's jaw and the way he shifted uncomfortably under her gaze only intensified her confusion and dread. Linda's thoughts whirled, trying to make sense of this surreal tableau. Was this a vision? A parallel reality? Or had she somehow been transported to another time and place entirely?

9 - 10

Linda's voice cracked as she struggled against the restraints, desperation clawing at her throat. "Richard? What's going on? What is this?"

The metal bindings bit into her wrists as she wriggled, her heart pounding so loudly she could barely hear her own words. Vega's familiar face, now etched with lines of worry and guilt, remained turned away from her. His silence was deafening, more painful than any physical wound.

"Look at me, Richard!" Linda's mind raced. "How could you be involved in this? We were colleagues, friends..."

Vega's jaw tightened visibly, the muscles in his face working as he swallowed hard. His eyes, when they finally flicked towards her, were pools of regret. But just as quickly, they darted away, landing on Gabriel.

Linda followed his gaze, her breath catching as she saw the sinister smile spreading across Gabriel's disfigured face. The green glow from his emblem seemed to pulse in time with her racing heartbeat, casting grotesque shadows that danced across the walls.

"Oh, Richard," Linda thought, a wave of despair washing over her. "What have they done to you? What have they threatened you with?"

The silence stretched on, broken only by the faint hum of unseen machinery and Linda's own ragged breathing. She could feel the weight of unspoken words, of terrible choices made, hanging in the air between them.

11 - 12

Gabriel's scarred visage loomed closer, his eyes glinting with a mixture of triumph and curiosity. "You're important, Linda," he said, his voice calm and unnervingly soft. "More important than you realize. But importance comes with a cost."

The words sent a chill down Linda's spine, her mind reeling with their implications. What did he mean? How could she be important to this twisted figure from Drake's nightmares? She thought of her husband, of Harrison, wondering if they were searching for her even now.

"Let me go," she demanded, her voice trembling despite her best efforts to sound strong. The chair creaked as she strained against her bonds, the metal cutting deeper into her skin.

Gabriel's proximity made her skin crawl, his breath ghosting across her cheek as he leaned in. The green glow from his emblem cast eerie shadows across his face, accentuating every scar, every twisted line.

"Oh, Linda," he whispered, almost tenderly. "If only it were that simple."

Linda's thoughts raced, searching for a way out, for some understanding of the situation. She'd faced challenges before, had weathered the storm of loss and grief, but this... this was beyond anything she could have imagined.

"Drake will find me," she thought fiercely, clinging to hope. "He always does. He'll make this right."

But as Gabriel's smile widened, a seed of doubt took root in her heart. What if this time, there was no escape?

13 - 14

Gabriel's chuckle reverberated through the dim room, a sound that sent shivers down Linda's spine. He took another step closer, his scarred face now mere inches from hers. The acrid smell of burnt flesh filled her nostrils, making her stomach churn.

"I can't do that. Not yet," Gabriel said, his voice a silky whisper that belied the menace in his eyes. "We have so much to discuss, you and I."

Linda's heart raced, her mind frantically searching for a way out. She could feel the cold sweat beading on her forehead, hear the blood rushing in her ears. Every instinct screamed at her to run, but the restraints held firm, biting into her skin with every movement.

Her gaze darted to Richard Vega, standing silently in the shadows. His face was a mask of conflicted emotions, guilt and fear warring in his eyes. Linda felt a surge of anger, of betrayal, cutting through her fear.

"You're just going to stand there?" she demanded, her voice cracking with desperation. "Let him do this?"

Vega flinched at her words, his shoulders hunching as if under a physical blow. He opened his mouth as if to speak, but no words came out. Linda watched him, searching for any sign of the man she thought she knew, the friend who had stood by Drake's side.

"Richard, please," she thought, willing him to meet her eyes. "You can still make this right. Help me."

But as the silence stretched on, broken only by Gabriel's soft, mocking laughter, Linda felt the last threads of hope slipping away. She was alone here, trapped in a nightmare she couldn't understand, with no way to reach those she loved.

15 - 16

Vega's gaze finally met Linda's, his eyes swimming with a torment that belied his composed exterior. "I didn't have a choice," he muttered, his voice barely audible, a whisper of regret in the oppressive silence of the room.

Linda's heart sank, the weight of his words crushing what little hope remained. She wanted to scream, to rage against the injustice of it all, but found herself paralyzed by the gravity of the situation.

Gabriel's laughter shattered the moment, echoing off the walls with a sinister resonance that sent chills down Linda's spine. "Oh, but he did," Gabriel sneered, his scarred face twisting into a grotesque smile. "And now he's learning what it means to keep his promises."

The green dragon emblem on Gabriel's chest pulsed brighter, casting eerie shadows across his disfigured features. Linda's mind raced, trying to piece together the fragments of this twisted reality. What promises? What choice did Vega have?

"Richard," she pleaded, her voice trembling, "what does he mean? What did you do?"

Vega's face contorted with anguish, his carefully constructed facade crumbling under the weight of Gabriel's words. Linda could see the internal struggle playing out in his eyes, the desperation of a man caught between impossible choices.

As Gabriel's laughter faded, leaving behind a suffocating silence, Linda felt a cold dread settling in her stomach. Whatever game was being played here, she realized with growing horror, they were all just pawns in Gabriel's grand design.

17 - 18

The room suddenly lurched, reality warping around Linda like a funhouse mirror. Her vision blurred, the world spinning in a dizzying kaleidoscope of fractured images. She clenched her eyes shut, fighting against the nausea that threatened to overwhelm her.

When she opened them again, the scene had shifted violently. Gone was the sterile room with its oppressive atmosphere. Instead, flashes of chaotic visions assaulted her senses.

Drake's face materialized before her, bloodied and contorted with anguish. His once-steady voice now cracked with desperation as he shouted, "Linda! Linda, where are you?"

The raw pain in his tone tore at Linda's heart. She tried to call out to him, to reach for him, but her body refused to obey. "Drake," she whispered, her words lost in the maelstrom of shifting realities.

The image flickered and changed. Now she saw Harrison, his small face pale with terror, arms outstretched towards her. "Mom!" he cried, tears streaming down his cheeks. "Help me!"

Linda's maternal instincts surged, every fiber of her being screaming to protect her son. But as she struggled against invisible bonds, she watched in horror as Gabriel's looming figure appeared behind Harrison, his scarred hands gripping the boy's shoulders.

"No!" Linda choked out, her heart pounding furiously. "Let him go!"

Gabriel's lips curled into a cruel smile as he began to drag Harrison away. The boy's frightened eyes locked onto Linda's, silently pleading for help she couldn't provide.

As the visions swirled and fragmented, Linda's mind raced. What was happening? Were these glimpses of another reality, or nightmarish premonitions of what was to come? The uncertainty gnawed at her, threatening to unravel the last threads of her sanity.

19 - 20

The kaleidoscope of horrors intensified, each fragment more vivid and excruciating than the last. Linda's temples throbbed, a searing pain that threatened to split her skull. She squeezed her eyes shut, but the images persisted, burning themselves into her mind's eye.

Drake's bloodied face morphed into Harrison's terrified visage, then back again. Their voices, once distinct, now blended into a cacophony of fear and desperation. Linda's breath came in ragged gasps, her chest tight with an anguish that threatened to consume her.

"Please," she whimpered, her voice barely audible even to herself. "Make it stop."

As if in response to her plea, a new voice cut through the chaos—low, calm, and terrifyingly familiar.

"Oh, Linda," Gabriel's silky tone reverberated through her consciousness. "This is only the beginning."

Linda's eyes snapped open, searching frantically for the source of the voice. But there was only darkness, punctuated by fleeting images of her loved ones in peril.

"What do you want from us?" she cried out, her words tinged with equal parts fury and fear.

Gabriel's laughter echoed in the void. "It's not about what I want, Linda. It's about what you fear. What you can't escape."

Linda's fists clenched, her nails digging into her palms. "We'll find a way," she insisted, clinging to the determination that had seen her through countless trials. "Drake will—"

"Drake can't save you," Gabriel interrupted, his voice suddenly harsh. "He can't even save himself."

The pain in Linda's head crescendoed, threatening to overwhelm her. Through gritted teeth, she managed to gasp, "You're wrong. We'll stop you."

Gabriel's response was immediate and chilling. "You'll never escape me, Linda. You'll never escape this."

His words seemed to reverberate through every fiber of her being, a promise and a threat intertwined. Linda wanted to scream, to fight, to do anything to push back against the tide of despair threatening to engulf her. But the pain and the visions held her captive, leaving her trapped in a nightmare from which there seemed to be no awakening.

21 - 22

Linda's eyes flew open, her chest heaving as she gulped in air. The stark white tiles of the hotel bathroom swam into focus, a jarring contrast to the oppressive darkness of her vision. Her fingers gripped the cold porcelain of the sink, knuckles white with tension.

"It wasn't real," she whispered, her voice trembling. "It wasn't real."

But as her gaze met her reflection in the mirror, Linda's breath caught in her throat. A thin trickle of blood ran from her nose, vivid crimson against her pale skin.

Her mind raced, struggling to process what had just occurred. Was it a premonition? A glimpse into another reality? Or something far more sinister?

"Drake," she called out, her voice stronger now, tinged with urgency. "Drake, I need you!"

As she waited for a response, Linda's eyes never left her reflection. The woman staring back at her seemed both familiar and foreign – the same blue eyes and blonde hair, but haunted by a knowledge that transcended this reality.

"What's happening to me?" she murmured, reaching up to touch her face, half-expecting her hand to pass through her reflection like smoke. "How can I protect them if I can't even trust my own mind?"

The weight of responsibility settled heavily on her shoulders. Whatever was happening, whatever Gabriel's plans were, she knew she had to be strong – for Drake, for Harrison, for all the realities hanging in the balance.

Linda took a deep breath, steeling herself. "We'll find a way," she affirmed, echoing her words from the vision. "We have to."

23 - 24

Linda's fingers trembled as she reached up, gingerly touching her upper lip. The warm, sticky sensation confirmed her fears. She pulled her hand away, staring at the bright crimson staining her fingertips.

"No," she whispered, her voice barely audible. "This can't be happening."

The pounding in her head had subsided, but her heart raced wildly, each beat echoing in her ears. Her chest felt tight, constricted by an invisible band of fear that threatened to suffocate her.

Linda gripped the edge of the sink, her knuckles turning white as she struggled to steady herself. The bathroom suddenly felt claustrophobic, the walls closing in around her.

"Breathe," she commanded herself, inhaling deeply. "Just breathe."

As she exhaled, a shaky whisper escaped her lips. "What... what was that?"

Her mind reeled, trying to make sense of the vision. Gabriel's sinister smile, Richard's guilt-ridden face, the feeling of being bound and helpless – it had all felt so real, so tangible.

"It was just a hallucination," Linda reasoned, her voice trembling with uncertainty. "It had to be."

But the blood on her fingers told a different story. Something was happening to her, something beyond her understanding. And as she stared at her pale, frightened reflection, Linda couldn't shake the feeling that this was only the beginning.

25 - 26

Linda's hands shook as she turned on the faucet, the rush of water a stark contrast to the eerie silence that had enveloped her moments ago. She grabbed a tissue, pressing it firmly against her nose, wincing at the pressure. The white paper quickly bloomed with crimson, a visual reminder of the inexplicable experience she'd just endured.

"Get it together, Linda," she muttered, her voice muffled by the tissue. "You're stronger than this."

But even as she tried to reassure herself, the vivid details of her vision replayed in her mind with haunting clarity. The cold bite of metal restraints against her wrists, the stale air that seemed to cling to her skin, the faint hum of machinery that had sent chills down her spine – it all felt too real to dismiss.

Gabriel's face swam before her eyes, his scarred visage twisted into a mocking smile that made her stomach churn. "You'll never escape me, Linda," his voice echoed in her thoughts, as clear as if he were standing right beside her.

She shuddered, gripping the edge of the sink. "It wasn't real," she whispered fiercely. "He's not here. He can't hurt me."

But even as she spoke the words, doubt gnawed at her. The image of Richard Vega lingered, his face etched with guilt and fear. What did it mean? Was he truly involved in all of this?

"Why, Richard?" she found herself asking the empty bathroom. "What did Gabriel do to make you betray us?"

The silence that followed her question was deafening, broken only by the steady drip of the faucet and her own ragged breathing. Linda stared at her reflection, searching for answers in her own tired eyes, but finding only more questions.

27 - 28

Linda's blue eyes, rimmed with exhaustion, gazed back at her from the mirror. She took a shaky breath, willing her racing heart to slow. "Is this what Drake feels?" she murmured, her voice barely audible. "These... visions?"

She reached up, touching her nose gingerly. The bleeding had stopped, but the memory of it sent a shiver through her. It was too visceral, too intense to be a mere daydream or trick of an overactive imagination.

"What if..." she began, her mind racing with possibilities. "What if it's a glimpse of another reality? Or a warning?"

The thought made her pause, her brow furrowing with concern. She recalled Drake's determination to fix everything, his unwavering belief that he could set things right. But what if the cost was higher than they realized?

Linda closed her eyes, steadying herself against the sink. When she opened them again, her reflection seemed different somehow – stronger, more resolute. "Whatever this is," she said softly, her voice gaining strength, "we'll face it together. Drake, Harrison, and me."

She straightened up, squaring her shoulders. The past may not be finished with them, but Linda Miller was far from finished fighting. As she turned to leave the bathroom, a quiet determination settled over her. They would find answers, no matter where – or when – they had to look.

The Road to New Haven

1-2 The asphalt ribbon stretched endlessly before Drake, a black river cutting through the autumn-tinged landscape. His knuckles whitened on the steering wheel as memories and questions swirled like leaves in a tempest.

"Rachel Summers," he muttered, tasting the name on his tongue. It felt both foreign and achingly familiar, like a half-remembered dream.

The car's engine thrummed, a steady heartbeat beneath the cacophony of his thoughts. Drake's eyes flicked to the rearview mirror, studying his own haggard reflection. The man staring back seemed a stranger—hollow-eyed and desperate.

He cleared his throat, breaking the oppressive silence. "Who are you, Rachel? What do you know?"

The questions hung unanswered in the stale air of the car. Drake's mind raced, constructing and discarding theories with dizzying speed. Each possibility seemed more outlandish than the last, yet none could be dismissed in this new reality he found himself navigating.

A green highway sign flashed past: "New Haven 50 miles." Drake's stomach clenched, a mixture of anticipation and dread. He was hurtling towards... what? Answers? More questions? Or perhaps the final unraveling of his sanity?

"Get it together, Miller," he growled, shaking his head as if to dislodge the doubts. "One step at a time. Find Rachel. Then..."

Then what? The thought trailed off, lost in the vast unknown that stretched before him. Drake's jaw tightened, determination etching itself into the lines of his face. Whatever came next, he would face it. He had to—for his family, for the world he'd left behind, for the life he could barely remember but ached to reclaim.

The miles rolled by, each one bringing him closer to New Haven, to Rachel Summers, to the truth that waited like a coiled serpent, ready to strike.

3 - 4

Rachel Summers. The name pulsed through Drake's mind, each syllable a beacon in the fog of his fractured memories. He gripped the steering wheel tighter, his knuckles whitening as fragments of recollection flickered like dying embers in the recesses of his consciousness.

"The Codex," he muttered, the words tasting foreign on his tongue. "She showed me the Codex."

In his mind's eye, he saw a flash of red hair, heard the echo of an urgent voice. Rachel's face swam into focus, her eyes alight with a fervor that bordered on madness. The image was so vivid it made his breath catch.

Drake shook his head, trying to clear the cobwebs. "What did you show me, Rachel? What truths?"

The silence of the car offered no answers. He glanced at his reflection in the rearview mirror, searching for any hint of recognition in his own eyes. But the man staring back seemed a stranger—hollow-eyed and desperate.

"The multiverse," he whispered, the word sending a shiver down his spine. "She said... she said it was all connected. But how?"

Drake's mind raced, grasping at the tendrils of memory. Each revelation only spawned more questions, leaving him feeling like he was trying to piece together a puzzle in the dark.

"She's the key," he said firmly, his resolve strengthening. "Whatever's happening, whatever I've forgotten... Rachel Summers is at the center of it all."

The realization settled over him like a heavy cloak. Rachel wasn't just a name from his past; she was his lifeline to understanding, his only hope of unraveling the mystery that had become his existence.

"I have to find her," Drake muttered, his foot pressing harder on the accelerator. "Whatever it takes."

5 - 6

The imposing silhouette of the New Haven Institute of Advanced Research loomed before Drake, its sleek glass-and-steel facade a stark contrast to the verdant landscape surrounding it. Sunlight glinted off the building's mirrored surface, momentarily blinding him as he pulled into the parking lot.

Drake killed the engine, his hands lingering on the steering wheel. The weight of his mission pressed down on him, making each breath feel labored. He closed his eyes, willing his racing heart to slow.

"You can do this," he murmured to himself, his voice barely audible. "For them. For everyone."

With a deep inhale, Drake stepped out of the car. The afternoon sun beat down mercilessly, and he squinted against its glare. His fingers fumbled with his jacket, adjusting it nervously as he surveyed the pristine grounds.

"Rachel," he whispered, her name a talisman against the doubt gnawing at his insides. "What secrets are you hiding behind these walls?"

As he approached the entrance, Drake's mind whirled with possibilities. Would she remember him? Would she have answers to the fragments of memory that tormented him? Or would this be another dead end in a journey that seemed increasingly futile?

He paused at the foot of the steps leading to the main doors, his reflection distorted in the polished glass. The man staring back at him seemed both familiar and foreign – a testament to the fractured nature of his reality.

"Time to face the music," Drake muttered, steeling himself for whatever lay ahead. With a deep breath, he climbed the stairs, each step bringing him closer to the truth – or to another crushing disappointment.

7 - 8

Drake's determined stride faltered as a uniformed security guard emerged from a small booth near the main gate. The guard's face was a mask of hostility, his eyes narrowing as they locked onto Drake's approaching figure.

"This is it," Drake thought, his jaw clenching involuntarily. "The moment of truth."

He continued forward, each step deliberate and measured. The guard's hand instinctively moved to rest on his hip, inches from his holstered baton. The tension in the air was palpable, thick enough to choke on.

Drake's mind raced, searching for the right words, the perfect approach. He'd come too far to be turned away now, but the guard's demeanor suggested that wouldn't be an easy task. Memories of past confrontations flickered through his consciousness – some resolved peacefully, others... not so much.

"Stay calm," he coached himself silently. "There's too much at stake to lose control now."

As the distance between them closed, Drake forced his features into a neutral expression, hoping to mask the desperation churning inside him. The guard's stance widened slightly, a subtle but clear message: he was ready for anything.

Drake's heart pounded in his chest; each beat a reminder of the urgency of his mission. Rachel's face flashed in his mind – a beacon of hope in the swirling chaos of his fractured memories. He had to find her, had to get answers. The fate of not just his family, but potentially countless others across the multiverse, hung in the balance.

With a deep breath, Drake prepared to speak, knowing that his next words could either open doors or slam them shut forever.

9 - 10

"Can I help you?" the guard asked, his tone dripping with thinly veiled hostility. His eyes, cold and calculating, swept over Drake's form, searching for any sign of threat.

Drake's muscles tensed involuntarily, his body reacting to the guard's aggression even as his mind fought for control. He raised his hands slightly, palms out, a universal gesture of peace. The motion felt both necessary and futile, like trying to calm a storm with a whisper.

"I'm looking for someone who works here," Drake said, his voice steady despite the turmoil roiling beneath the surface. "Rachel Summers."

As the name left his lips, Drake scrutinized the guard's face, searching for any flicker of recognition. His heart raced; each beat a silent plea for a positive response. The weight of his quest pressed down on him, threatening to crush him under its magnitude.

In the tense silence that followed, Drake's mind wandered unbidden to the family he'd left behind – or rather, the family that existed in this reality but didn't truly know him. The ache of their absence, even as they lived and breathed in this world, threatened to overwhelm him. He pushed the thought away, focusing on the guard's impassive face.

"Rachel," he repeated internally, clinging to the name like a lifeline. "She's the key to all of this. She has to be here. She has to remember."

The guard's hand remained uncomfortably close to his baton, a silent threat that spoke volumes. Drake fought the urge to glance at it, knowing any sudden movement could escalate the situation. Instead, he held the guard's gaze, willing him to see the desperation, the need for answers that burned within him.

11 - 12

The guard's eyes narrowed, his gaze hardening like ice. "No one by that name works here," he said, each word falling like a hammer blow against Drake's fragile hope.

Drake's heart plummeted, a sickening sensation of freefall overwhelming him. He swallowed hard, fighting to maintain his composure. The weight of his mission, the fate of countless realities, seemed to press down on his shoulders with renewed force.

"Are you sure?" Drake asked, unable to keep a note of desperation from creeping into his voice. He ran a hand through his disheveled hair, a nervous habit he'd never quite shaken. "She's a scientist—mid-forties, maybe older. She's done work on multiverse theory."

As he spoke, memories of Rachel flashed through his mind—fragmented glimpses of her explaining complex equations, her eyes alight with the passion of discovery. The stark contrast between those vibrant recollections and the cold reality before him was jarring.

Drake's gaze darted past the guard to the gleaming institute beyond, its promise of answers now seeming cruelly out of reach. "This is the right place, isn't it?" he pressed, his tone a mixture of hope and mounting frustration.

Internally, Drake's thoughts raced. "It has to be here. She has to be here. Without Rachel, how can I hope to unravel this mess? How can I save them all?"

13 - 14

The guard's stance hardened, his arms crossing over his chest like an impenetrable barrier. His eyes, cold and unyielding, bore into Drake with unwavering certainty. "This is the New Haven Institute of Advanced Research," he declared, his voice carrying a note of finality that sent a chill down Drake's spine. "If she were here, I'd know. But I'm telling you—no Rachel Summers."

Drake's frustration, simmering beneath the surface, finally boiled over. His fists clenched at his sides, knuckles whitening with the strain of holding back his mounting desperation. The world seemed to narrow, the sprawling institute grounds fading into a blur as he focused on the immovable figure before him.

"Look," Drake growled, his voice low and intense, "I don't have time to argue." His mind raced, fragments of memories and half-formed theories colliding in a chaotic maelstrom. Rachel's face, her voice, the weight of the Codex in his hands—all of it felt so real, so vital. How could it all lead to nothing?

"I know she's connected to this place," he insisted, taking a step forward. The guard tensed, but Drake pressed on, his words tumbling out in a rush. "Can you just check the employee directory or something? Call someone inside?"

As he spoke, Drake's gaze darted past the guard, searching for any sign of movement within the institute. A flicker of a lab coat, a glimpse of red hair—anything to confirm that his journey hadn't been in vain. But the building remained impassive, its gleaming surfaces revealing nothing but his own desperate reflection.

"Please," Drake added, the word barely above a whisper. In that moment, he felt the full weight of his mission, the countless lives hanging in the balance. If Rachel wasn't here, if this lead turned out to be another dead end, where else could he turn?

15 - 16

The guard's face hardened, lines etching deeper around his eyes and mouth. "Sir, I've told you everything I know," he said, his voice carrying a note of finality that sent a chill through Drake's core. "Now, if you don't have an appointment or official business here, I'm going to have to ask you to leave."

Drake's hands clenched into fists at his sides, his knuckles turning white with the effort of restraining himself. The urge to lash out, to force his way past this obstacle, surged through him like a tidal wave. He could feel the muscles in his jaw tightening, a vein throbbing at his temple.

"You don't understand," Drake said, his voice strained with the effort of maintaining control. His mind raced, grasping for words that could convey the magnitude of what was at stake. "This is important—life or death. I need to talk to her."

As he spoke, images flashed through his mind: his family, blissfully unaware of the danger that threatened their very existence; the Codex, its pages filled with secrets that could unravel the fabric of reality itself; and Rachel Summers, the elusive key to unlocking it all.

Drake's gaze bore into the guard's, silently pleading for understanding, for any shred of compassion that might crack the man's stern facade. The weight of his quest pressed down on him, each second ticking by feeling like another opportunity slipping through his fingers.

17 - 18

The guard's eyes narrowed, his expression hardening into granite. He took a measured step forward, closing the gap between them. The subtle shift in his posture sent a chill down Drake's spine.

"And you don't understand, sir," the guard growled, his hand coming to rest on the baton at his hip. The casual threat hung in the air between them. "I'm not repeating myself. Turn around and get back in your car before I call the authorities."

Drake's heart hammered against his ribs, a war drum of frustration and desperation. He could feel the situation slipping away, like sand through an hourglass. His gaze darted from the guard's face to his hand on the baton, then back to the impenetrable facade of the research institute looming behind them.

Is this really it? Drake thought, a wave of despair threatening to engulf him. *A dead end, when I'm so close?* The weight of his family's fate pressed down on him, suffocating in its intensity. Linda's worried face flashed through his mind, followed by Harrison's trusting eyes. They were counting on him, even if they didn't know it.

"Look," Drake said, forcing his voice to remain calm despite the storm raging within. "I understand you're just doing your job. But there has to be someone else I can talk to, someone who might know—"

The guard cut him off with a sharp gesture. "This conversation is over. Leave. Now."

Drake took a reluctant step back, his mind racing. *There has to be another way in,* he thought frantically. *Some piece of information I'm missing.* But as he met the guard's unyielding stare, he realized that pushing further would only lead to disaster.

19 - 20

Drake took a deep breath, the crisp autumn air filling his lungs but doing little to calm the tempest of emotions swirling within him. His fingers curled into fists at his sides, nails biting into his palms. The pain grounded him, a sharp counterpoint to the frustration and despair threatening to overwhelm his senses.

"Fine," he said through gritted teeth, the words tasting like ash in his mouth. "I'm leaving."

As he turned away from the guard, Drake's mind raced, fragments of thought colliding like shards of broken glass. *Rachel, where are you?* he wondered, his inner voice tinged with desperation. *This can't be another dead end. Not when the fate of everything hangs in the balance.*

He took a few measured steps towards his car, each one feeling like a betrayal of his purpose. The crunch of gravel under his feet seemed to mock him, a reminder of how far he'd come only to be turned away at the threshold of answers.

Drake paused, casting one last glance over his shoulder at the gleaming institute. "This isn't over," he murmured, too low for the guard to hear. "I'll find you, Rachel. I have to."

With a heavy sigh, he continued his reluctant retreat, the weight of his quest pressing down on his shoulders like an invisible burden. The car awaited him, a symbol of both escape and continued pursuit. As he reached for the door handle, Drake steeled himself for the long road ahead, knowing that somewhere out there, the truth – and Rachel Summers – were waiting to be found.

21 - 22

Drake slid into the driver's seat, the leather creaking beneath him like a whisper of protest. His hands found the steering wheel, gripping it with an intensity that turned his knuckles white. The familiar touch did nothing to quell the storm raging within him.

"Dammit," he hissed, his voice barely audible over the pounding of his heart. His eyes darted to the rearview mirror, catching sight of the guard still watching him with unwavering suspicion.

Was Rachel really not here? The thought gnawed at him, refusing to let go. Drake's mind raced through possibilities, each one more unsettling than the last. *Or is this all part of some elaborate protection scheme?*

He closed his eyes for a moment, trying to center himself. When he opened them again, determination blazed in their depths. "I'm not giving up," he muttered, his jaw clenching. "Not when I'm this close."

Drake's fingers drummed against the steering wheel, a physical manifestation of his inner turmoil. He glanced once more at the imposing structure of the research institute, its gleaming facade now seeming more like a fortress designed to keep secrets locked away.

"What aren't you telling me, Rachel?" he whispered, his voice hoarse with frustration. "And why go to such lengths to hide?"

The questions hung in the air, unanswered, as Drake started the engine. The low rumble seemed to echo his own restlessness, a reminder that his journey was far from over.

23 - 24

Drake's gaze lingered on the research institute, its sleek lines and reflective surfaces now taking on a sinister quality. The afternoon sun glinted off the glass, momentarily blinding him, as if the building itself were trying to repel his scrutiny.

"If she's not here," he muttered to himself, his voice low and gravelly with frustration, "then where the hell is she?"

The question hung in the air, heavy with implications. Drake's fingers tightened on the steering wheel; his knuckles white with tension. His mind raced, replaying every fragment of memory he had of Rachel Summers. Her face, kind but determined, swam before his eyes. The weight of the Codex, the secrets it held, seemed to press down on him.

He glanced at his phone, considering his next move. "There has to be another lead," he murmured, more to himself than anyone else. "Rachel wouldn't just disappear without a trace."

The hum of the idling engine seemed to mock his indecision. Drake's eyes darted back to the institute one last time, searching for any sign, any clue that might have eluded him. But the building remained impassive, its secrets locked behind steel and glass.

25 - 25

Drake inhaled deeply, the scent of leather and faint car exhaust grounding him in the present. He turned the key, the engine's roar matching his internal turmoil.

"I'm not letting this go," he said aloud, his voice firm despite the tremor of uncertainty. "There's too much at stake."

As he pulled away from the curb, Drake's mind raced with possibilities. The familiar ache of guilt and responsibility settled in his chest, a constant companion since he'd found himself in this altered reality.

"Think, Drake," he muttered, eyes flicking to the rearview mirror. The institute receded, but its presence loomed large in his thoughts. "What would the old you do? What am I missing?"

He merged onto the highway, the rhythmic thrum of tires on asphalt a backdrop to his swirling thoughts. The afternoon sun cast long shadows across the road, reminding him of the time slipping away.

"Rachel's connected to this place somehow," Drake reasoned, his lawyer's mind latching onto the fragments of information he possessed. "Even if she's not here now, there must be a trail."

He drummed his fingers on the steering wheel, a habit from his courtroom days when piecing together a case. The action stirred something in his memory – a flash of Rachel's face, her eyes alight with purpose as she spoke of the multiverse.

"The Codex," Drake breathed, a spark of realization cutting through his frustration. "It's not just about where Rachel is now. It's about where she's been – and when."

The implications of this thought sent a shiver down his spine. If Rachel had access to multiverse travel, the search for her just became infinitely more complex – and dangerous.

Drake's determination solidified; his jaw set in a hard line. "I'm not giving up," he affirmed, his voice steady despite the enormity of the task ahead. "Not when the truth is so close. Not when my family's future hangs in the balance."

As the miles rolled by, Drake's mind churned with plans and possibilities, each turn of the wheels bringing him closer to unraveling the mystery that had upended his life. The road stretched out before him, an uncertain path leading to an even more uncertain future.

Fired for Seeking the Truth

1 -2   The sunlight glinted off the New Haven Institute's pristine facade, mocking Drake Miller's mounting frustration as Drake pulled back into the parking lot. He gripped the steering wheel, knuckles whitening, as he stared at the gleaming building that seemed to taunt him with its secrets. The security guard's evasive answers echoed in his mind, each word a reminder of how close yet far he was from the truth.

Drake's jaw clenched. "There has to be something I'm missing," he muttered, his brown eyes scanning the institute's grounds for any sign of movement, any clue that might lead him to Rachel Summers. The weight of his mission pressed down on him, a constant reminder of the lives at stake—not just in this world, but in countless others.

He closed his eyes, trying to focus. The faces of his family flashed before him; their smiles tinged with an eerie unfamiliarity that still made his heart ache. "I can't fail them again," he whispered, the words barely audible even in the silence of his car.

As Drake reached for the ignition, a soft knock on the window startled him. His heart raced, years of legal training kicking in as he assessed the situation in a split second. Outside stood a man—wiry and worn, his lab coat a stark contrast to the deep lines etched into his face.

Drake's mind raced. Could this be the break he needed? Or was it another dead end, another false hope in a world that seemed determined to keep its secrets? He hesitated, his hand hovering over the window control, weighing the risks against the desperate need for answers that had driven him to this point.

The stranger's eyes met his, and in them, Drake saw a reflection of his own weariness, his own desperation. It was a look he recognized all too well—the look of someone carrying a burden too heavy to bear alone.

With a deep breath, Drake made his decision. Whatever came next, he knew he had to face it. For his family, for Rachel Summers, and for all the worlds teetering on the brink of oblivion. He steeled himself, ready to confront whatever truths—or dangers—this encounter might bring.

3 - 4

Drake rolled down the window cautiously, the soft whir of the mechanism cutting through the tense silence. "Can I help you?" he asked, his voice low and measured, betraying none of the turmoil churning within him.

The man's eyes darted nervously, scanning the parking lot as if expecting shadows to leap from every corner. Drake recognized that look—the paranoia of someone who knew too much, who had seen things they couldn't unsee. It was a feeling he'd become intimately familiar with since his accident, since the world had fractured around him into a kaleidoscope of possibilities and dangers.

Leaning closer, the stranger's breath fogged the glass as he whispered, "You're looking for Rachel Summers, aren't you?"

The name hung in the air between them, charged with an electric intensity that made Drake's skin prickle. His mind raced, memories of Rachel—brilliant, determined, misunderstood Rachel—flooding back. He saw her in flashes bent over complex equations, eyes alight with the fervor of discovery, then later, wild-eyed and desperate as she spoke of worlds beyond their own.

Drake's fingers tightened on the steering wheel; his knuckles white with tension. How much did this man know? And more importantly, could he be trusted? In a reality where nothing was as it seemed, where even his own family walked through life oblivious to the bonds they once shared, caution was more than prudence—it was survival.

5 - 6

Drake's pulse quickened; each beat a reminder of the precarious tightrope he walked between worlds. He swallowed hard, his throat dry as sandpaper, before responding with a careful neutrality that belied the storm of emotions within.

"Who's asking?" Drake's voice was low, edged with a wariness born of too many betrayals.

The stranger's lips curved into a faint smile, but it was a brittle thing, never reaching his eyes. Those remained haunted, carrying the weight of secrets Drake could only imagine.

"I'm Dr. Jonathan Evans," the man said, his gaze flicking once more to the pristine facade of the New Haven Institute looming behind them. "I work here—or, well, I used to work with Rachel. I overheard your conversation with the guard."

Drake's mind raced, piecing together fragments of a puzzle he'd been struggling with since awakening in this distorted version of reality. Rachel Summers—the key to understanding, perhaps even fixing, the fractures in the multiverse. And now, standing before him was someone who claimed to know her.

He studied Evans, noting the deep lines etched into his face, the slight tremor in his hands. This was a man carrying a burden, one that seemed to have aged him beyond his years. Drake recognized that weight; he carried a similar one himself.

"Rachel," Drake breathed, the name both a question and a lifeline. "You knew her work?"

7 - 8

Drake's fingers tightened on the car door handle, the cool metal grounding him in this moment of unexpected revelation. With a swift, decisive movement, he stepped out of the vehicle, his towering frame casting a long shadow across the sunbaked asphalt.

"You know Rachel?" Drake asked, his voice a mixture of hope and trepidation. The name felt both foreign and achingly familiar on his tongue, a reminder of the fractured reality he now inhabited.

Evans' expression darkened, the lines on his face deepening like canyons carved by time and sorrow. He nodded slowly, his gaze distant as if seeing beyond the present moment. "I did," he replied, his voice barely above a whisper. "But she doesn't work here anymore."

The finality in Evans' tone sent a chill down Drake's spine. His mind raced, grappling with the implications. Rachel Summers, the brilliant scientist who might have held the key to unraveling the mystery of his displaced existence, was gone.

Drake swallowed hard, fighting back the wave of disappointment threatening to engulf him. He'd come so close, only to have his lead slip away like sand through his fingers. But he couldn't give up now, not when the fate of multiple realities hung in the balance.

"What happened to her?" Drake asked, his voice low and urgent. He leaned in closer to Evans, searching the older man's face for any clue, any fragment of information that might point him in the right direction.

9 - 10

Drake crossed his arms, his brow furrowing as he struggled to maintain composure. The weight of his quest pressed down on him, a constant reminder of the lives at stake—his family, his own fractured existence, and the very fabric of reality itself.

"The guard said she doesn't work here, but he didn't say why," Drake pressed, his voice tinged with a mixture of frustration and desperation. "What happened to her?"

Evans hesitated, his eyes darting nervously towards the gleaming institute behind them. The sunlight glinted off the windows, momentarily blinding Drake. In that flash of brightness, he caught a glimpse of another world—a cityscape bathed in crimson light—before it vanished, leaving him disoriented.

"Rachel's fall from grace wasn't sudden," Evans finally said, his voice barely above a whisper. "It was a slow descent into... well, what the board called madness."

Drake's heart raced, his palms growing clammy. He remembered his own struggles with reality, the disbelief he'd faced. "Madness?" he echoed, the word tasting bitter on his tongue.

Evans nodded grimly. "Her theories became increasingly... unconventional. She spoke of parallel worlds, of realities bleeding into one another. The board couldn't—or wouldn't—understand."

Drake's mind reeled. Rachel's experiences mirrored his own, confirming his suspicions and deepening the mystery. He opened his mouth to press further, but the words caught in his throat as a sharp pain lanced through his skull, bringing with it a fleeting vision of Rachel—her red hair wild, her eyes blazing with determination as she scribbled complex equations on a whiteboard.

As the vision faded, Drake steadied himself against his car, the cool metal grounding him in the present. He knew he was on the right path, but the road ahead seemed more treacherous than ever.

11 - 12

Evans sighed, his shoulders slumping slightly as he leaned against the car. "Rachel was brilliant—one of the best minds we had here. She was working on groundbreaking research into multiverse theory. At first, everyone was excited. She was making connections no one else could see, pushing boundaries we didn't even know existed."

Drake's breath caught in his throat, a mixture of hope and trepidation swirling in his chest. He'd been chasing shadows for so long, and now, finally, a glimmer of light. His fingers twitched, itching to reach out and grasp this thread of information.

"She saw what I've seen," Drake thought, his mind racing with possibilities. The weight of his quest pressed down on him, the faces of his family—strangers in this world—flashing before his eyes.

He swallowed hard, forcing his voice to remain steady. "What changed?" Drake asked, studying Evans' weary face. The lines etched deep around the scientist's eyes spoke of sleepless nights and heavy burdens.

As he waited for Evans to respond, Drake's gaze drifted back to the institute. Its gleaming facade now seemed to mock him, a fortress of secrets he desperately needed to breach. The sun's reflection off the windows momentarily dazzled him, and for a split second, he thought he saw a shimmering portal—a gateway to another world—before it vanished, leaving him questioning his own sanity.

13 - 14

Evans' gaze dropped to the ground, his shoulders sagging under an invisible weight. The scientist's fingers fidgeted with the hem of his lab coat, a nervous habit that spoke volumes. Drake leaned in, every muscle in his body taut with anticipation.

"Her experiments started failing," Evans muttered, his voice barely above a whisper. "The data she presented didn't make sense—or rather, it made too much sense." He paused, swallowing hard. "It suggested things that were impossible. Parallel worlds, colliding timelines, people crossing between realities..."

Drake's breath hitched, a jolt of recognition surging through him. The words echoed in his mind, painfully familiar. He could almost see the swirling vortex of realities he'd witnessed, feel the gut-wrenching sensation of being torn between worlds.

"And no one believed her," Drake breathed, his voice thick with understanding and a hint of bitterness. The words hung in the air between them, heavy with implication.

As he spoke, Drake's fingers unconsciously traced the outline of the scar on his temple—a physical reminder of his journey across realities. His mind raced, connecting dots that had eluded him for so long. Rachel Summers wasn't just a scientist; she was a kindred spirit, someone who had glimpsed the truth he'd been desperately trying to prove.

The wind picked up, rustling the leaves of nearby trees. To Drake, it sounded like whispers from another world, calling him back to his mission. He clenched his fists, steeling himself for the challenges ahead. Rachel's path had led to ridicule and dismissal, but he couldn't—wouldn't—let that stop him. There was too much at stake.

15 - 16

Evans nodded grimly, his weathered face a map of deep-set lines and shadows. "At first, the institute supported her," he said, his voice barely above a whisper. "But as her experiments grew more... erratic, the board lost patience." He paused, glancing over his shoulder as if the very walls of the institute might be listening. "Her theories became more outlandish, and when she started claiming she had 'seen' these other worlds, they decided she was a liability."

Drake's heart raced, a mixture of excitement and dread coursing through his veins. He leaned in closer, his eyes searching Evans' face for any hint of deception. "What do you mean, 'seen' them?" he asked, his voice low and urgent.

As he waited for Evans' response, Drake's mind whirled with possibilities. Had Rachel truly witnessed what he had experienced? The thought both thrilled and terrified him. If she had seen the other worlds, maybe she held the key to understanding his own fractured reality.

Evans hesitated, his gaze darting nervously between Drake and the looming facade of the institute. The weight of unspoken truths hung heavy in the air between them. Drake could almost feel the tendrils of a vast, hidden knowledge brushing against the edges of his consciousness, tantalizing and just out of reach.

17 - 18

Evans took a deep breath, his eyes clouding with a mixture of awe and fear. "Rachel said her experiments opened... windows," he began, his voice quivering slightly. "That she could look into other realities. She described them in vivid detail—burning cities, endless forests, sterile machines. She called them the Red World, the Green World, and the Blue World."

As Evans spoke, Drake's vision swam, memories flooding back in a torrent of sensory overload. The acrid smell of smoke from the burning metropolis, the earthy dampness of the infinite forest, the cold sterility of the machine world—all of it crashed over him like a tidal wave.

His chest tightened, breath catching in his throat. "She was telling the truth," Drake whispered, more to himself than to Evans. His hands trembled as he gripped the car door, knuckles turning white with the effort to steady himself.

The weight of confirmation settled on Drake's shoulders, heavy and unyielding. He'd known, deep down, that his experiences were real, but hearing it from someone else—someone connected to Rachel—made it undeniable. The worlds he'd glimpsed, the realities he'd touched, they weren't fever dreams or delusions. They were real, tangible, and potentially within reach.

Drake's mind raced, piecing together the implications. If Rachel had found a way to see these worlds, could she have found a way to travel between them? And if she had, where was she now? The questions multiplied, each one carrying with it the promise of answers and the threat of even greater mysteries.

19 - 20

Evans's eyes narrowed, his initial skepticism morphing into a mix of curiosity and concern. "You know about these worlds?" he asked, his voice barely above a whisper.

Drake's gaze snapped back to Evans, the older man's weathered face swimming into focus. He hesitated, weighing the risks of revealing too much against the potential of gaining an ally. The memory of the burning city flashed behind his eyes, acrid smoke seeming to fill his nostrils even now.

"I've... seen them too," Drake admitted, his voice hoarse. He ran a hand through his disheveled hair, a nervous habit he'd never quite shaken. "I don't know how, but I have."

The confession hung in the air between them, heavy with implication. Drake's mind raced, trying to anticipate Evans's reaction. Would he believe him? Or would he, like the board had with Rachel, dismiss it as the ravings of a madman?

Drake's fingers twitched, itching to reach for the car door handle, to flee from this conversation and the truths it threatened to unveil. But he held his ground, muscles tense, ready for whatever came next. He'd come too far, sacrificed too much, to back down now.

21 - 22

Evans studied him for a moment, his expression shifting from skepticism to something softer, more pitying. The lines around his eyes deepened as he sighed, his shoulders sagging under the weight of unspoken burdens.

"Then you'll understand," Evans said, his voice tinged with a mixture of regret and resignation, "why the board thought she was losing her mind."

Drake's stomach clenched, a cold dread seeping through his veins. He'd known, deep down, that Rachel's fate couldn't have been pleasant, but hearing it confirmed made it painfully real.

Evans continued, each word falling like a hammer blow. "They fired her, citing failed experiments and delusions. She was put on medical leave, and we haven't heard from her since."

Drake's mind reeled, trying to process the implications. Rachel, brilliant and dedicated Rachel, cast aside like a faulty piece of equipment. The injustice of it burned in his chest, mingling with a growing sense of desperation.

"But she wasn't delusional," Drake insisted, his voice low and intense. "She saw what I've seen. What we've both seen." He gestured between them, a frantic energy building in his movements.

Evans's eyes darted nervously towards the institute, as if afraid someone might overhear. "Maybe so," he conceded, "but that doesn't change what happened. Rachel's gone, Mister. And I'm not sure anyone knows where to find her."

The words hit Drake like a physical blow. Rachel was his best hope, his only link to understanding the chaos that had become his life. Without her...

He clenched his fists, nails digging into his palms. "There has to be something," he pressed, fighting to keep the desperation from his voice. "Some lead, some clue. Anything."

23 - 24

Drake felt a sinking feeling in his chest, a cold weight that seemed to pull at his very core. The bustling parking lot faded away, leaving only the stark reality of Evans's words echoing in his mind. He swallowed hard, his throat tight with unspoken fear.

"You don't know where she went?" Drake asked, his voice barely above a whisper. He searched Evans's face, desperately hoping for a flicker of hope, a hint of knowledge withheld.

Evans shook his head, his weathered features etched with a mixture of regret and resignation. "She vanished after she was dismissed," he said, his gaze drifting towards the gleaming institute building. "She told a few of us she needed time to 'find the answers on her own.'" He paused, his shoulders sagging slightly. "After that, nothing. No calls, no emails—nothing."

Drake's mind raced, grappling with the implications. Rachel, his one link to understanding the impossible, had simply... disappeared. The weight of his own isolation pressed down on him, threatening to crush what little hope remained.

"But surely someone must have—" Drake began, only to be cut off by a sharp look from Evans.

"Listen," Evans said, his voice low and urgent, "you have to understand. Rachel wasn't just fired. She was erased. The institute wanted her gone, and they made it happen."

Drake's fists clenched at his sides, a familiar anger rising within him. It was the same fury he'd felt when he'd realized his family didn't remember him, when he'd first glimpsed the cracks in this false reality. He took a deep breath, forcing himself to focus.

"I need to find her," Drake said, his voice steady despite the turmoil within. "She's the only one who can help me make sense of... all of this." He gestured vaguely, encompassing not just the institute, but the entire world around them.

Evans studied him for a long moment, his expression unreadable. Drake could almost see the internal debate playing out behind the older man's eyes.

25 - 26

Drake pressed on; his voice tinged with desperation. "There must be something. A friend, a colleague, someone she might have trusted."

The words hung in the air between them, heavy with unspoken implications. Drake's mind raced, conjuring images of Rachel—brilliant, isolated, misunderstood. He saw himself in her, a kindred spirit lost in a world that no longer made sense.

Evans sighed, his shoulders slumping further. The lines on his face seemed to deepen as he spoke. "Rachel was... different. Brilliant, yes, but also guarded. She kept to herself, even before things started to unravel."

Drake's heart sank, but he refused to give up. He leaned in, his eyes searching Evans' face for any hint of hope. "But surely there must have been someone?"

Evans shrugged helplessly, his gaze dropping to the ground. "I wish I could tell you otherwise, but Rachel was a private person. She didn't share much about her personal life. If she wanted to disappear, she could've done it easily."

The finality in Evans' tone sent a chill through Drake. He closed his eyes, fighting back the wave of frustration threatening to overwhelm him. In his mind's eye, he saw Rachel—a solitary figure surrounded by equations and impossible theories, slowly fading from view as the world turned its back on her.

When Drake opened his eyes again, he found Evans watching him with a mixture of pity and curiosity. The silence between them stretched, filled with unasked questions and unspoken fears.

27 - 28

Drake clenched his fists, frustration bubbling to the surface. The cool metal of his wedding ring pressed against his palm, a stark reminder of what he stood to lose. "She's the only one who can help me," he said, his voice tight with desperation. "There has to be a way to find her."

The words hung in the air, heavy with the weight of Drake's unspoken fears. He could feel the seconds ticking away, each moment bringing him closer to a future he couldn't bear to face. In his mind, he saw his wife and son, their faces blurred and fading like a photograph left too long in the sun.

Evans studied Drake's face, his brow furrowing as if wrestling with an internal debate. The older man's shoulders sagged, and he let out a long, weary sigh. "I shouldn't be doing this," he muttered, more to himself than to Drake.

Drake held his breath, hope and dread warring in his chest as Evans reached into his coat pocket. The scientist's weathered hands trembled slightly as he pulled out a folded piece of paper.

"This is all I've got," Evans said, his voice barely above a whisper as he handed the paper to Drake. The exchange felt clandestine, as if they were trading state secrets rather than a scrap of information about a disgraced researcher.

As Drake's fingers closed around the paper, he felt a spark of possibility ignite within him. It was fragile, this tiny flame of hope, but it was all he had to light his way through the darkness that threatened to engulf him.

29 - 30

With hands that threatened to betray his inner turmoil, Drake carefully unfolded the paper. The creases were deep, as if it had been folded and refolded countless times, a secret kept close and protected. His eyes fell upon a string of characters scrawled in faded ink, the handwriting hurried and almost illegible.

"What's this?" Drake asked, his voice a mixture of confusion and desperate hope. He traced the letters with his fingertip, as if touch alone could reveal their significance.

Evans leaned in, his voice low and urgent. "She used that email to send us updates before the board shut her down," he explained, his eyes darting nervously towards the institute's imposing facade. "It's inactive now, but maybe it'll lead you to something."

Drake's mind raced, possibilities unfurling like a tapestry of interconnected threads. An email address – such a small thing, and yet it felt like a lifeline thrown into the chaotic sea of his quest. His fingers tightened on the paper, crinkling its edges.

"Inactive," Drake murmured, more to himself than to Evans. The word tasted bitter on his tongue, a reminder of how easily connections could be severed, lives disrupted. He thought of his own family, of the life he'd lost and found again in this strange, altered reality. Would this tenuous link to Rachel Summers prove just as ephemeral?

31 - 32

Drake nodded, tucking the paper into his pocket with a carefulness that belied its potential importance. "Thank you," he said, his voice low and gravelly, weighted with gratitude and the burden of what lay ahead.

As he spoke, Drake's hand lingered over the pocket, feeling the slight crinkle of the paper through the fabric. It was a tangible connection to Rachel, to answers, to hope – however faint. His jaw clenched, a muscle twitching beneath the skin as he fought to maintain his composure.

Evans straightened, his lab coat rustling softly in the breeze. His eyes darted towards the institute, a flicker of fear crossing his weathered features. When he turned back to Drake, his expression was grave, etched with lines of worry and warning.

"I've told you everything I know," Evans said, his voice barely above a whisper. He leaned in closer, the scent of antiseptic and coffee on his breath. "Be careful, sir. Rachel's work... it wasn't just controversial. It scared people."

Drake's breath caught in his throat. The weight of Evans' words settled over him like a shroud, cold and oppressive. He thought of Rachel, brilliant and determined, pushing against the boundaries of reality itself. What forces had she unleashed? What truths had she uncovered that could instill such fear?

Evans continued, his words tinged with a mix of awe and trepidation. "If you're following her path, you're likely to attract the same kind of attention."

The air around them seemed to thicken, charged with unspoken dangers. Drake's mind raced, imagining shadowy figures and clandestine organizations, all seeking to suppress the truths Rachel had discovered. He thought of his family, of the precious, fragile reality he'd fought so hard to protect. Was he putting them at risk by pursuing this?

But even as doubt gnawed at him, Drake felt a surge of resolve. He'd come too far, seen too much to turn back now. Whatever attention he might attract, whatever dangers lay ahead, he had to see this through – for Rachel, for his family, for the truth that lay hidden behind the veil of reality.

33 - 34

"I've already got attention," Drake muttered, more to himself than to Evans. His voice was low, tinged with a weariness that seemed to seep from his very bones. The weight of his past, of the lives he'd lived and lost, pressed down on him like a physical force.

Evans' eyes widened slightly, a flicker of concern – or was it fear? – crossing his weathered features. He opened his mouth as if to speak but seemed to think better of it. Instead, he gave Drake one last, long look, his gaze searching and heavy with unspoken questions.

Drake met his eyes, unflinching. In that moment, he felt the full weight of his journey, the impossible task that lay before him. The silence between them stretched, taut with unspoken understanding.

Then, without another word, Evans turned and walked briskly back toward the institute. Drake watched as the older man's lab coat fluttered in the breeze, a stark white against the gleaming facade of the building. With each step, Evans seemed to shrink, diminishing until he was swallowed by the yawning entrance of the institute, disappearing inside.

Left alone in the parking lot, Drake felt a chill that had nothing to do with the temperature. The enormity of his quest pressed in on him from all sides, threatening to overwhelm him. Yet beneath the fear and uncertainty, a fierce determination burned. He would find Rachel, unravel the mysteries of the multiverse, and somehow, someway, make things right.

35 - 36

Drake climbed back into his car, the leather seat creaking beneath him. His fingers curled around the steering wheel, knuckles whitening as he gripped it tightly. The slip of paper with Rachel's old email address felt impossibly light in his other hand, yet it carried the weight of his entire world.

He stared at the faded ink, tracing the loops and curves of the handwriting. "It isn't much," he murmured, his voice rough with emotion, "but it's a start."

The car's interior seemed to shrink around him, amplifying the thunderous beating of his heart. Drake closed his eyes, allowing himself a moment of vulnerability that he rarely showed to others. The faces of his family flashed behind his eyelids – his wife's smile, his son's laugh. Both so close, yet impossibly far away in this twisted version of reality.

"I'm sorry," he whispered, his words barely audible even in the silence of the car. "I'll make this right. I have to."

Opening his eyes, Drake carefully folded the paper and tucked it into his pocket. His gaze fell on his reflection in the rearview mirror, noting the deep lines of worry etched into his face. He hardly recognized himself anymore.

"You've made a mess of things, Miller," he said to his reflection, a hint of his old, sardonic humor creeping into his voice. "Time to clean it up."

With a deep breath, Drake started the engine. The car hummed to life beneath him, a reminder that despite everything, the world kept turning. As he pulled out of the parking lot, leaving the imposing silhouette of the New Haven Institute behind, a mix of dread and determination settled in his gut.

"Rachel Summers," he muttered, tasting the name on his tongue. "Wherever you are, whatever you've discovered... I'm coming. And God help anyone who tries to stop me."

37 - 38

Drake's hands tightened on the steering wheel as he navigated the winding roads away from the institute. The pristine façade of the building gradually shrank in his rearview mirror, its gleaming surfaces now seeming less like a beacon of scientific progress and more like a polished mask concealing dark secrets.

He glanced back one final time, the sunlight glinting off the institute's windows in a way that made them look like eyes – watchful, calculating, and utterly devoid of warmth. The pit in his stomach deepened as he realized how much the place had changed in his perception over the course of a single conversation.

"A fortress," Drake murmured, his voice barely audible over the hum of the engine. "Not guarding knowledge but burying it."

The weight of the folded paper in his pocket seemed to grow heavier with each passing moment. It was a tenuous lead at best, but it was all he had. His mind raced with possibilities, trying to piece together the fragments of information he'd gathered.

"Rachel Summers," he said softly, tasting the name on his tongue. The woman he'd never met but whose fate seemed inexorably intertwined with his own. "What did you see that scared them so much? What truths did you uncover?"

Drake's grip on the wheel tightened, his knuckles whitening. "I'm going to find you," he vowed, his voice low and intense. "One way or another. And together, we'll unravel this mess – even if it means tearing apart the very fabric of reality to do it."

As he drove on, the shadows of the trees lining the road seemed to stretch towards him, like grasping fingers trying to pull him back. But Drake pressed on, his jaw set with determination. The road ahead was uncertain, fraught with danger and the unknown, but he had no choice but to follow it to its end.

Closing the Net

1-2   Detective Holly Kierstead's stomach churned as she stood at the edge of the dimly lit basement, the stench of death and decay assaulting her senses. The funhouse's once-cheerful atmosphere had been perverted into a grotesque tableau of horror. Beside her, Franklin Bird's weathered face looked ashen as he flipped through his notepad, his hands trembling ever so slightly.

Seven bodies. Seven witnesses from the Parker deposition. The grim reality of what they'd uncovered weighed heavily on Holly's shoulders.

"Jesus," Bird muttered, his voice barely above a whisper. "I've never seen anything like this in all my years on the force."

Holly's sharp eyes scanned the room, taking in every gruesome detail. Her analytical mind was already piecing together the puzzle, even as her heart raced with a mix of adrenaline and dread.

"The precision," she said, her tone measured despite the turmoil within. "Look at how they're arranged. This wasn't some random act of violence."

Bird's skeptical gaze met hers. "You thinking what I'm thinking?"

Holly nodded, her long black hair swaying with the movement. "Someone wanted to send a message. And they wanted it found."

As she spoke, Holly couldn't shake the feeling that they were standing on the precipice of something far larger and more sinister than a typical murder case. The multiverse theories Drake had spouted seemed less fantastical with each passing moment.

"We need to secure the scene," Bird said, his years of experience evident in his calm demeanor. "Get forensics down here ASAP."

Holly's mind raced, considering the implications. If Drake was right about alternate realities, could this gruesome scene be connected to those other worlds? She pushed the thought aside, focusing on the immediate task at hand.

"Agreed," she replied, her voice steady despite the chaos of her thoughts. "And we need to track down Drake Miller. He's at the center of this somehow, I can feel it."

As they turned to leave the basement, Holly cast one last glance at the bodies. In that moment, she silently vowed to uncover the truth, no matter where it led her – across this world or any other.

3 - 4

Holly's sharp eyes scanned the chaotic scene, her trained gaze taking in every detail. Forensic technicians in white suits moved methodically through the basement, their cameras flashing in the dim light. The air was thick with tension and the acrid smell of death.

"Look at the positioning, Bird," Holly said, her voice low and measured. She gestured towards the bodies, careful not to disturb the crime scene. "It's too precise. Too... intentional."

Franklin Bird furrowed his brow, his skepticism evident in the set of his jaw. "What are you seeing, Kierstead?"

Holly took a step closer to the edge of the taped-off area, her mind racing. "The way they're laid out. It's almost... ritualistic. And look at their hands."

As she spoke, Holly's thoughts drifted to Drake's wild theories about alternate realities. She pushed the idea aside, focusing on the concrete evidence before her. Yet, a nagging feeling persisted that there was more to this case than met the eye.

"I'm telling you, Bird," she said, her voice steady but intense, "this isn't random. This was methodical. Deliberate."

Bird's eyes narrowed as he surveyed the scene again. "You think it's connected to the Parker case?"

Holly nodded, her posture tense. "It has to be. Seven witnesses, all arranged like this? Someone's sending a message."

As the words left her mouth, Holly felt a chill run down her spine. Whatever they had stumbled upon, she knew it was only the beginning of a much darker mystery.

5 - 6

Bird closed his notepad with a soft snap, glancing at Holly with a mixture of concern and apprehension. "You're thinking Drake Miller," he said, his voice low and gravelly.

Holly's arms crossed instinctively, her gaze drawn to the far corner of the basement where a crudely painted green dragon symbol loomed on the wall. The sight of it made her stomach churn, a visceral reaction to the mounting evidence before her.

"Think about it," she said, her voice tight with barely contained frustration. "He's been acting erratic for weeks now. We have footage of him alone at the amusement park the night of his so-called 'attack.'"

As she spoke, Holly's mind raced through the timeline they'd pieced together. The disappearances, Drake's increasingly bizarre behavior, the inconsistencies in his story. It all pointed to a troubling conclusion.

"And now we know he's been seen in this area multiple times over the past few weeks," she continued, her eyes never leaving the dragon symbol. "The same timeframe these witnesses started disappearing."

Holly felt a heaviness settle in her chest. She'd wanted to believe Drake, to find some explanation for his outlandish claims. But the evidence was mounting, and her instincts as a detective were screaming at her to follow the facts.

"I don't want to believe it either, Bird," she said softly, finally turning to meet her partner's gaze. "But we can't ignore what's right in front of us."

7 - 8

Bird's frown deepened, etching new lines into his weathered face. He shifted his weight, the floorboards creaking beneath him, a sound that echoed ominously in the dank basement. "But attacking himself?" he asked, his voice hesitant, tinged with disbelief. "Creating this whole story about a disfigured man and loops? That's... a lot, even for someone desperate."

Holly felt a chill run down her spine, not from the cold of the basement, but from the weight of her own suspicions. She turned to face Bird, her eyes glinting with resolute determination in the dim light. The musty air seemed to thicken around them as she spoke.

"Not if you're trying to cover your tracks," she countered, her voice low but firm. Her mind raced, connecting dots that had been scattered across their investigation. "What if the entire thing—his manic episode, the burns, the head injury—was staged?"

She paused, letting the implications of her words hang in the air. The silence was punctuated only by the distant hum of forensic equipment and the muffled voices of officers above. Holly's heart pounded in her chest as she voiced the theory that had been gnawing at her.

"What if he's working for NovaTech?"

As she said it aloud, Holly felt a mix of dread and certainty settle in her gut. It was a horrifying thought, but one that explained so much. She watched Bird's face, noting the flicker of shock in his eyes, the tightening of his jaw.

'How deep does this go?' she wondered, her mind already racing ahead to the next steps of their investigation. 'And how many more lives are at stake if we're right?'

9 - 10

Bird's eyebrow arched, his weathered face a mixture of disbelief and dawning realization. "NovaTech? The company Parker's suing?" His voice carried a note of caution, but Holly could see the gears turning behind his eyes.

She began to pace, her footsteps echoing in the dank basement. The green dragon symbol on the far wall seemed to mock her, its crude lines a stark reminder of the brutality they'd uncovered. Holly's mind raced, piecing together the puzzle that had eluded them for so long.

"Think about it," she said, her voice barely above a whisper. The weight of her theory pressed down on her, making each word feel like a struggle. "NovaTech has everything to lose if this case goes to court. The evidence Parker has could ruin them."

She paused, her eyes meeting Bird's. The seasoned detective's skepticism was still evident, but there was a glimmer of something else now—a grudging acknowledgment that her theory held water.

Holly continued, her words gaining momentum. "If NovaTech wanted to stop this, they'd need someone close to the witnesses. Someone who could earn their trust—and then eliminate them."

The implications of her words hung heavy in the air. Holly's stomach churned as she considered the depths of betrayal and desperation such a plan would require. She thought of Drake, of his family, of the tangled web of lies and violence that seemed to ensnare them all.

'How far would someone go to protect everything they have?' she wondered, a chill running down her spine. 'And how do we stop them before it's too late?'

11 - 12

Bird's brow furrowed, his weathered face a canvas of doubt and concern. He shifted his weight, the floorboards creaking beneath him like a hesitant protest. "Drake's a lawyer, not a hitman," he said, his deep voice tinged with skepticism.

Holly felt a surge of frustration course through her veins. She stopped her restless pacing, pivoting sharply to face her partner. Her eyes locked onto Bird's, fierce and unyielding. "He's also a father," she countered, her voice sharp enough to cut through the musty air of the basement.

The dim light cast long shadows across Holly's face, accentuating the determination etched into every line. She drew in a deep breath, the scent of decay and secrets filling her lungs. "What if they threatened his family?" she pressed on, her mind racing ahead of her words. "What if they told him he had no choice?"

As she spoke, Holly's thoughts turned to Drake's frantic behavior, his paranoid ramblings about keeping his wife and son safe. The pieces were falling into place, forming a picture as chilling as it was plausible. "That would explain why he's so obsessed with keeping his wife and son safe," she concluded, her voice softening slightly with the weight of realization.

Bird's skepticism wavered, uncertainty creeping into his expression. Holly could almost see the gears turning in his mind, reevaluating every interaction they'd had with Drake. She felt a pang of sympathy for her partner, knowing how difficult it was to reconcile the image of a desperate father with that of a potential killer.

'How many lines would I cross to protect the ones I love?' Holly wondered, a knot forming in her stomach. The question hung in the air, unspoken but palpable, as she and Bird stood in silent contemplation of the dark possibilities before them.

13 - 14

Bird ran a hand down his face, his weathered fingers tracing the deep lines etched by years of grim cases. The dim light of the basement cast long shadows across his features, accentuating the weariness in his eyes. "That's a hell of a theory, Holly," he muttered, his voice a low rumble that seemed to echo the unease churning in his gut. "But we don't have proof."

Holly's gaze swept across the macabre scene before them, the air heavy with the weight of lives cut short. Her heart raced, each beat a reminder of the urgency that thrummed through her veins. With a deliberate gesture, she motioned toward the bodies strewn about the room, each one a silent testament to the brutality that had unfolded here.

"This is proof," she declared, her voice steady despite the tremor of emotion she fought to suppress. The sight of the victims, once vibrant individuals now reduced to cold evidence, sent a chill down her spine. "Seven dead witnesses. And Drake's name keeps coming up. We can't ignore that."

As she spoke, Holly's mind raced through the connections, the seemingly disparate threads weaving together into a tapestry of deceit and desperation. She couldn't shake the image of Drake's haunted eyes, the frantic energy that seemed to consume him. 'What drives a man to such extremes?' she wondered, a mixture of pity and revulsion coiling in her chest.

Bird shifted uncomfortably beside her, his skepticism wavering in the face of the grim reality before them. Holly could sense his internal struggle, the battle between his cautious nature and the mounting evidence. She understood his hesitation; after all, accusing a colleague of multiple murders was no small matter.

"I know it's hard to swallow, Bird," Holly said softly, her tone gentler now. "But we have to follow where the evidence leads us, no matter how ugly the truth might be."

15 - 16

Holly's hand moved to her phone, her fingers hesitating for a fraction of a second before gripping it tightly. The weight of her decision pressed down upon her, a burden as tangible as the stench of decay that still clung to her nostrils. She drew in a deep breath, steeling herself for what needed to be done.

"This ends now," she murmured, more to herself than to Bird. With practiced efficiency, she dialed dispatch, her eyes never leaving the grotesque tableau before her. Each ring seemed to echo in the cavernous basement, a countdown to a point of no return.

"This is Detective Kierstead," Holly spoke into the phone, her voice carrying a resolve that belied the turmoil within. "I need an APB put out on Drake Miller. Suspected connection to the Parker deposition witness murders." She paused, the image of Drake's muscular frame and troubled expression flashing through her mind. "Approach with caution—he may be armed."

As she ended the call, Holly felt a peculiar mixture of relief and dread wash over her. She turned to Bird, noting the conflicted look on his face. "It had to be done," she said, her tone softer now, tinged with a sadness that surprised even her. "If we're right about this, God knows how many more lives are at stake."

Bird nodded solemnly, his usual skepticism momentarily set aside in the face of the gravity of their situation. Holly's gaze drifted back to the green dragon symbol on the wall, its crude lines seeming to mock her with their implications. She couldn't help but wonder what dark path had led Drake to this point, what pressures had twisted a once-respected colleague into a suspected murderer.

"What now?" Bird asked, breaking the heavy silence that had settled between them.

Holly's eyes hardened, her resolve strengthening. "Now," she said, "we find Drake before he can hurt anyone else—or before someone hurts him."

17 - 18

Bird shifted uncomfortably beside her, his weathered face creased with concern. The dim light of the basement cast long shadows across his features, accentuating the doubt in his eyes. "Holly, are you sure about this? If we're wrong—"

Holly felt a sharp pang of frustration cut through her chest. She turned to face Bird, her dark eyes blazing with conviction. The weight of seven bodies pressed upon her conscience, fueling her determination. "I'm not wrong," she interrupted, her voice low and intense. The musty air of the basement seemed to thicken around them as she spoke, carrying the gravity of her words.

She took a step closer to Bird, her gaze never wavering. "Drake's been lying to us from the start. Every lead, every clue—it all points back to him." Holly's mind raced through the evidence, each piece fitting together like a macabre puzzle. The green dragon symbol loomed in her peripheral vision, a constant reminder of the stakes.

Her hand instinctively moved to her holster, fingers brushing against the cool metal of her weapon. "If we don't stop him, more people could die." The words hung in the air, heavy with the promise of future victims.

As she spoke, Holly couldn't help but feel a twinge of regret. She and Drake had worked cases together, shared meals, even laughed over drinks. But now, those memories felt tainted, overshadowed by the mounting evidence of his deceit.

Bird's skepticism was palpable, but Holly knew she couldn't let doubt cloud her judgment. Not now, not with so much at risk. She took a deep breath, steadying herself for the challenging path ahead. The hunt for Drake Miller had begun, and Holly was determined to see it through to its bitter end.

19 - 20

Bird sighed, his broad shoulders sagging under the weight of their grim reality. "Alright," he conceded, his voice a low rumble that seemed to echo in the cavernous basement. "What's next?"

Holly's mind raced, calculating their next move with the precision of a chess master. The stench of death clung to her nostrils, a constant reminder of the lives already lost. She clenched her fist, her nails digging into her palm, grounding her in the moment.

"Get a judge to sign off on an arrest warrant," she replied, her tone sharp and decisive. "We can't let him slip through our fingers."

As she spoke, Holly's gaze drifted to the far corner where the green dragon symbol leered at her, its crude lines a mockery of justice. The image burned itself into her retinas, a constant reminder of the twisted game they were playing.

She turned back to Bird, noting the apprehension etched into the lines of his weathered face. Despite his reservations, she knew he would back her play. It was what made them an effective team, even in the face of such insurmountable odds.

"I'll make the call," Bird offered, already reaching for his phone. "Judge Hernandez owes me a favor. He'll push it through."

Holly nodded, a surge of determination coursing through her veins. As Bird stepped away to make the call, she found herself alone with her thoughts, the weight of their decision pressing down on her like a physical force.

21 - 22

The funhouse loomed behind them, its garish colors a stark contrast to the grim reality within. Holly's boots crunched on gravel as she and Bird stepped out into the crisp night air, the change in atmosphere palpable. The carnival music, once jovial, now seemed to mock their grim discovery.

Holly inhaled deeply, trying to cleanse her lungs of the basement's fetid air. Her mind raced, piecing together the puzzle that Drake Miller had become. Was he truly capable of such methodical brutality? The evidence pointed that way, but something nagged at the edges of her consciousness, a detail just out of reach.

Suddenly, her phone buzzed against her hip, the vibration jolting her from her reverie. Holly pulled it out, her brow furrowing as she read the notification. The screen's glow cast eerie shadows across her face, highlighting the sharp angles of her cheekbones and the tension in her jaw.

"Damn it," she muttered, her fingers tightening around the device. The message's implications sent a chill down her spine, colder than the night air around them. She glanced at Bird, who was still on his call with the judge, his back to her.

Holly's mind raced. This new development could change everything. She closed her eyes briefly, centering herself. When she opened them again, determination blazed in their depths. Whatever was coming, she would face it head-on. She always did.

23 - 24

Bird ended his call and turned back to Holly, his weathered face etched with concern. He paused, noticing the rigid set of her shoulders and the intensity in her gaze.

"What is it?" Bird asked, his gravelly voice tinged with apprehension.

Holly's eyes narrowed, her mind already racing through the implications. "A breach," she said, her tone clipped and taut. "Someone used my police login credentials to access restricted information."

The weight of her words hung in the air between them, as oppressive as the lingering stench of death that clung to their clothes. Holly's hand instinctively moved to her holster, her fingers brushing against the cool metal of her weapon. It was a habit born of years on the force, a physical manifestation of her racing thoughts.

Who could have accessed her credentials? And why? The questions swirled in her mind, each possibility more alarming than the last. Could it be Drake? Or was there someone else involved, someone they hadn't considered yet?

Bird's brow furrowed, the lines on his face deepening. "How the hell did that happen?" he asked, his voice low and guarded.

Holly shook her head, frustration evident in the tightness of her jaw. "I don't know," she admitted, her eyes scanning their surroundings as if the answer might materialize from the shadows. "But whoever did this, they're after something specific. And they're willing to compromise a police officer's account to get it."

The implications of her words settled over them like a heavy fog, obscuring the path forward. Holly felt the weight of responsibility pressing down on her shoulders, a familiar burden that seemed to grow heavier with each passing moment.

25 - 26

Holly's fingers danced across her phone screen, her eyes narrowing as she delved deeper into the breach notification. The dim light from the device cast harsh shadows across her face, accentuating the determination etched in her features.

"Restricted how?" Bird pressed, leaning in closer, his breath visible in the cool night air.

Holly's jaw clenched, her mind racing through the possibilities. She could feel the tension radiating from Bird, mirroring her own growing unease. "Location data," she finally said, her voice barely above a whisper. She continued scrolling, the soft blue glow illuminating her furrowed brow. "Specifically... for a Rachel Summers."

The name hung between them, heavy with implications Holly couldn't yet fully grasp. She felt a chill that had nothing to do with the temperature, a creeping sense that they were standing on the edge of something far more complex than they'd initially believed.

Who was Rachel Summers? And why would someone risk breaching a detective's credentials to find her? Holly's mind raced, trying to connect the dots between this mysterious woman and the gruesome scene they'd just left behind in the funhouse basement.

"Rachel Summers," Holly murmured, more to herself than to Bird. The name felt significant, like a key piece of a puzzle she couldn't quite see. She looked up at her partner, her dark eyes reflecting a mix of determination and concern. "We need to find out who she is, and fast. If someone's willing to compromise police systems to locate her, she's either in danger or..."

She left the alternative unspoken, but it hung in the air between them. *Or she's involved in this somehow.* The possibility sent another chill down Holly's spine.

27 - 28

Bird's eyebrow arched, his weathered face creasing with a mix of confusion and recognition. "Rachel Summers?" he echoed, his deep voice laced with a hint of uncertainty. "Why does that name sound familiar?"

Holly's mind raced, fragments of past conversations flitting through her thoughts like leaves caught in a sudden gust. Her eyes widened as the pieces clicked into place, a surge of adrenaline coursing through her veins.

"Drake mentioned her," she said, her words tumbling out faster than usual. Holly's normally composed demeanor cracked slightly, revealing the intensity beneath. "He claimed she was connected to this whole mess. Said she knew something about the multiverse or whatever nonsense he was spouting."

As she spoke, Holly's gaze darted around the dimly lit parking lot, half-expecting Drake or some unseen threat to materialize from the shadows. The weight of her service weapon at her hip offered little comfort against the growing unease in her gut.

Bird's skeptical frown deepened, etching new lines into his already careworn face. "Multiverse? Holly, you can't seriously be considering—"

"I don't know what to believe anymore, Frank," Holly interrupted, her voice tight with frustration. She ran a hand through her hair, disheveling her usually neat ponytail. "But whatever's going on, it's bigger than we thought. And this Rachel Summers... she's at the center of it somehow."

29 - 30

Bird crossed his arms, his imposing frame seeming to grow even larger as he shifted his weight. The fluorescent lights of the funhouse cast eerie shadows across his face, deepening the concern etched in his features. "You think Drake's the one who breached your login?"

Holly's jaw tightened, the muscle in her cheek twitching as she clenched her teeth. Her eyes, normally sharp and focused, now held a storm of conflicting emotions. She took a deep breath, the scent of stale popcorn and rusted metal filling her lungs.

"Who else would it be?" she replied, her voice low and taut with tension. "He's desperate, Frank. We've seen how erratic he's been acting." Her hand unconsciously moved to her holster, fingers tracing the familiar outline of her weapon. "If he's trying to find this Rachel Summers, then she's either an accomplice—or his next target."

The weight of her words hung heavy in the air, mingling with the distant echoes of carnival music that seemed to mock the gravity of their situation. Holly's mind raced, images of the seven bodies they'd just discovered flashing before her eyes. She couldn't shake the feeling that they were running out of time.

"We need to move fast," she muttered, more to herself than to Bird. Her partner's skepticism was palpable, but she couldn't afford to doubt herself now. Not when lives were at stake. Holly's fingers curled into fists at her sides, her nails digging into her palms as she steeled herself for what was to come.

31 - 32

Bird's weathered face creased with concern, his eyes searching Holly's determined expression. "So what's the plan?" he asked, his deep voice carrying a note of resignation.

Holly slipped her phone into her pocket, her movements deliberate and controlled despite the urgency thrumming through her veins. Her expression hardened, a grim mask settling over her features as she mapped out their next steps in her mind.

"I'm going to find Drake's family," she stated, her tone brooking no argument. The image of Drake's wife and son flashed in her mind, innocent bystanders caught in a web of deceit and danger. "If he's working with Summers—or going after her—they're not safe."

She paused, considering the implications of her decision. Was she acting on solid evidence, or was her intuition leading her astray? The doubt gnawed at her, but she pushed it aside. There was no time for second-guessing.

"You stay here and make sure the warrant goes through," Holly continued, her gaze locked on Bird's face. She could see the conflict in his eyes, the hesitation warring with his trust in her judgment. "We need to cover all our bases, Frank. If I'm wrong about this..."

She left the thought unfinished, the weight of potential consequences hanging between them. Holly's hand unconsciously moved to her badge, fingers tracing the cold metal as if seeking reassurance. The carnival sounds seemed to fade into the background, leaving only the pounding of her heart in her ears.

33 - 34

Bird's weathered face creased with concern, his eyes searching Holly's with a mix of trepidation and grudging respect. He nodded slowly, though the tension in his shoulders betrayed his unease. "Be careful, Holly," he said, his voice low and gravelly. "If Drake's as dangerous as you think, this could get messy."

The words hung in the air, heavy with implication. Holly felt a chill run down her spine despite the warm evening air. She inhaled deeply, tasting the lingering scent of carnival popcorn and cotton candy, now tinged with a bitter undercurrent of fear and uncertainty.

Her eyes hardened, steely determination replacing any last vestiges of doubt. "It already is," she replied, her voice barely above a whisper.

As she spoke, Holly's mind raced through the gruesome scene they'd just left behind. The basement, the bodies, the sinister green dragon symbol - all pieces of a puzzle that seemed to point squarely at Drake Miller. But was she seeing the full picture, or just the parts that fit her theory?

She squared her shoulders, pushing the nagging doubts aside. "I'll call for backup once I locate Drake's family," she said, already turning towards the parking lot. "Keep me updated on the warrant."

Bird's response faded into the background as Holly strode away, her steps purposeful. The carnival lights cast eerie, elongated shadows across her path, a stark reminder of the darkness they were up against. Whatever the truth might be, she knew one thing for certain: time was running out, and the next few hours could make all the difference between justice and catastrophe.

Tensions Boil Over

1[-2] The shadows lengthened across the plush carpet of the Lexington Hotel suite, stretching like grasping fingers in the fading afternoon light. Richard Vega's thumb hovered over his phone screen, trembling slightly as he contemplated sending the message that could change everything. He glanced up, meeting Linda's piercing gaze from across the room. Her blue eyes, usually so warm and reassuring, now blazed with a fury that made his insides twist.

I've done this to protect them, Richard reminded himself, but the words rang hollow even in his own mind. The weight of his choices pressed down on him, threatening to crush what little resolve he had left.

"How much longer are we going to sit here in silence?" Linda's voice cut through the tension, sharp as a blade.

Richard's jaw clenched. "Until I hear back from my contact. We need to be sure it's safe before we move."

Linda scoffed, folding her arms across her chest. "Safe? Nothing about this situation is safe, Richard. You've made sure of that."

From the corner of his eye, Richard saw Harrison flinch at his mother's words. The boy sat hunched on the edge of the couch, his lanky frame seeming to shrink with each passing moment. Richard's heart ached at the sight.

"Harrison," he said softly, "why don't you go check what's on TV? Maybe there's a movie playing."

Harrison's eyes darted between his mother and Richard, uncertainty etched across his young face. "I... I'm okay here," he mumbled, picking at a loose thread on his jeans.

The silence stretched between them once more, thick and suffocating. Richard's mind raced, searching for the right words to diffuse the situation. But how could he explain the impossible choices he'd been forced to make? How could he make Linda understand that every betrayal, every lie, had been to keep her and Harrison alive?

"I know you're angry," Richard began, his voice low and measured. "You have every right to be. But please believe me when I say—"

"Don't," Linda interrupted, her voice trembling with barely contained rage. "Don't you dare try to justify what you've done. Not now. Not after everything."

Richard's fingers tightened around his phone, the plastic case creaking under the pressure. He wanted to argue, to make her see reason, but the words died in his throat. Instead, he turned back to the window, watching as the city lights began to flicker to life in the gathering dusk.

Behind him, he heard the soft rustle of fabric as Harrison shifted on the couch. The boy cleared his throat hesitantly. "Mom? Maybe... maybe we should hear him out?"

Linda's sharp intake of breath was audible in the stillness of the room. "Harrison, you don't understand what's happening here. What he's done—"

"I know it's bad," Harrison interrupted, his voice small but determined. "But Dad always said we should listen to both sides of a story before we judge."

Richard's chest tightened at the mention of Drake. He closed his eyes, fighting back the surge of guilt and regret that threatened to overwhelm him. When he opened them again, he found Linda staring at him, her expression a complex mix of anger, fear, and something else—a flicker of uncertainty that hadn't been there before.

For a moment, hope fluttered in Richard's chest. Maybe, just maybe, there was still a chance to make things right.

3 - 4

Linda's piercing blue eyes bore into Richard, her gaze unwavering as she spoke. "I don't trust you, Vega," she said, her voice sharp, slicing through the silence. "Not after what I just remembered."

The words hung in the air, heavy and oppressive. Richard's jaw tightened, the muscles in his face working as he struggled to maintain his composure. He couldn't bring himself to look at her, couldn't bear to see the accusation, the betrayal in her eyes. Instead, he kept his gaze fixed on the cityscape beyond the window, watching as the last rays of sunlight painted the sky in hues of orange and purple.

His mind raced, searching for the right words, the perfect explanation that would make her understand. But how could he explain the impossible choices he'd been forced to make? How could he make her see that every decision, every action, had been driven by a desperate need to keep her safe?

"I'm here to protect you, Linda," he finally said, his voice low and strained. "That's all I've ever tried to do."

As the words left his mouth, Richard felt a wave of exhaustion wash over him. How many times had he repeated this mantra? How many times had he tried to convince himself that his actions were justified, that the ends justified the means?

He could feel Linda's eyes on him, could sense the skepticism radiating from her. In his peripheral vision, he saw her take a step closer, her slender frame taut with tension.

"Protect me?" she repeated, her voice laced with disbelief. "Is that what you call it?"

Richard's fingers tightened around his phone, the device a cold, unyielding presence in his hand. He wanted to turn to her, to make her understand, but fear held him in place. Fear of what he might see in her eyes, fear of the truth he might have to confront.

In the oppressive silence that followed, Richard found himself wondering how it had come to this. How had he gone from being Linda's protector to the person she feared most? And more importantly, was there any way back from this precipice they now stood upon?

5 - 6

Linda's scoff cut through the air like a knife, her voice trembling with barely contained rage. "Because what I remember is you standing there, watching as that monster—Gabriel—dragged me away. You didn't do a damn thing to stop him!"

The accusation hung heavy in the room, each word a dagger piercing Richard's carefully constructed facade. His mind raced, images of that fateful night flashing before his eyes—Linda's terrified face, Gabriel's cruel smirk, the cold metal of the gun pressed against his own temple. The weight of his choices, of his perceived cowardice, threatened to crush him.

Unable to bear the pressure of Linda's gaze any longer, Richard stood abruptly. The chair scraped harshly against the floor, the sound grating on his already frayed nerves. He turned to face her, his dark eyes meeting her accusatory blue ones.

"You don't understand what was happening, Linda," he said, his voice a mix of desperation and frustration. "I didn't have a choice!"

As the words left his mouth, Richard realized how hollow they sounded. He had rehearsed this explanation countless times in his head, but now, faced with Linda's raw pain and anger, his justifications felt weak and inadequate.

His hands clenched at his sides, knuckles white with tension. How could he make her understand the impossible situation he had been in? How could he explain the intricate web of lies and threats that had bound his actions that night?

7 - 8

Linda's eyes blazed with a fury Richard had never seen before. The soft, nurturing woman he once knew seemed to have vanished, replaced by a fierce, unyielding force of nature. Her blonde hair, usually so carefully styled, hung in disheveled strands around her face, framing the intensity of her gaze.

"There's always a choice," she hissed, her voice low and dangerous. Each word dripped with venom, laced with the pain of betrayal and the strength of a mother protecting her child.

Richard felt his resolve crumbling under the weight of her accusation. He opened his mouth to speak, to defend himself once more, but found no words. The air in the room grew thick, suffocating, as if all the oxygen had been sucked out by the intensity of their confrontation.

Linda took a step closer, her slender frame radiating a power that belied her physical stature. "You chose to stand by and watch," she continued, her voice barely above a whisper now. "You chose to let that monster take me, to put my son in danger. Those were your choices, Richard."

The truth of her words hit him like a physical blow. Richard staggered back, his legs hitting the edge of the chair behind him. He gripped the armrest for support, feeling the world tilt beneath his feet.

"Linda, please," he managed, his voice hoarse. "You have to understand—"

But Linda was beyond understanding. The dam had broken, and years of suppressed fear, anger, and resentment came pouring out. "Understand what?" she shouted, her calm facade shattering. "That you were a coward? That you valued your own life over ours?"

Richard felt something inside him snap. The careful control he had maintained for so long crumbled away, leaving only raw, exposed nerves. This was the breaking point.

9 - 10

Harrison's heart thundered in his chest, each beat a deafening drum that threatened to drown out the heated exchange between his mother and Richard. The air in the hotel suite felt thick, heavy with tension and unspoken accusations. He watched, wide-eyed, as his mother's face contorted with a fury he had rarely seen.

"Mom, maybe we should just—" Harrison began, his voice cracking. He desperately wanted to diffuse the situation, to find some middle ground in this storm of emotions. But the words died on his lips as Linda whirled around, her blue eyes blazing with determination.

"We're leaving," she interrupted, her voice brook no argument. Her hand shot out, fingers wrapping around Harrison's arm with surprising strength. "Get your things. We're getting out of here."

Harrison stumbled as she pulled him towards the door, his mind reeling. They couldn't just leave, could they? What about the danger his mother had spoken of, the mysterious Gabriel that seemed to lurk in the shadows of their fractured reality?

As he fumbled to grab his backpack, Harrison's gaze darted between his mother's resolute face and Richard's stricken expression. A part of him wanted to protest, to remind them both of the risks that awaited them beyond the relative safety of the hotel room. But the words stuck in his throat, held back by the fear of disappointing his mother and the lingering doubt about Richard's true motives.

"Mom," he managed to whisper, "are you sure this is the right thing to do?"

Linda's grip on his arm loosened slightly, and for a moment, Harrison caught a glimpse of vulnerability in her eyes. But it was quickly replaced by steely determination. "We can't stay here, sweetheart," she said, her voice softening. "Not with him. We'll figure this out together, just you and me."

As they moved towards the door, Harrison couldn't shake the feeling that they were leaping from the frying pan into the fire. The unknown terrors that awaited them outside seemed to pale in comparison to the emotional maelstrom they were leaving behind. Yet, as always, he found himself carried along by his mother's unwavering resolve, hoping against hope that she knew what was best for them both.

11 - 12

Richard Vega's lean frame filled the doorway, his shoulders tense as he planted himself firmly between them and escape. The room seemed to shrink, the air growing thick with unspoken accusations and barely contained fury.

"You can't leave," he said firmly, his voice a low rumble that sent a shiver down Harrison's spine.

Linda's fingers tightened around Harrison's arm, her knuckles whitening. The air crackled with tension as she locked eyes with Richard, her gaze as sharp as a blade.

"Move, Richard," she hissed, each word dripping with venom.

Harrison's heart hammered in his chest, his thoughts a whirlwind of confusion and fear. He wanted to believe in Richard, to trust that the man who had been their protector truly had their best interests at heart. But the memory of his mother's earlier words echoed in his mind, casting a shadow of doubt over everything he thought he knew.

Linda took a step forward, pulling Harrison with her. "I won't ask again," she warned, her voice trembling with a mix of anger and desperation.

Richard's jaw clenched, his eyes darting between Linda and Harrison. For a moment, Harrison thought he saw a flicker of genuine concern in the man's expression, quickly masked by his usual inscrutable demeanor.

"Linda, please," Richard said, his tone softening slightly. "You don't understand the dangers out there. If you'd just let me explain-"

"Explain what?" Linda cut him off, her voice rising. "How you've been lying to us this whole time? How you're no better than the monsters we're running from?"

Harrison felt torn between the two adults, each pulling him in opposite directions. He wanted to speak up, to find some way to bridge the chasm that had opened between them, but the words wouldn't come. Instead, he watched helplessly as the fragile alliance that had kept them safe began to crumble before his eyes.

13 - 14

Richard's shoulders tensed, his lean frame silhouetted against the door like a sentinel. The air in the room grew thick with unspoken accusations and fear.

"No," Vega said, his tone low and resolute. His dark eyes locked onto Linda's, a storm of emotions swirling within them. "It's not safe out there. If Gabriel finds you—"

The name hung in the air like a curse, sending a shiver down Harrison's spine. He could feel his mother's grip tightening on his arm, her fingers digging into his flesh. The pressure was almost comforting, a reminder that she was still there, still fighting.

"Then we'll take our chances," Linda snapped. Her voice rose, sharp and brittle, like glass about to shatter. "I'm not staying in this room with you, not after everything you've done!"

Harrison's gaze darted between his mother and Vega, his heart pounding in his chest. The tension in the room was suffocating, pressing in on him from all sides. He wanted to speak, to find some way to diffuse the situation, but his voice seemed trapped in his throat.

Linda's words echoed in his mind. Everything you've done. What exactly had Vega done? Harrison's memories were a jumble of fragments, pieces of a puzzle he couldn't quite fit together. But the fear in his mother's voice, the steel in her eyes – they spoke of betrayals he couldn't begin to understand.

As Linda pulled him closer, Harrison caught a glimpse of Vega's face. For a moment, he thought he saw a flicker of something – regret? Pain? – cross the man's features. But it was gone in an instant, replaced by that impenetrable mask of determination.

The world outside their hotel room window suddenly seemed vast and terrifying. Gabriel was out there, somewhere, waiting. But was staying here, with Vega, any safer? Harrison didn't know anymore, and that uncertainty gnawed at him, threatening to consume him whole.

15 - 16

Vega's composure shattered like a dam breaking under too much pressure. His face contorted, eyes flashing with a mixture of fury and desperation. "Everything I've done has been to keep you alive!" he shouted, his voice ricocheting off the walls of the suite. The vein in his temple throbbed visibly as he continued, "You don't know what I've sacrificed to make sure you and your family stayed safe!"

The words hung in the air, heavy and charged. Harrison felt his mother's grip on his arm tighten, her nails digging into his skin. He winced, but didn't pull away, afraid any movement might ignite the powder keg of emotions in the room.

Linda's laugh was bitter, devoid of any warmth. She took a step closer to Vega, her blue eyes blazing with a cold fire. "Safe?" she spat, the word dripping with contempt. "You think tying me to that monster kept me safe? You think watching him terrorize us makes you a hero?"

As she spoke, Harrison's mind reeled. Flashes of memory assaulted him – his mother's terrified face, Gabriel's cruel smile, Vega standing in the shadows. The pieces were starting to fall into place, and the picture they formed made his stomach churn.

He wanted to close his eyes, to block out the world and pretend none of this was happening. But he couldn't look away from the two adults, locked in their battle of wills, each word another blow in a fight that seemed to have no end.

17 - 18

Harrison's heart raced, his palms slick with sweat as he watched his mother's fury build. The tension in the room was suffocating, pressing down on him like a physical weight. He could see the muscles in Linda's jaw clenching, her body coiled tight as a spring about to snap.

"Mom," he whispered, his voice cracking. He tugged gently at her sleeve, hoping to draw her attention away from Vega. "Mom, please—"

Linda's gaze never wavered from Vega's face, but her free hand reached back, gently pushing Harrison away. "Stay back, Harrison," she said, her voice low and controlled, but trembling with barely contained emotion. "This is between me and him."

Harrison stumbled back a step, his chest tight with fear and uncertainty. He wanted to argue, to plead with his mother to stop, to find another way. But the words lodged in his throat, choking him with their intensity.

As he watched, helpless, Harrison's mind raced. What if this was the moment everything fell apart? What if he lost his mother, just like he'd lost his father? The thought sent a chill through him, and he wrapped his arms around himself, trying to hold the pieces of his world together.

19 - 20

In a heartbeat, the tension snapped. Linda's body surged forward, her hands connecting with Vega's chest in a violent shove. The force caught him off guard, sending him stumbling backward. His back hit the wall with a dull thud, knocking a framed painting askew.

Harrison's breath caught in his throat. He'd never seen his mother like this—raw, unbridled fury etched into every line of her face. Her blue eyes, usually so warm and comforting, now blazed with an intensity that frightened him.

Vega's expression morphed from surprise to anger, his jaw clenching as he straightened. "Linda," he growled, his voice low and dangerous. "You don't want to do this."

"Don't I?" Linda spat back, her hands curling into fists at her sides. "You betrayed us, Richard. You stood by and let that monster take me!"

Harrison's mind reeled. What was she talking about? What had Vega done?

Vega's eyes darted to Harrison, then back to Linda. "You don't understand," he said, his tone softening slightly. "I had no choice. It was the only way to protect—"

"Protect?" Linda's laugh was bitter, cutting through the air like a knife. "Is that what you call it?"

Harrison pressed himself against the wall, his heart pounding. He wanted to intervene, to stop this before it escalated further, but fear kept him rooted in place. The adults he trusted were falling apart before his eyes, and he felt powerless to stop it.

21 - 22

Linda's fist flew through the air, aiming for Vega's face. The lawyer's reflexes kicked in, his hand shooting out to grasp her wrist mid-swing.

"Linda, stop!" Vega barked, his fingers tightening around her arm. His usually composed demeanor cracked, revealing a mix of desperation and frustration beneath.

Linda's eyes flashed with defiance, her blonde hair whipping around her face as she struggled against his grip. "Get out of my way!" she screamed, her voice raw with emotion. She twisted, trying to wrench her arm free, her other hand clawing at Vega's chest.

Harrison watched in horror, his mind racing. Mom never loses control like this, he thought. What did Vega do to make her so angry? The tension in the room was suffocating, pressing against his chest like a physical weight.

Vega's grip remained firm, his face a mask of grim determination. "You're not thinking clearly," he said, his voice strained. "If you'd just listen—"

"Listen?" Linda spat, her eyes brimming with unshed tears. "I've done enough listening to last a lifetime, Richard. I trusted you, and look where it got us!"

Harrison's heart ached at the pain in his mother's voice. He wanted to understand, to help somehow, but he felt lost in a storm of adult secrets and betrayals.

23 - 24

Harrison's breath caught in his throat as he watched the struggle intensify. His back pressed harder against the wall, the cool plaster a stark contrast to the heat of fear rising within him. The room seemed to shrink, closing in around the violent tableau before him.

Vega, his face contorted with effort, managed to twist Linda's arms behind her back. The move was swift, almost practiced, and Harrison felt a chill run down his spine. How many times had Vega done this before?

"Stop fighting, Linda!" Vega growled, his usually smooth voice roughened by exertion. "You're only making this worse!"

Linda thrashed against Vega's hold, her legs kicking out wildly. Each impact echoed in Harrison's ears like thunderclaps. He wanted to cover his eyes, to block out the sight of his mother's desperation, but he couldn't look away.

"Calm down!" Vega shouted, his breath coming in labored gasps. Sweat beaded on his forehead, trickling down his temple. "This isn't helping anyone!"

Harrison's mind raced. Why isn't Mom listening? She always said violence never solved anything. But the fury in her eyes, the raw desperation in her movements – it was like looking at a stranger wearing his mother's face.

"Let me go, you bastard!" Linda snarled, her words dripping with venom. "I'll never trust you again, not after what you did!"

The words hung in the air, heavy with unspoken history. Harrison felt dizzy with questions he was afraid to ask, secrets he wasn't sure he wanted to know. His fingers dug into the wall behind him, seeking an anchor in a world that suddenly made no sense.

25 - 26

Linda's elbow shot back with unexpected force, connecting solidly with Vega's ribs. The sharp crack of impact was followed by Vega's pained grunt, the sound jarring in the tense atmosphere of the hotel suite.

For a moment, hope flared in Linda's eyes, a fierce determination that Harrison recognized from countless soccer games and school presentations. It was the look she got when victory seemed within reach.

But the triumph was fleeting. Vega's face contorted, a mix of pain and grim resolve. His arms tightened around Linda, pinning her own to her sides with ruthless efficiency. The struggle continued, but now it seemed one-sided, Linda's movements growing more desperate as Vega's grip held firm.

Harrison's throat tightened, his voice trapped behind a wall of fear and indecision. He wanted to shout, to beg them both to stop, but the words wouldn't come. Instead, he watched, paralyzed, as his mother's strength seemed to drain away, her struggles becoming weaker with each passing second.

"Why are you doing this?" Linda gasped, her voice raw and ragged. "We trusted you, Richard. I trusted you."

The accusation hung in the air, heavy with betrayal. Harrison's mind raced, trying to piece together a puzzle with too many missing parts. What had happened between his mother and Vega? What dark history lay beneath this violent confrontation?

27 - 28

Vega's chest heaved, his breaths coming in short, sharp bursts. The strain of restraining Linda was evident in the taut lines of his face, but there was something else there too—a flicker of anguish, quickly buried beneath a mask of determination.

"Enough!" Vega roared, his voice echoing through the suite with such force that the windows seemed to rattle.

The sudden outburst startled Harrison, causing him to flinch and press himself further against the wall. His heart hammered in his chest; each beat a painful reminder of how powerless he felt.

Linda's struggles ceased abruptly, shock momentarily replacing her anger. In that instant of stunned silence, Vega's demeanor shifted. His grip on Linda remained firm, but his voice dropped to a low, intense whisper.

"Listen to me," he hissed, his words carrying a weight that seemed to press down on the room. "You don't understand what's at stake here. What I've done—what I'm still doing—it's all to keep you safe."

Harrison watched as his mother's eyes narrowed, disbelief etched across her features. "Safe?" she spat. "You call this safe?"

Vega's jaw clenched, a muscle twitching beneath the skin. His gaze flicked towards Harrison, and for a moment, the boy saw a flicker of something—regret, perhaps? —in the man's eyes.

"Harrison," Vega said, his tone brooking no argument. "There's a cord in the kitchenette drawer. Bring it to me. Now."

The command hung in the air, heavy and terrible. Harrison felt his stomach lurch, bile rising in his throat as he realized what Vega intended.

29 - 30

Linda's chest heaved, her breath coming in ragged gasps as she glared up at Vega. Her blonde hair, usually so meticulously styled, hung in disheveled strands around her face. Despite her compromised position, her eyes blazed with an indomitable fire, a testament to her unwavering spirit.

"You can't keep us here," she snarled, her voice raw with emotion. "You don't own us."

Harrison felt a surge of pride at his mother's defiance, even as fear clawed at his insides. He watched, transfixed, as Vega's expression shifted, the hard lines of anger softening into something more complex.

Vega's grip on Linda's arms loosened slightly, but he didn't release her. When he spoke, his voice was quieter, though no less intense. "I'm not trying to own you, Linda," he said, his dark eyes searching her face. "I'm trying to keep you alive."

The words hung in the air, heavy with unspoken implications. Harrison's mind raced, trying to piece together the fragments of information he'd gathered. What did Vega mean? What danger were they in?

Vega continued; his tone tinged with a hint of desperation. "And until Drake gets back, this is where you're staying. It's the only way I can ensure your safety."

Linda scoffed, but Harrison noticed a flicker of uncertainty cross her features. He wondered if she, too, sensed the genuine concern beneath Vega's stern exterior. The tension in the room was palpable, a living thing that seemed to press in on them from all sides.

31 - 32

Linda's eyes flashed with a mixture of fear and fury, her voice dripping with venom as she spat, "You're insane. You're no better than Gabriel."

The words hung in the air, sharp and poisonous. Harrison felt his breath catch in his throat, his heart pounding so loudly he was sure the others could hear it. He watched as Vega's expression darkened, a storm gathering behind his eyes.

Vega's grip on Linda's arms tightened imperceptibly, his knuckles whitening. "You don't understand," he growled, his voice low and dangerous. "You have no idea what I've sacrificed to keep you safe."

Linda's laugh was bitter, tinged with hysteria. "Safe? You call this safe?"

Harrison pressed himself further into the corner, wishing he could disappear into the wall. He couldn't bear to see his mother like this – fierce and frightened all at once. His mind raced, trying to make sense of the fragments of information he'd gleaned. Who was Gabriel? What had Vega done?

Vega's jaw clenched, a muscle twitching in his cheek. He turned his head slowly, his gaze falling on Harrison. The boy trembled under the weight of that stare, feeling exposed and vulnerable.

"Harrison," Vega said, his voice unnervingly calm. "You need to understand—"

But Harrison didn't want to understand. He wanted to wake up from this nightmare, to be back in their old life where the biggest worry was a math test or a soccer game. The tension in the room was suffocating, pressing in on him from all sides.

33 - 34

Harrison's heart hammered against his ribs as Vega's cold, steady voice cut through the tension. "Harrison, tie her up."

The words hung in the air, heavy and incomprehensible. Harrison blinked; certain he must have misheard. His mouth went dry, and he struggled to form words. "What?" he finally managed, his voice cracking.

Vega's eyes bored into him, unrelenting. "You heard me. It's for her own good."

Linda thrashed in Vega's grip, her face contorted with rage and fear. "Don't you dare, Harrison! Don't listen to him!"

Harrison's gaze darted between his mother and Vega, his mind reeling. How did it come to this? Just yesterday, they were laughing over breakfast, and now... He felt sick, torn between the urge to protect his mother and the paralyzing fear of what might happen if he disobeyed Vega.

"I... I can't," Harrison whispered, his voice barely audible. He pressed his palms against the wall behind him, as if he could somehow sink into it and escape this impossible choice.

Vega's expression hardened. "You have to. If you don't, she'll run. And if she runs, Gabriel will find her. Is that what you want?"

The name 'Gabriel' sent a chill down Harrison's spine. He didn't know who this man was, but the fear in his mother's eyes whenever he was mentioned told him everything he needed to know.

35 - 36

Vega's jaw clenched, his patience visibly wearing thin. He jerked his head toward the kitchenette, his voice low and commanding. "There's a cord in there. Grab it and tie her hands."

Harrison's heart hammered in his chest as he took a hesitant step forward. The room seemed to tilt and sway around him, the distance to the drawer stretching impossibly. His mother's pleading voice cut through the haze.

"No!" Linda shouted; her struggle renewed with desperate vigor. "Harrison, please! Don't do this!"

He paused, torn between Vega's cold command and his mother's anguished plea. The weight of the decision pressed down on him, threatening to crush him beneath its impossible burden. His thoughts raced, searching for a way out, a solution that wouldn't betray either his mother or the man who claimed to be protecting them.

"I..." Harrison started, his voice trembling. "There has to be another way."

Vega's eyes flashed dangerously. "There isn't. This is how we keep her safe."

Safe. The word echoed in Harrison's mind, a cruel mockery of its true meaning. How could this be safety? How could tying up his own mother ever be the right thing to do? Yet the threat of Gabriel loomed large, an unseen specter that seemed to justify even this unthinkable act.

His feet carried him forward as if of their own accord, each step feeling like a betrayal. The drawer handle was cold beneath his fingers as he pulled it open, revealing the cord coiled inside like a sleeping snake.

37 - 38

Harrison's hand hovered over the cord, his fingers trembling as if repelled by an invisible force. The room felt too small, too hot, the air thick with tension and unspoken fears.

"Do it, Harrison!" Vega barked, his voice sharp and commanding.

The words sliced through Harrison's hesitation, but didn't dispel it. He lifted his gaze, meeting his mother's eyes. In them, he saw a mix of fear, anger, and something else—a fierce, unwavering love that made his heart ache.

"Mom..." he whispered, his voice cracking. The single word held a universe of questions, of apologies, of desperate pleas for guidance.

Linda's expression softened slightly, though the defiance never left her eyes. "It's okay, sweetheart," she said, her voice strained but steady. "Whatever happens, I love you. Remember that."

Harrison's mind raced, searching for a solution, a way out of this impossible situation. He thought of the strange language only he could understand, of the fractured realities they'd traversed. There had to be an answer hidden in the chaos, a key to unlocking this nightmare.

His hand closed around the cord, but he didn't move to tie his mother. Instead, he stood frozen, caught between Vega's demands and his own conscience, the weight of multiple worlds pressing down on his young shoulders.

39 - 40

Linda's voice softened, though her eyes were still fierce. "Don't listen to him, Harrison. Don't do this."

The words hung in the air; each syllable etched with maternal desperation. Harrison felt them wrap around his heart, tugging him away from the precipice of an unforgivable act. His mother's blue eyes, usually so full of warmth, now blazed with a protective fire that both comforted and terrified him.

Tears welled in Harrison's eyes as he looked between his mother and Vega. The world blurred, the hotel suite dissolving into a haze of indecision and fear. He blinked rapidly, trying to clear his vision, but the tears only fell faster, hot trails of anguish down his cheeks.

"I... I don't know what to do," Harrison choked out, his voice barely above a whisper. The cord in his hand felt heavier than any burden he'd ever carried, its weight threatening to drag him down into an abyss of regret.

Vega's voice cut through the room, sharp and insistent. "Think about what's at stake, Harrison. We're trying to protect her."

But Harrison couldn't tear his gaze from his mother's face. In her eyes, he saw not just fear, but trust—an unwavering belief in him that made his chest tighten with a mix of love and dread.

"Mom, I'm sorry," he whispered, his words barely audible. "I don't want to hurt you. I don't want any of this."

The tears flowed freely now, blurring the lines between right and wrong, between loyalty and betrayal. In that moment, Harrison felt the full weight of their fractured reality pressing down on him, a burden too heavy for his young shoulders to bear.

41 - 42

Vega's voice cut through Harrison's internal struggle, each word sharp and deliberate. "Do it," he commanded, his tone brooking no argument. "If you don't, she'll leave. And if she leaves, Gabriel will find her. Do you want that to happen? Do you want him to hurt her again?"

The questions hung in the air, heavy and suffocating. Harrison's mind raced, images of his mother in pain flashing before his eyes. He couldn't bear the thought of Gabriel getting his hands on her again. The memory of her screams from that terrible night still haunted his dreams.

"I... I don't..." Harrison stammered, his voice cracking under the weight of the decision before him.

His hands trembled as he took a hesitant step towards the kitchenette. Each movement felt like wading through molasses, his body resisting even as his mind pushed him forward. The drawer handle was cool beneath his fingers as he pulled it open, the soft scrape of wood against wood unnaturally loud in the tense silence of the room.

Harrison's heart pounded so hard he could feel it in his throat as his fingers closed around the cord. It was smooth and unyielding, a stark contrast to the turmoil roiling within him. He lifted it from the drawer, its weight seeming to increase with each passing second.

"Mom," he whispered, turning back to face her, the cord dangling from his shaking hand. "I don't know what else to do. I'm so scared."

43 - 44

"Good," Vega said, his voice a mix of approval and resignation. "Now tie her hands."

The command sliced through Harrison's hesitation, propelling him forward with a sickening lurch in his stomach. He approached his mother slowly, each step feeling like a betrayal. The cord hung heavy in his hand, a physical manifestation of the weight on his soul.

As he knelt beside her, Harrison's vision blurred with tears. They spilled over, hot trails of anguish down his cheeks. His mother's familiar scent - a mix of lavender and something uniquely hers - enveloped him, making this moment even more heart-wrenching.

"I'm sorry, Mom," he whispered, his voice breaking. The words felt inadequate, hollow in the face of what he was about to do. His hands shook as he raised the cord, his mind racing with desperate thoughts.

Maybe if I do this, it'll keep her safe. Maybe Vega knows something we don't. But what if he's wrong? What if this is all a mistake?

Harrison's gaze met his mother's, and he saw a mix of fear, anger, and - most devastatingly - a flicker of understanding in her eyes. It was that glimpse of comprehension that finally broke him, a sob escaping his lips as he fumbled with the cord.

"It's okay, sweetheart," Linda murmured, her voice strained but gentle. "You're just trying to protect me. I know that."

Her words, meant to comfort, only deepened Harrison's anguish. He wanted to throw the cord away, to stand up and declare that he wouldn't do this. But the fear of what might happen if he didn't keep his trembling hands moving.

45 - 46

Linda's eyes, those deep blue pools that had always been a source of comfort, now brimmed with a pain that Harrison had never seen before. Her voice cracked as she pleaded, "Harrison, don't."

The words hung in the air, heavy with desperation and maternal instinct. Harrison felt his resolve waver, his hands stilling for a moment as he wrestled with the enormity of what he was doing. The cord felt rough against his palms, a tangible reminder of the choice he was being forced to make.

I can't let Gabriel find her. I can't lose her again. Not after everything we've been through.

His heart pounded in his chest; each beat a painful reminder of the stakes. With a shaky exhale, Harrison steeled himself and began wrapping the cord around his mother's wrists. His voice trembled as he spoke, barely above a whisper, "I have to. I don't want anything to happen to you."

As he worked, Harrison's mind raced with memories of happier times - lazy Sunday mornings, his mother's laughter echoing through their old house in Bridgewater. How had they ended up here, in this nightmare where he was binding his own mother's hands?

The cord made a soft whisper as it looped around Linda's wrists, each turn feeling like a betrayal of everything Harrison held dear. He could feel his mother's pulse beneath his fingertips, rapid and afraid, mirroring his own racing heart.

47 - 48

Linda's shoulders slumped, the fight draining out of her like water from a broken vessel. Tears streamed down her face, leaving glistening trails that caught the dim light of the hotel room. Her blue eyes, usually so full of warmth and strength, now shimmered with a mix of sorrow and resignation as she stared at her son.

"It's okay, baby," she whispered, her voice cracking with emotion. "It's okay."

The words were meant to comfort, but they pierced Harrison's heart like shards of glass. He wanted to believe her, to find solace in her reassurance, but the weight of his actions pressed down on him, threatening to crush his spirit.

How can this be, okay? How can any of this be right? Harrison thought, his hands shaking as he finished securing the bindings.

Across the room, Richard Vega stood like a silent sentinel, his jaw clenched tight as he watched the scene unfold. His eyes, dark and unreadable, flicked between Linda and Harrison, assessing the situation with a cold calculation that belied the turmoil within.

"Is it tight enough?" Vega asked, his voice low and controlled, betraying nothing of the conflict that raged beneath his composed exterior.

Harrison looked up, meeting Vega's gaze with a mixture of resentment and desperation. "I think so," he replied, his voice barely audible.

Vega stepped forward, his movements precise and deliberate. He knelt beside Linda, his fingers probing the bindings with a detached efficiency that made Harrison's skin crawl.

"Mr. Vega," Harrison began, his voice trembling, "is this really necessary? She's my mom, she won't—"

"It's necessary," Vega cut him off, his tone brooking no argument. "For her safety. For yours."

49 - 50

Harrison's eyes stung with unshed tears as he watched his mother, her head bowed, her blonde hair falling like a curtain around her face. The sight of her bound wrists, the cord biting into her skin, made his stomach churn with guilt and shame.

"Mom?" he whispered, his voice cracking. "Are you... are you okay?"

Linda raised her head slowly, her blue eyes meeting Harrison's. Despite the tears that streaked down her cheeks, there was a fierce determination in her gaze that both comforted and unsettled him.

"I'm alright, sweetheart," she said softly, her words laced with a strength that defied her current state. "This isn't your fault. Remember that."

Harrison swallowed hard, fighting back a sob. "But I... I tied you up. I shouldn't have—"

"You did what you thought was right," Linda interrupted, her voice gentle but firm. "To keep us safe. That's what matters."

Vega cleared his throat, the sound harsh in the tense silence of the room. "Harrison, step back now. Give her some space."

Reluctantly, Harrison moved away from his mother, his legs feeling like lead as he retreated to the far corner of the room. His mind raced, replaying the events that had led to this moment, searching desperately for some way to make sense of it all.

How did we end up here? he wondered, his thoughts a whirlwind of confusion and fear. *One minute we were a normal family, and now... now everything's falling apart.*

51 - 52

Vega exhaled slowly, his shoulders relaxing slightly. The tension in his lean frame eased, but his eyes remained vigilant, darting between Linda and Harrison. "I didn't want it to come to this," he said quietly, his voice carrying a weight of regret that seemed at odds with his actions. "But you left me no choice."

Harrison watched as his mother's face hardened, her blue eyes flashing with a mixture of anger and determination. The soft, nurturing woman he knew had been replaced by someone fiercer, someone forged in the crucible of their current nightmare.

Linda raised her chin defiantly, her bound hands clenched into fists. "You'll regret this," she said, her voice low and venomous. "I promise you."

The words hung in the air, charged with an electric tension that made Harrison's skin prickle. He found himself holding his breath, caught between the two adults, each radiating a different kind of intensity.

Mom's never looked at anyone like that before, Harrison thought, a chill running down his spine. *It's like she's a different person.*

Vega's jaw tightened, his posture stiffening as if bracing for a physical blow. "Linda, you don't understand. There are things at play here that you can't—"

"Save it, Richard," Linda spat, cutting him off. "Your excuses mean nothing. Not anymore."

Harrison's gaze flicked between them, his heart pounding. He wanted to speak, to do something to diffuse the situation, but fear kept him rooted to the spot, a silent observer to the unfolding drama.

53 - 53

Vega's shoulders slumped almost imperceptibly, the weight of Linda's words seeming to press down on him. Without another word, he turned away, moving towards the expansive window that dominated one wall of the hotel suite.

The cityscape sprawled before him, a tapestry of lights and shadows. Vega's reflection stared back at him, ghostly and translucent against the backdrop of the urban night. His eyes, usually sharp and calculating, now held a haunted look.

What have I done? The thought echoed in Vega's mind, a relentless, accusing mantra. He placed a hand against the cool glass, as if seeking some form of absolution from the indifferent city beyond.

Behind him, he could hear Linda's ragged breathing, punctuated by the soft, muffled sobs of Harrison. The sounds twisted something inside him, a mixture of guilt and resolve that left a bitter taste in his mouth.

"You don't understand," Vega murmured, his words barely audible, meant more for himself than anyone else. "I never wanted any of this."

He turned slightly, catching Harrison's tear-stained face in his peripheral vision. The boy looked lost, broken in a way that no child should ever be. Vega's throat tightened.

"Harrison," he said, his voice hoarse. "I know you think I'm the villain here, but—"

"Don't you dare speak to my son," Linda hissed, her fury palpable even from across the room.

Vega's jaw clenched, his reflection in the window hardening. "This isn't about what any of us want anymore," he said, his tone low and resigned. "It's about survival. And sometimes... sometimes survival means making impossible choices."

The Librarians' Computer

1 The New Haven Public Library loomed before Drake, its weathered stone facade a silent sentinel against the fading afternoon light. He hesitated at the entrance, his hand hovering over the worn brass handle. The weight of his quest pressed down on him, as heavy as the guilt that had become his constant companion.

Drake pushed open the door, the musty scent of old books and polished wood enveloping him. Rows of towering bookshelves stretched upward, their contents holding countless stories—but not the one he desperately needed to unravel.

"Focus," he muttered to himself, scanning the cavernous room. The late sun slanted through arched windows, casting long shadows that seemed to reach for him like accusing fingers.

His footsteps echoed softly on the marble floor as he made his way deeper into the library. The search for Rachel Summers gnawed at him, a relentless ache that had only intensified since hitting a dead end at the research institute.

But now, an idea had taken root—fragile and dangerous, born from the fractured memories of another life. A life that felt both alien and achingly familiar.

Drake's gaze fell on a nearby computer terminal. His heart quickened. "This has to work," he thought, clenching his fists. "I need to find her. I need answers."

He approached the librarian's desk, forcing a smile that didn't reach his eyes. "Excuse me," Drake said, his voice low and urgent. "I was wondering if I could use one of the computers? It's... it's important."

The elderly librarian peered at him over her glasses, her expression a mix of suspicion and concern. "Do you have a library card, sir?"

Drake's smile faltered. "I'm afraid not. I'm not from around here, but—" He leaned in, his desperation bleeding through. "Please. I wouldn't ask if it wasn't crucial."

She studied him for a long moment, then sighed. "Very well. But keep it brief."

"Thank you," Drake breathed, relief washing over him. As he turned toward the computers, a pang of guilt twisted in his gut. How many more lies would he have to tell before this was over?

Settling into a chair, he flexed his fingers over the keyboard. The screen's glow illuminated his face, casting shadows that deepened the lines of worry etched there.

"Where are you, Rachel?" he whispered, as if she might somehow hear him across the vast, tangled web of realities. "What do you know about all of this?"

With a deep breath, Drake began to type, praying that this fragile thread of hope would lead him one step closer to unraveling the mystery that threatened to unravel everything he held dear.

3 - 4

Drake's fingers hovered over the keyboard, a kaleidoscope of memories flashing through his mind. In one reality—a life that now felt as insubstantial as smoke—he had been a detective, working cases alongside Holly Kierstead. The weight of that badge, the responsibility it carried, still phantom-pressed against his chest.

"Holly," he murmured, her name a talisman against the surreal nature of his current predicament. Though that life felt like a dream, one detail stood out with surprising clarity: Holly Kierstead's login credentials.

Drake closed his eyes, willing himself to focus. The sound of pages turning and hushed whispers faded into the background as he sifted through the fragments of that other existence. Slowly, carefully, he typed in Holly's badge number.

His finger paused over the 'Enter' key. Was he really going to do this? Use Holly's credentials without her knowledge or consent? The Holly he knew—observant, analytical, fiercely loyal—would be furious if she found out.

"I'm sorry, Holly," he whispered, guilt churning in his stomach. "But I need to find Rachel. I need answers."

With a deep breath, Drake pressed 'Enter'. The system whirred to life, granting him access to a wealth of information he had no right to possess. As he navigated through the database, a chill ran down his spine. How long before someone noticed this unauthorized access? How long before Holly herself realized what he'd done?

Time was running out. Drake knew he had to act fast, but caution warred with urgency. He glanced over his shoulder, half-expecting to see Holly's piercing gaze fixed upon him, her intuition having led her straight to his betrayal.

But the library remained quiet, oblivious to the desperate man mining secrets from a reality that wasn't quite his own.

5 - 6

Drake settled into the worn chair, its cracked leather creaking under his weight. The ancient computer before him hummed to life, the fan whirring like a labored breath. As the screen flickered awake, casting a pale blue glow across his face, Drake's fingers hovered over the keyboard, trembling slightly.

"This is it," he murmured to himself, his voice barely audible. "No turning back now."

With a deep breath, he began to type the URL for the Bridgewater Police Department's online database etched into his memory from a life that felt both distant and painfully close. The familiar interface materialized before him, a portal to a world he once knew intimately.

Drake's eyes darted nervously around the library, half-expecting to see accusatory glances or the librarian hovering nearby. But the room remained quiet, the only sound the soft tapping of his fingers on the worn keys.

As he worked, memories flooded his mind – the weight of a badge on his chest, the camaraderie of fellow officers, the satisfaction of solving cases. But with those memories came the crushing reminder of all he had lost, all he had sacrificed.

"Focus," he hissed through gritted teeth, forcing himself back to the present. "Rachel needs you. They all need you."

The database login screen stared back at him, a silent challenge. Drake's heart raced, the enormity of what he was about to do pressing down on him. But the faces of his family, of the world he was trying to save, flashed before his eyes.

"Whatever it takes," he whispered, resolve hardening his features as his fingers flew across the keyboard, accessing a system that no longer belonged to him.

7 - 8

The stark login screen materialized, its simplicity a stark contrast to the intricate web of realities Drake now navigated. The familiar interface transported him, and for a moment, he could almost hear the ambient sounds of the precinct – the rhythmic click-clack of keyboards, the low murmur of detectives conferring over cases, the distant ring of phones.

Drake's fingers hovered over the keys, a tremor running through them. He closed his eyes, taking a deep breath. "This has to work," he thought, the weight of his mission pressing down on him.

With practiced ease, he typed in Holly Kierstead's badge number. The cursor blinked expectantly in the password field, and Drake hesitated. His mind raced, fragments of memories from another life flickering like old film reels.

"Come on, Holly," he muttered, his brow furrowing in concentration. "What would you use?"

As if in response, snippets of conversation echoed in his mind – Holly's voice, confident and clear, discussing cases, sharing personal anecdotes. Drake's fingers twitched, poised above the keys as he sifted through the jumbled recollections.

"You always were meticulous about your passwords," he said under his breath, a sad smile tugging at his lips. "But I knew you, in that other life. I have to remember."

The weight of time pressed upon him, each second feeling like an eternity as he struggled to piece together the fragments of Holly's life from another reality.

9 - 10

"Rebekah," he muttered under his breath, the name materializing from the depths of his fractured memories.

Drake's fingers trembled as they hovered over the keyboard. The name resonated within him, carrying an emotional weight he couldn't fully comprehend. He closed his eyes, focusing on the shadowy recollections of Holly's life in another reality.

"Holly's girlfriend," he whispered, his voice barely audible. "She talked about her all the time. Rebekah was... her anchor."

As he opened his eyes, determination steeled his gaze. Drake began to type, his fingers moving with a mixture of certainty and desperate hope.

R-e-b-e-k-a-h

He paused, his brow furrowing. "It wouldn't be that simple," he thought. "Holly was too careful about that."

Drawing on instinct and fragmented knowledge, Drake added more characters: 1-2-3-!

The completed password stared back at him from the screen: Rebekah123!

"A steady presence in Holly's life," Drake murmured, his voice tinged with a mix of sadness and urgency. "The kind of person you'd build your world around. The kind of name you'd use to protect your most important information."

His finger hovered over the enter key, hesitation gnawing at him. "If I'm wrong about this," he thought, "I'm back to square one. And worse, I might alert Holly to what I'm doing."

The weight of his mission pressed down on him, the faces of those he was trying to save flashing through his mind. With a deep breath, Drake steeled himself for whatever came next.

11 - 12

Drake's finger descended on the enter key, the soft click echoing in his ears like a thunderclap. The screen before him flickered, and for an agonizing moment, time seemed to stretch into eternity. His breath caught in his throat, heart pounding against his ribcage as if trying to escape.

"Come on," he whispered, leaning forward, his eyes fixed on the monitor. "Please."

The cursor spun, a maddening dance of pixels that seemed to mock his desperation. Drake's fists clenched involuntarily, his nails digging into his palms. The pain was a dull counterpoint to the razor's edge of anticipation on which he balanced.

Then, like a veil being lifted, the login screen dissolved. In its place, the familiar interface of the police database materialized, its sterile blue background a stark contrast to the tumultuous emotions churning within Drake.

He exhaled sharply, a trembling hand running through his disheveled hair. "I'm in," he breathed, relief and trepidation mingling in his voice. "But at what cost?"

The database stretched before him, a digital labyrinth of information that held both promise and peril. Drake's eyes darted across the screen, taking in the various search options and tabs. It was eerily familiar, like a half-remembered dream.

"It's just like before," he murmured, his fingers hovering over the keyboard. "Another life, another me. But the stakes... they've never been higher."

As he prepared to navigate the database, a flicker of movement in his peripheral vision made him tense. The librarian was making her rounds, her footsteps a soft but insistent reminder of the precarious nature of his position.

Drake swallowed hard; his throat suddenly dry. "I need to be quick," he thought, his mind racing. "Every second I'm in here is another chance to get caught. To lose everything."

With renewed urgency, he turned back to the screen, ready to delve into the depths of the database. The answers he sought were tantalizingly close, but the shadow of consequence loomed large. Drake knew that each keystroke could bring him closer to salvation or damnation, and the line between the two had never seemed so thin.

13 - 14

Drake's fingers trembled as they hovered over the keyboard, the weight of his mission pressing down on him like a physical force. He took a deep breath, steadying himself, and began to type.

"Rachel Summers," he whispered, each letter appearing in the search field feeling like a step closer to unraveling the mystery that had consumed his life.

As he typed, memories of Rachel flickered through his mind - her determined gaze, her brilliant mind, the way she had challenged everything he thought he knew about reality. His heart raced, not just from the adrenaline of his illicit search, but from the possibility of finding her again.

"Where are you, Rachel?" Drake muttered; his eyes fixed on the screen. "What answers do you have for me?"

He hesitated for a moment before hitting enter, his finger hovering over the key. The weight of his choices - past, present, and future - seemed to converge on this single moment.

"I'm sorry, Holly," he thought, a pang of guilt twisting in his chest. "I hope you'll understand someday."

With a deep breath, Drake pressed enter. The database began to process his request, each passing second feeling like an eternity. He glanced nervously over his shoulder, half-expecting to see the librarian standing there, ready to confront him.

"Come on, come on," he urged under his breath, turning back to the screen. "Show me something, anything."

As the search results began to populate, Drake leaned in closer, his eyes scanning frantically for any mention of Rachel Summers. Each name that wasn't hers felt like a blow, chipping away at his fragile hope.

"She has to be here," he thought desperately. "She's the key to all of this. To saving everyone. To making things right."

15 - 16

The screen flickered, and Drake's eyes widened as a familiar name appeared amidst the sea of irrelevant results. His breath caught in his throat, the world around him fading into a muted haze as he focused on the crucial information before him.

"Rachel," he whispered, his voice barely audible. The entry stood out like a beacon of hope in the darkness that had been engulfing him:

Summers, Rachel – Former Employee, New Haven Research Institute. Current residence: 128 Willow Creek Lane, New Haven.

Drake's fingers trembled as they hovered over the keyboard. He wanted to reach out and touch the screen, as if doing so might somehow bring him closer to her. The weight of discovery pressed down on him, a mixture of elation and trepidation coursing through his veins.

"You're still here," he murmured, a ghost of a smile tugging at his lips. "You didn't disappear like the others."

His mind raced with possibilities. What had Rachel been doing since leaving the institute? Did she know about the fractures in reality, the dangers that loomed on the horizon? And most importantly, would she remember him?

Drake glanced around the library, suddenly acutely aware of his surroundings. The soft rustling of pages and muted conversations seemed distant, otherworldly. He turned back to the screen, committing the address to memory.

"I'm coming, Rachel," he thought, determination steeling his resolve. "Whatever answers you have, whatever truths we need to face – we'll do it together."

With a deep breath, Drake began the process of covering his tracks, erasing any evidence of his search. As he worked, a bittersweet realization settled over him: he was one step closer to unraveling the mystery, but also one step closer to a confrontation that could change everything.

17 - 18

Drake's fingers trembled slightly as he reached for a scrap of paper lying beside the computer. The yellowed edge caught against his calloused skin, a stark reminder of the physical reality he now inhabited. He scrawled the address quickly, each stroke of the pen feeling like a lifeline thrown into the murky waters of his fractured existence.

"128 Willow Creek Lane," he whispered, the words barely audible even to himself. "New Haven."

The weight of the moment pressed down on him, a mixture of relief and apprehension swirling in his chest. Drake stared at the hastily written address, his eyes tracing each letter as if they might disappear at any moment.

"I've found you," he murmured, a hint of wonder creeping into his voice. "After all this time, all these... realities."

He glanced around the library, suddenly hyper-aware of his surroundings. The soft rustling of pages and muted conversations seemed to fade away, leaving only the thunderous beating of his own heart.

"What will I say to you, Rachel?" Drake thought, his brow furrowing. "Will you even recognize me in this... version of myself?"

He folded the paper carefully, his movements deliberate and measured. As he slipped it into his pocket, a small smile tugged at the corners of his mouth.

"One step closer," Drake muttered, his voice a mix of determination and trepidation. "To answers to the truth... to you."

He stood from the computer, his legs feeling unexpectedly weak. The enormity of what lay ahead washed over him, a tidal wave of possibility and peril.

"Whatever comes next," he thought, steeling himself, "I'm ready. I have to be."

Drake took a deep breath, savoring the musty scent of old books that permeated the air. It grounded him, reminding him of the tangible world around him even as his mind raced with thoughts of alternate realities and multiversal consequences.

"Time to face the music," he said softly to himself, squaring his shoulders. "And hope it's not a requiem."

19 - 20

As Drake reached to log out of the database, a prickle ran down his spine. The air seemed to shift, carrying with it a sudden weight of scrutiny. He froze, his finger hovering over the mouse, as the hairs on the back of his neck stood up.

Slowly, he turned in his chair, his heart hammering against his ribs. The librarian stood just a few feet away, her arms crossed tightly over her chest. Her eyes, magnified behind thick lenses, bored into him with an intensity that made Drake's breath catch in his throat.

"I didn't mean to startle you," she said, her voice low and measured, but Drake could hear the undercurrent of suspicion.

He swallowed hard, forcing a smile that felt brittle on his face. "No, it's... it's fine. I was just finishing up."

The librarian's gaze flicked to the computer screen behind him, and Drake felt a surge of panic. Had he closed everything properly? Was there any trace of his illicit search still visible?

"I couldn't help but notice," she began, her words careful and deliberate, "you seemed quite... focused on your task."

Drake's mind raced, searching for a plausible explanation. "Just some urgent research," he managed, trying to keep his voice steady. "Family matter, you know how it is."

The woman's eyebrows arched slightly; skepticism etched in the lines of her face. "Indeed," she murmured, clearly unconvinced.

As Drake stood, he felt the weight of the scrap paper in his pocket like burning coal. He resisted the urge to touch it, to reassure himself it was still there. Instead, he met the librarian's gaze, summoning every ounce of his former lawyer's composure.

"Thank you again for your help," he said, injecting warmth into his tone. "It really means a lot."

The librarian's expression softened slightly, but her arms remained crossed. "Of course," she replied, her voice still carrying a note of wariness. "That's what we're here for."

As Drake moved to leave, his thoughts tumbled over each other. "She knows something's not right," he fretted internally. "But how much? And what if she reports this? Could it lead back to Holly?"

The weight of his actions pressed down on him, threatening to overwhelm the spark of hope he'd kindled. Yet beneath it all, a fierce determination burned. "It doesn't matter," he told himself. "I'm close now. Whatever comes next, I have to see this through. For Rachel, for my family... for all the realities hanging in the balance."

21 - 22

The librarian's cool tone cut through Drake's swirling thoughts. "You're done, right?" she asked, her eyes narrowing slightly as she studied him.

Drake felt a bead of sweat form at his temple, but he maintained his composure. He nodded, rising from the chair with deliberate casualness. As he stood, he slipped the paper into his pocket, acutely aware of its presence against his thigh. "Yeah, all done," he replied, forcing a smile that didn't quite reach his eyes. "Thanks for letting me use it."

His heart raced; each beat a reminder of the perilous path he trod. The weight of multiple realities pressed down on him, threatening to crush him beneath their impossible vastness. Yet he stood tall, shoulders squared against the burden.

"It was nothing," the librarian responded, her gaze still fixed on him. "I hope you found what you were looking for."

Drake's mind raced, calculating the risks of his next move. Should he leave quickly and arouse suspicion, or linger and potentially expose himself further? The familiar dance of legal strategy flickered through his consciousness, a ghost of his former life.

"More than I expected," he admitted, allowing a hint of truth to color his words. "Sometimes the smallest piece of information can change everything."

As he spoke, his fingers unconsciously brushed against the pocket containing Rachel's address. So close now, yet the journey ahead remained fraught with danger and uncertainty. Drake's resolve hardened, steeling himself for whatever challenges lay ahead in his quest to unravel the cosmic tapestry threatening to unravel around him.

23 - 24

The librarian's eyes narrowed imperceptibly, her tight-lipped smile a mask of professional courtesy. "No problem. Just make sure it was worth it."

Her words carried a weight that Drake couldn't ignore, settling in his chest like a stone. Was she suspicious? Or merely irritated by the breach in protocol? He searched her face for clues, his lawyer's instinct kicking in, dissecting every micro-expression.

"It was," Drake assured her, his voice steady despite the tumult of emotions churning within. He forced a smile, hoping it appeared genuine. "More than you know."

As he turned to leave, his mind raced. The fragility of his position struck him anew. One misstep, one moment of carelessness, and the tenuous thread connecting him to Rachel Summers—and possibly to answers about this fractured reality—could snap.

Drake's footsteps echoed in the cavernous space as he made his way toward the exit. Each step felt heavier than the last, the weight of his mission pressing down on him. He could feel the librarian's gaze boring into his back, and it took all his willpower not to increase his pace.

'Just a few more steps,' he thought, his hand reaching for the door. 'Just get out of here, and you're one step closer to the truth.'

As he pushed open the heavy wooden door, the cool evening air rushed in, carrying with it the promise of answers—and the threat of further complications. Drake stepped out into the gathering twilight, his resolve strengthened by the knowledge that, for better or worse, there was no turning back now.

25 - 26

The fading sunlight painted New Haven's streets in hues of amber and gold, casting long shadows that seemed to reach for Drake as he emerged from the library. He paused on the weathered stone steps, his hand trembling slightly as he unfolded the scrap of paper.

"128 Willow Creek Lane," Drake murmured, his voice barely above a whisper. The address burned itself into his mind, a beacon of hope in the murky sea of his fractured memories.

He glanced up, scanning the street with wary eyes. The world around him seemed both familiar and alien, a reminder of the precarious nature of his existence in this reality. A couple strolled past, their laughter floating on the evening breeze, oblivious to the weight of Drake's mission.

"Rachel," he breathed, his fingers tracing the hastily scribbled numbers. "What answers are you hiding?"

Drake's mind raced, possibilities unfolding like a complex legal argument. If Rachel was indeed connected to the research institute, she might hold the key to unraveling the mystery of the multiversal anomaly. But would she remember him? Would she understand the gravity of their situation?

He closed his eyes, memories of his family—of the life he'd sacrificed—washing over him. The ache of loss threatened to overwhelm him, but Drake steeled himself, his jaw clenching with determination.

"I have to do this," he said aloud, his voice rough with emotion. "For them. For everyone."

With a deep breath, Drake descended the library steps, each footfall bringing him closer to his uncertain future. The paper crinkled in his grip, a tangible link to his next move in this high-stakes game of cosmic chess.

As he reached the sidewalk, a nagging doubt tugged at him. "What if I'm wrong?" he wondered, the weight of potential failure pressing down on his shoulders. "What if this leads nowhere?"

But Drake pushed the thought aside, his stride purposeful as he headed towards his car. He had come too far, sacrificed too much, to let doubt derail him now. Whatever awaited him at 128 Willow Creek Lane, he would face it head-on—for the sake of his family, for the integrity of reality itself, and for the chance at redemption that had been so unexpectedly thrust upon him.

27 - 28

Drake's hand trembled slightly as he gripped the steering wheel, the car's engine humming to life beneath him. The address burned in his mind: 128 Willow Creek Lane. Rachel Summers, the key to unraveling this cosmic puzzle, was tantalizingly close.

"Just a little further," he murmured, his voice barely audible over the car's low rumble. "Hold on, Rachel. I'm coming."

As he pulled away from the curb, Drake's eyes flicked to the rearview mirror. The library's imposing facade receded, a silent sentinel to his desperate quest. His thoughts drifted to Holly Kierstead, her sharp gaze and analytical mind cutting through his memories like a knife.

"Damn it," he hissed, his knuckles whitening on the wheel. "If Holly finds out I used her credentials..."

The implications unfolded in his mind like a treacherous map. Holly's suspicion, already piqued by his erratic behavior, would surely explode into full-blown mistrust. And in this fragile web of realities, trust was a currency he couldn't afford to squander.

Drake navigated through the streets, each turn bringing him closer to Rachel and, he hoped, to answers. The setting sun painted the sky in hues of amber and crimson, a stark reminder of time's relentless march.

"What will I even say to her?" he wondered aloud, his brow furrowing. "'Hey, Rachel, remember me from another reality where we worked together to save the multiverse?' God, I sound insane."

A mirthless chuckle escaped his lips, the sound hollow in the confines of the car. The weight of his mission pressed down on him, a constant, suffocating presence. But beneath the fear and uncertainty, a spark of hope flickered stubbornly.

"She has to remember," Drake whispered, his eyes fixed on the road ahead. "She has to know something. Otherwise..."

He left the thought unfinished, unwilling to contemplate the alternative. As the streets gave way to more residential areas, Drake's anticipation grew, mingled with a gnawing anxiety. Whatever awaited him at Rachel's door, he knew with grim certainty that it would irrevocably alter the course of his fractured existence.

29 - 29

Drake's fingers tightened on the steering wheel as he turned onto Willow Creek Lane. The streetlights flickered to life, casting long shadows across manicured lawns and cookie-cutter houses. Each passing number brought him closer to his destination, closer to the precipice of truth or devastating disappointment.

"128," he murmured, slowing the car as he approached the address. "This is it."

He pulled over, killing the engine but remaining in the driver's seat. The house before him was unremarkable – a two-story colonial with white siding and navy shutters. No different from its neighbors, yet potentially holding the key to unraveling the mystery that consumed his every waking moment.

Drake closed his eyes, drawing in a deep breath. The scent of Rachel's perfume, a memory from another life, ghosted through his senses. "Focus," he chided himself. "You can't afford to lose it now."

With a final, steadying inhale, he opened the car door and stepped out. The evening air was cool against his skin, carrying the faint scent of freshly cut grass and upcoming rain. Each step toward the front door felt monumental, as if he were wading through invisible currents of time and possibility.

At the threshold, Drake hesitated. The weight of countless realities pressed down upon him, threatening to crush his resolve. But the faces of his family – of Emma and the kids – flashed through his mind, spurring him forward. He raised his hand and knocked, the sound echoing like thunder in his ears.

Seconds stretched into eternity as he waited, his heart a frantic drumbeat in his chest. Then, from within, the muffled sound of approaching footsteps. Drake swallowed hard; his mouth suddenly dry.

The door swung open.

The Meeting

1 - 2 The skeletal remains of New Haven's industrial past loomed before Drake, a graveyard of broken dreams and rusted ambitions. His eyes fixed on 128 Willow Creek Lane, a decaying edifice that seemed to sag under the weight of its own neglect. Cracked windows stared back at him like vacant eyes, while peeling paint revealed the building's weathered bones beneath.

Drake's fingers tightened on the steering wheel as he eased his car to a stop a short distance away. The silence here was different from the bustling city he'd left behind—heavier, more oppressive. It pressed against his ears, broken only by the whisper of wind through barren trees.

"This has to be it," he murmured, his voice barely audible even to himself. "Rachel's here. She has to be."

As he stepped out of the car, the crunch of gravel under his feet seemed unnaturally loud. Drake's heart raced, each beat a reminder of what was at stake. He'd come so far, sacrificed so much. The weight of his past mistakes, the lives he'd upended in his pursuit of the truth—it all converged on this moment.

The vines creeping up the building's facade caught his attention, their vibrant green a stark contrast to the lifeless gray surrounding them. "Life finds a way," Drake thought, a wry smile tugging at his lips. "Even here, at the edge of everything."

He took a deep breath, steeling himself for what lay ahead. The air tasted of dust and decay, with an underlying current of something else—something electric, as if the very fabric of reality was thinner here.

"Come on, Drake," he whispered to himself, clenching his fists. "You've faced worse than this. You've crossed worlds, for God's sake."

But as he approached the dilapidated structure, doubt crept in. What if Rachel wasn't here? What if this was another dead end, another failure to add to his growing list?

"No," Drake said aloud, his voice firm despite the tremor in his hands. "I can't think like that. For Linda, for Harrison... I have to keep going."

The weight of his family's absence pressed down on him, a constant ache that fueled his determination. He'd find a way back to them, no matter the cost. And it all started here, with Rachel Summers and the secrets she held.

Drake paused at the foot of the crumbling steps leading to the entrance. The wind picked up, carrying with it the faint scent of ozone—a smell that brought back flashes of swirling lights and tearing reality.

"Whatever's waiting for me in there," Drake muttered, his jaw set with resolve, "I'm ready. For my family, for the truth... for everything."

With that final thought, he ascended the steps, each creak of weathered wood bringing him closer to the answers he sought—and the dangers that lurked in the shadows of forgotten worlds.

3 - 4

Drake's hand hovered inches from the warped wooden door, his fingers trembling slightly. The peeling paint and splintered surface seemed to mock his hesitation. This was it—the culmination of sleepless nights and desperate leads. Rachel Summers had to be here.

"Come on, Miller," he whispered, his voice barely audible over the pounding of his heart. "You didn't come this far to chicken out now."

With a deep breath, Drake rapped his knuckles against the door. The sound echoed dully, seeming to reverberate through the empty street behind him. For a moment, nothing happened. The silence stretched, oppressive and thick with anticipation.

Then, without warning, a low groan emanated from within. The door creaked open on its own, swinging inward with an eerie, inviting gesture.

Drake's muscles tensed, ready for fight or flight. "Rachel?" he called out, his voice steady despite the adrenaline coursing through his veins. No answer came.

As he stood on the threshold, memories of his old life—of Linda's laugh, of Harrison's first steps—flashed through his mind. The weight of his mission, of the lives hanging in the balance, settled heavily on his shoulders.

"I didn't sacrifice everything just to turn back now," Drake muttered, steeling himself. With one last glance at the decaying world around him, he stepped forward into the unknown darkness of Rachel Summers' sanctuary, ready to face whatever truths—or horrors—awaited him inside.

5 - 6

The floorboards groaned beneath Drake's feet as he crossed the threshold, the sound reverberating through the silent house. Shadows clung to every corner, and the air hung heavy with the scent of dust and abandonment. Drake's eyes strained to adjust to the dim interior, his senses on high alert.

"Hello?" Drake called out, his voice a mixture of caution and determination. The word seemed to be swallowed by the oppressive stillness of the house. He took another step forward, wincing at the creak beneath his foot.

Is this really where Rachel's been hiding all this time? Drake thought, his gaze sweeping across the cluttered space. *What could have driven her to such extremes?*

The weight of his mission pressed down on him, a constant reminder of what was at stake. He couldn't afford to let his guard down, not when he was so close to finding answers.

"Rachel Summers?" he tried again, louder this time. "I need to speak with you. It's important."

As he ventured deeper into the house, Drake's mind raced with possibilities. What if Rachel wasn't here? What if this was another dead end? The thought sent a chill down his spine. He couldn't bear the idea of facing his family empty-handed again, of seeing the hope fade from their eyes.

"I'm not here to hurt you," Drake added, his voice softening. "I just need your help. Please."

The silence that followed was deafening. Drake's hand instinctively moved towards his pocket, where he kept the small notebook filled with his fragmented memories of the other realities. It was his lifeline, his proof that he wasn't losing his mind.

As he rounded a corner, a flicker of movement caught his eye. Drake's heart leapt into his throat. "Rachel?" he called out, hope and trepidation warring in his voice.

7 - 8

The oppressive silence settled back over the room, broken only by the soft creak of floorboards beneath Drake's cautious steps. His eyes strained in the dim light, searching for any sign of life amidst the chaos.

"Rachel, if you're here, I understand why you're hiding," Drake said, his voice low and steady despite the tension coiling in his chest. "I've seen things too—things that shouldn't be possible. I need your help to make sense of it all."

He paused, running a hand through his disheveled hair. The smell of stale coffee and moldy paper assaulted his senses, a stark reminder of how far the once-brilliant scientist had fallen.

What if I'm too late? The thought gnawed at him, threatening to unravel his resolve. *What if she's already gone, lost to whatever forces are tearing our reality apart?*

Drake's gaze fell on a discarded notebook, its pages filled with frantic scribbles and diagrams. He reached for it, his fingers trembling slightly.

"I know about the Codex, Rachel," he continued, flipping through the pages. "I've seen glimpses of other worlds—impossible worlds. And I think you're the only one who can help me understand why."

The sound of shifting papers made him freeze. Drake's heart pounded in his ears as he slowly turned, half-expecting to find himself face-to-face with the elusive Rachel Summers.

Instead, he found himself staring at a wall covered in intricate drawings and equations. At the center was a familiar symbol—a dragon eating its own tail.

"Ouroboros," Drake whispered, a chill running down his spine. "It's all connected, isn't it?"

9 - 10

Drake's fingers traced the edge of the Ouroboros symbol, his mind racing. The clutter around him took on new significance—not just the detritus of a reclusive life, but the scattered pieces of a cosmic puzzle.

"Rachel," he called out again, his voice lower this time, almost pleading. "I know you're here. I'm not leaving until we talk."

Silence answered him, broken only by the creak of settling floorboards. Drake sighed, his shoulders sagging under the weight of his mission. He turned away from the wall, carefully navigating through the maze of papers and discarded books.

How many realities has she seen? he wondered, eyeing a stack of notebooks. *How many versions of herself has she encountered?*

As he ventured deeper into the house, each step crunched against debris—broken glass, crumpled papers, the occasional shard of what might have been lab equipment. The further he went, the more oppressive the air became, thick with dust and unspoken secrets.

"I understand why you're hiding," Drake said to the empty rooms, his voice barely above a whisper. "I've seen things too—things that make you question your sanity. But we can't run from this, Rachel. The fate of everything depends on what we do next."

He paused in what might have once been a living room, now transformed into a makeshift laboratory. Whiteboards covered in equations lined the walls, and a tangle of wires snaked across the floor, connecting various devices Drake couldn't begin to comprehend.

Someone's still living here, he realized, noting the fresh coffee stains on scattered papers. *If you can call this living.*

"Rachel," he tried once more, desperation creeping into his voice. "I need your help. We need to fix what's broken—across all realities. Please."

11 - 12

Drake's voice echoed faintly through the cluttered space, desperation seeping into his words. "Rachel, I need to talk to you." His hand brushed against a dusty shelf, leaving a clean streak in its wake. The silence that followed felt oppressive, thick with unspoken secrets.

He rounded a corner, and his breath caught in his throat. Before him stood a desk, its surface a chaotic landscape of intellectual pursuit. Notebooks were stacked haphazardly, their pages dogeared and stained with coffee. Files bulged with loose papers, threatening to spill their contents onto the floor.

But it was the sketches that drew Drake's attention. Crude diagrams of intersecting circles and diverging lines covered every available surface. His eyes darted from one to another, recognizing theories of the multiverse he'd only begun to grasp.

How deep does this rabbit hole go? he wondered, a chill running down his spine.

Then he saw it. Nestled among the scientific scrawls was a symbol that made his heart skip a beat. A dragon, its serpentine body coiled into an impossible knot, etched in shaky pen lines. The same symbol that had haunted his dreams, that had appeared in flashes across realities.

Drake's fingers hovered over the sketch, not daring to touch it. "Rachel," he whispered, his voice barely audible even to himself. "What have you discovered?"

The silence of the house seemed to press in around him, heavy with the weight of knowledge that shouldn't exist. Drake felt a sudden, overwhelming certainty that he stood on the precipice of something vast and terrifying—a truth that could unravel everything he thought he knew about reality itself.

13 - 14

A floorboard creaked behind him, sending a jolt of adrenaline through Drake's body. His muscles tensed, instincts honed by years of experience screaming danger. The hairs on the back of his neck stood on end as he sensed a presence lurking in the shadows.

I've walked right into it, Drake thought, his heart hammering against his ribs. *Stupid, so stupid.*

He started to turn, but it was too late. The air shifted, carrying with it the faintest whisper of movement. Drake's hand instinctively reached for a weapon that wasn't there, cursing his lack of preparation.

"Rachel?" he called out, his voice steady despite the fear clawing at his throat. "Is that you?"

Silence answered him, thick and oppressive. Drake's eyes darted around the room, searching for anything he could use to defend himself. The cluttered desk offered nothing but papers and pens—useless against whatever threat lurked in the darkness.

Think, Drake. What would Linda do? The thought of his wife, her calm presence in the face of danger, steadied him. He took a deep breath, forcing his racing mind to focus.

"I'm not here to hurt anyone," Drake said, slowly raising his hands in a gesture of surrender. "I just want to talk. About the Codex, about the multiverse—about everything that's happening."

The silence stretched on, unbearable in its intensity. Drake's muscles screamed with the effort of remaining still, every instinct urging him to run, to fight, to do something.

Then, a voice—low, raspy, and tinged with a desperation that sent chills down Drake's spine.

"How do you know about the Codex?"

15 - 16

Before Drake could formulate a response, pain exploded through his skull. The world tilted violently as something heavy struck the back of his head. Stars burst behind his eyelids, and he stumbled forward, his body moving on pure instinct. His hands shot out, barely catching the edge of the desk as he fought to remain upright.

Not like this, he thought, his mind reeling. *Not when I'm so close.*

Drake's vision swam, the room blurring and doubling before him. He tried to turn, to face his attacker, but his legs wouldn't cooperate. The taste of copper filled his mouth, and he realized he'd bitten his tongue.

"Wait," he managed to croak, the word barely audible over the ringing in his ears. "Please, I can explain—"

His plea was cut short as something cold and hard pressed against his temple. The unmistakable feel of a gun barrel sent a jolt of adrenaline through his system, momentarily clearing the fog of pain.

"Don't," a voice hissed, trembling with a mixture of fear and determination. "Don't move. Don't speak."

Drake's heart hammered against his ribs, each beat a painful reminder of how quickly things had spiraled out of control. He'd come seeking answers, hoping to unravel the mystery that had consumed his life. Now, he stood on the precipice of losing everything—again.

Linda, Harrison, I'm sorry, he thought, a wave of regret washing over him. *I should have found another way.*

17 - 18

Drake froze, his breath catching in his throat. The voice was sharp and unsteady, tinged with a frantic edge that suggested desperation more than control. He could feel the barrel trembling against his skin, a silent testament to the speaker's state of mind.

Calm, Drake told himself, fighting to keep his own panic at bay. *Stay calm. You've faced worse.*

But had he? The memories of other realities, of other dangers, felt distant and hazy. Here, now, with cold metal pressed against his temple, Drake felt acutely mortal.

"I'm not here to hurt you," he said, his voice low and steady despite the fear coiling in his gut. "I'm looking for answers. About the Codex, about the multiverse."

The gun pressed harder, eliciting a sharp intake of breath from Drake.

"How do you know those things?" the voice demanded, cracking with tension.

Drake's mind raced, weighing his options. Truth had always been a shifting concept in his journey through the multiverse, but now it felt like his only lifeline.

"Because I've seen them," he said, carefully. "In other realities. Other versions of this world."

A beat of silence followed, heavy with the weight of impossibility.

"That's not possible," the voice whispered, more to itself than to Drake. "The crossings erase memory. No one remembers."

Drake seized on the hesitation. "But I do. And I think you know why."

19 - 20

The tension in the air thickened, a palpable force pressing against Drake's skin. He could hear the ragged breathing of his unseen assailant, could feel the slight tremor in the gun barrel still pressed against his temple. The musty scent of neglect and desperation filled his nostrils, a stark reminder of how far they'd both fallen.

"Who are you?" the voice demanded, a brittle edge of fear cutting through the hostility. "Why are you here?"

Drake's heart raced, his mind frantically searching for the right words. He'd faced death before, in other realities, other lives. But this moment felt painfully, terrifyingly real. The weight of his choices, of the lives he'd lived and lost, threatened to crush him.

Slowly, deliberately, he raised his hands in surrender. "Rachel?" he said cautiously, his voice barely above a whisper. The name hung in the air between them, a fragile bridge across a chasm of distrust and confusion.

As he spoke, Drake's thoughts whirled. *This is it,* he realized. *The moment everything changes. Again.* The irony wasn't lost on him - how many times had he stood on the precipice of revelation, only to have reality shift beneath his feet?

He waited, breath held, for Rachel's response. In that suspended moment, Drake found himself hoping - not just for his own survival, but for answers. For a chance to finally understand the tangled web of realities that had become his existence.

21 - 22

The pressure of the gun increased against Drake's temple, the cold metal biting into his skin. His pulse quickened, each heartbeat a thunderous reminder of his mortality.

"Answer me!" Rachel's voice cracked, a mixture of desperation and determination.

Drake inhaled deeply, steadying himself. The musty air filled his lungs, grounding him in this precarious moment. He chose his words carefully, knowing they could mean the difference between life and death.

"My name's Drake Miller," he said, his tone calm despite the tension coiling in his muscles. He fought the urge to turn and face her, instead keeping his gaze fixed on the cluttered desk before him. Papers covered in complex equations and diagrams swam in his vision, tantalizing hints of the knowledge he sought.

"I'm not here to hurt you," Drake continued, his voice low and steady. "I'm here because I need your help."

As he spoke, memories of Linda flashed through his mind – her gentle smile, her unwavering support. The thought of her gave him strength, even as it twisted like a knife in his gut. *I'm doing this for her,* he reminded himself. *For Harrison. For all of us.*

Drake's fingers twitched, aching to reach for the papers on the desk, to unravel the mysteries that had haunted him across realities. But he remained still, acutely aware of the weapon pressed against his head and the fragile trust he was trying to build.

"Help?" Rachel's voice wavered, a mix of skepticism and curiosity. "What could you possibly need my help with?"

Drake closed his eyes briefly, steeling himself for what came next. When he opened them, his gaze fell on a crude sketch of intertwining realities. *How fitting,* he thought grimly.

23 - 24

The silence stretched between them, heavy and oppressive. Drake's heart thundered in his chest, each beat a reminder of how precariously his life hung in the balance. Slowly, almost imperceptibly, he felt the pressure of the gun barrel shift against his temple.

Taking a carefully measured breath, Drake turned his head just enough to glimpse the person holding him at gunpoint. His eyes widened, a mixture of shock and recognition washing over him.

Before him stood a woman, her appearance as disheveled as the cluttered room around them. Her hair, once a vibrant auburn, now hung in unkempt strands streaked with premature gray. Dark circles ringed her eyes, which darted nervously between Drake and the door. She wore a wrinkled lab coat over a tattered sweater, the ensemble a far cry from the polished scientist he remembered from another life.

"Rachel," Drake breathed, his voice barely above a whisper. He hadn't meant to speak her name aloud, but the sight of her – so changed, so haunted – had startled the word from his lips.

Her hands trembled as she gripped the weapon, knuckles white with tension. "How do you know my name?" she demanded, fear and suspicion warring in her voice.

Drake's mind raced, weighing his options. How much could he reveal without pushing her over the edge? "It's... complicated," he began cautiously. "But I promise, if you'll hear me out, I can explain everything."

As he spoke, Drake's gaze swept over the room, taking in the scattered papers and discarded coffee cups. *What happened to you, Rachel?* he wondered. *What nightmares have you seen?*

25 - 26

"Rachel Summers," Drake said softly, his voice tinged with a mixture of relief and apprehension. The name felt both familiar and foreign on his tongue, a reminder of the surreal nature of his current reality.

Her eyes narrowed, the haunted look in them intensifying. Her finger tightened on the trigger, causing Drake's heart to skip a beat. "Who sent you?" she demanded, her voice a hoarse whisper. "Was it NovaTech? The board?" A flicker of raw fear crossed her face. "Or was it him?"

Drake's mind raced, trying to process the rapid-fire questions. The mention of NovaTech sent a chill down his spine, memories of corporate intrigue and ethical dilemmas flooding back. He raised his hands slowly, palms out in a gesture of peace.

"No one sent me, Rachel," he said, fighting to keep his voice steady. "I came here on my own. I need your help."

As he spoke, Drake's gaze darted around the cluttered room, taking in the chaos of papers and equipment. *This isn't just a hideout*, he realized. *It's a fortress of obsession*. The air felt thick with tension and the faint scent of ozone, as if the very fabric of reality was stretched thin here.

Rachel's grip on the gun wavered slightly, confusion momentarily replacing the fear in her eyes. "Help?" she repeated, her voice cracking. "You have no idea what you're asking. No idea what's at stake."

Drake swallowed hard, weighing his next words carefully. The wrong move could shatter this fragile moment, but he knew he had to push forward. "I know more than you think, Rachel," he said softly. "About the Codex, about the multiverse. About the price of crossing between worlds."

27 - 28

Drake's words hung in the air, heavy with implication. Rachel's eyes widened, a flicker of recognition passing across her haggard features. Her grip on the gun tightened once more, knuckles whitening.

"Him?" Drake echoed, confusion furrowing his brow. The tremor in Rachel's voice had stirred something deep within him, a primal fear he couldn't quite place. "Who are you talking about?"

Rachel's lips curled into a snarl, her whole body seeming to recoil at the mere thought of uttering the name. "Gabriel," she spat, her voice trembling with a mixture of rage and terror.

The name hit Drake like a physical blow, memories cascading through his mind in a dizzying rush. Gabriel – the specter that had haunted his dreams, the shadow lurking at the edges of every reality he'd encountered. His throat constricted, pulse quickening as he struggled to maintain his composure.

How does she know him? Drake wondered, fighting to keep his expression neutral. *What has Gabriel done to her?*

"Rachel," he said softly, taking a cautious step forward. "I need you to tell me everything you know about Gabriel. He's the key to all of this, isn't he?"

29 - 30

Drake's blood ran cold, the name reverberating through his core like a death knell. The room seemed to darken, shadows creeping in at the edges of his vision. His mouth went dry, tongue sticking to the roof of his mouth as he forced out the words.

"Gabriel? You've seen him?"

The question hung in the air, laden with unspoken dread. Drake's mind raced, conjuring images of Gabriel's scarred face, that twisted sneer that had haunted his nightmares. He clenched his fists, nails digging into his palms as he fought to stay grounded in this reality.

Rachel's expression shifted, the fear in her eyes momentarily replaced by confusion. Her grip on the gun loosened slightly, brow furrowing as she studied Drake's face with newfound intensity.

"You know Gabriel?" she asked, her voice a mixture of disbelief and cautious hope.

Drake swallowed hard, weighing his words carefully. How much could he reveal without putting Rachel – or himself – in even greater danger? The weight of multiple realities pressed down on him, memories of other lives, other choices, threatening to overwhelm his senses.

"I've... encountered him," Drake said finally, his voice low and measured. "He's been a shadow in my life, always just out of reach. But you – you've actually seen him here, in this reality?"

He watched Rachel closely, searching for any sign of deception or madness in her eyes. But all he saw was a mirror of his own haunted expression, a shared understanding of the terror Gabriel represented.

31 - 32

Drake's heart pounded in his chest, each beat a reminder of the fragile nature of his existence. He took a deep breath, steeling himself for the conversation ahead.

"I've seen him," Drake said, his voice low and husky with suppressed emotion. "He's been following me, haunting me. He's why I'm here." He paused, the weight of his next words pressing down on him like a physical force. "I need answers, Rachel. About the Codex, the multiverse—everything."

The air in the room seemed to thicken, charged with tension and unspoken revelations. Drake watched as Rachel's eyes widened, her grip on the gun faltering slightly. Her gaze darted to the cluttered desk behind him, lingering on a stack of papers covered in complex equations and diagrams.

"How do you know about the Codex?" Rachel whispered, her voice barely audible over the pounding of Drake's heart.

Drake's mind raced, memories of alternate realities flashing through his consciousness. He could almost taste the metallic tang of fear on his tongue, the same fear he'd experienced in countless other versions of this moment. But this time was different. This time, he had to get it right.

He opened his mouth to respond, but the words caught in his throat. How could he possibly explain the impossible? The weight of multiple lifetimes pressed down on him, threatening to crush him under the burden of knowledge no single person was meant to bear.

33 - 34

Drake swallowed hard, his Adam's apple bobbing visibly. The room seemed to spin around him, the cluttered walls closing in as he struggled to find the right words. Finally, he spoke, his voice low and measured.

"Because I've seen it, Rachel. I've seen the Red World, with its crimson skies and seas of blood. The Green World, where nature has reclaimed every inch of civilization. And the Blue World, where technology reigns supreme." He paused, his eyes locking onto hers. "I remember you showing it to me... in another reality."

The words hung in the air between them, heavy with implication. Drake watched as Rachel's face transformed, disbelief warring with a flicker of recognition in her eyes. Her hand trembled violently, the gun lowering slightly as her breathing quickened.

"That's... impossible," Rachel whispered, her voice cracking. "No one's supposed to remember. The crossings erase memory."

Drake's mind reeled, grappling with the implications of her words. He had suspected as much, but hearing it confirmed sent a chill down his spine. How many times had he crossed? How many versions of himself had been erased, forgotten?

"And yet, here I am," Drake said softly, spreading his hands in a gesture of vulnerability. "Remembering everything."

35 - 36

Drake took a cautious step back from the desk, his fingers brushing against the rough edge of a weathered notebook. The touch grounded him, a stark reminder of the precarious reality he now inhabited. His heart pounded, each beat echoing the weight of his next words.

"I'm not supposed to be here either," he said, his voice barely above a whisper. The admission felt like a stone lodged in his throat, a truth he'd been carrying for far too long. "But here I am. And I think you know why."

Rachel's eyes, wide and haunted, bore into him. Her lips pressed into a thin line, the gun in her hand wavering uncertainly. For a moment, Drake thought she might raise it again, might decide that silencing him was easier than facing the implications of his presence.

In that suspended moment, memories flooded Drake's mind—fragments of a life he'd lived and lost, of mistakes made and redemption sought. The weight of it all threatened to crush him, but he stood firm, waiting.

Then, with a defeated sigh that seemed to deflate her entire being, Rachel lowered the gun completely. She stepped back, her shoulders slumping as if Atlas had finally shrugged off the world.

"You're right," she murmured, her voice thick with resignation. "I do know why. God help me, I wish I didn't."

Drake's breath caught in his throat. Here, at last, was the precipice of truth he'd been seeking. But as he stood on the edge, he wondered if he was truly prepared for the fall that would follow.

37 - 38

"Close the door," Rachel said, her voice weary, the words hanging in the stale air like cobwebs.

Drake moved slowly, each step deliberate, as if traversing a minefield. The ancient hinges groaned in protest as he pushed the door shut, sealing them both in this forgotten pocket of reality. He turned back to face Rachel, his heart a thunderous rhythm in his chest.

Rachel's shoulders slumped further, if that was even possible. With trembling fingers, she placed the gun on the cluttered desk, the metallic clunk echoing in the silence. Her hand, now free of its deadly burden, ran through her tangled hair, leaving it even more disheveled.

"Rachel," Drake began, his voice low and careful, "I need to understand. What's happening to me, to us, to... everything?"

She let out a bitter laugh, the sound sharp and discordant. "Understanding? That's a luxury we can't afford, Drake. Not anymore."

Her words sent a chill down his spine. Drake's mind raced, piecing together fragments of memory and intuition. "The multiverse," he pressed, taking a tentative step forward. "It's unraveling, isn't it?"

Rachel's gaze snapped to his, a spark of her old brilliance flaring in those tired eyes. "How much do you remember?" she demanded.

Drake hesitated, sorting through the jumble of images and sensations in his mind. "Flashes," he admitted. "Glimpses of other worlds, other lives. And always, always that damn dragon symbol."

Rachel's breath hitched. "The Ouroboros," she whispered. "It's the key to everything."

As she spoke, Drake's gaze wandered to the scattered papers on her desk. Crude sketches of intertwining realities, equations that defied conventional physics, and there—stark against the chaos—the familiar coils of the dragon devouring its own tail.

"We've done this before, haven't we?" Drake asked, the realization settling like lead in his stomach. "In another reality, another time."

Rachel nodded, her expression a mixture of awe and dread. "You shouldn't remember," she said. "The crossings are supposed to erase everything."

Drake's fists clenched at his sides, frustration bubbling up. "Then why do I? Why am I here, Rachel? What went wrong?"

She turned away, her gaze fixed on some distant point beyond the grimy window. "Everything," she murmured. "Everything went wrong."

39 - 39

The weight of Rachel's words hung in the air, heavy and oppressive. Drake's chest tightened, a cold dread seeping into his bones. He watched as Rachel's fingers traced the outline of the Ouroboros on a nearby sketch, her touch almost reverent.

"What do you mean, everything?" Drake asked, his voice hoarse. He swallowed hard, trying to quell the rising panic. "Rachel, please. I need to understand."

She turned to face him, her eyes haunted. "The boundaries between realities are collapsing," Rachel explained, her words barely above a whisper. "Every time we cross, every time we manipulate the fabric of the multiverse, we weaken it further."

Drake's mind reeled. He remembered Linda's face, twisted with fear and confusion. How could he explain this to her? How could he protect her from something he barely understood himself?

"But there has to be a way to fix it," Drake insisted, desperation creeping into his voice. "That's why I'm here, isn't it? To set things right?"

Rachel's laugh was bitter, devoid of humor. "Fix it? Drake, we're way past fixing. The best we can hope for now is containment."

As she spoke, Drake's gaze was drawn to a series of complex diagrams on the far wall. Lines and circles intersected in dizzying patterns, like a mad spider's web of reality. In the center, the Ouroboros symbol pulsed with an almost hypnotic intensity.

"What happens if we can't contain it?" Drake asked, though part of him dreaded the answer.

Rachel's eyes met his, filled with a terrible certainty. "Then everything ends. Not just our world, but all worlds. The entire multiverse, snuffed out like a candle in the wind."

Fragments of Truth

1 -2 Rachel's frenzied movements blurred before Drake's eyes, her form a whirlwind of restless energy. Papers rustled and fluttered in her wake as she paced the cramped room, her muttered words an incomprehensible stream of consciousness. Drake watched, muscles tense, as her trembling hands skimmed over scattered documents and weathered tomes.

The air hung heavy with the musty scent of old books and desperation. Drake's heart hammered in his chest as he observed Rachel's manic search, her eyes wild and unfocused. What had happened to the brilliant scientist he remembered? The woman before him seemed a mere shadow of her former self, worn down by isolation and relentless pursuit of forbidden knowledge.

He raised his hands slowly, palms out in a gesture of peace. "Rachel," he began, his voice low and steady despite the turmoil roiling within him. The weight of his mission pressed down upon him, the fate of multiple realities balanced on a knife's edge.

Rachel's gaze snapped to him, her movements freezing mid-step. For a moment, recognition flickered in her eyes, quickly replaced by suspicion. Drake's breath caught in his throat. Would she remember him? Or had the distortions of this fractured reality erased all traces of their shared past?

"Who are you?" Rachel demanded, her voice hoarse from disuse. "How did you find me?"

Drake's mind raced, searching for the right words to bridge the chasm between them. How could he explain the inexplicable? That he had lived and died and lived again, all in pursuit of a truth that threatened to unravel the very fabric of existence?

"I'm here because I need your help," he said finally, each word carefully chosen. "Because I remember you, Rachel. I remember the Codex."

Rachel's eyes widened, a mix of fear and desperate hope etched across her features. Drake pressed on, knowing that every second counted. "I know it sounds impossible, but I've crossed lines that shouldn't be crossed. And now, I'm trapped. We're all trapped."

As he spoke, Drake's gaze swept the room, taking in the chaos of Rachel's makeshift sanctuary. Equations scrawled on crumpled papers, diagrams of intertwining realities, and fragments of ancient texts all pointed to one inescapable truth: the world they knew was an illusion, a construct hiding a far more terrifying reality.

Rachel's lips parted, poised to speak, and Drake held his breath. Would she believe him? Or had he come too late, the brilliant mind he once knew lost to paranoia and isolation? The fate of everything he loved hung in the balance, waiting for her response.

3 - 4

Rachel's body tensed, her fingers curling into fists at her sides. The soft light filtering through the dusty windows cast shadows across her face, highlighting the sharp angles of her cheekbones and the dark circles under her eyes. For a moment, the only sound in the room was the soft rustling of papers stirred by an unseen draft.

"Rachel," Drake said softly, his voice steady but gentle, "I'm not here to hurt you. I need your help."

The words hung in the air between them, heavy with unspoken implications. Drake's heart pounded in his chest, each beat a reminder of the precious seconds ticking away. He could almost feel the fabric of reality shifting around them, threatening to unravel at any moment.

Rachel froze mid-step, turning sharply to face him. Her eyes narrowed, lips curling into a sneer. "Help? You want my help?" Her voice dripped with bitterness and barely contained fury. "That's what they all say, right before they put a bullet in your head."

Drake flinched at the raw pain in her words. He remembered a different Rachel – confident, brilliant, fearless. The woman before him now was a shadow of that former self, worn down by isolation and the weight of terrible knowledge. Yet beneath the anger, he sensed a flicker of the same determination that had once driven her to unravel the mysteries of the multiverse.

'She's our only hope,' Drake thought, desperately searching for a way to reach her. 'If I can't convince her, everything we've fought for will be lost.' The faces of his wife and son flashed through his mind, their fates hanging in the balance of this fragile moment.

5 - 6

Drake raised his hands, palms out, in a gesture of peace. His voice was low and steady, belying the turmoil churning within. "No one sent me," he assured her, meeting Rachel's wild gaze. "I came here on my own. I'm just trying to figure out what's happening to me."

A flicker of uncertainty crossed Rachel's face, but it was quickly replaced by a sharp, humorless laugh that sent a chill down Drake's spine. The sound was tinged with hysteria, echoing off the cluttered walls of the small room.

"What's happening to you?" Rachel's voice rose, her words tumbling out in a frenzied cascade. "What's happening to you? Do you have any idea what I've seen? What I know?"

She whirled around, her frayed lab coat swirling about her like tattered wings. With frantic energy, Rachel gestured wildly at the papers strewn across her desk. Drake's eyes followed her movements, catching glimpses of complex equations and bizarre diagrams that seemed to swim before his eyes.

'What am I looking at?' he wondered, a growing sense of unease settling in his gut. 'How deep does this rabbit hole go?'

Rachel's next words cut through his thoughts like a knife. "They don't want me to talk. The Codex—it's not just a book. It's a key. A key to everything, to everywhere." Her voice dropped to a hoarse whisper, her eyes wide with a mix of fear and defiance. "And they'll kill me before they let me use it!"

Drake felt the weight of her words settle over him like a shroud. The Codex. The name stirred something in the depths of his fragmented memories, a sense of both hope and dread. He knew, with a certainty that chilled him to his core, that whatever this Codex was, it held the answers he so desperately sought.

'But at what cost?' he wondered, studying Rachel's haggard face. 'How many lives have already been destroyed by this knowledge?'

7 - 8

Drake took a cautious step forward, the floorboards creaking softly beneath his weight. The sound seemed to echo in the cramped, paper-strewn room, a stark reminder of the fragility of their situation. He lowered his voice, aware of the tremor in his own words as he spoke.

"Rachel, I believe you."

Her eyes snapped to his, wide with surprise and a flicker of something else—hope, perhaps, or the desperate need to be understood. Drake felt a tightness in his chest, a mixture of empathy and his own burning need for answers.

"I remember the Codex," he continued, the words tasting both familiar and foreign on his tongue. "That's why I'm here. I need you to help me remember what it is and what it does."

Rachel's frantic energy seemed to still for a moment, her gaze searching his face with an intensity that made Drake want to look away. But he held firm, knowing that this moment of connection was crucial.

'How much can I trust her?' he wondered, even as he maintained eye contact. 'And how much can she trust me, when I barely know myself?'

The silence stretched between them, heavy with unspoken questions and the weight of shared, yet fragmented, knowledge. Drake could almost feel the pieces of the puzzle shifting, realigning in his mind. But the picture was still far from complete.

"You remember?" Rachel finally whispered, her voice a mix of awe and suspicion. "But how? The Codex... it's not something you simply recall. It's—"

"Dangerous," Drake finished for her, the word rising unbidden from some locked corner of his memory. "Powerful. And the key to everything that's happening to me, isn't it?"

9 - 10

Rachel's eyes widened, her frantic energy faltering as confusion softened her features. "You... you remember the Codex?" Her voice trembled, a mix of disbelief and cautious hope.

Drake nodded slowly, his brow furrowing as he tried to grasp the elusive threads of memory. "Yes," he said, his voice low and measured. "It's not all clear, but I remember enough to know it's important."

He paused, running a hand through his disheveled hair. The weight of his experiences pressed down on him, making each word feel like a struggle. "I was in a car accident," he continued, his gaze distant. "It left me... stuck between two worlds."

As he spoke, Drake's mind flashed with fragmented images - the screech of tires, the shattering of glass, and then... darkness. And light. And darkness again. He shook his head, trying to clear the jumbled memories.

"I lived two different lives," he explained, his voice tinged with a mixture of wonder and dread. "Going to sleep in one and waking up in another."

Rachel leaned forward, her earlier hostility replaced by intense curiosity. Drake could almost see the gears turning in her brilliant mind, piecing together the impossible puzzle he presented.

'How much should I tell her?' Drake wondered, acutely aware of the delicate balance between trust and caution. 'Every word could change everything - or lead us closer to the truth.'

11 - 12

Rachel's eyes widened slightly, but she said nothing, letting him continue. The silence in the cluttered room felt oppressive, broken only by the soft rustling of papers as a draft whispered through the window.

Drake took a deep breath, steeling himself for what came next. His hand trembled slightly as he reached out to steady himself against the edge of Rachel's desk. The wood felt cool beneath his fingers, grounding him in this reality - for now.

"In both of those worlds," Drake said, his voice dropping to a near-whisper, "there was someone chasing me." He swallowed hard, the memory of his pursuer sending a chill down his spine. "A man - if you can call him that. His face was... burned, twisted."

As he spoke, Drake's mind conjured vivid images of the nightmarish figure that had haunted his dual existence. The smell of scorched flesh seemed to fill his nostrils, making his stomach churn.

"He hunted me across both realities," Drake continued, his eyes locked on Rachel's face, searching for any flicker of recognition. "Always one step behind."

'But why?' Drake thought, frustration building within him. 'What does he want from me? What am I missing?'

The weight of his words hung in the air between them, heavy with implications neither of them fully understood. Drake waited, his heart pounding, for Rachel's response. Would she believe him? Or had he just sealed his fate as another raving lunatic in her eyes?

13 - 14

Rachel's face drained of color, her freckles stark against her pallid skin. Her hands, once steady and sure in the lab, now trembled visibly as she gripped the edge of the desk for support. The scattered papers beneath her fingers rustled softly, a whisper of secrets yet untold.

"Gabriel," she murmured, the name escaping her lips like a prayer - or a curse.

Drake's stomach clenched at the sound, a cold dread seeping through his veins. The weight of that single word settled heavily in the air between them, thick with unspoken history and shared terror. He fought to keep his voice steady as he asked, "You know him?"

His mind raced, piecing together fragments of memory. The burn-scarred face that haunted his nightmares now had a name, and Rachel's reaction confirmed his worst fears. This wasn't just his nightmare anymore.

'What connection does she have to Gabriel?' Drake wondered, studying Rachel's face. The lines etched around her eyes seemed deeper now, speaking of sleepless nights and relentless pursuit. 'And how deep does this rabbit hole go?'

He watched as Rachel's gaze darted to the window, checking for unseen threats. Her paranoia was palpable, infecting the air around them. Drake found himself mirroring her actions, the hairs on the back of his neck standing on end.

"Rachel," he pressed gently, fighting to keep the desperation from his voice. "Please. I need to understand. Who is he?"

15 - 16

Rachel let out a shaky breath, her shoulders sagging under the weight of knowledge she'd carried for far too long. The fading sunlight caught the strands of her dulled red hair, casting shadows across her worn features.

"He's not just a man," she said, her voice barely above a whisper. Drake had to lean in to catch her words, the urgency in her tone sending a chill down his spine. "He's a... remnant. A fracture in the fabric of the multiverse, tied to the Codex."

Drake's mind reeled, struggling to process the implications of her words. The Codex – that elusive key to everything – suddenly felt more tangible, more dangerous.

Rachel's eyes met his, a fierce intensity burning within them. "He's the embodiment of everything broken, everything wrong. And if he's chasing you, it means you've crossed lines that shouldn't be crossed."

Drake swallowed hard, his throat dry. "What kind of lines?" he asked, dreading the answer.

Rachel's gaze drifted to the scattered papers on her desk, her fingers tracing the edge of a complex diagram. "Temporal lines, dimensional boundaries," she explained, her voice taking on the crisp, authoritative tone of the scientist she once was. "The Codex... it's not just a book. It's a map, a key to navigating the multiverse."

Drake's heart raced. This was it – the missing piece he'd been searching for. "And Gabriel? What's his connection to all this?"

Rachel's expression darkened. "He's the enforcer, the failsafe. When someone like you disrupts the natural order, he appears to... correct the anomaly."

The implications hit Drake like a physical blow. 'I'm the anomaly,' he realized, a cold sweat breaking out across his skin. 'My very existence is a threat to reality itself.'

As the gravity of the situation settled over him, Drake couldn't help but wonder: in trying to save his family, had he inadvertently put the entire multiverse at risk?

17 - 18

Drake ran a hand through his disheveled hair, his mind reeling with the weight of Rachel's words. The small room seemed to close in around him, the scattered papers and books on her desk now appearing less like academic clutter and more like the remnants of a desperate search for answers.

"I think I've been crossing lines my whole life," Drake admitted, his voice barely above a whisper. "I just didn't know it until the accident." He paused, meeting Rachel's intense gaze. "But here's the thing—I remember you. Not clearly, but I remember you helping me before."

Rachel's eyes widened, a flicker of recognition passing across her face.

"You had the Codex," Drake continued, the words tumbling out as fragmented memories surfaced. "Somehow, it helped me solve... something. Something about the multiverse."

As he spoke, Drake's mind raced, trying to piece together the elusive fragments of his past. Had he truly navigated the complexities of multiple realities before? The thought both thrilled and terrified him.

Rachel stared at him, her eyes searching his face as though trying to piece together a puzzle of her own. The silence stretched between them, heavy with unspoken questions and half-remembered truths.

"You're not supposed to remember," she said finally, her voice a mixture of awe and concern. "Crossings erase memory. They wipe away everything—past lives, past selves." She took a step closer, her gaze never leaving his face. "But you... you're different."

Drake felt a chill run down his spine at her words. Different. The word hung in the air, laden with implications he couldn't fully grasp. Was this why Gabriel was hunting him? Because he retained memories he shouldn't have?

"What does that mean for me?" Drake asked, his voice tight with apprehension. "For my family?"

Rachel's expression softened, a flicker of sympathy passing across her features. "It means you're a wild card, Drake. A variable the multiverse didn't account for." She gestured to the papers on her desk. "And in my experience, the multiverse doesn't like variables."

As Drake processed her words, a fierce determination welled up within him. He may not fully understand the forces at play, but one thing was clear: he would do whatever it took to protect his family and unravel the mystery of his fractured existence.

19 - 20

Drake's hands clenched at his sides, his knuckles whitening as he struggled to articulate the horrifying reality he'd been living. The weight of countless repeated days pressed down on him, each one ending in the same devastating loss.

"My memories are fragmented," he admitted, his voice rough with emotion. "I can't remember everything, but I know enough to realize that I'm stuck." He swallowed hard, forcing himself to meet Rachel's gaze. "I keep living the same day over and over again, and no matter what I do, my wife and son end up dying. Every time."

The words hung in the air, heavy and oppressive. Drake could almost see the ghosts of his family, their faces etched with fear and confusion in those final moments. He blinked hard, trying to banish the image.

Rachel's scrutiny softened, her earlier suspicion melting into something closer to sympathy. Her brow furrowed as she processed his words, her brilliant mind no doubt racing to connect the dots he couldn't yet see.

"You're trapped in a loop," she said, almost to herself. Her voice was barely above a whisper, tinged with a mixture of fascination and sorrow. "A temporal correction."

Drake's heart raced at her words. A correction? Was that what this hell was? Some cosmic force trying to set things right? He opened his mouth to ask, desperate for more information, but Rachel was already moving, her hands flying over the papers on her desk with renewed purpose.

As she worked, Drake's mind reeled. He thought of Linda's smile, of Harrison's laughter. How many times had he watched them slip away? How many more times would he have to endure it? The weight of it all threatened to crush him, but he steeled himself. He had to find a way out of this loop, not just for himself, but for them.

21 - 22

Drake's frown deepened, etching lines of worry across his forehead. The word "correction" echoed in his mind, a sinister whisper that sent a chill down his spine. His voice, when he finally found it, was hoarse with tension.

"What does that mean?"

Rachel's eyes met his, and in them, he saw a reflection of his own fear and desperation. She took a deep breath, her slender fingers tracing the edge of a worn leather-bound book on her cluttered desk. When she spoke, her voice was tinged with a sorrow that seemed to age her beyond her years.

"It means the universe is trying to fix a mistake," she explained, each word falling heavily between them. "Somewhere along the way, something happened that wasn't supposed to. A fracture. A deviation."

Drake's mind raced, grasping at fragments of memory. A car crash, a flash of light, the sickening crunch of metal. Had that been the mistake? Or was it something deeper, more fundamental?

Rachel continued, her gaze distant as if seeing beyond the confines of the small, paper-strewn room. "And now the loop is trying to correct it by erasing everything that shouldn't exist."

The implications of her words hit Drake like a physical blow. He staggered slightly, steadying himself against the edge of the desk. Everything that shouldn't exist. His family, his life, perhaps even himself. The room seemed to spin around him, the scattered papers and books blurring into a chaotic whirl.

"So, what you're saying," Drake began, his voice barely above a whisper, "is that my wife, my son... they're being erased because they're part of this mistake?"

The silence that followed was deafening. Drake could hear his own heartbeat, thundering in his ears like a countdown to oblivion. He watched Rachel's face, searching for any sign of hope, any indication that he had misunderstood. But her expression remained grave, her eyes filled with a mixture of pity and grim determination.

23 - 24

Drake's chest tightened, a vise of dread constricting his heart. He ran a hand through his disheveled hair, his fingers trembling. "And I'm part of that 'everything,'" he said, the words catching in his throat like shards of glass.

The weight of this realization pressed down on him, threatening to crush the last vestiges of hope he clung to. His mind reeled, flashing back to the countless iterations of that fateful day, each ending in tragedy. Had it all been leading to this? Was he nothing more than a glitch in the fabric of reality, destined to be erased?

Rachel nodded solemnly, her red hair catching the dim light as she moved. "If Gabriel is after you, then yes," she confirmed, her voice a mix of scientific detachment and genuine concern. "He's part of the correction. He's trying to make sure the loop succeeds."

Drake's fists clenched involuntarily, his knuckles turning white. The image of Gabriel's twisted, burned face floated before his mind's eye, a nightmarish visage that had haunted him across realities. He had thought the man—if he could be called that—was his personal demon. Now, he understood Gabriel was something far worse: an agent of a universe bent on his annihilation.

"So, every time I've tried to save them," Drake muttered, more to himself than to Rachel, "I've been fighting against... what? The very fabric of reality?"

He looked up at Rachel, searching her face for answers. The lines of exhaustion etched around her eyes seemed deeper now, mirroring his own weariness. In that moment, Drake felt the full weight of his isolation, adrift in a sea of fractured timelines and parallel worlds.

25 - 26

Drake took a step closer to Rachel, his heart pounding with a desperate urgency. The scattered papers on her desk rustled in the wake of his movement, a whisper of secrets yet to be uncovered. He could feel time slipping away, each second bringing him closer to another reset, another loss.

"Then help me stop it," Drake pleaded, his voice raw with emotion. He swallowed hard, fighting back the lump in his throat. "You did before—somehow, you did. I need you to do it again."

His eyes locked with Rachel's, searching for a glimmer of recognition, a spark of the alliance they must have forged in a timeline he could barely remember. The air between them felt charged, heavy with the weight of countless lives and realities hanging in the balance.

Drake's mind raced, recalling fragments of memories—Rachel's face illuminated by the glow of the Codex, her hands deftly manipulating its pages. He had trusted her once, relied on her expertise to navigate the labyrinth of the multiverse. Now, he needed that trust again, more than ever.

"I know it's asking a lot," Drake continued, his voice softening. "But I've seen my family die too many times. I can't—" His voice cracked, and he paused, gathering himself. "I can't let it happen again. Not if there's even a chance we can stop it."

He waited, breath held, as Rachel's expression shifted from wariness to consideration. The clock on the wall ticked loudly, each second an eternity as Drake silently willed her to understand, to remember, to help.

27 - 28

Rachel's eyes darted to the chaos of papers and books strewn across her desk, her gaze lingering on a tattered journal with faded leather binding. She took a deep breath, the weight of countless realities pressing down on her shoulders.

"The Codex," she began, her voice low and tinged with a mixture of awe and trepidation. "It's the only thing that can explain what's happening to you. The only thing that can break the loop. But..."

Rachel's words trailed off, leaving the air thick with unspoken implications. Drake's heart raced, his mind conjuring a thousand possible endings to that sentence, each more dire than the last.

"But what?" he pressed, fighting to keep his voice steady. His hands clenched at his sides, knuckles white with tension.

As he waited for Rachel's response, Drake's gaze swept over the cluttered room. Equations scrawled on whiteboards, star charts pinned to walls, and stacks of arcane tomes created a labyrinth of knowledge that seemed both comforting and overwhelming. This was the lair of a brilliant mind grappling with impossible truths.

Rachel's fingers traced the spine of the leather-bound journal, her touch reverent. "The Codex isn't just a book, Drake," she murmured, her eyes distant. "It's a key to the multiverse, a map of realities. In the wrong hands, it could unravel everything."

Drake's stomach churned with a mix of hope and dread. The Codex held the answers he desperately needed, but at what cost? He thought of his wife's smile, his son's laughter—echoes from a life that kept slipping through his fingers. Whatever the risk, he had to take it.

"I understand the dangers," Drake said, his voice barely above a whisper. "But I've lost them too many times. If there's even a chance..."

29 - 30

Rachel's shoulders slumped, her once-vibrant red hair falling limply around her face. She looked up at Drake, her eyes filled with a mix of regret and fear. "I don't have it anymore," she admitted, her voice trembling. "After they fired me, I hid it. I didn't want them—NovaTech, Gabriel, anyone—to get their hands on it. But I don't know if it's still safe."

Drake's heart plummeted. He clenched his fists, frustration mounting as he fought to keep his composure. The weight of countless lost days, of watching his family die over and over, threatened to crush him. He took a deep breath, steadying himself.

"Where did you hide it?" he asked, his voice low and urgent.

Rachel shook her head, her gaze darting nervously around the room. "I can't... I shouldn't tell you. It's too dangerous."

Drake stepped closer, his imposing frame casting a shadow over Rachel's hunched form. He didn't want to intimidate her, but desperation clawed at his insides. "Rachel, please," he implored. "Every moment we waste is another chance for me to lose them again. I can't... I can't keep living that nightmare."

As he spoke, images flashed through his mind: his wife's lifeless eyes, his son's small body crumpled on the pavement. The memories, real or imagined, tore at his soul. He swallowed hard, pushing back the tide of grief.

Rachel studied him, her expression softening. "You really do remember, don't you?" she murmured. "The loop hasn't erased everything."

Drake nodded, a glimmer of hope rising in his chest. "That has to mean something, right? Maybe I can break the cycle, but I need your help."

For a long moment, Rachel was silent, her internal struggle evident in the furrow of her brow. Finally, she sighed, her shoulders straightening with resolve.

"Alright," she said, her voice gaining strength. "If anyone has a chance of using the Codex without destroying reality, it's you."

Drake's heart leapt. He reached out, grasping Rachel's shoulder gently. "Then we'll find it. Together."

31 - 32

Rachel's eyes met Drake's, her gaze intense and conflicted. The dim light of the cluttered room cast shadows across her face, accentuating the lines of worry etched there. She took a deep breath, her fingers absently tracing the edge of a nearby book.

"If we do this—if we try to break the loop—it won't be easy," she said, her voice barely above a whisper. "Gabriel will come for us. The loop will fight back. And if we fail, it won't just be your reality that's erased."

Drake felt a chill run down his spine at her words. The weight of what they were about to attempt settled over him like a heavy cloak. He could almost feel the fabric of reality straining around them, as if the very air knew they were about to challenge its fundamental laws.

His mind raced, images of his wife and son flashing before his eyes. Their laughter, their warmth, their love—all of it hanging by a thread, trapped in an endless cycle of death and rebirth. The pain of losing them, over and over again, threatened to overwhelm him.

But beneath that pain, a fierce determination burned. Drake straightened his shoulders, meeting Rachel's gaze with unwavering resolve. "I've already lost everything once," he said, his voice steady despite the storm of emotions within. "I'm not afraid to fight for it again."

As he spoke, Drake could feel the truth of his words resonating through his very being. The fear was still there, a constant companion, but it no longer controlled him. He had faced the abyss of loss and come back, changed but unbroken.

Rachel studied him, her expression a mix of admiration and concern. "You don't fully understand what you're up against," she warned. "The multiverse doesn't like to be tampered with. It will resist."

Drake nodded, his jaw set. "Then we'll have to be stronger," he replied, his voice low and determined. "Whatever it takes, Rachel. I can't keep living this nightmare. And if what you're saying is true, it's not just about me and my family anymore. We have a responsibility to fix this, don't we?"

33 - 33

Rachel's eyes softened, a flicker of something—respect, perhaps, or shared resolve—passing across her weary features. She ran a hand through her tangled red hair, her gaze drifting to the scattered papers on her desk. The weight of knowledge, of responsibility, seemed to press down on her shoulders.

"Alright," she said finally, her voice barely above a whisper. "I know what we need to do next."

Drake's heart raced, a mixture of anticipation and dread coursing through him. "What is it?" he asked, leaning forward.

Rachel turned back to him, her eyes sharp and focused. "We need to find the Codex," she said, her words crisp and deliberate. "It's not just a book, Drake. It's a map, a key to the very fabric of the multiverse."

As she spoke, Rachel's hands moved with precise, almost frenetic energy, shuffling through papers and pulling out a worn leather journal. Drake watched, mesmerized by the sudden transformation in her demeanor.

"But where is it?" he asked, his mind racing with possibilities. "You said you hid it."

Rachel nodded, a wry smile tugging at the corner of her mouth. "I did," she confirmed. "In the last place they'd ever think to look."

Drake's brow furrowed. "Which is?"

"The past," Rachel replied, her voice tinged with a hint of pride. "I used the Codex itself to hide it in a timeline that no longer exists."

The implications of her words hit Drake like a physical blow. Time travel. Alternate timelines. The scope of what they were dealing with suddenly seemed impossibly vast. He swallowed hard, trying to steady his racing thoughts.

"How do we even begin to find it, then?" he asked, his voice hoarse.

Rachel's eyes gleamed with a mixture of excitement and trepidation. "That's where it gets complicated," she said, her fingers tracing the worn cover of the journal. "We'll need to recreate the conditions of a temporal rift. It's dangerous, but it's our only chance."

Drake nodded slowly, absorbing the information. "Whatever it takes," he repeated, more to himself than to Rachel. The faces of his wife and son flashed through his mind, driving home the stakes of their mission.

"Drake," Rachel said softly, her tone causing him to look up sharply. "You need to understand. This isn't just about saving your family. If we succeed, we could unravel the very fabric of reality itself."

The weight of her words settled over him like a shroud. Drake closed his eyes for a moment, drawing in a deep breath. When he opened them again, his gaze was steady, resolute.

"Then we'll have to be careful," he said simply. "Where do we start?"

Visions of the Codex

1 -2 The fluorescent light flickered overhead, casting erratic shadows across Rachel's haggard face as she slumped into the worn-out chair. Drake's eyes traced the chaotic landscape of papers and forgotten coffee mugs strewn across her desk, a stark reflection of the brilliant mind unraveling before him. The air hung heavy with the acrid scent of stale cigarettes and desperation.

Rachel's frail hands trembled as she rubbed her temples, her once-vibrant red hair now a dull tangle framing her gaunt features. Drake watched her carefully, his own bone-deep exhaustion momentarily forgotten as he waited for her to speak. The silence stretched between them, punctuated only by the soft tick of a clock marking the relentless march of time.

He found himself cataloging the changes in her appearance since he'd last seen her—the deepened lines around her eyes, the slight tremor in her hands that hadn't been there before. A pang of guilt twisted in his gut. How much of this was his fault? How many realities had he warped in his desperate attempts to save his family?

Finally, Rachel exhaled, her voice barely above a whisper. "The Codex... it's haunted me for weeks now. Visions, whispers, dreams—I can't escape it."

Drake leaned forward, his brow furrowing. The mention of the Codex sent a chill down his spine, memories of its power—and the devastation it had wrought—flooding back. "Rachel, I—" he began, but the words caught in his throat. What could he possibly say to make this right?

Rachel's eyes, once sharp with scientific curiosity, now held a haunted look that made Drake's chest tighten. He watched as her fingers absently traced patterns on the desk's surface, wondering if she was seeing symbols that weren't there.

"I never wanted this for you," Drake said softly, the weight of his choices pressing down on him. "I thought I could fix everything, but I just made it worse, didn't I?"

Rachel's gaze snapped to his, a flicker of her old determination cutting through the fog of exhaustion. "We're beyond blame now, Drake. The question is, what are we going to do about it?"

Her words hung in the air between them, a challenge and a lifeline. Drake felt the familiar surge of resolve, tinged with the ever-present fear of failure. He nodded, squaring his shoulders. "Whatever it takes," he said, meaning every word. "We'll figure this out together."

As Rachel began to speak again, Drake steeled himself for what was to come. The path ahead was fraught with danger, but he'd face any terror to make things right. He only hoped it wouldn't be too late for either of them.

3 - 4

Drake frowned, his curiosity mingling with concern. "Visions? What kind of visions?" The words left his mouth slowly, each syllable heavy with the weight of their shared burden. His eyes traced the lines of exhaustion etched into Rachel's face, a stark reminder of the toll their quest had taken.

Rachel leaned forward, resting her elbows on the desk and cradling her head in her hands. The movement sent a stack of papers cascading to the floor, but neither of them moved to retrieve them. "It started as flashes," she began, her voice barely above a whisper. "Images that didn't make sense. A book, ancient and worn, with a dragon emblazoned on its cover."

Drake's breath caught in his throat. The description sparked a memory, fragmented and elusive, from another life. He opened his mouth to interject, but Rachel continued, her words gaining momentum.

"Then... it became more vivid. Pages flipping on their own. Symbols I didn't recognize glowing in the dark." Her fingers trembled as she mimed the motion of turning pages. "And voices... faint at first, but louder as the weeks went on."

As Rachel spoke, Drake found himself transported, seeing the visions through her eyes. The musty scent of ancient parchment filled his nostrils, and for a moment, he could almost hear the whispered voices she described. He shook his head, trying to clear it.

"Rachel," he said softly, reaching out to touch her arm. "I'm so sorry. I never meant for any of this to happen." The guilt that constantly simmered beneath the surface threatened to overwhelm him. How many lives had he upended in his desperate quest to save his family?

5 - 6

Drake's breath caught, a sharp intake that seemed to echo in the cluttered room. "What did they say?" he asked, his voice low and urgent. The weight of his past mistakes pressed down on him, making each word feel like a struggle against an unseen force.

Rachel's eyes darted to his, wild and desperate. In that moment, Drake saw the toll this ordeal had taken on her—the dark circles under her eyes, the tremor in her hands, the haunted look that seemed to have etched itself permanently onto her features.

"They weren't words," she whispered, her gaze unfocusing as if she were reliving the experience. "Not ones I could understand, anyway. It was like the Codex was calling to me, pulling me toward something I couldn't reach."

Drake's mind raced, trying to piece together the fragments of his own memories with Rachel's account. He remembered the Codex, remembered its power, but the details were frustratingly vague, like trying to grasp smoke.

"I thought if I could just find it, the visions would stop," Rachel continued, her voice cracking. "But every time I tried, it slipped further away."

The desperation in her tone resonated deeply with Drake. How many times had he felt that same desperation, chasing after a solution that always seemed just out of reach? He clenched his fists, fighting back the wave of hopelessness that threatened to engulf him.

"We'll find it," he said, infusing his words with a conviction he didn't entirely feel. "Together. We have to."

7 - 8

Rachel stood abruptly, her lab coat swirling around her like a tattered banner. She began to pace the room, her movements erratic, each step a testament to her frayed nerves. The floorboards creaked beneath her feet, a discordant symphony accompanying her frenzied thoughts.

"I tried everything," she said, her voice tight with frustration. Her hands moved in sharp, agitated gestures as she spoke. "Retracing my steps, digging through old files at the institute, reaching out to colleagues who might have known where it ended up."

Drake watched her, his heart heavy. The brilliant scientist he once knew had been reduced to this—a woman on the brink, haunted by visions and failures. He wondered if he was looking at a mirror of his own future.

Rachel paused by the window, her silhouette stark against the fading light. "Nothing," she whispered, her voice barely audible. "It was like it had vanished into thin air."

"Could it have been moved?" Drake asked, grasping at straws. "Or hidden deliberately?"

Rachel turned to face him, her eyes blazing with a mix of determination and despair. "If it was, I couldn't find a trace. I exhausted every lead, every possibility." She ran a hand through her tangled hair, her fingers catching on knots. "The Codex doesn't want to be found, Drake. At least, not by me."

Drake felt a chill run down his spine at her words. The idea of the Codex having agency, of it choosing who could and couldn't find it, was unsettling. He pushed the thought aside, focusing instead on the practicalities.

"There has to be something we've missed," he insisted, leaning forward in his chair. "Some connection we haven't made yet."

Rachel's laugh was bitter, devoid of humor. "You sound like me, six months ago. Before—" She cut herself off, shaking her head. "Before everything fell apart."

The weight of unspoken words hung heavy in the air between them. Drake wanted to ask, to understand what had happened to her, but he held back. There would be time for that later. For now, they needed to focus on the Codex.

"Then we start over," he said firmly. "From the beginning. Tell me everything you remember about the last time you saw it." Rachel's pacing slowed, her footsteps echoing softly in the cluttered room. She closed her eyes, brow furrowing in concentration as she reached back into the recesses of her memory. Drake watched her intently, noting the way her hands trembled slightly at her sides.

"It was late," she began, her voice barely above a whisper. "I'd been working in the lab, running simulations on multiversal theory. The Codex was there, on my desk, just like always." She paused, swallowing hard. "I remember the weight of it in my hands, the way the dragon on the cover seemed to shimmer in the low light."

Drake leaned forward, hanging on her every word. "What happened next?"

Rachel's eyes snapped open, a haunted look crossing her face. "That's where it gets... strange. I blinked, and suddenly the lab was different. Books were floating, defying gravity. Equations I'd never seen before were scrawling themselves across the walls." She shook her head, as if trying to dislodge the memory. "When everything settled, the Codex was gone."

"And you're sure it wasn't just a dream?" Drake asked gently, even as he felt the truth of her words resonating within him.

Rachel's laugh was sharp, brittle. "Oh, I wished it was. But the equations remained, Drake. Impossible equations that challenged everything we thought we knew about reality."

9 - 10

Drake's mind raced, piecing together the fragments of Rachel's story. The weight of her words settled heavily in his chest, a mixture of dread and hope battling for dominance. He watched as she resumed her frantic pacing, her lab coat swishing around her ankles with each turn.

"And that's why you were fired?" he asked, his voice low and careful.

Rachel stopped abruptly, her laughter sharp and bitter, cutting through the tension-filled air like a knife. "Fired. Institutionalized. Labeled delusional. Take your pick." Her hand swept across the cluttered desk, papers rustling beneath her fingertips. "I tried to explain it to them, tried to make them see, but they couldn't—or wouldn't—understand. They thought I was losing my mind."

Drake's gaze followed her gesture, taking in the chaos of equations and diagrams spread before them. Each scrap of paper seemed to hold a piece of the puzzle, a fragment of the truth that had cost Rachel everything. He felt a twinge of guilt, wondering if his own inability to remember had somehow contributed to her downfall.

"But you weren't," he said softly, more statement than question. "Losing your mind, I mean."

Rachel's eyes met his, a flicker of gratitude passing across her face before being swallowed by the haunted look that seemed to have taken up permanent residence there. "Sometimes I wonder," she admitted, her voice barely audible. "But then I remember the feeling of the Codex in my hands, the way it seemed to pulse with its own energy. That was real, Drake. As real as you and I standing here now."

11 - 12

Drake hesitated, the weight of his next question hanging heavily in the air. His fingers drummed against his thigh, a nervous habit he'd never quite shaken. The room seemed to close in around them, the scattered papers and dimming light creating an atmosphere of claustrophobic intensity.

"Were you?" he asked quietly, his voice barely above a whisper.

The effect on Rachel was immediate and visceral. Her body went rigid, shoulders stiffening as if bracing for a physical blow. For a long moment, she remained motionless, her back to Drake, and he found himself holding his breath, waiting.

Then, with agonizing slowness, Rachel turned to face him. The look in her eyes was one of raw vulnerability, a stark contrast to the confident scientist he'd first met. "I don't know," she admitted, her voice trembling. "Some days, I feel like I'm holding onto my sanity by a thread."

Drake felt a surge of empathy, recognizing the struggle in her words. How many times had he questioned his own grip on reality since waking up in this distorted version of his life?

Rachel's gaze hardened suddenly, a spark of her old determination flaring to life. "But the Codex... it's real. I know it is." Her eyes locked onto his, intense and unwavering. "And so do you."

The conviction in her voice stirred something in Drake's memory – a fleeting image of an ancient book, its cover emblazoned with a dragon. He blinked, trying to hold onto the fragment, but it slipped away like smoke through his fingers.

13 - 14

Drake nodded, his brow furrowing as he struggled to piece together the elusive memories. "I've seen it," he said, his voice low and gravelly. "I remember you showing it to me, in another life." The words felt strange on his tongue, laden with the weight of experiences he couldn't fully grasp.

He ran a hand through his disheveled hair, frustration and determination warring within him. "It helped me then, and I believe it can help us now." Drake's eyes met Rachel's, a silent plea for understanding. "But if you don't have it anymore, where do we even begin?"

The question hung in the air between them, heavy with implications. Drake's mind raced, trying to connect the scattered fragments of his past – or was it his future? – with the desperate reality of their present situation.

Rachel's gaze flickered, a mix of hesitation and resolve playing across her features. She seemed to be weighing her words carefully, as if deciding how much to reveal. Drake felt the tension in his shoulders increase, recognizing the precipice they stood upon.

"We begin," Rachel said slowly, "by trusting each other." She extended her hand, the gesture both an offer and a challenge.

Drake stared at her outstretched palm, his heart pounding. The simple act of reaching out to shake her hand felt monumental, as if it would irrevocably alter the course of his fractured existence. He swallowed hard, acutely aware of the weight of his choices – past, present, and future.

"An uneasy alliance," he murmured, more to himself than to Rachel. With a deep breath, Drake clasped her hand, feeling the tentative beginnings of a partnership that could either save him or condemn him further.

15 - 16

Rachel sank back into her chair, her fingers gripping the worn edges as if anchoring herself to reality. The dim light cast shadows across her face, accentuating the lines of exhaustion etched deep into her skin. Drake watched her intently, his own weariness momentarily forgotten as he sensed the gravity of what she was about to reveal.

"The Codex," Rachel began, her voice barely above a whisper, "it's tied to the multiverse." She paused, her brow furrowing as if piecing together a complex puzzle in real-time. "It doesn't just exist in one place. It moves, shifts."

Drake leaned forward, his heart rate quickening. The air in the cluttered room seemed to thicken, charged with the weight of Rachel's words. He could almost feel the boundaries of reality bending around them, the veil between worlds growing thin.

"It's drawn to..." Rachel hesitated, her eyes meeting Drake's with a mix of fear and fascination. "Anomalies."

The word hung in the air, pregnant with meaning. Drake's mind raced, connecting dots he hadn't even realized existed. His own existence, his fractured memories, the sense of displacement that had haunted him since waking in this distorted reality – it all suddenly clicked into place.

"Like me," Drake said, his voice hoarse with realization. The words tasted of both revelation and damnation on his tongue. He was an anomaly, a glitch in the fabric of the multiverse. The thought both terrified and exhilarated him.

Rachel nodded slowly, her gaze never leaving his face. "Yes, Drake. Like you."

17 - 18

Rachel's eyes bore into him with an intensity that made Drake shift uncomfortably in his seat. Her voice, when she spoke again, carried a mixture of scientific curiosity and an undercurrent of something deeper—perhaps concern, or even fear.

"If you're stuck in a loop, if you're crossing realities without even realizing it," she said, her words measured and deliberate, "the Codex might be trying to find you as much as you're trying to find it."

Drake's mind reeled at the implication. The idea that this mysterious artifact might have a will of its own, that it might be seeking him out across the vastness of the multiverse, sent a shiver down his spine. He tried to process this information, his thoughts a whirlwind of possibilities and questions.

After a moment of heavy silence, Drake leaned forward, his hands gripping the edge of the desk. "Then how do we track it down?" he asked, his voice tight with a mixture of anticipation and dread.

As he waited for Rachel's response, Drake couldn't help but feel like he was standing on the edge of a precipice, about to plunge into unknown depths. Whatever her answer, he knew it would change everything—again.

19 - 20

Rachel's expression darkened, her face a canvas of conflicting emotions. She hesitated, her fingers tracing invisible patterns on the worn surface of the desk. The air in the cluttered room seemed to thicken, charged with unspoken tension.

"There's only one way I can think of," she finally said, her voice barely above a whisper. Drake watched as she swallowed hard, steeling herself for what came next. "We have to go back to the place where it first appeared to me. A place I swore I'd never return to."

The weight of her words hung heavy in the air. Drake felt a chill creep up his spine, his mind racing with possibilities. What could have happened at this mysterious location to elicit such a visceral reaction from the usually composed scientist?

He leaned forward, his eyes narrowing as he studied Rachel's face. The lines of fatigue etched around her eyes seemed to deepen, and for a moment, he caught a glimpse of the toll this knowledge had taken on her.

"Where?" Drake asked, his voice low and urgent. He could feel his heart pounding in his chest, a mix of anticipation and dread coursing through his veins. Whatever this place was, he knew it held the key to unraveling the mystery that had consumed his life.

As he waited for Rachel's response, Drake couldn't help but wonder if he was truly prepared for what lay ahead. The path to redemption, he realized, was rarely a straight or easy one.

21 - 22

Rachel's gaze drifted to the window, her eyes unfocused as if looking at something far beyond the cluttered room. "The ruins at Camelot's Crossing," she said, her voice barely above a whisper.

The words hung in the air, laden with an almost tangible weight. Drake felt a shiver run through him, though he couldn't explain why. The name evoked images of ancient stones and forgotten legends, but it held no specific meaning for him.

He frowned, his brow furrowing as he tried to place the unfamiliar location. "Camelot's Crossing? What is that?"

As he spoke, Drake studied Rachel's face, searching for clues. The tension in her jaw, the slight tremor in her hands as she gripped the edge of her desk – these subtle signs spoke volumes about the significance of this place.

His mind raced, piecing together fragments of their earlier conversation. The Codex, the visions that had haunted Rachel, the multiverse – somehow, this mysterious location tied it all together. But how? And why did the mere mention of it seem to drain the color from Rachel's face?

Drake leaned forward, his voice softening. "Rachel, what happened there? What makes this place so important – and so terrible?"

23 - 24

Rachel's eyes snapped back to focus, fixing on Drake with an intensity that made him lean back instinctively. The frayed edges of her lab coat rustled as she shifted, her voice taking on a clipped, almost clinical tone.

"It's not what—it's where," she said, her words precise despite the slight tremor in her voice. "A site tied to ancient legends, supposedly linked to the Codex. It's where I first discovered its existence... and where everything went wrong."

Drake's breath caught in his throat. The air in the room seemed to thicken, charged with the weight of Rachel's admission. He watched as her fingers traced absent patterns on the desk's worn surface, her gaze distant once more.

"What do you mean, everything went wrong?" he asked, his voice low, almost reverent in the face of Rachel's obvious distress.

She didn't answer immediately. Instead, she stood, her movements stiff and deliberate as she crossed to a battered filing cabinet. Drake observed her in silence, noting the slight tremor in her hands as she rifled through a drawer.

Finally, Rachel extracted a worn leather folder, its edges frayed and discolored. She returned to the desk, placing it between them with the care one might afford a bomb.

"This," she said, her voice barely audible, "is what I found at Camelot's Crossing. The first clue that led me to the Codex – and the beginning of my descent into..." She trailed off, gesturing vaguely at the chaos surrounding them.

Drake's fingers itched to open the folder, to uncover its secrets, but he held back. The fragility of the moment, the tenuous trust building between them, felt too precious to risk.

Instead, he met Rachel's gaze, his voice steady. "We don't have to go back there if it's too painful. There must be another way to find the Codex."

25 - 26

Rachel's eyes locked onto his, a maelstrom of emotions swirling within their depths. Fear, resolve, and something darker – a haunted look that spoke of sleepless nights and unshakable memories.

"If you want my help, I'll give it," she said, her voice low and intense. "But you have to understand something, Drake. Finding the Codex won't just stop the loop. It will force you to confront things you might not want to see—truths about yourself, about what you've done."

Drake felt a chill crawl up his spine, his mind racing with possibilities. What truths? What had he done in those lost timelines, those alternate realities he couldn't remember? The weight of unknown sins pressed down on him, threatening to suffocate.

He swallowed hard, his throat suddenly dry. "What kind of truths?" he managed to ask, his voice hoarse.

Rachel's gaze softened slightly, a flicker of sympathy crossing her face. "I don't know the specifics," she admitted. "But the Codex... it doesn't just reveal information. It shows you possibilities, paths not taken. And sometimes, those paths are darker than we'd like to admit."

Drake's stomach churned at her words, a cocktail of fear and anticipation swirling within him. He clenched his fists, feeling his nails dig into his palms. The pain grounded him, a reminder of the reality he was fighting to preserve.

"I've already lost everything once," he said, forcing the words past the lump in his throat. "I don't care what I have to face, as long as it ends this nightmare."

27 - 28

Rachel studied him for a long moment, her piercing gaze seeming to peel back the layers of Drake's resolve. The room fell silent, save for the gentle hum of the ancient radiator in the corner. Drake held his breath, feeling as if he were balancing on a knife's edge between hope and despair.

Finally, Rachel nodded, her shoulders relaxing infinitesimally. "Alright," she said, her voice barely above a whisper. "Then we start tomorrow."

The words hung in the air, heavy with promise and peril. Drake exhaled slowly, feeling a curious mix of relief and trepidation wash over him. Tomorrow. It seemed both an eternity away and far too soon.

Without thinking, Drake extended his hand across the cluttered desk. It was an instinctive gesture, born from years of sealing deals in boardrooms and courthouses. But this was no ordinary agreement, and Rachel was no ordinary partner.

For a heartbeat, Rachel hesitated, her eyes darting from Drake's outstretched hand to his face. He saw the conflict play out in her expression—the wariness of a woman who had been betrayed by the world, warring with the desperate need for connection, for purpose.

Then, with a barely perceptible nod, she took his hand. Her grip was surprisingly strong, a flicker of determination cutting through her frail exterior. Drake felt a jolt of energy pass between them, as if by joining hands, they had set in motion forces beyond their comprehension.

As their hands clasped, Drake's mind raced. What am I getting myself into? he wondered. And more importantly, what have I already done that I can't remember? The questions swirled in his mind, a dizzying maelstrom of doubt and determination.

29 - 30

"Thank you," Drake said softly, his voice barely above a whisper. The words felt inadequate, unable to convey the tumult of emotions churning within him. Gratitude, yes, but also fear, hope, and a gnawing sense of guilt for dragging Rachel back into a world she'd clearly tried to escape.

Rachel's lips quirked into a faint, humorless smile. Her eyes, once bright with scientific curiosity, now held a shadow of wariness. "Don't thank me yet," she cautioned, her tone a mixture of resignation and grim determination. "You might not like what we find."

The weight of her words settled over Drake like a shroud. He suppressed a shiver, remembering flashes of his other lives, other choices. What horrors lay hidden in the gaps of his memory? What version of himself would he have to confront?

"I understand," Drake replied, his jaw tightening. "But whatever it is, whatever I've done... I need to know. I can't keep living in this loop, this... half-life."

Rachel nodded, her expression softening slightly. "It won't be easy," she warned. "The Codex... it has a way of revealing truths we're not always ready to face."

Drake's mind conjured images of his family—smiling, laughing, alive. But were they real? Or just echoes from another reality? The thought sent a pang of longing through his chest. "Some truths are worth the pain," he said, more to himself than to Rachel.

As he spoke, Drake noticed the tremor in Rachel's hands, the dark circles under her eyes. She had paid a price for her knowledge, one he was only beginning to understand. And yet, here she was, willing to risk everything again.

"Get some rest," Rachel advised, her voice tinged with exhaustion. "Tomorrow, we face the unknown."

Drake nodded, feeling the weight of their impending journey settle onto his shoulders. As he turned to leave, he couldn't shake the feeling that he was walking towards a precipice—one from which there might be no return.

On the Hunt

1^{- 2} Detective Holly Kierstead's hands trembled as she gripped the steering wheel, her knuckles white against the black leather. The amusement park's neon lights faded in her rearview mirror, replaced by the eerie glow of a blood-orange sunset. The day's revelations churned in her stomach like acid, each gruesome discovery etching itself into her memory.

"Damn it, Drake," she muttered, her voice hoarse. "What have you gotten yourself into?"

She closed her eyes for a moment, inhaling deeply. The scent of cotton candy and popcorn still clung to her clothes, a stark contrast to the death that permeated the park. When she opened them again, determination blazed in her gaze.

"I'll find you," she promised the empty car. "Whatever it takes."

As Holly reached for the ignition, her phone buzzed insistently. She fished it out of her pocket, her heart racing as she read the alert. The breach of her police login had been traced – a search for Rachel Summers.

"Rachel?" Holly whispered, her brow furrowing. "Why would Drake be looking for her?"

Memories of late-night conversations with Drake flooded her mind. He'd mentioned Rachel before, always with a mixture of admiration and guilt in his voice. Holly had never pressed for details, respecting the pain that seemed to linger beneath the surface.

She tapped her fingers against the dashboard, her analytical mind whirring into action. "What's the connection, Drake? What aren't you telling me?"

The sky deepened to a rich purple, stars beginning to peek through the twilight veil. Holly's reflection stared back at her from the windshield, her eyes haunted by the weight of unsolved mysteries and the bodies left in their wake.

"I can't let this go," she said quietly, resolve hardening her features. "Not when there's so much at stake."

With a deep breath, Holly started the car. The engine's rumble seemed to echo the determination coursing through her veins. As she pulled away from the curb, leaving the amusement park's false cheer behind, she made a silent vow to uncover the truth – no matter where it led her.

3 - 4

"New Haven," she muttered, her grip tightening around the steering wheel. The name hung in the air, heavy with implications. Holly's mind raced, piecing together fragments of information. If Drake had gone after Summers, she knew she couldn't waste any time.

Her fingers danced across the car's onboard GPS, muscle memory guiding her as she keyed in the coordinates for New Haven. The screen illuminated, casting a soft blue glow across her face, highlighting the tension in her jaw.

"What are you thinking, Drake?" she whispered, shifting the car into gear. The engine roared to life, its vibrations rumbling beneath her feet like a caged beast eager for release. "Why Rachel? Why now?"

Holly's hand hovered over the switch for the lights, hesitation flickering across her features. Protocol demanded full lights and sirens for a pursuit, but instinct whispered caution. After a moment's deliberation, she hit the lights but kept the siren off, not wanting to draw unnecessary attention.

As the car pulled away from the curb, Holly's eyes darted to the rearview mirror, half-expecting to see shadows lurking in the gathering darkness. The city lights began to blur around her, a kaleidoscope of neon and streetlamps painting streaks across her windshield.

"Hold on, Rachel," she murmured, her voice barely audible over the engine's purr. "Whatever's happening, I'm coming. And Drake..." She paused, conflict etching lines around her eyes. "I hope you know what you're doing."

The road stretched before her, a ribbon of asphalt leading into uncertainty. Holly took a deep breath, steeling herself for whatever lay ahead in New Haven.

5 - 6

The streetlights streaked past in a blur as Holly accelerated onto the main road, her knuckles white against the steering wheel. Her jaw clenched, a muscle twitching beneath the skin as determination blazed in her eyes. The memory of Drake Miller's enigmatic smile flashed in her mind, fueling a mixture of frustration and resolve.

"If you're behind this, Drake," she muttered, her voice low and taut with tension, "I swear I'll make you face justice. No matter how complex this web you're weaving."

The car hummed beneath her, a steady vibration that matched the thrumming of her pulse. Holly's mind raced, piecing together the fragments of information she'd gathered. Drake's brilliance had always been a double-edged sword, his intellect as capable of destruction as salvation.

"What's your endgame?" she wondered aloud, her brow furrowing. "Rachel's involved somehow, but why? What could a disgraced scientist offer you?"

As if in response to her questioning, the GPS chimed softly, updating the estimated time of arrival. Holly's eyes flickered to the display, noting the miles stretching between her and New Haven. Between her and answers.

"Hang on, Rachel," she said under her breath, her tone softening with a hint of protective concern. "I'm coming. Whatever storm you're caught in, I'll find a way through it."

The words hung in the air, a promise and a prayer mingled together. Holly pressed down on the accelerator, the engine's roar a testament to her determination. The night seemed to part before her, a dark sea giving way to the beacon of her headlights as she raced toward the unknown.

7 - 7

The city lights dwindled in her rearview mirror, fading like dying embers against the encroaching darkness. Holly's eyes flicked between the road ahead and the shadowy landscape rushing past her windows, her mind churning with possibilities and fears.

"New Haven," she murmured, tasting the name on her tongue. "What secrets are you hiding?"

The car's headlights carved a path through the night, illuminating stretches of empty highway that seemed to stretch endlessly before her. Holly's fingers drummed a restless rhythm on the steering wheel, her body taut with anticipation.

"If I were Drake," she mused aloud, her voice barely audible above the engine's hum, "where would I go? What would be my next move?"

She inhaled deeply, the scent of leather and faint traces of coffee filling her nostrils. The familiar smells grounded her, a stark contrast to the surreal nature of the case unfolding around her.

"Rachel's involved, but how?" Holly's brow furrowed as she spoke to the empty car, her words a lifeline in the isolating darkness. "Is she a victim or an accomplice?"

The question hung unanswered in the air, joining the growing list of mysteries that seemed to multiply with each passing mile. Holly's grip tightened on the wheel, her knuckles whitening with determination.

"Whatever I find in New Haven," she vowed, her voice low and resolute, "I'll face it head-on. For the victims, for justice... and for the truth."

The car sped on, a solitary beacon of light racing through the night, carrying Holly closer to the answers that awaited her in New Haven – and the dangers that lurked in the shadows of discovery.

A Confession of Betrayal

1 -2   The air in the Lexington Hotel suite hung thick with tension, each breath a struggle against the suffocating atmosphere. Richard Vega's footsteps echoed hollowly as he paced, his trembling hands betraying the turmoil within. He couldn't bring himself to meet Linda's gaze, knowing the fire that burned there would sear right through him.

Linda sat bound to the chair, her wrists chafing against the coarse rope. Her shoulders remained rigid, a physical manifestation of her unwavering defiance. Her blonde hair fell in soft waves around her face, a stark contrast to the hardness in her eyes. On the couch, Harrison's wide brown eyes darted nervously between his mother and Vega, his young face etched with fear and confusion.

Vega's mind raced, searching for words that could somehow justify his actions. But how could he explain the impossible choice he'd been forced to make? The weight of his decisions pressed down on him, threatening to crush what little resolve he had left.

Finally, he halted his relentless pacing. Running a shaking hand through his disheveled hair, Vega turned to face his captives. His face was ashen, dark circles under his eyes speaking of sleepless nights and haunted dreams.

"I never meant for it to come to this," he said, his voice barely above a whisper.

Linda's eyes narrowed, her voice dripping with venom as she spat, "And yet, here we are."

Vega flinched at her words, feeling their sting as keenly as a physical blow. He opened his mouth to respond, but the words died on his lips. What could he possibly say to make this right?

Harrison whimpered softly, drawing Vega's attention. The boy's vulnerability struck him like a knife to the heart. In that moment, Vega saw his own son reflected in Harrison's frightened eyes, and the full weight of his actions came crashing down upon him.

"I'm sorry," Vega breathed, the words feeling woefully inadequate. "I'm so sorry."

But as he looked at Linda's unyielding expression and Harrison's trembling form, Vega knew that sorry would never be enough. The choices he'd made, the lines he'd crossed – they had brought them all to this point of no return. And now, trapped in this suffocating hotel room, the consequences of his actions were closing in around them all.

3 - 4

Linda's blue eyes flashed with a mix of fury and desperation, her blonde hair disheveled from her struggles against the bindings. She leaned forward in her chair, her voice low and dangerous, cutting through the tense silence of the hotel room.

"Then untie us," she demanded, each word sharp as a blade. "Right now."

Vega's shoulders sagged under the weight of her gaze. He ran a trembling hand through his hair, his mind racing with conflicting emotions. The urge to comply, to make this right, warred with the fear of what awaited him if he did.

"I can't," he whispered, more to himself than to Linda. "I wish I could, but..."

Linda's eyes narrowed, her maternal instincts flaring as she glanced at Harrison. The boy sat quietly, his wide eyes darting between the adults, fear evident in every line of his small body. Linda's heart ached at the sight.

"Look at him, Richard," she said, her voice softening slightly. "Look at what you're doing to my son. To my child. Is this really what you want?"

Vega's gaze shifted to Harrison, and for a moment, he saw his own son reflected in those frightened eyes. The realization hit him like a physical blow, nearly driving the breath from his lungs. What had he become?

"I never wanted this," he muttered, his voice thick with regret. "Any of this. But I don't know how to stop it now."

5 - 6

Vega shook his head, his lips pressing into a thin line. The weight of his decisions hung heavy on his shoulders, visible in the tightness around his eyes and the slight tremor in his hands. "I can't. Not this time," he said, his voice barely above a whisper.

Linda's jaw tightened, the muscles in her neck straining against the force of her anger. She leaned forward in her chair, her bound wrists resting on her lap, fingers curling into fists. Her blue eyes, usually so full of warmth, now blazed with a fierce intensity.

"You have no right to keep us here," she hissed, her voice rising with each word. The sound echoed off the walls of the hotel suite, filling the space with her righteous fury. "Drake will come back, and when he does, you'll regret this."

Vega flinched at the mention of Drake's name, a flicker of fear crossing his face. He turned away from Linda, pacing the length of the room. His mind raced, searching for a way out of this impossible situation. How had it come to this? He'd only wanted to protect his family, but now...

"You don't understand," he muttered, more to himself than to Linda. "If I let you go, he'll..."

He trailed off, unable to finish the thought. The image of his own family, held captive by Gabriel, flashed through his mind. He squeezed his eyes shut, trying to block out the haunting vision.

7 - 8

At the mention of Drake, Vega's expression twisted with a mix of anger and sorrow. He exhaled sharply, the sound cutting through the tense silence like a knife. With shoulders slumped, he sank into the chair across from Linda, his elbows resting heavily on his knees. The weight of his actions seemed to press down on him, etching deep lines into his forehead.

Linda watched him, her eyes narrowed, searching for any sign of deception. But all she saw was a man drowning in his own regret.

"You think I don't already regret it?" Vega said softly, his voice barely above a whisper. He raised his head, meeting Linda's gaze with eyes that spoke of sleepless nights and haunted dreams.

The silence that followed was thick with unspoken accusations. Linda's chest heaved with each breath, her anger palpable in the air between them. She wanted to lash out, to make him feel even a fraction of the pain he'd caused her family. But something in Vega's demeanor gave her pause.

What could have driven this man, once a respected colleague of Drake's, to such desperate measures? The question burned in her mind, mingling with her fury and fear for her son.

Vega's hands trembled slightly as he ran them through his disheveled hair. "Every decision, every choice," he murmured, his gaze distant, "it all seemed so clear at the time. But now..." He trailed off, lost in the labyrinth of his own memories.

Linda's voice, when she finally spoke, was low and controlled. "Regret doesn't change what you've done, Richard." The use of his first name hung in the air, a reminder of the trust he'd shattered.

A bitter laugh escaped Vega's lips. "No," he agreed, "it doesn't." His eyes flickered to Harrison, still bound on the couch, then back to Linda. "But maybe... maybe it can change what happens next."

9 - 10

Linda narrowed her eyes, her piercing blue gaze fixed on Vega. "Regret what?" The words came out as a challenge, laced with the quiet strength that had sustained her through countless trials.

Vega's shoulders sagged under the weight of her scrutiny. He looked up, meeting her eyes with a mixture of shame and resignation. "Everything," he whispered, the word hanging heavy in the air between them.

Linda's hands clenched involuntarily, the rope biting into her wrists. She could feel Harrison's frightened gaze on her, a silent plea for reassurance she couldn't give. Her mind raced, trying to piece together the fragments of Vega's cryptic statements.

"You're going to have to do better than that," she said, her voice steady despite the storm of emotions roiling within her. "What exactly are you confessing to, Richard?"

Vega leaned forward, elbows on his knees, his face a mask of anguish. "I've made so many mistakes, Linda. Choices that seemed right at the time, but..." He trailed off, swallowing hard.

Linda's patience wore thin. "Stop dancing around it," she snapped, her nurturing nature giving way to the fierce protectiveness of a mother. "What have you done?"

As Vega opened his mouth to respond, Linda's heart raced. Whatever he was about to say, she knew it would change everything. The air in the room seemed to thicken, time slowing to a crawl as she waited for the truth that would reshape their world once again.

11 - 12

Vega's gaze dropped to the floor, his shoulders slumping under an invisible weight. The room fell silent, save for the soft hum of the air conditioner and Harrison's muffled whimpers. Linda's eyes bored into Vega, willing him to speak, to explain the carnage he'd wrought upon their lives.

When Vega finally looked up, his eyes were hollow, haunted by the ghosts of his choices. "Gabriel has my family again," he said, his voice barely above a whisper. His hands clenched into fists, knuckles whitening with the strain. "And I'm not going to let you Millers get away this time. Not when I have a second chance to save them."

Linda's breath caught in her throat, a cold dread seeping into her bones. "What do you mean, 'again'?" she demanded, her mind reeling with implications.

Vega stood abruptly, pacing the room like a caged animal. "You don't understand," he muttered, more to himself than to Linda. "I've seen what happens if I don't comply. The consequences..."

Linda struggled against her bonds, fury and fear battling for dominance. "Consequences? You're talking about our lives, Richard! My son's life!"

Harrison's soft sob cut through the tension, reminding them both of the innocent caught in this web of deceit. Vega paused, his expression softening for a moment as he glanced at the boy.

"I'm sorry," Vega said, his voice cracking. "But I have to protect my own. You'd do the same if you were in my position."

Linda's thoughts raced, trying to find a way out of this nightmare. She knew she had to keep Vega talking, to find a weakness in his resolve. "Tell me about your family, Richard," she said, forcing her voice to remain calm. "What has Gabriel done to them?"

13 - 14

Linda's eyes widened slightly, the subtle shift betraying her growing unease. Yet her voice remained sharp as steel, cutting through the tension in the room. "What are you talking about?"

Vega leaned back in his chair, his gaze drifting to some unseen point beyond the confines of the hotel suite. The weight of memory seemed to press down on him, etching new lines of worry across his face. His fingers drummed an erratic rhythm on the armrest, a physical manifestation of his inner turmoil.

"I remember it now," he began, his voice barely above a whisper. "Being choked to death. The pain..." He swallowed hard, his Adam's apple bobbing beneath the stubble on his throat. "It felt like my soul was being ripped apart."

Linda watched him intently, her mind racing to make sense of his words. Was this some sort of twisted metaphor, or had Vega truly experienced death? The possibility sent a chill down her spine, but she remained silent, waiting for him to continue.

"And then I woke up," Vega said, his eyes refocusing on Linda. "This life, this second chance—it's not an accident. It's a test." His voice grew stronger, tinged with a mix of desperation and determination. "A test to see if I can fix what I broke."

The words hung in the air between them, heavy with implication. Linda's heart pounded in her chest, a deafening rhythm that threatened to drown out all other sound. What could he possibly mean? What had he broken that was so terrible it required a second chance at life to fix?

As she struggled to formulate a response, Linda's gaze flickered briefly to Harrison. Her son sat motionless on the couch, his eyes wide with fear and confusion. The sight of him, bound and vulnerable, reignited the fierce protective instinct within her. Whatever game Vega was playing, whatever cosmic test he believed he was undertaking, she would not let it harm her child.

15 - 16

Linda's eyes narrowed, her jaw clenching as she refocused on Vega. The room seemed to shrink around them, the air thick with tension. She leaned forward as much as her bonds would allow, her voice low and dangerous.

"What did you break, Richard?"

The words hung in the air, a challenge and an accusation rolled into one. Linda's heart raced, her mind conjuring a thousand horrifying possibilities. What could be so significant that it warranted this elaborate charade of kidnapping and confession?

Vega's face contorted, a flicker of pain crossing his features. He met Linda's gaze, his eyes filled with a mixture of guilt and resignation. For a moment, he seemed to struggle with himself, as if wrestling with the weight of his next words.

"Your life," he finally said, his voice barely above a whisper.

Linda felt as if she'd been struck. The room spun around her, and she blinked rapidly, trying to process what she'd just heard. Your life. The words echoed in her mind, each repetition bringing a fresh wave of confusion and anger.

"What are you talking about?" she demanded, her voice rising. "How dare you sit there and claim you've broken my life? You have no right—"

"I'm sorry," Vega interrupted, his voice cracking. "I never wanted it to come to this. But you have to understand, I had no choice."

Linda's thoughts whirled, a maelstrom of questions and accusations. What had Vega done? How could he possibly claim to have broken her life? And what did any of this have to do with their current situation?

As she opened her mouth to voice these questions, a small sound from the couch caught her attention. Harrison shifted uncomfortably, his eyes darting between his mother and Vega. The sight of her son's fear-stricken face tempered Linda's rage, replacing it with a steely resolve.

"Explain yourself, Richard," she said, her voice low and controlled. "Now."

17 - 18

Linda's breath hitched, her body stiffening as if bracing for impact. "What?" The word escaped her lips in a whisper, barely audible over the pounding of her heart.

Vega's shoulders slumped, the weight of his confession seeming to physically press him down. He ran a hand through his disheveled hair, his eyes distant and haunted. "Gabriel came to me," he admitted, his voice raw with emotion. "Months ago. He found me when I was at my lowest."

Linda watched him, her mind reeling. The room felt smaller suddenly, the air thick and oppressive. She could feel Harrison's eyes on her, sense his fear and confusion, but she couldn't bring herself to look at him. Not yet.

Vega continued, each word seeming to cost him. "My family—Emily, the kids—they'd been taken. He said he could save them, but only if I helped him."

The implications of his words crashed over Linda like a tidal wave. Her fingers gripped the arms of her chair, knuckles turning white. She wanted to scream, to lash out, but the words caught in her throat.

How long had Vega been working with Gabriel? What had he done? The questions swirled in her mind, each more terrifying than the last. She thought of Drake, of the accident that had torn their family apart. Had Vega played a role in that too?

"Your family," Linda finally managed, her voice trembling with a mix of anger and disbelief. "You're telling me you betrayed us—betrayed Drake—for your family?"

Vega met her gaze, his eyes filled with a mixture of shame and desperation. "I had no choice, Linda. You have to understand. They were everything to me."

Linda felt a surge of bitter laughter bubbling up inside her. "And what about my family, Richard? What about Harrison? What about Drake?"

19 - 20

Linda's voice trembled with anger, the words escaping her lips like venom. "Helped him do what?"

The air in the room grew thick, suffocating. Linda's heart pounded in her chest, each beat a painful reminder of the betrayal unfolding before her. She watched as Vega's Adam's apple bobbed, his discomfort palpable.

Vega swallowed hard, his eyes darting away from Linda's piercing gaze. The weight of his confession seemed to press down on his shoulders, aging him years in mere moments. When he finally spoke, his voice was barely above a whisper.

"Find Drake."

The words hung in the air, heavy and damning. Linda felt as if she'd been struck, the breath leaving her lungs in a rush. Her mind reeled, trying to process the implications of Vega's admission. Drake, her husband, the man she'd fought so hard to protect – he had been the target all along.

She wanted to scream, to lunge at Vega despite her bonds, but found herself paralyzed by shock and rage. Her thoughts raced, piecing together fragments of their shared history, seeing every interaction with Vega in a new, horrifying light.

"All this time," Linda thought, her jaw clenching, "he was working against us, against Drake. How could we have been so blind?"

21 - 22

Vega's hand trembled as he ran it over his face, his fingers catching on the stubble that had grown during their ordeal. When he spoke again, his voice broke, raw with emotion.

"Gabriel wanted Drake, and he needed me to get close to him." Vega's eyes, filled with a mixture of shame and desperation, met Linda's. "That's why I set up the meeting at the diner. I lured you and your family out onto the open road so Gabriel could cause the crash."

Linda's breath hitched, memories of that fateful day flooding back. The warmth of the rain on her skin as they drove, Harrison's laughter from the backseat, Drake's hand on hers. Then, the screeching of tires, the shattering of glass, the world turning upside down.

"You bastard," Linda hissed, her voice low and dangerous. "We trusted you. Drake considered you a friend."

Vega flinched at her words, his shoulders sagging under the weight of his confession. "I didn't want to," he murmured, more to himself than to Linda. "But Gabriel... he had my family. I thought I didn't have a choice."

Linda's mind raced, trying to reconcile the man before her with the friend they had known. She thought of Drake, of his unwavering determination to protect those he loved, even in the face of impossible odds. Would he have made the same choice as Vega?

"There's always a choice," Linda said, her voice trembling with a mix of anger and pity. "Drake would have found another way. He would have fought."

23 - 24

Linda's mind raced, the pieces falling into place with horrifying clarity. The diner, the seemingly innocuous meeting, the open road - it had all been a carefully orchestrated trap. Her heart pounded in her chest, each beat a painful reminder of the life they'd lost.

"You..." she whispered, her voice barely audible as she struggled to form the words. "You're the reason we were in that accident?"

Vega's eyes darted away, unable to meet her piercing gaze. His fingers twitched nervously at his sides, a physical manifestation of the guilt that seemed to radiate from him.

"I didn't know what he was planning," Vega said quickly, his words tumbling out in a desperate rush. "Not exactly. But I knew enough to realize that it wasn't going to end well for you."

Linda's mind reeled, trying to process the enormity of his confession. She thought of Harrison, so young and innocent, caught in the crossfire of this betrayal. Of Drake, who had trusted Vega implicitly. The weight of it all threatened to crush her.

"How could you?" she breathed, her voice thick with emotion. "We were your friends, Richard. Your family."

Vega's shoulders slumped, the fight seeming to drain out of him. "I know," he murmured, his voice barely above a whisper. "And I'll carry that guilt for the rest of my life."

25 - 26

Linda's eyes burned with fury, her vision blurring as tears of rage threatened to spill over. The room seemed to pulse with the intensity of her anger, the walls closing in around them. She pulled against her restraints, the rough cord biting into her wrists, but she barely felt the pain.

"You bastard!" she spat, her voice rising to a fever pitch. The words echoed in the suite, hanging in the air between them like a physical barrier.

Vega flinched as if he'd been struck, his carefully constructed facade crumbling before her eyes. His hair, usually so meticulously styled, fell in disarray across his forehead. Linda watched as he swallowed hard, his Adam's apple bobbing with the effort.

"I'm sorry," Vega said, his voice trembling. The words seemed to catch in his throat, choking him. "For what it's worth, I didn't think he'd go this far. I thought he just wanted to... I don't know. Warn Drake. Scare him."

Linda's jaw clenched, her teeth grinding together as she fought to contain her rage. She could see the moment etched in Vega's face, the realization of what he'd done hitting him like a physical blow.

"But when I saw the aftermath," he continued, his voice barely above a whisper, "when I realized what I'd done..."

He trailed off, leaving the horror of that moment unspoken. Linda's mind raced, filling in the blanks with vivid, terrible images. The screeching of tires, the shattering of glass, the sickening crunch of metal. Her family, broken and bleeding on the asphalt.

"Sorry doesn't begin to cover it, Richard," Linda hissed, her voice low and dangerous. "You've destroyed everything. And for what?"

27 - 28

Vega's shoulders slumped, the weight of his actions pressing down on him like a physical force. He leaned forward, burying his head in his hands. The dim light of the hotel suite cast long shadows across his face, accentuating the deep lines of guilt etched into his features.

"I didn't want any of this," he murmured, his voice muffled by his palms. Linda strained to hear him, her anger momentarily eclipsed by a morbid curiosity. "But Gabriel had my family. And I—I didn't have a choice."

The name 'Gabriel' hung in the air like a toxic cloud. Linda's mind raced, trying to reconcile the man she thought she knew with this new, terrible revelation. She could almost see the specter of Gabriel looming over Vega, his scarred face twisted in a cruel sneer, pulling the strings that had led them all to this moment.

"There's always a choice," Linda spat, her voice trembling with barely contained fury. She tugged at her bonds, the rough cord biting into her wrists. "You chose to betray us. To put your family above mine."

Vega looked up, his eyes red-rimmed and haunted. "You don't understand. Gabriel, he's not—he's not human. Not anymore. The things he can do, the power he has... He would have killed them, Linda. My children."

Linda's heart constricted, torn between empathy for a father's desperation and the raw, bleeding wound of her own family's suffering. She glanced at Harrison, slumped on the couch, his young face etched with fear and confusion. The sight steeled her resolve.

"And now my child might die because of your choice," she said, her voice low and dangerous. "There's no forgiveness for that, Richard. Not now. Not ever."

The finality in her tone seemed to echo in the oppressive silence of the room, a death knell for whatever friendship or trust had once existed between them.

29 - 30

Linda's words hung in the air, heavy and final. Vega's shoulders slumped, the weight of his choices visibly crushing him. He ran a trembling hand through his disheveled hair, his eyes fixed on a point somewhere beyond the hotel room's faded wallpaper.

"I don't expect you to forgive me," he said quietly, his voice barely above a whisper. "I just... I needed you to know the truth."

Linda watched him, her chest still heaving with anger, but a flicker of something else—pity, perhaps—stirred within her. She remembered the Richard Vega she had once known: confident, principled, a man who seemed incapable of the betrayal he had just confessed. How far they had all fallen in this twisted reality.

"The truth," she echoed, tasting the bitterness of the word. "And what good does that do us now, Richard? How does your truth help my son?"

Vega's gaze snapped back to her, a spark of desperate determination in his eyes. "Maybe it doesn't," he admitted. "But knowing the full extent of Gabriel's influence, understanding how he operates—it might be the key to stopping him."

Linda closed her eyes, fighting against the hope that threatened to rise in her chest. Hope was dangerous in this world; it had betrayed her too many times before. And yet, she couldn't quite extinguish it entirely.

"Even if that's true," she said, her voice softer now but no less resolute, "it doesn't change what you've done. The choices you've made."

Vega nodded, a single, sharp movement. "I know," he said. "And I'll carry that guilt for the rest of my life. However long or short that might be."

31 - 32

The tension in the room hung thick and heavy, like a fog that refused to dissipate. Linda's words echoed in the silence, a reminder of the irreparable damage done. Vega's confession had left them all raw, exposed, and vulnerable.

It was then that Harrison, who had been uncharacteristically quiet throughout the exchange, suddenly let out a soft whimper. The sound, barely audible, cut through the stillness like a knife.

"Mom," he said, his voice trembling with an unfamiliar weakness. His usual curiosity and optimism were notably absent, replaced by something that sent a chill down Linda's spine. "Something's wrong."

Linda's head whipped around to face her son, her anger at Vega momentarily forgotten. Harrison's face had gone pale, his normally bright eyes now dulled with an inexplicable fear. She could see him struggling against his bonds, his lean frame shaking with an effort that seemed beyond mere physical exertion.

"Harrison?" Linda's voice cracked with concern. She strained against her own restraints, desperate to reach her son. "What is it, sweetheart? What's happening?"

Harrison's gaze darted around the room, as if searching for something unseen. When he spoke again, his words were laced with a confusion that belied his usual perceptiveness. "I don't... I can't..." He swallowed hard, his Adam's apple bobbing in his throat. "It feels like... like everything's shifting. Like the world is coming apart at the seams."

Linda's heart raced, her mind frantically trying to make sense of Harrison's words. Was this another cruel twist in their already fractured reality? Or was it something worse, something tied to the virus that had caused so much chaos across the multiverse?

She looked to Vega, her earlier anger now mixed with a desperate plea for help. "Richard," she said urgently, "what's happening to my son?"

33 - 34

Linda's eyes widened in horror as she saw the first crimson droplet trickle from Harrison's nostril. It wound its way down his upper lip, a stark contrast against his ashen skin. His hands, bound tightly in front of him, twitched uselessly as he tried to reach for his face.

"Harrison!" Linda cried out, her voice breaking with a mother's anguish. The sound echoed in the hotel suite, bouncing off the walls and reverberating through her very core. She thrashed against her restraints, the cord biting into her wrists as she fought to reach her son.

"Mom," Harrison whimpered, his brown eyes wide with fear. "I can't... I can't stop it."

Linda's heart pounded in her chest, each beat a reminder of her helplessness. She could feel the tears welling up in her eyes, hot and stinging. "It's okay, baby," she said, trying to keep her voice steady. "Just stay calm. We'll figure this out."

But even as the words left her lips, Linda felt a wave of dread wash over her. This wasn't like anything they'd faced before. The blood trickling from Harrison's nose wasn't just a nosebleed – it was a sign of something far more sinister. Something tied to the fractured realities they'd been navigating, perhaps even to the virus that had caused so much chaos.

"Richard!" Linda shouted, her gaze snapping to Vega. "For God's sake, do something! Help him!"

35 - 36

Harrison's eyelids fluttered, his lashes matted with crimson. "I don't feel good," he murmured, his voice barely above a whisper. As if to underscore his words, blood began to seep from the corners of his eyes, leaving scarlet trails down his pale cheeks.

Linda's heart clenched, a visceral pain that threatened to tear her apart. She could feel the rough fibers of the cord digging into her wrists as she strained against her bonds, her maternal instincts screaming at her to reach her son, to comfort him, to save him.

"Richard, untie him! Do something!" The words erupted from her throat, raw and desperate. Linda's mind raced, grasping for solutions, for anything that might help Harrison. Was this the virus manifesting? Or something worse, some consequence of their reality-hopping that they'd never anticipated?

Her eyes darted around the room, searching for anything that might help. The opulent hotel suite, with its plush furnishings and gleaming surfaces, now seemed like a gilded cage. She thought of Drake, wishing fervently for his presence, for his ability to bend reality to his will. But he wasn't here. It was just her, Harrison, and the man who had betrayed them all.

"Please," Linda pleaded, her voice dropping to a hoarse whisper. "I know you've done terrible things, Richard, but he's just a boy. You can't let him suffer like this."

37 - 38

Vega sprang to his feet, his lean frame coiled with tension. The polished facade he'd maintained crumbled as he rushed to Harrison's side, revealing the conflicted man beneath. He crouched before the boy, his hands hovering uncertainly over Harrison's trembling form.

"Harrison, can you hear me? Stay with me, kid," Vega urged, his voice uncharacteristically gentle. His dark eyes, usually sharp with calculation, now held a glimmer of genuine concern.

Linda watched, her heart pounding a frantic rhythm against her ribcage. She could see the internal struggle playing out on Vega's face - the man who had orchestrated their tragedy now faced with its consequences.

"Do something!" Linda demanded, her voice raw with anguish. "You caused this, now fix it!"

Vega's hands shook as he reached for the cord binding Harrison's wrists. "I-I don't know how," he admitted, fumbling with the knots. "This wasn't supposed to happen. Not to him."

Harrison's breathing grew more labored, each shallow gasp a dagger in Linda's heart. Blood continued to trickle from his eyes and nose, staining the expensive upholstery of the couch. The metallic scent filled the air, a cruel reminder of their predicament.

"Mom," Harrison whimpered, his voice barely audible. "I'm scared."

Linda's screams filled the room, primal and heart-wrenching. The sound of a mother's anguish reverberated off the walls, seeming to shake the very foundations of the hotel suite. She thrashed against her restraints, feeling the skin of her wrists tear, but the physical pain was nothing compared to the agony of watching her son suffer.

"It's okay, baby," she managed between sobs, trying to infuse her voice with a calm she didn't feel. "Mommy's here. Just hold on."

As Linda's cries echoed around them, Vega's face contorted with a mix of guilt and desperation. He muttered under his breath, "What have I done? What have I done?" The weight of his choices seemed to crush him, the carefully constructed justifications crumbling in the face of Harrison's pain.

The Key to Remembering

1-2 The acrid scent of mildew clung to Drake's nostrils as he shifted uncomfortably in the tattered armchair. Its frayed fabric scratched against his skin, a constant reminder of the decay surrounding him in Rachel's dilapidated home. His eyes followed her pacing form, her worn lab coat swishing with each turn, a ghost of her former scientific prestige.

Rachel's muttered words drifted in and out of coherence, fragments of multiversal theories and temporal anomalies that made Drake's head spin. He ran a hand through his disheveled hair, trying to piece together the puzzle she'd laid before him. The weight of his family's fate pressed down on his shoulders, a burden he'd carried through countless iterations of this hellish day.

"What if I can't fix this?" Drake's voice was barely above a whisper, more to himself than to Rachel. The thought of failing again, of watching his wife and son slip away, threatened to consume him.

Rachel's pacing halted abruptly. She turned to face him, her eyes alight with a mix of fear and fierce determination. The intensity of her gaze bore into Drake, momentarily silencing the chorus of doubts in his mind.

"We don't have the luxury of 'what ifs,' Drake," Rachel stated, her tone sharp and unwavering. "The very fabric of reality is at stake. Your family, this world, everything hangs in the balance."

Drake's jaw clenched, a familiar surge of determination rising within him. "Then tell me what I need to do. Whatever it takes, I'll do it."

Rachel's expression softened slightly, a flicker of empathy crossing her features. "It won't be easy. The answers we seek are buried deep, perhaps in places you've tried to forget."

As she spoke, Drake's mind raced, grasping at fragments of memories that seemed just out of reach. What had he done? What mistake could have possibly led to this nightmarish loop?

"I'm ready," Drake declared, rising from the chair with renewed purpose. "Whatever it takes, whatever I need to face – I'll do it. For them. For all of us."

Rachel nodded, a grim smile tugging at the corners of her mouth. "Then let's begin. The path ahead is dark, Drake, but remember – you're not walking it alone."

3-4 Rachel's eyes locked onto Drake's, her gaze unwavering. "You're caught in a loop," she said bluntly, her voice cutting through the silence like a blade.

The words hung in the air, heavy and oppressive. Drake's shoulders tensed, his fingers digging into the worn fabric of the armchair. He could almost taste the bitter truth of her statement, mingling with the musty air of the room.

"I know that already," Drake replied, his voice rough with frustration. He ran a hand through his disheveled hair, the gesture betraying his inner turmoil. "I've been living the same day over and over, watching my wife and son die no matter what I do."

The image of their lifeless bodies flashed before his eyes, a cruel reminder that haunted his every waking moment. He swallowed hard, forcing the words past the lump in his throat. "That's why I came to you—for a way out."

As he spoke, Drake's mind raced, grappling with the weight of his predicament. How many times had he relived this nightmare? How many more times would he have to endure it? The thought of facing another cycle, another failure, sent a shiver down his spine.

Rachel's expression softened slightly, a flicker of sympathy crossing her features. But her voice remained firm as she replied, "It's not that simple, Drake. Breaking free from this loop will require more than just finding an escape route."

Drake leaned forward, his eyes blazing with a mix of desperation and determination. "Then tell me what I need to do. Whatever it takes, I'll do it. I can't—" his voice cracked, "I can't watch them die again."

5 - 6

Rachel shook her head, her tangled red hair swaying with the motion. "It's not just a loop, Drake. It's a temporal anomaly. And I don't think this is your first time in it."

The words hung in the air, heavy and ominous. Drake felt the blood drain from his face, his heart pounding against his ribcage. The room seemed to tilt, the mildew-scented air suddenly thick and oppressive.

"What are you saying?" he managed, his stomach tightening into a painful knot. His mind raced, grasping at fragments of memories that felt just out of reach. Had he been here before? Had he forgotten?

Rachel's eyes, sharp and knowing, bore into him. "I'm saying that your experience goes beyond a simple time loop. This anomaly... it's more complex, more insidious. And I believe you've been caught in its web far longer than you realize."

Drake's hands clenched involuntarily, his knuckles turning white. He struggled to process her words, to reconcile them with the hellish cycle he'd been living. "But how? I remember everything so clearly - the accident, the deaths, every failed attempt to save them. How could I forget other cycles?"

As he spoke, a flicker of something - a memory? a dream? - danced at the edges of his consciousness. It felt like grasping at smoke, ephemeral and elusive. Drake closed his eyes, trying to focus, to capture that fleeting sensation.

"The human mind is remarkably adaptable," Rachel replied, her voice softer now. "It can create barriers, shields to protect itself from trauma. But those barriers aren't impenetrable, Drake. And I think they're starting to crack."

7 - 8

Rachel leaned against the cluttered desk, her worn lab coat rustling against stacks of papers. The dim light cast deep shadows across her face, accentuating the lines of exhaustion etched there. Her voice lowered, taking on an urgent timbre that sent a chill down Drake's spine.

"I think you've been in this loop for far longer than you realize. You're only starting to remember because the multiverse itself is breaking down, forcing fragments of your past lives to surface."

Drake's breath caught in his throat. Past lives? The concept was both alien and oddly familiar, like a half-remembered dream. He could feel something stirring in the depths of his mind, memories struggling to break free from the fog that shrouded them.

"But this... this loop?" Rachel continued, her eyes never leaving his face. "It's your prison. And it's not letting you go until you figure out why you're here."

The words hit Drake like a physical blow. He stumbled back, gripping the edge of a nearby bookshelf for support. The room seemed to spin around him, the air heavy with the weight of this revelation.

"A prison," he whispered, the word tasting bitter on his tongue. "But why? What did I do to deserve this?"

Rachel's expression softened, a flicker of sympathy crossing her features. "That's what we need to uncover, Drake. The answer lies somewhere in those buried memories."

As she spoke, the ancient clock on the wall began to chime, its deep, resonant tones filling the room. Drake's gaze was drawn to it instinctively, watching as the hands ticked past midnight. Each chime felt like a hammer blow, driving home the reality of his situation.

Past midnight. Another day begun, another chance to save his family. Or was it? If Rachel was right, if this went beyond a simple time loop, what did that mean for his desperate quest?

9 - 10

Drake ran a hand through his disheveled hair, frustration simmering beneath the surface. His fingers trembled slightly, betraying the turmoil within. "I made it past midnight last night," he said, his voice low and strained. "That should've broken the loop, right?"

The hope that had briefly flickered in his chest began to wane as he met Rachel's unwavering gaze. Her red hair, dulled by years of isolation, framed a face etched with the weight of forbidden knowledge.

Rachel crossed her arms, her worn lab coat rustling with the movement. "Not necessarily," she replied, her tone measured but tinged with urgency. "Making it past midnight doesn't mean it's over. The loop isn't tied to time—it's tied to your choices."

Drake's mind reeled at her words. He paced the cluttered room, his footsteps echoing in the silence. Fragments of memories flashed before his eyes—his wife's smile, his son's laughter, their lifeless bodies. Each cycle, each desperate attempt to save them, had led him here.

"My choices," he muttered, more to himself than to Rachel. "But I've tried everything. I've changed every decision, explored every possibility. What am I missing?"

Rachel's voice cut through his spiraling thoughts. "It's trying to correct something, Drake. And until you fix the mistake you made, it's going to keep resetting."

The word 'mistake' hung in the air between them, heavy with implication. Drake's chest tightened, a familiar guilt gnawing at his insides. What had he done? What cosmic error was he being forced to rectify?

He turned to face Rachel, his eyes searching her face for answers she couldn't provide. "How do I fix something I can't even remember?" he asked, his voice barely above a whisper.

11 - 12

Drake's jaw tightened, the muscle twitching beneath his skin. "What mistake?" he asked, his voice low and strained. The weight of countless repeated days pressed down on him, each one a reminder of his failure to save his family.

Rachel sighed, her shoulders slumping slightly. The flickering light cast shadows across her face, accentuating the weariness etched into her features. "I don't know," she admitted, her eyes meeting his with a mix of sympathy and determination. "That's something only you can remember."

Drake turned away, his gaze sweeping over the cluttered room. Books on quantum physics and temporal mechanics lay scattered across every surface, silent witnesses to Rachel's relentless pursuit of answers. He ran a hand through his disheveled hair, frustration and fear battling within him.

"But it's tied to your family, Drake," Rachel continued, her voice softer now. "Protecting them is part of the equation, but it's not the whole solution."

The mention of his family sent a sharp pain through Drake's chest. In his mind's eye, he saw them again—laughing, alive, unaware of the danger that stalked them through time itself. How many times had he watched them die? How many more times could he endure it?

"You have to remember what you did," Rachel pressed, her words cutting through his anguished thoughts. "What set this all in motion."

Drake's fists clenched at his sides. "And if I can't?" he asked, his voice barely above a whisper. The enormity of his task loomed before him, a mountain of forgotten memories and unintended consequences.

13 - 14

Rachel straightened, her expression resolute. The faded lab coat she wore seemed to regain a measure of its former dignity as she squared her shoulders. "Come with me," she said, her voice cutting through the heavy silence. "There's something I want to show you."

Drake hesitated, his eyes darting to the cluttered desk where a replication of Sir Mordred's codex lay half-hidden beneath a stack of papers. What other secrets did Rachel harbor? His heart raced, a mix of anticipation and dread coursing through his veins.

"What is it?" he asked, his voice hoarse with fatigue and uncertainty.

Rachel's gaze softened for a moment, a flicker of empathy crossing her worn features. "It's a tool," she explained, her words precise and measured. "One that might help you access those buried memories."

Drake's brow furrowed. "And you think it'll work?" He couldn't keep the skepticism from his voice, even as hope stirred in his chest.

Rachel's lips tightened into a thin line. "I can't guarantee anything, Drake. But in my experience, when conventional methods fail, we must push the boundaries of what's possible."

As she spoke, Rachel moved towards a door at the far end of the room. Her steps were purposeful, each movement deliberate as if she carried the weight of countless failed experiments on her shoulders.

Drake followed, his mind racing. What lay beyond that door? And more importantly, was he ready to face whatever memories it might unlock? The thought of delving deeper into the twisted reality of his existence sent a shiver down his spine.

"Rachel," he called out, just as her hand reached for the doorknob. "What if... what if I don't like what I remember?"

She turned to face him, her eyes filled with a mixture of determination and something darker—a shadow of the burdens she carried. "Sometimes, Drake," she said softly, "the truth hurts. But it's the only way forward."

With those words hanging in the air, Rachel opened the door, revealing the path to whatever lay ahead—and possibly, to the key that would unlock Drake's fractured past.

15 - 16

Drake's heart thundered in his chest as he followed Rachel through the doorway. The floorboards beneath their feet groaned, a discordant symphony of age and neglect. Each step into the unknown sent a jolt of anticipation through his body, mingling with the ever-present fear that had become his constant companion.

"Watch your step," Rachel warned, her voice barely above a whisper. "The stairs are treacherous."

As they descended into the murky depths, Drake's mind raced. What secrets lay hidden in this cellar? Would they hold the key to breaking his torturous loop, or merely add another layer to the enigma that had become his existence?

The air grew thick and heavy, laden with the musty scent of decay. Drake's fingers trailed along the damp wall, seeking balance in the darkness. "Rachel," he called out, his voice tight with tension, "how much further?"

"Just a few more steps," she replied, her tone reassuring yet tinged with an edge of anticipation.

At the bottom of the stairs, Rachel paused. Drake could hear her fumbling in the darkness, and then suddenly, with a sharp click, dim light flooded the space.

As his eyes adjusted, Drake took in the cluttered expanse of the cellar. Shelves lined the walls, overflowing with an eclectic array of equipment and weathered tomes. In the center of the room stood something covered by a large tarp, its shape indistinct yet somehow ominous.

"What is all this?" Drake asked, his gaze darting from object to object, trying to make sense of the chaotic assemblage.

Rachel's eyes gleamed in the low light, a mixture of pride and trepidation evident in her expression. "This, Drake, is where we start unraveling the mystery of your existence."

17 - 18

Rachel stepped forward, her hand grasping the edge of the tarp. With a swift motion, she yanked it away, revealing the object beneath.

In the center of the room sat a deprivation chamber, its sleek, metallic surface a stark contrast to the otherwise decrepit surroundings. The chamber was rectangular, its edges rounded, with a small control panel on one side. The polished surface reflected the dim light, creating an otherworldly glow in the musty cellar.

Drake stared at it, his brow furrowing. "What is this?" he asked, his voice barely above a whisper. He took a hesitant step forward, drawn by a mixture of curiosity and apprehension.

The chamber seemed to pulse with potential, a silent promise of answers that had long eluded him. Drake's mind raced, memories of countless failed attempts to save his family flashing before his eyes. Could this strange device hold the key to breaking the cycle?

"It's... unexpected," Drake admitted, circling the chamber slowly. His fingers hovered just above the cool metal surface, not quite touching. "I've seen a lot of strange things since this all began, but nothing quite like this."

Rachel watched him intently, gauging his reaction. "It's more than just a piece of equipment, Drake. It's a tool that might help us unravel the mystery of your situation."

Drake's jaw clenched, a familiar determination settling over him. "And you think this can help me save my family? Break this infernal loop?"

He placed his palm flat against the chamber's surface, feeling a faint vibration beneath his skin. The sensation sent a shiver down his spine, a mix of hope and fear coursing through him.

19 - 20

Rachel stepped closer, her expression intense, eyes gleaming with a mixture of scientific curiosity and cautious hope. "A sensory deprivation chamber," she explained, her voice low and steady. "It's designed to cut off all external stimuli—sight, sound, touch—so your mind can focus inward. It's a tool for accessing deep memories, ones that are buried or blocked."

Drake's throat tightened as he took another step closer, his hand still resting on the cool metal surface. The chamber seemed to hum beneath his touch, as if responding to his presence. He swallowed hard, his mind racing with possibilities and fears.

"And you think this will help me remember?" he asked, his voice barely above a whisper. The weight of countless repeated days pressed down on him, each failure to save his family a fresh wound in his psyche.

Rachel's eyes met his, unflinching. "It's our best shot, Drake. Your mind holds the key to breaking this loop, but something's blocking those crucial memories."

Drake closed his eyes, inhaling deeply. The musty air of the cellar filled his lungs, grounding him in this moment. When he opened them again, determination had replaced the fear in his gaze.

"If there's even a chance," he murmured, more to himself than to Rachel, "I have to try. For Linda. For Harrison. For all of us trapped in this nightmare."

His fingers traced the edge of the chamber's entrance, his resolve strengthening with each passing second. The thought of delving into the depths of his own mind terrified him, but the alternative—watching his family die again and again—was unthinkable.

"How does it work?" Drake asked, his voice steadier now. "What should I expect?"

21 - 22

Rachel's expression softened, a flicker of compassion breaking through her usual stoic demeanor. She stepped closer to the chamber, her worn lab coat rustling softly in the stillness of the cellar.

"If the loop is tied to your mistake, then remembering it is the first step to breaking free," she explained, her voice low and urgent. "The deprivation chamber can help you access those memories—fragments from past cycles, things you might not even realize you've experienced."

Drake's brow furrowed, his hand still resting on the cool metal of the chamber. The weight of countless repeated days pressed down on him, each one a reminder of his failures. He could almost hear Linda's screams, see Harrison's terrified eyes. The memories threatened to overwhelm him, but he pushed them back, focusing on Rachel's words.

"Fragments," he repeated, his voice hoarse. "You mean I might remember other attempts? Other... deaths?"

Rachel nodded solemnly. "It's possible. The human mind is resilient, Drake. It might be protecting you from the full weight of your experiences."

Drake hesitated, his gaze lingering on the chamber. It looked like a coffin, he thought, and immediately regretted the comparison. How many times had he seen his family in coffins? How many funerals had he attended in this endless loop?

"How does it work?" he asked finally, forcing himself to focus on the present. His heart raced, a mix of fear and desperate hope coursing through him.

23 - 24

Rachel's eyes met Drake's, her expression a mixture of determination and concern. "You'll lie inside, and the chamber will seal shut," she explained, her voice steady but tinged with caution. "The lack of sensory input will force your mind to focus on itself, and if you're ready, the memories should start to surface."

Drake's fingers traced the edge of the chamber, feeling every cool, smooth contour. His chest tightened as he imagined being enclosed in the darkness, cut off from everything. Would he hear Linda's voice? See Harrison's smile? Or would he confront horrors he'd buried deep within his subconscious?

"It won't be pleasant, Drake," Rachel continued, her words cutting through his thoughts. "You'll see things you might not want to. But if you want to end this, it's the only way."

Drake nodded slowly, his jaw clenched. The weight of countless repeated days, of watching his family die over and over, pressed down on him. He'd endured so much already. Could he handle more?

"I've seen them die a thousand times," he murmured, more to himself than to Rachel. "How much worse can it get?"

Rachel's expression softened, a flicker of sympathy crossing her face. "This isn't just about reliving trauma, Drake. It's about uncovering the truth – the mistake that started all this. Are you ready to face that?"

Drake took a deep breath, steeling himself. The chamber loomed before him, a portal to his own fractured psyche. He thought of Linda and Harrison, of the chance to save them, to break free from this hellish cycle.

"I have to be," he said finally, his voice low but resolute. "For them. For all of us."

25 - 26

Drake's chest tightened, a mixture of apprehension and determination constricting his breath. The deprivation chamber loomed before him, its sleek surface reflecting the dim light of the cellar. He ran a hand through his disheveled hair, his lawyer's instinct pushing him to consider every angle.

"What if it doesn't work?" he asked, his voice barely above a whisper. The weight of countless repeated days hung heavy on his shoulders, each one ending in the same tragic loss of his family. He couldn't bear the thought of another dead end.

Rachel's gaze met his, her eyes softening with a compassion that seemed at odds with her usual assertive demeanor. The frayed edges of her lab coat caught Drake's attention, a stark reminder of the toll their pursuit had taken on both of them.

"Then we'll find another way," she replied, her voice quiet but firm. "But I believe this is your best shot."

Drake nodded, his jaw clenching as he wrestled with the decision. The thought of delving into the depths of his fractured memories terrified him, yet the alternative – remaining trapped in this nightmarish loop – was unthinkable.

"You've faced worse," he reminded himself silently, thinking of the countless times he'd watched his family slip away. "At least this time, there's hope."

He took a step toward the chamber, his hand brushing against its cool surface. "Alright," he said, steeling himself for what lay ahead. "Let's do this."

27 - 28

Drake's fingers trailed along the smooth metal of the chamber, his reflection distorted in its polished surface. He saw a man haunted by grief, driven by desperation, and clinging to a sliver of hope. The weight of countless iterations pressed down on him, each failed attempt to save his family etched into the lines of his face.

"I've watched them die so many times," Drake murmured, his voice thick with emotion. He turned to Rachel, his eyes searching for reassurance. "Will this really help me remember what I need to break free?"

Rachel stepped closer, her presence a steadying force in the dim cellar. "The mind is complex, Drake. But if there's a key to unlocking this loop, it's buried in your subconscious. This chamber... it's our best chance at excavating those memories."

Drake nodded slowly, his gaze drawn back to the ominous pod. The thought of being sealed inside, cut off from all sensory input, sent a shiver down his spine.

"I've faced courtrooms and criminals," he thought, a wry smile tugging at his lips. "How bad can a little sensory deprivation be?"

Taking a deep breath, Drake squared his shoulders. "Alright," he said, his voice steady despite the tremor in his hands. "Let's do it. Whatever it takes to save them, to end this nightmare... I'm ready."

29 - 30

Rachel gave a small nod, stepping aside to activate the control panel. The chamber hummed softly as it powered up, its lid sliding open to reveal the dark, padded interior. The sound reminded Drake of a heartbeat, steady and ominous, echoing in the musty cellar.

"It's like a coffin," Drake thought, his throat tightening. He swallowed hard, forcing the macabre image from his mind. "No, it's a way out. It has to be."

Drake stepped forward, his hands brushing against the cool metal as he prepared to climb inside. The smooth surface sent a jolt through him, as if the chamber itself was alive, waiting to swallow him whole.

"Rachel," he said, hesitating at the edge of the pod. "If something goes wrong... if I can't—"

"You can," Rachel interrupted, her voice firm but tinged with compassion. "You've survived worse, Drake. This is just another step towards the truth."

Drake nodded, drawing strength from her confidence. He took a deep breath, filling his lungs with the damp cellar air. As he exhaled, he muttered, "For Linda. For Harrison. For all of us."

With a final glance at Rachel, Drake lowered himself into the chamber. The padding enveloped him, soft yet unyielding, as if the very fabric of reality was preparing to reshape itself around him.

Into the Tank

1 ^{- 2}
The dim light of the cellar flickered, casting eerie shadows across the room. Drake ran his hand along the smooth surface of the deprivation chamber, feeling the cool metal beneath his fingertips. The hum of its internal mechanisms filled the silence, a low vibration that seemed to settle in his chest, reminding him of the precarious nature of his existence in this unfamiliar world.

As he stood there, transfixed by the machine that held the potential to unlock the mysteries of his fractured reality, Drake couldn't help but reflect on the twisted path that had led him to this moment. The weight of his past mistakes pressed down upon him, a constant reminder of the lives he had inadvertently destroyed in his quest for redemption.

He glanced over his shoulder at Rachel, her once-vibrant red hair now dulled and tangled, cascading loosely around her shoulders as she hunched over the small control panel. Her frayed lab coat, a remnant of her former life as a celebrated scientist, hung loosely on her frame. Drake couldn't help but feel a pang of guilt for the role he had played in her current circumstances.

"Why do you even have something like this?" he asked, his voice tinged with curiosity and unease. The question hung in the air, heavy with the implications of what they were about to attempt.

Rachel's fingers paused over the controls, her eyes fixed on the panel before her. "Necessity breeds innovation, Drake," she replied, her tone measured and precise. "When the world turns its back on you, you find ways to push forward, to seek answers where others see only darkness."

Drake nodded, understanding all too well the drive that had led Rachel to create such a device. He ran a hand through his disheveled hair, feeling the weight of their shared burden. "And you think this will help us unravel the truth about the anomaly? About why I'm here?"

Rachel turned to face him, her eyes reflecting a mixture of determination and exhaustion. "It's our best chance," she said, her voice carrying the conviction of a scientist on the brink of a breakthrough. "Your presence here defies the laws of our reality, Drake. This chamber might just be the key to unlocking the memories that could save us all."

As Drake contemplated her words, he felt a surge of resolve coursing through him. Despite the risks, despite the gnawing fear of what he might discover about himself and this distorted world, he knew he had to press on. For his family, for Rachel, and for the countless lives hanging in the balance across the multiverse, he would face whatever truths lay hidden in the depths of his fractured mind.

3 - 4

Rachel's fingers danced over the control panel, her movements precise and deliberate. The soft glow of the electronics cast eerie shadows across her face, accentuating the lines of fatigue etched into her skin. She didn't look up as she worked, her voice barely audible over the hum of the machinery. "It was supposed to help me remember," she said.

Drake's brow furrowed, his mind racing with possibilities. The chamber loomed before him, a metallic cocoon promising answers and nightmares in equal measure. He swallowed hard, his throat suddenly dry. "Remember what?" he asked, his voice a mixture of curiosity and trepidation.

As he awaited her response, Drake's gaze swept across the dimly lit cellar. The damp air clung to his skin, a constant reminder of the depths they had descended to in their quest for truth. He couldn't shake the feeling that they were teetering on the edge of something monumental, something that could shatter their perception of reality itself.

Rachel's hands stilled on the panel, her shoulders sagging slightly as if under an invisible weight. Drake found himself holding his breath, acutely aware of the tension crackling in the air between them. Whatever Rachel was about to reveal, he sensed it would irrevocably change the course of their journey.

5 - 6

"The Codex," she replied, her tone flat and devoid of emotion. The words hung in the air, heavy with unspoken implications. Drake's mind raced, trying to grasp the significance of this revelation.

Rachel's fingers hovered over the panel, trembling slightly. "I thought if I could clear my mind, focus on the visions, I'd be able to understand them. To find it again." She paused, her eyes distant, as if seeing something beyond the confines of the cellar. "But it didn't work. The Codex isn't calling to me. It never was."

Drake felt a chill run down his spine, his lawyer's instincts kicking in. Something about her words didn't add up, and he couldn't shake the feeling that they were missing a crucial piece of the puzzle. He ran a hand through his disheveled hair, buying time as he formulated his next question.

The weight of his past mistakes pressed down on him, a constant companion in this strange journey. He couldn't help but wonder if this Codex held the key to his redemption, to fixing the fractures in reality he'd unwittingly caused.

"Then why do you think it'll work on me?" Drake finally asked, his voice laced with a mixture of skepticism and hope. He studied Rachel's face, searching for any sign of deception or uncertainty.

As he awaited her response, Drake's mind whirled with possibilities. Was he truly different? Could he unlock the secrets that eluded Rachel? The thought both thrilled and terrified him, knowing that the answers he sought might come at a terrible cost.

7 - 8

Rachel's eyes snapped up, locking onto Drake's with an intensity that made him take a step back. The fluorescent light overhead flickered, casting shifting shadows across her face, accentuating the determination etched in her features.

"Because you're the anomaly, Drake," she said, her voice barely above a whisper but filled with conviction. "You're the one who shouldn't be here. I think you're the only one who really remembers, and the rest of us... we're just echoes. Shadows forced to remember because of you."

The words hit Drake like a physical blow, forcing the air from his lungs. He gripped the edge of the deprivation chamber, steadying himself as the implications of Rachel's statement washed over him. The cool metal beneath his fingers grounded him, a stark contrast to the surreal nature of their conversation.

Memories flashed through his mind – disjointed images of a life he both recognized and didn't. His family, whole and happy, yet somehow wrong. A world familiar but off-kilter, like a painting slightly askew. And always, always, that gnawing sense of guilt that had followed him since he'd awakened in this distorted reality.

Drake swallowed hard, his throat suddenly dry. "So, if this works..." he began, his voice hoarse with emotion, "I'll be dragging those memories to the surface?"

As he spoke, Drake's gaze drifted to the deprivation chamber, its smooth surface now seeming more ominous than before. What truths lay hidden in the recesses of his mind? And more importantly, was he ready to face them?

9 - 10

Rachel nodded, her eyes filled with a mixture of determination and apprehension. "If my hypothesis is correct, yes. You're the key to all of this, Drake. Whatever you've forgotten—it's the linchpin of the loop."

The weight of her words settled heavily on Drake's shoulders, a burden he hadn't asked for but knew he couldn't shirk. He ran his hand through his disheveled hair, feeling the slight tremor in his fingers. The damp cellar air clung to his skin, a constant reminder of the surreal nature of their situation.

"The linchpin," Drake repeated softly, more to himself than to Rachel. His mind raced, grappling with the enormity of what she was suggesting. He was both the cause and the potential solution to this fractured reality. The thought was terrifying, exhilarating, and utterly overwhelming.

He closed his eyes for a moment, trying to center himself. When he opened them again, his gaze fell on Rachel's worn lab coat, a stark reminder of her own sacrifices in pursuit of the truth. The sight stirred something within him—a mixture of gratitude and resolve.

Drake exhaled slowly, his breath visible in the cool air of the cellar. "Alright," he said finally, his voice steadier than he felt. "Let's do it."

As the words left his mouth, Drake felt a strange sense of inevitability wash over him. Whatever lay ahead—whatever truths or horrors he might uncover—he knew there was no turning back. The path forward, as uncertain and dangerous as it might be, was the only one left to take.

11 - 12

Rachel stepped aside, her movements deliberate and focused. The dim light caught the frayed edges of her lab coat, casting long shadows across the cellar floor. She motioned toward the deprivation chamber, its sleek surface a stark contrast to the rough stone walls surrounding them.

"You'll need to strip down to your boxers," she said, her voice steady and clinical. "The less distraction, the better."

Drake's heart hammered in his chest as he eyed the tank. It looked more like a coffin than a scientific instrument, and the thought of being sealed inside made his skin crawl. Still, he knew this was necessary. He had to remember, had to understand his role in this twisted reality.

"Right," he muttered, fingers fumbling with the buttons of his shirt. "Any other instructions before I climb into that thing?"

Rachel's eyes softened for a moment, a flicker of empathy breaking through her professional demeanor. "Just try to clear your mind," she advised. "Let the memories come naturally. Don't force them."

As Drake began to undress, he couldn't help but ponder the absurdity of their situation. Here he was, preparing to submerge himself in sensory deprivation, all in the hopes of unlocking memories that could unravel the very fabric of their existence. The weight of responsibility settled heavily on his shoulders, and he found himself longing for simpler times—times that might never have existed at all.

13 - 14

Drake hesitated for a moment, his hands hovering at the waistband of his pants. The chill of the cellar air prickled his exposed skin, raising goosebumps along his arms. With a deep breath, he steeled himself and finished undressing, carefully folding his clothes and placing them on a nearby chair. The cold concrete floor bit at his feet as he stepped towards the chamber, each movement deliberate and tinged with apprehension.

"I feel like I'm preparing for some bizarre alien abduction," Drake quipped, attempting to mask his nervousness with humor. His voice echoed slightly in the underground space, amplifying the tension he felt coursing through his body.

Rachel didn't respond to his jest. Her focus remained on the control panel, fingers dancing across the buttons and switches with practiced precision. "Once you're inside," she explained, her tone serious, "I'll seal the lid. The tank will eliminate all sensory input—no light, no sound, no touch. Just you and your mind."

Drake swallowed hard, his throat suddenly dry. "And if my mind decides to show me something I'm not ready for?" he asked, unable to keep the tremor from his voice.

Rachel paused, her hand hovering over the controls. She turned to face him, her eyes locking with his. "That's exactly what we're hoping for, Drake. Whatever you've forgotten—it's the key to all of this. Are you prepared to face it?"

As he stood there, vulnerable and exposed, Drake couldn't help but wonder if he truly was ready for what lay ahead. The weight of universes seemed to rest on his shoulders, and the thought was almost paralyzing. But he knew he had no choice. For his family, for Rachel, for the countless lives hanging in the balance—he had to do this.

"As ready as I'll ever be," he replied, mustering every ounce of determination he could find within himself. With a deep breath, he approached the chamber, ready to plunge into the depths of his own mind.

15 - 16

The padded interior of the chamber embraced Drake's body with an icy chill, sending a shiver down his spine. As he reclined, the curved surface cradled him like a frozen cocoon. His chest tightened, each shallow breath a battle against the rising tide of anxiety threatening to overwhelm him.

"Easy now," Drake whispered to himself, his voice barely audible over the thrumming of his pulse in his ears. He closed his eyes, desperately trying to steady his racing heart. The weight of countless realities pressed down upon him, a burden he alone could bear.

Rachel's face appeared above him, her features cast in shadow by the dim cellar light. Her expression was a mask of scientific detachment, but Drake caught a flicker of something else in her eyes—concern, perhaps even fear.

"Are you ready?" she asked, her voice steady despite the gravity of the moment.

Drake's mind raced, fragments of memories and doubts swirling in a dizzying maelstrom. Was he truly prepared to confront whatever lay buried in the recesses of his consciousness? The fate of universes hung in the balance, yet he felt achingly human, vulnerable, and afraid.

"I have to be," he replied, surprising himself with the resolve in his voice. "For my family, for everyone. Whatever I find in here," he tapped his temple, "it's the key to fixing all of this, right?"

Rachel nodded, her red hair catching the light as she moved. "Remember, Drake, you're our anomaly. Our hope. Whatever happens in there, know that you're not alone in this fight."

Her words settled over him like a comforting blanket, providing a small measure of warmth against the cold uncertainty that lay ahead. Drake took a deep, centering breath, steeling himself for the journey into the depths of his fractured memories.

17 - 18

Drake nodded, his voice steady despite the apprehension in his chest. "Let's find out."

The words hung in the air, heavy with the weight of countless lives and realities. Drake's gaze locked onto Rachel's, searching for reassurance in her eyes. He found only determination there, a mirror of his own resolve.

Rachel's hand hovered over the control panel, her fingers poised above a single button. "Remember," she said, her voice low and urgent, "focus on the Codex. It's the thread that connects everything."

Drake swallowed hard, his throat suddenly dry. "And if I can't find it?"

"You will," Rachel replied, a hint of her old confidence seeping into her tone. "You have to."

With a decisive motion, Rachel pressed the button. The lid of the deprivation chamber began to slide shut, its mechanism emitting a soft hiss that seemed to grow louder in Drake's ears. As the gap narrowed, he caught one last glimpse of Rachel's face, her expression a mix of hope and fear.

The seal engaged with a final, muffled thud, cutting off the outside world. Darkness enveloped Drake, absolute and consuming. The sudden absence of sensory input was jarring, leaving him adrift in a void of his own making.

In the silence, Drake's thoughts echoed loudly. 'What if I'm not the key?' he wondered, doubt creeping in. 'What if I'm just another shadow, like the others?'

But as the isolation settled around him like a heavy blanket, Drake steeled himself. He had come too far, sacrificed too much to falter now. Whatever truths lay hidden in the recesses of his mind, he would face them. For his family, for Rachel, for all the realities hanging in the balance.

19 - 19

Drake inhaled deeply, the sound of his breath amplified in the enclosed space. The darkness pressed against his eyes, a tangible weight that seemed to seep into his very being.

"Focus," he whispered to himself, his voice oddly muffled. "Remember."

As he lay there, suspended in nothingness, Drake's mind began to wander. Fragmented images flashed behind his closed eyelids: a courtroom, a car's headlights, his son's smile. Each memory slipped away as quickly as it appeared, like sand through an hourglass.

'Is this how it ends?' he thought, a wave of frustration washing over him. 'Trapped in a box, chasing ghosts?'

But then, something shifted. A subtle change in the air, a tingling at the base of his skull. Drake's breath caught in his throat as a new sensation washed over him.

"What's happening?" he murmured, his words swallowed by the void.

The darkness around him began to pulse, a rhythm that matched his heartbeat. With each throb, a new image flashed in his mind, clearer and more vivid than before. A book bound in ancient leather. Symbols etched in gold. The Codex.

Drake's fingers twitched, reaching out instinctively. "I can see it," he breathed, excitement and fear mingling in his chest. "It's right there, just beyond my reach."

As the visions intensified, Drake felt a pull, as if his very essence was being drawn into the memories. He surrendered to it, allowing himself to fall into the depths of his subconscious, ready to confront whatever truths awaited him.

The Flood of Memories

1 -2 The void swallowed Drake whole, an inky blackness that pressed against his skin like a living thing. He floated, suspended in nothingness, his body weightless yet heavy with the burden of his thoughts. The silence was deafening, a vacuum that seemed to suck the very air from his lungs.

"Linda," he whispered, the word lost in the endless dark. Her smile flickered in his mind, a beacon of warmth in the cold emptiness. But it faded too quickly, replaced by the echo of Harrison's laughter, bright and carefree.

Drake's heart clenched. He tried to reach out, to grasp these fleeting memories, but his arms moved sluggishly through the water. The sensory deprivation tank had stripped away all external stimuli, leaving him alone with the whirlwind of his mind.

"You can't save them, Drake," Gabriel's voice slithered through his consciousness, a serpent coiling around his thoughts. "You've already failed."

"No," Drake muttered, his brow furrowing. He could almost feel Gabriel's presence, that smug smile and cold eyes boring into him. "You're wrong."

But doubt gnawed at him, persistent as the water lapping at his skin. What if Gabriel was right? What if all his efforts, all his sacrifices, had been for nothing?

The memories swirled faster now, a dizzying kaleidoscope of moments. Linda's soft touch on his cheek, Harrison's small hand in his, Gabriel's mocking laughter. Drake squeezed his eyes shut, trying to make sense of it all.

"I have to solve this," he thought, his mind racing. "There's a connection, a key to understanding what's happening across the multiverse."

But the pieces refused to fit together. Each time he thought he grasped a thread of understanding, it slipped away like smoke. The weightlessness that had initially felt freeing now seemed suffocating, as if the very absence of anything solid was crushing him.

"Linda, Harrison," Drake whispered their names like a prayer. "I'll find a way. I'll protect you, no matter what it takes."

Yet even as he made this vow, Gabriel's mocking voice echoed in the recesses of his mind: "At what cost, Drake? How many worlds will you sacrifice for your precious family?"

The question hung in the darkness, unanswered and terrifying in its implications.

3 - 4

"It's hopeless," he whispered to himself, his voice swallowed by the emptiness.

The words seemed to hang in the void, mocking him. Drake's muscular frame tensed, his fists clenching beneath the water. The weight of his failures pressed down on him, heavier than the liquid surrounding his body.

"Dad, you can't give up," Harrison's voice echoed in his mind, a memory of unwavering faith. "You always find a way."

Drake's throat tightened. "I'm sorry, Harrison. I don't know if I can this time."

He could almost see Rachel's determined face, her red hair framing intense eyes. "Drake, every problem has a solution. We just haven't found it yet."

"But what if the cost is too high?" Drake thought, his inner voice tinged with desperation. "What if saving everyone means losing you all?"

The silence stretched on, oppressive and absolute. Drake's thoughts spiraled, each loop bringing him closer to the edge of despair. He floated there, suspended between realities, feeling the weight of countless worlds on his shoulders.

But then, like a switch flipping in his mind, a sudden spark ignited.

Drake's eyes snapped open, though the darkness remained absolute. His heart raced, pumping adrenaline through his veins. "Wait," he whispered, his voice hoarse with realization. "The nexus. The choice. It's all connected."

The pieces began to fall into place, a frenetic energy coursing through him. "Rachel!" he called out, his voice echoing in the confines of the tank. "I need to get out. Now!"

5 - 6

The darkness shifted, giving way to a cascade of vivid images, each one striking Drake with the force of a hammer blow. He gasped, his body jerking in the sensory deprivation tank as memories flooded his consciousness.

"Linda," he whispered, her face materializing before him, radiant and alive. The scent of her perfume, a delicate blend of jasmine and vanilla, filled his senses. "I remember... I remember everything."

His mind reeled as fragments of his past life coalesced. The courtroom victories, the late nights poring over case files, the stolen moments of joy with his family. Each memory was a dagger of bittersweet nostalgia, piercing through the fog of his current reality.

"The accident," Drake muttered, his voice thick with emotion. "It wasn't just an accident, was it?"

He saw himself behind the wheel, Linda beside him, Harrison in the backseat. The screech of tires, the shattering of glass, the world spinning out of control. But there was something else, something beyond the chaos of the crash.

"A choice," he realized, his heart pounding. "I made a choice."

The image of a shadowy figure loomed in his mind, its features indistinct but its presence undeniable. Drake's fists clenched involuntarily, his muscles tensing against the weightlessness of the tank.

"Who are you?" he demanded of the apparition. "What did you make me do?"

The figure remained silent, but Drake felt a surge of understanding wash over him. He had bargained for something, sacrificed something immeasurably precious. But the details remained frustratingly out of reach, like trying to grasp smoke with his bare hands.

"Rachel!" Drake called out, his voice echoing in the confined space. "I need to get out. There's more to this than we thought. So much more."

As the memories continued to assail him, Drake struggled to make sense of the fragments. He was close to unraveling the mystery, he could feel it. But with each revelation came a growing dread, a sense that the truth might be more terrible than he could imagine.

"What have I done?" he whispered, his voice barely audible even to himself. "And how do I make it right?"

7 - 8

The darkness swirled, coalescing into a kaleidoscope of horrors. Drake's breath caught in his throat as the first world materialized before him - the Red World. Towering skyscrapers crumbled under a blood-red sky, their jagged silhouettes like broken teeth against the horizon. Flames licked at the streets, devouring everything in their path.

"No," Drake whispered, his voice hoarse. "It can't be."

But the vision didn't stop. It shifted, melting into a verdant landscape - the Green World. Lush forests stretched as far as the eye could see, but something was wrong. The leaves withered and blackened before his eyes, decay spreading like a cancer through the once-vibrant ecosystem.

"I remember this," Drake muttered, his fists clenching. "We tried to save them all."

The scene changed again, revealing the sterile expanse of the Blue World. Cold, metallic structures dominated the landscape, and figures moved with robotic precision, their humanity stripped away.

Drake's mind raced, fragments of memory assaulting him. "The virus," he gasped. "It was everywhere, in every reality."

He saw himself running, always running. Through burning cities, decaying forests, and sterile corridors. The desperation clawed at him, threatening to overwhelm.

"We can't let it win," Drake's past self shouted, his voice echoing across the worlds. "There has to be a way!"

Present-day Drake felt the weight of that desperate chase, the bone-deep exhaustion and the gnawing fear that it might all be for nothing.

"Did we find it?" he asked the void, his voice trembling. "Did we find the cure?"

But the memories offered no comfort, only the relentless pursuit and the crushing responsibility of trying to save not just one world, but an entire multiverse teetering on the brink of annihilation.

9 - 10

A blinding light pierced through the darkness, coalescing into a figure of ethereal radiance. Drake squinted, his heart pounding as recognition dawned.

"The Chosen One," he whispered, awe and trepidation mingling in his voice.

The figure approached, its form shimmering with an otherworldly energy. Luminous blood pulsed through its veins, a stark contrast to the devastation surrounding them.

"You know what must be done," the Chosen One spoke, its voice resonating with power and sorrow.

Drake's past self nodded, jaw set with grim determination. "I do."

The memory shifted, and Drake felt a phantom warmth spreading through his body. He watched as his past self drank deeply from a chalice filled with the Chosen One's blood, the liquid glowing as it passed his lips.

"God," Drake muttered, his hand instinctively reaching for his throat. "I can still taste it."

The warmth intensified, becoming a searing heat that coursed through every fiber of his being. Drake's past self stumbled, gasping as the power to traverse worlds flooded his system.

"It's working," his past self croaked, eyes wide with a mixture of pain and wonder.

Drake's mind reeled, overwhelmed by the memory of that raw, unbridled power. "I remember now," he said, his voice barely above a whisper. "I could feel every world, every reality."

His past self straightened, a newfound resolve hardening his features. "I was their last hope," he declared, the words echoing across time and space.

Present-day Drake felt the weight of that statement settle in his chest. "I was their last hope," he murmured, the words tasting bitter on his tongue. "But at what cost?"

11 - 12

The memory shifted, plunging Drake into a maelstrom of sensations. He found himself standing in the heart of the nexus of torment, a place where reality itself seemed to writhe in agony. The air crackled with an otherworldly energy, sending shivers down his spine.

"This is it," Drake's past self whispered, his voice hoarse and strained. "The final stand."

Drake watched as his former self stumbled forward, body battered and broken. Blood – both his own and that of the Chosen One – trickled from countless wounds, leaving a trail of luminescent droplets in his wake.

"I can't..." Drake muttered, his present-day consciousness recoiling from the memory. "I can't watch this again."

But he had no choice. The scene unfolded before him, as vivid and visceral as the day it happened. His past self approached a pulsating vortex at the center of the nexus, its swirling mass a nightmarish blend of colors that shouldn't exist.

"Is this truly the only way?" Drake's past self called out, his voice barely audible over the cacophony of the nexus.

A disembodied voice, ancient and weary, responded: "You know it is, Drake Miller. Your sacrifice is the key."

Drake felt his throat tighten as he relived the moment of decision. His past self nodded, a single tear trailing down his cheek. "For Linda... for Harrison... for everyone."

With a deep breath, his past self stepped into the vortex. The nexus erupted in a blinding flash of light, and Drake felt every nerve in his body ignite with pain.

"I remember now," Drake gasped, the memory threatening to overwhelm him. "I offered myself willingly. To stop the virus. To save... everyone."

13 - 14

Drake's voice trembled as he whispered, "I gave my life... to save everyone." The words hung in the stillness of the deprivation tank, echoing in his mind like a solemn prayer.

He expected the memory to fade, for the crushing weight of his sacrifice to lift. But instead, the flood of recollections intensified, each new image more vivid than the last.

"No," Drake murmured, his body tensing. "There's more. Why is there more?"

In his mind's eye, he saw himself drifting in a void, formless and weightless. A voice, neither male nor female, resonated through his being. "Your sacrifice has been noted, Drake Miller. But your journey is not yet complete."

Drake's hands clenched into fists, his nails digging into his palms. "What do you mean?" he called out to the disembodied voice. "I died. I gave everything!"

"Death is not always the end," the voice replied, cryptic and calm. "Sometimes, it is merely a transition."

A kaleidoscope of images assaulted Drake's senses – glimpses of alternate realities, paths not taken, lives unlived. He saw himself in a world where the virus had won, another where it had never existed, and countless variations in between.

"Why show me this?" Drake demanded, his voice cracking with emotion. "What more do you want from me?"

The silence that followed was deafening, leaving Drake alone with the weight of his thoughts and the endless parade of possibilities.

15 - 16

The void shimmered, coalescing into a familiar yet alien landscape. Drake found himself standing on solid ground once more, his senses overwhelmed by the pulsating energies of the nexus. The air crackled with an electric tension, each breath carrying the weight of countless realities.

Before him loomed a figure cloaked in shadows, its presence both alluring and terrifying. Lucian. Drake's heart raced, his palms slick with sweat as he faced the embodiment of cosmic manipulation.

"Welcome back, Drake Miller," Lucian's voice slithered through the air, neither entirely masculine nor feminine. "How does it feel to stand at the crossroads of existence once more?"

Drake swallowed hard, his throat dry. "I thought... I thought it was over," he managed, his words barely above a whisper.

Lucian's form seemed to ripple, as if laughing without sound. "Oh, Drake. Nothing is ever truly over. The tapestry of reality is far more complex than you can imagine."

As they spoke, Drake's mind raced. Had his sacrifice been in vain? Was there no end to this cosmic game? He clenched his fists, determination rising within him.

"What do you want from me?" Drake demanded, his voice stronger now. "Haven't I given enough?"

Lucian glided closer, the shadows of their cloak seeming to reach out towards Drake. "We stand at a precipice, Drake Miller. Your actions have set events in motion that even we cannot fully predict."

Drake's eyes narrowed, suspicion gnawing at him. "We? Who's 'we'?"

"That," Lucian replied, their voice tinged with amusement, "is a question for another time. For now, you face a choice."

The air around them shimmered, and Drake felt the weight of countless possibilities pressing down upon him. He steeled himself, knowing that whatever came next would change everything.

17 - 18

The nexus around them pulsed with an otherworldly energy, each beat sending ripples of iridescent light across the void. Drake's heart raced in tandem, his mind struggling to process the enormity of the moment.

Lucian's voice slithered through the air, smooth and seductive, yet laced with a power that made Drake's skin crawl. "You've done your part, Drake. The multiverse owes its survival to you. But now, you stand at a crossroads."

Drake's breath caught in his throat. He'd been here before, hadn't he? The familiarity of the situation sent a chill down his spine. "What do you mean, crossroads?" he asked, his voice barely above a whisper.

The cloaked figure seemed to grow, shadows stretching out impossibly far. "Two paths lie before you, Drake Miller. Two futures, two fates."

As Lucian spoke, images flickered in the air around them. Drake saw flashes of his family—Linda's smile, Harrison's laughter—but also glimpses of destruction, of worlds burning and realities collapsing.

"I don't understand," Drake said, his voice trembling. "I made my choice. I sacrificed everything to save—"

"To save the multiverse?" Lucian interrupted, a note of amusement in their voice. "Perhaps. Or perhaps you merely delayed the inevitable."

Drake's mind raced, trying to piece together the fragments of memory that danced just out of reach. He remembered the offer—two paths laid before him. But the details were hazy, slipping away like smoke whenever he tried to grasp them.

"What are you offering me?" Drake asked, his fists clenching at his sides. "What's the catch this time?"

Lucian's form rippled, as if chuckling silently. "Always so suspicious, Drake. Is it so hard to believe that you might be given a true choice?"

But Drake knew better. There was always a price, always a consequence. He'd learned that lesson the hard way.

19 - 20

Lucian's towering form shifted, and with a fluid motion, they gestured towards a shimmering portal that materialized to their left. The air around it crackled with an otherworldly energy, sending tendrils of electricity dancing across Drake's skin.

"One leads to judgment," Lucian intoned, their voice echoing with an eerie resonance. "You will face the scales of the nexus, your heart weighed against a feather. The other..."

Drake's breath caught in his throat as he stared at the portal. Images of ancient Egyptian mythology flashed through his mind—Anubis, the weighing of the heart, the devourer waiting to consume the unworthy. He swallowed hard, his mouth suddenly dry.

"And if my heart is found wanting?" Drake asked, his voice barely audible.

Lucian's hood tilted, as if considering. "Then oblivion awaits. But perhaps that is preferable to the weight of your choices."

Before Drake could respond, Lucian glided closer, their presence enveloping him like a suffocating shroud. When they spoke again, their voice had softened to a seductive whisper that seemed to caress Drake's very soul.

"The other gives you what you've fought for all this time. Your family. A world where Linda and Harrison live, untouched by tragedy. No viruses, no sacrifices. Just peace."

Drake's heart leapt at the words, even as his mind screamed caution. He saw Linda's face, her eyes bright with life instead of dulled by grief. He heard Harrison's laughter, free from the shadow of loss that had haunted them for so long.

"How?" Drake breathed, torn between hope and disbelief. "How is that possible?"

21 - 22

Drake's hands trembled at his sides, his fingers flexing as if trying to grasp the intangible choice before him. The weight of guilt pressed down on his chest, a constant reminder of the lives lost, the worlds shattered in his wake. Yet the pull of his family—their faces etched in his mind—was an irresistible force.

"I've already sacrificed so much," Drake murmured, his voice thick with emotion. "Haven't I earned some peace?"

Lucian remained silent, a patient shadow waiting for Drake's decision.

Drake closed his eyes, memories flooding his consciousness. The acrid smell of burning cities, the screams of the dying, the cold sterility of a world reduced to mechanical existence—all of it swirled in his mind, a cacophony of suffering he had witnessed across realities.

"But if I choose judgment," he said, opening his eyes to meet Lucian's hidden gaze, "what becomes of Linda and Harrison? Will they be safe?"

"Their fate is not part of this bargain," Lucian replied, their tone neutral. "You must choose for yourself alone."

Drake's jaw clenched, a muscle twitching beneath the skin. The enormity of the decision weighed on him, threatening to crush his resolve. He thought of all he had endured, all he had lost. The chance to reclaim his family, to live in a world untouched by the horrors he had seen—it was everything he had fought for.

With a deep, shuddering breath, Drake straightened his shoulders. "I choose my family," he said, his voice gaining strength with each word. "I choose peace."

As soon as the words left his lips, Drake felt a shift in the air around him. The nexus seemed to pulse, acknowledging his decision. He remembered reaching out, his fingertips brushing against the promise of a new reality—a world where love triumphed over duty, where the warmth of family awaited him.

In that moment, as the choice solidified, Drake felt a mixture of relief and unease settle in his gut. He had made his decision, for better or worse. The path ahead was uncertain, but the promise of reuniting with Linda and Harrison propelled him forward into the unknown.

23 - 24

The memory crystallized with brutal clarity, each detail etching itself into Drake's consciousness. His stomach churned violently, a cold sweat breaking out across his forehead. The weight of his decision crashed down upon him, suffocating in its intensity.

"God, what have I done?" Drake whispered, his voice hoarse with dawning horror.

He stumbled backward, his legs weak beneath him. His hands trembled as he ran them through his disheveled hair, tugging at the strands as if the physical pain could distract from the emotional anguish.

"I thought... I was so sure..." Drake's words trailed off, his eyes unfocused as he replayed the moment of choice over and over in his mind.

The realization hit him like a physical blow. He had been so consumed by his desire to reclaim his family, to find some semblance of peace after all he'd endured, that he'd failed to see the bigger picture. The truth he now understood threatened to tear him apart.

"Linda... Harrison..." Drake murmured their names, a mixture of longing and guilt coloring his tone. "I wanted to save you, to give us the life we deserved. But at what cost?"

He paced the room, his movements erratic and charged with nervous energy. Each step felt like a betrayal of the sacrifice he had once made, of the duty he had sworn to uphold.

"I was their last hope," Drake said, his voice rising with a manic edge. "The chosen one's blood, the nexus, the virus – it all led to that moment. And I threw it away for... for what? A selfish dream?"

He stopped abruptly, his fists clenching at his sides. The enormity of his mistake pressed down on him, threatening to crush his very soul.

"I thought I was claiming my reward," Drake whispered, his voice breaking. "I thought I deserved it after everything I'd been through. But now..."

He trailed off, unable to finish the thought. The truth was too painful, too overwhelming to put into words. Drake had sacrificed the balance of the universe for his own desires, and the consequences of that choice were only beginning to unfold.

25 - 26

Drake's mind reeled as the full implications of his actions crashed over him like a tidal wave. The deprivation tank's silence now felt oppressive, a physical manifestation of the void he had created in the fabric of reality.

"The multiverse," he breathed, his voice barely audible even in the stillness. "I've fractured it all."

Images flashed before his mind's eye: countless worlds, countless versions of himself, all trapped in an endless loop of his own making. The peace he had so desperately sought for his family had come at an unimaginable cost.

Drake's hands trembled as he ran them through his damp hair, his muscular frame tensed with the weight of his realization. "I was so blind," he muttered, his lawyer's mind frantically trying to piece together a defense that didn't exist. "So desperate to have them back that I..."

He trailed off, unable to finish the thought. The truth was too heavy, too damning. Drake's eyes, usually sharp and focused, now darted around the tank as if searching for an escape from his own guilt.

"It was my fault," Drake finally whispered, his voice breaking. The words hung in the air, a confession to the universe he had unwittingly betrayed. "I broke it all."

27 - 28

The darkness of the tank shattered like glass, and Drake shot upright, gasping for air. His lungs burned as if he'd been drowning, each breath a desperate attempt to anchor himself in reality. The cool water that had once cradled him now felt like a thousand icy fingers clawing at his skin.

"No, no, no," Drake muttered, his voice hoarse and unfamiliar to his own ears. His muscular arms trembled as he gripped the edges of the deprivation chamber, knuckles white with the effort. The world spun around him, a kaleidoscope of fractured realities colliding in his mind.

His heart thundered in his chest, each beat a painful reminder of the choice he'd made. Drake's eyes, wide and haunted, darted around the dim room, struggling to focus on anything solid, anything real.

"Linda," he whispered, the name catching in his throat. "Harrison. What have I done to you?"

The weight of his actions pressed down on him, threatening to drag him back into the inky depths of the tank. Drake's lawyer's mind, once so sharp and decisive, now reeled with the implications of his choice.

"I thought I was saving them," he said to the empty room, his words echoing off the cold walls. "But I've damned us all."

With a groan, Drake hauled himself to the edge of the tank, water cascading off his body. He paused there, caught between worlds, the chill air raising goosebumps on his skin.

"How do I fix this?" he wondered aloud, his voice tinged with desperation. "How do I undo a mistake that's shattered the entire multiverse?"

29 - 30

Rachel's voice cut through the chaos of Drake's thoughts, sharp and urgent. "Drake! What's happening?"

Her words jolted him into action. With a strangled gasp, Drake heaved himself over the edge of the tank, his muscular frame suddenly uncooperative. Water sluiced off his body, pattering against the cellar floor in a cacophony that seemed to mirror the fragmented memories swirling in his mind.

He stumbled forward, legs giving way beneath him. The cold concrete rushed up to meet him, and Drake collapsed, his breath coming in ragged gasps. The chill of the floor seeped into his bones, grounding him in this reality—this fractured, broken reality he had unwittingly created.

"I can't—" Drake choked out, his hands flying to his head. He clutched at his temples, fingers digging into his scalp as if he could physically hold onto the flood of memories threatening to overwhelm him. "It's too much. Too many worlds, too many choices."

His eyes squeezed shut, but it did nothing to stem the tide of images flashing behind his eyelids. Red skies, green forests, blue sterility—all of it mixing and blending into a nauseating swirl of what-ifs and could-have-beens.

"Linda," he whispered, the name a prayer and a curse on his lips. "Harrison. I thought I was saving you. I thought—"

Drake's words caught in his throat, replaced by a low, guttural sound of anguish. The weight of his decision pressed down on him, heavier than any burden he'd carried in the courtroom, more devastating than any case he'd lost.

"What have I done?" he moaned, his body curling in on itself, water still dripping from his trembling form. "What have I done to us all?"

31 - 32

Drake's fingers clawed at the concrete, seeking purchase in a world that suddenly felt like it was spinning out of control. His chest heaved as he struggled to contain the torrent of emotions threatening to tear him apart.

"I remember," he said hoarsely, his voice rising into a scream. "I remember my mistake!"

The words echoed off the cold cellar walls, reverberating through Drake's skull like an accusation. In his mind's eye, he saw Lucian's shadowy form, heard the seductive whisper of an impossible choice. Family or duty. Love or balance. The weight of the multiverse or the warmth of Linda's embrace.

Rachel rushed to his side, her face pale with concern. The frayed edges of her lab coat brushed against Drake's arm as she knelt beside him. "What did you see?" she demanded, her voice steady despite the fear evident in her eyes.

Drake looked up at her, his vision blurred by unshed tears. How could he explain the magnitude of what he'd done? How could he convey the crushing guilt of choosing personal happiness over universal harmony?

"I chose wrong," he whispered, the words barely audible. "I chose... and I broke everything."

33 - 33

Drake's hands trembled as he pushed himself up, water pooling beneath him on the cold floor. His eyes locked onto Rachel's, wild with a newfound clarity that burned like fire.

"I chose my family over the balance of the universe," he said, his voice cracking under the weight of his confession. "And now we're all paying for it."

The words hung in the air, heavy and oppressive. Drake's mind reeled, flashing between memories of Linda's smile, Harrison's laughter, and the horrifying realization of what his choice had cost.

"What do you mean?" Rachel asked, her brow furrowed in confusion and concern.

Drake ran a shaking hand through his wet hair, struggling to articulate the enormity of his revelation. "There was a virus," he began, his words tumbling out in a rush. "It was destroying everything, not just our world, but all of them. I sacrificed myself to stop it, but then..."

He trailed off, lost in the memory of Lucian's offer. The temptation had been overwhelming, a chance to reclaim everything he'd lost.

"I was given a choice," Drake continued, his voice barely above a whisper. "Judgment or... or a world where my family was alive and safe. I chose them, Rachel. I chose them, and I fractured reality itself."

As he spoke, Drake's hands clenched into fists, nails digging into his palms. The pain was grounding, a reminder that this moment was real, that his memories weren't just another illusion.

"How could I have been so selfish?" he murmured, more to himself than to Rachel. "I thought I was claiming a reward, but I was just running from the consequences of my actions."

Ready for Anything

1-2   Detective Holly Kierstead's fingers tightened on the steering wheel as she eased her sedan to a halt, the cracked asphalt of the derelict neighborhood crunching beneath the tires. The fading sunlight cast long shadows across the dilapidated houses, their peeling paint and sagging roofs a testament to years of neglect. But it wasn't the rundown residence at 128 Willow Creek Lane that captured her attention. No, her gaze was fixed on the sleek black Toyota Corolla parked haphazardly in front of the house, its presence as incongruous as a diamond in a coal mine.

"Drake," she whispered, her voice barely audible over the idling engine. "What are you doing here?"

Holly's mind raced, piecing together the puzzle before her. Rachel Summers' connection to this address, Drake's unexpected appearance – it all pointed to something far more complex than a simple missing persons case. She leaned forward, squinting through the windshield at the house's darkened windows.

"This can't be a coincidence," she muttered, her analytical mind already formulating theories. "But why would he come here alone? And why now?"

With a deep breath, Holly killed the engine and opened her car door. The warm evening air rushed in, carrying with it the faint scent of decay and forgotten dreams. As she stepped out, her hand instinctively moved to her holster, the cool metal of her service weapon a reassuring presence against her hip.

"Drake?" she called out, her voice cutting through the eerie silence of the street. "Drake, are you in there?"

No response came from the house, but Holly could have sworn she saw a curtain twitch in one of the upstairs windows. Her partner's penchant for rash decisions and solo investigations had led them into dangerous situations before, but this felt different. There was an undercurrent of desperation in Drake's recent behavior that set her nerves on edge.

"Damn it, Miller," she growled, taking a cautious step towards the house. "What kind of mess have you gotten yourself into this time?"

3 - 4

Holly's heart quickened, a mix of apprehension and determination flooding her senses. She glanced at her reflection in the rearview mirror, her sharp eyes meeting their own gaze. The face staring back at her was a mosaic of emotions - concern for her partner, resolve to uncover the truth, and a flicker of fear at the unknown dangers that might await.

"You've got this, Kierstead," she whispered to herself, her voice barely audible. "Whatever's in there, you can handle it."

Her fingers traced the outline of her badge, a reminder of her duty and the oath she'd sworn to uphold. The weight of responsibility settled on her shoulders, familiar yet always daunting.

Reaching into the backseat, Holly retrieved her bulletproof vest, the fabric heavy and reassuring as she strapped it on. Her hands moved with practiced precision, checking the fit before securing her holster and drawing her weapon.

"I hope I won't need this," she murmured, feeling the comforting heft of the gun in her palm. "But with Drake involved, who knows?"

As she adjusted the vest, Holly's mind raced through possible scenarios. Was Drake in danger? Had he stumbled upon something bigger than they'd anticipated? Or was this another impulsive move on his part, driven by his relentless pursuit of justice?

"Whatever you're up to, partner," she said to the empty car, her voice tinged with a mix of exasperation and fondness, "I'll bring you to justice."

With a final deep breath, Holly steeled herself for what might come next. The house loomed before her, its secrets waiting to be uncovered, and she was ready to face them head-on.

5 - 6

The gravel crunched beneath Holly's boots as she stepped out of the car, the sound jarringly loud in the eerie silence of the street. The air hung thick with tension, heavy and oppressive, broken only by the faint rustle of leaves in the breeze.

Holly's eyes darted from shadow to shadow, her senses on high alert. "Stay focused," she whispered to herself, her grip tightening on her weapon. The weight of it was reassuring, grounding her in the moment.

As she approached the house, Holly's mind raced through her training, analyzing every detail of her surroundings. The peeling paint, the overgrown lawn, the drawn curtains - all potential clues, all potential dangers.

"Drake, what have you gotten yourself into this time?" she muttered under her breath, a mixture of concern and frustration coloring her words.

Her steps were measured, deliberate, each placement carefully chosen to minimize noise. The porch creaked under her weight, and Holly froze, listening intently for any reaction from within the house.

Silence.

Holly's heart pounded in her chest, but her hands remained steady. Years of experience had taught her to channel her adrenaline, to use it rather than be overwhelmed by it.

"Okay, Holly," she thought, steeling herself. "Whatever's behind that door, you're ready for it. Trust your instincts."

With one final, deep breath, Holly reached for the doorknob, prepared to face whatever - or whoever - awaited her inside.

The Revelation

1⁻²   The frigid water seeped into Drake's clothes, chilling him to the bone, but he barely noticed. His mind reeled, memories cascading through his consciousness like a torrent. The cellar's damp air clung to his skin, mingling with the acrid scent of fear and desperation.

Rachel's presence nearby was a faint comfort, but even her concerned gaze couldn't penetrate the fog of his thoughts. Drake's chest heaved, each breath a labored gasp as he struggled to process the weight of his newfound awareness.

"I remember," he rasped, his voice raw and unfamiliar to his own ears. "I remember everything."

The words hung in the air, heavy with implication. Drake's eyes, once clouded with confusion, now burned with a terrible clarity. He saw it all—the accident, the sacrifice, the choice that had led him to this distorted reality.

His fingers curled against the rough concrete, seeking purchase in a world that suddenly felt unstable. How could he have forgotten? How could he have lived in this construct, this prison of his own making, for so long without realizing the truth?

"Drake," Rachel's voice cut through his spiraling thoughts, steady and grounding. "What do you remember?"

He looked at her, really looked at her for the first time since emerging from the deprivation chamber. Her red hair, usually so vibrant, seemed dull in the dim light of the cellar. The lines of worry etched on her face spoke of a burden she'd carried far too long.

"Everything," Drake repeated, his voice gaining strength. "The accident, the virus, the choice I made. This world—" he gestured weakly at their surroundings, "—it's not real. None of it is."

Rachel's sharp intake of breath was audible in the stillness of the cellar. Her eyes widened, a mix of fear and something else—hope, perhaps?—flashing across her face.

Drake struggled to sit up straighter, wincing as his waterlogged clothes clung to his skin. "I was supposed to die, Rachel. That was the price for stopping the virus. But I chose... I chose wrong."

The weight of his decision pressed down on him, threatening to crush him beneath its enormity. How many lives had he altered? How much damage had he done in his selfish desire to live?

"We need to fix this," he said, his voice thick with determination and regret. "I need to set things right."

As the words left his mouth, Drake felt a shift in the air. The cellar seemed to flicker, its edges blurring for a moment before snapping back into focus. A reminder, perhaps, of the fragile nature of this constructed reality.

Rachel reached out, her hand hovering just above his shoulder, as if unsure whether to offer comfort or maintain distance. "Drake, if what you're saying is true... the implications are staggering. We need to think this through carefully."

But Drake knew, with a certainty that resonated in his very bones, that there was no time for careful consideration. The cracks in this world were widening, and soon, they would shatter completely.

"There's no time," he said, struggling to his feet. Water cascaded off him, pooling at his feet. "We have to act now, before it's too late."

As he stood, facing Rachel and the uncertain future that lay ahead, Drake felt a resolve settle over him. He had made a terrible mistake, but now he had the chance to correct it. Whatever the cost, he would see this through to the end.

The weight of his memories, of the truth he now carried, threatened to overwhelm him. But Drake stood tall, ready to face the consequences of his actions and restore the balance he had so carelessly upset.

3 - 4

Rachel leaned closer, her hands gripping the edge of the desk for support. The metal creaked under her weight, a stark reminder of the fragility surrounding them. "Tell me," she urged, her voice barely above a whisper, yet charged with an intensity that filled the dank cellar.

Drake's gaze drifted past her, focusing on some distant point only he could see. His voice trembled as he spoke, each word seeming to cost him dearly. "I was supposed to die. The accident, the sacrifice—I gave my life to stop the virus. That was the way it was supposed to end."

He paused, swallowing hard. The sound echoed in the silence, a painful reminder of the weight of his revelation. Rachel's knuckles whitened as she gripped the desk harder, her scientific mind racing to process the implications.

"But when I reached the nexus of torment," Drake continued, his words now coming in a rush, as if afraid they might slip away again, "Lucian gave me a choice."

The name hung in the air between them, heavy with unspoken significance. Drake's chest tightened, memories of that moment flooding back. He could almost feel the searing heat of the nexus, hear the whispers of countless souls judged before him.

Rachel's eyes widened, a mix of fascination and horror etched across her features. She opened her mouth to speak, but Drake pressed on, needing to expel the truth that had been buried for so long.

"I thought I was doing the right thing," he said, his voice cracking. "I thought I could save them all. But now... now I see the price of my choice."

As he spoke, the cellar seemed to waver, its edges blurring momentarily before snapping back into focus. Drake felt a chill run down his spine, wondering if Rachel had noticed it too. How much longer could this construct hold?

5 - 6

Rachel's brow furrowed, her scientific mind grappling with the implications of Drake's words. "Lucian?" she asked, her voice a mixture of disbelief and dawning realization. "The same Lucian from the Codex?"

The name hung in the air, heavy with portent. Drake could almost see the gears turning in Rachel's mind, her brilliant intellect connecting disparate threads of information. He remembered her countless hours poring over Sir Mordred's enigmatic text, searching for answers that always seemed just out of reach.

Drake nodded slowly, his gaze unfocused as he retreated into the memory. The nexus of torment materialized in his mind's eye, a swirling vortex of light and shadow that defied description. He could almost feel the weight of Lucian's presence, an oppressive force that seemed to bend reality itself.

"He offered me two paths," Drake said, his voice barely above a whisper. The words tasted bitter on his tongue, laden with the consequences of his choice. "One to judgment in the nexus, where my heart would be weighed, and the other..." He paused, swallowing hard against the lump in his throat. "To this. A world where my family was alive, where the accident never happened."

As he spoke, Drake's hands trembled, and he clenched them into fists to still the shaking. The magnitude of his decision crashed over him anew, threatening to drown him in a sea of regret and self-recrimination. How could he have been so blind?

Rachel leaned forward, her eyes searching Drake's face. "And you chose this world," she said softly, her voice tinged with a mixture of compassion and something else – fear, perhaps, at the implications of his revelation.

7 - 8

Drake's hands curled into fists, his knuckles whitening as he struggled to contain the maelstrom of emotions threatening to overwhelm him. The cold, damp concrete beneath him seemed to leech away what little warmth remained in his body, leaving him feeling hollow and exposed.

"I thought I was saving them," he rasped, his voice thick with self-loathing. The memory of his family's faces flashed before him – vibrant, alive, untouched by the tragedy that had haunted his every waking moment. "I thought I deserved this after everything I'd done."

His gaze drifted to the shadows lurking in the corners of the cellar, as if searching for answers in the darkness. The weight of his choice pressed down on him, a crushing burden that threatened to suffocate him.

"But now I see it for what it is," Drake continued, his words barely audible over the thundering of his heart. He turned to Rachel, his eyes filled with a mixture of despair and dawning realization. The truth of his situation crashed over him like a tidal wave, leaving him gasping for air.

Rachel's brow furrowed, her analytical mind working to process the implications of Drake's words. "What do you mean?" she pressed, her voice steady despite the tremor in her hands.

Drake opened his mouth to respond, but the words caught in his throat. How could he explain the enormity of his mistake? How could he convey the horror of realizing that everything he thought he'd saved was nothing more than an elaborate illusion?

9 - 10

Drake's hollow eyes met Rachel's, the weight of millennia seeming to press down upon his broad shoulders. The damp cellar air clung to his skin, a constant reminder of the deprivation chamber's cold embrace. He drew a ragged breath, the sound echoing in the oppressive silence.

"A prison," he whispered, his voice raw with emotion. "A purgatory."

Rachel leaned closer, her red hair catching the dim light as she searched Drake's face for answers. The frayed edges of her lab coat brushed against the concrete floor, a testament to the countless hours she'd spent unraveling this mystery.

Drake's fists clenched and unclenched, his knuckles white with tension. "I was always meant to die, Rachel. That was the balance." The words tasted like ash in his mouth, bitter with the knowledge of his own hubris. "But I chose to live instead, and now I'm trapped in this... this construct."

His mind reeled, recalling the moment of his fateful decision. The nexus of torment, Lucian's otherworldly presence, the promise of a second chance – it all seemed like a cruel joke now.

"Lucian built this to punish me," Drake continued, his voice barely above a whisper. The name hung in the air between them, heavy with malevolence. He could almost feel Lucian's insidious influence seeping through the cracks in reality, a constant reminder of the price of his choice.

Rachel's eyes widened, her scientific mind grappling with the implications of Drake's revelation. "Lucian?" she breathed, the name carrying a weight she couldn't fully comprehend.

Drake nodded, his gaze distant as he contemplated the true nature of his prison. Every happy moment, every glimpse of the life he thought he'd saved – it was all part of an elaborate tapestry of deception, woven by hands far more cunning than his own.

11 - 12

Rachel sat back, her face draining of color as the full weight of Drake's words settled upon her. The cellar seemed to close in around them, the damp air thick with the scent of mold and long-buried secrets. She ran a trembling hand through her tangled red hair, her mind racing to process the implications.

"If this world isn't real," she said slowly, her voice barely above a whisper, "then everything here—your family, me, even Gabriel—it's all part of the construct." The realization hit her like a physical blow, stealing the breath from her lungs.

Drake watched her, his hollow eyes reflecting a pain that went beyond the physical realm. He could see the gears turning in Rachel's brilliant mind, piecing together the fragments of their shattered reality.

"A design meant to keep you here," Rachel continued, her scientific instincts kicking in despite the horror of the situation, "repeating the same day over and over."

Drake nodded, a mirthless chuckle escaping his lips. "A perfect prison," he mused, his gaze sweeping across the cellar. "Every happiness a reminder of what I've lost, every moment of hope another turn of the screw."

Rachel's fingers twitched, longing for the comfort of Sir Mordred's codex. "But why?" she pressed, her brow furrowing. "Why create such an elaborate illusion?"

Drake's jaw clenched, the muscles in his neck standing out like cords. "To make me understand the cost of my choice," he said, his voice thick with regret. "To force me to confront the truth, over and over again, until I..."

He trailed off, unable to finish the thought. The silence that fell between them was heavy with unspoken possibilities and the weight of a world built on lies.

13 - 14

Drake's shoulders sagged, the weight of his revelation pressing down on him like a physical force. He ran a trembling hand through his disheveled hair, his eyes unfocused as he stared into the middle distance.

"He wanted me to remember," Drake rasped, his voice thick with regret. "That's the whole point of this loop. To make me relive my mistake until I understand what I've done."

The words hung in the air, heavy and oppressive. Rachel felt a chill run down her spine, her analytical mind racing to process the implications. She swallowed hard, her throat suddenly dry.

"If Lucian built this," she began, her voice barely above a whisper, "then breaking the loop won't just free you. It'll destroy this entire world. Everyone in it."

Drake's gaze snapped to hers, a flicker of pain crossing his features. He opened his mouth to speak, but no words came out. Instead, he clenched his fists, knuckles turning white with the effort.

Rachel's mind whirled with possibilities, each more terrifying than the last. She thought of her research, her colleagues, the life she had built. All of it, a carefully crafted illusion. The realization made her feel hollow, as if she were made of spun glass, ready to shatter at the slightest touch.

"How can we be sure?" she asked, her scientific instincts kicking in despite the horror of the situation. "Is there a way to test the boundaries of this... construct?"

Drake's laugh was bitter, bordering on hysterical. "Test the boundaries?" he repeated, shaking his head. "Rachel, we've been testing them every day. Every time we tried to break the loop, every anomaly we encountered – it was all part of the design."

Rachel's brow furrowed, her mind racing through equations and probabilities. "But if we could find a flaw, a weak point in the fabric of this reality..."

"And then what?" Drake interrupted, his voice sharp with anguish. "Tear it all down? Destroy everything and everyone in it?"

The silence that followed was deafening. Rachel stared at Drake, seeing not just the man before her, but the weight of countless loops etched into every line of his face. She wondered, with a pang of existential dread, how many times they had had this very conversation, only to forget and start anew.

15 - 16

Drake's eyes flickered with pain, the haunted depths reflecting the harsh fluorescent light of the cellar. "It's not real, Rachel. None of it is," he said, his voice barely above a whisper. The words seemed to physically pain him, each syllable a shard of glass in his throat. "I have to end this, no matter what."

Rachel opened her mouth to protest, but the words died on her lips. She watched as Drake's muscular frame sagged against the damp wall, his broad shoulders hunched under an invisible burden. The silence stretched between them, heavy with unspoken grief.

In that moment, Drake's mind raced through a kaleidoscope of memories - his family's laughter, the warmth of his son's embrace, the pride in his wife's eyes. All fabrications, exquisitely crafted to ensnare him in this purgatory. The realization twisted like a knife in his gut.

"You don't know what you're asking," Rachel finally said, her voice trembling. "To erase everything, everyone..."

Drake's fists clenched at his sides, knuckles whitening. "Don't you think I understand that?" he snapped, his tone raw with anguish. "But continuing this charade, this... this mockery of life. It's not a kindness, Rachel. It's torture."

Before Rachel could respond, a sound from above froze them both in place. The unmistakable creak of floorboards, followed by the soft thud of approaching footsteps. Drake's body tensed, every muscle coiled and ready for action. His eyes darted to Rachel, a silent question passing between them.

"Who else knows we're here?" he whispered urgently, his mind racing through possibilities, each more alarming than the last.

Rachel shook her head, her face pale in the dim light. "No one," she mouthed back, her eyes wide with a mixture of fear and confusion.

As the footsteps drew nearer, Drake's hand instinctively reached for a weapon that wasn't there. He cursed silently, berating himself for his lack of preparedness. The construct had made him soft, complacent. Another of its cruel designs, no doubt.

"Get behind me," he ordered Rachel, his voice low and firm. As she complied, he positioned himself between her and the staircase, ready to face whatever – or whoever – was about to descend into their sanctuary of terrible truths.

17 - 18

The footsteps grew louder, each one echoing in Drake's ears like a thunderclap. His heart raced, pounding against his ribs as if trying to escape the confines of his chest. He could feel Rachel's presence behind him, her breath quick and shallow, mirroring his own tension.

Then, emerging from the shadows of the staircase, Detective Holly Kierstead appeared. Her gun was drawn, its muzzle aimed squarely at Drake's chest. She moved with the fluid grace of a predator, each step deliberate and controlled as she descended into the cellar.

Drake's mind reeled. Holly's presence here, now, couldn't be a coincidence. Was she another construct, a new obstacle thrown in his path? Or had she somehow broken through the illusion?

"Detective Kierstead," he said, his voice steadier than he felt. "I didn't expect to see you here."

Holly's eyes, sharp and focused, never left Drake as she reached the bottom of the stairs. "Funny," she replied, her tone clipped and professional, "I could say the same about you, Miller."

Drake raised his hands slowly, palms out in a gesture of surrender. But his mind was racing, calculating. How much did Holly know? How much could he risk telling her?

"This isn't what it looks like," he began, knowing how cliché the words sounded even as they left his mouth.

Holly's grip on her gun tightened imperceptibly. "Oh? And what exactly does it look like, Drake? Because from where I'm standing, it looks like you're in a whole lot of trouble."

19 - 20

The cellar's damp air clung to Drake's skin, a constant reminder of the water chamber's lingering presence. Holly's gun gleamed in the dim light, an extension of her unwavering resolve.

"Drake Miller," she said firmly, her voice cutting through the tension. "Step away from her. Hands where I can see them."

The words hung in the air, heavy with authority and an undercurrent of something else—concern, perhaps? Drake's mind whirled. Even now, even here, Holly's dedication to her duty shone through. Was it possible that some essence of the real Holly had broken through the construct?

Slowly, deliberately, Drake raised his hands higher, his fingers splayed wide. His suit jacket, once crisp and tailored, now hung heavy with moisture, a physical manifestation of the weight pressing down on him.

"Detective Kierstead," he said, his voice calm despite the turmoil within. "You're a little late to the party."

A wry smile tugged at the corner of his mouth, unbidden. How many times had they been here before, locked in this dance of suspicion and half-truths? But this time was different. This time, Drake knew the true nature of their reality.

As he met Holly's piercing gaze, Drake wondered if she could see the change in him. Could she sense the newfound understanding that set him apart from the construct she believed herself to be?

21 - 22

Holly's eyes narrowed, her analytical mind working overtime. The tension in the room was palpable, thick as the humidity that clung to Drake's skin.

"I don't know what kind of game you're playing," Holly said, her gaze flicking to Rachel. "But you've got a lot of explaining to do. Both of you."

Drake watched as Rachel slowly rose to her feet, her hands mirroring his own raised position. The frayed edges of her lab coat caught the dim light, a stark reminder of the toll their twisted reality had taken on her. Despite everything, her voice remained steady, unwavering.

"He's telling the truth," Rachel said, her words cutting through the tension like a scalpel.

Drake's heart clenched. Even now, even knowing the truth of their existence, Rachel stood by him. He wondered, not for the first time, how much of her was real and how much was construct. The thought sent a wave of guilt crashing over him.

As Holly's gaze darted between them, Drake could almost see the gears turning in her mind. She was piecing together the fragments, just as she always did. But would she be able to see beyond the illusion this time? Or was she too deeply embedded in Lucian's construct?

The weight of his choices pressed down on Drake, threatening to crush him. He had to make her understand, had to find a way to break through the carefully crafted facade. But how could he convince her of a truth that defied everything she believed to be real?

23 - 24

Holly's sharp eyes narrowed, her grip on the gun unwavering. The fluorescent light flickered overhead, casting harsh shadows across her face. "About what?" she demanded, her voice a mixture of skepticism and underlying fear. "That he's stuck in some kind of purgatory? That this world isn't real?"

Drake's chest tightened. He could hear the doubt in Holly's voice, but beneath it, a flicker of something else. Recognition, perhaps? Or the stirring of long-buried memories?

Rachel stepped forward, her movements careful but determined. "Yes," she said firmly, her voice carrying the weight of countless hours of research and revelation. "It sounds insane, but it's the only thing that makes sense."

Drake watched as Rachel's hands clenched at her sides, her knuckles white with the intensity of her conviction. She continued, her words tumbling out in a rush, "The loop, the anomalies, the Codex—they're all part of a construct designed to trap him."

As Rachel spoke, Drake's mind raced. He could see Holly's resolve wavering, could almost feel the cracks forming in her perception of reality. But would it be enough? Or would the construct's safeguards kick in, erasing this moment of clarity like so many others before it?

The cellar suddenly felt claustrophobic, the weight of unseen eyes pressing down on them. Drake fought the urge to look over his shoulder, knowing that Lucian's presence lurked just beyond the edges of perception, always watching, always waiting.

25 - 26

Holly's grip on her gun tightened, her knuckles turning white against the dark metal. Her jaw clenched, muscles working beneath her skin as she fought against the tide of doubt rising within her. "You expect me to believe that?" she demanded, her voice a mixture of incredulity and barely concealed fear.

Drake felt a surge of empathy for Holly. He remembered his own disbelief, the vertigo of realizing everything he knew was a carefully constructed lie. Slowly, deliberately, he lowered his hands, taking a cautious step forward. The cold concrete beneath his feet grounded him, a stark reminder of the physical reality they inhabited – real or not.

"I don't expect you to believe anything, Holly," Drake said softly, his voice rough with exhaustion and the weight of his memories. He met her gaze, searching for a flicker of the partner he'd known in another life. "But think about it—doesn't anything about this world feel... off to you?"

As he spoke, images flashed through Drake's mind: the way shadows sometimes moved when no one was looking, the inexplicable déjà vu that plagued him daily, the eerie silence that fell over the city at precisely 3:17 every afternoon. "Haven't you noticed the cracks?" he pressed, willing her to see what he saw.

Drake's heart raced, pounding against his ribs like a caged animal seeking freedom. He knew he was treading dangerous ground. If Holly rejected this truth, if she retreated into the false safety of the construct, all might be lost. But if she could just see, just for a moment...

"The inconsistencies," he continued, his voice gaining urgency. "The way certain memories don't quite fit. The dreams that feel more real than waking life. Holly, you're not just a detective here. You're the key to unraveling all of this."

27 - 28

Holly's brow furrowed, her gun wavering slightly as uncertainty crept into her expression. "What cracks?" she asked, her voice barely above a whisper.

Drake felt a surge of hope at her question. He took a careful step forward, his hands still raised in a placating gesture. The damp chill of the cellar seemed to intensify, raising goosebumps on his skin as he spoke.

"The missing witnesses, the strange symbols, the way time keeps slipping," Drake said, his voice gaining strength with each word. He could see it now – the subtle shifts in Holly's posture, the flicker of recognition in her eyes. "Remember the Carlson case? How the key witness vanished without a trace, and no one seemed to care?"

As he spoke, Drake's mind raced through a kaleidoscope of memories – both real and constructed. The symbols etched into abandoned buildings that seemed to change when he looked away. The way clocks sometimes ran backwards, if only for a moment.

"And it's not just the cases," he continued, his voice urgent. "Haven't you felt it? The way sometimes the world seems to... stutter? Like a skipping record or a glitch in a video game?"

Drake took another step closer, his eyes locked on Holly's. "You're part of it too, Holly. You just don't realize it yet."

The weight of his words hung in the air, heavy with implication. Drake held his breath, watching Holly's face for any sign of breakthrough, any crack in the facade of this carefully constructed reality.

29 - 30

Holly's gun wavered slightly, the barrel dipping as doubt flickered across her face. Her sharp eyes darted between Drake and Rachel, searching for deception but finding only grim certainty. The cellar air grew thick with tension, each breath seeming to draw the walls closer.

"If this is true," Holly said slowly, her voice barely above a whisper, "then what are you planning to do about it?"

Drake's heart hammered in his chest. He could see the struggle playing out behind Holly's eyes – the detective's instinct to question, to analyze, warring with the impossible truth before her. He weighed his words carefully, knowing that his next sentence could tip the scales.

"I'm going to set things right," he replied, his tone measured but resolute. "But I need you to trust me, Holly. To really look at this world and see it for what it is."

As he spoke, Drake's mind raced through possibilities. How much could he reveal without shattering the construct entirely? Would Holly's realization accelerate the collapse, or could her insight be the key to unraveling Lucian's design?

Holly's grip on her weapon tightened, her knuckles white against the dark metal. "Trust you?" she said, a bitter laugh escaping her lips. "After everything that's happened?"

Drake took a careful step forward, his hands still raised. "I know it sounds insane," he said, his voice low and urgent. "But think about it, Holly. Really think. Haven't you felt it? The wrongness just beneath the surface of everything?"

He watched her closely, saw the flicker of uncertainty in her eyes. For a moment, the cellar seemed to shimmer around them, reality itself wavering under the weight of their shared epiphany.

31 - 32

Drake's grim expression deepened, the lines on his face etched with the weight of his decision. "I'm going to end it," he declared, his voice a low rumble that seemed to resonate through the damp cellar air.

The words hung heavy in the silence that followed, each person in the room processing their implications. Drake could feel the weight of Holly's gaze, her gun still trained on him, but his focus had shifted inward. He saw flashes of memory – his family's faces, moments of joy and pain, all tinged with the knowledge that they were constructs in this elaborate prison.

Rachel's sudden movement broke the tension. She stepped forward, her lab coat swishing against her legs, her eyes wide with a mixture of fear and determination. "If he breaks the loop," she said, her voice carrying an urgency that cut through the air like a knife, "this world will collapse. Everyone in it will cease to exist."

Drake watched as Holly's expression shifted, confusion giving way to a dawning horror. He could almost see the pieces falling into place in her mind, the reality of their situation becoming clearer with each passing second.

"Is that true?" Holly asked, her voice barely above a whisper, the gun in her hand wavering slightly.

Drake nodded slowly, feeling the weight of his words before he spoke them. "It's the only way," he said softly, his heart heavy with the knowledge of what must be done. "This world... it's not real. It's a construct, a prison built to keep me trapped in an endless cycle of guilt and regret."

As he spoke, Drake's mind raced with possibilities. How could he make them understand? How could he bear the burden of destroying this world, even knowing it wasn't real? The faces of his family flashed before his eyes, and he felt a deep, aching pain in his chest.

"There has to be another way," Rachel interjected, her scientific mind clearly racing for alternatives. "We could try to—"

"There isn't," Drake cut her off, his voice firm but tinged with sadness. "I've seen the truth now. I remember everything. This world... it's a beautiful lie, but a lie nonetheless. And the longer it exists, the more damage it does to the fabric of reality itself."

33 - 34

Holly's eyes darted between them, her grip tightening on the gun. "And you're okay with that?" The tension in her voice was palpable, a mixture of disbelief and growing unease.

Drake felt the weight of her words like a physical blow. He closed his eyes for a moment, memories of laughter with his family, of quiet evenings with Linda, flashing through his mind. When he opened them again, his gaze was steady, but filled with an ocean of pain.

"It's not real, Holly," he said, his voice thick with emotion. "It's an illusion. And it's the only way to fix what I broke." The words tasted bitter on his tongue, each syllable a reminder of his past mistakes and the impossible choice before him.

He took a step forward, hands raised in a placating gesture. "I know how it sounds. Believe me, I've fought against this truth with everything I have. But the cracks in this reality are growing. If we don't act, the consequences could be catastrophic beyond just this construct."

Holly's gun remained trained on him, but doubt flickered across her face. "How can you be sure? How do you know this isn't just some... delusion?"

Drake's mind raced, searching for the right words to make her understand. "Because I remember dying, Holly. I remember the sacrifice, the virus, the choice Lucian gave me. This world... it's a beautiful dream, but it's one we have to wake up from."

35 - 35

The room fell into silence, the weight of Drake's words hanging heavily in the air as Holly considered her next move. The faint drip of water from Drake's soaked clothes echoed in the cellar, a constant reminder of the surreal nature of their situation.

Holly's sharp eyes narrowed, her analytical mind working overtime. She lowered her gun slightly, but kept it at the ready. "If what you're saying is true," she began, her voice steady but tinged with uncertainty, "then everything I know, everything I am... it's all part of this construct?"

Drake nodded slowly, his chest tightening with the weight of the revelation. "I believe so, yes. But Holly, you're more than just a construct. Your intuition, your ability to piece things together - that's real. It's why you're here now."

Holly's grip on her gun tightened, her knuckles whitening. "And what happens if you 'end it,' Drake? What becomes of us?"

The question hung in the air, heavy and suffocating. Drake swallowed hard, his mind racing through the implications. "I don't know," he admitted, his voice barely above a whisper. "But I do know that staying here, trapped in this loop, isn't the answer."

Rachel stepped forward, her eyes darting between Holly and Drake. "There has to be another way," she pleaded. "Something we haven't considered yet."

Drake shook his head, a wave of weariness washing over him. "I've been through this loop countless times, Rachel. Every path leads back here, to this moment, this choice."

Holly's analytical mind kicked into overdrive, processing the information. "If this is all a construct," she mused, lowering her gun further, "then maybe... maybe ending it isn't destruction. Maybe it's liberation."

The words hung in the air, a glimmer of hope in the darkness that surrounded them. Drake felt a flicker of something - not quite hope, but a sense of purpose - ignite within him. "Maybe you're right, Holly," he said, his voice growing stronger. "Maybe this is the key to breaking free, for all of us."

A Shattered Illusion

1 ^{- 2} The dim light of the cellar cast long shadows across Drake's face, etching deep lines of weariness into his features. His heart pounded, each beat a painful reminder of the weight pressing down on him—the weight of worlds colliding, of realities unraveling.

Detective Holly Kierstead's gun gleamed coldly in the half-light, her stance rigid and uncompromising. Her voice cut through the heavy silence like a blade.

"Get on your knees, now. You're under arrest for the murders of the Parker deposition witnesses and for hacking into federal police accounts."

Drake's muscles tensed, the urge to run, to escape, thrumming through his veins. But he knew better. He had run far enough, across realities and timelines. Now, face-to-face with Holly—a woman who had once been his partner, his confidante in another life—he felt the crushing futility of it all.

He remained rooted to the spot, his expression a battlefield of exhaustion and defiance. The weight of unspoken truths hung heavy in the air between them.

"Holly," Drake said, his voice low and urgent, "I'm telling you, this isn't what you think."

He searched her face for any flicker of recognition, any hint of the bond they had once shared. But her eyes were cold, unfamiliar. In this reality, he was nothing more than a suspect, a murderer.

The irony of it all threatened to overwhelm him. Here he stood, accused of crimes he hadn't committed, while the real threat—Gabriel, the virus, the collapsing multiverse—loomed just beyond their understanding. How could he make her see? How could he bridge the chasm between their realities?

Drake's mind raced, grasping for words that could pierce through the veil of this world's illusions. But as he looked into Holly's unwavering gaze, he realized the magnitude of his task. He wasn't just fighting for his innocence; he was fighting for the very fabric of reality itself.

3 - 4

"On your knees!" Holly barked, her finger twitching against the trigger.

The command cut through Drake's thoughts like a knife. He could see the tension in Holly's stance, the barely contained fury in her eyes. This wasn't the partner he knew, the woman who had once shared late-night stakeouts and early morning coffee runs with him. This Holly was a stranger, poised to end him without a second thought.

Drake's heart pounded in his chest as he slowly lowered himself to the ground. The cold, hard floor pressed against his knees, a stark reminder of the precarious position he found himself in. He raised his hands in surrender, feeling the weight of countless worlds on his shoulders.

"You're not listening to me," Drake said, his voice steady despite the turmoil within. He looked up at Holly, willing her to see beyond the surface, to recognize the truth in his words. "I'm not from this world. In another reality, I was a detective—your partner."

The words hung in the air between them, heavy with implications that Drake knew would be hard for Holly to accept. He watched her face carefully, searching for any sign of recognition, any crack in her resolute facade.

Inside, Drake's mind raced. How could he make her understand? The multiverse, the impending collapse, Gabriel's manipulations—it all seemed too fantastical, too far-fetched. And yet, it was the truth that bound them all together, a truth that threatened to unravel everything they knew.

As he knelt there, under the barrel of Holly's gun, Drake felt the crushing weight of his choices. Every decision, every step that had led him to this moment seemed to converge, creating a tapestry of regret and determination. He had to find a way to break through, to make Holly see. Their lives—and the fate of countless realities—depended on it.

5 - 6

Holly's brow furrowed, her sharp eyes narrowing as she studied Drake's face. The dim light cast shadows across his features, accentuating the lines of worry etched into his skin. Her voice cut through the tense silence, laced with a mixture of confusion and anger.

"You're delusional," she spat, her grip tightening on the gun. "You've been lying since the moment this case started. How did you do it, Drake? How did you kill those people?"

Drake felt a pang in his chest at her words. The accusation stung, not because it was true, but because it revealed how far they'd drifted from the partnership they'd once shared in another world. He took a deep breath, steadying himself against the tide of emotions threatening to overwhelm him.

"I didn't kill anyone," Drake said, his voice calm but insistent. He met Holly's gaze unflinchingly, willing her to see the truth in his eyes. "I'm trying to stop this world from falling apart. I'm trying to save my family and fix my mistake."

As he spoke, memories flashed through his mind—glimpses of the life he'd left behind, the family he was desperately trying to protect. The weight of his choices pressed down on him, a constant reminder of the stakes at play.

Holly's expression wavered for a moment, a flicker of uncertainty crossing her face. Drake seized on that hesitation, his heart racing. Could he be getting through to her? He longed to reach out, to bridge the chasm between them, but he remained still, acutely aware of the gun still trained on him.

7 - 8

Holly's eyes narrowed, her jaw tightening as she processed Drake's words. The skepticism in her voice was palpable, cutting through the tension-filled air. "Your mistake?" she asked, her tone dripping with disbelief. "You mean the mistake of covering your tracks?"

Drake felt a surge of frustration, the weight of his impossible situation bearing down on him. He shook his head, his brown hair falling across his forehead as he struggled to find the right words. How could he make her understand?

"No," he said, his voice low and urgent. "The mistake of choosing this world over my death." The memory of that fateful decision flashed through his mind, a kaleidoscope of regret and determination. He took a deep breath, steeling himself for what he had to say next.

"Holly, you know me—even if you don't remember," Drake continued, his eyes searching her face for any sign of recognition. "In another world, we worked together. You were my partner, and we solved cases side by side."

As he spoke, Drake's mind raced with memories of their shared past—a past that existed only in his mind now. He remembered late nights poring over case files, the thrill of cracking a difficult case, the easy camaraderie they'd shared. The stark contrast between those memories and the distrust in Holly's eyes now was almost too much to bear.

Drake's heart pounded in his chest, hope and desperation warring within him. If only he could make her see, make her remember. But as he watched Holly's face, he saw only confusion and growing alarm. The gulf between them seemed insurmountable, and Drake felt the weight of his isolation more keenly than ever.

9 - 10

Holly's eyes narrowed, her grip tightening on the gun as she rolled them dismissively. The cool metal of the weapon anchored her to reality, a stark contrast to the absurd claims spilling from Drake's lips. Her analytical mind raced, searching for any logical explanation for his words, but found none.

"You expect me to believe that?" she scoffed, her voice laced with incredulity. The dim light of the room cast long shadows across Drake's face, accentuating the desperation in his eyes. Holly felt a flicker of doubt, quickly suppressed by years of training and instinct.

Drake's gaze softened, his shoulders sagging slightly as if under an invisible weight. When he spoke again, his voice was gentle, almost tender. "I know about you and Rebekah Sharp."

The words hit Holly like a physical blow. Her breath caught in her throat, memories of Rebekah flooding her mind—stolen moments, shared laughter, and the bittersweet ache of a love kept hidden. How could he possibly know? She'd guarded that secret fiercely, tucking it away in the deepest recesses of her heart.

Holly's fingers trembled almost imperceptibly on the trigger, her mind reeling. The certainty she'd felt moments ago began to crumble, replaced by a creeping sense of unease. What if there was truth to Drake's wild claims? What if the world she knew was not as solid as she'd always believed?

11 - 12

Holly's breath hitched, but she didn't lower her weapon. The cold metal of the gun felt like an anchor, tethering her to reality as her world tilted on its axis. "What did you just say?" she demanded, her voice a hoarse whisper.

Drake's eyes met hers, unflinching. The room seemed to narrow, the air thick with tension. He spoke slowly, deliberately, each word carrying the weight of another world. "In my world, I remember you two fighting over a coffee machine."

Holly's mind raced. How could he know about Rebekah? About their relationship? She'd never breathed a word to anyone, not even her closest confidants. The barrel of her gun wavered slightly, her resolve cracking under the impossible knowledge Drake possessed.

"She wanted that $600 espresso maker," Drake continued, his voice steady but tinged with a hint of sadness. "And you told her, 'If you wanted a $600 coffee machine, you should've married a CEO.'"

The words hung in the air, a perfect echo of a moment Holly had thought lost to time. She could almost smell the rich aroma of coffee, feel the warmth of Rebekah's laughter. The memory, so vivid and unexpected, threatened to overwhelm her.

Holly's throat constricted, her chest tight with a mixture of fear and longing. How could Drake know this? What did it mean for everything she thought she understood about her life, her world? The gun in her hand suddenly felt heavier, its purpose less certain.

13 - 14

Holly's lips parted, her mind reeling. The room seemed to spin around her, the familiar contours of her reality blurring at the edges. She blinked hard, trying to focus on Drake's face, but his features began to waver and distort.

"How..." she began, but the words died in her throat as a searing pain lanced through her temple.

The dingy cellar dissolved, replaced by a kaleidoscope of fractured images. Holly gasped, her gun clattering to the floor as she stumbled backwards. The world tilted and shifted, reforming into a nightmarish tableau.

She found herself standing before a dilapidated funhouse, its once-cheerful facade now twisted and grotesque. The air crackled with an unnatural energy, making the hairs on the back of her neck stand on end. From the shadows emerged a figure that made her blood run cold.

Gabriel.

His scarred face contorted into a cruel smile, eyes gleaming with malevolent intent. "Detective Kierstead," he purred, his voice like oil on water. "How nice of you to join us... again."

Holly's heart hammered in her chest. This couldn't be real, and yet every detail was achingly vivid – the acrid smell of decay, the chill wind that cut through her jacket, the weight of dread settling in her stomach.

"What is this?" she demanded, her voice trembling despite her efforts to remain calm. "What's happening to me?"

Gabriel's laughter echoed unnaturally, seeming to come from everywhere and nowhere at once. "Oh, Holly," he said, shaking his head in mock disappointment. "You're asking the wrong questions. The real question is: how many times will you dance this dance before you finally remember?"

15 - 16

Holly's fingers trembled as they closed around the cold metal in her pocket. She withdrew the bullet, its weight familiar yet suddenly ominous in her palm. Her heart raced, each beat a thunderous reminder of her mortality.

The bullet gleamed dully in the dim light, a talisman from a case that had nearly cost her everything. She'd carried it as a reminder of her fallibility, of how close she'd come to losing it all. Now, as she stared at it, memories and doubts swirled in her mind like a maelstrom.

"Enough with the games," she said, her voice wavering slightly despite her best efforts to maintain control. The words felt hollow in her throat, a feeble attempt to cling to a reality that was rapidly unraveling around her. "How do you know that?"

Her eyes darted between Drake and the bullet, searching for answers in both. The cool metal against her skin grounded her, a tangible link to the world she thought she knew. But Drake's words, his impossible knowledge, tugged at the edges of her perception, threatening to unravel everything.

'This can't be real,' she thought, her analytical mind racing to make sense of it all. 'But if it's not real, how does he know about Rebekah? About that stupid coffee machine?'

The room seemed to pulse around her, shadows stretching and contracting in impossible ways. Holly fought to keep her composure, years of detective training warring against the surreal nature of the situation.

"I need you to explain," she said, her tone a mixture of demand and plea. "Now. Every detail. And so help me, if I catch even a hint of a lie..."

She left the threat unfinished, her free hand instinctively reaching for the gun she'd dropped. The familiar motion brought a modicum of comfort, a reminder of who she was – or who she thought she was.

17 - 18

Drake's lips parted, his eyes reflecting a deep, haunting sadness. "Holly, I—"

But his words never materialized. Holly's vision suddenly blurred, the world around her losing focus as if she were peering through a rain-streaked window. She blinked hard, trying to clear her sight, but the distortion only intensified.

"What's happening?" she gasped, her voice sounding distant and muffled to her own ears.

The dim cellar began to dissolve, its concrete walls and musty air giving way to something else entirely. Colors swirled and bled into one another, shapes warping and reforming in a dizzying kaleidoscope of sensory input. Holly's heart raced, her analytical mind struggling to process the impossible transformation occurring before her eyes.

'This isn't real,' she thought desperately, clinging to her training, her logic. 'It can't be real.'

But as the room continued to shift, a creeping dread settled in her stomach. The bullet in her hand seemed to grow heavier, its presence a stark reminder of the thin line between what she knew and what she feared.

"Drake?" she called out, her voice trembling despite her efforts to remain calm. "What's going on?"

But Drake's form had vanished in the swirling chaos, leaving Holly alone in a rapidly changing landscape of horror and uncertainty.

19 - 20

The swirling chaos coalesced into a nightmarish scene. Holly found herself standing outside a dilapidated funhouse, its once-vibrant paint now peeling and faded. The air hung heavy with the scent of rust and decay, a stark contrast to the cheerful memories such places were meant to evoke.

Her gun was drawn, its familiar weight a small comfort in this unsettling reality. Holly's eyes darted around, searching for any sign of movement in the encroaching shadows. Her heart pounded, each beat echoing in her ears like a warning drum.

'This isn't right,' she thought, her mind racing. 'How did I get here? Where's Drake?'

A flicker of movement caught her attention, and from the inky darkness emerged a figure that made her blood run cold. Gabriel stepped into view, his disfigured face twisting into a grotesque parody of a smile. The scars that marred his features seemed to dance in the dim light, creating an ever-shifting landscape of horror.

"Detective Kierstead," Gabriel's voice slithered through the air, calm and menacing. "So good of you to join our little game."

Holly's grip on her weapon tightened, her training kicking in despite the surreal circumstances. "Freeze!" she commanded, her voice steadier than she felt. "Don't move!"

Gabriel's laugh was a harsh, grating sound that set her teeth on edge. "Oh, Holly," he mocked, "when will you learn that your rules don't apply here?"

With a movement so swift it seemed almost inhuman, Gabriel raised a stolen gun, its barrel glinting ominously in the fading light. Holly's finger tensed on the trigger, but before she could react, a deafening crack split the air.

Pain exploded in her chest, a white-hot agony that radiated outward, stealing her breath and clouding her vision. Holly staggered, her mind reeling as she tried to process what had just happened.

'I've been shot,' she realized, the thought distant and detached. 'But how? This can't be real...'

As darkness began to encroach on the edges of her vision, Holly's last conscious thought was of Rebekah. Of gentle hands and soft words, of a love that had always felt like home. And as she slipped into unconsciousness, a part of her wondered if she would ever find her way back to that warmth again.

21 - 22

Holly gasped, her lungs burning as if she'd been holding her breath underwater. The vision of Gabriel lingered, his scarred face etched into her mind like a nightmare refusing to fade. Her knees buckled, the phantom pain in her chest still achingly real.

"Don't worry, Detective," Gabriel's voice echoed, cold and mocking. "You'll wake up again. They always do."

The words sent a chill down Holly's spine, her analytical mind struggling to make sense of what she'd just experienced. 'How can this be happening?' she thought, her heart racing. 'It felt so real, but...'

Her vision swam, the cellar coming back into focus. Holly stumbled, her hand grasping desperately for support. She found the edge of a desk, her fingers curling around the worn wood as she fought to steady herself.

"Holly?" Drake's voice cut through the haze, concern evident in his tone. "Are you alright?"

She turned to face him, her breath coming in short gasps. "I... I saw him," Holly managed, her voice barely above a whisper. "Gabriel. He shot me, but it wasn't real. It couldn't have been real."

Drake's expression softened, a mix of understanding and sadness crossing his features. "It was real, Holly. Just not in this reality."

Holly shook her head, her analytical nature rebelling against the impossibility of it all. "That's not possible," she insisted, even as doubt crept into her voice. "Alternate realities, time travel... it's the stuff of science fiction, not real life."

"And yet," Drake said gently, "you saw it. You felt it. Your instincts are telling you there's more to this, aren't they?"

Holly's grip on the desk tightened, her mind racing. She'd always prided herself on her observational skills, on her ability to piece together complex puzzles. But this... this defied everything she thought she knew about the world.

"I don't understand," she admitted, her voice barely audible. "How can any of this be true?"

23 - 24

The room seemed to spin around Holly, the familiar contours of the precinct office blurring into an indistinct haze. She blinked hard, trying to regain her composure, but the lingering echoes of Gabriel's mocking voice still rang in her ears.

"What's wrong?" Rachel asked, her voice laced with concern.

Holly turned to face the red-haired scientist, noting the worry etched across her face. She opened her mouth to respond, but found herself at a loss for words. How could she possibly explain what she had just experienced?

"I... I'm not sure," Holly finally managed, her voice trembling slightly. "I saw something. Something impossible."

Rachel's eyes narrowed, a spark of understanding igniting within them. "Impossible by the standards of this reality, perhaps," she said, her tone measured and precise. "But Holly, you must consider the possibility that what you've witnessed is a glimpse into a truth far more complex than you've been led to believe."

Holly's mind raced, grappling with the implications of Rachel's words. Could it be true? Could everything she thought she knew about the world be just a fraction of a much larger, more intricate reality?

"This is insane," Holly muttered, more to herself than to Rachel. "I'm a detective. I deal in facts, in evidence. Not... not visions and alternate realities."

Rachel stepped closer, her lab coat rustling softly. "Sometimes, Detective," she said, her voice low and urgent, "the most crucial evidence is that which challenges our fundamental understanding of the world."

25 - 26

Holly's chest heaved as she stared at the bullet in her hand, her mind reeling from what she had just seen. The cold metal pressed against her palm, a stark contrast to the vivid, searing images that still burned behind her eyelids. Gabriel's twisted face, the funhouse, the searing pain of a bullet tearing through her chest—it all felt so real, so visceral.

She blinked rapidly, trying to clear her vision and ground herself in the present moment. The dim cellar came back into focus, the musty scent of damp earth filling her nostrils. Her fingers trembled slightly as they curled around the bullet, its weight suddenly seeming to carry the burden of untold truths.

"I don't understand," Holly whispered, her voice barely audible. She looked up, her gaze settling on Drake, still on his knees before her. The man she had been ready to arrest moments ago now seemed like a lifeline to sanity in a world rapidly unraveling around her.

Drake's eyes met hers, filled with a mixture of empathy and resigned understanding. His voice was soft, gentle, as if speaking to a frightened animal. "You saw him, didn't you? Gabriel."

The name sent a shiver down Holly's spine. How could Drake possibly know? She hadn't spoken a word about her vision, yet here he was, naming the very specter that had haunted her moments before.

"How..." Holly started, her throat constricting around the words. She swallowed hard, trying to regain her composure. "How could you know that?"

Drake's shoulders sagged slightly, the weight of unseen burdens evident in his posture. "Because I've seen him too, Holly. More times than I can count, across more realities than you can imagine."

Holly's mind reeled, struggling to process the implications of Drake's words. Part of her wanted to dismiss it all as the ravings of a madman, to cling to the familiar certainties of her world. But the bullet in her hand, the lingering echo of Gabriel's mocking laughter in her ears, they spoke of a truth far stranger than she had ever dared to consider.

"Tell me," she said, her voice barely above a whisper. "Tell me everything."

27 - 28

Holly's wide eyes met Drake's, her grip on the gun faltering as the weight of her confusion pressed down upon her. The cold metal suddenly felt foreign in her hands, a stark contrast to the familiar confidence she usually carried as a detective.

"How... how do you know his name?" she asked, her voice trembling with a mixture of fear and disbelief. The name 'Gabriel' hung in the air between them, heavy with unspoken implications.

Drake's expression softened, a flicker of pain crossing his features as he slowly rose to his feet. His movements were careful, deliberate, as if he feared startling Holly out of this moment of vulnerability.

"I've been running from him across worlds," Drake said, his voice heavy with the weight of countless memories. The words seemed to physically pain him as he spoke, each syllable etched with exhaustion and despair. "He's the one who's been pulling the strings, hunting me, and keeping us all trapped in this cycle."

Holly's mind raced, trying to make sense of Drake's words. Worlds? Cycles? It all sounded like something out of a science fiction novel, yet the conviction in Drake's voice was undeniable.

She found herself lowering her guard, her instincts as a detective warring with the impossibility of what she was hearing. "What do you mean, 'across worlds'?" she asked, her analytical mind grasping for solid ground in this sea of uncertainty.

Drake ran a hand through his disheveled hair, his eyes distant as if seeing beyond the confines of the room. "It's a long story, Holly. One that spans multiple realities, multiple versions of us. But Gabriel... he's the constant. The puppeteer behind it all."

Holly's heart pounded in her chest, the echo of her vision still fresh in her mind. She couldn't reconcile the Drake she thought she knew with this man before her, speaking of impossible things with such conviction. Yet, a part of her yearned to believe, to find an explanation for the inexplicable vision she had experienced.

"I don't understand," she admitted, her voice barely above a whisper. "How can any of this be real?"

29 - 30

Holly's hand shook as she tried to steady herself, the cold metal of her gun a stark contrast to the warmth of the bullet clenched in her other palm. The vision of Gabriel's twisted face and the phantom pain in her chest lingered, a ghostly reminder of a reality she couldn't comprehend. Drake's words echoed in her mind, each syllable resonating with a truth she didn't want to accept.

"It can't be real," she murmured, more to herself than anyone else. But even as the words left her lips, doubt crept in, insidious and persistent.

Rachel stepped forward, her frayed lab coat rustling in the tense silence. "Holly," she said, her voice low and urgent, "listen to him. Whatever you just saw, it's part of the truth. This world isn't what you think it is."

Holly's gaze snapped to Rachel, taking in the scientist's disheveled appearance and the fervent gleam in her eyes. "And how would you know?" she demanded, her detective instincts kicking in despite her inner turmoil.

Rachel's lips curved into a sad smile. "Because I've seen it too. The cracks in our reality, the inconsistencies that shouldn't exist. I've been studying them for years, trying to understand why our world feels... wrong."

Holly's mind reeled, grasping for solid ground in a reality that seemed to be crumbling around her. She thought of her life, her career, her memories. Were they all fabrications? A part of some grand illusion?

"If what you're saying is true," Holly said, her voice barely above a whisper, "then what is real? Who am I, really?"

31 - 32

Holly shook her head vigorously, her eyes darting between Drake and Rachel like a cornered animal. The dim light of the cellar cast long shadows across their faces, deepening the lines of worry etched into their expressions. "No," she said, her voice cracking. "This doesn't make sense. None of this makes sense!"

Her fingers tightened around the gun, the cold metal a stark contrast to her clammy skin. The bullet she'd pulled from her pocket earlier felt impossibly heavy in her other hand, as if it carried the weight of all the impossible truths she was being asked to accept.

Drake moved then, rising from his knees with the slow, careful movements of someone approaching a spooked horse. His eyes, filled with a mix of determination and empathy, never left Holly's face. "I know it doesn't," he said softly, his deep voice carrying an undercurrent of shared pain. "But it will. Just trust me, Holly. I'm trying to fix it."

Holly's mind raced, grappling with the implications of Drake's words. Fix it? Fix what? Her entire world? The very fabric of reality? She felt a hysterical laugh bubble up in her throat but swallowed it down.

"Trust you?" she managed to choke out, her analytical mind desperately seeking solid ground. "You're asking me to believe that everything I know is a lie. That you're some... interdimensional traveler? That we were partners in another life?"

Drake took a cautious step forward, his hands still raised in a gesture of peace. "I know how it sounds," he said, his eyes pleading. "But think about what you saw, Holly. About Gabriel. How else could I know about that?"

The name sent a shiver down Holly's spine, the phantom pain from her vision flaring in her chest. She found herself lowering her gun slightly, uncertainty replacing some of the fear in her eyes.

"I don't know," she admitted, her voice barely above a whisper. "But if what you're saying is true... what does that mean for us? For this world?"

Is This my Hell

1 -2 The fluorescent lights flickered overhead, casting eerie shadows across Holly's face as she stared at Drake. Her chest heaved, each breath a labored effort against the crushing weight of the vision that had just assaulted her senses.

Holly's hands trembled, her fingers instinctively reaching for the comfort of her service weapon, but finding only empty air. She swallowed hard, her throat constricting around the words she needed to force out. "What... what did I just see?" Her voice cracked, barely above a whisper. "How can I remember dying?"

The words hung in the air between them, heavy and accusatory. Holly's mind raced, desperately trying to reconcile the flood of memories—the searing pain of a bullet tearing through her flesh, the metallic taste of blood on her tongue, the encroaching darkness—with the reality of her standing here, alive and whole.

Drake's broad shoulders sagged, the weight of countless worlds and decisions visibly pressing down upon him. His brown eyes, usually sharp and determined, now softened with a sadness that seemed to age him beyond his years. He ran a hand through his disheveled hair, a gesture that spoke volumes of his inner turmoil.

"Because you did," he said quietly, each word carefully measured, as if speaking them aloud might shatter the fragile reality around them.

Holly's knees weakened, threatening to buckle beneath her. She gripped the edge of the metal table, its cold surface anchoring her to the present. Her mind reeled, grasping at the fragments of memories that didn't belong to her—or did they? The lines between realities blurred, leaving her dizzy and disoriented.

Drake took a tentative step forward, his hand half-raised as if to offer comfort, but he hesitated, the gulf between them suddenly vast and insurmountable. The fluorescent light caught the anguish etched into the lines of his face, a map of guilt and regret that Holly found herself desperate to decipher.

3 - 4

Holly's grip on the table loosened, her fingers unfurling as if in slow motion. The weapon slipped from her grasp, clattering to the floor with a jarring metallic echo that reverberated through the room. Her arms fell limply to her sides, her voice barely above a whisper as she asked, "What are you talking about?"

The words hung in the air between them, heavy with unspoken implications. Holly's mind raced, trying to reconcile the impossibility of Drake's statement with the undeniable weight of her own memories. How could she have died? How could she be standing here, alive and breathing, if what he said was true?

Drake hesitated for a moment, his eyes searching Holly's face as if gauging her readiness for the truth. Then, with a deep breath that seemed to carry the weight of countless worlds, he stepped closer. His voice, when he spoke, was calm but laden with a sorrow that seemed to permeate the very air around them.

"You died protecting me," he began, each word carefully chosen. "It was in another world—one of the many I crossed. Gabriel was trying to stop me from ending the virus that was destroying the multiverse. You stood in his way; gave me the time I needed to finish it."

As Drake spoke, Holly felt a chill course through her body. The certainty in his voice, the pain etched into every line of his face, left no room for doubt. Yet her mind rebelled against the notion, struggling to process the enormity of what he was saying.

"Another world?" she whispered, more to herself than to Drake. The concept of a multiverse, once relegated to the realm of science fiction, now loomed before her as an overwhelming reality. Holly's detective instincts kicked in, desperate to make sense of this new information. "And Gabriel... the virus... How is any of this possible?"

5 - 6

Holly's breath caught in her throat, her chest constricting as if an invisible hand had wrapped around her lungs. The world around her blurred, replaced by fragmented images that flashed through her mind with startling clarity. She saw herself running, her long black hair whipping behind her as she sprinted through shadowy alleyways, the echo of her footsteps mingling with the pounding of her heart.

"Gabriel," she gasped, the name tasting bitter on her tongue. In her mind's eye, she caught glimpses of a figure always just out of reach, always one step ahead.

The memories came faster now, more intense. The deafening roar of an explosion ripped through her consciousness, and Holly instinctively flinched. She could feel the heat on her skin, smell the acrid scent of smoke and burning debris.

Then came the pain—sharp, searing, and all-consuming. Holly's hand flew to her chest, her fingers desperately searching for a wound that wasn't there. Yet the phantom agony persisted, a vivid reminder of a bullet that had torn through her in another life, another world.

Her legs trembled, no longer able to support her weight. Holly sank to the floor, her knees hitting the hard surface with a dull thud. Her hands moved from her chest to her head, fingers tangling in her hair as she tried to anchor herself against the flood of memories threatening to sweep her away.

"No," she whimpered, hot tears spilling down her cheeks. "This can't be real. It can't be."

But even as she denied it, more details surfaced. The pursuit, the desperate race against time, the knowledge that something far greater than herself hung in the balance.

"I remember," Holly choked out, her voice barely above a whisper. "The pursuit... the virus..." She looked up at Drake, her vision blurred by tears, seeking answers, comfort, anything to make sense of the chaos in her mind. "How? How is this possible?"

7 - 8

Drake's face contorted with a mixture of sorrow and compassion as he lowered himself to the floor beside Holly. His brown eyes, usually sharp and focused, now held a softness that spoke volumes of the weight he carried. He reached out, his hand hovering near Holly's shoulder, unsure if his touch would be welcome in this moment of raw vulnerability.

"You were a hero, Holly," Drake said, his voice soft but steady, each word carefully chosen. "You sacrificed everything to save countless lives."

The gentleness in his tone contrasted sharply with the turmoil raging inside Holly. Her mind reeled, struggling to reconcile the memories of her death with the very real sensation of her heart pounding in her chest. She could feel the cool floor beneath her, the air filling her lungs with each ragged breath. How could she be dead when everything felt so visceral?

Holly shook her head violently, her long black hair whipping across her tear-stained face. "I don't want to be dead," she whispered, her voice cracking under the strain of emotion. Her analytical mind, usually so adept at piecing together complex puzzles, now failed her completely. She looked up at Drake, her eyes wide with fear and confusion. "Is this... is this my hell?"

The question hung in the air between them, heavy with implications. Holly's mind raced, trying to make sense of it all. If this was the afterlife, why did it feel so real? And if it wasn't, how could she remember dying? The detective in her wanted answers, but the human in her recoiled from the truth, afraid of what it might mean.

9 - 9

Drake's shoulders slumped, the weight of countless worlds pressing down upon him. His gaze dropped to the floor, unable to meet Holly's desperate eyes. The room seemed to shrink around them, the air thick with unspoken regrets and impossible choices.

"No, Holly," Drake's voice was barely audible, a whisper that carried the weight of universes. "It's mine."

The words hung in the air, each syllable a dagger to his heart. Drake's mind raced, memories of countless iterations of Holly flashing before his eyes. Every sacrifice, every loss, every version of her that had died because of his choices.

Holly's brow furrowed, her analytical mind struggling to process his words. "What do you mean?" she asked, her voice steadier now, the detective in her pushing through the emotional fog.

Drake's hands clenched involuntarily, knuckles white with tension. He forced himself to look up, meeting Holly's gaze. "I've watched you die a thousand times," he said, his voice cracking. "In a thousand different worlds. And each time, it's because of me."

The confession tore from his throat, raw and painful. Drake's eyes burned with unshed tears; the guilt of countless lifetimes etched into every line of his face. He wanted to reach out to Holly, to offer some comfort, but he held back, afraid that even his touch might somehow bring her harm.

Racing Against Time

1-2 The biting cold sliced through Drake's jacket as he rushed towards his car, the wind carrying a hint of impending snow. Rachel's labored breathing and Holly's frustrated muttering punctuated the eerie silence of the night. Drake's heart pounded; each beat a reminder of the precious seconds ticking away.

Holly's fingers flew over her phone's screen, her brow furrowed in concentration. The soft glow illuminated her face, casting harsh shadows that emphasized the tension in her jaw. Drake watched her, a knot forming in his stomach. What if they were too late?

"Come on, pick up," Holly hissed, her words barely audible over the howling wind. Drake clenched his fists, wishing the universe to cooperate just this once. The fate of his family, of the entire world, hung in the balance.

Rachel's voice cut through his spiraling thoughts. "Perhaps they're in an area with poor reception?" Her scientific mind, ever rational, sought logical explanations even in the face of mounting dread.

Holly's sharp intake of breath drew his attention. "They're not picking up," she muttered, shoving the phone back into her pocket with more force than necessary. The finality in her tone sent a chill down Drake's spine that had nothing to do with the frigid air.

Time seemed to stretch and compress simultaneously as they reached the car. Drake's fingers trembled as he fumbled with the keys, his mind racing through possibilities, each more terrifying than the last. He had to focus, had to push past the paralyzing fear. His family needed him.

"We need to move," he said, his voice rough with suppressed emotion. "Every second counts." As he spoke the words, Drake realized the truth of them. In this moment, faced with the potential loss of everything he held dear, nothing else mattered. Not his past mistakes, not the weight of the future. Only the present, and the desperate need to protect those he loved.

3-4

Drake's knuckles whitened as he gripped the steering wheel, his voice taut with barely contained panic. "They might be in trouble," he said, the words hanging heavy in the air. "We have to go now."

Rachel slipped into the backseat; her movements swift yet eerily silent. The rustle of her worn lab coat seemed amplified in the tense atmosphere. Drake caught a glimpse of her in the rearview mirror, noting the determined set of her jaw that belied the fear in her eyes. He wondered fleetingly what secrets she held, what knowledge burned behind those haunted eyes.

As Drake slid into the driver's seat, the leather creaked beneath him, a stark reminder of normalcy in a world rapidly spinning out of control. His mind raced, cataloging every possible scenario, every potential threat. The weight of responsibility pressed down on him, threatening to crush his resolve.

Holly paused outside the car, her silhouette stark against the night sky. Drake watched as she pulled out her phone again, her expression hardening into a mask of grim determination. The detective's instincts were kicking in, he realized, a small spark of hope igniting in his chest. Perhaps her analytical mind could unravel this nightmare before it was too late.

"What are you thinking?" Drake called out, his voice barely above a whisper, as if speaking too loudly might shatter their fragile chances.

5-6

Holly's eyes met Drake's through the windshield, a silent understanding passing between them. "I'll call Bird," she said, stepping away to speak privately. The gravel crunched under her feet as she moved, each step deliberate and measured.

Drake's fingers tightened on the steering wheel, knuckles turning white with the pressure. He could feel the urgency coursing through his veins, every second ticking by a potential threat to his family's safety. The weight of his past mistakes pressed down on him, threatening to suffocate his resolve. He couldn't fail them again, not when the stakes were so impossibly high.

Through the rearview mirror, he watched Holly's tense posture as she made the call. Her free hand clenched and unclenched at her side, a tell-tale sign of her own inner turmoil. Drake's mind raced, piecing together the fragmented reality they found themselves in. Could Bird be trusted in this world? Was he still the seasoned detective Drake remembered, or had the multiversal anomaly twisted him into something unrecognizable?

"Tell him to head to the Lexington," Drake called out, his voice rough with emotion. "That's where they're staying." The words felt like sandpaper in his throat, each syllable a reminder of the precious time slipping away.

As Holly nodded in acknowledgment, Drake closed his eyes briefly, allowing himself a moment of vulnerability. The faces of his family flashed before him – smiling, unaware of the danger that lurked in the shadows of this illusory world. He drew a shaky breath, steeling himself for whatever lay ahead.

7 - 8

Holly's jaw tightened as she stepped away from the car, her phone pressed firmly against her ear. The cold night air whipped around her, carrying the weight of their impending mission. Drake watched her intently, his fingers drumming an anxious rhythm on the steering wheel.

As Holly began to speak, her voice low and urgent, Drake strained to catch her words. The muffled conversation drifted through the car's open window, fragments of urgency and concern coloring the air.

"Bird, we need you at the Lexington. Now." Holly's tone brooked no argument, her usual analytical demeanor giving way to raw necessity.

Drake's mind raced, calculating distances and probabilities. Would Bird arrive in time? Could they trust him in this reality? The questions swirled in his head, a maelstrom of doubt and hope.

Holly's free hand clenched at her side; her knuckles white with tension. Even from a distance, Drake could see the furrow in her brow, the set of her shoulders that spoke volumes about the gravity of their situation.

"No, listen," Holly insisted, her voice rising slightly. "This isn't about Miller. It's about preventing a catastrophe."

Drake winced at the mention of his name, the weight of suspicion still hanging over him like a shroud. He longed to prove himself, to show Holly and the others that he was fighting for the right side. But time was a luxury they couldn't afford, and trust was a currency in short supply.

As Holly continued her terse conversation, Drake closed his eyes, allowing himself a moment of silent prayer. "Please," he whispered to the universe, to whatever cosmic force might be listening. "Keep them safe until we get there."

9 - 10

The tension in Holly's voice coiled tighter with each passing second. Her free hand raked through her dark hair, a rare display of agitation from the usually composed detective. "Bird, I swear on my badge, this is critical. Lives are at stake."

Drake's eyes flicked to the rearview mirror, catching a glimpse of Rachel's pale face in the backseat. The weight of responsibility pressed down on him, threatening to crush his resolve. He drew a deep breath, steadying himself for whatever lay ahead.

Holly's jaw clenched, her words clipped and urgent. "I need you to trust me on this. Get to the Lexington Hotel, now. We'll explain everything when we arrive."

The car's engine thrummed beneath them, a steady counterpoint to the frantic beating of Drake's heart. He gripped the steering wheel tighter, knuckles white with tension. Every traffic light seemed to stretch into eternity, each second lost a potential nail in their collective coffin.

"Thank you," Holly breathed, relief evident in her voice as she ended the call. She turned to Drake, her eyes glinting with determination in the dim light. "Bird's on his way. Let's hope we're not too late."

Drake nodded, swallowing hard against the lump in his throat. The city blurred past them, a kaleidoscope of neon and shadow. In the quiet of the car, the weight of their mission hung heavy, a silent prayer for salvation echoing in every heartbeat.

11 - 12

Bird's voice crackled through the phone, taut with concern. "The Lexington? What's going on?"

Holly's grip on her phone tightened, her knuckles whitening as she fought to keep her voice steady. The car's interior felt claustrophobic, the weight of their mission pressing in on all sides. "Drake's family is there, and so is Vega," she explained, her words clipped and precise. "Something feels off. I need you to put them under surveillance until I get there."

As she spoke, Holly's gaze darted to Drake, noting the rigid set of his jaw, the way his fingers flexed on the steering wheel. The streetlights cast intermittent shadows across his face, highlighting the lines of worry etched deep into his features.

Drake's mind raced, a torrent of fears and possibilities cascading through his thoughts. His family, trapped in a hotel room with Vega – a man whose loyalties were as shifting as desert sands. The image of his families faces, wide-eyed and afraid, flashed before him, spurring him to press harder on the accelerator.

"We're on our way," Holly continued, her voice barely above a whisper. "But we need eyes on that suite now. Anything could be happening in there."

The city streaked by outside, a blur of muted colors and harsh neon. Drake felt each second ticking away like a physical blow, every moment of delay another chance for disaster to strike. He drew a shaky breath, willing the universe to bend to his desperate need for speed.

13 - 14

A beat of silence stretched over the line, pregnant with tension. Holly could almost see Bird's furrowed brow, his weathered hand rubbing his chin as he processed her request.

"You're trusting Miller now?" Bird's gravelly voice finally crackled through the phone, heavy with skepticism. "I thought he was our suspect."

Holly's grip on the phone tightened, her knuckles whitening. She glanced at Drake, noting the tightness around his eyes, the subtle clench of his jaw. The car swerved slightly as he took a corner too fast, the urgency of their mission palpable in every movement.

"Just do it, Bird," Holly snapped, her patience fraying like an overworked rope. Her free hand clenched into a fist, nails digging into her palm. "We'll sort everything out later. Right now, I need eyes on that suite."

As she spoke, Holly's mind raced, calculating probabilities and potential outcomes. The pieces of this puzzle were shifting, realigning in ways she hadn't anticipated. Drake Miller, once a prime suspect, now seemed like their best hope of unraveling this mystery. The irony wasn't lost on her, but there was no time for dwelling on past suspicions.

"Lives are at stake," she added, her voice dropping to a near-whisper. "We can't afford to hesitate."

15 - 16

Bird sighed, a deep, weary sound that seemed to carry the weight of his years on the force. "Alright, I'm on it," he conceded, his tone a mixture of resignation and determination. Holly could picture him now, his imposing frame already in motion, grabbing his coat and keys. "What about you?"

Holly's gaze darted to the car's dashboard clock, its green digits a stark reminder of the precious minutes ticking away. She swallowed hard, her throat tight with anxiety. "I'll be there as soon as I can," she said, her voice clipped and tense.

Without waiting for a response, Holly ended the call abruptly, her thumb pressing the screen with more force than necessary. The sudden silence in the car felt oppressive, broken only by the hum of the engine and the rhythmic thud of her own heartbeat in her ears.

She turned to Drake, noting the white-knuckled grip he had on the steering wheel. His eyes were fixed on the road ahead, but Holly could see the storm of emotions raging behind them. Fear, determination, and a fierce protective instinct battled for dominance in his expression.

As they sped through the darkened streets, Holly's mind raced, piecing together fragments of information, searching for patterns and connections. The weight of responsibility settled heavily on her shoulders. She had set things in motion, trusting her instincts and Drake's desperate plea. Now, all they could do was hurry towards an uncertain outcome, hoping they weren't already too late.

17 - 18

Holly slid into the passenger seat, the leather creaking beneath her as she slammed the door shut. The sound echoed in the tense silence of the car, a stark punctuation to the gravity of their situation. She turned to Drake, her eyes searching his face for any sign of hope or despair.

"Bird's on his way to the Lexington," she said, her voice low and urgent. "Let's hope your family's still safe."

Drake's jaw tightened, a muscle twitching beneath the skin. His hands gripped the steering wheel tighter, knuckles turning white with the pressure. He didn't respond verbally, but Holly could feel the wave of anxiety and determination radiating from him.

As they pulled away from the curb, tires screeching against the asphalt, Holly's mind raced. She thought of Bird, heading into a potentially dangerous situation on her word alone. The weight of her decision pressed down on her, a suffocating blanket of responsibility.

"How long until we reach the hotel?" she asked, breaking the heavy silence.

Drake's eyes never left the road as he replied, "Thirty minutes, if traffic's on our side."

Thirty minutes. Holly's heart rate quickened. In thirty minutes, anything could happen. She closed her eyes briefly, willing herself to focus, to prepare for whatever they might find at the Lexington. When she opened them again, her gaze was steely, her resolve hardened.

"We'll make it," she said, as much to reassure herself as Drake. "We have to."

19 - 20

Drake's hands gripped the wheel, his knuckles bone white as he navigated the car through the darkened streets. The engine's low rumble echoed his inner turmoil, a constant reminder of the urgency that propelled them forward. His mind raced, conjuring images of his family in peril, each scenario more horrifying than the last.

"We should've never left them alone," he muttered, more to himself than to his passengers. The words tasted bitter on his tongue, laced with self-recrimination.

Rachel leaned forward from the backseat, her voice cutting through the tense atmosphere. "Drake, you couldn't have known. We're doing everything we can now."

He caught her gaze in the rearview mirror, noting the determination etched in her features. It was a stark contrast to the disheveled scientist he'd first encountered, and for a moment, he felt a flicker of hope.

"I just can't lose them again," Drake said, his voice barely above a whisper. The weight of his past mistakes, of lives lost in another reality, pressed down on him. "Not after everything we've been through."

The car swerved around a corner, the inertia pushing them all against their seats. Holly gripped the dashboard, her knuckles white, mirroring Drake's own tension.

"We won't let that happen," Holly assured him, her tone firm despite the uncertainty that gnawed at her. "Bird's already there. He'll keep them safe until we arrive."

Drake nodded, trying to draw strength from her words. The streets blurred past them, a dizzying kaleidoscope of neon signs and shadowy alleyways. With each passing moment, the Lexington drew closer, and with it, the answers they desperately sought.

As they approached their destination, Drake's heart pounded in his chest, a deafening rhythm that seemed to drown out everything else. He steeled himself for what lay ahead, knowing that whatever they found, it would irrevocably change the course of their lives.

Betrayal at the Lexington

1^{-2} The Lexington Hotel loomed before Detective Franklin Bird, its weathered brick façade a stark contrast to the pulsing red and blue lights of his unmarked cruiser. As he killed the engine, the silence seemed to amplify the churning unease in his gut. Holly's call echoed in his mind, her usually steady voice tinged with an urgency he'd rarely heard before.

"Something's not right, Frank," she'd said. "The Millers... I think they're in danger."

Bird's weathered hands tightened on the steering wheel. He'd learned long ago to trust Holly's instincts, even when they defied logical explanation. With a deep breath, he stepped out of the car, the cool night air carrying a hint of impending rain.

As he adjusted his holster, Bird's keen eyes scanned the area, searching for any sign of disturbance. The hotel's windows stared back at him, dark and inscrutable. He couldn't shake the feeling that somewhere behind those panes of glass, a clock was ticking down to something irreversible.

"Get a grip, old man," he muttered to himself. "You've seen stranger things."

But had he? Lately, the world seemed to be tilting on its axis, reality bending in ways that defied his decades of experience. Drake's wild theories about alternate worlds and multiversal anomalies... Bird had dismissed them at first, but now? He wasn't so sure.

With measured steps, Bird entered the lobby, the sudden warmth a stark contrast to the chill outside. The front desk clerk looked up, eyes widening at the sight of the detective's determined approach.

Bird's badge flashed in the muted light as he leaned in close. "Detective Bird, Bridgewater PD. Suite 214—where are the Millers?"

His voice was low, urgent, carrying the weight of too many unsolved mysteries and the creeping dread that this case might be the one to finally break him. As he waited for the clerk's response, Bird's mind raced, piecing together the fragments of information he'd gathered.

The Millers. Richard Vega. Holly's cryptic warnings. It was like trying to assemble a jigsaw puzzle in the dark, each piece potentially belonging to a different reality. And somewhere in the tangle of it all was the truth – a truth that Bird feared might shatter everything he thought he knew about the world.

3 - 4

The clerk's hesitation was palpable, his Adam's apple bobbing as he swallowed hard. "Second floor, west wing," he stammered, his eyes darting nervously between Bird and the elevator.

Bird's weathered features hardened, lines deepening around his eyes as he processed the clerk's reaction. Something was off, the air thick with an unspoken tension that set his nerves on edge. Years of experience had honed his instincts, and right now, they were screaming at him.

Without another word, Bird headed for the elevator, his hand resting lightly on his sidearm. The weight of the weapon was reassuring, a cold certainty in a world that seemed increasingly uncertain. As he waited for the elevator doors to open, Bird's mind raced through possible scenarios, each more unsettling than the last.

"What am I walking into?" he muttered under his breath, the words barely audible over the soft ding of the arriving elevator. As he stepped inside, Bird caught a glimpse of his reflection in the polished metal doors – a man on the edge of something big, something that could change everything.

The elevator began its ascent, and with each floor, Bird felt the pressure mounting. He'd seen his fair share of horrors in his career, but lately, the cases had taken on a surreal quality that left him questioning the very nature of reality. Drake's words echoed in his mind, a persistent whisper about alternate worlds and the fragility of the barriers between them.

"Get it together, Franklin," he chided himself, squaring his shoulders as the elevator slowed. "One step at a time. Find the Millers, get answers."

But as the doors slid open to reveal the second floor, Bird couldn't shake the feeling that he was stepping into something far beyond his understanding – a mystery that would challenge not just his skills as a detective, but his entire perception of the world.

5 - 6

The hallway stretched before him, a silent tunnel of muted beige and flickering fluorescent lights. Bird's footsteps echoed softly on the worn carpet, each step bringing him closer to Suite 214. The air felt heavy, charged with an unseen tension that made the hairs on the back of his neck stand on end.

As he approached the door, slightly ajar, Bird's hand instinctively moved to his holster. He paused, taking a deep breath to steady his nerves. Years of experience had taught him to trust his instincts, and right now, every fiber of his being screamed that something was terribly wrong.

"Richard Vega?" Bird called out, his voice firm despite the unease churning in his gut. "Detective Franklin Bird. Open the door."

He waited, straining to hear any movement from within. The silence that followed was deafening, broken only by the faint hum of the air conditioning.

'What if this is another dead end?' Bird thought, frustration and doubt creeping into his mind. 'How many more realities do we have to sift through before we find the truth?'

Shaking off the thought, Bird raised his hand to knock again. As his knuckles met the wood, the door creaked open further, revealing a sliver of the room beyond.

"Mr. Vega?" Bird called again, his tone sharpening. "I'm coming in."

With practiced caution, Bird pushed the door open, his other hand hovering near his weapon. The room slowly came into view, and Bird's eyes widened at the scene before him.

"Jesus," he whispered, his stomach dropping as he took in the sight of the bound Millers. "What the hell happened here?"

7 - 8

The creak of the door echoed in the hallway, punctuating the tense silence. Richard Vega's disheveled figure emerged from the shadows, his once-pristine shirt now a map of wrinkles and worry. The pallor of his face spoke volumes, a canvas of stress and sleepless nights. Yet, as his eyes met Bird's, a faint smile flickered across his lips - a mask slipped on with practiced ease.

Bird's gaze swept over Vega, cataloging every detail. The loosened tie, the faint tremor in Vega's hands, the beads of sweat dotting his forehead. 'He's unraveling,' Bird thought, 'but from what?'

"Detective," Vega said, his voice a study in forced calm. He stepped aside, the reluctance in his movement as palpable as the tension in the air. "Come in."

The invitation hung between them, heavy with unspoken truths. Bird hesitated, his instincts screaming caution. He could almost taste the wrongness of the situation, bitter on his tongue.

"Mr. Vega," Bird began, careful to keep his tone neutral. "I appreciate you seeing me. Mind if I ask a few questions about recent events?"

Vega's smile tightened, a fracture in his composed facade. "Of course, Detective. Although I'm not sure how much help I can be."

As Bird crossed the threshold, the air seemed to thicken, laden with secrets and lies. He couldn't shake the feeling that he was walking into something far more complex than he'd anticipated. The weight of multiple realities, of paths not taken and choices unmade, pressed down on him.

'What game are you playing, Vega?' Bird wondered, studying the man's face. 'And who's really pulling the strings?'

9 - 10

Bird's eyes scanned the room, his seasoned instincts prickling. The suite was immaculate, almost unnaturally so. The coffee table gleamed, devoid of even a single magazine or coaster. Heavy curtains were drawn tight against the windows, blocking out the afternoon light and casting the room in an eerie twilight.

"Quite a tidy place you've got here, Mr. Vega," Bird remarked, his tone casual but eyes sharp. "Not what I'd expect from someone who's been... preoccupied."

Vega's laugh came out forced, brittle. "Ah, well, I've always believed in keeping things in order. Helps me think clearly."

Bird nodded, unconvinced. The air felt thick, oppressive, as if the very atmosphere was conspiring to conceal something. He took a few steps further into the room, every sense on high alert.

"And the Millers?" Bird asked, turning slightly to keep Vega in his peripheral vision. "Have they been helping you keep things tidy too?"

A flicker of something—fear? guilt?—passed across Vega's face before it was quickly masked. "They... stepped out for a bit. Needed some air."

Bird's jaw tightened. The wrongness of the situation intensified, a discordant note in an already unsettling symphony. His gaze swept the room once more, searching for any sign of disturbance, any clue to unravel this increasingly complex puzzle.

And then he saw them.

11 - 12

The sight before him struck Bird like a physical blow. In the far corner of the room, partially obscured by shadows, sat Linda and Harrison Miller. Their limp forms were bound tightly to chairs, heads lolling forward in a grotesque parody of sleep. But it was the blood that made Bird's stomach heave—vivid streaks of crimson cascading from their noses, ears, and eyes, staining pale skin and matting once-lustrous hair.

"Jesus Christ," Bird muttered, his professional detachment crumbling as he rushed forward. The metallic scent of blood assaulted his nostrils, mixing with the acrid tang of fear that permeated the room. "What the hell is going on here?"

His mind raced, struggling to reconcile the horrific scene with the mundane hotel suite. Linda's usually vibrant blonde hair hung in sticky, rust-colored clumps around her face. Harrison's lanky frame seemed impossibly small, crumpled in on itself like a discarded marionette.

Bird's hand hovered over Linda's neck, searching for a pulse. "Mrs. Miller? Harrison? Can you hear me?" His voice sounded strained, even to his own ears.

A weak groan escaped Harrison's lips, barely audible. Bird's heart clenched, a mixture of relief and renewed dread flooding through him. They were alive, but for how long?

"Vega!" Bird barked, not taking his eyes off the Millers. "Call an ambulance, now!"

He fumbled with the ropes binding Linda's wrists, his fingers clumsy with adrenaline. How had it come to this? The case that had seemed so straightforward—a missing persons investigation—had spiraled into something far darker, far more sinister than he could have imagined.

As he worked to free the Millers, a part of Bird's mind couldn't help but whisper: What if Drake had been right all along? What if there really were other realities, other versions of events bleeding into their own? The thought sent a chill down his spine, even as he tried to focus on the immediate crisis at hand.

13 - 14

The silence that met Bird's command was deafening. He turned, his weathered face etched with a mixture of confusion and growing suspicion. Vega stood motionless, his lean frame taut with an almost palpable tension. The air in the room seemed to thicken, charged with an unspoken menace.

"Vega?" Bird's voice was low, tinged with a wariness that came from years on the force. His hand moved instinctively towards his holster, fingers brushing against the cool metal of his weapon. "What's going on here?"

Vega's eyes darted between Bird and the Millers, a storm of emotions swirling in their depths. His usual smooth demeanor had cracked, revealing glimpses of fear, guilt, and something else—a cold, hard resolve that sent a chill down Bird's spine.

"I can't let you do that, Detective," Vega finally spoke, his words carefully measured. "You don't understand what's at stake here."

Bird's mind raced, piecing together fragments of information, trying to make sense of the nightmare unfolding before him. He thought of Drake's wild theories, of realities bleeding into one another, of choices echoing across dimensions. For a fleeting moment, he wondered if this was how it felt to stand at the precipice of madness.

"Talk to me, Richard," Bird said, his tone softening slightly. "Whatever's going on, we can figure this out. But those people need help, now."

Vega's lips twisted into a bitter smile. "It's not that simple, Franklin. It never was."

As Bird's fingers tightened around his gun, a part of him mourned for the man he thought he knew, for the friend he believed Vega to be. The weight of betrayal settled heavy on his shoulders, mingling with the crushing responsibility of the lives hanging in the balance.

15 - 16

Bird's weathered eyes narrowed, his jaw clenching as he struggled to keep his composure. "What did you do, Vega?" he demanded, his voice sharp enough to cut through the tension-filled air.

The words hung between them, heavy and accusatory. Vega's gaze flickered, a kaleidoscope of emotions playing across his face—fear, guilt, and something darker, more resolute. It was a look Bird had seen before, in the eyes of desperate men pushed to their limits.

"I had no choice," Vega whispered, his voice barely audible. "You have to understand, Franklin. My family—"

But Bird wasn't listening anymore. His instincts, honed by years on the force, screamed danger. He watched, as if in slow motion, as Vega's hand inched towards the nearby table.

I should've seen this coming, Bird thought, a wave of self-recrimination washing over him. *All the signs were there.*

Before Bird could react, Vega's fingers closed around the base of a heavy lamp. In one fluid motion, born of desperation and fear, Vega swung the improvised weapon with all his strength.

"Richard, don't—" Bird started to say, but the words died in his throat as he realized it was already too late.

17 - 18

The heavy base struck Bird on the side of the head with a sickening thud. Pain exploded through his skull, white-hot and all-consuming. His world tilted, the room spinning in a nauseating blur of colors and shapes. Bird's knees buckled, and he crumpled to the floor with a groan that seemed to come from somewhere deep within him.

This can't be happening, he thought, his usually sharp mind struggling to process the betrayal. The cool hardwood pressed against his cheek, anchoring him as his consciousness threatened to slip away.

Through the haze of pain, Bird was dimly aware of Vega standing over him, chest heaving, the lamp still clutched in his trembling hand. The detective's vision swam, but he could make out the conflicted expression on Vega's face—a mixture of horror at what he'd done and grim determination to see it through.

"I'm sorry," Vega muttered, his voice barely above a whisper. It was as if he was speaking more to himself than to Bird. "I don't have a choice."

Bird wanted to respond, to demand answers, to understand how they'd arrived at this moment. But the words wouldn't come. Instead, he found himself thinking of all the cases he'd left unresolved, all the loose ends he might never tie up now.

"Your family," Bird managed to rasp, fighting against the encroaching darkness. "They wouldn't... want this..."

Vega's face contorted, a flash of anguish crossing his features. "You don't understand," he said, his grip tightening on the lamp. "I have to protect them. No matter the cost."

As consciousness began to slip away, Bird's last coherent thought was of the irony. He'd spent his career unraveling mysteries, and now he might die in the middle of the biggest one yet.

19 - 20

The metallic clatter of the lamp hitting the floor echoed through the room, jolting Bird back to painful awareness. Through blurred vision, he watched as Vega's trembling hands reached down, fumbling at his holster. The weight of Bird's service weapon lifted from his side, and a cold dread settled in his stomach.

Vega hefted the gun, its gleam catching the dim light as he checked the chamber with practiced ease. "Never thought I'd be on this side of the law," he muttered, his voice thick with regret.

Bird's mind raced, grasping for words that might defuse the situation. "Vega," he croaked, tasting blood, "there's always... another way. We can figure this out."

A bitter laugh escaped Vega's lips. "Figure it out? You have no idea what's at stake here, Detective. The things I've seen... the choices I've had to make..."

"Then explain it to me," Bird urged, fighting to keep his voice steady. "Help me understand."

Vega's gaze flickered between Bird and the bound Millers, indecision etched across his face. "I wish I could," he whispered. "But some truths are too dangerous."

As Bird struggled to formulate a response, his eyes locked onto the gun in Vega's hand. He couldn't help but think of all the times that weapon had been a source of comfort, of security. Now, in the wrong hands, it represented a terrifying unknown. What would Vega do next? And more importantly, could Bird find a way to stop him before it was too late?

21 - 22

Vega's eyes darted to Linda and Harrison, his knuckles whitening around the grip of the gun. Sweat beaded on his forehead, catching the dim light as he wiped it away with a trembling hand. His chest heaved with shallow, rapid breaths.

"This is for my family," he whispered, the words barely audible. His voice wavered, as if he were trying to convince not just the others, but himself as well. The weight of his actions pressed down on him, threatening to crush what remained of his resolve.

In the corner, Linda stirred faintly. Her blonde hair, matted with blood, clung to her swollen face as she turned towards Vega. Her blue eyes, once vibrant, now dulled by pain and betrayal, locked onto his.

"Richard..." she rasped, her voice a haunting mixture of anger and despair. The single word carried the weight of their shared history, of trust betrayed and innocence lost.

Vega flinched at the sound of his name. "I never wanted this, Linda," he said, his voice cracking. "You have to believe me. If there was any other way..."

He trailed off, unable to finish the thought. The gun felt impossibly heavy in his hand, a physical manifestation of the choices that had led him to this moment. Vega's mind raced, replaying the events that had brought him here, wondering if there had been another path, another choice he could have made.

"Your family?" Linda spat, each word a struggle. "What about mine? What about Harrison?"

At the mention of her son's name, Vega's gaze flickered to the boy's unconscious form. A wave of nausea washed over him, threatening to bring him to his knees. What had he become?

23 - 23

Vega's fingers tightened around the cold metal of the stolen gun, his knuckles whitening with the force of his grip. He paced the room like a caged animal, each step measured and tense. The weight of his actions pressed down on him, threatening to crush what remained of his resolve.

"I don't have a choice," he muttered, more to himself than to Linda. His eyes darted nervously between the door and the window, anticipating the moment when everything would come crashing down. "Gabriel... he has my family. My little girl..."

He paused, swallowing hard against the lump in his throat. The image of his daughter's smiling face flashed in his mind, a stark contrast to the horror surrounding him now.

"There's always a choice, Richard," Linda whispered, her words slurred but filled with conviction. "You're making it right now."

Vega's pacing quickened, his breath coming in short, sharp bursts. "You don't understand," he hissed, running a hand through his disheveled hair. "I've tried to break free, to do the right thing. But every time, every reality, it ends the same way. I can't... I can't lose them."

He glanced at the unconscious form of Detective Bird on the floor, a pang of guilt twisting in his gut. "I never meant for it to go this far," Vega said, his voice barely above a whisper. "But I'm in too deep now. There's no going back."

As he spoke, Vega's mind raced through possible scenarios, each more desperate than the last. He knew time was running out, that soon he would have to make a decision that would change everything. The gun in his hand seemed to grow heavier with each passing second, a constant reminder of the choices that had led him to this moment.

Just as Fun the Third Time

1-2 The Lexington Hotel loomed before them, a monolith of weathered brick and faded grandeur. Drake's hands trembled slightly as he gripped the steering wheel, his eyes fixed on the dim, flickering streetlights that cast eerie shadows across the building's facade. He could feel his heart pounding against his ribcage, each beat a reminder of the urgency that propelled them here.

With a deep breath, Drake maneuvered the car into a hasty park, the tires screeching softly against the asphalt. In the rearview mirror, he caught sight of Rachel Summers, her eyes darting nervously between the hotel and the shadowy streets surrounding them. The weight of their mission hung heavily in the air, suffocating in its intensity.

Drake's mind raced, memories of his past life as a lawyer intertwining with the surreal nature of his current reality. How had he ended up here, trapped between worlds, tasked with unraveling a multiversal mystery that threatened all of existence? The guilt of his past mistakes gnawed at him, a constant reminder of the redemption he sought.

"Rachel," Drake said, his voice low and measured, betraying none of the turmoil within. "I need you to stay here."

He watched as Rachel's brow furrowed, her lips parting as if to protest. The determined set of her jaw reminded him of the brilliant scientist she once was, now reduced to a pariah in this distorted world. Her presence both comforted and unnerved him, a stark reminder of the sacrifices that lay ahead.

"But Drake," Rachel began, her tone laced with urgency, "you can't go in there alone. We don't know what—"

"I said stay here," Drake interrupted, his tone firmer this time. He softened slightly, adding, "Please. It's safer this way."

As he spoke, Drake couldn't help but marvel at the strange twist of fate that had brought them together. Here he was, a man out of time and place, working alongside a disgraced scientist to save a world that had forgotten them both. The irony wasn't lost on him.

With a resigned nod, Rachel settled back into her seat, her fingers absently tracing the worn edges of Sir Mordred's codex. Drake's gaze lingered on the ancient book, a tangible link to the mysteries they sought to unravel. He wondered, not for the first time, if the answers they sought would bring salvation or damnation.

Taking a deep breath, Drake steeled himself for what lay ahead. The hotel loomed before him, a silent sentinel guarding secrets he both dreaded and desperately needed to uncover. As he reached for the door handle, a flicker of movement in the shadows caught his eye, sending a chill down his spine. Whatever awaited him inside, he knew with grim certainty that nothing would ever be the same again.

3 - 4

Rachel's mouth opened, her eyes flashing with defiance, but Holly's authoritative voice sliced through the tension. "Do what he says," she ordered, her tone brooking no argument. "We'll handle this."

Drake felt a surge of gratitude for Holly's support, even as guilt gnawed at him for dragging her into this tangled web of time and deception. He cast a final glance at Rachel, her red hair a dull flame in the dim light of the car, before stepping out into the night.

The air hit him like a physical force, heavy with the promise of rain and the weight of their mission. As Holly joined him, her detective's uniform a stark contrast to his disheveled appearance, Drake found himself searching her face for any sign of doubt or hesitation.

"You sure about this?" he murmured, his voice barely audible above the distant hum of traffic.

Holly's eyes met his, steely with determination. "No," she admitted, "but we're out of options. Whatever's waiting for us in there, we face it together."

As they approached the hotel entrance, Drake's mind raced with possibilities and fears. The weathered brick seemed to loom over them, its shadows concealing untold dangers. With each step, the urgency that had driven them here battled against the creeping dread of what they might find.

"Holly," Drake started, his hand hovering over the door handle, "if anything happens in there—"

"Don't," she cut him off, her voice softer now. "We both knew the risks when we started this. Let's just focus on getting the answers we need."

Nodding grimly, Drake pushed open the door, the hinges groaning in protest. As they stepped into the dimly lit lobby, the musty air closed around them like a shroud, and Drake couldn't shake the feeling that they were walking into the maw of something far greater and more terrible than they could imagine.

5 - 6

The ancient elevator groaned and shuddered as it ascended, its rusted cables straining against the weight of its passengers and their unspoken burdens. Drake stood rigidly in the corner, his eyes fixed on the flickering numbers above the door, each illuminated digit bringing them closer to an uncertain confrontation. The cramped space amplified every sound—the ragged breath catching in Holly's throat, the soft rustle of fabric as she shifted her weight, the thunderous pounding of Drake's own heart.

As they passed the first floor, Holly's voice cut through the suffocating silence, barely above a whisper. "Drake, I'm sorry."

The words hung in the air, heavy with unspoken regret. Drake turned his head slightly, catching a glimpse of Holly's reflection in the tarnished elevator door. Her usual composure had cracked, revealing a vulnerability he'd rarely seen.

"Holly, I—" Drake began, his voice hoarse. He swallowed hard, fighting against the tide of emotions threatening to overwhelm him. "We don't have time for this now."

But even as he said it, Drake's mind raced. Sorry for what? For doubting him? For the years lost between them in this twisted reality? For the weight of responsibility they both carried?

The elevator lurched to a stop, the doors creaking open to reveal the dimly lit second-floor hallway. As they stepped out, Drake's hand instinctively moved towards the concealed weapon at his hip. Every shadow seemed to pulse with potential danger, every closed door a barrier between them and the truth they sought.

"Whatever happens," Drake murmured, his eyes scanning the corridor, "we stick together. No heroics, no solo plays. Agreed?"

Holly nodded, her earlier moment of vulnerability replaced by the sharp focus of a seasoned detective. "Agreed. Now, let's find out what Gabriel's been hiding."

As they moved towards Suite 214, Drake couldn't shake the feeling that they were walking into a trap—one that had been centuries in the making.

7 - 8

Drake's brow furrowed, his eyes searching Holly's face. "For what?" he asked, his voice low and gravelly. The flickering fluorescent lights cast harsh shadows across his features, accentuating the weariness etched into every line.

Holly's gaze dropped momentarily, her fingers fidgeting with the hem of her jacket. When she looked up again, her eyes were filled with a mix of regret and determination. "For not believing you," she admitted, the words tumbling out in a rush. "For thinking you were part of this mess instead of a victim of it."

Drake felt a twinge in his chest, a complex cocktail of emotions he couldn't quite name. Part of him wanted to feel vindicated, but mostly he just felt tired. So damn tired. He ran a hand through his disheveled hair, buying time as he formulated a response.

"I don't blame you," he finally said, his voice barely above a whisper. "Hell, half the time I don't even believe myself." A humorless chuckle escaped his lips, echoing softly in the narrow hallway.

Holly opened her mouth to respond, but Drake held up a hand, silencing her. His mind raced, replaying every moment that had led them here, every decision, every missed opportunity. The weight of it all threatened to crush him, but he steeled himself, drawing on reserves of strength he didn't know he possessed.

"What matters now," he continued, his tone gaining resolve, "is that we're on the same page. We need to focus on stopping Gabriel and saving Harrison. Everything else..." he trailed off, leaving the thought unfinished.

9 - 10

Drake's expression softened, a faint smile tugging at his lips. "You were doing your job. I don't blame you." The words hung in the air, heavy with unspoken understanding.

Holly nodded, her eyes flickering with a mix of relief and lingering concern. The elevator doors slid open with a soft ding, revealing the second-floor landing. As they stepped out, the hallway stretched before them, eerily quiet and bathed in dim, flickering light.

Drake's senses heightened, every shadow seeming to conceal a potential threat. The faded carpet muffled their footsteps as they moved towards Suite 214, the air thick with tension and the musty scent of an aging building.

We're so close, Drake thought, his heart hammering against his ribs. *But at what cost?* Images of Harrison, of Rachel waiting anxiously in the car below, flashed through his mind, fueling his determination.

Suddenly, Holly hesitated, her hand brushing Drake's arm. He turned, meeting her questioning gaze. "What happened to Gabriel?" she asked, her voice barely above a whisper.

The question hit Drake like a punch to the gut. Memories of that night flooded back – the struggle, the knife, Gabriel's body falling. He swallowed hard, fighting the urge to look away. *How do I explain something I don't even understand?*

"I..." Drake began, his voice catching. He cleared his throat, buying time as he grappled with how much to reveal. The weight of his past actions, of the inexplicable events that followed, threatened to overwhelm him.

11 - 12

Drake's jaw tightened, his eyes darkening as he finally spoke. "I killed him," he said quietly, the words heavy with a mixture of guilt and disbelief. "At least, I thought I did. But nothing about him stays dead."

Holly's eyes widened, her hand instinctively moving towards her holstered weapon. "What do you mean?" she pressed, her voice a mix of concern and skepticism.

Drake ran a hand through his disheveled hair, frustration etching lines across his face. "I don't understand it myself," he admitted, his voice barely above a whisper. "It's like he's a ghost, or something worse. Every time I think it's over, he's back, always one step ahead."

As if summoned by his words, a chill swept through the hallway. Drake's muscles tensed, every instinct screaming danger. He glanced at Holly, seeing his own apprehension mirrored in her eyes.

"We need to move," Drake urged, his hand reaching for Holly's arm. But before he could take a step, a familiar, chilling laugh echoed down the corridor.

Drake's blood ran cold. *No, not here. Not now.* He turned slowly, dread coiling in his stomach as he faced the source of that haunting sound.

13 - 14

From the shadows at the end of the hallway, a figure emerged. Drake's breath caught in his throat as Gabriel's disfigured face came into view, half-hidden beneath the hood of his white robe. The green dragon symbol emblazoned across his chest seemed to writhe in the dim light, a testament to the twisted nature of its wearer.

Gabriel's scarred lips twisted into a grin that sent a shiver down Drake's spine. The sight of his former self, now warped into this monstrous visage, filled Drake with a nauseating mix of horror and guilt. He fought the urge to look away, to deny the reality of what stood before him.

"Well, well," Gabriel drawled, his voice a chilling blend of familiarity and otherworldly menace. "Drake Miller and Detective Kierstead. Together again. It's almost touching."

Drake's fists clenched at his sides, his mind racing. How had Gabriel found them so quickly? What new torment did he have planned? The weight of responsibility for Holly's involvement, for the danger he'd brought into her life, pressed down on him like a physical force.

"Gabriel," Drake managed, his voice hoarse. "How—"

"How am I here?" Gabriel interrupted, his tone mocking. "Oh, Drake. You should know by now. I'm always here, always watching. Your feeble attempts to rid yourself of me are... amusing, at best."

Drake felt Holly tense beside him, her presence both a comfort and a source of anxiety. He had to protect her, had to find a way out of this nightmare. But as Gabriel's twisted grin widened, Drake couldn't shake the sinking feeling that they were trapped in a game where the rules kept changing, and Gabriel always held the winning hand.

15 - 16

Holly's sharp intake of breath cut through the oppressive silence. Drake could sense her analytical mind working overtime, trying to reconcile the impossible figure before them with her understanding of reality.

"Gabriel," Holly muttered, her grip tightening on her gun. "So you're real."

The words hung in the air, heavy with implication. Drake felt a surge of conflicting emotions: relief that Holly finally believed him, fear for what that belief might cost her. He wanted to reach out, to shield her somehow from the malevolent presence that loomed before them, but found himself rooted to the spot.

Gabriel's disfigured face contorted into what might have been a smile, the scarred tissue stretching grotesquely. "More real than you'd like to admit," he said, his grin widening.

The green dragon symbol on Gabriel's chest seemed to writhe in the dim hallway light, hypnotic and threatening. Drake's mind raced, searching for a way out, a strategy to protect Holly and himself. But Gabriel's presence seemed to fill the space, suffocating hope and reason alike.

"Holly," Drake whispered, his voice barely audible. "Whatever happens, don't—"

But before he could finish, Gabriel took a step forward, his limp somehow making his approach more menacing rather than less. The air grew thick with tension, and Drake's heart hammered in his chest, each beat a countdown to an inevitable confrontation.

17 - 18

Gabriel's movement was a blur, defying the laws of physics and human capability. One moment he stood at the end of the hallway, the next his hand connected with Holly's face in a brutal backhand. The crack of flesh meeting flesh echoed through the corridor, followed by the dull thud of Holly's body slamming against the wall.

Drake's mind reeled, struggling to process the inhuman speed of the attack. "Holly!" he cried out, his voice raw with fear and rage.

But there was no time for concern or retaliation. Gabriel pivoted, his scarred visage now inches from Drake's own. Those eyes, cold and calculating, bore into him with an intensity that spoke of eons of malice.

"Your turn, old friend," Gabriel sneered, his breath hot against Drake's face.

Drake's police training kicked in, muscles tensing to defend, but it was futile against Gabriel's supernatural strength. The punch came swiftly, a bone-jarring impact to his temple that sent him crashing to the floor. Pain exploded behind his eyes, and the world tilted sickeningly.

As Drake lay there, his vision swimming and darkness encroaching, a single thought cut through the haze of pain and disorientation: Rachel. He had to protect Rachel. But his body refused to respond, limbs heavy as lead.

"Is this... how it ends?" Drake thought, fighting against the encroaching darkness. "No... not like this. Not while she's still in danger."

But despite his determination, consciousness slipped away, leaving him helpless before the monster he'd tried so hard to stop.

19 - 20

Holly's fingers scrabbled against the rough carpet, her mind racing as she fought to regain control of her battered body. The metallic taste of blood filled her mouth, and she could feel a warm trickle running down her chin. Her gun. Where was her gun?

As if in answer to her frantic thoughts, a shadow loomed over her. Gabriel crouched beside her, his disfigured face twisting into a grotesque parody of a smile. Holly's heart hammered in her chest, her police instincts screaming danger even as her analytical mind struggled to process the impossibility of Gabriel's existence.

"Looking for this, Detective?" Gabriel's voice was a chilling whisper as he held up her service weapon, its polished surface gleaming in the dim hallway light.

Holly's eyes widened, a surge of anger cutting through her pain. "You won't... get away with this," she managed to grit out, her voice hoarse.

Gabriel's laugh was a dry, mirthless sound that sent shivers down her spine. "Oh, but I already have. Multiple times, in fact."

As Holly stared into those cold, calculating eyes, a horrifying realization dawned on her. The nexus, the merging of realities – it wasn't just affecting her and Drake. Gabriel was playing a game across dimensions, and they were merely pawns on his twisted chessboard.

"Why?" Holly asked, desperately trying to buy time, to understand. "What do you want?"

Gabriel leaned in closer, his scarred face filling her vision. "Want? My dear detective, it's not about what I want. It's about what must be."

Holly's mind raced, piecing together fragments of information from across realities. The virus, the collapse of worlds – Gabriel was at the center of it all. But before she could voice her revelation, Gabriel's hand shot out, snatching her gun with inhuman speed.

"No!" Holly cried, her fingers grasping futilely at the air where her weapon had been.

Gabriel stood, towering over her prone form, the gun now a menacing silhouette in his grip. "I'm afraid our time is up, Detective Kierstead," he said, his tone almost regretful. "But don't worry. In another reality, perhaps you'll fare better."

As Gabriel's finger tightened on the trigger, Holly closed her eyes, bracing for the impact. In that final moment, her thoughts weren't of fear or regret, but of determination. Somewhere, in some reality, she would find a way to stop this madness. She had to believe that.

21 - 22

Gabriel's twisted grin widened, his burn-scarred face cast in eerie shadows by the dim hallway light. "You're persistent," he said with a chuckle, his voice a low, menacing rumble. "But I do love a good repeat performance."

Holly's heart raced, her analytical mind desperately searching for a way out of this nightmare. She could feel the cold sweat beading on her forehead, hear the ragged sound of her own breathing in the oppressive silence of the hotel corridor.

"This isn't just about Drake, is it?" she managed to gasp out, buying time as she tried to push herself up. "You're playing a much bigger game."

Gabriel's eyes glinted with cruel amusement. "Clever girl," he murmured, pressing the barrel of the gun against her chest. Holly froze, feeling the cold metal through her shirt, a chilling reminder of her mortality.

As Gabriel's grin turned predatory, Holly's mind raced through possibilities. She thought of the nexus, of the knowledge she'd gained across realities. There had to be a way to turn this around, to use what she knew against him.

"You can't kill all of me," Holly said, her voice steadier than she felt. "There are versions of me across realities that will stop you."

Gabriel's laugh was like ice down her spine. "Oh, Detective," he said, leaning in close, his scarred face filling her vision. "That's exactly what makes this so entertaining."

23 - 24

Gabriel's twisted smile widened, his eyes gleaming with a malevolent light that made Holly's blood run cold. She could smell his acrid breath, a mixture of decay and something otherworldly that made her stomach churn.

"Third time's the charm, isn't it?" he said, his tone dripping with malice.

Holly's mind raced, desperately trying to process the implications of his words. Third time? Had this happened before? The weight of alternate realities pressed down on her, memories she couldn't quite grasp flickering at the edges of her consciousness.

She opened her mouth to speak, to buy more time, to understand, but Gabriel's finger tightened on the trigger. Time seemed to slow, stretching like taffy as Holly saw the minute movement of his hand, the flash of the muzzle.

The gunshot exploded in the hallway, deafening in its intensity. Holly felt the impact like a sledgehammer to her chest, her body jerking violently as the bullet tore through her. Pain blossomed, hot and sharp, radiating outward as she gasped for air that wouldn't come.

As darkness began to encroach on her vision, Holly's last coherent thought was of Drake. She hoped he would understand, that he would find a way to stop this cycle of violence across realities. With her fading strength, she clung to the belief that her sacrifice would not be in vain.

25 - 26

Gabriel stood over Holly's crumpled form, his disfigured face twisting into a grotesque smile as he watched the life drain from her eyes. The crimson pool beneath her expanded, seeping into the worn carpet of the hallway. He crouched down, his white robe brushing against the blood, the green dragon emblem on his chest seeming to writhe in the dim light.

Leaning in close, Gabriel's scarred lips nearly touched Holly's ear as he whispered, "It was even more fun doing that a third time." His voice carried a perverse satisfaction, each word dripping with malice and dark amusement.

Holly's consciousness flickered like a dying flame. Her once sharp, observant eyes now struggled to focus, the world around her blurring into a haze of muted colors and indistinct shapes. She fought to keep her eyes open, her detective's instinct pushing her to gather every last detail, even as her body betrayed her.

"Dr-Drake," she managed to rasp, her voice barely audible. "He'll... stop you."

Gabriel's mocking grin widened, revealing teeth that seemed unnaturally sharp in the shadows. "Oh, I'm counting on him to try," he sneered, his calm demeanor belying the chaos he represented.

As the darkness encroached further, Holly's mind raced through fragmented memories - glimpses of other realities, other versions of herself merging into one. She clung to these fleeting images, desperate to make sense of the cosmic puzzle she found herself a part of.

"Why?" she breathed, her final question hanging in the air between them.

Gabriel's eyes glinted with malevolent glee as he responded, "Because, my dear detective, chaos is the only constant across all realities."

As Gabriel left, heading towards where the Millers were held captive, Holly slowly embraced the darkness that took hold once again.

The Reckoning

1 The muffled sound of a gunshot echoed through the walls of the Lexington Hotel suite, sharp and startling in the oppressive quiet. Richard Vega froze mid-step, the tension in his posture betraying his growing unease. His heart pounded in his chest, each beat a reminder of the precarious situation he found himself in.

"No," Richard whispered, his voice barely audible. "Not now."

He glanced around the opulent room, his eyes darting from the ornate wallpaper to the heavy curtains, searching for any sign of movement. The air felt thick, charged with an electric anticipation that made the hairs on the back of his neck stand on end.

Richard's hand instinctively moved to the concealed weapon at his waist, his fingers brushing against the cold metal. He took a deep breath, trying to steady his nerves. The weight of his choices pressed down on him, a constant reminder of the path he'd chosen.

"Gabriel?" he called out, his voice wavering slightly despite his efforts to maintain composure. "Is that you?"

Silence answered him, broken only by the faint ticking of an antique clock on the mantelpiece. Richard's mind raced, replaying the events that had led him to this moment. The promises made, the alliances formed, all in the name of protecting those he loved. But at what cost?

He took a cautious step forward, the plush carpet muffling his footsteps. "I know you're here," Richard said, his tone a mixture of resignation and defiance. "Show yourself."

As if in response to his challenge, a chilling laugh emanated from the shadows, sending a shiver down Richard's spine. He recognized that laugh, a sound that had haunted his dreams and waking moments alike.

"Well done, Richard," Gabriel's voice slithered through the room, seeming to come from everywhere and nowhere at once. "You've played your part admirably."

Richard's jaw clenched, his fingers tightening around the grip of his gun. "I've done everything you asked," he said, his words laced with bitter resentment. "What more do you want from me?"

Gabriel stepped into view, his scarred face twisted into a mockery of a smile. "Oh, Richard," he purred, his eyes gleaming with malevolent amusement. "We're only just getting started."

As Gabriel approached, Richard felt the weight of his choices bearing down on him. He had aligned himself with this monster, all for the sake of his family. But as he looked into Gabriel's eyes, he wondered if he had made a deal with the devil himself.

3 - 4

The acrid smell of gunpowder lingered in the air, mingling with the metallic tang of blood. Linda and Harrison Miller stirred in their chairs, the ropes biting into their flesh as they struggled weakly against their bonds. Richard Vega's gaze flickered between them and Gabriel, his heart pounding a frantic rhythm against his ribs.

Linda's once-pristine blonde hair hung in matted strands around her face, streaked with crimson. Her blue eyes, usually so full of warmth, now brimmed with fear and desperation as they locked onto Richard. "Please, Richard," she pleaded, her voice barely above a whisper, cracked and raw from screaming. "Let us go. You don't have to do this."

The words hit Richard like a physical blow, causing him to flinch. He'd known Linda for years, had shared meals and laughter with her family. Now, here she was, begging for her life and the life of her son. Richard's grip on the gun tightened, his knuckles turning white.

"I..." Richard's voice faltered. He swallowed hard, trying to steel himself. "I have no choice, Linda. You don't understand what's at stake."

His mind raced, replaying the events that had led him to this moment. The threats, the promises, the impossible choices he'd been forced to make. He'd told himself it was all for his family, but standing here now, faced with the consequences of his actions, doubt gnawed at him.

"There's always a choice," Linda insisted, her words tinged with a desperate hope. "Whatever they have on you, whatever they've threatened – we can help. Drake will understand. We can protect you."

Richard's laugh was hollow, bitter. "Protect me? Like Drake protected my family in the other world?" The words tasted like ash in his mouth. "No, Linda. It's too late for that."

As he spoke, Richard's eyes darted to Harrison. The boy's silent tears carved clean paths through the blood on his cheeks, his brown eyes wide with terror. For a moment, Richard saw his own son reflected in Harrison's face, and his resolve wavered.

"What about Harrison?" Richard asked, his voice barely audible. "He's just a kid. He doesn't deserve this."

Gabriel's cold laugh cut through the tension like a knife. "Sentiment, Richard? How disappointing. I thought you understood what needed to be done."

Richard's jaw clenched, torn between the mercy Linda begged for and the ruthlessness Gabriel demanded. In that moment, standing in the blood-stained hotel room with the weight of lives in his hands, Richard Vega realized that no matter what choice he made, he would never be able to wash the blood from his conscience.

5 - 6

Harrison's voice cracked, raw with fear and desperation. "Mom," he croaked, tears mingling with the blood on his cheeks, "I don't want to die." His lanky frame trembled in the chair, unruly blonde hair matted with sweat against his forehead.

The words pierced through Richard Vega's fragile composure. He turned to face them, his grip tightening on the stolen gun until his knuckles blanched white. His expression contorted, a battle between guilt and grim determination etched across his features.

Vega's mind raced, memories of his own family flashing before his eyes. How many times had he been in this position, forced to make an impossible choice? The weight of countless realities pressed down on him, each one a reminder of his failures.

"Harrison," Vega said, his voice barely above a whisper, "I never wanted it to come to this." He took a shaky step forward, the gun wavering slightly in his hand. "But you don't understand. None of you do. The things I've seen, the choices I've had to make..."

His eyes darted between Linda and Harrison, searching for understanding, for absolution. But all he saw was fear and confusion reflected back at him.

"Please," Linda pleaded again, her voice hoarse but determined. "Whatever's happening, whatever you're afraid of, we can face it together. Just put the gun down."

Vega's laugh was bitter, tinged with a desperation that chilled the room. "Together? There is no 'together' anymore. Not in this world, not in any world." His hand trembled, the gun's aim shifting between mother and son. "I have to do this. For my family. For the chance to make things right."

As the words left his mouth, Vega felt the hollow echo of his own lies. How many times had he told himself this was the only way? How many more innocent lives would be sacrificed on the altar of his misguided hope?

7 - 8

Vega's throat constricted, his breath coming in short, ragged gasps. The weight of his choices, of the lives he'd already taken, pressed down on him like a physical force. He could feel the gun growing slick in his palm, his finger twitching against the trigger.

"I'm sorry," Vega murmured, more to himself than to them. The words hung in the air, heavy with the finality of what was to come. He could see the fear in Linda's eyes, the silent plea for mercy, for understanding. But there was no turning back now.

With a trembling hand, Vega raised the gun, aiming it directly at Linda. The barrel seemed to stretch endlessly between them, a chasm of broken trust and shattered possibilities. His mind raced, memories of other timelines, other choices, flashing before his eyes.

"I can't let Gabriel down again," he said, his voice cracking under the strain. "Not this time." The words tasted like ash in his mouth, a bitter reminder of all he'd sacrificed to reach this point.

Linda's gaze never wavered, even as tears streamed down her face. "Richard," she whispered, her voice a mixture of sorrow and compassion, "whatever Gabriel's holding over you, it's not worth this. You're better than this."

For a moment, Vega's resolve faltered. The gun dipped slightly, his finger easing off the trigger. Could she be right? Was there still a chance for redemption, for a different path?

But then the memory of his own family's faces flashed before him - their fear, their pain, their silent accusation of his failure. And he knew, with a sickening certainty, that he had no choice. The multiverse had brought him to this moment, this terrible crossroads, and he had to see it through.

9 - 10

The air in the room grew thick with tension, each second stretching into an eternity as Vega's finger tightened on the trigger. Linda's eyes widened, a silent plea for mercy reflected in their depths.

Suddenly, the world exploded into chaos.

The door crashed open with a thunderous bang, wood splintering as it slammed against the wall. The sound reverberated through the room, shattering the oppressive silence and freezing Vega in place.

Drake Miller stood in the doorway, his imposing figure silhouetted against the hallway light. His chest heaved with exertion, and for a moment, time seemed to stand still.

Vega's mind reeled. How was this possible? Drake shouldn't be here – couldn't be here. Yet there he stood, a living, breathing impossibility.

"Drake?" Vega's voice was barely a whisper, disbelief etched into every syllable.

Drake's eyes locked onto Vega, burning with an intensity that seemed to pierce through the very fabric of reality. "It's over, Richard," he said, his voice low and steady despite the obvious strain in his posture.

Vega's thoughts raced, fragments of memories from other timelines colliding in his mind. In how many realities had he faced Drake like this? How many times had he failed? The weight of countless possibilities pressed down on him, threatening to crush him beneath their burden.

"You don't understand," Vega pleaded, his gun hand wavering. "I have to do this. For my family. For everything I've lost."

Drake took a step forward, his presence filling the room. "There's always another way, Richard. Always."

As Vega stood frozen between past and future, between duty and redemption, he realized that the true battle wasn't in the room around him, but in the war raging within his own soul.

11 - 12

The silence in the room was shattered as Drake Miller staggered forward, his left leg dragging across the carpet with a soft, scraping sound. Blood glistened on his temple, a stark contrast to his ashen face. Despite his battered appearance, his eyes burned with an intensity that seemed to defy his physical state.

Vega's grip on the gun tightened, his knuckles turning white. How had Drake survived? The question echoed in his mind, mingling with a cocktail of fear and grudging admiration.

"Vega," Drake said, his voice steady but laced with exhaustion. The single word carried the weight of their shared history, of countless timelines and realities where they had been allies, enemies, and everything in between.

Vega's thoughts raced. He could end this now, pull the trigger and be done with it all. But something in Drake's unwavering gaze gave him pause. "You shouldn't be here," he muttered, more to himself than to Drake.

Drake's lips twitched in a mirthless smile. "Yet here I am."

The air between them crackled with tension, decades of unspoken words and buried emotions threatening to burst forth. Vega found himself torn between the mission he had sworn to complete and the man before him – a man who, in another life, might have been his savior.

"Why did you come back?" Vega asked, his voice barely above a whisper. "You know what I have to do."

13 - 14

Drake's limp was pronounced as he stepped further into the room, each movement a testament to his determination. The gun in his hand gleamed dully in the dim light, a stark reminder of the stakes at play.

"It's over, Richard. Let them go," Drake said, his voice carrying a weight that seemed to fill the entire room.

Vega's mind reeled, caught between the shock of Drake's appearance and the fear of what it meant for his plans. He glanced back at Linda and Harrison, their terrified faces a silent plea for mercy. The weight of his choices pressed down on him, suffocating in its intensity.

"You don't understand," Vega said, his voice cracking. "I can't just let them go. Gabriel—"

"Gabriel doesn't control you," Drake interrupted, taking another painful step forward. "Not here, not now. We can end this, Richard. Together."

Vega's hand trembled, the gun wavering in his grip. He wanted to believe Drake, wanted to think there was a way out of this nightmare. But the memory of his family's fate in other realities haunted him, a constant reminder of what he stood to lose.

"And what then?" Vega asked, bitterness seeping into his words. "We go back to our normal lives, pretending none of this ever happened? That's not how it works, Drake. You know that better than anyone."

Drake's eyes softened, a flicker of understanding passing across his face. "No, we can't go back. But we can move forward. Make things right."

The words hung in the air, heavy with promise and possibility. Vega felt the resolve that had driven him this far begin to crumble, replaced by a desperate hope he hardly dared to acknowledge.

15 - 16

Vega's arm lowered further, the barrel of the gun now pointing at the floor. The harsh lines of determination on his face softened, giving way to a vulnerability he'd long buried beneath layers of guilt and fear. His eyes, usually sharp and calculating, now held a glimmer of something almost forgotten – hope.

"I..." Vega began, his voice barely above a whisper. The words caught in his throat, choked by the weight of countless realities where he'd made the wrong choice. He swallowed hard, fighting against the instinct to retreat behind his carefully constructed walls.

Drake's unexpected presence had shattered the fragile equilibrium of Vega's plans, leaving him adrift in a sea of uncertainty. The room seemed to close in around him, the muffled sobs of Linda and Harrison a stark reminder of the lives hanging in the balance.

"How are you even standing?" Vega asked, his voice trembling with a mixture of awe and disbelief. "You should be dead." The words escaped him before he could stop them, betraying the depth of his shock at Drake's survival.

As he spoke, Vega's mind raced, desperately trying to reconcile this new reality with the carefully laid plans that now lay in ruins at his feet. The gun in his hand felt heavier with each passing moment, a physical manifestation of the choices that had led him to this point.

17 - 18

Drake's jaw clenched, his eyes never leaving Vega's face. The weight of countless decisions, of lives lost and saved across multiple realities, pressed down on him like a physical force. He pushed aside the searing pain in his leg, focusing on the man before him with unwavering intensity.

"Put the gun down," Drake commanded, his voice low and steady. The words hung in the air, heavy with unspoken history and the possibility of redemption.

Vega's hand trembled, the gun wavering in his grip. "I can't," he whispered, his voice cracking. "You don't understand what's at stake."

Drake took a measured step forward, ignoring the protest of his injured leg. "I understand more than you know, Richard," he said, his tone softening slightly. "But this isn't the way."

The air in the room grew thick with tension, the silence broken only by the ragged breathing of the hostages. Drake's mind raced, calculating the odds, weighing the consequences of every possible move. He'd been here before, in countless iterations of reality, but never with so much on the line.

"We can fix this," Drake continued, his voice barely above a whisper. "But you have to trust me."

Vega's eyes darted between Drake and his captives, indecision etched across his features. The gun in his hand dipped slightly, then rose again, mirroring the conflict raging within him.

Drake's heart pounded in his chest, each beat a reminder of the precious seconds ticking away. He knew that in this moment, balanced on the knife's edge of possibility, the fate of not just this world, but countless others, hung in the balance.

19 - 20

Vega's grip on his weapon tightened again, his knuckles turning white as he looked back at Linda and Harrison, their faces etched with fear and desperation. His gaze then snapped back to Drake, eyes blazing with a mixture of anger and anguish.

"Why should I?" he spat, his voice trembling with barely contained emotion. "You've always been the hero, right? Always saving the day. But not for me. Never for me."

The words hung in the air, heavy with unspoken history and accusation. Drake felt each syllable like a physical blow, the weight of Vega's pain pressing down on him. He took another step forward, his injured leg nearly buckling beneath him. The room swam for a moment, black spots dancing at the edges of his vision, but he forced himself to focus on Vega's face.

"What are you talking about?" Drake asked, his voice low and strained. His mind raced, trying to piece together the fragments of memory from countless realities, searching for the key to unlock Vega's anguish.

As he waited for Vega's response, Drake's thoughts turned inward. What had he missed? What crucial moment had slipped through the cracks of his fractured existence? The weight of every decision, every branching path of reality, seemed to converge on this single, fragile moment.

21 - 22

Vega's face contorted, a dam of emotion finally breaking. His voice cracked, tears welling in his eyes as he spoke, each word laden with grief and accusation. "You never saved my family. Not in the other world. Not when it mattered. You let them die, Drake!"

The revelation struck Drake like a physical blow, forcing the air from his lungs. Memories cascaded through his mind—fragments of other realities, glimpses of choices unmade and paths untaken. He saw Vega's family, faces blurred by the fog of alternate timelines, their fates sealed by his own inaction.

Drake's jaw clenched, his expression hardening into a mask of cold detachment. It was a look he knew well, one he had worn countless times in courtrooms and boardrooms. But now, it felt like a shield against the crushing weight of his own failures.

"Because I never cared about anyone but me," Drake replied, his voice devoid of emotion. The words tasted bitter on his tongue, a truth he had long denied but could no longer ignore.

As he spoke, Drake's mind raced. Had he truly been so callous, so self-absorbed? The Drake of that other world seemed like a stranger, yet he recognized the seeds of that selfishness within himself. It was a stark reminder of how far he had come, and how easily he could have remained that man—indifferent to the suffering of others, blind to the consequences of his actions.

The air in the room grew thick with tension, the weight of unspoken regrets and shattered trust hanging between them like an invisible barrier. Drake's fingers twitched, acutely aware of the gun in his hand and the precarious balance of the moment. One wrong move, one misplaced word, and everything could unravel.

23 - 24

Richard Vega's face crumpled, the fight draining from his eyes as Drake's words hit him like a physical blow. His shoulders sagged, the gun in his hand wavering, lowering slightly. The weight of betrayal seemed to crush him, bending his spine and robbing him of his resolve.

Drake watched, his heart pounding, as Vega's grip on the weapon loosened. In that fleeting moment of hesitation, a window of opportunity yawned open. Time seemed to slow, each heartbeat stretching into eternity.

Without conscious thought, Drake's body moved. His finger squeezed the trigger, the sound of the gunshot shattering the heavy silence. The recoil vibrated through his arm, a stark reminder of the finality of his action.

As the echo of the shot faded, Drake's mind raced. Had he just crossed a line he could never uncross? Was this the moment that would define him in this new reality? The guilt that had been his constant companion threatened to overwhelm him, but he pushed it aside. There would be time for introspection later. Now, he had to focus on the immediate aftermath of his decision.

"Richard," Drake called out, his voice hoarse. "It's over. Just... just stay down."

25 - 26

The gunshot's echo faded, replaced by an eerie stillness. Vega stumbled backward, his eyes wide with shock and disbelief. His free hand clutched at his chest, fingers splaying over the rapidly spreading crimson stain on his shirt.

"I... I didn't..." Vega gasped, his words trailing off as he struggled to process what had just happened.

Drake watched, frozen in place, as Vega's knees buckled. The man who had once been his colleague, his friend in another reality, crumpled to the floor. The gun slipped from Vega's grasp, clattering against the hardwood with a finality that seemed to punctuate the moment.

A wave of nausea washed over Drake. He'd pulled the trigger, but the consequences felt surreal, as if happening to someone else. His mind raced, grappling with the weight of his actions.

"Richard," Drake managed, his voice barely above a whisper. "I... God, I didn't want it to end like this."

Vega's breath came in ragged gasps, each one seeming to require more effort than the last. His eyes, once filled with determination and desperation, now held a mixture of pain and resignation.

Drake took a halting step forward, his own injuries momentarily forgotten in the face of this new, terrible reality. The room felt oppressively silent, save for Vega's labored breathing and the muffled sobs of Linda and Harrison.

"Why?" Vega wheezed, his voice weak and fading. "Why couldn't you... save them?"

The question hung in the air, unanswered, as Vega's eyes slowly lost focus. Drake stood there, the weight of multiple realities pressing down on him, watching as the life ebbed from the man at his feet.

27 - 28

Vega's gaze, once sharp and calculating, now clouded with pain and betrayal, locked onto Drake's. Blood trickled from the corner of his mouth as he struggled to form words. "Why?" he whispered, his voice barely audible above the pounding in Drake's ears. "Why didn't you ever save them?"

The question hit Drake like a physical blow, forcing him to confront the demons he'd been running from across realities. He felt the weight of his gun, still warm in his hand, a stark reminder of the choices that had led them both to this moment.

Drake's jaw clenched, memories of his past failures flashing through his mind. The car accident, the countless realities where he'd put his own interests first, the faces of those he'd failed to protect. He swallowed hard, tasting bile.

"Because I didn't know how to care for anyone but myself," Drake admitted, his voice steady despite the tumult of emotions threatening to overwhelm him. He met Vega's fading gaze, forcing himself to face the consequences of his actions. "That's my mistake, Richard. One I'll live with for the rest of my life."

As the words left his lips, Drake felt a shift within himself. The admission was both a condemnation of his past and a promise for his future. He realized, with a clarity that cut through the chaos of the moment, that this was the turning point he'd been searching for across countless realities.

29 - 30

Vega's lips parted, a final retort or perhaps a plea for forgiveness forming on his blood-flecked lips. But the words never came. His eyes, once filled with pain and betrayal, now glazed over, the light within them extinguished like a candle in a gust of wind. With a soft thud, his body slumped to the floor, the last whisper of life escaping him in a barely audible sigh.

Drake stood motionless, his chest heaving with labored breaths. The gun in his hand felt impossibly heavy, a physical manifestation of the weight now settling on his conscience. He stared at Vega's lifeless form, his mind reeling.

"I didn't want this," Drake thought, a wave of nausea washing over him. "But how many more would have suffered if I hadn't acted?"

The room fell into an eerie silence, broken only by the muffled sobs of Linda and Harrison. Their cries pierced through Drake's shock, reminding him of the family he had nearly lost – the family he had sworn to protect.

"Dad?" Harrison's voice wavered, thick with tears and uncertainty.

Drake turned slowly, his eyes meeting the frightened gazes of his wife and son. The sight of them, bound and bloodied, ignited a fierce protectiveness within him.

"It's over," he said softly, moving towards them with deliberate steps. "You're safe now. I'm here."

As he began to untie their bonds, Drake's mind raced. The multiverse stretched before him, infinite possibilities branching out from this moment. But for the first time in what felt like lifetimes, he knew exactly where he belonged.

A Familiar Limp

1-2 Drake's calloused fingers worked feverishly at the coarse ropes binding Linda and Harrison, his heart pounding a frantic rhythm against his ribcage. The dim light of the room cast long shadows across their faces, highlighting the dried blood and bruises that marred their once-familiar features. A lump formed in Drake's throat as he took in the sight of his family, battered and broken before him.

He swallowed hard, pushing down the surge of guilt and anguish that threatened to overwhelm him. There would be time for self-recrimination later—if they survived this.

"Almost there," he murmured, more to himself than to them. The final knot came loose under his trembling hands, and he exhaled sharply. "Can you stand?"

Linda nodded weakly, her eyes unfocused. Harrison remained silent, his gaze fixed on some distant point beyond Drake's shoulder. The sight of his son's vacant stare sent a chill down Drake's spine.

"We need to go," Drake said, his voice low but firm. He glanced nervously at the door, half-expecting it to burst open at any moment. "Holly and Dr. Summers are waiting for us downstairs. We'll be safe once we're out of here."

As he spoke, Drake's mind raced through the possibilities that lay ahead. Would Holly's sharp instincts be enough to keep them all alive? Could Dr. Summers truly unravel the mysteries that had brought them to this point? And most pressingly—how much time did they have before Gabriel realized his prisoners were escaping?

"Dad," Harrison's voice broke through Drake's spiraling thoughts, barely above a whisper. "Are you... are you really you?"

The question hit Drake like a physical blow, forcing him to confront the chasm that had grown between them. How many versions of himself had his son encountered in these endless loops? How many times had hope turned to betrayal?

"It's me, son," Drake replied, fighting to keep his voice steady. "I know I've let you down before, but I swear to you, I'm here now. And I'm going to get us all out of this."

As he spoke the words, Drake prayed they were true. The weight of his past mistakes pressed down on him, threatening to crush what little resolve he had left. But the sight of his family—battered but alive—ignited a fierce determination within him.

"Let's move," he said, helping Linda to her feet while Harrison struggled to stand on his own. "Every second counts."

With one last glance at the room that had been their prison, Drake ushered his family towards the door and what he hoped would be their salvation. The path ahead was fraught with danger, but for the first time in what felt like an eternity, Drake allowed himself to feel a glimmer of hope.

3-4 Linda leaned heavily on Drake as she stood, her legs shaky beneath her. The warmth of her body against his side was a bittersweet reminder of all they had endured. Her blonde hair, matted with sweat and grime, fell across her face, obscuring the weariness etched into her features.

Drake's heart constricted as he felt Linda's trembling. How many times had he failed to protect her? The weight of his guilt threatened to overwhelm him, but he pushed it aside. There would be time for recrimination later—if they survived.

Harrison rubbed his sore wrists, the angry red marks a stark contrast against his pale skin. His eyes darted nervously between his parents, a silent testament to the trauma he had endured. The sight of his son's lanky frame, hunched with exhaustion and fear, made Drake's chest ache with a mixture of love and regret.

"Are you okay, Dad?" Harrison asked hesitantly, his voice barely above a whisper.

The question hung in the air, laden with unspoken fears and a desperate hope for reassurance. Drake felt the weight of his son's gaze, searching for any sign of the strength and certainty that had once defined their relationship.

How could he answer? The truth—that he was far from okay, that he was terrified and uncertain—would only add to their burden. But lies had brought them to this point, and Drake was tired of deception.

"I'm..." he began, his voice catching. He swallowed hard, forcing himself to meet Harrison's eyes. "I'm doing what needs to be done. We're going to get through this together."

It wasn't the answer Harrison wanted, Drake knew. But it was all he could offer in that moment—a promise, fragile but sincere, that he would not abandon them again.

5 - 6

Drake waved off the concern, gesturing for them to follow. "I'm fine. Let's move," he said, his voice gruff with the effort of maintaining composure. The words felt hollow in his mouth, a lie he told himself as much as them.

He turned towards the door, his mind racing with plans and contingencies. They needed to get out, to find Holly and Dr. Summers, to escape this nightmare. But as he took his first step, a searing pain shot through his left leg. Drake stumbled, his body betraying him at the worst possible moment.

His left leg dragged, the limp pronounced and unmistakable. Drake gritted his teeth, fighting against the weakness that threatened to overwhelm him. He could feel Harrison's eyes on him, knew that his son's keen mind was piecing together a puzzle Drake desperately wanted to keep hidden.

'Just a few more steps,' Drake thought, willing his uncooperative limb to obey. 'Just get them out of here, and then...' He couldn't bring himself to complete the thought. The future was a luxury he couldn't afford to contemplate, not when the present was so fraught with danger.

As he reached for the door handle, Drake's mind reeled with the implications of his injury. How much had he revealed? How much did Harrison suspect? The weight of his secrets pressed down on him, threatening to crush what little resolve he had left.

7 - 8

Harrison's voice cut through the silence, cautious and tinged with concern. "Dad," he said, his words hanging in the air like a fragile thread. "What happened to your leg?"

Drake's hand froze on the door handle, his back to his son and Linda. The question pierced through him like a cold blade, forcing him to confront the very thing he'd been desperately trying to conceal. He could almost feel Harrison's inquisitive gaze boring into him, searching for answers that Drake wasn't ready to give.

For a fraction of a second, Drake remained motionless, his mind racing. The urge to protect his family warred with the need to maintain the façade he'd so carefully constructed. He drew a deep breath, steeling himself against the rising tide of emotions threatening to overwhelm him.

"It's nothing," Drake said dismissively, his voice betraying a hint of strain despite his efforts to sound nonchalant. He half-turned, offering a weak smile that didn't quite reach his eyes. "Just something from one of the loops."

As the words left his mouth, Drake felt a pang of guilt. The lie tasted bitter, a necessary evil in this twisted game of survival. He watched Harrison's face, seeing the flicker of doubt in his son's eyes. The weight of his deception pressed down on him, a constant reminder of the impossible choices he faced.

'If only you knew, Harrison,' Drake thought, his heart heavy with unspoken truths. 'If only I could tell you everything without putting you in danger.' But he knew that wasn't an option. Not here, not now, when every second counted and the shadows of their pursuers loomed ever closer.

9 - 10

Harrison froze, his eyes narrowing as pieces clicked into place in his mind. The air in the room seemed to thicken, charged with a sudden, palpable tension. Drake could almost see the gears turning behind his son's thoughtful brown eyes, so much like his own.

"You never hurt your leg in one of the loops," Harrison said slowly, his voice barely above a whisper. "Not once."

The words hung in the air, heavy with accusation and dawning realization. Drake felt a chill run down his spine, his carefully constructed façade threatening to crumble. He fought to keep his expression neutral, even as his mind raced, searching for a way out of this unexpected confrontation.

'He's too clever,' Drake thought, a mixture of pride and fear coursing through him. 'Just like his old man. But I can't let him piece it together. Not now. Not when we're so close.'

Drake turned to face Harrison fully, summoning every ounce of his lawyer's composure. A faint smile tugged at his lips, deliberately casual, though it felt more like a grimace. "What are you talking about?" he asked, infusing his tone with just the right amount of confusion and amusement.

As he spoke, Drake's mind whirled with possibilities. How much did Harrison suspect? How much danger were they in if the truth came out now? The weight of his choices, of the lies he'd told to protect them all, pressed down on him like a physical force.

11 - 12

Harrison's gaze dropped to Drake's limp, then back up to his face. His brown eyes, so much like Linda's, widened with a mixture of dawning horror and disbelief. The boy's lanky frame seemed to tense, as if bracing for impact.

"Gabriel had that same limp," Harrison said, his voice barely above a whisper. Each word fell like a hammer blow in the tense silence. "The burns... the way he moved..." He swallowed hard, his Adam's apple bobbing. "Dad, you're not... you're not him, are you?"

The question hung in the air, charged with an electric tension that seemed to suck all the oxygen from the room. Drake felt his heart hammering against his ribs, a cold sweat breaking out across his forehead. He opened his mouth to speak, to deny, to explain—but no words came.

In that moment of paralyzing silence, Drake's mind raced. He saw the fear in Harrison's eyes, the desperate hope that he was wrong. He felt the weight of Linda's gaze on him, confused and wary. The carefully constructed reality he had built was crumbling around him, and he was powerless to stop it.

'How did it come to this?' Drake thought, a wave of despair washing over him. 'All I wanted was to protect them, to fix what I broke. But at what cost?'

The room fell deathly silent, the only sound the ragged breathing of its occupants. In that silence, the truth hung unspoken but undeniable, a chasm opening between father and son that no words could bridge.

13 - 14

Drake's faint smile spread into a sinister grin, the transformation sending a chill through the room. His posture shifted ever so slightly, the tension in his muscles melting away like ice under a scorching sun. Where moments ago he had been a picture of urgency and concern, now he exuded an eerie calm that seemed to suck the warmth from the air.

Harrison took an involuntary step back, his eyes widening in horror as he watched the familiar features of his father morph into something alien and terrifying. The burns that marred Drake's face seemed to deepen, casting grotesque shadows across his visage.

'This is it,' Drake thought, a strange mix of relief and regret washing over him. 'The moment of truth. The end of the charade.'

His gaze locked onto Harrison, drinking in the dawning realization in the boy's eyes. When he spoke, his voice carried a mocking edge that cut like a razor.

"You always were too clever for your own good," Drake said, each word dripping with cruel amusement. He cocked his head to the side, studying Harrison as if he were an interesting specimen under a microscope. "I suppose I should be proud. After all, you are my son... in a manner of speaking."

The words hung in the air, heavy with implication. Drake's mind raced, memories of countless loops flashing before his eyes. How many times had he tried to outmaneuver Gabriel? How many times had he failed? And now, here he stood, wearing the face of the man he had once been, tasting the bittersweet victory of becoming his own worst enemy.

15 - 16

Linda's sharp intake of breath cut through the tension like a knife. Her blue eyes, once filled with hope at the sight of her husband, now widened with dawning horror. She stumbled backward, her hand flying to her mouth as if to stifle a scream.

"Drake... what's going on?" Her voice trembled, barely above a whisper.

The man who wore Drake's face turned to her, his eyes glittering with malevolent amusement. A soft chuckle escaped his lips, the sound sending chills down Linda's spine. It was Drake's laugh, but twisted, devoid of warmth.

"Oh, Linda. Sweet, loyal Linda." His tone dripped with mock affection, each word a cruel caress. "You really thought I'd let him win? Let him outsmart me?"

As he spoke, memories of countless loops flooded his mind. The frustration, the rage, the burning desire to best Drake Miller at his own game. Now, standing here in Drake's skin, he savored the sweet taste of victory.

He took a step toward Linda, relishing the way she flinched. "Your precious Drake," he sneered, "he tried so hard. But in the end, he was just another pawn in my game."

The room seemed to shrink around them, the air thick with fear and betrayal. In that moment, as he stood before the woman who had loved Drake Miller, Gabriel felt a twisted sense of completion. He had won, truly and utterly, and the despair in Linda's eyes was the sweetest reward of all.

17 - 18

Harrison's heart pounded in his chest, each beat a thunderous reminder of the danger they faced. He moved swiftly, positioning himself between his mother and the man who wore his father's face. The lanky teenager's muscles tensed, his fists clenching so tightly his knuckles turned white.

"What did you do to my dad?" Harrison demanded, his voice cracking with a mixture of fear and determination. His wide brown eyes, usually filled with wonder, now blazed with a fierce protectiveness.

The man's grin widened, a sinister parody of Drake's once-comforting smile. "Let's just say," he drawled, savoring each word, "your father and I have gotten... very close over the loops. Closer than you'd think."

As the words hung in the air, Harrison's mind raced. Loops. The word echoed in his head, conjuring fragmented memories of alternate realities and fractured timelines. He thought of the virus, the chaos it had caused across the multiverse. Was this connected? Had his father fallen victim to some twisted merging of realities?

"No," Harrison whispered, more to himself than anyone else. "That's not possible. Dad wouldn't... he couldn't..." But even as he spoke, doubt crept in, cold and insidious. The man before him moved like his father, spoke with his voice, but there was something fundamentally wrong, a darkness that had never been there before.

19 - 20

Linda's trembling voice cut through Harrison's tumultuous thoughts. "Gabriel..." she breathed, the name falling from her lips like a leaden weight. Her blue eyes, usually so warm and reassuring, now swam with a mix of recognition and horror.

The figure—Gabriel—tilted his head, his burned face twisting into an expression of dark satisfaction. The scarred tissue pulled taut across his cheeks, accentuating the cruel curve of his lips. "It's so good to be home," he purred, his gaze sweeping over Linda and Harrison with predatory intensity.

Harrison's stomach lurched. Home. The word felt like a mockery, a perversion of everything he held dear. This wasn't home—not with this monster wearing his father's skin. He glanced at his mother, noting the way her hands shook, her slender frame seeming to shrink under Gabriel's piercing stare.

"You're not welcome here," Harrison spat, mustering every ounce of courage he possessed. "Where's my real dad? What have you done with him?"

Gabriel's laugh was a low, unsettling rumble. "Oh, Harrison," he said, taking a step closer. "Always so quick to assume there's a simple answer. Your father and I... we've become something new. Something beyond your limited understanding."

As Gabriel advanced, Harrison felt his mother's hand on his shoulder, squeezing gently. It was a gesture he'd felt a thousand times before—a silent signal of support, of unity. But now, it carried a desperate edge, as if Linda was anchoring herself as much as she was steadying her son.

"Please," Linda whispered, her voice barely audible. "Just let us go. We won't interfere with whatever you're planning."

Harrison's mind raced, grappling with the implications of Gabriel's words, the terror in his mother's voice. What did she know about this man that he didn't? How deep did this nightmare truly go?

Its Always Been Me

1-2   A swirling vortex of shadows enveloped Drake, his senses reeling as he struggled to orient himself in the oppressive darkness. Flashes of light pulsed through the gloom, revealing fleeting glimpses of a familiar scene—the nexus of Torment, a place that haunted his nightmares.

Drake's heart pounded as he watched a ghostly version of himself materialize before him, locked in combat with Gabriel. The spectral Drake's face was contorted with rage, his movements fueled by desperation and hatred. With a sickening crunch, Drake saw himself plunge a jagged shard of reality into Gabriel's chest.

"No," Drake whispered, his voice hoarse. "This can't be happening again."

He squeezed his eyes shut, trying to block out the memory, but it persisted, burning behind his eyelids. The weight of his actions pressed down on him, threatening to crush his very soul.

When Drake opened his eyes, he found himself face to face with Gabriel, whole and unharmed. The burn scars that marred the man's face seemed to writhe in the flickering shadows, his sneer more pronounced than ever.

Drake's mind reeled. How could this be? He distinctly remembered the feeling of Gabriel's life slipping away, the warmth of his blood on his hands. Yet here he stood, as real and menacing as ever.

"How..." Drake began, his voice trailing off as he struggled to form coherent thoughts.

Gabriel's eyes gleamed with malicious amusement, his very presence a mockery of Drake's sanity. Drake felt the familiar tendrils of doubt creeping into his mind, questioning everything he thought he knew.

As he stared at his nemesis, Drake's thoughts raced. Had he imagined killing Gabriel? Was this all part of some elaborate illusion, another trick of the multiverse? Or had he somehow failed, allowing Gabriel to cheat death once again?

The uncertainty gnawed at Drake, threatening to unravel the fragile threads of his resolve. He had sacrificed so much, endured countless horrors, all in the name of protecting his family and saving reality itself. And yet, here stood the embodiment of his failure, alive and seemingly triumphant.

Drake's fists clenched at his sides, a mixture of anger and fear coursing through his veins. He had to find answers, had to understand how Gabriel could be standing before him. The fate of everything he held dear hung in the balance, and Drake knew he couldn't afford to falter now, no matter how impossible the situation seemed.

3 - 4

A chilling chuckle pierced the shadowy limbo, sending shivers down Drake's spine. He whirled around, his heart pounding, to find Gabriel standing mere feet away, a twisted smirk playing on his scarred lips.

"Surprised to see me alive?" Gabriel's voice dripped with mock amusement. "Crazy we made it this far together, isn't it?"

Drake's mind reeled, struggling to reconcile the impossibility before him. His voice came out hoarse, barely above a whisper. "How? I killed you. I saw you die."

Gabriel's eyes glinted with malevolent glee. "Don't you remember, Drake? My blood is your blood now." He took a step closer, his presence suffocating. "You may have killed my body, but a part of my spirit lives through you."

The words hit Drake like a physical blow. He stumbled back, memories of the blood ritual flooding his consciousness. The implications were staggering, threatening to shatter what little remained of his sanity.

"No," Drake muttered, more to himself than to Gabriel. "That's not possible. I'm not you. I can't be."

But even as he spoke, doubt gnawed at him. How many times had he felt that sinister whisper in the back of his mind, urging him towards darkness? How often had he questioned his own actions, wondering if they were truly his own?

Gabriel's laughter echoed through the void, a haunting reminder of the bond they now shared. Drake clenched his fists, fighting against the wave of despair threatening to engulf him. He had to find a way to break this connection, to reclaim his identity and protect his family from the monster that now resided within him.

5 - 6

Drake's world shattered as the realization struck him. "So all this time... this killing has been me?" His voice trembled, heavy with the weight of his newfound understanding.

Visions assaulted him, vivid and merciless. He saw himself crouched in the basement, methodically cutting the gas line to the stove. The memory of his son's terrified face flashed before him as he recalled pushing the boy into oncoming traffic. His hands, once instruments of protection, now appeared before him stained with the blood of Bird and Kierstead.

"No," Drake whispered, his throat constricting with horror. "It can't be."

But the memories continued their relentless assault. He felt the sharp pain in his thumb as he dislocated it to escape the handcuffs, the act now tainted with the knowledge of his true motives.

Gabriel's scarred face twisted into a cruel smile. "It's a lot to take in, isn't it?" he taunted, circling Drake like a predator. "The truth can be... liberating."

Drake's legs gave way, and he sank to his knees, overwhelmed by the enormity of his actions. "All this time... it was me," he murmured, his voice hollow with disbelief.

"Correct," Gabriel purred, his tone dripping with satisfaction. He knelt beside Drake, his breath hot against his ear. "Now, how about we deal with your family and do this loop over again? This day's been going on forever, after all."

The suggestion sent a chill down Drake's spine. He looked up at Gabriel, seeing his own reflection in those malevolent eyes. The loop, the endless cycle of violence and despair – it all made a twisted kind of sense now. But as he grappled with this horrifying revelation, a spark of defiance ignited within him. He might be tainted, but he wasn't lost. Not yet.

Rematch

1⁻² The air crackled with tension as Drake lunged at Gabriel, his fist cutting through the stagnant atmosphere of the abandoned funhouse. The impact never came. Gabriel sidestepped with an eerie grace, his scarred face twisting into a cruel smirk.

"Still so predictable, Drake," Gabriel taunted, his voice a chilling whisper. "Your guilt makes you weak."

Drake's jaw clenched, memories of his past mistakes flashing before his eyes. He shook them away, focusing on the present. "You won't win this time," he growled, circling his nemesis.

Gabriel's laugh echoed off the corrugated metal walls. "I already have. Your family, your world—they're all mine now."

Rage boiled within Drake, fueling his next attack. He feinted left, then drove his right fist into Gabriel's midsection. The satisfying thud of flesh meeting flesh filled the air, but Gabriel barely flinched.

As they grappled, Drake's mind raced. How could he defeat this embodiment of his own failures? The weight of worlds pressed down on him, threatening to crush his resolve.

"You can't save them, Drake," Gabriel hissed, his breath hot against Drake's ear. "You couldn't even save yourself."

Drake broke free, panting heavily. "You're wrong," he spat, blood trickling from a split lip. "I won't let you destroy everything I love."

Gabriel's eyes glinted with malice. "Love? You abandoned them, remember? Left them to my tender mercies."

The words cut deeper than any physical blow. Drake faltered, his guard dropping for just a moment. It was all Gabriel needed.

With lightning speed, Gabriel struck, his fist connecting with Drake's jaw. The world spun, and Drake stumbled backward, struggling to maintain his footing.

"Face it, Drake," Gabriel sneered, advancing slowly. "You're outmatched. Always have been."

Drake's vision blurred, his legs trembling beneath him. He couldn't let it end like this. His family, the very fabric of reality it all depended on him.

"No," Drake whispered, more to himself than his adversary. "I won't give up. Not again."

With a surge of desperate strength, Drake launched himself at Gabriel once more. Their bodies collided, a tangle of limbs and fury. For a moment, it seemed Drake might prevail, his hands closing around Gabriel's throat.

But then, with a twist of his body and a knee to Drake's stomach, Gabriel reversed their positions. The cold concrete floor slammed against Drake's back, knocking the wind from his lungs.

Gabriel loomed over him, a triumphant gleam in his eyes. "It's over, Drake. Time to face your failures."

As darkness crept into the edges of his vision, Drake's last coherent thought was of his family—their faces fading like smoke on the wind.

3 - 3

Gabriel's fist connected with Drake's temple, sending a shockwave of pain through his skull. The world tilted, colors bleeding into a nauseating swirl. Drake's legs buckled, his body suddenly heavy as lead.

"You never could see the bigger picture, could you?" Gabriel's voice echoed, distant and distorted.

Drake struggled to focus, his thoughts fragmented. "My family... I have to..."

"They're not real, Drake. None of this is." Gabriel's words cut through the haze, sharp as a blade.

With monumental effort, Drake raised his head, meeting Gabriel's gaze. "No... you're wrong. I can feel them. They're real to me."

Gabriel sighed, a flicker of something—pity?—crossing his face. "And that's always been your weakness."

Drake's vision darkened at the edges, consciousness slipping away like sand through his fingers. He reached out, grasping at empty air, trying to hold onto the image of his wife's smile, his son's laugh.

"I'm sorry," he whispered, unsure if the words even left his lips.

The last thing Drake saw was Gabriel's hand, fingers splayed, descending towards his face. Then, darkness claimed him, dragging him down into a void where neither reality nor illusion held sway.

As Drake's body went limp, Gabriel stood over him, a mix of triumph and regret etched on his features. "Rest now, old friend. The real fight is yet to come."

Bird Down

1-2 The room swam into focus, a kaleidoscope of shadows and muted colors. Drake's eyes, now vessels for Gabriel's malevolent consciousness, swept across the space with predatory precision. Every object, every flicker of movement, registered with heightened clarity.

A soft groan pierced the silence. Drake's head snapped toward the source, his lips curling into a cruel smile as he spotted Franklin Bird stirring on the floor. The older man's distinguished features were contorted in pain, his silver hair matted with sweat and grime.

"Ah, Franklin," Drake's voice purred, a unsettling blend of his own timbre and Gabriel's mocking tone. "How kind of you to rejoin us."

As he approached, Drake's thoughts raced with a mixture of Gabriel's cold calculation and lingering echoes of his own consciousness. *How easy it would be to end this now,* Gabriel mused within him. *To snuff out this tiresome obstacle.*

Franklin's eyes widened as he took in Drake's altered demeanor. "Drake," he croaked, struggling to push himself up. "You need to fight this. Whatever's controlling you—"

"Controlling?" Drake chuckled, the sound devoid of warmth. "Oh, Franklin. You always did underestimate the power of true conviction."

With fluid grace that belied the inner turmoil, Drake withdrew the gun from his waistband. The weight of it felt different now, an extension of Gabriel's will rather than the burden it had once been to Drake.

"Wait," Franklin pleaded, his usual commanding presence diminished by fear. "Think about what you're doing. The consequences—"

Drake tilted his head, studying Franklin with detached fascination. "Consequences? I'm afraid you won't be around to witness those, old friend."

As he raised the gun, a fleeting image of his family flashed through Drake's mind—a reminder of what he once fought for. But Gabriel's influence crushed it mercilessly, leaving only cold resolve.

"Goodbye, Franklin," Drake whispered, his finger tightening on the trigger. "May your next life be less... troublesome."

The gunshot echoed through the room, a stark punctuation to the end of Franklin Bird's story. Drake watched dispassionately as the light faded from the man's eyes, feeling neither triumph nor remorse. There was only the next move in Gabriel's grand design, and the growing anticipation of what was to come.

3-3

Gabriel turned to face Linda and Harrison, his eyes gleaming with a predatory satisfaction. Linda instinctively pushed Harrison behind her, her slender frame a fragile barrier against the looming threat. The air seemed to thicken, heavy with the weight of unspoken fears and shattered hopes.

"Let's end this before it gets too painful," Gabriel said, his voice a chilling blend of Drake's familiar timbre and something alien, something cruel.

Linda's heart raced, her breath catching in her throat. She fought to keep her voice steady, to project a calm she didn't feel. "Drake, please. This isn't you. Think of your family, think of Harrison."

Gabriel's lips curled into a mirthless smile. "Oh, Linda. Always the optimist, aren't you? Clinging to hope even when it's long gone."

Behind her, Harrison's fingers dug into her arm, his voice barely a whisper. "Mom, what's happening to Dad?"

Linda's mind raced, searching for words to explain the inexplicable. How could she tell her son that the man before them wasn't his father anymore? That the multiverse they'd sought to explore had birthed this nightmare?

"Your father..." she began, her voice faltering. "He's... lost right now, sweetheart. But we're going to help him find his way back."

Gabriel laughed, the sound sharp and discordant. "Find his way back? There's no going back, Linda. Only forward. Into a new reality, one where the constraints of your petty morality don't apply."

As he spoke, Linda's gaze darted around the room, desperately seeking an escape route. But Gabriel's imposing figure blocked the only exit, his presence a suffocating reminder of their vulnerability.

"You don't have to do this," Linda pleaded, her calm facade cracking. "Whatever Gabriel's promised you, whatever power he's offering, it's not worth destroying everything you've built, everything you love."

For a moment, something flickered in Gabriel's eyes—a hint of doubt, a glimmer of the man Linda once knew. But it vanished as quickly as it appeared, replaced by a cold, unyielding resolve.

"Love?" Gabriel spat the word like a curse. "Love is a weakness, a chain that binds us to this flawed reality. I've seen beyond it now, Linda. And I'm offering you and Harrison the chance to see it too."

He raised the gun, its barrel glinting in the harsh light. "One last time, Linda. Join me, or face the consequences of your shortsightedness."

Linda's mind reeled, torn between her instinct to protect Harrison and her desperate hope that somewhere, deep inside, Drake was still fighting. She tightened her grip on Harrison, feeling his rapid heartbeat against her back.

"I won't let you hurt our son," she said, her voice finding strength in maternal ferocity. "And I won't give up on you, Drake. Not now, not ever."

The Battle for Control

1 -2
The room seemed to grow colder, the air thick with a suffocating tension as Gabriel—inhabiting Drake's body—took a deliberate step toward Linda and Harrison. His sinister grin never wavered, and his eyes, once familiar and warm, now burned with a malevolent gleam.

Harrison's breath caught in his throat as he watched the figure of his father approach. But it wasn't his father anymore, not really. The way Gabriel moved in Drake's body was all wrong—a predator's stalk, smooth and calculated, nothing like his dad's familiar gait. Harrison's gaze flicked to the family photo on the mantle, his father's warm smile frozen in time, a stark contrast to the cruel twist of his lips now.

The floorboards creaked under Gabriel's weight, each step echoing in the oppressive silence. Harrison's heart thundered in his chest, a desperate rhythm urging him to run, to hide. But he couldn't leave his mother. He couldn't abandon his father.

"You're not welcome here," Harrison said, his voice barely above a whisper. He cleared his throat, trying to summon courage he didn't feel. "This isn't your home."

Gabriel's laugh was a low, menacing rumble that sent shivers down Harrison's spine. It was his father's voice, but the sound was all wrong, like nails on a chalkboard.

"Oh, but it is now, boy," Gabriel purred, his eyes—Drake's eyes—gleaming with malice. "Your father was kind enough to invite me in."

Harrison's fists clenched at his sides, nails digging crescents into his palms. The pain grounded him, cutting through the fog of fear that threatened to overwhelm him. He thought of all the times his father had protected him, had stood strong in the face of danger. Now it was Harrison's turn.

"Get out of my dad," he growled, his voice trembling with both fear and determination. The words hung in the air between them, a challenge and a plea.

For a moment, something flickered in Gabriel's eyes—a flash of recognition, perhaps, or a hint of the man trapped within. But it was gone in an instant, replaced by cold amusement.

"Your father can't hear you," Gabriel taunted, taking another step forward. "He's gone, little one. And soon, you will be too."

3 - 4
Gabriel chuckled darkly, the sound reverberating through the room like distant thunder. "Your dad? Oh, Harrison. He's not coming back. This body belongs to me now."

The words struck Harrison like a physical blow, stealing the breath from his lungs. He stared at the thing wearing his father's face, searching desperately for any sign of the man he knew. But there was nothing—only the cold, calculating gaze of a predator.

Time seemed to slow as Harrison's mind raced. He thought of all the moments he'd shared with his dad—camping trips, late-night talks, the comforting weight of his hand on Harrison's shoulder. Was it all gone? Just like that?

"No," Harrison whispered, more to himself than anyone else. "I don't believe you."

He took a half-step forward, driven by a desperate need to reach the father he knew was still in there somewhere. But before he could move any further, he felt his mother's hand close around his arm.

"Harrison, don't—" Linda's voice was tight with fear, her fingers digging into Harrison's skin. He could feel her trembling, her maternal instinct warring with her own terror.

Harrison turned to look at his mother, seeing the fear in her wide blue eyes. But beneath that fear was something else—a fierce determination that mirrored his own. She was trying to protect him, just as she always had. But this time, Harrison knew he couldn't stand back and let her face this alone.

"Mom," he said softly, his voice steadier than he felt. "We can't give up on Dad. He's still in there. I know it."

5 - 6

Harrison's heart pounded in his chest, each beat a thunderous reminder of what was at stake. With a sudden, violent twist, he wrenched his arm free from his mother's grasp. The world blurred around him as he launched himself forward, propelled by a fury he'd never known before.

"Give him back!" Harrison roared, his voice cracking with raw emotion. He collided with Gabriel's chest, the impact jarring every bone in his body. But Harrison didn't care about the pain. All he could focus on was the cold, unfamiliar gleam in his father's eyes.

Gabriel's lips curled into a sneer. "Such spirit," he taunted, easily absorbing the force of Harrison's attack. "Your father would be proud. If he were still here, that is."

Harrison's fists pummeled against Gabriel's torso, each blow fueled by desperation and love. "He is here," Harrison panted, tears stinging his eyes. "Dad, I know you can hear me! Fight him!"

As they grappled, Harrison's mind raced. Is this what it means to fight for someone you love? he wondered. The thought both terrified and emboldened him.

Gabriel's hand shot out, gripping Harrison's shoulder with bruising force. "Your faith is admirable," he hissed, "but misplaced. Your father is gone, boy. Accept it."

"Never," Harrison growled, twisting in Gabriel's grip. He locked eyes with the entity possessing his father's body, searching for any flicker of recognition. "Dad, please. Remember who you are. Remember us."

The struggle continued, a desperate dance of wills. Harrison fought with every ounce of strength he possessed, driven by the unshakeable belief that somewhere, beneath Gabriel's malevolent presence, his father was fighting too.

7 - 8

The collision reverberated through Harrison's body, a dull thud that seemed to echo the pounding of his heart. Gabriel's form barely moved, a mountain unmoved by the tempest of Harrison's fury. The boy's palms stung from the impact, his breaths coming in ragged gasps.

"Is that all you've got?" Gabriel taunted, his voice a cruel mimicry of Drake's familiar tones. "Your father's strength clearly didn't pass down to you."

Harrison gritted his teeth, pushing harder. "You don't know anything about my dad," he spat, his muscles straining. "Or me."

For a brief moment, hope flared in Harrison's chest as Gabriel stumbled, his limp causing a momentary loss of balance. Is this it? Harrison thought. Is Dad fighting back?

But the hope was short-lived. Gabriel's lips twisted into a malevolent grin as he regained his footing. "Nice try, boy," he sneered, hands shooting out to grasp Harrison's shoulders. "But it'll take more than that to best me."

Time seemed to slow as Harrison felt himself lifted off the ground. He caught a glimpse of his own wide-eyed reflection in Gabriel's cold, unfamiliar eyes before the world spun around him.

"Dad, please!" Harrison cried out as he flew through the air. "I know you're in there!"

The impact with the floor drove the air from Harrison's lungs. Pain exploded through his ribs, each breath a sharp agony. He lay there, gasping, his mind reeling. How can I fight something that isn't even human? he wondered desperately. How can I save Dad when I can't even stand up to his body?

9 - 10

"Harrison!" Linda's voice pierced the air, thick with maternal anguish. Her blue eyes, wide with terror, fixed on her son's crumpled form.

Harrison's vision swam, the room tilting as he struggled to focus on his mother's approaching figure. The soft patter of her footsteps seemed to echo in his ears, each one bringing a mixture of relief and dread. Don't come closer, Mom, he thought desperately. He's too dangerous.

But Gabriel moved with startling speed, his scarred face contorting into a mask of malevolence as he whirled to face Linda. The tattered white robe with its green dragon emblem swirled around him, lending an eerie, otherworldly quality to his movements.

"Stay back," Gabriel growled, his voice a low, menacing rumble that seemed to vibrate through the very air.

Harrison's heart hammered in his chest, fear for his mother momentarily eclipsing his own pain. He tried to call out, to warn her, but his voice caught in his throat, strangled by the agony in his ribs.

Linda froze, her slender frame taut with tension. Harrison could see the conflict raging in her eyes – the primal urge to protect her child warring with the very real danger that Gabriel posed.

"Please," Linda whispered, her voice trembling. "He's just a boy."

Gabriel's lips curled into a cruel smirk. "A boy who needs to learn his place," he snarled, taking a threatening step towards Linda.

Harrison's mind raced, searching desperately for a way to help, to intervene. But his body refused to cooperate, each attempt to move sending fresh waves of pain coursing through him. Is this how it ends? he thought bitterly. Are we going to lose everything to this... this thing wearing Dad's face?

The air in the room seemed to grow thicker, heavier with each passing second. Harrison's gaze darted between his mother's terrified face and Gabriel's menacing form, silently willing her to run, to save herself. But he knew she wouldn't. She'd never abandon him, no matter the cost.

And in that moment, as Gabriel loomed over them both, Harrison realized with chilling clarity that their fight was far from over. It had only just begun.

11 - 12

Suddenly, Gabriel's body convulsed. His hand, poised to strike, trembled violently as if battling an invisible force. Harrison's breath caught in his throat, his pain momentarily forgotten as he watched the impossible unfold before him.

Gabriel's eyes widened, a flicker of confusion—or was it fear?—passing across his face. "What... what is this?" he growled, his voice strained and unfamiliar.

Harrison's heart raced. Could it be? He didn't dare to hope, and yet...

"Dad?" he whispered, barely audible.

Gabriel's head snapped towards him, but the malevolent gleam in his eyes had dimmed, replaced by a desperate struggle. His lips parted, and when he spoke, it was as if two voices fought for dominance.

"No," Gabriel-Drake muttered, the words grating against each other. "This is my body."

Harrison watched, transfixed, as his father's familiar tone battled against Gabriel's sinister drawl. The sound sent chills down his spine, a confusing mix of hope and terror coursing through him.

What's happening? Harrison thought, his mind reeling. Is Dad fighting back? Can he actually win?

He wanted to move, to help somehow, but fear and uncertainty kept him rooted to the spot. All he could do was watch as the internal struggle played out before him, praying that somehow, someway, his father would find the strength to break free.

13 - 14

Gabriel staggered backward, his hands clutching at his head as if trying to contain an explosion within. His face contorted in agony, eyes squeezed shut, mouth twisted in a silent scream. Harrison's heart thundered in his chest as he watched, paralyzed by a mixture of fear and desperate hope.

Then, like a mirage shimmering into existence, a faint, ghostly image began to form behind Gabriel. Harrison blinked hard, certain his eyes were playing tricks on him. But no—there it was, growing clearer by the second: the translucent outline of his father, Drake.

"Dad?" Harrison whispered, his voice barely audible even to himself. He wanted to shout, to run to the apparition, but his body refused to move, pinned to the floor by shock and disbelief.

The spectral form of Drake flickered, his features etched with determination. His eyes, though ghostly, burned with the same protective fire Harrison remembered from countless childhood moments.

Gabriel's body convulsed violently, his voice emerging as a guttural growl. "Impossible! You can't—"

"I can," Drake's voice echoed, seeming to come from everywhere and nowhere at once. "And I will."

Harrison's mind raced. Is this real? Can Dad actually come back? The hope that bloomed in his chest was almost painful in its intensity.

"Harrison," Drake's spectral form called out, his voice strained but resolute. "Stay back. I need to—"

But before he could finish, Gabriel's body lurched forward, face twisted in a snarl of rage and desperation. "No!" he roared. "I won't be cast aside again!"

Harrison scrambled backward, his eyes darting between the writhing form of Gabriel and the determined specter of his father. The air crackled with an otherworldly energy, and Harrison could almost taste the desperation of both entities fighting for control.

This is it, Harrison realized, his heart in his throat. The moment that decides everything.

15 - 16

Drake's spectral form surged forward, his ethereal hands grasping at Gabriel's shoulders. "Get out of my body!" he roared, his voice reverberating with a power that seemed to shake the very foundations of the room. His translucent fingers sank into Gabriel's flesh like mist meeting stone, the collision of two realities made visible.

Harrison watched, transfixed, as his father's ghostly form wrestled with the physical manifestation of Gabriel. The air around them shimmered, distorting like a heat haze. Is this really happening? he wondered, his mind reeling. Can Dad actually win this?

Gabriel's body twisted violently, his movements jerky and unnatural as he tried to shake off Drake's spectral grip. His eyes, once cold and calculating, now blazed with a mixture of fury and fear. "You're nothing but a remnant!" he spat, his words dripping with venom. "You don't belong here anymore!"

The raw hatred in Gabriel's voice sent a chill down Harrison's spine. He clenched his fists, willing his father to prevail. Come on, Dad, he thought desperately. You can do this. You have to.

Drake's face, though ghostly, contorted with effort. "This is my body," he growled, his voice echoing with determination. "My family. My world. And I'm taking it back."

Harrison felt a surge of pride at his father's words, mixed with a gnawing fear. What if this doesn't work? What if Gabriel's too strong? The thought of losing his father again, just when hope had been rekindled, was almost unbearable.

17 - 18

"And neither do you," Drake shot back, his voice filled with steely resolve. The words seemed to reverberate through the room, carrying the weight of a man who had traversed realities and faced the abyss of his own guilt.

Gabriel's body lurched, slamming against the wall with a sickening thud. Picture frames crashed to the floor, glass shattering in a cacophony that mirrored the fractured reality before them. Drake's ethereal form clung tenaciously, his spectral fingers digging deeper into the physical plane.

Harrison's heart raced as he watched the surreal struggle unfold. Is this what it means to fight for your soul? he wondered, a mixture of awe and terror coursing through him.

Gabriel's movements became increasingly erratic, his limbs flailing wildly as he fought against Drake's incorporeal assault. "You can't... win," he snarled through gritted teeth, his words punctuated by ragged breaths.

Drake's response was not in words, but in the intensifying of his efforts. His ghostly visage flickered, determination etched into every translucent feature. I won't let you take this from me, he thought fiercely. Not my family. Not my chance at redemption.

The struggle raged on, Gabriel's body careening across the room like a marionette with tangled strings. A bookshelf toppled, sending volumes cascading to the floor in a literary avalanche. The air crackled with an otherworldly energy, the very fabric of reality seeming to warp around the battling entities.

19 - 20

Harrison pushed himself to his feet, his lanky frame trembling with a mixture of fear and determination. His breath came in ragged gasps as he stumbled forward, drawn inexorably toward the supernatural melee before him. The room spun, debris crunching beneath his feet, but his focus remained laser-sharp on the ghostly form of his father.

"Dad!" he shouted, his voice cracking with emotion. The word hung in the air, heavy with all the unspoken fears and hopes that had built up over their fractured existence.

Drake's spectral visage turned, his translucent features contorting with effort. For a moment, father and son locked eyes across the chasm of realities. Harrison saw the man he remembered – the lawyer, the protector, the father who had always been there to chase away the monsters under the bed. Now, that same father was battling a monster far more terrifying than any childhood nightmare.

"Harrison, help me!" Drake's voice echoed with an otherworldly resonance, strained but filled with a fierce determination.

The plea hit Harrison like a physical blow. How can I help? he thought desperately. I'm just a kid. This is so far beyond anything I've ever faced. But as he looked at his father's struggle, a surge of resolve welled up within him. No matter what, I have to try. We're in this together.

21 - 22

Harrison's eyes darted around the chaos-strewn room, searching for anything that might help. His gaze settled on a shattered lamp, its heavy ceramic base lying intact amidst the wreckage. A spark of inspiration ignited in his mind, tinged with both hope and trepidation.

"I... I don't know if this will work," he muttered, his fingers closing around the cool, smooth surface of the lamp base. The weight of it in his hand felt reassuring, a tangible anchor in this surreal battle.

He looked up at his father's spectral form, still locked in combat with the malevolent presence of Gabriel. The sight of Drake's familiar features, now ghostly and translucent, sent a pang through Harrison's heart.

"Dad," he called out, his voice trembling but growing stronger with each word. "I'm here. We're going to fight this together, just like we always have."

Drake's ethereal form seemed to flicker, his attention momentarily divided between the battle and his son. "Harrison," he managed, his voice strained but filled with warmth. "You've always been braver than you know."

The boy's grip tightened on the lamp base, his knuckles whitening. "I learned from the best," he replied, a ghost of a smile playing across his lips. "Now, let's show this creep what the Millers are made of."

As Harrison steeled himself for what came next, a flood of memories washed over him – lazy Sunday mornings, bedtime stories, shoulder rides through the park. Each moment a testament to the unbreakable bond between father and son, a bond that transcended even the boundaries of reality itself.

23 - 24

With a deep breath, Harrison charged forward, his heart pounding in his ears. The lamp felt heavy in his hands, but his determination made it weightless. He swung with all his might, aiming for Gabriel's temple.

The impact reverberated through Harrison's arms as the lamp base struck true. A sickening thud echoed in the room, followed by Gabriel's howl of pain. The sound sent chills down Harrison's spine, but he stood his ground, ready to strike again if necessary.

"You little brat!" Gabriel snarled, his voice a distorted mixture of rage and agony. He staggered backward, his movements jerky and uncoordinated.

Harrison watched in awe as his father's spectral form surged forward, pushing harder against Gabriel's weakening presence. "That's it, son!" Drake's voice echoed, filled with pride and urgency. "We've got him on the ropes!"

As Gabriel's grip on the body faltered, Harrison felt a glimmer of hope. Could they really win this? He tightened his grip on the lamp, ready to swing again if needed. "Get out of my dad!" he shouted, his voice cracking with emotion.

The air around them seemed to thicken, charged with an otherworldly energy. Harrison's skin prickled, and he could almost taste the metallic tang of fear and desperation in the air. But beneath it all, there was something else – the warm, familiar presence of his father, growing stronger with each passing moment.

25 - 26

"Harrison, again!" Drake's spectral voice rang out, urgent and commanding.

Without hesitation, Harrison swung the lamp once more. This time, his aim was true, the heavy base connecting solidly with Gabriel's chest. The impact sent shockwaves through Harrison's arms, and he stumbled back, nearly losing his grip on the makeshift weapon.

Gabriel's body – his father's body – crashed to the floor with a sickening thud. Harrison's heart lurched, torn between triumph and terror. Had he hurt his dad? But there was no time for doubt.

"Dad?" Harrison called out, his voice trembling. He watched, transfixed, as his father's body convulsed on the ground. It was as if two forces were warring within, each struggling for dominance.

Gabriel's face contorted, twisting between expressions of rage and determination. "You... can't... win," he spat out, his words a guttural growl.

Harrison's mind raced. Was it working? Was his dad winning? He gripped the lamp tighter, ready to strike again if needed. "Fight him, Dad," he whispered, willing his father to hear him. "I know you can do it."

The internal battle raged on, visible in every twitch and spasm of the body on the floor. Harrison stood frozen, the weight of the moment pressing down on him like a physical force. He'd never felt so helpless, yet so crucial, in his entire life.

27 - 28

Drake's spectral form shimmered into view, a ghostly silhouette hovering over Gabriel's prone body. With grim determination etched across his translucent features, Drake leaned in, his ethereal hands pressing against Gabriel's chest.

"You're done, Gabriel," Drake growled, his voice a mix of desperation and resolve. "This is my body, my family, and you're not taking them from me."

Gabriel's eyes, cold and malevolent, locked onto Drake's. "You can't... expel me," he hissed, his words strained. "I'm... part of you now."

Drake's spectral form flickered, doubt threatening to unravel his concentration. He thought of Harrison, of Linda, of the life he'd fought so hard to reclaim. No, he couldn't let Gabriel win. Not now, not ever.

"You're wrong," Drake retorted, pushing harder. He could feel Gabriel's presence, a writhing, oily darkness within him. "I've made mistakes, Gabriel. God knows I have. But I won't let you use them against me anymore."

With each word, Drake felt a surge of strength. He pressed his advantage, channeling every ounce of love and determination he possessed. Gabriel's hold began to weaken, his presence receding like a tide pulled back to sea.

"No!" Gabriel roared, his voice fading. "You can't—"

But Drake was beyond listening. With a final, herculean effort, he forced Gabriel's presence out, feeling his own spectral form merge back into his physical body. The sensation was overwhelming – a rush of sensations, emotions, and memories flooding back into place.

Drake gasped, his eyes flying open as he regained full control. He lay there, panting, every muscle trembling with exertion. The room swam into focus, and he saw Harrison standing over him, lamp still clutched in his shaking hands.

"Dad?" Harrison's voice was barely a whisper, hope and fear warring in his eyes.

Drake managed a weak smile. "It's me, kiddo," he rasped. "It's really me."

29 - 30

Drake's body stilled, his chest heaving as he struggled to his knees. The room spun around him, a kaleidoscope of familiar shapes and shadows. He blinked hard, trying to focus, but his vision kept blurring, alternating between crystal clarity and a hazy, red-tinged nightmare.

"Linda," he gasped, reaching out a trembling hand. "Harrison."

His family's faces swam before him, etched with concern and fear. Drake's heart ached at the sight, a surge of love and protectiveness welling up within him. But beneath that warmth, a cold, insidious presence lurked.

Gabriel's voice echoed in his mind, a silky whisper that sent chills down his spine. "You can't keep me out forever, Drake. We both know that."

Drake gritted his teeth, fighting to maintain control. "Get out," he hissed, his voice barely audible.

"Dad?" Harrison's voice cut through the fog. "What's happening?"

Drake looked up, meeting his son's gaze. His eyes flickered, shifting between his own warm brown and Gabriel's icy blue. "I'm... fighting him," Drake managed, his voice strained. "He's still here, but I've got him... for now."

Linda took a cautious step forward. "Drake, is it really you?"

He nodded, swallowing hard. "Mostly. But Gabriel... he's not gone completely. I can feel him, like a shadow at the edge of my mind."

Drake's hands clenched into fists, his knuckles white with the effort of maintaining control. He could feel Gabriel probing, searching for weaknesses, for any crack in his resolve.

"I won't let you win," Drake muttered, his jaw set in determination. "This is my life, my family. You have no place here."

Gabriel's laughter echoed in his mind, cold and mocking. "Oh, Drake. You forget – I am you. Every dark thought, every selfish impulse. I'm the part of you that you try so hard to ignore."

Drake shook his head violently, trying to dispel the voice. He looked up at his family, his anchor in this storm of conflicting identities. "I need your help," he said, his voice hoarse. "I can't fight him alone."

31 - 32

Harrison knelt beside him, gripping his arm tightly. "Dad?" he asked cautiously. The boy's touch was warm, grounding, a lifeline in the tumultuous sea of Drake's mind.

Drake looked at him, his gaze softening slightly. The battle within him raged, but Harrison's presence acted as a beacon, guiding him back to himself. "It's me," he said, his voice strained but sincere. A flicker of Gabriel's influence threatened to surface, but Drake pushed it down, clinging to the love he felt for his son. "At least... mostly me."

The words hung in the air, heavy with implication. Drake's mind raced, torn between relief at regaining control and the gnawing fear that Gabriel could resurface at any moment. He focused on Harrison's face, memorizing every detail as if it might slip away.

"Harrison," Drake thought, his inner voice a mix of pride and anguish, "you shouldn't have to see me like this. To fight battles meant for adults. But you're so brave, so strong. I need that strength now more than ever."

He wanted to reach out, to pull his son into an embrace, but uncertainty held him back. Was he truly in control? Could he trust himself not to harm Harrison if Gabriel suddenly took over?

"I'm sorry," Drake whispered, the words escaping before he could stop them. "For everything you've had to endure because of me."

33 - 34

Linda's tentative approach drew Drake's attention. Her steps were measured, careful, as if treading on unstable ground. The fear in her eyes pierced him, a stark reminder of the danger he now posed to his own family. Yet beneath that fear, a glimmer of hope shone through, tugging at Drake's heart.

"Drake?" Linda's voice wavered, a mixture of longing and apprehension.

He met her gaze, drinking in the sight of her. How many times had he dreamed of this moment, of being reunited with his family? But not like this, never like this.

Drake nodded, the simple motion sending tremors through his body. His hands shook as he tried to brace himself against the floor, muscles straining with the effort of maintaining control. "I've got him... for now," he managed, his voice rough with exertion. "But he's still here."

The admission hung heavy in the air. Drake's mind raced, grappling with the implications of his words. Gabriel's presence lurked just beneath the surface, a malevolent undercurrent threatening to pull him under at any moment.

"Linda," he thought, his inner voice a torrent of conflicting emotions, "I wish I could tell you it's over, that we're safe. But I can't. I don't know how long I can hold on."

The trembling in his hands intensified, a physical manifestation of the war raging within him. Drake clenched his fists, fighting for every second of control, determined to protect his family for as long as he could.

35 - 36

Harrison's grip tightened on Drake's arm, his fingers digging into the fabric of his father's shirt. The boy's touch anchored Drake, a lifeline in the tumultuous sea of his consciousness.

"Then we'll fight him. Together," Harrison declared, his voice steady despite the fear that flickered in his eyes.

Drake's heart swelled with a bittersweet mixture of pride and anguish. His son's unwavering loyalty was both a balm and a burden. He wanted nothing more than to shield Harrison from this nightmare, yet here the boy stood, ready to face the darkness head-on.

A faint smile tugged at Drake's lips, his features softening for a moment. "You're a brave kid, Harrison," he said, his voice tinged with pride and a hint of resignation. "Too brave for your own good."

As the words left his mouth, Drake felt a surge of memories – moments of Harrison's courage throughout their fractured existence. The way his son had navigated this altered reality with a resilience that belied his years. It was inspiring and terrifying in equal measure.

"I can't let him face this," Drake thought, his inner voice tight with resolve. "I have to find a way to end this, to keep him safe. But how?"

The weight of responsibility pressed down on Drake, threatening to crush him. He struggled to his feet, every movement a battle against the darkness that sought to reclaim control.

37 - 37

Drake's vision swam, the room's edges blurring as he fought to maintain his grip on reality. Gabriel's presence churned within him, a malevolent undercurrent threatening to pull him under at any moment. He clenched his fists, nails digging into his palms, using the sharp sting to anchor himself.

"Dad?" Harrison's voice cut through the internal tumult, laced with concern.

Drake forced a smile, though it felt more like a grimace. "I'm okay, son," he lied, his voice rough. "Just... adjusting."

Linda approached cautiously, her eyes searching Drake's face. "How much of you is... you?" she asked, her words barely above a whisper.

The question hung in the air, heavy with implications. Drake closed his eyes, taking stock of the war raging within. Gabriel's essence pulsed at the edges of his consciousness, a dark, insidious presence.

"Mostly me," Drake finally answered, opening his eyes to meet Linda's gaze. "But he's still here, lurking. Waiting."

As if summoned by the acknowledgment, Gabriel's voice slithered through Drake's mind. "You can't keep me out forever, Drake. This body will be mine again."

Drake's jaw clenched, a visible tension rippling through him. "No," he growled, both to Gabriel and aloud. "I won't let you."

Harrison's hand found Drake's, squeezing tightly. "We're with you, Dad. All the way."

The touch grounded Drake, reminding him of what he was fighting for. He looked at his son, then at Linda, drawing strength from their presence. The room came into sharper focus, the shadows receding slightly.

"We need to find a way to exorcise him completely," Drake said, his mind racing. "There has to be a solution, something we're missing."

As he spoke, Drake felt the weight of his past mistakes pressing down on him. The choices that had led to this moment, the lives he'd inadvertently put in danger. But with that guilt came a steely determination. He would make this right, no matter the cost.

"Whatever it takes," he thought, his resolve hardening. "I'll protect them, even if it means losing myself in the process."

A World of Regret

1 ^-2 The shattered remains of the chandelier crunched beneath Drake's feet as he stood in the center of the ruined hotel suite. Smoke curled from charred furniture, and the acrid stench of burnt fabric filled his nostrils. His muscular frame trembled as he looked at Linda and Harrison, their faces illuminated by the flickering emergency lights.

Drake's heart constricted, a physical ache that threatened to consume him. The weight of his choices, the pain he had caused, and the torment this fractured world had inflicted upon his family bore down on him like a crushing tide.

He swallowed hard, his throat tight with unshed tears. "I'm sorry," Drake said, his voice raw with emotion. The words felt inadequate, a paltry offering in the face of such devastation. "For everything. This... this isn't the world I wanted for you."

His gaze swept over Linda's slender figure, her blonde hair matted with dust and debris. The strength in her blue eyes, even now, pierced his soul. Harrison stood beside her, his lanky frame seeming so fragile in this moment. The boy's unruly hair reminded Drake of happier times, of ruffling those locks after a game of catch in the backyard.

How had it come to this? Drake's mind raced, recalling the choices that had led them here. The hubris of thinking he could manipulate reality itself, the desperation to save Linda from a fate he couldn't accept. And now, the bitter irony of having caused even greater suffering in his attempts to prevent it.

"I never meant for any of this to happen," Drake continued, his voice barely above a whisper. "I thought I could fix everything, make it perfect for us. But I was wrong. So terribly wrong."

He took a shaky step forward, his hands clenching and unclenching at his sides. The urge to embrace them, to shield them from the horrors of this world, warred with the knowledge that he was the source of their pain.

"Can you ever forgive me?" Drake asked, the question hanging in the smoke-filled air between them. He held his breath, awaiting their response, knowing he had no right to ask for absolution.

3 - 4

Linda's tear-streaked face softened, her blue eyes shimmering with a complex mixture of emotions. She stepped toward Drake; her movements unsteady but determined. Her trembling hand reached out, fingers stretching towards him like a lifeline.

"Drake..." she whispered, her voice hoarse from crying. The single word carried the weight of their shared history, of love tested by unimaginable circumstances.

Drake's heart constricted, torn between hope and the crushing guilt that threatened to overwhelm him. He wanted nothing more than to take her hand, to feel the warmth of her touch and believe that somehow, they could find their way back from this nightmare.

Harrison's grip on his father's arm tightened, drawing Drake's attention. The boy's brown eyes, so like his own, were wide with a tumultuous blend of fear and hope. His dirty blonde hair fell across his forehead, reminding Drake of how young and vulnerable his son truly was.

"We'll get through this, Dad," Harrison said, his voice cracking slightly. "Together."

The words hit Drake like a physical blow. How could his son still have faith in him after everything that had happened? He didn't deserve such unwavering support, and yet here it was, freely given.

"I don't know if we can," Drake admitted, his voice barely audible. "I've made such a mess of everything. How can we possibly-"

But as he looked at Linda and Harrison, standing there amidst the ruins of their lives, a flicker of something - not quite hope, but perhaps resilience - sparked within him. Maybe, just maybe, if they faced this together...

5 - 6

Drake's lips quivered, his chest heaving as he fought back tears. The weight of his past mistakes and the surreal reality of their situation pressed down on him, threatening to crush his resolve. Yet, the sight of Linda and Harrison, their faces etched with a mixture of fear and unwavering love, compelled him to act.

"I've failed you both so many times," Drake whispered, his voice raw with emotion. "But I swear, I'll make this right."

He reached out, his arms trembling as he moved to embrace them. The desire to feel their warmth, to anchor himself in the love of his family, overwhelmed him. But as his fingers brushed against Linda's shoulder, a sickening jolt of energy coursed through the air.

"What's happening?" Harrison cried out, his eyes widening in terror.

Drake's heart hammered in his chest as he watched in horror. The very air around them seemed to ripple and distort, like heat waves rising from scorched pavement. Linda's form began to flicker, her outline blurring as if she were a faulty hologram.

"No," Drake breathed, panic rising in his throat. "No, no, no!"

He tried to grab hold of them, to somehow keep them tethered to reality, but his hands passed through their bodies as if they were made of smoke. The room around them groaned, the walls seeming to bend and warp in impossible ways.

"Drake!" Linda's voice echoed strangely, as if coming from far away. "What's going on?"

Tears streamed down Drake's face as he watched helplessly. "I don't know," he choked out. "I'm sorry, I'm so sorry. This isn't what I wanted!"

His mind raced, desperately searching for a solution, for any way to stop the terrifying transformation that was beginning to consume his family. But as the world twisted around him, Drake could only watch in abject horror as the nightmare he'd feared most began to unfold before his eyes.

7 - 8

Linda's body seized violently; her eyes wide with terror as she froze mid-step. Her hands flew to her chest, clutching desperately as if trying to hold herself together. A guttural gasp escaped her lips, her knees buckling beneath her.

"Mom!" Harrison cried, his voice cracking with fear. He lunged forward, reaching out to catch her falling form.

Drake watched in helpless horror, his heart shattering at the sight of his wife's pain and his son's desperation. The air around them seemed to thicken, pressing against his skin like an oppressive weight.

"Linda!" Drake's voice was raw with anguish. "What's happening to you?"

Linda's eyes met his, filled with a mixture of confusion and agony. "Drake," she whispered, her voice trembling. "I can't... I can't feel..."

Harrison wrapped his arms around his mother's shoulders, trying to support her. "It's okay, Mom," he said, his words brave despite the tremor in his voice. "We're here. We've got you."

Drake's mind raced, searching frantically for a solution. This wasn't supposed to happen. Not here, not now. Not when he'd finally found them again. The guilt threatened to overwhelm him as he realized the horror he'd inadvertently brought upon them.

"Stay with us, Linda," Drake pleaded, his hand hovering inches from her face, afraid to touch her lest she shatter completely. "Fight it. Please, you have to fight it."

Linda's body continued to convulse; her blonde hair matted with sweat against her forehead. Her blue eyes, once so full of warmth and hope, now clouded with pain and fear.

"I'm trying," she gasped, her fingers digging into Harrison's arm. "But it hurts... everything hurts..."

Drake felt utterly powerless, watching the woman he loved suffer while their son tried desperately to hold her together. The weight of his choices, of the worlds he'd traversed and the chaos he'd unleashed, pressed down upon him with crushing force.

"I'm sorry," he whispered, tears streaming down his face. "I'm so sorry. This isn't the world I wanted for you. I never meant for this to happen."

As Linda's body continued to convulse and Harrison clung to her, Drake could only watch, his heart breaking anew with each passing second. The reality he'd fought so hard to create was unraveling before his eyes, and he was powerless to stop it.

9 - 10

Harrison's desperate lunge toward his mother faltered mid-stride. His body jerked violently, limbs twisting at unnatural angles as if manipulated by some unseen puppeteer. A strangled cry escaped his lips as blood began to seep from his nose, ears, and eyes, mingling with the sweat that now drenched his trembling form.

Drake's heart seized in his chest, his breath catching painfully as he watched the horrific scene unfold before him. His son, his precious boy, was being torn apart by the very forces he had unwittingly unleashed.

"Harrison!" Drake cried out; his voice raw with anguish. He took an involuntary step forward, every fiber of his being screaming to protect his child.

But as Harrison's body continued to contort, Drake found himself stumbling backward, his legs nearly giving out beneath him. The weight of his guilt threatened to crush him, his mind reeling with the consequences of his actions.

"No... no, no, no!" he shouted, his voice breaking. The words tore from his throat, a desperate plea to a universe that seemed determined to punish him for his hubris.

Drake's thoughts raced, a maelstrom of regret and desperation. How could he have been so blind? So arrogant to think he could manipulate reality without consequence? He had only wanted to save them, to give them the life they deserved. Instead, he condemned them to this nightmarish fate.

"Dad..." Harrison's voice, distorted and pained, cut through Drake's spiraling thoughts. "What's... happening to us?"

Drake's heart shattered anew at the fear in his son's eyes. He wanted to reassure him, to promise that everything would be alright. But the lies died on his lips, choked by the overwhelming guilt that threatened to consume him.

11 - 12

Linda's piercing screams shattered the air, her body writhing in agony as her skin rippled like water disturbed by a stone. Her once-gentle features twisted into grotesque shapes, her blonde hair seeming to melt and reform in chaotic patterns. Drake watched in horror as his wife's body began to stretch and contort, her limbs elongating unnaturally.

"Linda!" Drake cried out; his voice hoarse with desperation. "Fight it! Please, you have to fight it!"

But his pleas fell on deaf ears as Harrison's body succumbed to the same terrifying transformation. The boy's lanky frame shuddered violently, his arms and legs bending at impossible angles.

"Dad," Harrison gasped, his wide brown eyes filled with terror and confusion. "What's happening to us? Make it stop!"

Drake's heart shattered at the sound of his son's plea. He wanted nothing more than to rush to their aid, to somehow reverse the nightmarish process unfolding before him. But he remained rooted to the spot, paralyzed by the horrific spectacle.

"I'm sorry," he whispered, tears streaming down his face. "I'm so sorry. I never meant for this to happen."

As he watched, helpless and devastated, Drake's mind raced against the weight of his choices. He had sought to create a better world, to undo the tragedy that had torn his family apart. Instead, he had unleashed something far worse, something beyond his comprehension or control.

The room seemed to pulse with an otherworldly energy as Linda and Harrison's bodies continued their grotesque metamorphosis. Drake could only stand there, a broken man, witness to the unthinkable consequences of his actions, as the very fabric of reality began to unravel around them.

13 - 14

The cacophony of their agonized screams crescendoed, blending into a horrifying symphony that tore through Drake's soul. Linda and Harrison's bodies, once separate entities, now lurched towards each other with an unnatural magnetism. Their flesh, no longer bound by the laws of nature, stretched and warped like molten wax.

"No, please!" Drake cried out; his voice hoarse with desperation. He lunged forward, fingers grasping at the air between them, as if he could somehow pull them apart by sheer force of will. "Linda! Harrison!"

But his efforts were futile. Before his eyes, their forms began to meld, skin fusing in grotesque patterns that defied comprehension. Harrison's youthful features momentarily surfaced in the writhing mass, contorted in pain, before being swallowed by the undulating flesh.

Drake's mind reeled, unable to process the horror unfolding before him. This was worse than any nightmare he could have imagined. The guilt that had been his constant companion now threatened to crush him entirely.

"Stop it!" he screamed, tears streaming unchecked down his face. His hands clawed at his hair; eyes wild with despair. "Leave them alone! Take me instead!"

But there was no entity to bargain with, no force he could plead with. This was the cruel, unintended consequence of his own actions, the price of his hubris in thinking he could reshape reality without dire repercussions.

As Linda and Harrison's merged form continued to twist and contort, Drake fell to his knees, overwhelmed by the weight of his failure. "I'm sorry," he whispered, his voice breaking. "I only wanted to save you. I never meant for this to happen."

The room seemed to pulse around him, reality itself straining under the weight of this abomination. And still, the horrifying transformation continued, unabated and merciless.

15 - 16

The amalgamation of flesh and bone before Drake pulsated sickeningly, growing larger with each passing second. Linda's graceful features briefly surfaced; her blue eyes wide with terror before being subsumed once more into the undulating mass. Harrison's lanky form stretched and distorted, his limbs melting into the grotesque entity that now dominated the ruined hotel suite.

"Dad... help us..." Harrison's voice, now warped and inhuman, echoed from within the writhing blob. The sound tore at Drake's heart, a cruel reminder of his son's unwavering faith in him.

Drake stumbled backward, his legs trembling beneath him. "I don't know how," he choked out, his voice barely above a whisper. "I don't know how to fix this."

Linda's soothing tone, now twisted into something unrecognizable, joined the cacophony. "Drake... why?"

The question hung in the air, heavy with accusation and sorrow. Drake's mind raced, searching desperately for an answer, for some way to undo the horror he had wrought.

"I wanted to give you a better world," he said, his words tumbling out in a frantic rush. "I thought I could change things, make it right. But I was wrong. So terribly wrong."

The entity shuddered, its surface rippling as if in response to his words. Drake watched, transfixed by the grotesque spectacle, as the last vestiges of his family's humanity dissolved into the monstrous creation before him.

17 - 18

Drake's legs gave way beneath him, and he crashed to his knees, his hands flying up to clutch at his hair. The rough carpet bit into his skin, but the pain was nothing compared to the anguish that tore through his chest.

"No... please, no..." he whispered, his voice cracking under the weight of his despair. His eyes, wide with horror, remained fixed on the pulsating mass that had consumed his family.

The entity before him shifted and writhed, a living nightmare born from his misguided ambitions. Drake's fingers tightened in his hair, pulling at the roots as if the physical pain could somehow anchor him to reality.

"I never meant for this," he said, his words barely audible over the sickening sounds emanating from the blob. "I was trying to save you, to give you the life you deserved."

His mind reeled, recalling the fateful decisions that had led to this moment. The car accident, the alternate realities, the desperate attempts to manipulate the fabric of existence – it all seemed so foolish now, in the face of this abomination.

"What have I done?" Drake's voice trembled, thick with self-loathing. "How could I have been so blind?"

The grotesque entity continued its unholy transformation, oblivious to Drake's anguish. He watched, paralyzed by guilt and fear, as the last traces of Linda and Harrison's individuality were swallowed by the writhing mass.

19 - 20

The amorphous blob shuddered violently, its gelatinous surface rippling like a disturbed pond. Drake's breath caught in his throat as it stretched towards him, tendrils of viscous matter reaching out with unsettling purpose. Within its undulating mass, he glimpsed fleeting impressions of familiar features - Linda's gentle eyes, Harrison's crooked smile - flickering in and out of existence like cruel phantoms.

"God, no," Drake choked out, his muscular frame trembling uncontrollably. He wanted to run, to flee from this nightmare, but his legs refused to obey. "This can't be real. It can't be."

His thoughts raced, a maelstrom of regret and desperation. How had his quest to save them led to this abomination? The weight of his choices pressed down on him, threatening to crush his very soul.

Suddenly, a sound emerged from the entity - a haunting amalgamation of voices that sent chills down Drake's spine.

"Drake..." it called, the distorted tones carrying echoes of Linda's warmth and Harrison's youthful enthusiasm. The name hung in the air, a ghostly reminder of all he had lost.

Drake's chest tightened, his heart pounding so hard he thought it might burst. "Linda? Harrison?" he whispered, hope and horror warring within him. "Are you... are you still in there?"

The blob pulsated, as if in response to his words. Drake leaned forward, torn between the instinct to flee and the desperate need to reconnect with his family.

"I'm here," he said, his voice breaking. "I'm so sorry. I'll find a way to fix this, I swear."

But even as the words left his lips, Drake wondered if there was any way to undo the horror he had unleashed. The faces within the mass seemed to blur and shift, a cruel reminder of the irreversible nature of his actions.

21 - 22

Drake recoiled, his body shaking as he crawled backward. The plush carpet beneath his hands felt like sandpaper against his skin, every nerve in his body screaming for escape. His breath came in ragged gasps, tears streaming down his face as he stared at the monstrosity before him.

"I'm sorry," he sobbed, the words tearing from his throat. "I'm so sorry..."

The weight of his guilt crushed him, memories of his past mistakes flashing through his mind. How many times had he tried to fix things, only to make them worse? His determination to save his family, to unravel the mystery of this twisted reality, had led to this grotesque outcome.

The entity before him trembled violently, its amorphous form collapsing inward with a sickening squelch. Drake's stomach lurched as he watched, unable to look away. Then, with a horrifying suddenness, it expanded outward, filling the room with its presence.

An unbearable sound erupted from the creature - a cacophony of wails and guttural groans that seemed to come from everywhere at once. It was as if the very air was screaming, the pain of a thousand souls condensed into a single, agonizing moment.

Drake clapped his hands over his ears, but it did nothing to block out the noise. "Please," he whispered, his voice lost in the din. "Please, make it stop."

But there was no reprieve, no escape from the nightmare he had created. As the sound washed over him, Drake could only curl into himself, haunted by the knowledge that this was the price of his ambition, the cost of his desperate attempts to save those he loved.

23 - 24

Drake's chest heaved as he struggled to breathe, each inhalation a ragged gasp that tore at his lungs. The monstrous abomination before him pulsated and writhed, its form a grotesque mockery of the family he had sought to protect. He could barely discern Linda's delicate features or Harrison's youthful countenance within the shifting mass, their essence dissolving into the nightmarish creation.

"What have I done?" Drake choked out, his voice barely audible over the entity's wails. His fingers dug into the plush carpet, anchoring him to reality as his world crumbled around him.

The creature lurched forward, tendrils of flesh reaching out towards him. Drake flinched but found himself unable to move, paralyzed by the weight of his guilt and the horror before him.

"I never wanted this," he whispered, tears streaming down his face. "I just wanted to save you."

As if in response, the entity shuddered, emitting a sound that was part sob, part roar. Drake's heart shattered at the realization that somewhere within that mass, his wife and son might still be aware, might still be suffering.

"I'm sorry," he repeated, the words hollow in the face of such monstrosity. "I thought I could fix everything. I thought I could be the hero."

Drake's mind raced, desperately searching for a solution, a way to undo the damage he had caused. But as the abomination continued to grow and change, he knew with crushing certainty that there was no going back. This was the consequence of his actions, the price of his hubris.

"Linda... Harrison..." he murmured, reaching out a trembling hand towards the entity. "I failed you. I failed everyone."

25 - 26

The walls of the hotel suite began to waver, shimmering like a mirage in the desert heat. Drake's vision blurred, reality itself seeming to bend and warp around the monstrous entity that had once been his family. The ornate chandelier above flickered erratically, casting dancing shadows across the room that seemed to take on a life of their own.

"What have I done?" Drake choked out, his voice hoarse and barely audible. He watched in horror as the wallpaper peeled away in strips, revealing glimpses of an impossible void beyond. The very fabric of this constructed world was unraveling before his eyes.

The creature let out a haunting wail, its amorphous form pulsating with an otherworldly energy. Drake's heart raced, his lawyer's mind frantically searching for a solution, a loophole in the cosmic contract he'd unwittingly signed.

"There has to be a way," he muttered, pushing himself to his feet despite the room's violent tremors. "I can't let it end like this. I won't."

But even as determination surged through him, Drake felt the crushing weight of inevitability. He had played with forces beyond his understanding, and now the bill had come due. The floor beneath him rippled like water, and he struggled to maintain his balance.

"I'm sorry," he whispered again, the words falling from his lips like a mantra. "I'm sorry. I'm sorry."

With each repetition, Drake's voice grew softer, drowned out by the cacophony of a dying reality. He closed his eyes, unable to bear witness to the destruction he had wrought, but unable to escape the guilt that consumed him.

27 - 27

"I'm sorry. I'm so, so sorry." Drake's words hung in the air, each syllable a leaden weight upon his soul. He opened his eyes, meeting the grotesque, shifting gaze of the entity that had once been his family. The room continued to disintegrate around them, reality fraying at the edges like worn fabric.

"I never meant for this," he whispered, his voice cracking. Drake took a tentative step forward, his hand outstretched towards the writhing mass. "Linda... Harrison... if you're in there, please..."

The creature shuddered, emitting a low, mournful sound that seemed to reverberate through Drake's very bones. He flinched but didn't retreat, his lawyer's resolve steeling him against the horror before him.

I have to fix this, Drake thought desperately. There has to be a way to undo what I've done. His mind raced, grasping at fragments of memories, searching for a clue, a loophole, anything that might salvage this nightmare.

"Dad..." The word emerged from the creature, a warped echo of Harrison's voice. "Why?"

Drake's heart clenched, tears streaming down his face. "I wanted to give you everything," he choked out. "A perfect world. I was wrong. So terribly wrong."

As he spoke, Drake's gaze darted around the disintegrating room, searching for an anchor in the chaos. The void beyond the crumbling walls seemed to pulse with malevolent energy, hungry to consume what remained of this fractured reality.

The Universe Takes Control

1 ^{- 2} Rachel's heart pounded in her chest as she pressed her back against the cold concrete wall of the stairwell. The cacophony from above assaulted her senses—gunshots cracking like thunder, screams piercing the air, and a sickening, wet sound she couldn't quite place. It was as if reality itself was being torn apart.

She closed her eyes, trying to steady her breathing. "I should have stayed in the car," she whispered to herself, her voice barely audible over the chaos. But the sudden silence that followed had been too much to bear. The quiet had pulled at her, an invisible force drawing her from the safety of the vehicle and into this nightmare.

As Rachel began her ascent, each step felt heavier than the last. The dread in her stomach twisted and churned, a physical manifestation of her fear. Her mind raced with possibilities, each more terrifying than the last.

"Drake," she muttered, her voice trembling. "What have you done?"

The stairwell seemed to stretch endlessly before her, a cruel illusion born of her anxiety. Rachel's fingers trailed along the wall, seeking some anchor to reality as she climbed. The rough texture beneath her fingertips was a stark contrast to the surreal situation unfolding above.

"I should have insisted on coming with him," she thought, guilt gnawing at her insides. "I knew the risks. I knew what could happen if he made the wrong choice."

As she neared the top of the stairs, Rachel paused, her breath catching in her throat. The sounds had ceased, replaced by an eerie stillness that seemed to pulse with potential energy. She stood there, frozen, her scientific mind grappling with the impossible situation before her.

"This isn't just about Drake anymore," she realized, her eyes widening. "This is about the very fabric of our reality."

With trembling fingers, Rachel reached for the door handle. The cool metal against her skin sent a shiver down her spine, a final warning from her instincts to turn back. But she knew she couldn't. Whatever lay beyond that door, whatever horror Drake had unleashed, she had to face it.

"Please," she whispered, though to whom or what, she wasn't sure. "Please let there be a way to fix this."

Taking a deep breath, Rachel steeled herself for what was to come. The weight of Sir Mordred's codex seemed to press against her, a reminder of the knowledge she carried and the responsibility that came with it. With one final moment of hesitation, she turned the handle, ready to step into the unknown and face the consequences of Drake's actions.

3 - 4

Rachel pushed the door open slowly, her heart pounding in her chest. As it swung inward, the scene before her unfolded like a nightmare made flesh. Her breath caught, and for a moment, the world seemed to tilt on its axis.

"Oh god," she whispered, her voice barely audible over the wet, pulsing sounds emanating from within the room.

The horror that greeted her defied explanation, a grotesque amalgamation of flesh and bone that writhed in the center of the suite. Rachel's scientific mind reeled, desperately trying to categorize and understand what she was seeing, even as her instincts screamed at her to run.

"Drake?" she called out, her eyes scanning the room for any sign of him. "Drake, where are you?"

A muffled groan answered her, and she spotted him kneeling near the abomination, his face a mask of anguish and disbelief. Rachel took a cautious step forward, her mind racing with possibilities and theories.

"This is it," she thought, her heart sinking. "The universe's correction. We've pushed too far, and now it's pushing back."

As she approached Drake, Rachel's eyes never left the pulsating mass before them. Her scientific curiosity warred with her revulsion, and she found herself analyzing its movements, its very existence.

"It's trying to reconcile conflicting realities," she realized, the pieces falling into place. "But at what cost?"

Rachel knew that whatever happened next would determine not just their fate, but the fate of countless realities. The weight of that knowledge pressed down on her, threatening to crush her resolve. But she steeled herself, drawing on the determination that had carried her through years of isolation and ridicule.

"We can fix this," she said, as much to herself as to Drake. "We have to."

5 - 6

Rachel's gaze swept across the devastated suite, her mind struggling to process the carnage before her. Shards of shattered glass crunched beneath her feet as she stepped over a toppled lamp, its shade askew and stained with something dark and viscous. The acrid smell of copper and decay assaulted her nostrils, making her eyes water.

"My God, Drake," she whispered, her voice trembling. "What happened here?"

Drake didn't respond, his attention fixed on the horror at the room's center. Rachel followed his gaze, and her breath caught in her throat. Where Linda and Harrison should have been, there was only a writhing mass of flesh, pulsing and undulating like some grotesque, living sculpture.

"Linda? Harrison?" Rachel's scientific mind raced, trying to make sense of the impossible. "How... what is this?"

As if in response, the blob shifted, and for a moment, Rachel caught a glimpse of Linda's face emerging from the mass, her blue eyes wide with terror before being swallowed again by the undulating flesh.

Drake's voice was hollow when he finally spoke. "I did this. I brought them here, and now... now the universe is trying to correct itself."

Rachel's heart ached at the pain in his words. She wanted to comfort him, to tell him it wasn't his fault, but the truth of the situation was undeniable. Instead, she asked, "How long has it been like this?"

"Minutes? Hours?" Drake shook his head. "I don't know anymore. Time feels... wrong here."

As Rachel watched, Harrison's features briefly surfaced, his youthful face contorted in a silent scream before disappearing once more. The sight sent a chill down her spine, reminding her of the urgency of their situation.

"We need to do something," she said, her mind already racing through possibilities. "There has to be a way to separate them, to undo this."

But even as the words left her mouth, Rachel knew the truth. This was beyond science, beyond reason. This was the fabric of reality coming undone, and they were at its epicenter.

7 - 8

The entity writhed, its amorphous form twisting and contorting in ways that defied logic. Suddenly, it let out a blood-curdling scream, a sound that resonated at a frequency that seemed to vibrate the very air around them. The noise was unlike anything Rachel had ever encountered in her years of scientific research—a haunting amalgamation of human agony and something utterly alien.

Rachel's stomach churned violently, her body's instinctive reaction to the horror before her. She swallowed hard, fighting against the nausea that threatened to overwhelm her. Her analytical mind struggled to process the scene, to find some rational explanation for the abomination that Linda and Harrison had become.

"Oh my God," she whispered, her hand flying to her mouth. The words escaped her lips unbidden, a rare display of raw emotion from the usually composed scientist. Her fingers trembled against her lips, and she could taste the acrid tang of fear on her tongue.

As she stood there, frozen in shock, Rachel's mind raced. This was the consequence of their actions, the price of meddling with the fabric of reality. She had warned Drake about the risks, had tried to make him understand the delicate balance they were disrupting. But even she hadn't anticipated something this horrific.

"This isn't just a simple temporal anomaly," Rachel managed to say, her voice barely audible over the entity's agonized wails. "It's a complete breakdown of spacetime cohesion. The multiverse is... it's trying to rectify the paradox we've created."

She took a shaky step forward, her scientific curiosity warring with her instinct for self-preservation. "Drake," she called out, her eyes never leaving the pulsating mass, "we need to act fast. This isn't just about Linda and Harrison anymore. If we don't find a way to stabilize this, the effects could ripple out across multiple realities."

9 - 10

Drake's knees hit the floor with a dull thud, his body surrendering to the weight of despair. The once-confident lawyer, now a broken man, knelt before the writhing mass that had been his family. Tears carved glistening trails down his ashen cheeks, mixing with the blood and grime that caked his face.

"What's happening? What's happening to them?" His voice cracked, raw with anguish and disbelief. Drake's eyes, wild with panic, sought Rachel's, desperately searching for answers, for hope, for anything to cling to in this nightmare.

Rachel's heart clenched at the sight of Drake's utter devastation. The man who had defied death, who had traversed realities to save his family, now looked utterly lost. She opened her mouth to respond, but the words caught in her throat.

The entity before them pulsed grotesquely, Linda and Harrison's distorted features emerging and submerging in a horrific dance. Drake reached out a trembling hand towards the abomination, his fingers stopping just short of touching it.

"I did this," he whispered, his voice barely audible over the entity's tortured moans. "I thought I was saving them, but I've damned them to... to this."

Rachel took a cautious step forward, her scientific mind racing to process the impossible scene before her. The air crackled with an otherworldly energy, raising goosebumps on her skin. She knew they were witnessing something beyond the scope of conventional physics—a correction on a cosmic scale.

11 - 12

Rachel's voice shook but remained steady as she spoke, her words carrying the weight of a profound realization. "It's the universe," she said, her eyes fixed on the writhing mass before them. "It's trying to correct itself."

Drake's head snapped up, his gaze locking onto Rachel. His brow furrowed, desperation and disbelief etched into every line of his face. "What does that mean?" he asked, his voice hoarse and tinged with a desperate hope for understanding.

Rachel's mind whirled, trying to find the right words to explain the incomprehensible. She could feel the pull of cosmic forces in the room, an invisible tide threatening to sweep them all away. The air seemed to thicken, making each breath a conscious effort.

"The fabric of reality," she began, her hands gesturing as if trying to grasp the concept physically, "it's been stretched too thin. Your choices, Drake, they've created paradoxes, inconsistencies that the universe can't sustain."

Drake's eyes darted between Rachel and the grotesque amalgamation of his family. His jaw clenched, muscles working beneath his skin as he struggled to process her words. "But I was trying to save them," he whispered, more to himself than to Rachel. "How could saving them be wrong?"

Rachel took another step closer, her lab coat rustling in the eerie stillness of the room. She could see the weight of guilt crushing Drake, his broad shoulders hunched under an invisible burden. Part of her wanted to offer comfort, but she knew the harsh truth was their only hope now.

13 - 14

Rachel's eyes locked onto the pulsating mass of flesh that had once been Drake's family. Her voice wavered, tinged with a sorrow that seemed to seep into the very air around them. "They weren't supposed to be here, Drake. They were meant to die—and keep dying—until you found a way to break the cycle. But you didn't. You made the wrong choice, and now the universe is taking control."

The words hung heavy in the air, each syllable a hammer blow to Drake's already fractured psyche. He stared at the writhing entity, his mind reeling as he tried to reconcile the horror before him with the family he had fought so desperately to save.

Suddenly, the mass let out a piercing wail that seemed to shake the very foundations of reality. Its form twisted violently, distorted faces emerging and submerging in a nightmarish dance. Drake clutched his head in anguish, his own scream joining the cacophony.

"I remembered my mistake!" he shouted, his voice raw with pain and desperation. Tears streamed down his face, cutting through the grime and blood. "I chose this world when I was supposed to die. I know that now." His eyes, wild with a mix of realization and terror, locked onto Rachel. "But what do I do to stop this?"

As he spoke, Drake's mind raced through a kaleidoscope of memories—the accident, the choices, the countless iterations of failure. He could feel the weight of every wrong decision pressing down on him, threatening to crush him beneath their collective guilt.

15 - 16

Rachel's gaze softened, her eyes reflecting a mixture of sorrow and understanding. The chaos of the room seemed to fade into the background as she focused solely on Drake, her voice dropping to an almost whisper. "You need to finish what you started. You were supposed to die, Drake. That's the only way to fix this."

Her words hit Drake like a physical blow, forcing the air from his lungs. He stumbled backwards, his legs threatening to give out beneath him. The room spun, and for a moment, he thought he might be sick.

"That's why the injuries carried over," Rachel continued, her voice barely audible over the entity's muffled wails.

Drake's mind whirled, trying to process her words. He glanced down at his body, suddenly hyper-aware of every ache and pain that had plagued him since his arrival in this world. The phantom burns that sometimes flared across his skin, the persistent limp he could never quite shake—all of it suddenly took on a new, terrifying significance.

He looked up at Rachel, confusion and pain etched deeply into the lines of his face. "The injuries?" he asked, his voice cracking. "What are you talking about?"

As he spoke, Drake's hand unconsciously moved to his side, where an old wound throbbed with renewed intensity. He couldn't shake the feeling that his body was trying to tell him something—a message written in scars and lingering pain that he had been too blind to read until now.

17 - 18

Rachel knelt beside him, her hand hovering near his shoulder, not quite touching. Her eyes, filled with a mix of compassion and scientific certainty, locked onto his. "Every injury you've carried over—the burns, the limp, the pain—they weren't just coincidences. They were signs. The universe has been telling you what you needed to do all along."

Drake's mind reeled, each word hitting him like a hammer blow. He could feel the phantom pain of every injury flaring to life, as if his body was corroborating Rachel's theory. The burn on his arm tingled, his knee ached, and a dull throb pulsed behind his eyes. He closed them, trying to shut out the cacophony of sensations.

"No," he whispered, more to himself than to Rachel. "That can't be right. I survived. I'm here."

But even as he spoke, a part of him knew. The nagging feeling that had followed him since he'd arrived in this world, the constant sense of displacement—it all suddenly made a horrifying kind of sense.

Drake's breath hitched as Rachel's words sank in, the weight of his realization pressing down on him like a crushing tide. His eyes snapped open, meeting Rachel's gaze with a look of dawning comprehension and terror.

"I was always meant to die," he whispered, his voice trembling. The words felt foreign on his tongue, as if speaking them aloud made them irrevocably true.

His mind raced, replaying every moment since his arrival in this world. The joy of seeing his family alive, the desperate attempts to make things right—all of it now tainted by the knowledge that it was never meant to be.

Drake's hands clenched into fists, his knuckles white with tension. "How?" he asked, his voice barely audible. "How could I have been so blind?"

19 - 20

Rachel's eyes glistened, a single tear tracing a path down her cheek. "Yes," she said softly, her voice barely above a whisper. "That's the balance. That's the only way this ends."

The words hung heavy in the air, each syllable a leaden weight upon Drake's shoulders. He felt his chest constrict, his breath coming in short, ragged gasps. The room seemed to spin around him, the grotesque mass that was once his family pulsating in his peripheral vision.

"Balance," Drake repeated, the word tasting bitter on his tongue. His mind raced, memories flashing before his eyes—every moment of joy, every fleeting embrace with his family, now tainted by the cruel reality of his situation. He clenched his fists, feeling the familiar ache in his knuckles, a reminder of injuries that should have healed long ago.

Rachel reached out, her hand hovering near his shoulder but not quite touching, as if afraid he might shatter at her touch. "Drake, I—"

"No," he cut her off, his voice steadier than he felt. "I understand now. I've been fighting against the current this whole time, haven't I?" He let out a bitter laugh, running a hand through his disheveled hair. "Some lawyer I am, arguing with the universe itself."

Drake pushed himself to his feet, wincing at the twinge in his knee—another sign he'd been too blind to see. He turned to face the writhing mass in the center of the room, his jaw set in determination. The screams had lessened, but the air still thrummed with an otherworldly energy.

"I chose this world when I was supposed to die," he said, more to himself than to Rachel. "I thought I was saving them, but I was just prolonging their suffering." His voice cracked on the last word, but he pressed on. "And mine."

Drake's resolve crystallized, a cold certainty settling in his chest. He turned back to Rachel, his eyes burning with a mix of sorrow and determination. "I know what I have to do now," he said, his voice low but unwavering. "It's time to set things right."

21 - 22

Drake turned back to the writhing mass that had once been his family, his heart constricting painfully in his chest. The grotesque blob pulsated, and for a brief, horrifying moment, he saw Linda's face emerge from the fleshy horror. Her eyes, wide with terror and pain, locked with his before being swallowed back into the undulating mass.

"I can't lose them again," Drake choked out, his voice cracking under the weight of his anguish. His hands clenched into fists at his sides, knuckles white with the strain of holding himself together. The coppery scent of blood and decay assaulted his nostrils, a grim reminder of the reality he'd been desperately trying to avoid.

Rachel stepped closer, her presence a steady anchor in the chaos. "You already lost them," she said gently, her words cutting through the air like a knife. "And you're going to keep losing them, over and over, until you do what's right."

Drake's mind reeled, memories of countless iterations flashing before his eyes. How many times had he watched them die? How many times had he tried to save them, only to fail again and again?

"This world isn't real, Drake," Rachel continued, her voice tinged with a mix of sorrow and urgency. "It's a prison. And the only way to set them free is to set yourself free."

The truth of her words settled over Drake like a heavy shroud. He stared at the nightmarish entity before him, his throat tight with unshed tears. "How?" he whispered, the single word laden with desperation and fear. "How do I end this?"

23 - 24

Drake closed his eyes, the weight of his decision pressing down on him like a physical force. Tears streamed down his face, etching paths through the grime and blood that caked his skin. The room seemed to spin around him, the air thick with the scent of decay and the echoes of his family's distorted screams.

"If that's what it takes," he said, his voice barely more than a whisper, heavy with resignation. The words tasted bitter on his tongue, a final admission of defeat in a battle he'd been fighting across countless realities.

He felt a gentle touch on his shoulder and opened his eyes to see Rachel standing before him, her expression grim but resolute. The determination in her eyes sparked a flicker of hope in Drake's chest, a fragile lifeline in the maelstrom of his emotions.

"I'll help you, Drake," Rachel said, her voice steady despite the tremor in her hand. "But you have to make the choice."

Drake's mind raced, memories of his past lives flashing before him in a dizzying kaleidoscope. The weight of his injuries – the burns, the limp, the constant pain – suddenly took on new meaning. They weren't just remnants of past failures; they were signposts, guiding him towards the truth he'd been too afraid to face.

"I've been running for so long," Drake murmured, more to himself than to Rachel. He turned his gaze to the writhing mass that had once been his family, feeling a surge of love and sorrow that threatened to overwhelm him. "But I can't keep living this lie, can I?"

Rachel shook her head, her red hair catching the dim light. "No, you can't. The universe demands balance, Drake. It's time to restore it."

Drake took a deep, shuddering breath, steeling himself for what was to come. The room seemed to pulse around him, reality itself holding its breath in anticipation of his decision.

"Tell me what I need to do," he said, his voice growing stronger with each word. "I'm ready to end this, once and for all."

25 - 26

Drake's legs trembled as he rose to his feet, the weight of countless lifetimes bearing down on his shoulders. He faced the grotesque entity that had once been Linda and Harrison, his heart constricting at the sight. The mass pulsated weakly, its agonized screams now reduced to pitiful whimpers. It was as if the very fabric of reality sensed the impending resolution.

"It's almost over," Drake whispered, a mixture of relief and dread coursing through him. He ran a hand through his disheveled hair, feeling the phantom pain of burns that had long since healed. "They won't suffer much longer."

Rachel stepped closer, her presence a comforting anchor in the chaos. "Are you sure you're ready for this, Drake?" she asked, her voice laced with concern and scientific curiosity.

Drake turned to face her, his brown eyes meeting her penetrating gaze. In that moment, he felt the full weight of his decision, the crushing responsibility of setting right what he had unwittingly distorted.

"I've never been more certain of anything in my life," he said, his voice steadier than he felt. "Or should I say, in all my lives?"

A wry smile tugged at the corner of his mouth, a final nod to the dark humor that had sustained him through this ordeal. With a deep breath that seemed to fill his entire being, Drake squared his shoulders and locked eyes with Rachel.

"Let's end this," he declared, his tone resolute. The words hung in the air, heavy with finality and the promise of redemption. "Tell me what I need to do to set them free – to set us all free."

A Dark Intervention

1^{-2} Drake's gaze lingered on the gun lying on the bloodstained floor, its dark metal gleaming faintly in the dim light. The weight of Rachel's words and the grotesque horror of what his family had become pressed down on him like a suffocating force. His mind reeled, struggling to reconcile the reality before him with the life he once knew.

"Drake," Rachel's voice cut through the oppressive silence, tinged with a mixture of fear and determination. "You don't have to do this. We can find another way."

He couldn't bring himself to look at her, his eyes fixed on the weapon that promised an end to this nightmare. The memory of his family's twisted forms flashed through his mind, a cruel reminder of his failure to protect them.

"What other way is there, Rachel?" Drake's voice was barely above a whisper, raw with emotion. "I've tried everything. I've failed them. I've failed everyone."

His fingers twitched, longing to reach for the gun. The weight of his guilt, the burden of his knowledge about the multiversal anomaly, it all seemed too much to bear. He could feel Rachel's eyes on him, pleading silently.

Taking a shaky breath, he reached for the weapon, his fingers curling around the cold steel. The familiar weight of it in his hand brought a perverse comfort. He stood, trembling, and raised the gun to his temple.

"Please," Rachel's voice cracked, her scientific detachment crumbling in the face of his despair. "Your blood, your very existence, it's the key to everything. We can't lose you now."

Drake's hand shook, the barrel of the gun pressing against his skin. He closed his eyes, memories flooding his mind – the car accident, the alternate realities, the lives he'd lived and lost. The cold metal against his temple was a stark contrast to the warmth of tears he hadn't realized were falling.

"I'm sorry, Rachel," he choked out, his finger tensing on the trigger. "I can't bear to see them suffer anymore. I can't keep fighting when every choice I make seems to make things worse."

The room fell silent, save for the sound of Drake's ragged breathing. In that moment, suspended between life and death, between universes, he felt the full weight of his existence pressing down upon him.

3 - 4

"This has to end," Drake whispered, his voice barely audible over the faint, agonized sounds coming from the blob that had once been Linda and Harrison. The grotesque mass of flesh pulsated in the corner, a horrific reminder of what his choices had wrought. Each whimper and gurgle from the amalgamation of his wife and son sent a fresh wave of nausea through him.

His finger trembled against the trigger, the cold metal a stark contrast to the feverish heat of his skin. In his mind's eye, he saw Linda's warm smile, heard Harrison's carefree laughter – memories now tainted by the abomination before him. How had it come to this? The weight of his failures crushed down upon him, each breath a struggle against the tide of despair threatening to drown him.

"I'm sorry," he murmured, though whether to Rachel, his family, or the universe itself, he couldn't say. "I can't fix this. I can't—"

But before he could pull the trigger, a mocking voice pierced the air, shattering the moment of terrible resolution. The words sliced through the room like a knife, dripping with malice and dark amusement.

Drake's eyes snapped open, his body going rigid. The gun wavered in his grip as a chill ran down his spine, recognition and dread mingling in his gut. He knew that voice, knew it all too well, and its presence here could only mean one thing: whatever hell he'd thought he'd escaped had found him once again.

5 - 6

"You really think I'd let you kill me again?"

The words hung in the air, heavy with menace and dark amusement. Drake's breath caught in his throat, his hand trembling as he lowered the gun. His mind reeled, struggling to process the implications of that chilling statement.

"Gabriel," he whispered, the name tasting like ash on his tongue. "How... how are you here?"

A low, mirthless chuckle echoed through the room, seeming to come from everywhere and nowhere at once. Drake's eyes darted around, searching for the source, but found only shadows.

"Oh, Drake," Gabriel's disembodied voice crooned, "I'm always here. In every reality, every timeline. You can't escape me."

Drake's jaw clenched, a mixture of fear and defiance surging through him. "No," he growled, "I won't let you control me again. This ends now."

He raised the gun once more, determination steeling his resolve. But as his finger tightened on the trigger, an invisible force seized him. It was as if icy tendrils had wrapped around his limbs, freezing him in place.

Panic clawed at Drake's chest as he struggled against the unseen grip. His muscles strained, tendons standing out on his neck, but he couldn't move an inch. The gun remained fixed in his outstretched hand, a cruel mockery of his impotent defiance.

"What's happening?" he gasped, his voice barely above a whisper. "I can't... I can't move."

Gabriel's laughter filled the room, a sound that sent shivers down Drake's spine. "Did you forget so quickly, Drake? Your body, your will – they belong to me now."

7 - 8

As if summoned by his own malevolent laughter, Gabriel's figure materialized from the shadows. The dim light caught the twisted landscape of his scarred face, casting eerie shadows that seemed to dance across his disfigured features. His lips curled into a sadistic grin, revealing teeth that gleamed unnaturally white against his burned flesh.

Drake felt his stomach lurch. The very air around Gabriel seemed to thicken, pressing in on him from all sides. It was as if the room itself was bending to the will of this nightmarish apparition. Every instinct in Drake's body screamed at him to run, to fight, to do anything but stand there frozen in place.

"Gabriel," Drake managed to choke out, his voice barely more than a whisper.

Gabriel's eyes locked onto Drake's, and in that moment, Drake felt as if he were falling into an abyss of endless malice. The oppressive energy emanating from Gabriel's presence made Drake's skin crawl, each hair standing on end as if electrified.

"Look at you," Gabriel sneered, his voice a grating whisper that seemed to scrape against Drake's eardrums. "Still clinging to the illusion of control."

Drake's mind raced, searching desperately for a way out of this nightmare. But even as he struggled, a part of him knew the futility of his efforts. He had been here before, trapped in Gabriel's twisted game.

Gabriel's burned lips curled upward, his expression a mockery of amusement. When he spoke again, his tone dripped with malice, each word a venomous barb aimed directly at Drake's heart. "I told you before, Drake. You don't get to make the rules here. This is my game."

The words hung in the air between them, heavy with the weight of their shared history and the horrors yet to come. Drake felt a chill run down his spine as he realized that once again, he was nothing more than a pawn in Gabriel's cruel machinations.

9 - 10

Drake's muscles seized, his body going rigid as if gripped by an invisible vise. The gun in his hand felt impossibly heavy, his fingers locked around its cold metal. He strained against the unseen force, every fiber of his being fighting for control, but his limbs refused to obey.

Panic surged through him, his heart thundering in his chest. Each breath came in short, sharp gasps as the reality of his situation crashed over him. He was trapped, not just in this nightmarish world, but within his own body.

"This can't be happening," Drake thought, his mind reeling. "I was supposed to end this, to protect them all."

His eyes darted frantically around the room, seeking escape, seeking help, but finding only the grotesque remains of what had once been his family and the impassive face of Rachel watching from afar.

"Fight it," he commanded himself silently. "You've faced worse. You've sacrificed everything before. You can do it again."

But even as he rallied his willpower, a cold dread settled in the pit of his stomach. This felt different, more absolute than before. The oppressive weight of Gabriel's control seemed to press down on his very soul.

"No," Drake murmured, his voice trembling with a mix of fear and defiance. "No, not again." The words came out barely above a whisper, a desperate plea to a universe that seemed bent on his suffering.

As he stood there, paralyzed by forces beyond his comprehension, Drake's mind raced through memories of his past life, of the family he'd lost and found again, of the weight of guilt that had driven him to this moment. He had thought he was ready to end it all, to make the ultimate sacrifice once more. But now, faced with the terrifying prospect of becoming a puppet in Gabriel's twisted game, he realized how desperately he wanted to live, to fight, to make things right.

11 - 12

Gabriel stepped closer, his scarred face twisting into a grotesque parody of a smile. The smell of burnt flesh and decay wafted from him, making Drake's stomach churn.

"Oh, but yes, Drake," Gabriel's voice slithered through the air, each word dripping with malice. "You see, you're not just trying to end your misery. You're trying to end mine. And we can't have that, now can we?"

Drake's jaw clenched, his eyes burning with a mixture of fury and despair. He wanted to lash out, to scream, to fight back against this monstrous apparition from his nightmares. But his body remained frozen, a prisoner in its own skin.

"You're wrong," Drake managed to grunt out, his words strained as if fighting against an invisible gag. "This isn't about you. It's about saving them... saving everyone."

Gabriel's laughter echoed through the room, a sound devoid of mirth. "Always the hero, aren't you, Drake? But you forget – your actions ripple across realities. Your death here doesn't just end your story. It unravels mine."

As Gabriel spoke, Drake felt a horrifying shift in his arm. The gun, still clutched in his rigid fingers, began to move of its own accord. Panic flooded his system as he realized what was happening.

"No," he thought desperately. "Not this. Anything but this."

The barrel of the gun slowly turned away from his own head, seeking a new target. Drake's heart pounded in his chest, each beat a desperate prayer that he could regain control before it was too late.

13 - 14

Drake's arm trembled violently, his muscles straining against the invisible force guiding his movements. The gun, once a potential instrument of his own demise, now became a terrifying threat to others. His fingers, white-knuckled and rigid, tightened around the grip as if trying to anchor the weapon in place.

"This can't be happening," Drake thought, his mind racing. Images of his family, of the world he was trying to save, flashed before his eyes. The weight of his responsibility, the lives hanging in the balance, pressed down on him with suffocating intensity.

Sweat beaded on his brow as he fought against Gabriel's control. His arm continued its agonizing trajectory, each inch of movement a battle lost. The cool metal of the gun seemed to burn against his palm, a constant reminder of the danger it posed.

"Stop it," Drake gasped, his voice strained and raw with desperation. The words clawed their way out of his throat, a plea to both Gabriel and himself. "Let me go!"

His eyes darted around the room, searching for any sign of help, any chance of breaking free from this nightmare. But he knew, with a sinking feeling in his gut, that this was a battle he might not be able to win alone.

15 - 16

Gabriel's laughter cut through the tense silence, a chilling sound that sent shivers down Drake's spine. It echoed off the walls, filling the room with an oppressive, malevolent energy.

"You've always been stubborn, Drake," Gabriel's voice dripped with cold amusement, each word a dagger of ice. "But you're not in control anymore."

Drake's heart raced, pounding against his ribcage like a caged animal desperate for escape. He could feel the weight of Gabriel's presence, an invisible force guiding his every move. His arm continued its inexorable motion, muscles trembling with the effort of resistance.

Rachel's sharp intake of breath drew Drake's attention. He saw her standing a few feet away, her face a mask of horror as she watched the gun's barrel slowly turn towards her. The sight of fear in her eyes, usually so confident and determined, sent a fresh wave of anguish through Drake.

"No," he thought desperately, "not Rachel. Please, not her."

Rachel took a hesitant step backward, her lab coat rustling softly in the stillness of the room. Her voice, usually so steady and assured, trembled as she spoke. "Drake... what are you doing?"

The question hung in the air, heavy with accusation and fear. Drake wanted to scream, to explain that this wasn't him, that he would never willingly threaten her. But Gabriel's control was absolute, leaving him trapped in his own body, a prisoner watching helplessly as events unfolded around him.

17 - 18

Drake's face contorted with anguish, every muscle straining against the invisible force controlling him. Sweat beaded on his forehead, his brown hair plastered to his skin. The gun in his hand felt impossibly heavy, a leaden weight of impending tragedy.

"I can't stop it," he choked out, his voice raw with desperation. The words scraped against his throat, each syllable a battle against Gabriel's iron grip. "I'm sorry. I can't control myself."

Drake's mind raced, searching frantically for a way out of this nightmare. He'd faced impossible odds before, fought against the very fabric of reality, but this – this helplessness was a new kind of terror. The guilt of his past mistakes, the weight of his family's fate, all paled in comparison to the horror of becoming a weapon against the one person who still believed in him.

Rachel's eyes widened, realization dawning in their depths. Her gaze darted from Drake's trembling form to the shadows beyond, where Gabriel's presence lurked. The fear in her expression hardened, transforming into something fiercer, more defiant.

"Gabriel," she hissed, her voice a mixture of fear and fury. The name hung in the air like a curse, charged with the weight of all they'd endured.

Drake watched as Rachel's brilliant mind worked, connecting the pieces of their twisted reality. Even now, faced with imminent danger, her determination shone through. It was that unwavering spirit that had drawn him to her, that had given him hope when all seemed lost.

"Fight it, Drake," he silently urged himself, desperate to break free of Gabriel's control. "For Rachel, for your family, for everything we've been through – fight!"

19 - 20

Drake's hand steadied, the invisible force guiding his movements with cruel precision. The gun, once a potential escape from his torment, now aimed squarely at Rachel's chest. Tears streamed down Drake's face, each drop a testament to his internal struggle against the puppeteer pulling his strings.

Rachel's lab coat fluttered as she took a step back, her eyes never leaving Drake's. In them, he saw not just fear, but a glimmer of the brilliant mind working overtime, searching for a solution even in this dire moment.

"Don't do this!" Rachel cried, her voice cracking with desperation. The sound tore at Drake's heart, reminding him of all they'd been through together, all the mysteries they'd unraveled.

Drake's throat constricted, choking back words he longed to say. 'I'm trying,' he thought frantically, 'God, Rachel, I'm trying.' His fingers trembled against the trigger, fighting against the inexorable pressure building there.

"Rachel," he managed to gasp out, "the codex... there has to be something..."

Even as he spoke, Drake's mind raced. The multiversal anomaly, the constructed reality, the sacrifices he'd made – all of it seemed to converge on this moment. He'd given his life once to save everything. Now, trapped in this nightmare, he feared he might take a life instead.

21 - 21

Gabriel's grin widened, his scarred face twisting into a grotesque mask of triumph. The dim light cast deep shadows across his disfigured features, accentuating the malice in his eyes.

"Say goodbye, Doctor Summers," he mocked, his voice low and dripping with cruel satisfaction.

Drake's heart hammered against his ribs, each beat a desperate plea for control. He could feel Gabriel's presence like a suffocating shroud, pressing in on all sides. The gun in his hand felt impossibly heavy, a leaden weight of impending tragedy.

"No," Drake choked out, his voice barely above a whisper. "Rachel, I... I can't stop it."

Rachel's eyes darted between Drake and Gabriel, her brilliant mind clearly racing. "Drake, listen to me," she said urgently, her tone steady despite the fear etched on her face. "This isn't you. Remember the codex, the patterns we discovered. You're stronger than his influence!"

Gabriel laughed, the sound grating against Drake's nerves. "Touching, Doctor. But your science can't save you now."

Drake's finger twitched on the trigger, a bead of sweat rolling down his temple. 'Fight it,' he screamed internally. 'For Rachel, for Harrison, for everything we've sacrificed.' The memory of his son, lost in an uncertain future, surged through him, igniting a spark of defiance against Gabriel's control.

The Return of Holly Kierstead

1‑2 The world swam into focus, a blur of muted colors and sharp edges. Holly's chest burned, each breath a desperate struggle against the weight crushing her ribs. The acrid tang of gunpowder lingered in the air, mingling with the metallic scent of her own blood.

"Breathe," she commanded herself, forcing air into her aching lungs. "Just breathe."

As consciousness fully returned, memories flooded back—the frantic chase, the confrontation, the deafening crack of gunfire. Holly's hand instinctively moved to her chest, fingers probing the dented fabric of her bulletproof vest. Relief washed over her as she realized the extent of her luck.

"Thank God for small favors," she muttered, her voice hoarse and unfamiliar to her own ears. The words carried a bitter irony; how many times had she narrowly escaped death in pursuit of the truth?

Holly winced as she slowly pushed herself into a sitting position, her body protesting every movement. The world tilted dangerously, and she closed her eyes, willing the dizziness to pass. In the darkness behind her eyelids, Rebekah's face swam into view—worried, loving, pleading with her to be careful.

"I'm sorry, love," Holly whispered, guilt twisting in her gut. How many times had she promised Rebekah she'd come home safe? How many more close calls could their relationship endure?

As the initial shock began to fade, Holly's analytical mind kicked into gear. She surveyed her surroundings, noting potential escape routes and points of cover. The detective in her couldn't help but catalog evidence, even as her body screamed for rest.

"Focus, Kierstead," she chided herself, pushing aside the flood of emotions threatening to overwhelm her. There would be time for introspection later. For now, she had a job to finish.

With a grimace, Holly forced herself to her feet, swaying slightly as she found her balance. The pain in her chest was a constant reminder of her mortality, but also of her determination. She had come too far, sacrificed too much, to give up now.

"One step at a time," she murmured, her voice steadier now. "Just keep moving forward."

As Holly steeled herself for what lay ahead, she couldn't shake the feeling that this was more than just another case. Something fundamental had shifted, and she stood on the precipice of a truth that would change everything. With a deep breath and a silent prayer, she took her first step into the unknown.

3‑4

Holly's fingers closed around the familiar grip of her backup weapon, the cool metal grounding her in the chaos. She drew it from her ankle holster with practiced ease, its weight a comforting anchor as she rose unsteadily to her feet.

"Get it together," she muttered, willing her legs to stop shaking. Each breath sent a fresh wave of pain through her chest, but Holly pushed it aside, her mind sharpening with focus.

The cacophony of screams and a distant gunshot propelled her forward, her detective instincts overriding the body's protests. As she approached the hotel suite, Holly's analytical mind raced, piecing together the fragments of information she'd gathered.

"What the hell have you gotten yourself into this time, Drake?" she wondered, her voice barely above a whisper. The bond between partners ran deep, but Holly couldn't shake the feeling that this case was unraveling into something far beyond their usual fare.

With each step, the sounds of chaos grew louder. Holly's grip tightened on her weapon, her senses heightened to a razor's edge. She paused at the suite's entrance, taking a final steadying breath.

"Into the fire," she murmured, steeling herself for whatever horrors awaited beyond. With a swift, decisive motion, Holly pushed open the door, her gun raised and ready as she stepped into the maelstrom of carnage that lay within.

5 - 6

The scene inside the suite froze Holly in her tracks, her seasoned detective's eyes struggling to comprehend the nightmarish tableau before her. The acrid stench of copper and something far more alien assaulted her nostrils, causing her stomach to lurch.

"Christ almighty," she breathed, her voice barely audible over the cacophony of screams that filled the room.

Her gaze was inexorably drawn to the center of the chaos, where a grotesque, pulsating mass dominated the space. Its fleshy, undulating surface defied natural law, writhing and contorting in ways that made Holly's mind recoil.

As she watched, paralyzed by the sheer impossibility of what she was witnessing, the blob's surface rippled. For a fraction of a second, Linda Miller's face emerged from the viscous mass, her features contorted in a silent scream of anguish before being swallowed once more by the undulating flesh.

Holly's breath caught in her throat. "Linda?" she whispered, her analytical mind desperately grasping for an explanation that could make sense of this horror.

Before she could process further, another face materialized within the blob—Harrison, his young features twisted in confusion and terror. The sight of the boy trapped within this unnatural prison ignited a fierce protective instinct in Holly.

"Hold on, kid," she muttered, her grip tightening on her weapon as she fought against the urge to rush forward. "We're going to get you out of there."

The rational part of Holly's mind screamed that this was impossible, that she was witnessing something beyond the realm of science or reason. Yet the detective in her, the part trained to observe and analyze, couldn't help but search for patterns, for some thread of logic in this madness.

"What the hell are we dealing with here?" she wondered aloud, her eyes darting around the room, seeking any clue that might shed light on this grotesque phenomenon. "And how in God's name do we stop it?"

7 - 8

"Oh my God," Holly whispered, her grip tightening on the gun. The weight of it anchored her to reality as her mind reeled from the grotesque spectacle before her.

Her gaze shifted, taking in the carnage that surrounded her. Blood streaked the walls in violent arcs, a macabre Jackson Pollock painting come to life. Shattered furniture littered the floor, wood splinters and fabric scraps testament to a struggle of unimaginable intensity.

Near the pulsating blob, Holly's eyes locked onto a familiar figure. Drake stood unsteadily, his usually commanding presence diminished by the tremor in his hand as he clutched a gun. The sight of him, so changed from the man she knew, sent a chill through her core.

"Drake," she called out, her voice barely audible above the ambient horror of the room. "What have you done?"

He didn't respond, his gaze fixed on the writhing mass. Holly's mind raced, piecing together the fragments of the scene before her. The blood, the destruction, the monstrous blob that had consumed Linda and Harrison - all of it pointed to a nightmare beyond comprehension.

"This can't be real," Holly thought, her detective's instincts warring with the impossible reality before her. "But if it is, how do I even begin to make sense of it?"

She took a cautious step forward, her gun raised. "Drake," she tried again, louder this time. "Talk to me. What's happening here?"

9 - 10

Holly's eyes fell upon a crumpled form on the floor, her heart sinking as she recognized the vibrant red hair, now dulled and matted with blood. Rachel Summers lay motionless, a dark pool spreading beneath her still body. The sight of the woman who had sacrificed so much in her pursuit of truth struck Holly like a physical blow.

"Oh God, Rachel," Holly whispered, her voice breaking. The churning in her stomach intensified, a mix of horror and grief threatening to overwhelm her.

She forced herself to look away, her gaze snapping back to Drake. To her dismay, he was raising the gun once more, his eyes fixed on Rachel's prone form with an unsettling intensity.

"Drake, stop!" Holly shouted, her voice echoing in the blood-splattered room. "What are you doing?"

Drake's hand trembled, but his aim remained steady. "I have to finish this, Holly," he said, his voice hollow. "It's the only way to set things right."

Holly's mind raced, trying to reconcile the man before her with the partner she once knew. "This isn't you, Drake. Think about what you're doing!"

"You don't understand," Drake replied, his eyes never leaving Rachel. "None of this was supposed to happen. We were never meant to survive."

Holly inched closer, her own weapon raised. "Then help me understand. Talk to me, Drake. What did Rachel know? Why are you doing this?"

As she spoke, Holly's gaze darted between Drake and Rachel, her heart pounding. She silently willed Rachel to move, to show any sign of life, but the woman remained still.

"I'm sorry, Holly," Drake said, his finger tightening on the trigger. "But this is bigger than all of us."

11 - 12

Without hesitation, Holly stepped forward, her voice firm and commanding. "Drake!"

The word hung in the air, heavy with urgency and desperation. Holly's heart pounded in her chest, each beat a reminder of the precious seconds ticking away. She watched Drake intently, searching for any sign of recognition in his haunted eyes.

He didn't respond. His arm moved almost mechanically, the barrel of the gun steady as it pointed toward Rachel once more. The sight sent a chill down Holly's spine. This wasn't the partner she knew, the man who'd shared countless cups of coffee and late-night stakeouts with her. This was someone—something—else entirely.

"Drake, please," Holly tried again, her voice softer now, tinged with a vulnerability she rarely allowed herself to show. "Look at me. Whatever's happening, we can figure it out together."

She took another cautious step forward, her own weapon a reassuring weight in her hand. The acrid smell of gunpowder and the metallic tang of blood filled her nostrils, threatening to overwhelm her senses. Holly pushed the nausea aside, focusing on the task at hand.

What happened to you, Drake? The thought flashed through her mind as she studied his impassive face. The man before her was a far cry from the passionate detective she'd known, the one who'd fight tooth and nail for justice. Now, he seemed more like a puppet, strings pulled by an unseen force.

"I know you're in there somewhere," Holly said, her voice barely above a whisper. "The Drake I know wouldn't do this. He wouldn't give up on finding the truth, no matter how ugly it might be."

She held her breath, hoping against hope for a flicker of recognition, a moment of hesitation—anything that might give her an opening to reach him.

13 - 14

Holly's finger tensed on the trigger, her heart thundering in her chest. Time seemed to slow, each second stretching into an eternity as she watched Drake's finger tighten on his own trigger. The weight of the moment pressed down on her, the knowledge that her next action would irrevocably alter the course of their lives.

"I'm sorry, Drake," she whispered, her voice barely audible over the blood rushing in her ears.

In one fluid motion, honed by years of training and countless hours at the range, Holly squeezed the trigger. The gun kicked in her hand, the sharp report echoing off the walls of the hotel suite.

As the bullet left the chamber, Holly's mind raced. Images flashed before her eyes: Drake's easy smile on their first day as partners, the determined set of his jaw as they worked late into the night on a tough case, the warmth in his eyes when he'd told her she was the best partner he'd ever had.

The shot rang out, crisp and final, cutting through the cacophony of screams from the grotesque blob and the labored breathing of the room's occupants. Holly watched, her chest tight with a mix of dread and resolve, as the bullet found its mark.

"God forgive me," she thought, her eyes never leaving Drake's form. "Because I'm not sure I can forgive myself."

15 - 16

The gunshot's echo reverberated through the room, a haunting resonance that seemed to stretch time itself. For a heartbeat, Drake stood motionless, his eyes wide with shock and betrayal. Then, as if the strings holding him upright had been suddenly cut, he stumbled backward.

Drake's hand flew to his chest, fingers splaying across the rapidly spreading crimson stain on his shirt. His mouth opened, but no sound emerged, only a soft, pained gasp. The gun he'd been holding slipped from his grasp, clattering against the floor with a metallic finality that seemed to punctuate the gravity of the moment.

As he sank to his knees, Drake's mind raced, grappling with the surreal turn of events. This wasn't how it was supposed to end. He'd sacrificed everything, crossed realities, all in a desperate attempt to save his family, to save the world. And now...

"Holly," he managed to choke out, his voice a ragged whisper. "You don't... understand. I had to... had to stop it."

His vision began to blur, the room tilting sickeningly around him. Drake could feel the warmth of his blood seeping through his fingers, each heartbeat pushing him closer to the edge of consciousness. As darkness crept in at the edges of his sight, one thought burned brightly in his fading mind:

"I failed. God help us all, I failed."

17 - 18

Holly's heart thundered in her chest as she advanced, each step measured and deliberate. The weight of her gun felt heavier than usual, her hands trembling almost imperceptibly as she kept it trained on Drake. The acrid scent of gunpowder hung thick in the air, mingling with the metallic tang of blood.

"Don't move," she commanded, her voice steadier than she felt. Her eyes darted around the room, assessing the carnage, before settling back on Drake's crumpled form.

Drake's gaze lifted to meet hers, his eyes clouded with pain yet tinged with an unsettling relief. "Holly..." he murmured, his voice barely more than a whisper.

The familiar way he said her name sent a chill down Holly's spine. This man, this version of Drake, was both familiar and utterly foreign to her. She wrestled with the conflicting emotions surging through her – sympathy for his obvious suffering warred with the horror of what she'd witnessed.

"I need answers, Drake," Holly thought, her mind racing. "What drove you to this? What could possibly justify... this?" The questions burned in her throat, unspoken, as she maintained her defensive stance.

As she stood there, gun unwavering, Holly couldn't shake the feeling that she was standing at the precipice of something far larger and more terrifying than she could comprehend. The room seemed to pulse with an otherworldly energy, and the weight of countless realities pressed down upon her shoulders.

19 - 20

Holly's jaw tightened, her voice sharp as broken glass. "Don't you dare say my name."

The words hung in the air, heavy with unspoken accusations and shattered trust. Holly's grip on her gun tightened, her knuckles white against the dark metal. Her heart hammered against her ribs, each beat a reminder of how close she'd come to death.

Her eyes darted to Rachel, who lay motionless on the floor, red hair splayed out like a halo of blood. "Rachel," Holly thought, a wave of dread washing over her. "Please, don't be dead. We need you. I need you."

Then her gaze snapped back to the monstrous blob, its pulsating mass defying all logic and reason. The writhing flesh seemed to mock her, faces she once knew and loved now twisted into grotesque parodies of themselves. Linda's terrified eyes, Harrison's contorted mouth – snippets of humanity trapped in an abomination.

"Focus, Holly," she commanded herself silently, even as nausea threatened to overwhelm her. "You can't fall apart now. There's too much at stake."

The horrific reality of the situation settled over her like a suffocating weight, each breath a struggle against the crushing pressure of what she'd witnessed. Yet beneath the fear and revulsion, a spark of determination burned. Holly forced herself to stay focused, to push aside the trembling of her hands and the screaming of her instincts to run.

"What have you done, Drake?" she asked, her voice barely above a whisper, eyes never leaving the grotesque blob. "What have you unleashed?"

21 - 21

Holly's gaze locked onto Drake, her gun still trained on his kneeling form. The blood seeping through his shirt was a stark reminder of the shot she'd just fired, but she couldn't afford to let sympathy cloud her judgment now.

"Drake," she said, her tone steady despite the turmoil within her. "What the hell is going on?"

Drake's eyes, filled with a mix of pain and something darker – regret, perhaps? – met hers. He opened his mouth to speak, but only a ragged cough emerged, flecks of blood staining his lips.

Holly's finger tightened on the trigger. "Answer me, damn it!" she demanded, her voice cracking with the strain of maintaining control.

"I... I didn't mean for this to happen," Drake finally rasped, his words barely audible over the inhuman sounds emanating from the blob. "The multiverse... it's collapsing. I thought I could fix it, Holly. I thought I could save everyone."

A humorless laugh escaped Holly's lips. "Save everyone? Look around you, Drake. This isn't salvation. It's a nightmare."

As she spoke, Holly's mind raced. The Drake she knew – or thought she knew – had always been driven by a need to protect his family. But this... this was beyond comprehension. What could have pushed him to such extremes?

"The anomaly," Drake continued, his voice growing weaker. "It's spreading faster than I anticipated. I had to act... had to try..."

Holly's eyes narrowed, her suspicion warring with a desperate need for answers. "Try what, exactly? What did you do to Linda and Harrison?"

The blob pulsed violently at the mention of their names, and Holly felt her stomach lurch. She forced herself to focus on Drake, on the truth she needed to extract from him before it was too late.

The Final Shot

1 -2 The metallic scent of blood filled the air, mingling with the acrid smell of gunpowder. Drake Miller lay sprawled on the floor, his life seeping away with each labored breath. The polished hardwood beneath him, once pristine, now bore witness to the violent struggle that had unfolded mere moments ago.

Drake's eyes, once sharp and determined, now flickered with a mixture of pain and resignation as they darted between Holly and Rachel. He tried to speak, to warn them, but his voice failed him. The weight of his choices, the burden of his secrets, pressed down upon him with crushing force.

Rachel knelt beside him, her trembling hands desperately trying to stem the flow of blood from his chest. Her once-vibrant red hair hung limp and tangled around her face, framing eyes wide with fear and desperation.

"Holly, listen to me," Rachel pleaded, her voice thick with urgency and despair. "Gabriel was inside him. He wasn't in control."

Drake's mind raced, even as his body grew weaker. He wanted to tell them everything—about the entity that had possessed him, about the terrible things he had been forced to do. But the words wouldn't come. Instead, he focused on Rachel's face, memorizing every detail as if it were the last time he'd ever see her.

Holly stood nearby, her presence a mixture of strength and uncertainty. Drake could sense her internal struggle, the conflict between her duty and her loyalty to him. He wished he could reassure her, tell her that she had made the right choice in shooting him. It was the only way to stop Gabriel, to protect them all.

As his vision began to blur, Drake's thoughts turned to his family, to the life he had fought so hard to protect. He had always known that his pursuit of answers might lead to this moment, but he had never truly been prepared for it. Now, as he lay dying, he realized that some questions would remain forever unanswered.

With the last of his strength, Drake reached out, his bloodied fingers brushing against Rachel's arm. He hoped that somehow, in that fleeting touch, she would understand all that he couldn't say—his love, his regret, his final plea for forgiveness.

The room began to fade around him, the voices of Holly and Rachel growing distant. Drake's last conscious thought was a fervent wish that his sacrifice would be enough, that somehow, they would find a way to stop Gabriel and end this nightmare once and for all.

3 - 4

Holly's expression hardened, her jaw clenching as she kept her gun trained on Drake's head. The weight of the weapon felt heavier than usual in her hands, a tangible reminder of the gravity of the situation. Her detective's instincts, honed over years of experience, had served her well once again.

"I know," she said flatly, her voice devoid of emotion.

The words hung in the air, heavy and suffocating. Holly's mind raced, recalling all the subtle signs she had noticed—the slight changes in Drake's mannerisms, the unfamiliar glint in his eyes. She had seen through Gabriel's façade, recognizing the malevolent presence lurking beneath Drake's familiar exterior.

Rachel's eyes widened, her hands freezing over Drake's wound. The realization hit her like a physical blow, her breath catching in her throat. "You knew?" she whispered, her voice a mixture of disbelief and dawning comprehension.

Holly's gaze remained fixed on Drake, her finger resting lightly on the trigger. She couldn't afford to let her guard down, not when Gabriel could resurface at any moment. The weight of her knowledge pressed down on her, a burden she had carried alone until now.

I should have said something sooner, Holly thought, a flicker of regret passing through her. But there had been no time, no opportunity to voice her suspicions without potentially endangering them all. Now, as she stood poised to make the ultimate decision, she wondered if her silence had cost them dearly.

5 - 6

Holly nodded, her jaw clenched tight. "I saw it in the way he moved, in his eyes," she explained, her tone sharp as a razor's edge. "That wasn't the Drake I knew. That was Gabriel wearing his skin."

The words tasted bitter on her tongue, each syllable a painful admission of the truth she'd been grappling with. Holly's grip on the gun tightened imperceptibly, her knuckles whitening as she fought to maintain her composure. She'd seen countless horrors in her career, but nothing could have prepared her for this moment—facing down the hollow shell of a man she once trusted, now inhabited by a malevolent force.

Drake's eyes flickered at her words, a spark of recognition—or was it desperation?—igniting in their depths. His lips parted, struggling to form words that refused to come. Holly watched, her heart constricting, as Drake's bloodied hand twitched weakly. It reached out, trembling fingers stretching towards Rachel in a silent plea before falling limp at his side.

The gesture hit Holly like a physical blow. Even now, with Gabriel's presence lurking just beneath the surface, some part of Drake was fighting to break through. She swallowed hard, pushing back the tide of emotions threatening to overwhelm her. This isn't Drake, she reminded herself sternly. Not anymore.

"Rachel," Holly said quietly, her eyes never leaving Drake's prone form. "Step back. We don't know when Gabriel might resurface."

7 - 8

Holly's boots crunched against shards of broken glass as she stepped closer, each crackle a discordant note in the heavy silence. The acrid scent of gunpowder and blood hung in the air, a grim reminder of the violence that had brought them to this moment. She knelt beside Drake, her movements fluid and controlled despite the turmoil raging within her.

Her gun remained steady in her hand, a cold extension of her will. As she looked into Drake's eyes, Holly's jaw clenched, a muscle twitching beneath the taut skin. There, in the depths of his gaze, she saw a faint flicker—a ghost of the man she had once doubted, the partner she had fought beside through countless realities.

"Drake," she murmured, her voice barely above a whisper. "If you're still in there, if you can hear me..."

Her words trailed off as Drake's eyes locked onto hers, a desperate intensity burning within them. For a fleeting moment, Holly felt a surge of hope—maybe, just maybe, they could reach him.

But then his expression shifted, a cruel smirk twisting his features. Holly's grip on the gun tightened instinctively.

Is this really how it ends? she thought, a wave of sadness washing over her. After everything we've been through, all the worlds we've traversed...

"Holly," Rachel's voice broke through her reverie, trembling with fear and uncertainty. "What are you going to do?"

Holly took a deep breath, steeling herself for what she knew had to come next. "What needs to be done," she replied, her voice steady despite the turmoil in her heart. "For all our sakes."

9 - 10

Holly's grip on the gun loosened slightly, her knuckles no longer white with tension. She leaned in closer to Drake, her voice softening to a whisper that only he could hear.

"I'm sorry, friend," she said quietly, her tone carrying a surprising gentleness that belied the gravity of the situation. The words hung in the air between them, heavy with unspoken regret and shared history.

Drake's eyes, once wild with Gabriel's malevolent presence, now seemed to clear. His gaze locked with Holly's, a silent understanding passing between them. A single tear slipped down his cheek, leaving a glistening trail on his blood-stained skin.

His lips moved, forming words that Holly strained to hear. Was it her name? A final plea? Or perhaps a message meant only for her? Whatever it was, the sound was too faint to reach her ears, lost in the deathly silence of the room.

Holly's mind raced, memories of their shared adventures flashing before her eyes. She thought of the Drake she knew—brilliant, conflicted, always striving for redemption. How many realities had they traversed together? How many times had they saved each other?

"Drake," she whispered, her voice thick with emotion. "I wish there was another way. I wish I could save you one last time."

As she watched the life slowly ebb from his eyes, Holly felt a profound sense of loss. This was more than just the death of a comrade; it was the end of a journey that had spanned countless worlds and realities.

Rachel's quiet sobs filled the background, a reminder of the pain that rippled outward from this moment. Holly knew what she had to do next, but for now, she allowed herself this final goodbye to the man who had been both her greatest ally and her most complex adversary.

11 - 12

Holly rose to her feet, her muscles taut with tension. The weight of the gun in her hand felt heavier than ever, a cold reminder of the grim task ahead. She inhaled deeply, steeling herself for what came next.

"I know you're in there, Gabriel," she said, her voice cutting through the oppressive silence. Her eyes, once soft with sorrow, now blazed with determination. "And I know you can hear me."

She tightened her grip on the weapon, her finger ghosting over the trigger. The room seemed to darken around her, as if Gabriel's presence was consuming the very light. Holly felt a chill run down her spine, but she refused to show any sign of fear.

"You really think I'd let you kill me a third time?" she spat, her words laced with defiance. Her heart pounded in her chest, each beat a reminder of the lives she'd lived and lost at Gabriel's hands.

As she stood there, poised on the precipice of action, Holly's mind raced. How many realities had she traversed to reach this point? How many versions of herself had fallen victim to Gabriel's machinations? The weight of all those lost lives, all those shattered worlds, pressed down on her.

But with that weight came resolve. Holly knew that this moment, this confrontation, was the culmination of everything she had endured. She was no longer just Holly Kierstead, rookie detective. She was the sum of all her experiences, all her sacrifices, across the multiverse.

"Not this time," she thought, her inner voice steely with determination. "This ends here, Gabriel. For Drake, for Rachel, for every version of myself you've destroyed. I'm ready for you."

13 - 14

A chilling sound filled the room, sending shivers down Holly's spine. Gabriel's cruel laughter echoed faintly through Drake's lips, a haunting melody that seemed to warp the very air around them. Holly watched as Drake's familiar features contorted, twisting into something unnatural and alien. His eyes, once warm and determined, now gleamed with a malevolent light that didn't belong to her friend.

"You can't stop me," Gabriel hissed, his voice a discordant blend of Drake's baritone and his own sinister timbre. The words dripped with malice, each syllable a promise of destruction.

Holly's grip on her weapon tightened, her knuckles turning white. She fought to keep her expression neutral, even as her mind raced with memories of past defeats, of worlds torn asunder by Gabriel's machinations. The weight of countless lost realities pressed down on her shoulders, threatening to crush her resolve.

But beneath the fear, a spark of defiance ignited in Holly's chest. She thought of Drake, of the man he truly was beneath Gabriel's cruel puppetry. She thought of Rachel, of all the innocent lives hanging in the balance. With each heartbeat, her determination grew stronger.

"Watch me," Holly said coldly, her voice carrying a sharp edge that could cut through dimensions. Her eyes locked onto Gabriel's, unflinching in the face of his otherworldly malevolence. In that moment, she was more than just Holly Kierstead - she was the culmination of every version of herself that had fallen, every reality that had crumbled. And she was ready to end this, once and for all.

15 - 16

The room held its breath, suspended in a moment of terrible anticipation. Holly's finger curled around the trigger, her analytical mind calculating trajectory even as her heart ached with the weight of what she must do. The gun's report shattered the silence like a thunderclap, deafening in the confined space.

Time seemed to slow as Holly watched the bullet's path, her enhanced perception - a gift from the nexus of her selves - allowing her to track its deadly arc. She saw Drake's eyes widen, a flicker of something - relief? gratitude? - passing through them before Gabriel's influence snuffed it out.

"I'm sorry, Drake," Holly whispered, the words barely audible over the ringing in her ears. Her arm remained steady, the gun still trained on the spot where she'd fired. "In every reality, you were my friend. I hope you can forgive me."

The silence that followed was oppressive, broken only by Rachel's ragged breathing and the faint, sickening drip of blood on tile. Holly's senses, honed through multiple lifetimes, strained to detect any lingering trace of Gabriel's presence. She couldn't afford to lower her guard, not when the stakes were so impossibly high.

"Is it... is it over?" Rachel's voice quavered, thick with shock and disbelief.

Holly didn't answer immediately. Her eyes remained fixed on Drake's now-still form, searching for any sign of the malevolent entity that had possessed him. The air felt charged, as if reality itself was holding its breath, waiting to see if Gabriel's threat had truly been neutralized.

17 - 18

Holly's shoulders sagged as she finally lowered the gun, her exhale sharp and ragged. The weight of what she'd done settled over her like a leaden shroud, threatening to crush her beneath its enormity. Yet she remained upright, her spine rigid with the same determination that had carried her through countless iterations of this cosmic struggle.

"I don't know," Holly admitted, her voice low and rough. She holstered her weapon with practiced efficiency, but her hands trembled slightly as she did so. "Gabriel's... persistent. We can't assume anything."

She knelt beside Drake's body, her movements careful and controlled despite the storm of emotions raging within her. Holly's analytical mind cataloged every detail: the stillness of his chest, the vacant stare of his eyes, the way his blood mingled with the shattered remnants of their shared past scattered across the floor.

"I'm sorry it came to this, old friend," she murmured, gently closing Drake's eyes. "In another life, we might have..."

Holly's voice caught, the weight of infinite possibilities and lost chances threatening to overwhelm her. She swallowed hard, forcing herself to focus on the present – on this reality, where hard choices had to be made.

"We need to move," she said, her tone firmer as she addressed Rachel. "Gabriel may be gone, but his plans won't unravel themselves. There's still work to be done."

As Holly rose, her gaze lingered on Drake's face. In death, free from Gabriel's influence, she could see echoes of the man she'd known across countless realities – brave, loyal, and ultimately caught in a web far beyond his understanding. A pang of guilt twisted in her chest, but Holly pushed it aside. There would be time for mourning later, if they survived what was to come.

19 - 20

Rachel sat back, her face ashen and hands trembling as she stared at Drake's lifeless form. "Is it over?" she whispered, her voice breaking. The once-vibrant scientist looked utterly shattered, her red hair matted with sweat and blood, her lab coat a tattered reminder of the life she'd left behind.

Holly's sharp eyes darted from Rachel to the grotesque mass that had once been Linda and Harrison. The detective's jaw clenched as she watched the monstrous blob shudder violently, then begin to dissolve. Its flesh liquefied, dripping onto the floor in a nauseating display.

"I don't know," Holly admitted, her voice low and tense. She fought to keep her composure, but the sight of the melting abomination made her stomach churn. "This feels like an ending, but with Gabriel, I've learned nothing is ever truly finished."

She took a steadying breath, her analytical mind already racing ahead. "Rachel, we need to focus. What do you know about this... process?" Holly gestured towards the dissolving mass, careful not to step in the expanding puddle of viscous fluid.

Rachel's scientific instincts seemed to kick in, momentarily overriding her shock. "It's unprecedented," she murmured, her eyes widening. "The cellular structure appears to be breaking down at an accelerated rate. But why? And what happens when it's completely liquefied?"

Holly's hand tightened on her gun. "Whatever the answer, I doubt it's good news for us. We should—"

She was cut off by a sickening gurgle from the rapidly disintegrating blob. Holly's instincts screamed danger, but a part of her couldn't look away. She thought of all the realities she'd seen, all the horrors she'd faced, and wondered if this would be the one that finally broke her.

21 - 21

Holly's eyes narrowed as she watched the horrifying scene unfold. "I hope so," she muttered, her voice barely audible over the nauseating sounds of liquefying flesh. The acrid stench of decay filled her nostrils, making her eyes water.

She took a cautious step back, her mind racing through possibilities. "Rachel," she said, her tone clipped and professional despite the churning in her gut, "we need to contain this. Any ideas?"

Rachel's scientific mind seemed to snap into focus. "We could try to neutralize it with a strong base, but without knowing its composition..."

Holly's gaze darted around the room, assessing. "No time for lab work. We improvise." She spotted a fire extinguisher in the corner. "This might slow it down."

As she moved to retrieve it, a memory flashed through her mind – another reality, another version of herself facing a similar horror. The weight of all her experiences across dimensions pressed down on her, a burden she alone could bear.

"What if it's not over?" Rachel's voice quavered. "What if Gabriel—"

"Then we'll face it," Holly cut her off, her voice steely with determination. "We've come too far to give up now." She hefted the extinguisher, aiming it at the writhing mass. "Stand back," she ordered, "and be ready for anything."

Back to the Nexus of Torment

1 -2   Drake's eyes fluttered open, his senses immediately assaulted by the oppressive atmosphere. The stench of decay mingled with a sulfuric tang, coating his tongue and making him gag. As he became aware of his surroundings, the cold, jagged ground beneath him dug into his back, each point of contact a fresh reminder of his vulnerability.

"Where am I?" he muttered, his voice hoarse and barely audible. The words seemed to dissipate into the thick air around him, swallowed by the oppressive silence.

With great effort, Drake pushed himself upright, grimacing as pain lanced through his body. Every muscle protested, every joint creaked as if he'd aged a hundred years in an instant. As he struggled to sit up, his mind raced, grasping for any memory that might explain his current predicament. ""Linda? Harrison?" he called out, his voice stronger now but tinged with desperation. The names of his wife and son echoed in the emptiness, unanswered.

Drake's heart pounded in his chest; each beat a painful reminder of his isolation. He squinted, trying to pierce the gloom that surrounded him. As his vision slowly cleared, the world around him came into sharp, terrible focus.

And then, he froze.

The landscape before him was alien, nightmarish. Jagged stones stretched as far as the eye could see, their surfaces glinting with an otherworldly sheen. The air itself seemed to shimmer, distorting reality in a way that made Drake's head spin.

"This can't be real," he whispered, his lawyer's mind desperately trying to rationalize what he was seeing. "I was just... I was..."

But the memory slipped away like smoke, leaving him grasping at fragments of his past. The weight of his confusion pressed down on him, threatening to crush his spirit.

Drake's hands clenched into fists, his nails digging into his palms. The pain grounded him, gave him something to focus on beyond the overwhelming sense of wrongness that permeated this place.

"Think, Drake," he commanded himself, his voice low and determined. "How did you get here? What's the last thing you remember?"

But as he searched his memories, all he found were glimpses of a life that felt both familiar and foreign. A courtroom, the faces of his family, a car's headlights bearing down on him – each image flashed through his mind, disconnected and hazy.

Drake forced himself to his feet, swaying slightly as he stood. His muscles screamed in protest, but he ignored the pain. He had to move, had to find answers. With each step, he felt a growing sense of urgency, a nagging feeling that time was running out.

"I'll find a way out," he promised himself, his voice barely above a whisper. "I'll find my way back to you, Linda. Harrison. Whatever it takes."

As Drake took his first tentative steps into the unknown landscape, he couldn't shake the feeling that he was walking into something far beyond his understanding. But the face of his son, the memory of his wife's touch, drove him forward. Whatever trials lay ahead, whatever nightmares this place held, he would face them.

For his family. For redemption. For a chance to make things right.

3 - 4

Drake stumbled forward; his eyes wide with horrified recognition. The Nexus of Torment stretched before him, a hellscape that haunted his deepest nightmares. The crimson sky churned overhead, violent storms lashing out with jagged bolts of lightning that illuminated the desolate expanse.

"No," he whispered, his voice hoarse. "Not here. Not again."

The air crackled with an otherworldly energy, and in the distance, the haunting wails of unseen souls sent chills down Drake's spine. He clenched his fists, fighting against the wave of despair threatening to overwhelm him.

"Focus," Drake muttered to himself, his brown eyes scanning the horizon. "There has to be a way out. There's always a way out."

But even as he spoke the words, doubt gnawed at him. How many times had he been here before? How many cycles of torment had he endured?

A particularly loud crack of lightning startled him, and Drake instinctively ducked. As he straightened, his gaze fell upon a twisted formation of rocks in the distance. Something about it tugged at his memory.

"The portal," he breathed, hope flickering to life within him. "If I can just reach it..."

Drake set off toward the rocks, each step a battle against the uneven terrain. As he walked, memories of his family flooded his mind – Harrison's laugh, Linda's determined gaze. They were counting on him, even if they didn't know it.

"I won't fail you again," Drake promised, his voice carrying on the sulfuric wind. "I'll find a way to fix this. To save you all."

But as he pressed on, a nagging voice in the back of his mind whispered doubts. What if this was just another illusion? Another trick of this Nexus?

Drake shook his head, pushing the thoughts aside. "It doesn't matter," he growled. "I'll keep fighting. I'll keep trying. Until I make it right."

5 - 6

Drake's foot caught on a jagged outcropping, nearly sending him sprawling. As he regained his balance, his gaze fell to the ground beside him, and his breath caught.

Gabriel's body lay sprawled there, motionless. Blood pooled around the disfigured man's form, staining the dark stone. His face, twisted in a permanent grimace, was eerily silent now.

"Gabriel," Drake whispered, his voice a mixture of shock and revulsion. He took an involuntary step back, his mind reeling. How had he not noticed the body before?

The sight of his nemesis, once so formidable, now reduced to a lifeless husk, stirred a maelstrom of emotions within Drake. Relief warred with a perverse sense of loss, as if a vital piece of his own identity had been stripped away.

"Is this real?" Drake muttered; his eyes fixed on Gabriel's disfigured visage. "Or just another trick of the Nexus?"

He crouched beside the body, his hand hovering uncertainly over Gabriel's chest. Part of him wanted to check for a pulse, to confirm what his eyes were telling him. But another part recoiled at the thought of touching the man who had caused so much pain.

"You manipulated me," Drake said, his voice growing stronger. "You twisted everything. My family, my life, reality itself." His fists clenched at his sides. "And for what? What was it all for, Gabriel?"

Only the distant wails of trapped souls answered him. Drake stood, his gaze sweeping across the desolate landscape. The finality of Gabriel's death seemed to cast the Nexus in a new light, somehow more threatening and yet more conquerable.

"It doesn't end here," Drake declared, his resolve hardening. "Your games, your machinations – they're done. But I'm still here. And I'm going to find a way out, for all of us."

He cast one last look at Gabriel's body, a complex mix of emotions churning within him. Then, with a deep breath, Drake turned away, his eyes fixed on the distant rocks that might hold the key to his escape.

"Linda, Harrison," he murmured, their names a talisman against the horrors of the Nexus. "I'm coming. Whatever it takes, I'm coming home."

7 - 8

The sight of Gabriel's lifeless body sent a chill down Drake's spine, his muscles tensing as if to ward off the cold reality before him. "No," he whispered, shaking his head in disbelief. "This can't be happening." His voice trembled, barely audible above the haunting wails echoing through the Nexus.

Drake's hands shook as he ran them through his disheveled hair, his mind reeling. "I've been here before," he muttered, his eyes darting around the desolate landscape. "But it's different this time. Why is it different?"

He paced, his footsteps crunching on the blackened stone. The oppressive air seemed to press in on him, making each breath a struggle. "Linda," he called out, his voice cracking. "Harrison. Are you out there?"

Only the eerie silence of the Nexus of Torment answered him. Drake's shoulders slumped as he turned back to Gabriel's body. "You were supposed to have all the answers," he said bitterly. "But even in death, you're just another dead end."

As he spoke, something caught Drake's eye – a faint shimmer in the distance, barely visible through the crimson haze. His heart raced as recognition dawned. "The portal," he breathed, a mix of hope and dread washing over him. "It's still here."

Drake took a hesitant step forward, then stopped, torn between the pull of the portal and the weight of his past choices. "I can't make the same mistake again," he said, his voice low and determined. "But I can't stay here either. There has to be another way."

He closed his eyes, trying to center himself amidst the chaos of his thoughts. When he opened them again, his gaze was resolute. "I'm coming, Linda. Harrison. This time, I'll make it right."

9 - 10

A metallic glint caught Drake's eye, drawing his attention to the jagged ground near Gabriel's lifeless form. His breath hitched as he recognized the object. With trembling fingers, he reached out and grasped the cold, familiar weight of the gun.

"I thought I'd never see this again," Drake murmured, his voice barely audible over the distant wails echoing through the Nexus. The weapon felt heavier than he remembered, as if burdened by the weight of his past actions. He turned it over in his hands, memories of that fateful moment flooding back.

"Was it really justice?" he asked himself, thumb tracing the trigger guard. "Or just another selfish choice?"

Drake's introspection was cut short as a chill ran down his spine. Something had changed in the air around him, a shift in the oppressive atmosphere that set his nerves on edge. Slowly, he raised his head, gun still clutched tightly in his hand.

As his gaze lifted, Drake's entire body went rigid. His eyes widened in disbelief, and the words caught in his throat as he tried to process what he was seeing. The gun nearly slipped from his grasp as his mind reeled, struggling to reconcile the impossible scene before him.

"This can't be real," he whispered, his voice hoarse with shock and confusion. "How is this happening?"

11 - 12

In the distance, near the swirling edges of a shimmering portal, two figures stood in stark relief against the churning crimson sky. Drake's breath caught in his throat as he recognized them both.

Lucian towered there, a seven-foot monolith of darkness. The being's cloak seemed to devour the very light around it, leaving only the eerie glow of otherworldly eyes visible beneath the hood. Beside this imposing figure stood... himself. Drake's past self, looking hesitant and uncertain, poised on the precipice of a life-altering decision.

"No," Drake whispered, his voice cracking. "Not this moment. Not again."

His heart thundered in his chest; each beat a painful reminder of the choice he'd made. Memories crashed over him like a tidal wave, threatening to drown him in regret.

"You stand at a crossroads, Drake Miller," Lucian's voice echoed in his mind, a perfect recollection of that fateful conversation. "Judgment in the Nexus... or a world where your family lives, untouched by tragedy."

Drake's grip on the gun tightened, his knuckles white. "I was a fool," he thought, watching his past self's inner struggle play out. "I chose selfishly. I chose wrong."

He took a stumbling step forward, desperation clawing at his insides. "Don't do it!" he tried to shout, but his voice emerged as barely a whisper. "You don't know the cost!"

But his past self couldn't hear him. Drake watched, helpless, as the scene unfolded exactly as he remembered. The weight of inevitability pressed down on him, suffocating in its finality.

"The Grey World," his past self said, sealing their fate. "I choose the Grey World."

13 - 14

Drake's muscles tensed; his body coiled like a spring ready to unleash. The gun felt heavy in his hand, a cold reminder of the choices that had led him to this moment. He raised it, aiming at his past self with trembling fingers.

"I can stop this," he muttered, his voice raw with emotion. "I have to."

But even as he steadied his aim, doubt gnawed at him. What would happen if he pulled the trigger? Would he cease to exist? Or would he create yet another fractured timeline, another version of himself doomed to repeat this cycle?

His past self-took a step towards the shimmering portal, unaware of the internal struggle raging just yards away. Drake's finger hovered over the trigger, his breath coming in short, ragged gasps.

"Wait!" he called out, his voice stronger now, fueled by desperation. "You don't understand what you're doing!"

To his astonishment, his past self-paused, turning slightly as if he'd heard something. For a moment, their eyes met across the desolate expanse of the Nexus. Drake felt a jolt of recognition, a nauseating sense of déjà vu as he stared into his own eyes, seeing the confusion and fear reflected there.

"Listen to me," Drake pleaded, lowering the gun slightly. "The Grey World isn't what you think. It's a trap, a twisted version of reality. You'll lose everything you're trying to save."

His past self-frowned, clearly conflicted. "Who are you?" he asked, his voice echoing strangely in the oppressive atmosphere of the Nexus.

Drake swallowed hard, his mind racing. How could he explain? How could he make himself understand the magnitude of this decision?

"I'm you," he finally said, his voice breaking. "I'm what you become if you step through that portal. And believe me, it's not worth the cost."

15 - 16

Drake's legs trembled as he traversed the jagged terrain, each step sending shockwaves of pain through his battered body. The pulsating light from the portal cast eerie, dancing shadows across the blackened stone, distorting his perception and making the ground seem to shift beneath his feet.

"Stop!" he shouted, his voice raw and desperate. The words tore from his throat, carrying with them the weight of countless regrets and the bitter taste of failure.

His past self-hesitated, turning slightly at the sound. Drake's heart pounded in his chest, hope and dread warring within him. Could he really change things this time? Or was he doomed to watch himself make the same catastrophic mistake again?

"Please," he croaked, taking another unsteady step forward. "You don't know what you're about to do. The consequences... they're unimaginable."

The air grew thick with tension as his past self-regarded him warily. Drake could see the conflict in his own eyes, the desperate desire for a world where his family was whole battling against the instinctive fear of this strange, haggard version of himself.

"Who are you?" his past self-demanded, voice laced with suspicion and a hint of fear.

Drake's mind raced. How could he possibly explain? The words tumbled out, urgent and pleading. "I'm you. I'm what you become if you step through that portal. And trust me, the price is too high."

He watched as disbelief and horror flickered across his past self's face. It was surreal, arguing with himself, trying to prevent a tragedy he had already lived through. But he had to try. He couldn't bear the thought of reliving that nightmare again.

17 - 18

The cacophony of the Nexus swelled, drowning out Drake's desperate pleas. His past self-turned back to Lucian, their conversation continuing as if Drake's intrusion had never occurred. The towering, cloaked figure of Lucian loomed over Drake's past self, their words lost in the howling winds and anguished cries that echoed through the desolate landscape.

Drake's heart sank, a cold dread seeping into his bones. He watched helplessly as his past self-nodded, seeming to come to a decision. The gun in Drake's hand felt impossibly heavy, a stark reminder of the choices that had led him to this moment.

With trembling fingers, he raised the weapon, aiming it squarely at his past self. The irony wasn't lost on him – to save himself, he might have to destroy himself. "Don't do it!" he screamed, his voice raw with desperation. "You don't know what you're about to unleash!"

As he shouted, Drake's mind raced. Could he really pull the trigger? Would killing his past self-erase the nightmare he'd been living? Or would it create an even worse paradox? The weight of the multiverse seemed to press down on him, each second stretching into an eternity as he grappled with the impossible choice before him.

19 - 20

A flicker of movement caught Drake's eye. His past self-hesitated, head turning slightly as if he'd heard something. Drake's breath caught in his throat, a surge of hope mingling with his terror. Had his warning finally broken through?

Drake's heart pounded so fiercely he could feel it in his temples. He took another step closer, his hands trembling as he kept the gun trained on his target. The jagged stones beneath his feet shifted, sending small cascades of pebbles skittering into the abyss.

"Listen to me!" he begged, his voice cracking with emotion. "I've seen what happens. I've lived it." Memories of the Grey World flashed through his mind – the hollow shell of his family, the emptiness that permeated every moment. "You can't go through that portal. You have to stay here!"

As he spoke, Drake's mind raced. Would his past self believe him? Could he make him understand the weight of the choice he was about to make? The fate of not just their family, but entire realities hung in the balance.

"Please," Drake whispered, more to himself than to his past self. "Don't make the same mistake I did. Don't let your guilt and desperation cloud your judgment." He took a shaky breath, realizing how much of himself he still saw in that past version, standing on the precipice of a decision that would shatter worlds.

21 - 22

The figure before him turned fully now, his face a mirror of Drake's own – calm but unreadable. Their eyes locked, and Drake felt a jarring sense of déjà vu wash over him. It was like staring into a fractured reflection, seeing both who he was and who he'd become.

"You don't understand," Drake said, his voice low and urgent. "The price is too high. Our family—"

But his words trailed off as he saw the resolution harden in his past self's eyes. A chill ran down Drake's spine as he recognized that look – the same stubborn determination that had driven him to make countless mistakes in his quest for redemption.

"No," Drake breathed, taking another step forward. "Don't—"

Without a word, his past self-turned away. The shimmering portal pulsed, its ethereal light casting long shadows across the desolate landscape. Drake lunged forward, his free hand outstretched, but he was too late.

His past self-stepped through the portal. The shimmering light enveloped him, warping and bending reality around his form. In an instant, he was gone, leaving Drake alone in the oppressive silence of the Nexus.

"Damn it!" Drake shouted, his voice echoing across the barren expanse. He lowered the gun, his arm suddenly feeling leaden. "I was so close," he whispered, the weight of failure crushing down upon him once more.

23 - 24

The gun slipped from Drake's trembling fingers, clattering against the jagged stone with a hollow finality. His legs buckled beneath him, and he crashed to his knees, the impact sending shockwaves of pain through his body. But the physical discomfort paled in comparison to the anguish that clawed at his insides.

Drake's eyes remained fixed on the empty space where the portal had been, its absence a stark reminder of his failure. The air around him seemed to thicken, pressing down on him with an almost tangible weight. His breath came in ragged gasps, each inhalation a struggle against the crushing realization of what had just transpired.

"I failed," he whispered, his voice barely audible over the distant wails that echoed through the Nexus. "Again."

His hands, still shaking, clenched into fists against the unforgiving ground. Memories flashed through his mind – his family's smiling faces, untouched by the tragedy he knew awaited them. The illusory world he'd chosen, thinking he could outsmart fate.

"Why?" Drake growled, his voice rising with a mixture of anger and desperation. "Why couldn't I stop myself?"

He looked up at the roiling crimson sky, searching for answers in its violent churning. Lightning crackled overhead, illuminating the desolate landscape in brief, harsh flashes.

"I saw it all," he continued, his words tumbling out in a torrent of emotion. "I lived through the lies, the pain, the destruction. And still, I couldn't..."

Drake's voice trailed off as he struggled to articulate the magnitude of his failure. He closed his eyes, fighting against the wave of despair threatening to overwhelm him.

"What do I do now?" he asked, opening his eyes to stare at his trembling hands. "How do I fix this when I can't even change my own past?"

25 - 26

Drake's anguished question hung in the air, unanswered. The oppressive silence of the Nexus was broken only by the distant, haunting wails of trapped souls. He lifted his gaze from his hands, his eyes scanning the desolate landscape as if searching for a shred of hope in this realm of torment.

"No," he whispered, his voice breaking. "No... I was so close."

The words tasted bitter in his mouth, a stark reminder of his repeated failures. Drake's shoulders slumped, the weight of his choices pressing down on him with crushing force. He could still see the shimmering portal, the ghostly afterimage of his past self-stepping through it, sealing a fate he now desperately wished to change.

A shadow fell over him, and Drake tensed, recognizing the looming presence without needing to look up. Lucian's towering form seemed to absorb the very light around them, a void given shape and purpose.

Lucian turned to him then, their expression serene and inscrutable. "You can't change the past, Drake," they said, their voice calm but laced with a cruel edge. "You've tried before, and you'll try again. That's the nature of your torment."

Drake's jaw clenched, a surge of defiance rising within him despite his despair. He struggled to his feet, facing the enigmatic being that had orchestrated his suffering.

"There has to be a way," Drake insisted, his voice hoarse but determined. "I won't accept this... this cycle of failure."

Internally, Drake's mind raced. How many times had he been here? How many versions of himself had he watched make the same mistake? The thought sent a chill down his spine, but he refused to let it paralyze him.

27 - 28

Drake looked up at Lucian, his eyes filled with anguish, the crimson sky reflecting in their depths like pools of blood. "Why?" he demanded, his voice raw with emotion. "Why do you keep doing this to me?"

The words echoed across the desolate landscape, swallowed by the vastness of the Nexus of Torment. Drake's fists clenched at his sides, knuckles white with tension. He could feel the jagged stones beneath his feet, a constant reminder of the harsh reality he found himself in once again.

Lucian's smile was faint, barely visible beneath the shadow of their hood. Their gaze, steady and unblinking, seemed to pierce through Drake's very soul. "Because you made a choice, Drake," they intoned, their voice a melodic whisper that somehow carried over the distant wails of tormented souls. "And all choices come with consequences."

Drake's mind reeled, memories of that fateful decision flooding back. The promise of a world where his family lived, untouched by tragedy. The selfish hope that had driven him to step through that shimmering portal. He shook his head, trying to clear the fog of regret.

"But this... this endless cycle," Drake argued, gesturing wildly at the hellish landscape around them. "How is this justice? How is this fair?"

Lucian's form seemed to ripple, as if reality itself bent around them. "Fair?" they echoed, a hint of amusement in their tone. "The universe cares not for fairness, Drake Miller. It only responds to the choices we make."

The being's words hung in the air, heavy with implication. Drake's shoulders sagged, the weight of his actions pressing down upon him. But beneath the despair, a spark of determination still burned.

Lucian tilted their head, regarding Drake with what might have been curiosity. "The question is, Drake," they continued, their voice taking on an almost hypnotic quality, "are you ready to face them this time? Your consequences. Your true test."

Drake's breath caught in his throat. He stared at Lucian, searching for any hint of deception in their inscrutable features. Was this another trick? Another layer to his torment? Or was it... hope?

A Leap of Defiance

1 -2 The crimson sky churned above, a maelstrom of swirling clouds that seemed to pulse with malevolent energy. Drake's eyes widened as he took in the desolate expanse of the Nexus of Torment, his heart pounding in his chest. The air crackled with an otherworldly electricity, raising the hair on his arms.

Lucian's laughter shattered the eerie silence, low and menacing. It reverberated through the barren landscape like rolling thunder, each echoing peal sending a chill down Drake's spine. The towering figure loomed over him, a black void against the blood-red sky. Glowing eyes pierced the shadows beneath Lucian's hood, filled with cruel amusement as they bore into Drake's soul.

Drake swallowed hard; his throat suddenly dry. He fought to keep his voice steady as he spoke. "What have you done, Lucian?"

But Lucian merely chuckled, the sound grating against Drake's ears. When they finally spoke, their words dripped with mockery and condescension.

"You still don't understand, do you?" Lucian's head tilted slightly, regarding Drake as one might observe an insect. "You can't change destiny, Drake. You can only influence it. Nothing more."

The weight of those words pressed down on Drake, threatening to crush him. His mind raced, grasping for some argument, some shred of hope to cling to. He thought of his family—of Linda's smile, of little Harrison's laughter. The memory of their faces, now lost to him, sent a fresh wave of anguish through his heart.

No, he couldn't accept this. There had to be a way to set things right, to undo the damage he had caused. Drake's fists clenched at his sides; his jaw set with determination. He would find a way, no matter the cost. He had to.

3 - 4

Drake's knees dug into the harsh, unyielding ground of the Nexus, the pain a dull echo of the turmoil raging within him. His fists clenched tightly, knuckles white with strain, as if he could physically grasp the shreds of hope slipping through his fingers. Lucian's words hung in the air, a suffocating miasma of despair.

Yet, in the depths of his anguish, something stirred. A flicker of defiance, small but persistent, like a flame refusing to be extinguished.

"No," Drake whispered, his voice barely audible even to himself. Then, louder, with a tremor that spoke of both fear and resolve, he raised his head to meet Lucian's glowing gaze. "You're wrong."

The words hung between them; a challenge hurled into the face of inevitability. Drake's heart pounded in his chest, each beat a reminder of all he had to lose—and all he had to fight for. He waited, muscles tense, for Lucian's response, knowing that whatever came next would shape the course of not just his fate, but that of everything he held dear.

5 - 6

Lucian's smile widened, a predatory gleam in their eyes as they tilted their head slightly. The shadows beneath their hood seemed to deepen, swallowing any trace of mercy. "Oh? And what do you plan to do, Drake?" Their voice dripped with mockery, each word a dagger aimed at Drake's resolve. "You've already made your choice. It's written in the fabric of this existence. The Grey World is your creation. Your punishment."

The words hit Drake like a physical blow, threatening to shatter his newfound determination. For a moment, he teetered on the brink of despair, the weight of his past mistakes pressing down on him. The Grey World—a realm of emptiness and loss—flashed through his mind, a stark reminder of the consequences of his actions.

Slowly, painfully, Drake rose to his feet. His body protested, muscles screaming from the ordeal he'd endured, but he pushed through the pain. With each inch he gained, his resolve strengthened.

'I've made mistakes,' Drake thought, his jaw clenching. 'But I won't let them define me. Not anymore.'

As he straightened to his full height, Drake locked eyes with Lucian. The burning determination in his gaze was a stark contrast to the cruel amusement in Lucian's glowing orbs. In that moment, Drake felt a surge of defiance coursing through him, pushing back against the suffocating despair that had threatened to consume him.

'I may not be able to change the past,' Drake realized, his thoughts racing, 'but I'll be damned if I let it dictate my future. Or the future of those I love.'

7 - 8

"Watch me," he said, his voice low and charged with an intensity that surprised even him. The words hung in the air, a challenge and a promise wrapped into one.

Lucian's eyes narrowed, the amusement in them flickering for a moment. Drake could almost taste the tension crackling between them, electric and dangerous.

Without waiting for a response, Drake turned away. His muscles coiled, ready for action. In his mind's eye, he saw Linda's determined face, heard Harrison's hopeful voice. They were counting on him. The entire world—no, the entire multiverse—was hanging in the balance.

'This is for you,' he thought, his heart pounding. 'For all of us.'

With a surge of adrenaline, Drake launched himself forward. The world blurred around him as he moved, each step bringing him closer to his destiny. He could feel Lucian's presence behind him, a looming threat that spurred him on.

The portal shimmered ahead, its ominous light both terrifying and alluring. Drake's breath came in ragged gasps, his body protesting the sudden exertion. But he pushed on, driven by a force greater than his physical pain.

'I don't know what lies beyond,' Drake thought, his mind racing as fast as his feet. 'But whatever it is, I'll face it. I have to.'

As he neared the portal, time seemed to slow. Drake could hear his heartbeat thundering in his ears, feel the sweat beading on his brow. The air around him crackled with energy, the very fabric of reality seeming to bend and warp.

In that final moment before the leap, a strange calm washed over Drake. He thought of Gabriel's scarred face, a reminder of the consequences of failure. But instead of fear, he felt only determination.

'This is my choice,' Drake realized. 'My destiny.'

And with that thought, he leapt.

9 - 10

The shimmering portal loomed before Drake, its ominous light pulsing with an otherworldly rhythm. Each step brought him closer to judgment, the promise of redemption and damnation intertwined in its ethereal glow. His muscles burned with exertion, but Drake pushed on, his determination fueled by the faces of his family flickering in his mind.

"You can't escape fate, Drake!" Lucian's voice boomed across the Nexus, a mixture of fury and desperation. "This isn't how it's supposed to end!"

Drake's heart raced, his thoughts a tumultuous storm. 'Maybe not,' he mused internally, 'but I'm done playing by your rules, Lucian.'

He could feel the entity's presence looming behind him, a dark shadow threatening to engulf him. The air crackled with tension, reality itself seeming to warp around them.

"Drake, stop!" Lucian roared, their voice reverberating through the air like thunder.

But Drake didn't falter. His eyes remained fixed on the portal, its light growing brighter with each passing second. 'I'm sorry,' he thought, a pang of regret piercing through his resolve. 'I know this might mean losing you all again, but I have to make this right.'

The portal was now mere feet away, its energy washing over Drake in waves. He could feel it pulling at him, promising judgment, revelation, and perhaps, at long last, peace.

11 - 11

With a final burst of speed, Drake hurled himself towards the shimmering threshold. The world around him blurred into a kaleidoscope of crimson and shadow as he crossed the boundary between realms. Blinding light engulfed him, searing his retinas and flooding every cell of his being with an otherworldly energy.

'Linda... Harrison...' Their names echoed in his mind as he plunged into the unknown. The familiar weight of guilt and desperation that had driven him this far began to dissolve, replaced by an overwhelming sensation of weightlessness.

As the Nexus of Torment faded behind him, Drake felt a curious detachment from his physical form. His consciousness expanded, stretching across what felt like infinite possibilities. Fragments of realities flickered past – glimpses of lives unlived, choices unmade.

"What have you done?" Lucian's voice, now distant and distorted, reached him through the maelstrom of light and sensation.

Drake couldn't respond, couldn't even form coherent thoughts as the portal's energy coursed through him. He was being unmade and remade with each passing moment; his very essence scattered across the multiverse.

'Is this judgment?' he wondered, a fleeting thought in the chaos of his dissolving self. 'Or is this the price of defiance?'

The light intensified, threatening to consume what remained of Drake Miller. Yet, at his core, a small spark of determination still burned – a reminder of why he had taken this leap into the unknown. As consciousness began to slip away, Drake clung to that spark, hoping against hope that somehow, someway, this sacrifice would be enough to save those he loved.

A Voice in the Darkness

1‑2

Darkness enveloped Drake, an absolute void that seemed to swallow even the concept of light. He floated, weightless, his limbs drifting in nothingness. The silence pressed against his eardrums, a tangible force that threatened to crush him. As he struggled to orient himself in the endless black, Drake's mind raced.

How did I get here? What is this place?

The memories of his past life—his career as a lawyer, the car accident, the alternate realities—swirled in his thoughts, but felt distant, as if belonging to someone else. The crushing weight of guilt that had become his constant companion seemed amplified in this strange realm.

Suddenly, a voice shattered the oppressive quiet, startling Drake so severely that he would have jumped if his feet had purchase on solid ground.

"Well, well," the voice drawled, its timbre shifting unnaturally between tones. "Look who's finally arrived."

Drake's heart hammered in his chest. The voice was unlike anything he'd ever heard—a cacophony of familiar inflections blended into one unsettling whole. He recognized snippets: the warmth of his wife's laughter, the gruff baritone of his father, even the high-pitched giggle of his son.

"Who's there?" Drake called out, his own voice sounding thin and reedy in the vastness. "Show yourself!"

A chuckle rippled through the void, seeming to come from everywhere and nowhere at once. "Oh, Drake," the voice sighed, now taking on the disappointed tone his mother used when he'd disappointed her as a child. "Always so demanding, aren't you?"

Drake clenched his fists, frustration bubbling up inside him. "I'm tired of games," he growled. "I've been through too much, seen too many impossible things. Whatever you are, whatever this place is, I deserve answers!"

As he spoke, Drake realized the truth of his words. He had sacrificed everything—his life, his family, his very existence—in an attempt to save the multiverse. Now, suspended in this incomprehensible void, he felt a surge of determination. He would not be cowed by this disembodied voice, no matter how unsettling its nature.

"Answers?" the voice mused, now taking on a contemplative tone that reminded Drake of his old mentor from law school. "Oh, my dear boy. You'll have your answers soon enough. But first, you must remember."

Drake's brow furrowed. "Remember what?"

The silence stretched for a long moment before the voice responded, its words dripping with malevolent glee. "Everything."

3 ‑ 4

"Drake Miller," it drawled, smooth and ominous. "You came to me once, didn't you? You made a deal."

The words slithered through the void, wrapping around Drake like icy tendrils. His mind reeled, grasping for memories that seemed to dance just out of reach. A deal? When? With whom? The weight of forgotten choices pressed down on him, threatening to crush his resolve.

Drake spun in the endless darkness, his eyes straining against the impenetrable black. Panic clawed at his throat as he searched for any sign of the voice's source. His thoughts raced to Linda and Harrison; their faces etched with worry in his mind's eye. What had he done? What bargain could he have struck that would have torn him away from them?

"Who are you?" Drake demanded, his voice echoing faintly in the void. The words felt hollow, inadequate against the vastness surrounding him. "What deal?"

His own voice bounced back at him, mockingly empty. Drake's chest tightened, a familiar sensation of helplessness washing over him. It was the same feeling he'd had when he couldn't protect his family, when he'd watched worlds crumble before his eyes.

"I've made no deals," Drake insisted, more to himself than the disembodied voice. "I wouldn't... I couldn't have forgotten something like that."

But even as he spoke, a seed of doubt took root in his mind. How much had he truly forgotten in his journey across realities? What price might he have been willing to pay to save those he loved?

5 - 6

The voice chuckled, a cacophony of familiar tones that sent chills down Drake's spine. It was as if Linda's gentle laughter intertwined with Harrison's deep rumble, punctuated by Holly's lilting giggles and Gabriel's menacing sneer. The dissonance was jarring, each loved one's voice a knife twisting in Drake's gut.

"You don't even remember, do you?" The fragmented voice taunted, its words dripping with cruel amusement. "A world for your family. Peace in exchange for your soul. You came to me, Drake. You chose this."

Drake's mind reeled, grasping for any memory of such a bargain. His fists clenched involuntarily, nails digging into his palms. The pain was grounding, a reminder that this nightmarish void was real.

"I don't even know who you are!" Drake shouted, his words echoing in the endless dark. Frustration and fear battled within him, threatening to overwhelm his senses. "I never made any deal!"

But even as he denied it, a flicker of doubt ignited in his chest. Had he, in some desperate moment, struck a bargain he couldn't remember? The weight of countless realities pressed down on him, each one a reminder of the lengths he'd gone to protect his family.

"This can't be real," Drake whispered, his voice hoarse. "I wouldn't... I couldn't have forgotten something so important."

The silence that followed was deafening, filled with the unspoken possibility that perhaps, in his quest to save everything, he had damned himself.

7 - 8

The voice paused, letting the silence stretch unnervingly. Drake's thoughts raced, images of Harrison's trusting eyes and Linda's determined face flashing through his mind. The weight of their expectations, their faith in him, pressed against his chest like a physical force.

When the voice finally spoke again, it was softer but no less menacing. The shift in tone sent a chill down Drake's spine, his muscles tensing instinctively.

"Ah," it said, the sound a discordant blend of amusement and malice. "That's because you haven't made the deal... yet."

Drake's heart stuttered, his breath catching in his throat. The implications of those words crashed over him like a tidal wave, threatening to drown him in confusion and dread.

"What do you mean, 'yet'?" Drake demanded, his voice wavering despite his attempt at bravado. He squinted into the darkness, searching for any sign of the entity tormenting him. "Time doesn't work like that. It can't."

But even as he spoke, doubt crept in. After everything he'd seen, after jumping through realities and witnessing the impossible, could he really be certain of anything anymore?

The voice chuckled, a sound that seemed to reverberate through Drake's very bones. "Oh, Drake," it purred, using Linda's voice this time, a cruel mockery of her scientific certainty. "You of all people should know better than to put limits on reality."

9 - 10

The void around Drake pulsed, a rhythmic throbbing that seemed to echo his own racing heartbeat. The darkness grew thicker, more oppressive, as if it were a living entity intent on smothering him. Cold tendrils of fear slithered down his spine, wrapping around his chest and constricting his breath.

Drake's mind reeled, grappling with the implications of the entity's words. The weight of countless decisions, of paths not taken, pressed down on him. He thought of Linda, of his son, of the world he'd left behind and the one he was desperately trying to save. His voice, when he finally found it, was barely more than a whisper, trembling with a mixture of fear and defiance.

"What are you talking about?" he asked, the words escaping him in a shaky exhale. The darkness seemed to swallow his voice, muffling it as if he were speaking underwater.

As he waited for a response, Drake's thoughts raced. Had he unknowingly set something in motion? Was this entity offering him a deal he had yet to make, or warning him of a future he couldn't escape? The questions swirled in his mind, each more unsettling than the last.

"I've never made any deal," he insisted, his voice growing stronger as he clung to this certainty. "And I never would, not if it meant sacrificing everything I love."

But even as he spoke, a nagging doubt gnawed at him. How far would he go to protect his family, to save the world? The line between right and wrong, once so clear, now seemed blurred beyond recognition in this surreal darkness.

11 - 12

The voice laughed again, this time louder, as if reveling in his confusion. The sound reverberated through the void, each echo a distorted reflection of Drake's own laughter, his family's joy, and the sinister undertones of something inhuman.

"Time is irrelevant here, Drake," it drawled, the words slithering around him like tendrils of smoke. "You've always been here. You've never been here. But don't worry... you'll understand soon enough."

Drake's fists clenched, his nails digging into his palms as he fought against the disorientation. The entity's words seemed to twist reality itself, bending his perception of time and space until he could no longer trust his own memories.

"That's impossible," he growled, more to himself than to the voice. "I remember my life, my choices. I know who I am."

But did he? Doubt crept in, insidious and cold. What if his entire existence—his career, his family, his desperate quest to save the world—was nothing more than an illusion?

As if in response to his inner turmoil, the darkness around him began to shift. The oppressive void gave way to something else, something Drake's mind struggled to comprehend. It started as a pinprick, a minuscule spark in the distance, but it grew rapidly, expanding outward in all directions.

Light.

It was unlike anything Drake had ever seen—not warm or comforting, but searing and all-consuming. It burned away the darkness, revealing... what? The truth? A new reality? Or perhaps the ultimate deception?

As the light engulfed him, Drake's last coherent thought was of his family. Whatever came next, whatever choices he had made or would make, he knew one thing with absolute certainty: he would fight. For them. For himself. For the chance to understand the cosmic game in which he found himself an unwitting pawn.

13 - 14

The blinding light slammed into Drake with the force of a tidal wave, searing his retinas and threatening to overwhelm his senses. He instinctively threw his arm up to shield his eyes, but the radiance penetrated even that meager defense, burning through flesh and bone as if they were nothing more than gossamer.

"No!" Drake roared; his voice lost in the maelstrom of light. His mind reeled, desperately clinging to the fragments of his identity. Linda's smile, Harrison's laugh —he clung to these memories like a drowning man to driftwood.

The disembodied voice, now a cacophony of familiar tones, echoed around him. "Time unravels, Drake Miller. Past, present, future—all one."

Drake's thoughts raced, matching the frenetic pulse of the light. Was this what it felt like to be unmade? To have one's very essence scattered across the multiverse? He gritted his teeth, fighting against the dissolution of his being.

"I won't let you erase me," he snarled, each word a battle against the overwhelming brightness. "Whatever deal you think I made, whatever I'm supposed to become—I choose my own path!"

The light intensified, if such a thing were possible, and Drake felt himself stretched thin, his consciousness spread across an infinite expanse. Yet still, he fought, clinging to the core of who he was—a father, a husband, a man determined to right his wrongs.

As the voice faded, its final words barely audible above the roar of the light, Drake made a silent vow. Whatever came next, he would find a way back to his family, to his world. He would unravel this cosmic mystery, no matter the cost.

15 - 16

"Welcome to your reckoning, Drake Miller..."

The words reverberated through Drake's very being, each syllable a hammer blow against his soul. He wanted to scream, to rage against the cosmic injustice of it all, but the light stole his voice, his breath, his very essence.

In that moment of blinding intensity, Drake's mind raced through a kaleidoscope of memories and possibilities. Linda's face swam before him, her blue eyes filled with a sorrow he couldn't fathom. "I'm sorry," he thought desperately, hoping against hope that somehow, she could hear him across the vast expanse of realities.

The light pulsed, each wave threatening to tear him apart at the seams. Drake's fists clenched; his jaw set in defiance. He wouldn't go quietly into this cosmic abyss. "I don't accept this!" he roared internally, his thoughts a beacon of resistance against the overwhelming brilliance.

As the darkness faded completely, replaced by an endless sea of white, Drake felt himself being unmade and remade simultaneously. It was excruciating, exhilarating, terrifying. He thought of Harrison, of the lost years, of the promises he had yet to keep.

"Whatever this reckoning is," Drake vowed silently, his determination a burning core within the maelstrom of light, "I'll face it. For them. For all of us."

The brilliance crescendoed, and Drake Miller ceased to be—and began anew.

The Scales of Redemption

1 -2   Drake's eyes fluttered open, adjusting to the sudden absence of blinding light. The oppressive darkness that had enveloped him moments ago dissipated, replaced by a landscape that seemed to breathe with tranquility. Reeds swayed gently around him, their slender stalks brushing against his legs as he stumbled forward, disoriented.

"Where am I?" he muttered, his voice hoarse and unfamiliar to his own ears.

The sky stretched endlessly above, a canvas of gold and orange hues that cast a warm, ethereal glow over everything. Drake inhaled deeply, the sweet scent of wildflowers and morning dew filling his lungs. For the first time in what felt like an eternity, the crushing weight of guilt that had been his constant companion began to lift.

He ran a hand through his disheveled brown hair, his muscular frame tense with uncertainty. "Is this... peace?" The word felt foreign on his tongue, almost sacrilegious given the torment he'd endured.

Drake's feet carried him forward, aimlessly at first, then with growing purpose as he navigated the sea of reeds. Each step brought a soft whisper from the plants, as if they were sharing secrets he couldn't quite comprehend.

"I don't deserve this," he thought, the lawyer in him arguing against this unexpected reprieve. "After everything I've done, all the mistakes I've made..."

His internal dialogue was cut short as his gaze landed on an incongruous sight amidst the pastoral scene. A large, ornately carved door stood alone in the middle of the field, its presence both mystifying and somehow fitting in this surreal landscape.

Drake approached cautiously, his eyes widening as he took in the door's shimmering surface. Golden engravings pulsed with a faint light, as if alive with some inner energy. He reached out a tentative hand, fingers hovering just above the intricate patterns.

"What are you?" he whispered, voice tinged with awe and trepidation. "Another test? Another chance to fail?"

The door remained silent, its rhythmic pulsing the only response to his query. Drake's mind raced, memories of his past mistakes and the weight of his choices flooding back. The serenity of the moment began to crack under the pressure of his guilt.

"I was trying to save them," he said, his voice rising with a mix of desperation and defiance. "My family. The world. I didn't mean for any of this to happen!"

The door's pulsing seemed to intensify, as if responding to his emotional outburst. Drake took a step back, his fists clenching at his sides as he struggled to maintain composure.

"Is this my punishment?" he demanded of the silent sentinel before him. "To be taunted with peace I can never truly have?"

As the words left his lips, Drake felt a shift in the air around him. The fragile peace he'd experienced upon arriving began to solidify, taking on a tangible quality that seemed to envelop him. It was an alien sensation, one that both comforted and unsettled him in equal measure.

He closed his eyes, allowing himself a moment to bask in this unfamiliar feeling. When he opened them again, his gaze was resolute, fixed on the enigmatic door before him.

"Whatever you are," Drake said, his voice low and determined, "whatever test or trial you represent, I'm ready. I have to be. For my family, for the world... for a chance at redemption."

With a deep breath, he stepped forward, hand outstretched towards the shimmering surface of the door, prepared to face whatever lay beyond.

3 - 4

As Drake's hand hovered mere inches from the door's shimmering surface, his attention was suddenly drawn to a figure materialized before him. Sitting cross-legged in front of the ornate portal was a young man, his presence both ethereal and undeniably real. Drake's brow furrowed as he studied the stranger, whose very essence seemed to defy the laws of nature.

The man's complexion shifted subtly, his features morphing every few moments, as if he were a reflection of many people at once. One instant, Drake saw Harrison's youthful optimism in the curve of his smile; the next, Rachel's determined intelligence gleamed in his eyes. It was mesmerizing and disorienting all at once.

"What are you?" Drake whispered, his voice barely audible over the soft rustling of the reeds around them. He felt a strange pull towards this shape-shifting entity, a mixture of curiosity and caution warring within him.

The man's gaze settled on Drake, piercing and ancient despite his youthful appearance. "Sit," he said softly, his voice calm yet commanding. The single word carried the weight of eons, brooking no argument.

Drake hesitated, his muscles tensing instinctively. Part of him wanted to demand answers, to rage against this new mystery thrust upon him. But something in the man's serene demeanor gave him pause.

He's the key, Drake realized suddenly. Whatever this place is, whatever that door leads to... this being holds the answers.

With a deep breath, Drake lowered himself to the ground, mirroring the stranger's cross-legged position. The reeds bent gently beneath him, their sweet scent rising up to mingle with the otherworldly air of this realm.

"Who are you?" Drake asked, his voice steadier now. "And why am I here?"

5 - 6

The man's eyes seemed to pierce through Drake's very soul, kind yet unflinching. A breeze whispered through the reeds, carrying with it the faint scent of jasmine and something indefinable—perhaps the essence of time itself.

"You've committed many sins in your life, Drake Miller," the man began, his voice taking on a somber tone. Each word seemed to resonate in the air, heavy with significance. "One of the greatest of which is gluttony—for wanting to keep your family at the cost of the world."

Drake's breath caught in his throat, a mixture of indignation and shame washing over him. He opened his mouth to protest, but the words died on his lips as memories flooded his mind—Linda's smile, Harrison's laughter, the warmth of their embraces.

How could protecting them be wrong? he thought, his hands clenching involuntarily in the soft earth beneath him.

"I..." Drake started, his voice barely above a whisper. He swallowed hard, trying to steady himself. "I was trying to save them. To save everyone."

The man's features shifted again, momentarily taking on an expression of profound sadness. "Were you, Drake? Or were you saving yourself from the pain of loss?"

The question hung in the air between them, sharp and unyielding. Drake felt as if the ground beneath him had suddenly become unstable, his certainties crumbling like sand.

"I didn't want to lose them," he admitted, the words tearing from his throat. "But I never meant for any of this to happen. The virus, the collapse of reality—I was trying to prevent it all."

The man nodded slowly, his gaze never leaving Drake's face. "Intentions, Drake, are but a small part of the tapestry we weave with our choices. The path to destruction is often paved with the noblest of intentions."

7 - 8

Drake's chest tightened, a knot of anguish forming in his core. He straightened his back defiantly, the reeds rustling beneath him as he shifted. The ethereal glow of the endless sky cast shadows across his face, highlighting the lines of determination etched there.

"I was trying to save them," Drake insisted, his voice raw with emotion. "It was Gabriel who unleashed the virus! I did everything I could to stop it." The words tumbled out, laden with the weight of his past actions and the desperation to justify them.

As he spoke, memories of Gabriel's scarred face and haunting presence flooded his mind. The chaos unleashed across realities, the manipulation, the ever-present threat—it all seemed to converge in this moment of reckoning.

The man before him tilted his head, his ever-shifting features settling into an expression of infinite patience. "Did you?" he asked, his voice soft yet piercing.

Those two simple words cut through Drake's defenses like a knife through butter. He felt exposed, vulnerable, as if the man could see right through to the core of his being.

Doubt crept into Drake's mind, insidious and unwelcome. Had he truly done everything? Or had his actions, driven by love for his family, inadvertently paved the way for Gabriel's machinations?

Drake's gaze dropped to his hands, calloused and worn from his struggles across realities. "I... I thought I did," he murmured, uncertainty coloring his tone. The weight of his choices pressed down on him, heavier than ever before in this serene field of judgment.

9 - 10

Drake blinked, taken aback by the man's penetrating question. The serenity of the golden field suddenly felt oppressive, the swaying reeds a silent audience to his unraveling certainty.

"The blood you were given," the man continued, his tone measured, each word falling like a stone into still water, "was a gift—a divine chance to save the whole world."

Drake's breath caught in his throat. The memory of that viscous, shimmering liquid flooded his senses—its metallic scent, the weight of the vial in his palm, the desperate hope it had represented.

"But instead," the man went on, his ever-shifting features settling into a look of profound disappointment, "you used it to save your own family."

Drake's jaw clenched, his hands curling into fists at his sides. He wanted to argue, to defend his choice, but the words wouldn't come. Instead, he found himself transported back to that moment of decision, the world crumbling around him, his family's faces etched with fear.

"You drank what was meant to heal humanity," the man's voice cut through Drake's reverie, "and used it to cross worlds, selfishly tearing the multiverse apart in your pursuit of happiness."

The accusation hung in the air, heavy and undeniable. Drake's shoulders sagged under its weight, his mind racing. Had he truly been so blind? So selfish? The faces of countless strangers, lives he could have saved, flashed before his eyes, intermingling with those of his beloved family.

"I... I didn't realize," Drake whispered, more to himself than to the man before him. The enormity of his actions, the ripple effect across realities, crashed over him like a tidal wave. He staggered, overwhelmed by guilt and the shattering of his self-perception.

11 - 12

Drake's fists clenched, his knuckles turning white as he struggled to contain the tempest of emotions within him. The golden reeds around him seemed to whisper accusingly, their gentle swaying now a reproachful dance.

"I didn't mean for this to happen!" he burst out; his voice raw with anguish. The words echoed across the ethereal field, seeming to ripple the very fabric of this strange realm. Drake's chest heaved, his breath coming in short, sharp gasps as he fought against the crushing weight of his guilt.

The man before him remained unmoved, his ever-shifting features settling into a look of weary understanding. He sighed softly, the sound carrying an ancient sadness that seemed to transcend time and space.

"Intentions matter little when weighed against actions," the man said, his voice gentle yet unyielding. His eyes, pools of infinite wisdom, bore into Drake's soul. "Harrison was given the ability to find me, to fulfill the words of the chosen one and save his mother."

At the mention of his son's name, Drake felt a pang of longing so intense it was almost physical. He remembered Harrison's curious eyes, his unwavering belief in his father's ability to make things right. The memory was a double-edged sword, both comforting and excruciating.

The man's next words cut through Drake's reverie like a knife. "But you, blinded by your desire, took that from him."

Drake's mind reeled. He had robbed his own son of his destiny? The implications of this revelation threatened to overwhelm him, each new understanding another weight added to his already burdened conscience.

13 - 14

Drake's shoulders sagged, the weight of the man's words pressing down on him like an invisible hand. The reeds around him seemed to whisper accusations, their gentle swaying now a mocking reminder of the peace he'd stolen from the world. He swallowed hard, his voice barely above a whisper as he asked, "What happens now?"

The question hung in the air, heavy with the implications of his past actions and the uncertainty of what was to come. Drake's mind raced, imagining countless scenarios of punishment and retribution, each more terrible than the last.

But the man's response was not what Drake expected. Without a word, he gestured to his side, and suddenly, a small, gleaming scale materialized beside him. Its balance beam shimmered faintly in the ethereal light, casting dancing reflections across the swaying reeds. Drake's eyes were drawn to one of the pans, where a single white feather rested, so delicate it seemed to float rather than sit.

Drake stared at the scale, his brow furrowing in confusion. "I don't understand," he murmured, more to himself than to the man. The sight of the feather, so pure and weightless, stirred something within him – a faint glimmer of hope, perhaps, or the first stirrings of true understanding.

As he gazed at the mysterious apparatus, Drake's thoughts turned inward. What did this scale represent? Was it meant to measure the weight of his sins? The enormity of his mistakes? Or perhaps, he dared to hope, it offered a chance at redemption?

15 - 16

The man's voice broke through Drake's racing thoughts, calm yet laden with significance. "You must weigh your heart against the feather," he said, extending his hand toward Drake.

A sharp, sudden pull in Drake's chest made him gasp. His eyes widened in shock as he felt something vital, something integral to his very being, shift within him.

"My heart?" Drake whispered, his voice trembling. "But how can I—"

His words were cut short as the man's hand drew closer. Drake felt a strange sensation, as if his entire essence was being drawn out through his chest. He wanted to resist, to pull away, but found himself rooted to the spot, mesmerized by the otherworldly process unfolding before him.

With a strangled gasp, Drake watched in awe and terror as the man drew a glowing, crimson heart from his body. It hovered between them, pulsing faintly, its light dim and heavy with the weight of Drake's choices and regrets.

"Is that... me?" Drake asked, his voice barely audible. He stared at the heart, transfixed by its rhythmic beating. Each pulse seemed to echo the choices he'd made, the lives he'd affected, the worlds he'd torn apart in his desperate quest to save his family.

The man said nothing, his ever-shifting features impassive as he gently placed the heart onto the empty pan of the scale. Drake held his breath, his mind reeling with the implications of this moment. Would the weight of his actions condemn him? Or was there still hope for redemption?

As the heart settled onto the scale, Drake felt a profound sense of vulnerability. His entire life, his very essence, was laid bare for judgment. He closed his eyes, bracing himself for what was to come, silently praying for a chance to make things right.

17 - 18

The scales tipped immediately, the heart sinking low, the feather remaining untouched by even the faintest shift. The suddenness of the movement sent a jolt through Drake's body, his eyes snapping open to witness the damning result. The golden beam of the scale creaked under the weight of his heart, the sound reverberating through the ethereal field like a mournful dirge.

Drake's breath hitched, a cold dread seeping into his bones. "What does this mean?" he asked, his voice barely above a whisper. The words felt heavy on his tongue, laden with the fear of an answer he already suspected.

His gaze darted between the sunken heart and the pristine feather, untouched and light. In that moment, the weight of his actions crashed down upon him. Every decision, every selfish choice made in the name of love and family, now bore down on his soul with crushing force.

"I tried," Drake thought, his mind racing. "I only wanted to save them. To keep my family safe." But even as these justifications rose in his mind, he felt their hollowness. The scale before him told a different story - one of consequences that reached far beyond his intentions.

He clenched his fists, fighting against the urge to reach out and tip the scales himself. "There has to be a way to balance this," he said, desperation creeping into his voice. "Tell me how to make this right."

The reeds around them whispered in the breeze, seeming to echo Drake's plea. He stood there, heart pounding, awaiting judgment from the enigmatic figure before him, hoping against hope for a chance at redemption.

19 - 20

The man's eyes, deep and unfathomable, bore into Drake as he studied the scales. His face remained impassive, a mask of otherworldly serenity that only heightened Drake's growing sense of unease.

"Your heart is heavy with guilt, grief, and selfishness," the man finally spoke, his voice carrying the weight of ages. "You cannot pass into the Nexus of Peace until you right your wrongs and relieve yourself of this burden."

Drake's stomach churned, a nauseating mixture of shame and fear coursing through him. He could feel the enormity of his transgressions pressing down on him, threatening to crush him beneath their weight. The golden sky above seemed to darken, closing in around him.

"I never meant..." Drake began, but the words died in his throat. Excuses felt hollow in the face of such judgment. Instead, he asked the question that truly terrified him, his voice barely a whisper, "Am I to repeat this torment? To relive my family's death over and over until I learn to let them go?"

The reeds swayed gently, their rustling a stark contrast to the turmoil in Drake's mind. He thought of his wife's smile, his son's laughter – memories that had driven him to tear apart the very fabric of reality. Now, faced with the consequences of his actions, he wondered if he had the strength to endure losing them again.

"Is this my punishment?" Drake thought, his heart constricting painfully in his chest. "An eternity of loss, until I can finally accept it?"

21 - 22

The man's gaze softened, the ever-shifting features of his face settling into an expression of compassion. "You have one chance for redemption," he said, his voice carrying a hint of hope that pierced through Drake's despair.

Drake's head snapped up, his eyes wide with a mixture of disbelief and desperate longing. The golden light around them seemed to pulse, matching the sudden quickening of his heartbeat. He could feel the weight of countless decisions, countless mistakes, pressing down on him. But there, in the gentle eyes of this enigmatic being, he saw a glimmer of possibility.

"Redemption," Drake breathed, the word tasting both foreign and familiar on his tongue. His mind raced, recalling every moment that had led him to this point - the car accident, the virus, the frantic jumps between realities. He had been so focused on saving his family, on clinging to what he'd lost, that he'd never truly considered the concept of making amends.

His fists clenched in the soft earth beneath him, grounding him in this surreal moment. The sweet scent of wildflowers filled his nostrils, a stark contrast to the acrid smell of fear and desperation that had followed him for so long.

"What must I do?" Drake asked, his voice low and determined. He leaned forward, every muscle in his body tense with anticipation. The lawyer in him wanted details, wanted to know exactly what this 'redemption' would entail. But the man he had become – the man who had traversed realities and faced unimaginable horrors – knew that sometimes, the path forward was one of blind faith.

As he awaited the man's response, Drake felt a curious mix of emotions swirling within him. Fear, certainly – fear of what trials might lie ahead. But also, a glimmer of hope, fragile yet persistent, like the first ray of dawn breaking through a storm-darkened sky.

23 - 24

The man's features settled, his ever-shifting visage momentarily coalescing into a serene countenance. His eyes, deep and knowing, fixed upon Drake with an intensity that seemed to pierce through to his very soul.

"The world is still in danger, Drake," the man said, his voice carrying a weight that made the air around them feel heavy. "Humanity teeters on the brink, and it needs a prophet—someone to usher in the words of the chosen one and save mankind from its collapse."

Drake's breath caught in his throat. The enormity of the task before him crashed over him like a tidal wave, threatening to overwhelm his senses. His mind reeled, grappling with the implications of the man's words. A prophet? Him? The irony wasn't lost on Drake—a man who had spent his life manipulating words in courtrooms was now being called to deliver divine messages.

He closed his eyes, allowing the gentle breeze to caress his face. In that moment, he saw flashes of his past—his family's smiling faces, the chaos of the virus outbreak, the desperation of his multiversal journey. Each memory was a weight on his conscience, a reminder of his failures and the selfish choices that had led him here.

When Drake opened his eyes again, they blazed with a newfound determination. He swallowed hard, his throat dry with the gravity of his decision. "I'll do it," he said firmly, his voice carrying across the tranquil field. "Whatever it takes. Just tell me what to do."

The words left his lips with a finality that surprised even him. Gone was the hesitation, the self-doubt that had plagued him for so long. In its place was a resolute acceptance of his fate, a willingness to bear whatever burden necessary to right his wrongs.

As he awaited further instruction, Drake's mind raced with possibilities. What would being a prophet entail? How could he, a man with so much blood on his hands, possibly be the one to save humanity? Yet, beneath the doubt and fear, a small spark of hope flickered to life. Perhaps this was his true purpose—not to save his family, but to save everyone.

25 - 26

The man's smile widened slightly, and he nodded. The shifting features of his face settled into an expression of solemn approval. "So be it. But know this: your path will not be easy. There will be tests, and there will be great loss. Only through enduring these trials will you earn your peace."

Drake's heart raced, a mixture of anticipation and dread coursing through his veins. He clenched his fists, feeling the weight of his past mistakes pressing down on him. The sweet scent of the field around him seemed to intensify, as if nature itself was bearing witness to this pivotal moment.

"I understand," Drake said, his voice low and determined. He met the man's ever-changing gaze, searching for any hint of what lay ahead. "What kind of trials? What more could I possibly lose?"

The man remained silent; his enigmatic smile unchanged. Drake's mind whirled with possibilities, each more terrifying than the last. Would he have to watch his family die again? Face the consequences of the virus he'd unknowingly helped spread?

Despite the fear gnawing at his insides, Drake straightened his back, squaring his shoulders. He'd come too far, sacrificed too much to back down now. The image of his wife and son flashed before his eyes, reminding him of why he'd started this journey in the first place.

"I'll endure it," Drake declared, his resolve unshaken. His voice carried across the tranquil field, seeming to echo with the weight of his commitment. "All of it. If it means I can find peace... if it means I can make things right."

As the words left his lips, Drake felt a strange sense of calm wash over him. For the first time since this nightmare began, he felt like he was on the right path. Whatever trials lay ahead, whatever loss he might face, he would face it head-on. It was time to stop running, time to stop trying to change the past. It was time to save the future.

27 - 28

The man stood, his form towering yet serene. "Then it begins now," he intoned, his voice reverberating through Drake's very being.

Drake's heart thundered in his chest, a mix of anticipation and dread coursing through his veins. He watched, transfixed, as the man raised his hand, fingers poised to snap. Time seemed to slow, each second stretching into eternity.

"Wait," Drake began, a sudden urgency gripping him. "What about my fam—"

His words were cut short as the man's fingers snapped; the sound impossibly loud in the quiet field. In an instant, Drake was engulfed in a brilliant white light, so intense it seared his retinas even through closed eyelids.

The world around him dissolved, reality unraveling like frayed threads. Drake's mind reeled, grasping for something solid, something real. 'Is this what it feels like to be unmade?' he wondered, a fleeting thought in the chaos.

As quickly as it began, the light faded, leaving Drake disoriented and gasping. He blinked rapidly, trying to clear the spots from his vision. "What... where am I?" he muttered, his lawyer's instinct to gather information kicking in despite his confusion.

The serene field was gone, replaced by... something else. Drake struggled to make sense of his new surroundings; his senses overwhelmed. 'Focus,' he commanded himself. 'One thing at a time. You've faced the impossible before. You can do this.'

Epilogue

10 A.C – 10 years after the multiversal collision
1 - 2

Drake's eyes snapped open, his vision blurry and unfocused. The harsh fluorescent lights above him seared his retinas, forcing him to squint. He felt the cold, unyielding surface of the metal table beneath him, the same table where he had made the ultimate sacrifice. The acrid smell of antiseptic filled his nostrils, a stark reminder of the clinical nature of his surroundings.

As his senses slowly returned, Drake's mind raced with confusion. How am I alive? The last thing he remembered was the life draining from his body as his blood was extracted to save the world. He flexed his fingers, surprised to feel strength in them. The weight of his past decisions pressed down on him, threatening to suffocate him with guilt and regret.

Suddenly, the double doors at the far end of the room burst open with a thunderous crash. Drake's heart leapt into his throat, his muscles tensing instinctively. Dr. Rachel Summers strode in, her presence filling the sterile room with an air of urgency and purpose. Her white robe billowed behind her, and Drake's keen eyes immediately locked onto an unfamiliar symbol emblazoned on the fabric—a dragon, its scales shimmering with an almost lifelike quality.

"Dr. Summers?" Drake's voice came out as a hoarse whisper, his throat dry and raw. He struggled to reconcile the sight before him with his memories of the brilliant but isolated scientist he had known.

Rachel's eyes met his, a storm of emotions swirling within them. "Drake," she breathed, her tone a mixture of relief and apprehension. "You're back."

As Drake tried to process the situation, a nagging thought tugged at the corners of his mind. Something about this felt wrong, out of place. The dragon symbol, Rachel's demeanor—it all hinted at a reality far different from the one he had left behind.

"What's going on?" he managed to croak out, his lawyer's instincts kicking in despite his disorientation. "How am I here?"

Rachel hesitated, her fingers nervously tracing the dragon emblem on her robe. The action didn't escape Drake's notice, and he filed it away as another piece of this perplexing puzzle.

"It's... complicated," she finally said, her voice carrying the weight of untold secrets. "There's so much you need to know, Drake. So much has changed."

Drake's mind reeled, grappling with the implications of her words. What had he missed? How long had he been gone? The questions piled up, each one adding to the crushing weight of uncertainty that threatened to overwhelm him.

As he opened his mouth to demand answers, Drake couldn't shake the feeling that he had stepped into a world far more complex and dangerous than the one he had left behind. The dragon symbol seemed to mock him, a constant reminder that nothing was as it seemed in this new reality.

3 - 4

Drake's muscles protested as he pushed himself off the cold metal table, his body remembering the sacrifice he had made. He stood unsteadily, facing Rachel, her presence both familiar and alien in this sterile environment. The fluorescent lights cast harsh shadows across her face, accentuating the lines of worry etched there.

"""

"When and where am I?" Drake asked, his voice hoarse and uncertain. He glanced around the room, searching for any clue that might anchor him to this new reality. The walls seemed to pulse with an otherworldly energy, and he couldn't shake the feeling that time itself had become malleable.

Rachel's eyes flickered with a mixture of relief and apprehension. She took a deep breath, her fingers absently tracing the dragon symbol on her robe. "Drake," she began, her tone measured and careful, "He said you would return."

The words hung in the air between them, heavy with implication. Drake's mind raced, trying to piece together the fragments of his shattered existence. Who was 'he'? And what did his return mean for this world he no longer recognized?

As he grappled with these questions, Drake couldn't help but feel a sense of déjà vu. Had he been here before, in another life, another timeline? The weight of responsibility settled on his shoulders once more, a familiar burden that both comforted and terrified him.

5 - 6

Drake's brow furrowed, his heart pounding with a mixture of confusion and dread. "Who said I'd return? What's going on?" he demanded, his voice tinged with desperation. He ran a hand through his disheveled hair, trying to ground himself in this moment that felt so surreal.

Rachel opened her mouth to respond, but before she could utter a word, a familiar voice cut through the tension-filled air.

"Hello, Drake."

The sound sent a jolt through Drake's body, every muscle tensing as he whirled around. From behind Rachel emerged a figure he knew all too well – Justin – the chosen one. The ethereal being's presence seemed to alter the very fabric of reality, the harsh fluorescent lights softening to a warm glow around them.

Drake's mind reeled. How was Justin here? What did this mean for the timeline, for the multiverse he had sacrificed everything to protect? A maelstrom of emotions surged within him – relief, fear, hope, and an overwhelming sense of uncertainty.

As Justin stepped forward, their serene expression a stark contrast to the chaos in Drake's mind, he couldn't help but wonder: Was this the beginning of another impossible journey, or the final chapter of a story he thought he'd already concluded?

7 - 7

Justin's piercing blue eyes met Drake's, their gaze filled with a profound wisdom that seemed to transcend time and space. A gentle smile played on their lips as they spoke, their voice as soothing as a summer breeze.

"Are you ready to keep your promise and save the world one last time?"

The words hung in the air, heavy with implication. Drake's mind raced, memories of his past sacrifice flooding back in vivid detail. He could almost feel the cold steel of the table against his skin, taste the metallic tang of fear in his mouth.

"One last time?" Drake echoed, his voice barely above a whisper. He glanced between Justin and Rachel, searching for answers in their expressions. "I thought... I thought it was over. That I'd done enough."

Justin took a step closer, their presence both comforting and intimidating. "The multiverse is a complex tapestry, Drake. Sometimes, even the most selfless acts create ripples we cannot foresee."

Drake's hands clenched into fists at his sides, a mix of determination and resignation washing over him. He had given everything once before. Could he do it again? The weight of countless lives pressed down on his shoulders; a burden he thought he'd finally shed.

"What's at stake this time?" he asked, bracing himself for the answer.

To Be Continued....

Be on the lookout for Book 4 of the Drake Miller Saga: The Worlds Last Garden. Following the events of Harrison and Linda Miller and Rachel Summers after the stunning conclusion to Worlds Collide.

www.ingramcontent.com/pod-product-compliance
Lightning Source LLC
Chambersburg PA
CBHW082121180726

48291CB00011B/2795